NEW HORIZONS

Sequel to *End of the Line*

SHIRLEY HUGHES

First published in Australia 2023 by Shirley Hughes
This edition published 2023

Cover design, typesetting: WorkingType (www.workingtype.com.au)

ISBN: 978-1-922958-53-2

ABOUT THE AUTHOR

Shirley Hughes has 55 years of experience and knowledge of the opal industry under her belt.

Shirley was first employed in a small, end-of-the-line town in south-western Queensland.

In 1979 Shirley moved to Western Australia. She lives in Western Australia with her son, Russell.

This book is dedicated to Paul and Ross

CONTENTS

PART III

BOULDER OPAL

Word was out in all opal-producing areas in Australia—some drunken pharmacist from some little pin-prick-on-the-map town called Brolga in Queensland was searching for opal. Critical negative comments came from all and sundry.

'He's employed the town drunks! What a joke!'

'He's a bloody dreamer! A drunken, womanising one, at that.'

'He's got no hope.'

'He'll never do it. Better men than him have tried and failed.'

'He's an arrogant shit-head.'

These people were obsessively jealous of Vance and the chance that he may become a legend within the small exclusive opal industry of Australia. Many of them lost precious sleeping hours while consumed by thoughts of how they could cash in on this possible new find of a different type of opal.

On the other hand, there were a few old timers in the industry who secretly wished him well. It had been their good fortune to have seen some beautiful Queensland opal many years before when a German couple had given it a go and struck opal not far from Brolga. The couple had played their cards close to their chests and opted to send whatever they had found to Germany for processing. Truth was they had neither the facilities nor the know-how to process it themselves.

§

'Toughest, most beautiful opal I have ever seen,' said one of the old-timers. Bert Black lay in his bed in his tiny house in a small town in

New South Wales, just south of the Queensland Border.

'Is that right, sweetheart?' asked the pretty twenty-year-old girl lying beside him.

'Yes. If that chemist finds opal, we had best take a trip to Brolga, my lovely little Leanne.' They heard his wife cough in the bedroom next door.

'I'd best go see if she's all right,' said Bert Black with a sigh as he slowly and reluctantly got out of bed.

¶

Vance was unaware that rumours about his project had spread to far-flung places. He would soon learn that the opal industry was very similar to Brolga—all the news travelled at breakneck speed.

¶

Vance was on his way to the mine long before dawn. He hoped the kangaroos were all asleep instead of hopping all over the road.

¶

Yappy breathed a sigh of relief when he heard Vance's ute in the distance.

'The Boss is coming, men,' said Yappy as he turned to the kitchen table where the men were finishing their breakfast.

'We know that, Yappy,' replied Neil.

'Do you think we are deaf, Yappy?' added Faith.

'Smart mongrels. Finish your breakfasts,' snapped Yappy.

Vance purposely slowed the ute down to a snail's pace when he got near to the camp. He knew the men would be eating their breakfast. They did not need dust billowing all over it.

Vance made himself a mental note.

'Think I'll put a marker up back there to remind me to slow down in future before I get into camp.'

'What? No dust?' said Yappy with a "Gee, it's good to see you" smile.

'What? No hello?' replied Vance, feigning disappointment as he pulled up a chair and sat down.

Yappy placed a mug full of black coffee on the table in front of Vance, who was lighting a cigarette.

'Want some tucker, Vance?' asked Yappy.

'No, thanks, Yappy. I'll wait until smoko time. I ate a lot yesterday.'

'Who is going to tell him?' asked Yappy.

'Not you,' chorused Faith, Neil, and Little Joe.

'Tell me what?' enquired Vance.

'A couple of Yanks came and blew the hill,' replied Faith.

'Yes, they showed us the nitty-gritty on how to do it in the future,' added Neil. 'They left us a heap of ignites cord and ammonium nitrate.'

'You owe them an opal for each of their mothers,' said Faith.

'You also owe one of them a date with TC,' added Neil.

Little Joe surprised them all by laughing, then saying, 'Don't like your chances with that one, Boss.'

'He's a bit too worldly for TC. Think I'll have to give him more than one opal,' replied Vance, then added, 'That is, if we ever find any.'

'Time to go to work, men,' said Neil. 'Come with us, Boss. We want to show you something.'

'Yeah, the new dunny,' said Yappy as the others left the kitchen.

'We wanted to paint it pink, but we don't have any pink paint,' said Neil.

'Thank God for that,' said Vance with a laugh.

'We have got something else pink to show you,' he said as he lifted up a small tarpaulin near the wash bench.

'Look what we have, Boss,' he continued as he leaned over to pick up the chipped boulder which was about fifteen inches long, eight inches high, and perhaps ten inches through.

'Well, look at that. Still a lot of pale blue, but there definitely is pink in there. Pretty thick seam, too,' said Vance as he examined the exposed opal seams.

'Don't know if there's colour in the others, but they all came from the same spot,' said Neil as he pointed at the other boulders, which were a little smaller than the one Vance was holding.

'Mysterious buggers, aren't they. Who would think dust-encrusted rocks like these could hold so much mystery and beauty?' said Vance.

'I think you are in love, Boss,' said Faith.

'I think you could be right, Faith,' replied Vance. Vance reluctantly put the boulder back on the ground with the others. 'Now show me the new outhouse.'

'Well,' said Faith, 'it's not quite finished yet; it doesn't have a toilet seat to cover the pit.'

'That's handy,' replied Vance with a chuckle. 'I'll get old Jordan to create one of his masterpieces.'

'Make sure you get him drunk before he starts building it. That way he'll do a better job,' said Faith without thinking first. Immediately they all thought of grog. Vance was surprised that, until this moment, he had not thought of a drink since he had announced to Jake, TC, and Lou the night before that he had quit. Little Jo, Neil, and Faith were silently thinking how great it would be to be seated at the bar in the Majestic with a drink of anything in front of them.

'Come on, stop dreaming,' said Vance. Little Joe led the way through the trees to a small clearing on which the toilet was erected.

'We put it on higher ground so it doesn't get flooded when and if it rains,' said Neil. 'I'll have to knock down a few of these trees so there will be a clear path. I'll do that next time I bring the machine up to camp for a service.'

'What do you think, Vance?' came Yappy's voice from behind them.

'What are you doing here, Yappy?' asked Vance. 'You are supposed to be in the kitchen.'

'Yes, Yappy, a woman's place is in the kitchen,' said Neil with a smile.

'Smart bastard,' snapped Yappy. 'I helped build the bloody thing, so I'm entitled to be here for the bloody unveiling.'

'What did you build, Yappy?' asked Vance with a smile.

'The bloody sign is what,' replied Yappy indignantly as he pointed at a forty-four-gallon drum lid standing upright with the lower edge embedded in a roughly rendered concrete support slab which was situated a couple of feet to the right of the toilet door. On the yellowish lid perfect copper plate writing which read, in black, gloss paint—

Ladies only. Please check carefully for spiders, snakes, and lizards before being seated. Thank you. C.E.O.

'You did that, Yappy? That's incredible!' said Vance. 'It's beautiful. Where did you learn to write like that?'

'At school, of course,' replied Yappy with pride.

'You actually went to school, Yappy?' teased Neil.

'Oh, shut up. You are all mongrels. Not you, Vance,' retorted Yappy as he stormed off towards the campsite.

'Quite illustrious,' said Vance with fake interest.

He wanted to hear the loader in action and see the men walking alongside picking up opal-laden boulders as the loader bucket blade exposed them.

Anyway, first things first.

'Very innovative,' he said as he looked at the corrugated-iron structure with sloped, corrugated-iron roof and concrete floor with an eighteen-inch round hole in the centre. Halfway down the left wall there was a long nail sticking out of the horizontal wooden support. On the nail a dozen or so pieces of neatly cut squares of old newspaper were hanging. Vance burst into gales of laughter.

'We own a pharmacy, and we can't afford toilet rolls!'

'Yappy thought the old newspaper squares added a nice touch, Boss,' replied Neil seriously before he too burst into laughter.

'What I really love is the door,' said Faith.

'Me, too,' added Little Joe while moving his head from side to side.

'There isn't one,' said Vance before laughing as realisation struck home that the dunny was doorless.

'Exactly,' said Neil. 'That is why we like it.'

'It has to have a door,' said Vance seriously.

'We ran out of timber and iron,' replied Faith just as seriously.

'You got out of here in such a hurry last time, Boss, that you didn't give us time to check what we needed.'

'Fair enough. Let's get to work now. We'll make out a list tonight.' Then, 'Would like to have been here when they blew the hill,' said Vance.

'Hope we didn't do the wrong thing by telling those Yanks to go ahead,' replied Neil.

'No! Not at all. They did us a favour.'

'Just a lot of dirt and a few rocks flying everywhere,' said Faith.

'I can imagine,' replied Vance. 'I'll have plenty of opportunities to see it in the future. Where did we uncover those boulders?' asked Vance.

'Followed your hunch that the level runs across the hill, not along it,' replied Neil. 'I have a feeling the boulder level is running on a downward slope because those boulders were unearthed about six feet below the level of that blue stuff. What do you want me to do?'

Vance was silent for a moment or so before replying.

'Follow your feelings, Neil. We'll see what happens.'

Neil hesitated before climbing onto the ladder. Turning towards Vance, he said, 'We are going to need a lot more equipment to do this properly, Boss.'

'I know,' nodded Vance.

After the loader and the men moved off towards the site, Vance found his way to an overlooking mound on which he sat while observing and falling deep into thought until the men knocked off for smoko.

§

It was the men's habit at smoko and lunchtime to sit and enjoy a 'roll your own' cigarette before eating, after which they would have another cigarette while finishing their coffee.

Their rollies, as they called them, were prepared the night before to save precious time during their breaks. Each man carried his smokes neatly lined up in an old tobacco tin.

They were settling outside the kitchen about to have a cigarette after enjoying Yappy's freshly baked scones when Faith opened the tobacco tin to extract a cigarette.

'Bugger it, I've only got five fags left, and I'm out of tobacco to make more. Have any of you blokes got spare tobacco?'

'I can give you a couple, mate,' replied Faith as he counted the contents of his tobacco tin. 'I have eleven.' This discussion put Little Joe and Vance on alert.

'I have ten smokes and enough weed near my bed to roll maybe ten more,' said Little Joe with absolute panic in his voice.

'Gee, Joe, that would have to be the longest sentence I have ever heard you utter,' said Vance as he opened his packet of Craven A before almost running to his ute in search of, hopefully, another packet or two. He found none. He had only the half dozen or so left in his pocket, which he once again removed from his shirt pocket in order to count the contents accurately.

'I have fourteen tailor-mades,' announced Vance. Vance's mind was racing. 'Bloody hell, I have taken the grog away from these poor bastards. I can't take the nicotine away as well. Can't take it away from myself, either. Truth is, we are all dependent men. Can't give everything up at the same time and expect to remain sane.' With that, Vance quickly went into the kitchen where Yappy was washing up with a portable radio crackling on the bench.

'Wish I could get the racing tips on this bloody thing,' complained Yappy.

'Be quiet, Yappy. If you work your cards right, you can be in town this afternoon to place a bet, a real bet. You pick the horses; TC will give you fifty quid, you put in fifty; if we win, give my share to TC. She will take all of it.'

'You're crapping me, Vance,' replied Yappy as he immediately stopped washing up before collecting a tea towel from a stack piled on a sheet under the bench and dried his hands while looking at Vance in absolute shock.

'Yappy, get your pen and paper; make a list of everything you need provisions-wise; then top up the fuel in the ute before dressing yourself up so you impress everyone in Brolga when you make your grand entrance.' Vance then went outside to join Neil, Faith, and Little Joe.

'I am sending Yappy to town to get us some tobacco and cigarettes,' announced Vance. As he absorbed the, "You have got to be joking" and "Why not me?" looks, he shook his head before saying, 'I need you men here. Yappy is a cook; you are opal miners.'

Neil, Faith, and Little Joe knew very well why Vance was sending Yappy to town instead of one of them. Yappy would follow instructions. Get dressed up, drive to town, collect orders, place a couple of bets with the S.P. bookie at the Empire, then return to camp, that is, unless the thought of the woman who 'broke his heart a thousand years ago' popped into his head. That would put him on the grog; then, in all likelihood, he would not return to camp for quite a while.

Vance also knew this. He was prepared to take the gamble.

'Get some of that bloody dust off the seats of the ute,' directed Yappy as he wrote his list.

Less than an hour later, Yappy was on his way after Vance had whispered to him on departure, 'Need that tobacco and cigarettes back here with you tonight, Yappy. Also, Yappy, watch out for roos.'

'I know, Vance. I know,' Yappy replied with a smile. The smile was not only a smile of agreement with Vance's request but also a smile of unspoken thanks for Vance's trust.

Yappy was elated as he drove the ute along the track towards the road.

'Gee, it feels good to be wearing town clothes,' he said to himself. *I've always been known as a snappy dresser. Must hark back to my days as a jockey,* he thought as he glanced down at his mirror-polished brown leather shoes, beige trousers, brown leather belt, and long-sleeved, tan shirt with the cuffs folded up a couple of widths. *You've still got it, Yappy,* he thought as he looked at himself briefly in the rear-vision mirror. Yes, his hair was neatly parted as it had been when he left camp.

Yappy glanced at his watch as he turned off the track onto the road. *Good,* he thought. *Should be in town around lunch time.*

¶

Yappy went immediately to the grocery shop after reaching Brolga. The grocer's young son took the order and suggested they send it by mail truck next morning. That way, the fruit and vegetables would be fresher as they would arrive on the Flea that evening. Made sense to Yappy, who agreed but insisted on collecting on the spot the six tins of Havelock Tobacco and two cartons of Craven A. Yappy then went to the pharmacy to see TC, for whom he had a note from Vance.

TC was surprised to see Yappy. She immediately jumped to the conclusion that something was wrong.

'Hello, Little Flower. You look pretty enough to give poor old Yappy a peck on the cheek.'

'My privilege, Yappy,' replied TC with a smile before kissing him lightly on the side of his face. 'What's wrong, Yappy?'

'Nothing wrong. Vance asked me to come into town for a few things. We've found a few boulders. Think he wanted to stay at camp to see if and where we find anymore.' Yappy then reached into his pocket and extracted a piece of paper, which he handed to TC. 'Vance wants you to give me whatever is on the list plus fifty quid for some bets.' TC read Vance's short note and smiled at a postscript Vance had written at the bottom—

P.S. Give Yappy fifty from the till. He's going to place a couple of bets for me. If he picks winners, put the fifty back in the till and keep the winnings as a bonus for being such a hard-working girl.

P.P.S. Yappy has his own money. Little bugger is richer than I am! Then again just about everyone is at the moment.

TC took fifty pounds from the cash register, then gave it to Yappy as she said, 'This is for his bets, Yappy. I'll pack up what the Boss wants. It's his books on opal. I'll put it in the ute if you leave it parked out front. I'll be here doing mail orders until late. Be a good man, Yappy.'

'Of course, I'll be a good man, Little Flower. Always am. I'll be back after I've backed a few winners.' TC smiled and wished Yappy good luck as he left the shop and headed off towards the Empire.

¶

Jake was sitting alone in the ladies' lounge when Yappy walked past the door and spotted him.

'Jake, mate, what the bloody hell are you doing sitting in the ladies' lounge?'

'Trying to be invisible, Yappy,' replied Jake with a grimace.

'Why?' asked Yappy

'Nothing, Yappy. Are you going to have a bet?'

'Sure am, mate. Today I'm betting for Vance as well as myself.'

'I'm just about to phone my bets through to Sydney. Usually the odds are better than S.P.' said Jake.

'Will you phone a couple through for me, mate?' asked Yappy.

'Sure, Yappy. Here is the form. I have already made my selections,' replied Jake as he handed Yappy the racing section of the newspaper flown in that morning on the small plane from Curloo.

'Take your time, Yappy. My first race is not run for almost another hour,' added Jake. 'Would you like a beer, Yappy?'

'Not for me, mate. Wouldn't be fair to the other men if I get back to camp smelling of beer.'

'You're a good bloke, Yappy,' said Jake before lighting a Rothman and silently puffing while Yappy concentrated on the horses. After ten minutes or so, Yappy took a hundred pounds out of his wallet and handed it to Jake.

'Two outsiders, fifty quid on the nose for both of them, half for Vance and half for me. After you've phoned through our bets, how about having a feed with me at Con's? A man gets tired of his own bloody cooking.'

'You're on, Yappy,' agreed Jake. 'Let us go phone these bets through. We'll phone from the pharmacy as it's closer than my shop.'

'Want to phone some bets through, TC. Okay if I use your phone?' asked Jake.

TC nodded, then turned to Yappy. 'Have the things the boss ordered ready, Yappy. There're two parcels and that carton,' as she pointed to a large box marked, Toilet Paper Extra Soft. 'I'll put the parcels in the front of the ute, if you'll put the carton in the back,' continued TC. Yappy twigged immediately when he looked at the carton of toilet paper.

'Smart bloody Callahan,' he said under his breath.

'Well, on,' said Jake as he hung up the telephone and looked towards Yappy, who was picking up the huge box of toilet paper.

'Has someone at the camp got the runs, Yappy?' asked Jake while holding back a giggle.

'No!' snapped Yappy. 'It's Callahan's warped sense of humour.'

'Well, look on the bright side, Yappy, if you ever run out of tissues, you'll have plenty of super soft toilet rolls you can use to blow your nose,' said Jake with a smirk.

'You are a smart mongrel, too, Jake. You and Vance are the bloody same,' replied Yappy as he carried the toilet paper to the ute, threw it in the back, then made sure it was covered by the tarp.

'You and Vance got pretty good odds on your outsides, Yappy. One is forty-five to one, and the other is fifty-six to one.'

'Good let's go eat,' replied Yappy.

¶

As was Con's habit on Saturday afternoons, he had radio station 4CL blasting out in the café. Con loved to punt on the horses almost as much as he loved poker games. Radio station 4CL was reliable with broadcasting race results from Brisbane, Sydney, and Melbourne.

'Yappy is tired of eating the tucker he cooks, so here we are,' said Jake when Yappy and he walked into Con's Café.

'Had a bet?' asked Con.

'What do you think?' replied Jake with a smile. 'Yappy has backed a couple of outsiders. He'll be a rich man if they come home.'

'I'll have a large, thick, well-done rump steak with a couple of half-cooked eggs, some grilled tomato, and canned spaghetti, please, Con,' ordered Yappy.

'Sure you can fit all that in your little tummy, Yappy?' asked Jake.

'Mind your own bloody business, Jake,' replied Yappy. 'Order yours; the sooner you tell Con what you want to eat, the sooner he can start cooking it.'

As they waited for their food, the voice on the radio announced that Jake's first bet had romped in at ten to one.

'I just won a thousand quid,' announced Jake happily.

'Good on you, mate,' said Yappy.

Shortly after, it was announced that Jake's Brisbane bet had also won.

'Another five hundred quid, Yappy. I'm on a roll,' said Jake.

'Hope I roll with you,' laughed Yappy as Con placed their meals in front of them. 'How do you expect a man to eat all of that?' complained Yappy.

'Ssh, listen, Yappy. Your first horse has come home,' said Jake with a huge smile. 'You and Vance have just won a thousand and fifty quid each.'

'Good on you, mate,' said Con. 'Looks like we are all having a good day. I have backed two winners myself.'

Halfway through eating their meal, Jake's third and last bet won in Sydney.

'Another nine hundred and fifty quid,' said Jake. 'A good day! I've won nearly two-and-a-half thousand!'

'Now you can afford a game of poker, mate,' said Con. Jake laughed, hoping Con would not force the issue.

'Almost time for your second race to be run, Yappy,' said Jake as he checked his watch. 'We'll hear the results in a few minutes.' The three men listened intently, waiting for what seemed an eternity to Yappy.

When it was announced that Yappy's horse had won, Yappy jumped to his feet, slammed both hands on the table, and yelled, 'The bastard won, Jake! It won, Con! Bloody hell, I can't wait to tell Vance!'

'You and Vance have won another fourteen hundred quid each,' said Jake with a smile. 'Good on you, mate! We have all, in fact, cleared two thousand, four hundred and fifty quid each today. That's great!'

'I won only five hundred,' complained Con.

'That's because you are a rich Greek,' laughed Jake. 'You don't need money. You've got more than you need already,' said Jake with a chuckle.

'You are quick on your calculations, Jake,' said Yappy.

'Yes, mate, you should be a bookie,' said Con.

'Great feed, Con,' said Yappy as he paid Con for the meals. 'I'd best be going back to camp before it gets too late.'

§

When Jake and Yappy were outside, Jake told Yappy to go to the pharmacy and wait for him while he went to his shop.

'Why is that, mate?' asked Yappy.

'I'll give you your winnings. The bookie will credit them to my account today and wire me the money on Monday. I think I've got enough to cover it, Yappy. I won't be long,' said Jake as he walked away towards his shop.

'You look as if you won, Yappy,' said TC.

'Yes, Little Flower, I'm a happy Yappy,' replied Yappy with a beaming smile. 'Jake has gone to get the winnings. I'm going back to camp as soon as he comes. The men are almost out of fags, poor buggers. I'll wait for Jake out in the ute.'

'Say "hello" to everyone for me, Yappy. It was nice to see you. Please tell the boss everything is okay and I'm happy you found some opal,' said TC.

§

Lou was visiting her parents, and the mail orders were finished early for a change, so TC locked up and was leaving as Jake crossed the street towards the ute and Yappy.

'Drive carefully, Yappy,' said TC as she blew him a kiss, then waved.

'Wait a minute, Little Flower,' called Yappy, who spoke to Jake for a couple of minutes before getting out of the ute, walking up to TC, and handing her a bundle of money.

'Vance said to give his share to you if we won,' said Yappy. 'Here it is. I'll see you soon, I hope.'

'TC, I'll give you a lift,' called Jake as Yappy drove off.

'I can walk, Jake' replied TC, who was in shock as to the size of the bundle of money Yappy had given her.

'I know you can walk, woman,' said Jake. 'I'll still give you a lift. I feel like a beer, but I don't want to go to the pub. Maybe we can sit on the top step for a little while.' TC nodded.

'Okay, Jake. Thank you,' she said as she turned to walk with Jake across the street to his car, which was parked in front of the Empire.

As they seated themselves in Jake's car, Graham Sandler walked around the corner and saw them.

Oh, no! Don't tell me TC is going out with that bastard, he thought. *Why doesn't Carmichael stick to the bloody nurses and leave decent girls like TC alone? I'll book that mongrel Carmichael one day. Don't know where or when, but I will get him.*

Jake and TC were silent until Jake pulled into the driveway.

'Won over a couple of thousand today, TC. As a matter of fact, so did Vance and Yappy.'

'That's good, Jake,' replied TC.

When they were inside the house, TC put a Jerry Lee Lewis record on the stereo, then went to her bedroom, where she put the money Yappy had given her inside her pillows before gathering some fresh clothes.

'I'm going to take a shower, Jake,' she said as she walked past the kitchen where Jake was taking his first gulp of the beer he had just opened.

'Can I take a shower with you?' asked Jake.

'Don't be ridiculous, Jake. Just drink your beer,' commanded TC.

'Can't blame a man for trying,' mumbled Jake as he walked towards the front of the house, where he opened the door, then pushed himself down on the top step, where TC joined him after finishing her shower.

'Where are your rollers?' asked Jake.

'I'm warning you, Jake. I've had enough of you,' replied TC seriously.

'TC, I know for a fact you have not had any of me,' retorted Jake.

'Jake, stop now or leave,' replied TC with a scowling serious expression on her face.

'How long will Vance be out at the mine?' asked Jake.

'I don't know. He might stay there for a while. Yappy told me they found some opal,' replied TC matter-of-factly before continuing. 'So, I hope he finds tons and tons of opal. He deserves to. People shouldn't laugh at him, Jake. At least, he's having a go. I know he has his weaknesses; then again, most people do.'

'Is that why you quit all the time?' asked Jake.

'No, Jake, I just don't agree with some of the things he does. I hope with all my heart that he can manage to stay off the rum this time. That will put a few of his critics in their place.'

'I hope so, too, TC,' agreed Jake sincerely. 'He's a good man and a good mate.'

'He sure is,' replied TC softly.

As Jake and TC each drifted into silent thought, Vance was at the mine thinking about how to expose whatever colour was inside the boulders the men had found. They had hit the previous boulders with a hammer. Vance didn't want to do that with these because he had noticed that some of the veins of pale blue—*patch*, as he had read it was called—opal had cracks when exposed. He had a feeling that these cracks had occurred due to the impact of the hammer. He picked up the boulder, which had been chipped by the loader blade. There were no visible cracks in the seams of opal.

'Why would the impact of a hammer crack the opal when a loader bucket-blade could take the edge off a boulder and not do damage?' he asked himself repeatedly. He checked the time on his watch, decided to take a shower, then do something about a feed for the men's dinner as Yappy probably wouldn't be back for hours.

Wonder how Yappy went with our bets? he thought as he put the boulder down.

Vance was in the camp kitchen investigating options for the evening meal when he heard the loader approaching as Faith and Little Joe appeared in the doorway. They looked excited as Faith announced, 'We found some more boulders, Boss. We were about to call it a day when the blade unearthed them. One is a big bugger. Thought I was going to have to ask Little Joe to help me lift it into the bucket.'

'You were proving to yourself how strong you are, Faith; that is why you didn't call on Little Joe for help,' said Vance with a laugh.

'Come have a look, Boss,' said Little Joe.

Neil turned off the loader after pulling to a stop and lowering the bucket.

'We've got some more,' he said excitedly as his feet hit the ground. 'Can't see any colour. Let's have a smoke before we unload them,' he added.

'That's a big bugger, all right,' said Vance as he inspected the dozen or so boulders resting on the bucket blades. 'Must be three feet long and more than a foot through.'

'Felt a lot bloody bigger than that when I lifted it,' said Faith.

All of them desperately wanted to know if the boulders were opal bearing; instead, they all sat down to have a smoke and a chat.

As the men opened their tobacco tins and Vance his Craven A packet, they simultaneously thought, *Hope Yappy isn't too late getting back.*

¶

'Hope Yappy didn't get tied up in town,' said Faith.

'He'll be fine, Faith,' said Vance confidently. 'Don't know what I'm going to feed you men for dinner. That's my biggest worry at the moment.'

'Don't worry, Boss. We'll just help ourselves, okay, men?' said Neil. Little Joe and Faith nodded in agreement.

Vance was relieved as he said, 'The water is boiling if anyone wants coffee.'

'Well, Boss, we've found some boulders,' said Neil. 'Are we going to bash them with the hammer?'

'Not yet. Don't know what we'll do for sure. Don't want to crack the opal if there is any in there. I need to think about it.'

'That makes sense,' said Faith. The others agreed.

'Too bloody hard to find. We don't want to wreck it,' said Faith as he lit another roll-your-own.

Little Joe stood up as he said, 'I'm going to take a shower. There's a little bit of tobacco beside my bed if any of you need it.'

'Thanks, mate,' said Neil.

'You're a bloody good mate at that,' added Faith.

'So are both of you,' replied Little Joe as he unpegged a pair of shorts and his bath towel from the clothesline before walking towards the shower.

That is what real people are about. Sharing your last cigarette, slice of bread, or quid with your friends when they are in need, thought Vance.

'There's a car coming,' said Neil.

'Wonder who the bloody hell that is?' said Faith.

'It's Yappy! I'd know the sound of the ute anywhere,' said Vance as he got to his feet. 'Didn't expect the little bugger back this early.'

'Perhaps he's afraid of the dark,' said Neil with a smirk.

They heard the ute slow down to a snail's pace as it got closer to the campsite.

'Bright looking pair of drongos you are,' said Vance as Faith and Neil jumped to their feet and stood with their arms thrust out in an exaggerated welcoming gesture as Yappy pulled the ute to a stop in front of them.

As Yappy got out of the car he said, 'Smart bastards! Are you happy to see me or is the welcome for the tobacco I left behind in Brolga? It was a mistake. I left it in the pharmacy when I went to say goodbye to Little Flower. I'm sorry.' Vance was almost certain that Yappy was having them on, so he did not comment.

'You'd better bloody well not have left it behind,' said Neil seriously.

'Do you think a bloody man is stupid!' said Yappy as he laughed loudly while handing the cigarettes to Vance and the tobacco to Neil, who handed two tins to Faith and placed two tins for Little Joe on the wash bench.

'What's for dinner, Yappy?' asked Faith.

'I'm on strike,' replied Yappy. 'Strike a man pink. I have had a busy day. Help me here, Vance,' he continued with a begging gesture of his hands and a helpless expression on his face.

Vance laughed.

'I think we should let everyone get their own dinner tonight, Yappy.'

'Thought that was already decided,' said Little Joe, who had finished his shower and was collecting his tobacco from the washing bench.

'You mongrel, Faith. You always have to take the piss out of a man,' snapped Yappy before turning his attention to Vance.

'Your parcels from TC are on the front seat. You are a smart bastard, too.'

'Why is that, Yappy?' replied Vance feigning hurt innocence.

'That bloody great box of super-soft crapper paper in the back of the ute! That is why!'

'Come on, Yappy, mate, I was just having a go at you because I found your neatly cut pieces of paper in the women's toilet amusing.'

'Come into the kitchen with me while I throw a feed together. I'd rather not let everyone help themselves. They will upset my kitchen, and I won't be able to find anything tomorrow.'

'How are things in town?' asked Vance.

'Two outsiders I picked came in, mate,' said Yappy quietly as he danced a little mock jig. 'We won two thousand, four hundred and fifty quid each.'

'Well, I'll be buggered, Yappy! Good on you,' said Vance. 'Now tell me about things in town.'

'I was only there a couple of hours. TC said to tell you everything is fine. The order from the grocer's is coming by mail truck tomorrow morning. Jake and I had a feed at Con's café while we listened to the race results. Jake won the same amount but he backed different horses, three winners. I gave your money to TC. That's it! Now you tell me, Vance, how were things here during my absence?' Yappy finished with a broad smile.

'Found more boulders, Yappy. I have a feeling they have opal in them.'

'I bloody hope so, mate,' replied Yappy with an exuberant smile.

'Yappy, thank you for today. You didn't even have a beer, did you?' said Vance sincerely.

'Wouldn't be fair to the men, Vance,' replied Yappy. 'By the way, thank you for trusting me to go. Apart from that, I'm better off by nearly two-and-a-half thousand quid.'

Yappy bustled around the kitchen while Vance sat smoking, drinking coffee, feeling useless, and thinking.

TC must be over the moon. Poor little bugger will think she's rich. Bet she'll rush to the bank as soon as it opens on Monday. I imagine Claudia will be working tonight. What a woman! Suppose Delores has spent the three thousand by now. If she hasn't spent it all, I'd bet 'London to a brick' that she's put a huge bloody hole in it. Wonder how the kids are. Fancy having three kids. I hardly know them. They hardly know me. Probably never will. Wonder how Anna is. Dear, sweet Anna.

'Tell those mongrels the food is ready,' interrupted Yappy.

As instructed, Vance went to call the men, who were now all showered and sitting on their bunks, rolling tobacco carefully into cigarette papers.

Over dinner. Vance promised to buy a power generator when money was available.

'Great,' they all agreed.

'I would like you all to put your heads together and come up with suggestions on gear that would make life around the camp a bit better.' The men all knew Vance was sincere. They knew when and if the money was there, whatever was required for the camp would be high on his list of priorities.

'We already have one luxury,' quipped Yappy. 'We have a huge carton of super-soft toilet paper.' Everyone laughed.

§

Next day being Sunday, Neil, Faith, and Little Joe would start work at 8 a.m. instead of the usual 6 a.m. The alarm clocks within their heads did not differentiate between days. So, instead of lying in on Sundays, they would rise as usual around five-fifteen, wash their faces, clean their teeth, and have a smoke.

Neil and Faith had developed a habit of doing their washing on Sunday mornings while Little Joe preferred to take care of his after work a couple of days during the week.

That morning, Vance got out of bed the moment he heard Yappy mumbling to himself about how there must be a better life than this.

Poor Yappy, Vance had thought. *He always has to be up and at it long before the others.* When Vance heard Yappy mumbling, he recalled a recent conversation he had shared with Jake. Vance had been telling Jake about how hard and what long hours the men worked and how they never complained.

'Poor bastards really earn their twenty-five quid a week, mate.' At the time Vance had smiled at Jake before replying.

'They also get room and board thrown in, Jake.' Jake had simply shaken his head, then changed the subject. Vance was now feeling guilty as to how long and how hard the men worked for such little money. Neil, Faith, and Little Joe were doing at least seventy hours a week. Yappy worked even longer hours. 'These poor buggers' wages amount to much less than five bob an hour!' In self-justification, Vance told himself that, if he paid them more, they would only blow it on grog first chance they got. He then decided not to think about it anymore. Too hard!

'Got to stoke up the fire. Should have boiling water for coffee in five to ten minutes. The parcels from TC are still in the ute,' said Yappy as Vance followed him into the kitchen.

'Thanks, Yappy. I had forgotten,' replied Vance as he left the kitchen en route to the ute from which he returned less than a minute later.

'Shit, Yappy, we have all those bloody boulders out there, and I forgot about these,' said Vance as he cut the string on both packages, then began ripping off the brown paper.

'Bloody hell, Vance what is in there? A million quid?' asked Yappy in surprise to Vance's suddenly larger attitude towards the couple of packages which had been disregarded in the ute since last night.

'No, Yappy, just books on gem cutting,' replied Vance. 'Now that we have some opal, we need to find out what to do with it and how to do it.'

'You've got enough of the bloody things,' said Yappy as Vance placed the two piles of assorted books and lapidary magazines on the table.

'Yes, Yappy, we've got everything I've been able to track down,' replied Vance. 'Oh, stuff it, Yappy. The suspense is driving me insane. I have to know if there is opal in those boulders. I'm going to chip the ends off them. If I make a mess of it, I'll learn by my mistake.' Yappy was surprised at how quickly Vance left the kitchen. One second he was talking, next second he was gone.

'I'm surprised he lasted this long,' murmured Yappy to himself. 'Bet the men will be out of bed the minute they hear Vance mucking around with the rocks.' As almost always, Yappy was correct.

Within minutes, Neil, Faith, and Little Joe were on their haunches with Vance beside the heap of boulders.

'What took you so long, Boss?' asked Neil with a smile.

'Knew you would buckle,' added Faith.

'I am excited,' said Little Joe as Vance momentarily hesitated before gently tapping the end of one of the smaller boulders with a miniature pick.

'Will have to hit it just a little harder,' said Vance when the boulder remained intact. He hit the boulder again, and the end of the boulder broke off to expose thin, bright green seams of opal, which Vance scrutinised carefully as he held the chipped-off piece in shaking hands. There were no visible cracks. He then pushed the piece back against the bigger piece of the boulder. It joined together perfectly.

'You are like a bloody kid in a bloody lolly shop, Boss,' said Neil, who desperately wanted to have a close look at the two pieces of rock.

'Yes, Boss when do we get to hold it?' asked Faith.

'Be patient. We must be patient,' said Little Joe.

Vance reluctantly handed the small piece of boulder to Faith, and the larger piece to Neil.

'Incredible,' said Faith as he moved the piece of opal-bearing rock from side to side.

'Amazing!' said Neil. 'Just bloody amazing.'

Vance stood up and lit a cigarette as he observed the excitement on the men's faces. He was equally happy for them as he was for himself. After all, they were the ones who did all the hard work. 'All I have to do is worry about financing the project. Lord only knows how I'll do that. One way or another, I know it's going to happen.'

Yappy emerged from the kitchen while wiping his hands on a tea towel.

'Why aren't you doing your washing, Neil and Faith?' he asked with authority.

'Oh, shut up, Yappy,' replied Neil as he handed the piece of boulder he had been examining to Little Joe.

'This is why, Yappy,' said Faith as he handed over the piece he had been looking at.

Yappy placed the tea towel over his shoulder, then took the rock from Faith. Yappy was standing in the morning sun, the rays of which seemed to cause the veins of opal to dazzle.

'Bloody hell, it's alive! Look at it shine. It's bloody beautiful,' said Yappy, who, being an emotional man, was close to tears as he placed the boulder on the wash bench, then made a hasty retreat back to the kitchen.

Little Joe placed the end he had been looking at on the wash bench before picking up the piece Yappy had put down. He held it to the sun, then after a short silence, he said softly, 'Yappy is right! The sunshine does bring it to life. Truth be known, we all feel like shedding a tear or two. Difference between Yappy and the rest of us is that Yappy is an open book while we force ourselves not to cry even when we want to let a few tears fall. We're afraid it would be viewed as a sign of weakness instead of being an indication that we are normal human beings with feelings.'

Vance, Neil, and Faith stood in shocked silence as Little Joe replaced the rock on the wash bench before walking away towards the marquee. Vance broke the silence.

'Life sure is full of surprises, and Little Joe has to be one.'

'In all the time I have known Little Joe, I have never heard him utter so many words in one hit,' said Neil.

'Not only that, he strung the words together so bloody well,' said Faith.

'Come on, Faith, we'll do our washing, or at least soak it, before breakfast,' said Neil. 'Truth be known, I feel like crying myself. We are finally on our way, Boss.'

'Yes, Neil, I know, but our way to where?' replied Vance silently as he picked up the two pieces of rock, then placed them in the back of the ute. He returned to the rock heap and retrieved the larger boulder, which had been chipped by the loader bucket. He also put that in the back of the ute before going into the kitchen, where he flicked through a couple of lapidary magazines. His mind was racing, and he counted his blessings when for once Yappy did not start chatting.

Yappy called the men to breakfast at exactly seven-thirty. Conversation over breakfast was centred on opal as was to be expected. Every one of them was happy and extremely excited.

At seven-fifty on the dot, Neil, Little Joe, and Faith picked up their coffee mugs and moved outside to enjoy a smoke before work began. Vance followed them, sat down, and reached for his cigarette packet as Neil said, 'We'll find more boulders today, Boss.'

'That would be nice, Neil' replied Vance with a smile. He did not want to disillusion the men by telling them he didn't have a clue as to what they were going to do with the boulders.

'When is the machine due for a service, Neil?'

'Perhaps the end of the week. I've been working it pretty hard,' replied Neil as he got to his feet. 'Come on, men time to start work.'

Vance collected the men's coffee mugs, which he returned to the kitchen as Neil started up the loader while Faith and Little Joe made their way towards what was left of the hill.

¶

Vance decided to resume investigating whether or not there was opal present in the rest of the boulders on the heap. The truth was he was itching to get at it, yet afraid of disappointment should they prove to be void of opal seams. His fear was wasted as boulder after boulder turned out to be opal-bearing. The seams varied in colour and width. So far, the opal was mostly emerald green in colour. Some seams showed a little orange as well as green. Vance noticed that, for some reason unbeknown to him, the thin seams appeared to be much brighter than the wider ones.

¶

Due to the late start on Sundays, the men skipped smoko and worked through until lunchtime. Consequently, Vance was able to concentrate on his task uninterrupted except for when Yappy emerged from the kitchen to finish Faith and Neil's laundry.

'Poor Buggers didn't get time to finish. They are too bloody excited about finding opal,' said Yappy as he pegged the men's clothes on the line.

'Aren't we all, Yappy,' replied Vance.

'Too bloody right, Vance. Anyway, you are a man on a mission. I'll make myself scarce,' said Yappy. 'The mail truck should be here soon. I've got a fruit cake in the oven. I better keep an eye on it. I usually give the truckie a cup of coffee and something to eat. Those poor buggers have a lousy bloody life. May as well live in their trucks.'

¶

As Vance hit the ends off the boulders, he would look at them carefully, then line them up, then matching boulder with each end. He had them placed out in a row so the men could see them, touch them, and discuss them. Most of all, feel satisfaction knowing their relentless hard work had at last paid off.

When Vance heard the mail truck approaching, he decided to take a break. He did not want to leave off his project with the boulders as he had only a couple plus the huge one left to do. He did know it would be rude of him not to help the truck driver unload their order and have a yarn accompanied by a cup of coffee and a slice or two of Yappy's fruit cake.

The dust-covered, heavily-laden mail truck pulled to a halt. The young, blonde-haired, tired-looking truckie stepped down through the truck doorway. He was clad in normal truckie garb, that being khaki shirt and shorts, long socks rolled down over the top of his work boots, and, most importantly of all, a smile.

'G'day, Mr Callahan. Don't run into you here too often.'

'That is because we visit here at different times,' replied Vance cordially. 'Yappy cooked a fruit cake. I think he cooked it because we were expecting you and he wants to impress you.'

'What I would really like is a cold beer, Mr Callahan. Had a late night loading up for today's deliveries. As we load, we drink. Think by the way my head feels today, I must have drunk one too many last night.'

Vance ignored the part about a cold beer as the young truck driver climbed onto the back of his truck and lifted the tarp, revealing numerous boxes and parcels.

Vance said, 'Hope they are not all for us.'

'Wish they were, mate,' said the truckie. 'If they were all yours, that would mean I could unload, then head back to town.' Vance laughed as the truckie passed down open-topped fruit cases filled to the top with provisions.

'How are you, mate?' asked Yappy as he emerged to help.

'Hello, Yappy. As usual, you feed your men well here, by the looks of things,' said the truckie.

'Well-fed men are healthy and hardworking,' replied Yappy, who was wearing a grin all over his face.

'I must be very well fed, Yappy, because I'm healthy and work bloody hard,' answered the truckie with a genuine smile as he jumped down from the back of his truck, picked up the last fruit box, and headed towards the kitchen where Yappy had the kettle boiling and the smell of freshly baked fruit cake permeated the air. Vance made himself a coffee before seating himself at the kitchen table and cutting a slice of fruit cake.

'Help yourself, young fellow,' directed Yappy.

'Thanks, Yappy. The cake smells good,' said the young man as he seated himself opposite Vance, then cut himself a generous portion of cake.'

'Found any opal yet, Mr Callahan?' asked the young man with sincere interest.

'As a matter of fact, we have,' replied Vance while smiling and nodding his head. 'By the way, please call me Vance.'

'Thank you, Mr Callahan. I'm so happy you found opal. That will put the town's busybody gossips in their place.'

'They have to have something to talk about,' interrupted Yappy. 'May as well be Vance.'

'My mum says all small towns are like that. I'm running a bit late. I have to get back on the road. Thanks for the cake, Yappy.'

§

'Yappy, what is that kid's name?' asked Vance.

'Not sure. I always call him mate,' replied Yappy. Within a couple of minutes, the truck and the young man driving it were gone.

Vance went back to his precious boulders. He decided not to mess with the huge one. Because of its size, he believed he would have to hit it much harder than he had the smaller ones. He didn't want to risk cracking the opal if, indeed, there was any opal in it. Vance looked at the two remaining boulders, which were much smaller than all of the others. These two were about the size of the average potato. He decided to leave them alone for the time being; so, he put them in the back of the ute. He wanted to wait until the men came for lunch so someone could help him to put the huge boulder in the ute. But pride would not allow him to ask one of the men to assist him, so with great difficulty he picked it up and carried it to the ute, where he literally dropped it into the back, where it landed with loud crashing sound.

Yappy came racing out from the kitchen yelling, 'What the hell was that?'

'Just me! I dropped that big one into the back of the ute,' replied Vance with a restrained smile.

'You are bloody mad, Vance. You could have asked me to help you lift the bloody thing,' chastised Yappy in concern.

'I'm hungry, Yappy. How long until lunch?' replied Vance, who was not feeling at all hungry.

'As soon as the men come from work,' yelled Yappy. 'You are all mad. All of you.'

Vance slumped to the ground and leaned against an empty, upturned forty-four gallon drum while he lit a cigarette and took in his surroundings.

After a few moments his eyes and thoughts focused on Neil and Faith's work gear, which was drying on the clothes line.

How simple, thought Vance. *Shorts, singlets, underpants, and socks. If only my life were that simple. Oh, to be responsible only for myself. Now I have this opal thing started. God only knows where it will take me. I owe it to these simple, hard-working, honest men to give it my best. I hope my best is good enough. I wonder how Delores and my kids are doing. I wonder where my Anna is. I hope I haven't bitten off more than I can chew. I'm tired already.* Vance's thoughts were interrupted when he realised Faith and Little Joe were standing in front of him.

'We have found more boulders, Boss,' said Faith.

'Lots of them,' added Little Joe.

Both Faith and Little Joe were wearing broad smiles, and their eyes were sparkling with the joy of achievement while hoping for accreditation from Vance.

'Bloody hell, good on you! Where is Neil?' said Vance as he quickly stood up to shake the men's hands.

'You are going to be a rich man, Boss,' said Faith while patting Vance on the shoulder.

'There won't be any bloody thing if you don't all get your butts in here and eat this bloody tucker,' came Yappy's voice from the kitchen door. 'A man's been slaving all bloody day, and now you decide to glorify yourselves because you have found more opal. Get in here NOW!'

'The little man has spoken. We had best do as we have been told,' said

Vance with a laugh. 'Where is Neil?'

'I'm in here,' called Neil from the kitchen. 'I thought I would let Little Joe and Faith bask in the glory of our find.'

'No more work today,' announced Vance as Little Joe and Faith and himself joined Neil at the kitchen table.

'Bet that does not include me,' quipped Yappy.

'Spot on, Yappy,' replied Vance. Everyone laughed. *This is a memory worth filing,* thought Vance.

It's great to see them all happy, thought Yappy.

Wish I had a drink, thought Faith.

Bloody hell, the loader needs a service come the end of the week, thought Neil.

Glad we found more boulders, thought Little Joe.

¶

As Vance and his crew sat at the camp kitchen table, word of their opal find was on the grapevine. Brolga was buzzing with the news! The young truck driver, just for something to say, had spread the word to whoever would listen at every stop he had made. As usual in Brolga and the district, word travelled fast.

After listening in and repeatedly hearing about the find, the telephonist on duty at the exchange called Lou.

'The mad bloody chemist and his mob of drunks have found opal.'

'He's not mad!' replied Lou before hanging up immediately and turning towards TC, who was ironing. 'Vance and the men have found opal, TC,' said Lou excitedly doing a little dance and waving her arms around. TC nodded and smiled as she continued ironing.

'This will put a few of Vance's critics in their place,' continued Lou. 'The Seat of Knowledge gentry will have a ball with this one.' TC acknowledged with another nod.

'I'm going to call Jake. He'll be happy for Vance,' said Lou as she rushed to the telephone.

'I know. Yappy told me,' replied Jake after Lou gave him what she had thought would be surprising news.

'Why didn't you tell us?' asked Lou.

'Yappy told TC, too,' replied Jake. Lou put the telephone down, then turned to TC.

'Why didn't you tell me about them finding opal, TC?' enquired Lou with obvious disappointment in her voice.

'I thought I would let the Boss tell you, Lou. Now that the word is out, I hope it's good opal that they have found,' replied TC with a hopeful smile. 'Will give the Boss a new lease on life, and I hope with all my heart it will, at last, give him a reason to stay off the rum forever.'

'I do, too, TC,' agreed Lou with a sigh.

¶

Back at camp, Vance was carefully chipping the ends off the boulders unearthed that day while the men observed and chatted excitedly as more and more veins of colour were revealed.

The sun began to set, so one by one the men reluctantly shaved and showered. They didn't want to miss anything as the beautiful colours created by nature and entombed for millions of years within the boulders were exposed for the first time.

'I had better get cleaned up myself,' announced Vance. 'We'll do the rest tomorrow.'

'Hard to leave them, isn't it, Boss?' said Faith.

'You are not wrong there, Faith,' replied Vance with a laugh.

'Bloody incredible!' said Neil.

'Hope we find more tomorrow,' said Faith.

'I do, too,' said Little Joe as he took a rollie from his tobacco tin.

Yappy was in the kitchen, wishing Vance and the others would come inside to eat.

'A man will be here all bloody night,' he mumbled to himself. 'All right for them. They just eat, then go to bed. I have to wash up. Can't blame the poor buggers. They are excited. So am I, for that matter. Well, if they won't come inside, I'll go outside.'

'How long will you buggers be keeping me waiting?' he asked.

'What's wrong, Yappy? Have you got a date?' asked Neil.

'Yes, I have as a matter of fact, I have a date with my bloody bed sometime between now and 4 a.m. when a man has to get out of it to fix breakfast for you mongrels,' replied Yappy with a smile.

'We're waiting on the boss to finish his shower,' said Faith.

'Stuff the bloody boss,' replied Yappy.

'What did I hear you say, Yappy?' said Vance with a laugh as he emerged from the shower.

'You heard me, Vance. Now hurry up, all of you.'

'Yes, sir,' said Neil as they obeyed Yappy's command and entered the kitchen.

Surprisingly there was little conversation during meal time. Yappy surmised they were all overwhelmed by the reality of the fact that after all these months, their hard work had come to fruition. Even Yappy himself was quiet as he went about washing his cooking utensils. One by one, the men helped themselves to a mug of coffee, thanked Yappy for the great food, then made their way to their bunks.

Vance remained in the kitchen with Yappy. He drank his coffee and smoked a couple of Craven A as Yappy completed his nightly after-dinner chores.

'We finally found it, Yappy. We finally found it!' said Vance.

'This is only the beginning, Vance,' said Yappy as he checked that there was wood in the stove. 'That's it, Vance. It's been a long day. Let's hit the sack.' Yappy picked up a large torch from the bench, clicked it on, then extinguished the carbide light by placing the lid over the flame.

Little Joe, Neil, and Faith were already asleep.

'They must be buggered,' whispered Yappy. 'See you in the morning.' Both Vance and Yappy were also asleep within minutes of their heads hitting their pillows.

¶

In Brolga, Lou and TC decided to break the monotony of step-sitting by taking a walk up the street to Con's Café. They deliberately waited until the movies had started; that way they avoided the crowd.

'Here they are, my two favourite girls,' greeted Con as TC and Lou entered the café.

'Mine, too,' added Lisa. 'How are you, my darlings?'

'Not often we see you here after dark,' said Con.

Both girls adored Con and Lisa.

'We thought we needed a break from the house,' said Lou with a broad smile.

'So, my friend has found opal?' asked Con.

'Great news!' replied TC with a smile.

'The whole town is talking about it,' said Lisa.

'We missed you girls when you were in Sydney,' said Lisa.

Both girls laughed and replied in unison. 'Not as much as we missed you.'

'What would you like, whatever it is, it is on the house,' said Lisa. Con nodded in happy agreement with his wife.

'You never say that to me,' came a deep male voice from the doorway behind the girls, who both immediately turned to see who had spoken.

Movie star material, thought Lou. *He's as gorgeous as Elvis. I bet he can't sing or move like Elvis.*

TC's mind was blank as she attempted to avoid eye contact with Graham Sandler in his immaculate khaki police uniform. Graham stood there, holding his police hat in his hand and wearing a smile that would melt any woman's heart. He was twenty-two years old and stood around six feet in height, with thick, black, wavy hair, with slightly longer than police regulations side burns, beautiful brown eyes, and long, black eyelashes most women would covet. Despite all this, Graham wore a look of masculinity rather than soft prettiness, as did the new doctor.

As Graham stood in the doorway looking at Lou and TC, he was thinking how refreshing it was to see girls like these two. Neither wore make-up except for lipstick. Both wore their hair pulled back in pony tails. Lou was wearing a cute, green dress with cut-outs in the sleeves and flat, gold sandals. TC was wearing white pedal pushers with a modest pink blouse and white flatties with bows on the fronts. Girls like these would be few and far between in the cities.

'Come in, Constable Graham. Meet our lovely girls,' invited Con.

'Thought you would never ask, Con,' replied Graham, still smiling as he entered the café.

'Con and I just love these girls,' said Lisa.

'I can see why,' said Graham.

'This little redhead is Lynette but her friends call her Lou. Lou is Jordan's daughter.'

'I've given your father a lift home a couple of times, Lou,' said Graham with a smile.

'Was he drunk?' asked Lou.

'No, he was carrying a carton of beer on his shoulder, and I thought it the decent thing to do. I find your father intelligent and very amusing.'

'Amusing that is for sure,' replied Lou with a laugh. Everyone else laughed in agreement.

Lisa Kara walked around from behind the counter and, lightly tugging TC's pony tail, said, 'And this is TC, who works in the chemist shop for one of Con's gambling friends.'

'I know,' replied Graham with a smile. 'I saw you through the week when the sergeant and I dropped off Mr Callahan after his car ran out of fuel.'

'Sorry, Graham, I didn't notice you,' replied TC while thinking, *If I'd seen you, I certainly would remember.*

'It's movie night. I thought all Brolga girls would be at the movies with their boyfriends,' said Graham, testing the girls' reactions.

'Are you mad, Constable Graham? These girls don't have boyfriends,' said Con seriously.

'Nobody in Brolga is good enough for these two,' added Lisa with a beaming smile.

'Thought I had seen both of you with Jake Callahan,' said Graham casually. Everyone laughed except Graham, who displayed confusion on his face.

'Here, girls,' said Con as he placed two chocolate thick-shakes on the counter. 'What will you have, Constable Graham? I am shouting.'

'Thank you, Con, but I'm fine,' replied Graham, whose deep-voiced enunciation was in absolute contrast to the majority of regular, hard-working Brolgaites.

'Join us, Constable Graham,' invited Lisa as she and the girls sat down at a table. Graham looked at his watch before saying, 'Thank you,' and sitting down.

'The drunks are all really going to love you when you try to break up a brawl,' said Lou directing her attention towards Graham.

'Why do you say that Lou?' asked Graham.

'Just difficult to imagine you in amongst a mob of drunken, cursing madmen,' replied Lou.

'Time will tell, Lou. I was posted here because of trouble; yet, here I am in full uniform on a Sunday night when all I have to do is stand outside the picture theatre before the movies start, at interval, and when they finish. Quite frankly, when I'm not on duty, I'm bored and quite lonely. The sergeant has a family, so I work longer hours than I have to just for something to do.' Both TC and Lou nodded in agreement.

'I am with you all on that one,' said Lisa.

'Don't forget me,' interjected Con while waving a tea towel in the air above his head. Once more all of them including Graham laughed. Graham looked at his watch, then stood up as did the girls and Lisa.

'Interval in fifteen to twenty minutes,' said Graham.

'We'll walk with you,' said Lou.

'Thank you, Con and Lisa. See you tomorrow,' from TC as she returned the shake containers to the counter. 'Don't want to be here for the interval rush.'

Lisa patted the girls on their shoulders. 'Please come again next Sunday night girls.'

¶

'So, what do young people do here in Brolga?' asked Graham as they walked along the footpath towards Carmel's picture theatre.

'Depends on how high or how low they are on the social ladder,' replied Lou.

'I see,' replied Graham as they arrived out front of the picture theatre. 'Nice meeting you girls. Hope to see you around,' said Graham as he came to a halt and placed his hat on his head.

'How could you not see us around in Brolga?' asked Lou, looking over her shoulder as she and TC kept walking. Graham watched their backs as they crossed the street and continued walking towards the edge of town. He was more than a little confused as Lou seemed to be the talkative one whereas the sergeant had told him TC was a fiery little thing. He silently recalled how he had quizzed the sergeant for every bit of information he had regarding TC after she had come to the police car when they dropped off her boss. Hard to imagine a little thing like her storming to the pub window and screaming into a bar filled with drunks.

Suddenly the front door to the theatre was abruptly opened and out rushed half of Brolga's population. As Graham stood to attention with his arms behind his back, he did his best to appear official and take note of everyone who emerged, then hurried towards Con's Café to buy refreshments.

¶

'So, what do you think about Constable Graham, TC?' asked Lou as she and TC walked home.

'Gorgeous!' replied TC.

'I agree! But I bet he cannot play guitar like Elvis,' from Lou.

'Probably not!' laughed TC.

When TC and Lou got home, they could hear the telephone ringing as they walked up the front steps. By the time they unlocked the door and went inside, it had stopped.

'I wonder who that was,' said TC.

'I'll find out,' answered Lou as she picked up the telephone and got through to the telephone exchange.

'Hi, this is Lou. Who was calling TC and me?'

'Jake Carmichael has called four times,' came the reply.

'Please put me through to his mother's house,' requested Lou.

'Where the hell have you and TC been? I sat on your back steps for over half an hour! I have called and called and bloody well called,' demanded Jake.

'Jake, mind your own bloody business. You are no longer the best-looking young rat in town! Goodnight! Jake thinks he owns us, TC,' said Lou as she put the phone down.

'Let's go to bed, Lou,' replied TC, while rolling her eyes backwards.

'Good idea, I have to start work back at the exchange in the morning. It is what I live for,' said Lou sarcastically.

The girls headed towards their bedrooms as they heard Jake's car scream into the driveway. Both Lou and TC met him at the back door, which Lou opened as Jake was about to knock on it.

'Jake, you look frantic,' said Lou.

'Who is the new best-looking rat in town? Word is all over the bloody place that my mate and his men have found opal. We should be celebrating together for all of them. Instead, you two decided to piss off to God-knows-where without telling a man,' yelled Jake.

'We went to Con and Lisa's. Sure beats hanging around here all of the time. We don't exactly lead exciting lives,' replied TC.

'That is for sure,' added Lou.

'Jake, almost everyone obviously knows the boss has found opal. Of course, you and Lou and I are definitely excited for the boss and the men. He just simply does not know what he is going to do with it. That is his next problem. Please go home to bed, Jake,' said TC.

'I agree, Jake. We will see you later,' said Lou as she pushed the door closed and locked it.

Jake did as instructed by Lou and TC. He went home, told his mother he was safe and sound, then went to his bed in which he had great difficulty finding sleep. He kept thinking, *Shit, my best bloody mate is going to be famous. Where the bloody hell will that leave me? I just know everything is going to change from here on in.*

¶

Constable Graham was drinking coffee with Con and Lisa in the café as they waited for the movies to finish. Con and Lisa kept the café doors open because they could always rely on making a couple or three quid after the movies ended. Graham was there because he was on duty until after the movies ended, when he would once again have to prove police presence to the Brolgaites by being outside in full uniform for all to see when they exited Carmel's theatre.

'Please tell me about Mr Callahan,' requested Graham as he sat with Con and Lisa Kara.

'He and my husband play poker! Sometimes all night! Always with Jake Carmichael, as well. Sometimes I get very angry because Con loses money, lots of it, to those two people,' replied Lisa.

'Stop now, woman!' commanded Con. 'They are my friends. I love playing cards!'

'Do you like losing our hard-earned money?' asked Lisa heatedly as she stood up, grabbed her coffee cup, and stormed off towards the kitchen.

'Sorry I asked,' said Graham with sincerity.

'I am so sorry, Constable Graham. Women are women!' replied Con as he threw his arms up wide above his shoulders.

Graham checked his watch before standing up and saying, 'It's time to go, Con. Time to be a cop. See Lisa and yourself tomorrow. Hope everything is okay with Lisa.'

'Mate,' said Con whilst once again throwing his arms wide in a gesture of surrender. 'That's women! See you tomorrow at breakfast time.'

Graham went off to wear what he hoped was a stern, nothing-gets-past-me look while he stood out in front of the theatre as Brolgaites rushed out to their cars or towards Con, who tonight would have to handle the late-night rush by himself before locking up the café and going to join Lisa in their accommodation at the rear of the joint, as Con called the café.

This night is going to cost me, thought Con as he served chocolates, coffees, and cigarettes to the after-movie crowd. *I know my Lisa! She will demand a new piece of expensive jewellery or a trip back to Greece. Of course, I will give it to her. I love her! As my mother used to say, 'If the woman of the house is happy, everyone else in the house is happy.'*

Con bid goodnight to the last customer before walking around from behind the counter to lock up before going to tell Lisa he loved her and would try never to gamble again.

Graham drove the police car around and down the few Brolga streets. All was quiet apart from loud rock and roll music emanating from the bank employees' quarters, where there was obviously a party in progress. The song blasting out was, Johnny Be Good.

More like, Graham Be Good, thought Constable Graham as he wheeled the police car into the yard of the police station. He locked the police car, double-checked to make sure, then closed the gate to the police quarters yard.

This life is too bloody exciting for me, he thought as he walked into his room, threw his hat on the only chair, and loosened his tie. Graham took off his uniform meticulously, moved across the room, hung it on a hanger, then grabbed a Coke from the small refrigerator, moved his hat from the chair to a short, narrow bench running along one side of his room, picked up his guitar, which had been leaning against the chair, and thought of TC.

As he took a sip of his Coke, he wondered what song he would sing to her, if he ever got the opportunity, that is.

The sergeant and his wife were in bed almost asleep, his wife more so than the sergeant.

'Brolga is all right for the night, luv,' muttered the sergeant as he touched his wife's shoulder.

'How do you know?' answered his wife in a low, muffled, almost-asleep voice.

'Because he has locked up everything, including himself, and he's playing his guitar and singing along with it so softly he doesn't think we can hear.'

'Good. I feel safe the town is locked up. Now let us get some bloody sleep.'

In Sydney. the hotel owners' son who had invited and escorted Lou and TC to rock and roll shows, rugby league games, and after-show and game party activities found himself tired of the crap going on around him. Always the same scene, especially at the parties where everyone except himself was rotten drunk and screwing wherever they could find a bed, couch, space on the floor, against a wall, or even a table. He didn't drink much himself because his parents owned a pub. Deep down he knew the only reason he was invited to these shows was because a lot of the guys drank there.

He was verging on twenty-four and looking for a good girl. He had taken quite a liking to a lovely, auburn-haired girl named Lou who had worked in the pub's office for almost a year. When he had told his parents he wanted to ask her out, they said, 'No!' They had told him he was definitely not to become involved with any staff member because they would certainly be after the money he would eventually inherit.

He got around his parents by telling them he would ask Lou's friend to go as well. 'Safety in numbers, son. Good thinking,' agreed his mum and dad.

He had realised Lou and her friend, TC, were not the run-of-the-mill. They were different. The first after-show party to which he took them, he could see they were happy to meet the rock stars. He made a mistake by staying too long. When the real action began, he could see they were embarrassed and uncomfortable and wanted to get out of the place. He never made that mistake again. The moment things looked like they were going a bit wild, he would take the girls home, say goodnight, and then return to the party.

He was upset when Lou left a couple of months back. The way she said goodbye to him made him realise that he particularly liked her and that she thought of him only as the boss' son who had helped her and her friend meet a few rock stars and football players, none of whom appeared to have impressed them much.

Now, after years of countless one-night stands, he recalled almost word-for-word what he had heard a hot rugby league player say to Lou and TC.

'Almost extinct species; better go back to the bush.'

Just what I am looking for, thought Colin. Here I come, Lou. All I have to do is find you. If you don't like me, then at least I will have tried.'

One of Colin's mates, Johnny O'Keefe, was singing, She's My Baby on radio station 2UE.

Hope you are right, Johnny, thought Colin.

Next morning, after a sleepless night, Colin went to the hotel's office and looked through the wages books. He could not find anyone recorded in the books as Louise.

Why didn't I ask for her surname! Shit, thought Colin. *I'll have to suck up to the bloody bookkeeper and swear her to secrecy. My parents are so far up themselves they probably expect me to fall in love with and marry a movie star. Who knows? At the moment, I want to get in touch with Lou.*

'Her name is Lynette Blake. Nice kid. Beautiful long, auburn hair. Comes from some one-horse town in the outback of Queensland. Think it's called Brolga,' said the bookkeeper with a smile. 'There is no address here, Colin, just Brolga Road. Your mum and dad won't like this, so good luck. My lips are sealed. Oh, one thing, Colin. I seem to recall Lou inferred her dad was the town handyman as well as the undertaker when necessary,' added the bookkeeper.

'Holy shit!'

'Trust me.'

'Please don't dob me in to my parents. All I am going to do is write her a letter,' said Colin with a wink and a smile before pecking the bookkeeper on the cheek and taking the tiny piece of paper on which was written, Miss Lynette Blake, Brolga, QLD.

Colin immediately took the elevator to the top floor of his parents' hotel, closed and locked the door to his three-room apartment, turned on the radio, then sat down with pen and paper to compose his letter. After partially writing on, then crumpling, numerous pages, Colin was finally happy with his effort, so he folded his two pages, placed them in an envelope, which he sealed, then kissed the back tab while saying softly, 'There you go, Miss Lynette. If I do not hear from you within a month, my letter is not good enough to convince you of my feelings. I mean every word I wrote.'

¶

Next morning at the opal mine, Vance and Yappy arose from their bunks at the same time.

'How long are you staying in the camp, Vance?' asked Yappy as he filled a bucket of water from the water tank on the back of the water truck.

'When the back of the ute is full of boulders, Yappy,' replied Vance as he splashed his face with water Yappy had just poured into one of the washtubs. 'Who knows, mate? Could be today, could be next week. Depends if we run out of fags first,' laughed Vance as Yappy himself splashed water from another washtub on his face.

'Be this bloody week,' came Faith's voice from behind them.

'Probably tomorrow,' added Neil, who was also up and ready to find more boulders.

'Could be today,' said Little Joe.

'How long 'til breakfast is ready, Yappy?' asked Neil.

'Usual time! Probably an hour plus a bit. It's not even bloody daylight yet! You bastards are suddenly in a great bloody hurry,' replied Yappy.

'Yappy, we are on a roll. See you at smoko time,' said Faith.

'Yes, Yappy, make sure the scones are bloody good,' said Neil.

'We will fill the back of the ute today,' said Little Joe.

Neil, Faith, and Little Joe quickly washed their faces, brushed their teeth, then went off to find more boulders.

Vance watched them as, one by one, they paused to urinate en route to the hill.

'What do you reckon, Yappy? Are they dedicated men or what? They would probably give me their guts for garters if I asked them,' said Vance.

'They are bloody already doing that, Vance. So am I, by the way,' replied Yappy as he turned towards the kitchen while muttering, 'I'll give the bastards the best bloody scones they have ever tasted. Even going to surprise them with some bloody pancakes. Bloody bastards. They get all the bloody glory. Well, they wouldn't have the bloody energy to find the boulders unless they had me to cook their bloody tucker.'

Vance thought for a few seconds as he lit a Craven A. *Think I should show Yappy some appreciation*! Vance followed Yappy into the kitchen, then asked, 'What is for breakfast, Yappy?'

'Get stuffed, Vance! Get your bloody own,' replied Yappy as he threw pots and pans all over the place.

'I thought you would react something like that, Yappy. You are as important to this deal as are Neil, Faith, and Little Joe,' said Vance.

'No, I bloody well am not! I'm just the bloody cook,' replied Yappy, who was flinging flour into whatever utensils he had at hand, cracking eggs, then flinging the white and the yolks after the flour.

'Okay, mate,' said Vance. 'We are all a team. That is the way it is. You cook. Neil operates the machine. Faith and Little Joe walk beside or behind the bastard. I have to come up with the loot to finance it. We all have a job to do, Yappy. Hope you understand that, mate. Now, please let me help you get some tucker together for the other men.'

'Help by getting some sort of bloody reception on the radio,' replied Yappy with a smile. 'Bloody thing never works for me.'

¶

At North Sydney, Colin was posting his letter to Lou. He hoped it would reach her and eventually he would get a reply.

In Brolga, Lou was heading off to an early start at the exchange.

Delores was lying in her bed in Brisbane wondering when and if Vance would call her.

Graham Sandler was lying in his bed thinking how on earth he would spend his allocated time in Brolga. He was also thinking about TC and how he should approach her.

Jake was in bed thinking, *I hate this bloody place. Just another day, hopefully another dollar.*

The Romeo brothers and their wives were luxuriating in their beds, knowing full well they had at least a couple of hours in which to have the staff serve their breakfasts before they had by law to fling open the doors of their hotel.

Doctor Jackson lay in his bed, staring at the ceiling, wondering, *What on earth did I let myself in for, coming to this place? Perhaps I'll see two, maybe three, patients today. If I'm lucky, that is.* He reached the conclusion that he must be crazy.

Louise was rousing. She had to work with Jess that morning. Neither Jack nor Bert had reprimanded her regarding the tray of glasses she had thrown at Claudia. Consequently, she knew her job was safe.

§

Claudia was asleep in the staff quarters. She had spent a restless night wondering if there was any hope of a future for her with Vance. She was in love and desperate for him to return from the mine.

Con and Lisa were rising from bed. They were both happy. Con had promised not to gamble for two weeks. Lisa knew very well that Con would gamble at the drop of a hat should the opportunity present itself. However, he had given her a thousand pounds to spend on whatever she wished. He had promised his love forever. She didn't care if he gambled or not. After all, apart from work, there was not much else for her darling husband to do in Brolga.

§

With radio station 4CL playing some song she did not know, TC. was at home sipping tea in the kitchen. She was thinking about the boss and the men, happy they had found opal, hoping the pharmacy would bring in enough money to keep things going. *It's all in the Lord's hands,* she thought as she stood to rinse her tea cup. *Think I'll get an early start today. Nothing else to do; it's a bit lonely here without Lou.*

They had not had to be separated so early in the morning for a long time. TC finished making her bed as the phone rang. It was Lou.

'Do you miss me, TC?' asked Lou.

'I was just thinking that,' replied TC.

'It's almost a year since I have worked here, TC,' stated Lou.

'For thirteen months, we have been able to gossip, laugh, or cry together in the mornings.'

'That time just flew by, TC,' continued Lou.

'I know, Lou,' replied TC matter-of-factly.

'Now that I'm back here in this joint looking at the switchboard, I wish we had stayed in Sydney,' said Lou.

'We both know we didn't fit in there, Lou. Sad, but it's true,' replied TC.

'At least we got to meet a lot of rock stars. Nobody else around here can say that,' said Lou. 'That is something we've got up on the snooty miss perfects in this town. See you on my break; a couple of lights on the board are flashing,' finished Lou.

TC put down the telephone receiver while thinking how lucky she was to have Lou as her friend. In reality, meeting Lou and then becoming so close was probably the reason fate had brought her to Brolga.

We are as close as sisters. Perhaps closer than some, thought TC as she placed the two thousand, four hundred and fifty pounds in the brown paper bag. Wish Lou and I could have had that much money when we went to Sydney. Bad timing, I guess. Anyway, don't think it would have made much difference.

¶

TC arrived at the pharmacy as Con was opening the café door at 7 a.m.

'You're early, TC,' called Con from across the street. 'Come over and have some breakfast. I insist.' TC walked across to the café.

'I'm early because Lou started back at the exchange on daybreak shift, and I miss her,' said TC with a sigh.

'I know. Old Jordan says you and his daughter are like Siamese twins, joined at the hip,' replied Con with a laugh. 'Now come in. Have some tea and toast, at least. Lisa will like to chat with you. She doesn't like talking to too many people in this town. You and Lou are the chosen few.'

'Thank you, Con. You always make us feel special,' said TC as she followed him into the café.

'When is Vance coming back, luv?' asked Con over his shoulder.

'I don't know. Probably when they run out of cigarettes and tobacco or food,' replied TC to Con's back as he led the way through the café to the kitchen where Lisa was seated at a small table for two located in a corner of the huge kitchen. Lisa, who was holding a cup of coffee in one hand and flicking through a fashion magazine with the other, was delighted to see TC.

'Sit down, darling,' beamed Lisa. 'Would you like some breakfast?'

'No, thank you, Lisa. I had tea and a piece of toast at home with Lou before she went to work.'

'Look at this. Isn't it lovely?' said Lisa, pointing to a beautiful, white evening gown with seed pearls bordering the scooped neckline. 'I love this fashion magazine, and I love this gown.'

'It's beautiful, Lisa,' agreed TC as she thought, *Wish Lou and I could make something as lovely as that.*

'I don't know why I keep buying clothes. Nowhere here to wear them, but I keep buying them, anyway. They come in handy when I take my occasional vacation in Greece,' laughed Lisa with a shrug of her shoulders before looking around to make certain Con was not in the kitchen, then whispering, 'Con gave me a thousand pounds, and I am going to spend it on clothes. Naughty, aren't I, TC?' whispered Lisa with a wink and a mischievous smile. TC said nothing, just giggled quietly as she winked back at Lisa.

'Time for me to go,' said TC after Lisa flicked over the last page of the magazine.

'I'll walk you to the door,' said Lisa, as they both stood up and pushed their chairs under the table. 'By the way, TC, I think Constable Graham likes you,' said Lisa quietly with a mischievous smile as she tugged lightly on TC's pony tail.

'Why do you think that?' asked TC curiously.

'By the way he looked at you last night, TC,' replied Lisa, with a broad smile. 'I'm getting old. I know these things.' Lisa and TC were halfway through the café, walking towards the door when Graham Sandler came through the front door.

Good Lord, thought TC. *He looks as gorgeous in blue jeans and a T-shirt as he did in his uniform.* She wished she could disappear, especially after what Lisa had just told her.

'We were just talking about you, Constable Graham,' greeted Lisa with a beaming smile. Graham was momentarily taken aback with surprise when he saw TC with Lisa walking towards him.

'I hope it was all good,' replied Graham with his incredible smile.

'Well, let me tell you we did not say anything bad,' teased Lisa.

'Just your luck, Constable Graham. TC is leaving as you arrive,' said Con from behind the counter where he was scrubbing a large ice cream can. Both Lisa and Con laughed as TC smiled. Graham forced himself to smile as he thought, *Why the bloody hell didn't I get here earlier?*

'I have to open up, so I'll see you all later,' said TC with a smile as she left the café.

'You like her, don't you, Constable Graham?' said Lisa as her husband and Graham along with herself watched TC walk across the street and open the pharmacy door.

'I think you are correct, Lisa,' replied Graham quietly.

'My wife is always right,' laughed Con from behind the counter.

¶

In the dispensary, TC was busy placing the two thousand, four hundred and fifty pounds into envelopes, which she enclosed in a cloth bank bag. When she finished, she folded the bank bag around the envelopes, then secured the folded bag with two thick rubber bands, and pulled out the bottom drawer of the filing cabinet, and let the bag fall onto the floor beneath before locking the drawer and taping the key to the bottom of the top filing cabinet drawer. TC then proceeded to sweep and mop the floors. With the floors, finished she decided to collect the mail.

¶

Graham Sandler was standing at the counter in the café talking to Con, yet watching the pharmacy. As predicted by Con and Lisa, he now saw TC close the pharmacy door and turn towards the post office.

'Go on, mate. This is your chance,' urged Con.

Graham took a deep breath, then walked onto the footpath and called out to TC. 'I'm going that way. I'll walk with you.' TC nodded as she crossed the street to the café. Carmel, who was standing out front of her shop, thought, *Good. TC might wake Jake up to himself. Having a bit of competition will do him good.*

'So, TC, what brought you to Brolga?' asked Graham.

'Fate, I think. My old school friend and I decided to come to the end of the line.'

'You are not wrong about that,' chuckled Graham. 'Who did you come here with, TC?' enquired Graham with interest.

'Sam. She works in the house at the Empire. We seemed to have drifted apart from almost the moment we arrived here,' replied TC sadly as they arrived at the post office corner. I had best collect the mail and get back to the pharmacy,' said TC. 'Nice talking to you.'

'Same here, TC.' Replied Graham as he turned towards the police station. He was furious with himself for wasting the few precious minutes by asking with whom she had come to Brolga. He already knew that. The sergeant had told him about Sam, Brad Lester, and the drama Sam caused in the pharmacy.

¶

When TC returned to the pharmacy, Jake was sitting in his car waiting for her. He got out of his car and slammed the door.

'What were you doing talking to the cop?' he demanded.

'That is none of your business, Jake,' snapped TC as she flung open the door and stormed inside. You are not my father, and you are not the boss. Don't act as if you own me, Jake, because you don't,' said TC angrily as Jake followed her.

'I'm not trying to own you, TC. I am just looking out for you.'

TC threw the mail on the dispensary desk, then turned to face Jake. She was furious. Jake knew because she had both hands on her hips a-la her pub window stance.

'Jake Carmichael, why don't you and the boss get together, wrap me in cotton wool, enclose me in glass, and put me on a shelf? That way neither of you will need to worry about looking out for me. You will be in total control. It is perfectly all right for the boss, who is a married man with children, by the way, to parade his sluts through here while I sit on the Seat of Knowledge for hours, watching for the front door to open so I can return. It is all right for you to spend half your life doing God-knows-what down by the creek with the poor nurses. You use them, Jake.' Jake started to open his mouth to speak. 'Be quiet, Jake. I have not finished,' commanded TC in a controlled tone of voice and determination expressed on her face. 'You are both hypocritical, drunken, gambling, womanising, bullshit artists.'

'That is not fair to Vance. He's quit the grog,' interjected Jake.

'Well, then, he is an adulterous, hypocritical, gambling, womanising bullshit artist,' snarled TC. 'Lou and I lead the life of nuns! Lou's own father and mother credit her with being sensible. They allow her to make her own decisions because they know she will make the right ones. You and the boss must think I'm an idiot. At the rate you two are 'looking out for me,' I'll probably end up as a nun.

'Now, leave me alone, Jake. I'm responsible enough to look after this place. Surely that is a sign that I am not stupid. Not completely, anyway.

I must be slightly stupid because I'm talking to you.'

The telephone rang. Before TC picked up the receiver, she said firmly, 'Leave NOW, Jake!'

TC breathed deeply, put the phone to her ear, and spoke with as much normalcy as she could possibly muster.

§

'Good morning. Brolga Pharmacy.'

She knew it would be Delores.

'TC, is Vance back in town yet?'

'No, Mrs Callahan. I don't know when he'll be back.'

'Have you heard from him?'

'He sent Yappy in for supplies a few days ago.'

'He sent Yappy into town? Vance must be out of his mind.'

'No, Mrs Callahan. Yappy was fine.'

'Good. I'll call tomorrow. Should Vance show up, please ask him to call me.'

Click. Delores was gone.

'Precise and to the point, as usual, Mrs Callahan,' muttered TC to herself as she began filing gaps on the shelves.

§

As she did so, Jake pulled his car to a screeching halt down by the creek, where he began chain-smoking, soul-searching, and mulling over what TC had said.

§

At the mine, Vance and the men were enjoying smoko.

'You've outdone yourself, Yappy. These bloody pancakes are bloody beautiful,' said Faith.

'So are the scones, mate. Even my poor old mum couldn't do better than these. They are bloody great,' said Neil.

'Good, all right, Yappy,' from Little Joe.

'Yappy sure is a great cook,' added Vance.

'Stop sucking up to a man, you mob of bastards,' snapped Yappy. 'If you bloody well don't, the next feed I serve you will be laced with bloody arsenic.'

'You wouldn't do that to us, Yappy,' teased Vance.

'Oh, yes, I bloody well would do. Don't say you weren't warned. Now, shut up, all of you.'

Yappy was actually happy because that morning Vance had managed to get radio reception after he had fiddled for an hour or so with the copper, the so-called antenna attached to the back of the radio running through the gap between the roof and wall of the kitchen and attached to a tree about ten yards away. When Vance had finally achieved the connection successfully, Yappy clapped his hands and did his usual little jig.

'They can call you a mad bloody chemist, Vance, but I sure will vote for you as a magnificent bloody radio technician. I've been trying to get some response from that thing for months,' said Yappy excitedly as he continued clapping and jigging. 'Now I can listen to the races on Saturdays.'

After smoko, Vance, Neil, Faith, and Little Joe moved outside as usual to finish their coffees, smoke, and have a yarn. The men were disappointed. They had felt so confident when they went to work in the morning; now they felt flat and disillusioned.

'Don't know why we bothered to skip breakfast,' said Faith, exhaling smoke as he starred into space.

'Yeah, mate, I thought we were on a roll,' said Neil, hunched forward on his chair with both elbows on his knees as he gazed at the ground with his left hand cupping his chin and the side of his face while he took an occasional puff from the rollie he held in his right.

Little Joe said nothing, just alternated between a sip from his coffee mug and a drag on his cigarette.

Vance, although disappointed they had not found any boulders that morning, was more disappointed for his men.

§

'Listen, men, don't be so down unless you want Yappy to come out here and start crying,' said Vance. Begrudgingly, Neil and Faith made a feeble attempt at a smile. Little Joe didn't even try.

I'd best try another tack, thought Vance. 'The bottom line is, men, we know the opal is there. All we have to do is find it. We are not going to find it sitting around here feeling sorry for ourselves.'

'That is what I was thinking, Boss,' said Little Joe as he stood up and threw the dregs of his coffee on the ground.

'If you feel strongly enough about it to give an opinion, Little Joe, I suppose we had best get back to work,' said Neil matter-of-factly.

'I agree,' said Faith. 'We'll find those bloody boulders or die trying.'

'Don't do that. I can't afford to bury you,' laughed Vance.

§

Less than five minutes later Yappy and Vance heard the machine start up.

'Give me a haircut, will you Yappy?' asked Vance.

'You haven't got much bloody hair,' replied Yappy.

'Get rid of this, Yappy, this long stuff I sweep across my balding top. It drives me mad. It's always flying out to one side. I've wanted to get rid of it for ages, but Delores doesn't want me to bear a balding head to the world. I don't know why she worries about it. We hardly ever see each other.'

'Oh, Vance, I don't know. What if I make a bloody mess of it?' whined Yappy.

'You cut Neil and Faith's hair. They look all right,' replied Vance.

'Cut my own, too, Vance. Do you think mine looks all right, as well?' asked Yappy seriously. Vance burst into gales of laughter.

'Oh, yes, Yappy. Yours looks even better than theirs. Now get the damned scissors and cut my hair.'

'All right, all right, Vance. I just hope I don't make a mess of it,' said Yappy as he wondered why Vance was laughing.

'Look at it this way, Yappy. If you make a mess of it, you can shave it all off like Little Joe does his.'

'Oh, no, Vance, I don't think that would suit you,' said Yappy with utmost concern as Vance removed his shirt. Vance began laughing again. 'What's bloody funny, Vance?' asked Yappy as he tentatively ran the comb through to the end of the long piece of Vance's hair.

'Nothing, Yappy. Just cut my hair,' replied Vance with a broad smile.

'You must be bloody mad, then. That mob in Brolga must be right. Nobody laughs at nothing!' mumbled Yappy. 'Don't suppose any bastard apart from the men and I will have to look at it if I do make a bloody mess of it,' continued Yappy matter-of-factly as he made the first cut. Yappy snipped away in silence. When he had finished, he stood back and scrutinised his work before collecting his shaving mirror, which he handed to Vance.

'What do you think, Vance?' asked Yappy anxiously as Vance pretended to care.

'Very, very good job, Yappy. How much do I owe you, miss?' said Vance as he handed the shaving mirror back to Yappy.

'Smart bloody bastard, aren't you, Callahan. Don't bloody well call me "Miss",' snapped Yappy as he snatched the mirror from Vance.

'Sorry, Yappy, mate,' said Vance with an expression of mock sincerity on his face.

'Go take a shower, you smart mongrel,' directed Yappy. 'Otherwise you'll get itchy.'

'All right, Boss,' smiled Vance as he quickly stood up and went directly to the shower.

'Smart bloody mongrel, fancy calling me "Miss",' muttered Yappy as he swept Vance's hair into a metal dustpan.

Vance was in the shower telling himself how much he enjoyed teasing Yappy. He knew he shouldn't bait the poor little bugger so. He couldn't help himself. He thought the world of little Yappy, who was honesty and integrity personified. The only time poor little Yappy went off the rails was occasionally when something would spark memories of his lost love. That was not too often; as a matter of fact, rarely. *I know how the poor man feels,* thought Vance as Anna flashed into his mind.

When Vance joined Yappy in the kitchen, Up on the Roof Is Peaceful as Can Be was sounding from the radio.

'I climbed onto the roof of a pub in Longreach once,' said Yappy matter-of-factly. 'Of course, a man was as drunk as fifteen bastards. Just when I was about to jump, I fell backwards onto the roof and passed out. When I woke up next day, the sun was blazing, my head was aching something bloody terrible, my throat was dry as a bloody bone, and I wondered where the hell I was. Caused quite a commotion, I did. Still don't know how the bloody hell I got up there.

Vance was silently intrigued as he endeavoured to imagine how much Yappy must have been hurting when he found his way to the roof of a pub with the intention of jumping off. Vance wanted to tell Yappy that he understood because he, too, had lost the woman he loved. Instead, he reached for a Craven A, lit it, then inhaled before saying, 'Well, Yappy, I'm glad you fell asleep when you did; otherwise, we would have missed out on all your wonderful cooking, not to mention your great haircuts.'

'Smart bastard, can't help yourself, can you?' said Yappy with a slight grin. Vance stood up, patted Yappy on the shoulder, then walked outside.

'I'll go see what's happening with the men, Yappy. Be back soon.'

'Find out what time they want to eat,' called Yappy as he went about cleaning up after the smoko mess in the kitchen.

¶

Back in Brolga as always on weekdays, the radio was announcing it was ten o'clock and the Commonwealth Bank was open for business at the precise moment that Bert and Jack Romeo opened the pub doors.

'Few more cars than usual around today, Jess,' said Jack Romeo as he made his morning inspection of the Empire Bar.

'Yes, Jack, there's a C.W.A meeting on. A lot of the cow cockies' wives will go to that,' replied Jess matter-of-factly.

'Hope they brought their husbands with them,' said Jack as he left the bar.

'Old bugger never thinks of anything but bloody money,' said Louise, who had purposely busied herself scrubbing a fridge at the far end of the bar when Jack was talking to Jess.

'You mind your manners, Louise,' warned Jess. 'You are lucky you still have a job. I know why you threw the glasses at Claudia.'

'Is that so?' replied Louise angrily. 'You weren't here!'

'I know everything that happens in this joint, Louise. I also know why things happen. Also, please mind your tone of voice when you are speaking to me. I am older and hopefully wiser than you. I suggest you show me a little respect. If you don't, I promise you, I shall make things tough for you tonight.'

Old bitch, thought Louise as she smiled at Jess. 'Sorry, Jess. I'll try to keep me tongue under control.'

'Good,' replied Jess with a nod of her head.

TC was busy at the pharmacy. She had already served half dozen or so customers. She was relieved that only two of them were uppity; the rest were normal, friendly, down-to-earth women whose husbands' money and social standing had not gone to their heads. Probably, as Jess had always said, 'because they were born to it.'

Lou was at the telephone exchange listening to an interesting conversation concerning Vance. The conversation was between a Brolga stock and station agent and another man whose brother was obviously an opal miner in South Australia.

'So that bastard has struck opal? I'll tell my brother as soon as we finish talking. Unbelievable! Trust a bloody drunken asshole like him to strike it lucky. Get ready for an invasion, mate. Once word gets around, they'll come from everywhere.'

Lou had desperately wanted to interrupt to tell the man, whomever he was, that Vance had given up the booze and that he definitely was not an asshole Of course, she could not say a word. Her job would be gone.

Jake phoned TC late in the morning after returning from the sulking binge down by the creek.

'You are right. Okay?' Jake almost yelled before immediately hanging up.

'I know, Jake,' replied TC to herself. Doctor Jackson called almost immediately after Jake.

'TC, I have seen only one patient this morning. For some unknown reason to me, I have to see a heap of people after two.'

'That's because there is a Country Women's Association meeting today. A lot of people off the properties are in town,' replied TC.

'I see. That explains it,' said an enlightened Doctor Jackson. 'I was so concerned a plague had hit the place,' he added ever so seriously. TC stifled a laugh before replying.

'That would certainly put Brolga on the map, Doctor Jackson.'

'TC, I'm not certain what time I'll be finished with my last patient. I was wondering if you would mind staying back late if necessary?'

'Not at all,' replied TC while thinking, *Wait until you have been here for a while, Dr Jackson; then you will realise that I am frequently here very late.*

'All right, TC. I shall call you when my last patient has left,' said Doctor Jackson. 'Then, if necessary, I shall come to the pharmacy to help you with the prescriptions if you are bogged down.'

'That's fine, Dr. Jackson,' replied TC. 'I'll hear from you later.'

I wonder if the Doctor ever laughs, thought TC as she put down the telephone.

Claudia came into the Pharmacy a few minutes before siren time. Claudia was wearing one of her usual slightly flared skirt-style dresses with a wide belt at the waist, high-heeled shoes, and tons of make-up, and her hair piled on the top of her head.

'Is Vance back?' she demanded.

Here we go again, thought TC before replying, 'Sorry, he's not back in town yet.'

'Are you sure?' questioned Claudia with more than a little arrogance in her voice.

'If Mr Callahan is back in town, I have not seen him,' replied TC. 'Sorry. I am closing for lunch now,' continued TC as the siren sounded.

'Tell him Claudia wants him to contact her as soon as you see him,' commanded Claudia as TC held the door partly open, waiting for her to leave.

Mr Callahan, you sure can pick them. This one is perhaps worse than Louise, thought TC as she deliberated over whether or not she was hungry. She decided to wait for Lou, who would be there in an hour. She would use that hour to replenish the gaps on the shelves caused by the morning's rush. TC wondered what Vance and the men were doing.

¶

Little Joe and Faith were in the kitchen eating their lunch as they listened to Yappy prattle on. Vance and Neil were in deep conversation as they sat outside the kitchen. They were discussing whether or not they were once again looking in the wrong direction.

'Bloody hell, Boss. It's feast or bloody famine with the stuff. In all the months of every day working and hoping, all we found was a dozen or so boulders with pale blue colour; then suddenly we came across a heap with decent colour. At least it looks like pretty colour from where you chipped off the ends,' said Neil. 'All we found today was a few of those little potato-sized rocks. And we don't know if there is any colour in them or not,' continued Neil.

'Neil, I don't particularly want to chip the ends off those. They are too small and if they do contain colour, I might wreck it,' said Vance. 'My gut feeling tells me we should carry on as we are for a while, at least for a couple more weeks. We have been patient this long, so another week or two won't hurt. Until we strike the motherload, I honestly do not believe we can expect to find opal all day, every day.'

'That's just it, Boss. We thought we had struck the motherload,' replied Neil.

'Maybe we have. Perhaps we are on the edge of it,' reasoned Vance.

'The boys and I feel like going to town. We want to see civilisation,' replied Neil. 'We are pissed off at the moment.'

Holy hell, thought Vance, 'if they go to town, that will be the end of everything. Apart from that, I don't have the money to pay them.'

'I understand you are all disappointed, Neil,' said Vance. 'Summer is about six weeks away. What say you and the men hang in until then? Maybe close down the operation just before Christmas and come back towards the end of February?'

Neil looked Vance directly in the eyes.

'One thing is for certain, mate, we are definitely not spending another bloody summer out here. It's just too damned hot. Nearly killed us last year. It's too bloody hot already.'

'That was my mistake, Neil,' apologised Vance. 'I just didn't think. I thought once I had you men well and out here, it was best to stay here rather than go through the drying-out process all over again.' Neil stood up and laughed as he looked at Vance.

'Tell you what, Boss. You had best book a couple of rooms at the Majestic towards the end of February because I can guarantee there will be some drying out to be done.'

'All right, mate. I will have to warn Yappy, your baby sitter,' replied Vance with a laugh more of relief than joviality.

'It's a deal,' said Neil. 'Now, let's go eat what the babysitter has prepared for lunch.'

Lou arrived at the pharmacy a few minutes after two. She was carrying a loaf of bread.

'Well, this is a start,' she said as she placed the bread on the dispensary desk. 'I'll go to the grocery shop later.'

'How was your first day back at the gossip house?' asked TC.

'Piece of cake until I got cheesed off because I heard some guy running Vance down,' replied Lou seriously.

'Well, Lou, perhaps you shouldn't listen in. Sooner or later you are bound to hear something that will upset you,' said TC matter-of-factly.

'I know, TC. It's simply that the job is so damned monotonous without listening to other people banter. By the way, I invited Constable Graham to visit us tonight.'

'Lou, you could have asked me first!' replied a surprised TC. 'When did you do that?'

'He was posting some mail when I left work. We talked for a minute or two. He's lonely here, so I invited him to our place tonight around seven-thirty. I'm going to get us a shake. It's my turn to shout,' added Lou as she turned and headed for Con's.

The telephone rang. TC spoke the usual greeting.

A masculine voice asked, 'Is Vance Callahan there?'

'No, Mr Callahan is out of town,' replied TC.

'Look, luv, I'm an opal miner in Coober Pedy. Ask him to call me when he's got time. Here is my number.'

'Do you want to leave your name, sir?' asked TC.

'No!' The man hung up.

Ladies from the CWA meeting began coming in. Four came at once; one of them had a prescription from Doctor Jackson.

That would be right; they all come at once, thought TC as she counted tablets into a pill bottle. Lou returned as she was typing the label.

'Just as well you've got me for a friend,' whispered Lou as she put the milkshakes on the desk before returning inside to chat to the ladies and help out wherever she could. The rush on general cosmetics and other lines along with a few more prescriptions was over in an hour or so.

TC noted that Doctor Jackson's scripts were presented approximately every twenty-five minutes.

He's a pretty fast worker, she thought. *However, judging by the prescriptions, no one is too sick.*

Lou went off to the grocery shop, then home. Doctor Jackson phoned right on six o'clock.

'TC, sorry to keep you late. For whom was the last prescription you filled?' TC told him. There was a brief silence before he said, 'That's it, then, TC. Thank you very much. Obviously, Vance is not back yet? I may pop in to say hello tomorrow. Thank you, TC.'

'Any time, Doctor Jackson. Goodnight,' replied TC. *Poor Doctor Jackson is most likely lonely too,* thought TC as she collected her keys and switched off the lights. *Lord only knows in which part of Brolga society he will fit.*

⁊

At camp Vance and the men were about to have their evening meal.

'Hope you skipped the arsenic flavouring, Yappy,' said Neil jovially.

'Don't bloody start! That goes for all of you mongrels,' replied Yappy as he finished mashing potatoes.

'Yappy, mate, don't be like that! You know we all love you, Yappy,' said Faith.

'We love your cooking, too, Yappy,' said Neil.

'I already bloody told you not to start. You bloody bastards never let a chance go by. A man's sick of it. Now eat your bloody tucker and leave a man alone,' retaliated Yappy as he slammed cooking utensils onto the bench.

Little Joe was silent as almost always. He was thinking, *Why do they tease Little Yappy all the time? He's a good man. If I was Yappy, I would deck them. Yappy has a lot more patience and tolerance that I do, that is for certain. Never mind, it's none of my business.*

Vance waited silently until the others had helped themselves to food and sat down to eat before he put food on his plate and joined them at the table.

'So how are you feeling, men?'

'Better than we did at lunch time,' replied Faith. 'Neil told us we've only got nine weeks, then we are out of here for a couple of months.'

'First I bloody heard of it,' interjected Yappy. 'Still, I'm always the last to know any bloody thing around here.'

'Oh, come on, Yappy, mate. I was going to tell you in the morning,' said Vance. 'I wanted to wait until Faith and Little Joe told me what they thought of the plan.'

'Get stuffed, all of you,' replied Yappy quietly. 'That includes you, Vance. I'm going to bed,' as he threw down the tea towel he had been using and left the kitchen.

'Oh, shit, I sure as hell put my foot in my bloody mouth,' said Faith.

'He'll get over it,' said Neil.

'I don't blame him,' said Little Joe, who stood up, put his plate, knife, and fork in the dishwashing tub, poured himself a mug of coffee, then went outside to have a smoke.

'I feel like crap,' said Neil.

'Not your fault, Neil. I should have mentioned it to him,' said Vance. 'I'll fix it in the morning.'

'I still feel like bloody crap,' said Faith.

'You men go ahead. I'll clean up in here,' said Vance. *No wonder Faith feels like crap. I feel the same,* thought Vance as he performed Yappy's usual after-dinner chores. *I should have told the poor little bugger. I was too damned busy worrying about the others.*

¶

The police sergeant dropped Graham Sandler off at the girls' house at exactly seven-thirty.

'I'll pick you up after I've done the last round after the pubs close,' said the sergeant.

'I might not still be here, Sarge,' replied Graham.

'Easy. If you are still here, leave the verandah light on,' said the sergeant.

'Thanks, Sarge. I feel like a kid being dropped off at school by his dad,' laughed Graham.

'All I did was give you a lift, mate,' replied the sergeant. 'Apart from that, I have to know where you are so I can contact you if there is any trouble. Have a good time. It's your night off. Also stop being so bloody nervous. Lou and TC won't hurt you. Now, go get in there before your hair turns grey.'

Lou opened the front door as Graham closed the gate behind him.

'So, it is you,' said Lou. 'We could hear a car motor running.'

'Hello, Lou. The sergeant dropped me off,' replied Graham. 'The sergeant gave me a lift. He'll pick me up after he sees the pub's closed, that is, if you and TC haven't turfed me out by then.'

'I doubt that, Constable Graham,' said Lou with a laugh as she closed the door behind them and led the way to the dining room.

'Where's TC?' asked Graham.

'She's talking on the telephone,' replied Lou, 'She won't be long.' Graham handed Lou a thick, brown- paper bag containing six small bottles of Coke.

'I don't drink alcohol. I hope you and TC don't think I'm square.'

'If you are, we are,' replied Lou with a broad smile. 'We'll put some music on as soon as TC gets off the phone.' TC emerged from the lounge room.

'Hello, Graham. Nice to see you again. Auntie Flo says hello, too, Lou. What kind of music do you like, Graham?'

'Anything except opera,' replied Graham with a shrug of his shoulders and his million-dollar smile.

'You'll fit in just fine here,' said Lou. 'I'll put on that various-artists LP we bought in Sydney.'

As Lou was putting the record on the stereo, she called, 'Graham doesn't drink booze, TC.'

'What a relief and what a change from the other men who visit us,' said TC as Fats Domino began singing, I Want To Walk You Home.

'Do you have a lot of male visitors?' asked Graham in surprise.

'Only Vance and Jake,' answered Lou from the lounge room door.

'I see,' said a relieved Graham with a sigh. His police-trained mind had fleetingly and disbelievingly thought the two girls were on the game. He reprimanded himself silently. 'Bloody idiot. Look at them. Stop being a cop for a few hours.'

'How is this music, Constable Graham?' asked Lou.

'Great, Lou,' replied Graham with a smile. 'Lou, please, when I'm off duty, don't call me Constable Graham. Just Graham will be fine; otherwise, I'll think I'm on duty all of the time.'

'That works for me, Graham,' said Lou.

'We usually sit on the front stairs and listen to the music, have a Coke, and talk,' said TC. 'Except in winter time or during dust storms, that is.'

'Otherwise, we can play Scrabble or Monopoly. We bought the games in Sydney,' said Lou.

'I'll opt for a Coke and a talk on the front steps,' said Graham with a wink and a smile.

'You sure are beautiful, Graham,' said Lou. Graham was noticeably embarrassed as his face turned red.

'I'll get the Cokes,' said TC.

Graham regained his composure as TC handed him a bottle. 'Lou, you sure know how to embarrass a man.'

'Lou's like that, Graham,' said TC. 'I tell her she gets it from her dad.' They all laughed as they perched themselves on the stairs.

'So, this is where you hang out. It's nice, 'said Graham.

'Yes, lovely view of the truck depot across the road,' said Lou sarcastically.

'Well, it sure beats sitting by myself in my room,' said Graham. 'My room is so tiny and compact, I sometimes feel as if I'm living in a shoe box. That's why I like it here; it's open.'

'It's exciting, all right,' said Lou. 'Sometimes we even see a car or two drive past.'

'Don't forget the nights before mail days,' said TC seriously.

'Oh, yes, Graham, I forgot about that,' said Lou. 'Those are very exciting experiences. We get to watch the truckies across the road load their trucks as well as see the occasional car drive by.' Graham was in fits of laughter.

'Yes, Graham, you really hit the jackpot when you got stationed in Brolga,' said TC.

'Just one thrill after another,' added Lou. Johnny O'Keefe came on singing, Move, Baby, Move.

'We met him in Sydney, Graham,' said Lou.

'Who?' asked Graham.

'Johnny O'Keefe. He's singing now.'

'I know who it is,' replied Graham. 'How did you meet him?'

'We didn't only meet him,' replied Lou. 'We met a lot of rock stars. I worked at a hotel in Sydney. The owner's son took TC and me to a lot of shows and parties. He was nice to us.'

'That must have been exciting,' said Graham.

'No, not really,' replied Lou and TC in unison.

'Why not?' asked Graham.

'Far too boring for us, Graham,' replied Lou.

'Yes, we missed the go, go, go routine of life in Brolga,' said TC.

'You have to be joking,' said Graham in surprise.

'It's simple, Graham. Lou and I did not merge too well with the Sydney-siders of our generation. Not the ones we met. Too wild for us!'

'I can understand that,' nodded Graham. 'Anyway, I'm glad you didn't merge. If you had, I wouldn't be sitting on these stairs talking to you.'

Both Lou and TC looked at Graham. They could see by the expression on his face that he was absolutely sincere.

'You are not enjoying being in Brolga, are you, Graham?' asked TC.

'Until tonight the only people I have held a real conversation with are the sergeant and his wife, Lisa and Con, and occasionally the Romeo brothers and Carmel at the theatre.'

'Well, that has changed now because you have us,' said Lou. 'I'll get us another Coke.'

'How old are you, TC?' asked Graham after Lou went to fetch the Cokes.

'Lou's Dad always says a gentleman never asks a lady her age,' replied TC with a smile.

'Seriously, TC. How old are you?' repeated Graham seriously.

'Eighteen plus a few months. I lied about my age when I came here. I told people I was eighteen while in fact I was only sixteen. I think Jess told my boss. We don't discuss it.'

'Is that because you needed to be eighteen to work in the bar at the Empire?'

'Yes,' replied TC in surprise. 'I didn't last there very long.'

'Not even a full week.'

'Now, how come you know about that?'

'TC, I know just about everything about you since the day you set foot on Brolga soil,' replied Graham seriously. 'I asked the sergeant about you.'

'Why?'

'Here we go, lady and gentleman,' said Lou as she returned with the Cokes. 'The King is about to sing.' Sure enough, Elvis' voice came blasting from the stereo, singing, Oh, Baby, Won't You Be My Loving Teddy Bear.

'Anytime, Elvis darling,' said Lou. 'We love him, don't we, TC?'

'Why should we be different from every other girl in the world, Lou?' replied TC with a laugh. 'Of course, we love him.'

'I just love the way he sings and the way he looks so gorgeous with his guitar,' said Lou excitedly.

'What do you think of guitar players, TC?' asked Graham.

TC smiled, then thought for a moment before replying.

'I suppose I find myself drawn to the guitar-playing singers, something magnetic about them. To me the guitar men are sexy.'

'You can say that again,' said Lou. 'They are sexy, all right. Especially the King.'

Graham smiled as he thought to himself, *Well, that's one point I've got up my sleeve.*

❡

Time passed quickly as they chatted, laughed a lot, and listened to the music. Around eleven o'clock, they saw the police car come around the corner.

'There's my lift. Thanks for inviting me, Lou. Thanks for your hospitality, both of you. I'm on duty tomorrow night. Perhaps I'll cruise by and wave to you.'

The girls watched the police car until it disappeared from view.

'What do you think of him, TC?' asked Lou.

'I think he's very nice,' replied TC. 'A big change from Jake. Yes, I like him. What do you think of him?'

'I think he's gorgeous. I also think he's wrapped in you,' answered Lou.

TC stood up and stretched. 'Let's go to bed, Lou. Big day tomorrow with mail orders.'

'I'll help you after I knock off at the exchange,' replied Lou.

¶

As the girls climbed into their beds, the police sergeant and Graham bid each other good night, and once again the tiny town of Brolga was safely tucked in for the night.

¶

Vance got out of his bunk when he heard Yappy moving around. After the usual morning of teeth brushing, etc., he joined Yappy in the kitchen.

'Good morning, Yappy. I thought you'd have the radio on.'

'Stuff the radio, Vance,' replied Yappy. 'I considered not doing breakfast today. I'm shut out of everything else that goes on around here, so I may as well be shut out of the bloody kitchen, as well.'

'Oh, come on, Yappy,' replied Vance seriously. 'I spoke to Neil yesterday. I put the proposition to him because they were all feeling down in the dumps. The only excuse I have for not mentioning the plan to you is because I was worried about them and how disappointed they are about not finding more boulders. I'm sorry, Yappy, I really am.'

'Sure, Vance, until next time!' replied Yappy. 'The way I feel now I won't be coming back after the break. Perhaps you should start looking around for a new cook and camp joke.'

Vance reached for his cigarette packet as he always did when stalling for a little time in which to come up with the right words. He stared into space as he lit his cigarette, took a deep drag, then slowly exhaled.

'We both know I won't find another cook like you, Yappy. We know that because there is only one Yappy. I feel safe in speaking for the men as well as myself. You are the touchstone of this outfit, Yappy. I know we all tease you; that is because we know you will react and we love the way you react. We would all hate to lose you, Yappy.'

'We'll see, Vance,' replied Yappy seriously. 'Pour yourself a cup of coffee and take it outside while I get breakfast.'

Vance breathed a sigh of relief as he heard the radio come to life a few seconds after he left the kitchen.

The bond of closeness between Neil, Faith, Little Joe, and Yappy was so strong that if one of them was down, the rest were down with him. Due to Yappy's silence and body language, hardly a word was spoken at breakfast or when they moved outside for their usual routine of coffee and rollies. Apart from the obligatory good-morning greeting to the men, Vance had also remained silent, deep in thought most of the time.

Until today he had not realised just how strong this bond was of brotherhood between the men. They were much more than just mates who got on the grog together. They were true friends. What hurt one hurt the others. If one was happy, they would all be happy; and if one was sad, they would all be sad. From here on in, he would see these real men in a different perspective than that of the past.

Neil broke the silence. 'Let's go find some rocks.'

'We hope so,' replied Faith. Little Joe said nothing.

As Vance watched them walk slowly towards the hill, he thought, *I hope you find some rocks, too, Neil. Might put you all in brighter spirits as well as help get the back of the ute filled so I can get back to town and concentrate on what we do next. I can't go before the ute is full because I was stupid enough to say I wouldn't.*

❡

In Brolga life went on. Just another day as the Seat of Knowledge patrons would frequently say.

Lou called TC around eight-thirty.

67

'TC, don't think you'll need my help this afternoon.'

Why?' asked TC.

'Because, you fool, most of your mail-order customers shopped yesterday when they were in town for the CWA meeting.'

'I am a fool, Lou,' laughed TC. 'I didn't think of that. I was beginning to wonder why the phone hadn't been ringing.'

'See you after I finish work,' said Lou.

Delores called as usual at nine o'clock.

'Is Vance back yet, TC?'

'No, Mrs Callahan.'

'What on earth is he doing out there?'

'I heard they are finding opal, Mrs Callahan.'

'Who told you, TC?'

'Yappy told me when he was in town.'

'Why didn't you tell me before?'

TC wanted to reply, 'Because you didn't give me a chance!' Instead, she said, 'I don't know. I'm sorry, Mrs Callahan.'

'All right, tell him to call me the moment you see him.' Click. Delores was gone again.

TC put down the telephone, thinking, *If the boss didn't rely on me so much, I'd quit.*

In Brisbane, Delores was thinking, *Stupid little bitch! I hope Vance calls me soon. I want to go back to Brolga.*

Doctor Jackson arrived at the pharmacy a little while later.

'Thank you for yesterday, TC,' he said as TC made him a cup of coffee.

'No problem, Doctor Jackson. Sometimes I'm here until all hours of the morning. Nothing much else to do, so I may as well be working.'

'Yes, TC, Brolga is certainly a quiet little town,' replied the Doctor. 'I must say, it's quite a culture shock after the hustle and bustle of a big city.'

'You'll get used to it, Doctor Jackson. Everyone does,' said TC.

'Don't suppose you know when Vance is coming back to town,' asked Doctor Jackson. TC shook her head.

'Sorry. I don't know. They have found opal with colour at last, so

I can only guess he's staying at the mine because of that.' They sat in silence momentarily.

'You had a rush of patients yesterday, Doctor Jackson,' said TC just for something to say. The Doctor took a sip of his coffee before replying;

'TC, some of the patients I saw yesterday had nothing wrong with them. Do you think it's possible they simply wanted to check me out?' Doctor Jackson had spoken so seriously that TC didn't dare laugh.

'Believe me, Doctor Jackson, in Brolga anything is possible. You are the first permanently based doctor Brolga has ever had, so, of course, people are curious. I'm uncertain anyone would go to those lengths to check you out. Still, as my boss says, "Never be surprised by anything that happens around here".'

'I'll have to keep Vance's advice in mind,' said Doctor Jackson, seriously as usual. 'Thank you for the coffee, TC.'

Poor Doctor Jackson is sure in for a few shocks, thought TC as she watched him leave.

By siren time, TC realised Lou was right. Only a handful of phone orders came in for the mail truck. There were no prescriptions, so obviously Doctor Jackson had not seen any patients in the morning. TC had to admit to herself that she missed the boss coming and going. Forget the fact that they had a fight every other day, she missed him. She felt lonely with nothing to keep her company except the radio station 4CL, very little work to keep her busy, and nobody to talk with. She decided to go across to the café to see Lisa and Con. They probably wouldn't be busy. The three cars in the street were outside the Empire. TC noticed one of them was Jake's.

That would be right. Didn't take Jake long to find new drinking buddies, she thought as she walked over the median strip to the café.

¶

At camp Vance and the men had finished lunch and were having their coffee and smokes. They were all relieved that Yappy was more relaxed than he had been at breakfast and smoko. He was still not the Yappy they knew. Perhaps he was halfway to getting there.

'I don't want to get everyone's enthusiasm racing,' said Neil. 'I think we'll hit the motherload this afternoon.'

'Sure, Neil. Pigs might bloody fly, too, mate,' said Faith.

'What makes you think that, Neil?' asked Vance.

'My gut,' replied Neil, 'Just my gut feeling.'

'I hope your gut is on the ball, mate,' said Faith.

'Even I bloody well do,' came Yappy's voice from the kitchen door. 'Might put a bloody smile on your miserable, ugly, bloody faces.' They all turned towards Yappy.

'Yappy is back,' said Faith with exaggerated excitement as he jumped up, raced to Yappy, and hugged him before picking Yappy up and whirling him around.

'Put me down, you stupid bastard,' demanded Yappy. Vance and Neil were clapping. Little Joe was smiling.

'We missed you, Yappy, mate,' added Neil.

'We sure did, Yappy,' said Vance. Little Joe kept smiling as he nodded his head.

'No point in a man sulking for too bloody long. Makes you bastards too bloody sad. Now, go find this bloody motherload so a man can have some peace around here.'

'Sure thing, Boss,' said Neil as he stood to attention and saluted Yappy. Little Joe patted Yappy on the shoulder. Once again they headed off for the hill. Vance followed Yappy into the kitchen.

'Yappy, I have decided that any future plans of importance will be discussed with all of you at the same time.'

'Good idea, mate,' said Yappy. 'Now, go read your bloody lapidary books. I want to get finished here so I can lay down for an hour or so. I didn't get much sleep last night. I was too busy being pissed off.'

Vance laughed and did as instructed. He resumed looking through and reading his pile of gem-cutting and lapidary equipment journals while making notes on equipment of interest.

¶

Lou arrived at the pharmacy a little after two. With her was Graham Sandler. They both were laughing.

'What's so funny, you two?' asked TC.

'Nothing,' replied Graham.

'Liar,' said Lou. 'Graham's been wanting to come to see you all morning but wasn't game. I just told him all he had to do was pretend he needs some toothpaste or soap. He said you were too smart for that. You would know he was scamming. He reckons we are the most intelligent eighteen-year-olds he has ever met or is likely to meet. He says we are eighteen going on eighty.'

Graham was visibly embarrassed as he thought, *I must remember never again to tell Lou anything that I don't want TC to know.*

TC laughed.

'Why are you afraid of me, Graham? Nobody else is.'

'Except Mr Callahan when you yell at him through the Empire window,' said Graham. 'I hear that has happened more than a few times.'

'That's different; that's business,' replied TC. 'My boss made me so angry sometimes I had to take drastic measures to get his attention.'

'She got Vance's attention, all right, Graham. She also got the attention of everyone else in the bar, not to mention the rest of the town,' said Lou.

So, it is true, thought Graham. *I thought the sarge was exaggerating.*

'Real little spitfire, huh?' said Graham. 'I'll have to remember that.'

'I thought you were on duty today, Graham,' said TC, changing the subject.

'Start at four. From four on I'll be guarding Brolga until shut-down time.'

'Have you had lunch, TC?' asked Lou.

'Of course not. I went over and talked to Con and Lisa for a while, then came back here to wait for you.'

'I'll go get something,' said Lou.

'I'll come with you, Lou,' said Graham.

§

When Lou and Graham walked into the café, Con and Lisa were standing behind the counter talking.

'Lovely Lou,' said Lisa. 'This is my lucky day. I had TC here a little while ago; now I have you.' Con looked at Graham and winked.

'Making progress, mate?'

'I'm not sure yet,' whispered Graham with a smile. Graham insisted on paying Con for the girls' lunch as well as his own. When he and Lou returned to the dispensary with sandwiches and Cokes, Lou told TC.

'Graham paid, TC. So, next time I'll pay, then it will be your turn.'

'Sure,' agreed TC.

'That's not necessary,' said Graham.

'For us it is,' said TC.

While they were eating, Slim Dusty came on 4CL, singing, Pub with No Beer.

'God help us!' said Lou.

'Why is that, Lou?' asked Graham curiously.

'The pubs ran out of beer here once. What a mess!' replied Lou.

'What happened?' asked Graham.

'Ask the sergeant,' replied Lou with a laugh. 'It's a wonder he hasn't told you.'

'What do you do from four until shut-down time?' enquired TC with genuine interest.

'Good question, TC,' replied Graham. 'Well, I drive slowly around the streets on patrol a couple of dozen or so times; I drive to the end of the bitumen on the eastern side of town, turn around, come back over the bridge, drive up Brolga Street and continue on to the end of the bitumen on the western side of town. I probably do that ten or so times and, of course, I do so slowly. I park the car half a dozen or so times so I can stretch my legs, try walking slowly up and down the main block looking through the pubs' doors and windows as I pass them. Of course, when it's closing time, I get to go inside the pubs. Sometimes I get to chat to one or both Mr Romeos.'

'Sounds boring,' said Lou.

'Not really. It's as exciting as it is for you when you sit on your steps,' replied Graham with a smirk. Lou and TC giggled.

'Not only are you beautiful, you also have a sense of humour,' said Lou. Graham Sandler smiled. Once again he felt embarrassed.

'Lou, if you tell me I'm beautiful again, I shall have to book you. *Beautiful* is a word reserved for young women like yourself and TC or a beautiful experience, memory, dream, poem, lyrics in a song, etc., etc., etc. Apart from that, Lou, I am a police officer. The last thing I need is an ego the size of Australia. Badge and ego are a dangerous combination. Could see me in a lot of trouble.'

'How many nights a week do you work, Graham?' asked TC to change the subject.

'I have been working six because I have nothing else to do. As the sergeant has a family, it's nice for him to be home at nights with them. I can change it anytime I want except if something is happening in town or, of course, if there is trouble.'

'Don't think there'll be too much of either, Constable,' said TC with a smile while raising her eyebrows. 'Now that we have your routine, ethics, and schedule out of the way, you can put Constable Graham outside and bring Graham back in,' said TC quietly with a smile.

'Constable is done,' replied Graham, nodding his head, smiling and eyes twinkling. 'I have to go now. Constable Graham has to put on his uniform, then go on patrol.'

'I'm going home, TC. See you after you finish here,' said Lou.

¶

Jake's mother phoned late afternoon.

'TC, luv, I've got some mending needs to be done. Is that all right with you, luv?'

'Of course, Mrs Carmichael,' replied TC.

'I'll have Jake drop it to the house after work; he already has it in his car.'

'Lou is at home now, Mrs Carmichael. He can give it to her if he likes. We'll do it tonight.'

'There's a lot, luv. I haven't done any since you and Lou went to Sydney,' said Thel Carmichael apologetically.

'No problem, Mrs Carmichael. It's the least we can do for you. After all, we are using your sewing machine,' replied TC.

'All right, TC. I'll tell Jake to drop the things down to Lou now. I'll tell Jake to invite you for a meal here soon,' finished Thel Carmichael.

Don't know how such a lovely woman is the mother of someone like Jake, thought TC.

Ten minutes later, Lou heard Jake's car in the driveway. Jake got out of the car, collected a washing basket containing his mother's mending from the back seat, stormed up the back steps into the dining room, almost threw the basket onto the dining room table, and stormed out without speaking to a shocked Lou, who was sitting at the table varnishing her fingernails. Lou rushed to the back landing as Jake slammed his car door.

'What's wrong, Jake?' Jake glared at Lou as he turned the ignition key.

'Get stuffed! That goes for Miss Goody-Two-Shoes as well. Probably do you two the world of good. A pair of bitches, that's what you are.' With that Jake reversed out of the driveway at maniacal speed with the driveway gravel flying so high it hit the side of the house.

Lou was immediately on the telephone to TC to ask if TC knew what was wrong with Jake. TC explained to Lou what had happened and what she had said to Jake.

'Perhaps he doesn't like the truth,' said Lou.

'Obviously not,' agreed TC.

'See you soon.'

¶

About an hour before knock-off time, Vance heard the loader stop. He immediately headed for the hill. *Don't tell me it's broken down,* he thought. *That's the last thing we need at the moment. We can't afford parts or any other damned thing, for that matter. I was down there less than half an hour ago.*

Little Joe was running towards Vance.

'We got it, Boss! Neil's gut was spot-on. There are boulders everywhere! Come on, Boss!' said Little Joe as he turned and began running back to the cut in the hill.

Vance ran with him, silently thanking God. *At last,* he thought. *At last!*

Faith and Neil were beside themselves with excitement.

'I told you!' said Neil.

'We must have hit a pocket, Boss,' said Faith. 'A few rolled out, and then a heap came out behind them. Lucky they didn't hit Little Joe because he was walking behind.'

Vance was speechless. There were boulders of all shapes and sizes scattered all over the place.

'Looks like you've got enough to fill the back of the ute, Vance,' said Yappy as he joined them.

'Looks like it, all right, little man. It sure does look like it!'

'Neil, mate, any chance of borrowing your gut to pick a few winners for me when we go on holidays?' said Yappy.

'No problem, you mad little bugger,' replied Neil. They all laughed. They were all very, very happy. Their hard work had finally paid off.

'Well done, men. Well done. That includes you, Yappy,' said Vance, whose mind was racing here, there, and everywhere. 'That's enough for today! Early finish. Let's get cleaned up, relax, and have a coffee and a few smokes before we eat.'

'We can eat early, too,' said Yappy. Vance laughed with the others.

'Sounds good, Yappy,' said Vance.

'Yes, sounds good, Yappy,' agreed Neil and Faith. A smiling Little Joe nodded.

It was decided over their meal that they would load the boulders into the ute next morning. Neil would service the machine while Faith and Little Joe did a water run.

'What about you and me?' asked Yappy.

'Oh, yes, Yappy,' said Vance. 'I need you to write out a list on whatever we need from town.'

'Can I include a door for the toilet?' asked Yappy. Everyone laughed except Yappy.

'No, not yet, Yappy,' replied Vance.

¶

The girls were in the dining room doing Thel's mending. TC was using the sewing machine and Lou was hand-sewing. They both had their hair in rollers and were wearing their short, cotton dressing gowns. Lou wore pale green rollers and matching dressing gown with silver cute jiffy slippers. TC wore pink rollers, pink gown, and pink jiffy slippers. Little Richard was blasting out Tutti Frutti on the stereo. The girls were singing along with him.

Suddenly, they heard a deep, very loud cough at the back doorway. It was Graham.

'Well, don't you two look cute,' he said while smiling from ear to ear.

'This is as bad as it gets,' said TC.

'Bad looks pretty good to me,' replied Graham. 'I knocked on the front door, then realised you couldn't hear me because of the music.'

'Thought you were on duty,' said Lou.

'I am. It's my tea break. I hope you don't mind me just rocking up without an invitation. I drove past to wave to you, but you stood me up. You weren't on the stairs.'

'You can come visit anytime you want to, Graham,' said TC, 'as long as you don't come to arrest us.'

'Would you like a Coke?' asked Lou.

'No, thank you, Lou. I have to go on patrol,' replied Graham.

'Be sure to drive slowly,' said TC. They all laughed.

'You can wave to us later,' said Lou.

'We'll be finished sewing in less than an hour,' said TC. 'Then we'll be on the stairs as usual. At least we know we'll see one car drive past.'

'Yes, the police car,' said Graham with a wink as he turned to leave via the back stairs.

'I'll let you out the front door,' said Lou.

When Lou returned to the dining room, she said, 'Graham should be a movie star, not a cop. He certainly is something else in the looks department.'

'Lou, you've said it a million times,' replied TC. 'I think everyone knows Graham is handsome except Graham. I think he's shy and not at all egotistical. That's what I like about him. I also like the fact that he's not a drunk. Now, let's get this sewing finished.'

'I'll put the King on first,' said Lou.

¶

When TC finished the machine-sewing, she put Thel's machine away, then ironed the seams while Lou finished the hand-sewing.

Out of the blue, Lou said seriously, 'We are a great team, TC. I hope we will be friends for the rest of our lives. I'll hate it when we have to go our separate ways.'

'Of course, we'll always be friends, Lou,' replied TC just as seriously. 'We won't be going our separate ways for a long time. We are only eighteen.'

The girls sat on the stairs talking about anything and everything. They had bought heaps of patterns and fabrics in Sydney, so they decided they had best do some serious sewing soon before summer hit full-on.

Graham patrolled by every fifteen minutes or so and blinked the headlights of the police car every time he drove past. Just before ten, he drove by and blinked the lights twice.

'Guess that's Graham's way of saying goodnight,' said Lou.

'Yes, he's gone to see the pub's closed,' replied TC.

'I suppose having the cop car wink at us is something the other girls in Brolga don't have,' said Lou.

'You are incredible, Lou,' said TC with a laugh. 'Are you tired?'

'Not yet, TC. Let's play one more record. Perhaps Elvis will miraculously appear at the bottom of the stairs while we listen to him sing.'

'I'm sure he will, Lou, if we close our eyes and imagine him standing there,' laughed TC.

'I hope he's holding his guitar!' said Lou as she went to change the record and put Elvis on.

§

Next morning at camp everyone was in high spirits as they loaded the boulders into the back of the ute.

'If we fill it, they'll be too heavy,' said Neil when it was half full.

'I think you're right, Neil,' said Vance. 'We'll just stack the rest in a pile outside the marquee. Don't know where I'll put them in town, anyway. Probably throw them in the backyard. Well, I'm ready to go. Yappy, give me your list, mate.'

'It's in the kitchen, Vance. I want to discuss it with you,' replied Yappy. Vance followed Yappy into the kitchen.

'What is it, Yappy?' Yappy replied so quietly he was almost whispering.

'Here's a hundred quid, Vance. If you are still in town on the weekend, put in on a winner for me. If you are coming to the mine before then, would you give it to Jake to put on a winner for me?' Vance laughed.

'How do you know Jake or I will pick a winner, Yappy?'

'I'll take a punt on it,' replied Yappy seriously.

'You're something else, Yappy,' replied Vance with a laugh. 'All right, your hundred quid will go on a winner. I'm not sure when I'll be back. Could be a couple of days, could be a week. If I don't come back before next mail day, I'll send everything on the mail truck.'

'Don't send my bloody winnings on the mail truck,' said Yappy.

'I'm going now, Yappy,' said Vance while throwing his hands in the air.

'See you men later,' he waved to the other men as he got into the ute. 'Be good.' The men laughed.

'What bloody options do we have?' said Faith as Vance drove off at snail's pace as usual for the first hundred yards or so. He didn't want a dust cloud upsetting Yappy.

§

Vance arrived in town mid-morning. He felt drained. He still had not come to grips with the fact that they had found opal and lots of it. TC was tidying one of the lipstick stands with her back to the dispensary when she was startled by a tap on the shoulder. She quickly turned as Vance said, 'Just as well you're working. If I caught you slacking off, I'd have to fire you.'

'It's so good to see you, Boss,' said TC as she hugged him and pecked him on the cheek. 'Seems like you've been gone forever!'

'Feels like it, too. What has been happening here? Fill me in while you make me some coffee,' replied Vance all in one breath.

'Your hair looks better, Boss,' said TC as she switched on the kettle. 'Who cut it?'

'Yappy did. He cuts Neil's and Faith's and also his own,' replied Vance, who was now seated at his desk and in the process of lighting a Craven A.

'Yappy told me you found opal,' said TC as she placed the coffee on the desk in front of him.

'You can say that again, Little One. We found opal, all right,' replied Vance with a relieved smile. 'Tell me what has been happening here? We'll talk about the opal later.'

TC handed Vance a list—

1.   Mrs Callahan wants you to call her as soon as you get back (Please call her; she is your wife).
2.   Claudia wants you to contact her as soon as you get back (I think she's worse than Louise).
3.   A man from Coober Pedy called. He did not leave his name (He did leave his number).
4.   You might want to call Doctor Jackson. He has asked about you a few times (I think he's lonely).

Vance read it and laughed.

'You've got the answers to everything, haven't you, young lady? What else has been going on?' TC told him everything as it came to mind. She left the Jake bit until last.

'I had a row with Jake,' said TC. 'He told Lou we should both get stuffed.'

'He what?' said Vance with an angry, shocked expression on his face.

'He told Lou we should both get stuffed and that it would do us good,' replied TC. 'We figure he wants us to keep out of his way. We are both happy about that.'

'Why did Jake say that to Lou, TC?' asked Vance with great interest. TC thought for a moment before replying.

'Because I told him that I am tired of you and him looking out for me. I told him you were both hypocritical, drunken, womanising, gambling, bullshit artists. He said that wasn't fair to you because you have quit the booze. I then said you were an adulterous, hypocritical, gambling, womanising, bullshit artist.' Vance momentarily glared at TC in silent disbelief before going into fits of laughter.

'Why are you laughing? It's not funny,' said TC. Vance replied but TC could not decipher what he was saying because he was laughing too much.

'Why are you laughing?' repeated TC. Vance composed himself and lit another cigarette.

'The reason I was laughing is because you hit the nail right on the head. I could not possibly describe Jake and myself more appropriately if I tried. No wonder Jake's upset,' Vance began laughing again. 'The truth about himself must have been one hell of a blow to his ego,' said Vance with more laughter. 'Why was he looking out for you?'

'Because he saw me talking to Graham, the policeman,' replied TC.

'I've met him. He seems a nice, quiet young man,' said Vance matter-of-factly.

'He is and he doesn't drink, so you and Jake don't have to look out for me,' said TC.

'I see. So you like Graham, don't you?' replied Vance with a slight touch of concern.

'He's nice, Boss. Please call Mrs Callahan; otherwise, she'll think I didn't give you her messages.'

'In a minute, in a minute. Don't nag me, TC,' said Vance lightly.

'What did you buy with your winnings?'

'Nothing,' replied TC, who was embarrassed to tell him why she had kept it. 'Straight to the bank, I bet,' said Vance.

'You are wrong again, Boss,' replied TC while shaking her head.

'Well, what did you do with it?' demanded Vance in a strong, frustrated tone of voice.

'I put it away in case you need it,' admitted TC as she picked up a feather duster and went into the shop while fighting back tears.

Oh, shit, I'm a prick, thought Vance as he watched TC through the dispensary mirrored glass. *I wonder if I would be so interested in what she did with the money if Yappy had only won a hundred quid instead of twenty-four hundred quid. In reality, all I did was give her a fifty-pound bonus, which she got if Yappy picked a winner. As luck has it, Yappy picked more than one winner; so, TC's maybe fifty-pound-bonus turned into a two thousand and four hundred bonus. That pissed me off because I need the money. Then I interrogate her only to find out she hasn't spent a cracker but put the money aside in case I need it.* Vance concluded his self-analysis by telling himself that he must be the bastard of the century. *What a week,* he thought. *First, I nearly lose Yappy, then we find opal, and now I've been a prick to TC. Oh, well, what's done is done.*

Vance went back out to the ute to collect the lapidary journals and the list he had made. Back in the dispensary, he began calling lapidary supplies and equipment merchants in Adelaide, Sydney, and Melbourne.

Come siren time Vance was still on the telephone. TC took her keys and purse, closed the front door of the pharmacy, then walked home, where she threw herself on her bed and cried. When she was all cried out, she got up, straightened her bed, washed her face, and called Lou.

'Vance is back,' said Lou. 'I know that because he's been on the phone for ages. Delores has been trying to call him.'

'Lou, I didn't call you to talk about the boss. I called to tell you not to come to the shop after you finish work today. It's not a very nice atmosphere there today. I'll see you this afternoon when I come home.'

'Have you and Vance had a fight?' asked Lou.

'No, Lou, nothing like that, I'll see you later,' replied TC before collecting her keys and purse from her bedroom.

¶

Vance put the phone down as TC slid the door open. When TC entered the dispensary, Vance opened his mouth to say something when through the mirror windows he saw Claudia walk through the door. He met her at the shop counter, where they talked quietly for a few minutes before TC heard Claudia say quite loudly, 'Aren't you going to invite me in for a coffee?'

Vance replied just as loudly, 'Can't today. I'm a bit busy.' Then there was whispering and giggling and Vance saying loudly, 'All right, one coffee.'

When Vance and Claudia came into the dispensary, Vance said, 'TC, go and collect the mail,' in an off-handed manner.

'I already got it this morning, Mr Callahan,' replied TC icily.

'Well, get it again,' said Vance.

'Mr Callahan, I told you that I am not sitting on the Seat of Knowledge ever again during working hours,' said TC determinedly.

'Vance, this brat is an employee. She should do as she is told,' said Claudia in an outraged manner.

'TC, just this once, please,' said Vance softly.

'I'm going to the café. Open the door when I'm allowed back,' said TC. Once again, she picked up her purse and closed the pharmacy door. As she did so, Vance took the phone off the cradle, then locked the back door.

Lou was walking into Con's café as TC left the pharmacy.

'What's wrong, TC? You've been crying,' said Lou when TC joined her in the café.

'Not much, Lou. Just having a down day,' replied TC.

'Let's have something to eat. I doubt I'll be going back to work in a hurry.'

'Is Louise there?' asked Lou.

'No, this one's name is Claudia,' replied TC. 'Two toasted ham, cheese, and tomato sandwiches, please, Con, and two Cokes.'

'Make that three, please, Con,' came Graham's voice from the doorway.

'Good timing,' said Lou. 'Couldn't have timed it better if it was planned.'

'It was planned,' said Graham with a broad smile and a wink as they sat down at a table. 'How come you are not at work, TC?' asked Graham.

'My boss is back. He's in a meeting,' replied TC. Lou almost choked on the Coke she had just sucked through her straw.

'What's the problem, Lou? Are you all right?' asked Graham.

'Nothing wrong. I was just a little eager sucking my Coke.'

'Did you get my goodnight message last night?' asked Graham.

'Of course, we did—two winks and you were gone,' replied Lou.

'Every time I drove past, I wanted to park the patrol car and join you on the stairs,' said Graham wistfully. 'I asked the sergeant for Friday night off,' said Graham. 'He said it would be fine and I could take the day shift.'

'Yes, you come sit on our stairs Friday night if you wish to do so,' invited TC.

'I'll be there,' replied Graham elatedly. 'I was hoping you would say that.'

They chatted with each other and Con until Graham had to leave a little after three. Before leaving Graham moved to the counter to pay Con.

'No! A deal is a deal, Graham,' said TC. 'Lou pays today, I pay next time. Then it will be your turn again.'

'Okay, a deal certainly is a deal. See you on patrol,' said Graham as he left. He smiled all the way as he walked to his quarters.

No wonder they didn't merge in Sydney, he thought. *Too principled, amongst other things. Principles Personified, that's them. Friday night, please come soon!*

Con was keeping watch on the pharmacy door from his vantage point behind the counter while the girls sat chatting about girl things with Lisa. Come four o'clock, TC decided to wait no longer. Lou and she could be doing something constructive at home.

'The boss' meeting is taking longer than anticipated. Let's go home, Lou. Con, would you please tell him I went home? Would you please also tell him the time we left?'

'No problem, TC.' replied Con with a smile along with his usual arms-and-hands-spread gesture.

'Let's go,' said Lou.

When the girls had gone Con and Lisa were silent for a few minutes, both of them deep in thought. Lisa broke the silence as she stood up from the table where she had been sitting with the girls.

'The whole town knows what is going on over there in the dispensary, yet that girl never says a word about it.'

'I was just thinking the same thing,' replied Con. 'I hope my friend, Vance, realises how loyal the kid is to him.'

Lisa sighed heavily before agreeing, 'Me, too, Con, me, too.'

¶

In the dispensary, Vance and Claudia were taking a break from their energy-absorbing activities. Vance, clad only in his underpants, was sitting at his desk. Claudia's attire consisted of Vance's shirt with buttons undone and one side of the shirt front flung outside to expose one breast. She was sitting on Vance's lap, gazing into his eyes as she massaged the back of his neck with the fingers of both hands. Vance had one arm around Claudia and was slowly and gently rubbing the small of her back with his hand. In the other hand, he held a cigarette from which he intermittently deeply inhaled before blowing smoke over Claudia's shoulder.

'When is your wife coming back, darling?' asked Claudia softly.

'I don't know. All I know is that she will come back,' replied Vance in his normal tone of voice. 'She always does.'

'She must love you a lot,' said Claudia.

'Poor woman! I'm sure she does,' replied Vance. 'Let's not talk about my wife. Let's get back to what we were doing before.' He squashed his cigarette in the ashtray.

When the girls got home, TC called Jake's mother to tell her that the mending was finished.

'I'll tell Jake to collect it, luv,' said Mrs Carmichael.

'Mrs Carmichael, please tell Jake we'll leave the basket on the back landing,' replied TC.

'All right, luv. Thank you for doing it,' said Thel. 'I'll call Jake now.'

TC immediately placed the basket containing the mending on the back landing.

'Doing Mrs Carmichael's bits and pieces has given me the sewing bug,' said Lou.

'Me, too,' replied TC. 'Let's make a new dress each.'

They were in the dining room sorting through patterns when Jake's car screeched, then hurtled into the driveway. They heard him open his car door, bound the few stairs up and down, slam his car door, and leave as fast as he arrived.

'Jake is obviously still angry,' said TC as she continued scrutinising the cover of the pattern packet she held in her hand.

'He probably thinks we're busy getting stuffed,' said Lou flippantly. Neither of the girls was aware of their connotation of stuffed. They both thought it was simply Jake's way of telling them to leave him alone.

¶

Claudia left the dispensary via the back-door route. Vance walked across to Con's café. When he entered the café, he ignored Con, who was behind the counter putting drink straws into a stainless-steel container. Vance glanced around the empty café with a confused expression on his face.

'She's gone, mate,' said Con. 'She left for home at exactly nine minutes past four. Can't say I blame her.'

'Don't suppose I can, either, Con,' replied Vance. 'I'll see you later, Con.'

That was quick, thought Con as he continued with the drink straws.

¶

Damn it, thought Vance as he hurried back to the dispensary. *No wonder the kid gets pissed off with me. Twice in one day. If she had any brains, she would have taken that money, packed up, and left. Still, if she did have any brains, she wouldn't be here.* He picked up the telephone from the counter, clicked it onto the cradle, then picked it up, and put it to his ear, and asked the on-duty telephonist for TC's number.

Lou answered when the girls heard their telephone ringing.

'I'll get her,' said Lou the moment she heard Vance's voice. 'It's Vance,' mouthed Lou while rolling her eyes.

'Hello, Mr Callahan,' said TC indifferently into the phone.

'TC, I'm sorry,' said Vance sincerely.

'What for, Mr Callahan?' asked TC seriously. 'For breaking your word about having your girlfriends in the shop during work hours? I told you, I refuse to sit on the Seat of Knowledge ever again while I wait for you to finish with them in the dispensary.'

'I got caught off-guard, TC,' replied Vance apologetically. 'She just walked in. I didn't know she was coming.'

'You could have fled through the back door instead of rushing to meet her at the counter,' reprimanded TC.

'It won't happen again, TC. I promise!' said Vance.

'Sure, tell it to the fairies, Mr Callahan,' replied TC.

'Are you coming to work tomorrow, TC?' asked Vance, who couldn't think of anything else to say.

'I have nowhere else to go, Mr Callahan. I'll see you then,' replied TC before putting the telephone down.

'She's right,' thought Vance after TC ended their conversation. 'I could easily have escaped through the back door. My problem is the same as it has always been. I'm ruled by my no-conscience dick. I'll go home, take a real shower, then get Con to cook me one of his famous steaks. The rocks can stay in the ute 'til morning. I don't know what to do with them. No other bastard around here will.'

¶

'I miss Vance,' said Yappy as the men sat down to dinner.

'Bloody hell, Yappy! He only left this morning,' said Faith.

'I think you and the boss have a thing going,' said Neil.

'I'll give you a thing' said Yappy. 'I'll cut your bloody throat with this bloody thing,' as he waved around the carving knife. They all laughed, even Little Joe, who surprised everyone by saying, 'Do it, Yappy; that'll shut him up.'

'Thanks a lot, Little Joe,' said Neil in mock fear. 'I'll have to keep an eye on you. Let's finish eating, have a few smokes and a yarn, then get to bed. We've got another big day tomorrow. Don't know about you lot, but I can't wait for Christmas to come.' Faith, Yappy and Little Joe nodded and mumbled in agreement,

In Con's Café, Vance was eating his steak while conversing with Con between mouthfuls.

'Now that you've got opal, mate, what is the next step?' asked Con.

'Turn it into gemstones, I hope,' said Vance with a smile. 'I've got a little compact cutting machine set up at home. Delores used it when she was having a go at the stuff we found before. That gear won't be any good for the big boulders we've just found. I ordered new equipment today.'

'I'd like to come see how it's done once you get set up,' said Con. 'Anyway, mate, good on you. I might even buy Lisa a gem from you one day.' Vance laughed.

'I wish I had one to show you now, Con. Money is pretty tight at the moment but not for long I hope.'

'I'll lend you a few quid, mate,' said Con. It was a genuine offer.

'I appreciate your thought, Con,' replied Vance. 'Let's see how things go before I start borrowing your money. I'm already into Jake for a few quid.' Vance finished his meal. As he was paying Con, he saw the young cop, Graham, walk past.

'What's that kid like, Con?' he asked.

'Who?' enquired Con, who had not noticed Graham go by.

'The young policeman,' replied Vance.

'Constable Graham is a nice young man. Nice manners, too. He'll be here to eat soon.'

'I see. The steak was great, Con. I'm going home to bed. My body is still on mine time.' Vance walked out of Con's Café. He paused on the footpath, stretched his arms, then reached for a cigarette.

'I'm tired,' he said to himself as he yawned before lighting his Craven A.

'Hello, Mr Callahan,' said Graham, who was less than ten feet away, walking towards him.

'Graham, how are you?' asked Vance.

'Obviously on duty. I saw you yawning. I feel a bit that way myself,' replied Graham.

'You are too young to be tired this early in the night,' said Vance with a laugh.

'I've had a bit of trouble sleeping the last couple of nights,' replied Graham. 'My mind races. It won't switch off.'

'I know what that's like,' laughed Vance. *I bet the young prick can't sleep because he's been thinking about TC,* thought Vance, who couldn't stop himself from speaking.

'I hear you've been talking to TC, Graham,' said Vance.

'She's a nice girl, Mr Callahan,' replied Graham. 'So is Lou.'

'I know they are nice girls, Graham,' said Vance. 'That is what I am worried about. Lou has her father to protect her. TC only has me. If it's TC you are interested in, please tread lightly. Don't hurt her. She's vulnerable.'

'I know, Mr Callahan,' replied Graham. 'She's also smart.'

'They both are,' said Vance as he threw his cigarette butt into the footpath bin. 'Nice talking to you Graham. No doubt I'll be seeing you around.'

Vance seated himself in the ute laden in the back with boulders, then drove home while Graham, as usual, went into the café.

'What will you have tonight, Constable Graham?' asked Con.

'I don't think I'm hungry tonight, Con,' replied Graham, whose face was white as a sheet.

'Are you all right, Constable Graham? You look sick,' said Con.

'No, I'm fine, Con. If I feel hungry later, I'll come back. I'll get going now.'

I'd bet a thousand quid that Vance said something about TC to Constable Graham, thought Con as he watched Graham walk outside.

Consider yourself told to back off from TC, thought Graham as he got into the police car and started it up. He drove to the end of the bitumen on the western side of the town, where he turned off the car engine and sat deep in silent thought. After a while, he switched on the ignition, then turned the car around and drove back towards town. 'Sorry, it's too late, Mr Callahan,' he said aloud. 'I've already fallen for her.'

¶

Jake was in the Empire bar drinking Rum and Coke as if there were no tomorrow. He was well on the way to being plastered already, and the Empire would still be open for hours.

'Take it easy, Jake,' advised Jess, who was on duty by herself because it was quiet.

'Mind your own business, Jess,' replied Jake. 'I'll get drunk if I want.'

'You are doing a pretty good job of it, mate,' said one of the young truckies with whom Jake was drinking.

¶

They must be sewing again, thought Graham when he drove past and saw that the girls were not on the steps.

Just before ten, TC said, 'There we go, Lou, we each have a new dress. All we have to do is the hand-sewing and press them.'

'And,' said Lou, 'we have two more cut out. Let's leave the machine out in case we feel up to sewing again tomorrow night.'

'I need a shower, Lou,' said TC. 'Should have had one before we started sewing. How about you sit on snake guard while I take a shower, then we switch places?'

'Sounds good to me, TC. Go ahead,' replied Lou.

¶

Come ten o'clock, the Majestic and Brick were already closed. Jack Romeo closed the bar doors at the Empire. There were a few truckies and a very drunk Jake Carmichael still there.

Jess whispered to Jack Romeo. 'Get Jake out of here before the police come. He's drunk and mouthing off.'

Jake was so drunk that he was swaying backwards, then forwards, with his head wobbling all over the place.

'Come on, young Jake, let's get your face washed with cold water, then some coffee,' said Jack.

'I'm all right, Jack,' slurred Jake.

'At least sit in the smoking room. The cop will be here any minute.'

'Too late, Mr Romeo. I'm already here,' said Graham from the hallway door.

'Young Jake here had a few to many, Constable,' said Jack Romeo.

'I can see that, Mr Romeo,' replied Graham. 'You had best take his car keys, Mr Romeo. He can't drive in his condition.'

'Go to shithouse! No one's taking my keys,' slurred Jake, whose wobbly head appeared to be out of control.

'Are any of you sober enough to drive?' asked Graham.

'I am, mate. I don't drink booze, only Coke,' said the young, blonde-haired truck driver who worked at the truck depot opposite the girls. 'Jake's a mate of mine. We went to school together. I'll drive him home. I'll drive them all home.'

'Off you go, then,' said Graham.

'Bloody bastard cop,' mumbled Jake as his friend guided him through the door.

As they left, Graham was thinking, *If we were in the city, Jake Carmichael, you'd be heading for the slammer instead of home.*

Jake's mate was back in less than a minute.

'I'll drive them home in my car. Jake can pick his up in the morning.'

Graham said goodnight to Jess and the Romeo brothers, then left to do his final patrol of the streets before heading home for the night.

He did back streets first. As was his routine, he left Brolga Street until last. When he drove by the girls' house, they were sitting on the steps. He quickly reversed to a stop adjacent to their gate and got out of the patrol car.

'I missed you,' he said.

'We've been busy,' said TC.

'Will you be up for a while?' asked Graham.

'Till midnight, at least,' replied Lou.

'Okay. I'll put the car to bed, change out of uniform, and come back for a little while if that's okay with you,' said Graham.

'Sure. See you then,' replied TC.

Radio station 2UE in Sydney was playing in the background. Del Shannon was singing, Runaway Sue.

'Wish we could run away, TC.' said Lou.

'We've already tried that, Lou,' said TC matter-of-factly. 'Don't tell me you have forgotten already. It was a disaster.'

The girls were wearing their baby-doll pyjamas and jiffy slippers.

'We had best put on our dressing gowns,' said TC. 'Don't want Graham to get the wrong idea about us.'

'Good idea,' agreed Lou.

The girls were in the hallway buttoning up their dressing gowns when Graham arrived at the front door.

'Don't get dressed just for me.'

'That was quick,' said Lou. 'Come in.'

'Did you run?' asked TC with a little laugh.

'As a matter of fact, I did,' replied Graham. 'It's only two-and-a-half blocks.'

'Would you like a Coke?' asked TC as she walked towards the kitchen.

'Thank you, yes,' replied Graham. 'This is a good station you have on the radio.' Linda Ronstadt was singing, Distant Drum. 'Which one is it?'

'That, Graham, is radio station 2UE Sydney,' replied Lou. 'Can't get good reception until around ten at night and then only if the weather is calm.'

'Here we go,' said TC as she handed Lou, then Graham their drinks. 'Time to hit the stairs.'

Lou led the way. She seated herself on the third top stair with her back against one side rail and her slippered feet against the other. TC and Graham sat on the top stair with their feet on the second.

'Wish I'd thought of sitting this way before,' said Lou. 'It's pretty comfortable. Also gives me a good view of you two.'

'How was your night, Graham?' asked TC.

'Pretty much normal,' replied Graham with one of his smiles. He really wanted to say, *Well, TC, my night sucked. Your boss virtually told me to stay away from you, and Jake Carmichael called me a bastard cop.* Instead, he continued, 'The town is very quiet, no parties, hardly anyone in the pubs, and nobody in the main street. Even Con closed the café early around nine.'

'The lull before the storm,' said Lou.

'What do you mean, Lou?' asked Graham.

'Word is out on the telephone pipeline,' replied Lou. 'Come the end of next week, the town will be overrun with transients.'

'How do you know, Lou?' asked Graham.

'Don't ask,' said TC.

'I just know,' said Lou with a shrug of her shoulders.

Graham sat with a puzzled look on his face for less than a minute before bursting into laughter.

'What are you laughing for?' asked TC.

'You listen to people's phone calls, don't you, Lou?' said Graham. 'You do know that is illegal, don't you?'

'Well, Constable Graham, if you arrest me, you will have to arrest everyone else who works at the telephone exchange because they all listen in. Then there will be no telephone service into or out of Brolga.' Graham laughed again before replying.

'No, Lou, I shall just have to be *en garde* as to what I say when I'm on the phone. Now that you have confessed, please tell me why the town will be busy next week.'

'Well,' said Lou. 'There's a cattle sale on Thursday; one shed cuts out on Thursday and two other sheds cut out on Friday; also, the fettlers have a four-day weekend break. That's all I know so far.'

I wonder if the Sarge knows, thought Graham. *He can't know; he would have mentioned it.*

'Looks as if you will be very busy, Graham,' said Lou. 'I strongly suggest you get your next week's days or nights off before Thursday. I'm dry. I'll get us another Coke.' Lou stood up, collected the empty bottles, stepped between Graham and TC, and off she went to the kitchen.

Without warning, Graham took TC's face in his hands and kissed her lightly on the forehead. While looking into TC's eyes, he whispered seriously, 'Just something I needed to do. You don't realise how beautiful you are.'

TC whispered back with a hint of a smile,' I'm not beautiful. I'm too short.' They heard the fridge door slam.

Graham removed his hands from TC's face. 'Not for me,' he said softly as he ruffled her hair.

As Lou resettled herself on the steps, Graham winked and smiled broadly at TC, put one of his fingers to his lips, then touched the finger to TC's wrist. TC was experiencing great difficulty concentrating on what Lou was saying. Her young heart and mind were racing out of control. *So, Lisa and Lou are right,* she thought. *He does fancy me! I thought he preferred Lou. Oh, my God, I can't believe it! I hope the boss doesn't interfere. He can't. Graham doesn't drink alcohol.*

'TC, are you with us?' asked Lou while tapping TC on the knee.

'Sorry, Lou, what's wrong?' replied TC while shaking her head in confusion. 'I was deep in thought.'

'Graham and I have decided the three of us will play a few games of Scrabble tomorrow night,' said Lou. 'We want to find out which of us is the most intelligent.' TC began laughing.

'I think Graham is holding an ace up his sleeve,' said TC. 'Have you told Graham neither of us have played Scrabble before?'

'Of course!' replied Lou. TC looked at Graham suspiciously.

'I'll wager you have played before.'

'A few times,' he admitted with a smile. He didn't bother to tell them it was most likely he'd played the game a few hundred times. Growing up, he and his sister used to play Scrabble frequently in order, as their Mother said, 'to improve their vocabulary.'

Midnight came quickly. Graham reluctantly stood up to leave.

'I'll see you tomorrow night, young ladies,' as he patted the top of TC's head.

'Sure, pat TC's head. What about me?' said Lou, pretending hurt. Graham laughed, patted Lou on the head, closed the gate behind him, then ran up the street.

'Did Graham kiss you, TC?' asked Lou.

'On the forehead, Lou,' replied TC. 'I don't want to talk about it. Let's brush our teeth and go to bed.'

'Kitchen sink, here we come.'

¶

Vance was up early, unloading boulders from the back of the ute and throwing them into what used to be a fowl house situated thirty yards behind his home. The old fowl-house had corrugated iron roof, back, and side walls, a wired-in area which used to be a chicken run, and most importantly a gate which he padlocked shut when he had finished unloading.

Vance gave the ute a hose-down, got cleaned up, then drove to the shop, where he did some logistics as to where he could locate the equipment he had ordered yesterday. Tape measure in hand, he raced back and forth between the lapidary catalogues containing dimensions of the forthcoming cutting gear and the area to the rear of the dispensary shelves which housed the prescriptions and medications. By the time TC arrived, he had come up with a plan he thought would work.

'Good morning, TC,' said Vance sheepishly with half a smile.

'Good morning, Mr Callahan,' said TC as she immediately picked up the broom.

'TC, make me some coffee before you do that,' said Vance. TC made his coffee, placed it in front of him, then once more collected the broom.

'The joint doesn't need sweeping today,' said Vance. 'Just leave it. I want to talk to you. Now sit on the stool and listen.' TC sat on the stool as directed while she waited for Vance to speak. Vance blew smoke into the air, momentarily looked at the ceiling, then at TC.

'TC, I am sorry about yesterday. I should not have pushed you about the money and I should not have invited Claudia back here.'

'It's done, Mr Callahan. You are the one who tells me what's done is done. All I ask is that next time you bring your girlfriends into the dispensary, you simply tell me to go home, rather than tell me to collect the mail. Your girlfriends treat me worse than Mrs Callahan does.'

'As for the money, it's here in the office. I'll get it for you.'

TC unlocked and pulled out the bottom drawer of the filing cabinet, reached in, pulled out the bank bag, then passed it to Vance.

'Ingenious hiding place,' mused Vance with a smile.

'Please count it, Mr Callahan,' said TC.

Vance could not recall when he had felt so pissed off with himself. Yes, he could. It was yesterday. This was worse! Vance took the money out of the envelope and counted it before he handed it to TC.

'Better bank it this morning.' TC nodded as she picked up the bank deposit book.

'As soon as the bank opens,' she replied.

¶

TC was writing up the deposit slip when Vance said casually, 'I ran into that young policeman last night. He seems to be all right. He's a good-looking kid.' Vance paused for a moment before continuing in a more serious tone. 'Be careful, Little One. Don't rush into anything.'

'I'm not rushing into anything, Mr Callahan,' replied TC softly. 'I'm young; yet, I feel old. I want to know what it feels like to hold hands and be kissed. I want to know what it's like to laugh and be happy. I want to know what it's like to feel young.'

Oh, shit, thought Vance. *Talk about lambs to the slaughter. What on earth can I tell her?* Vance lit a Craven A, deliberated before taking the first puff, sighed, then said, 'TC, holding hands and kissing is fine. Unfortunately, holding hands and kissing usually leads to other, more adventurous sexual activities. I know you are a virgin; make sure you stay that way until you find someone you want to marry. No man likes spoiled goods. Just stay as you are. Brolga is a very small town, TC. Word travels at lightning speed in this place. Do one wrong thing to spoil your reputation and the whole town will know. That's why I tell you to be careful.' TC was staring at the floor. She was on the verge of tears. She was confused. Losing her virginity had not entered her mind.

The telephone rang.

'That will be Mrs Callahan.'

'I'll call her later. Don't tell her I'm here.'

'TC, is Vance back yet?' asked Delores. TC looked at Vance, who was shaking his head from side to side and had his lips clenched.

'He's not here, Mrs Callahan,' lied TC.

'I didn't ask if he was there; I asked you if he was back in Brolga,' said Delores.

'Yes, he is back,' said TC.

'Did you tell him to call me?'

'Yes, Mrs Callahan, I told him. He said he would call you later,' replied TC.

'Please tell him again when you see him.' Click. Once more Delores was gone. TC put down the telephone, then turned to Vance.

'Mrs Callahan would like you to call her. Please don't worry about me doing anything silly, Mr Callahan. I'm not stupid.'

'Good,' smiled Vance. 'I'm going to put Yappy's order in at the grocer's and butcher's. After that, I'm going to order some fuel for the loader. Then I'm going to see Lou's dad. I want him to knock together a toilet seat plus lid and a door for the toilet the men built. I'll be a while. If the doctor comes in, tell him I'm back and ask him what is the best time for me to call him. By the way, please start calling me Boss again. I hate it when you call me Mr Callahan because that means you are angry or disappointed with me. TC nodded.

'All right, Boss.'

Vance left via the back door as Claudia entered through the front door.

'Is Vance here?' demanded Claudia.

'No, sorry, he's not,' replied TC.

'I'll check, anyway,' snapped Claudia as she brushed past TC into the dispensary. She went to the back door and looked out to see if Vance's car was there before returning inside and turning on TC with a vengeance.

'Think you're a smart little bitch, don't you? Vance said I can't come here when the place is open, unless I want to buy something. I'm not paying money for anything I get from this joint. I'm screwing your boss, so I'm entitled to get whatever I want. So, little girl, I strongly suggest you keep your place. If you don't, I'll deck you.' Claudia pushed TC backwards with both hands. TC almost fell over a stacked display.

'Pity you didn't fall on your arse,' snarled Claudia as she charged out of the pharmacy.

What a day, thought TC as she went to answer the telephone.

'Is Vance there?' asked Jake gruffly.

'No, Jake,' replied TC.

'Tell him to give me a call!' Jake slammed down the phone.

'Just gets better and better,' mumbled TC to herself.

At camp the men were busy adding more rocks to the mounting heap near the marquee.

'The Boss will need a bloody truck, not a ute,' said Faith.

'We'll just have to make more tips, mate,' said Neil matter-of-factly. Little Joe said nothing. Yappy was in the kitchen happily listening to the radio while he prepared lunch.

Hope bloody Vance or Jake stick my money on a bloody winner, thought Yappy. *A man doesn't mean to be greedy, but it would be great if he happened to wager it on a long shot.*

⁋

Vance returned to the shop as the siren sounded.

'What's been happening, TC?'

'Jake wanted you to call him,' replied TC. 'No prescriptions, only two mail orders, and your new girlfriend came in and abused me.'

'Run the last bit by me again?' said Vance seriously.

'Your new girlfriend came in and abused me.'

'What did she say?' TC told him.

'Right!' said Vance, who was in the Empire bar in less than a minute.

'If you are looking for your new girlfriend, she's at lunch,' said Louise indifferently.

'Tell her to stay away from TC or she'll be the one who gets decked,' said Vance before turning on his heel and hurrying back to the shop.'

Bloody hell, he's furious! thought Louise. *Claudia has really upset him. Good*!

Vance was still fuming when he got back to the dispensary.

'If Claudia touches you or abuses you again, I want you to tell the sergeant. I'm taking my laundry to Neil's mother. As soon as she's got it ready for me, I'm going back to camp. Life is so much simpler out there.'

Wish I could go with you, Boss, thought TC as she heard Vance's car start up. *Life is anything but simple in this place. Think I'll go over and talk to Lisa.*

§

A few minutes later TC was seated at a table in the café talking to Lisa.

'I hear Constable Graham is visiting you and Lou tonight to play scrabble,' said Lisa.

'Who told you, Lisa?' asked TC in surprise.

'He did when he came for breakfast,' replied Lisa. 'He was hungry, poor darling. He didn't eat dinner last night. Con said he was white when he came in after talking to Vance out the front. Perhaps sometimes, luv, Vance is overprotective where you are concerned,' said Lisa with sincerity. 'I don't think he realises how sensible you are.'

'I know, Lisa. I got a lecture this morning,' replied TC. 'I don't think the boss wants me to grow up. Thank you, Lisa. I had better go now.'

TC went back to the dispensary. Vance was talking to Doctor Jackson on the phone when TC walked in.

'She told you that, did she, Jackson? She's always quoting me. All right, I'll see you at the café at seven.' Vance put the telephone down, turned to TC, and said, 'So, you told the doctor not to be surprised by anything that happens around here.'

'Yes,' replied TC. 'Was that wrong?'

'Not at all,' laughed Vance. 'Neil's mum will have my laundry ready tonight. Remind me to collect it. I'm leaving for camp in the morning. How much pay do I owe you?'

'Three weeks tomorrow,' replied TC. 'Don't worry about it. I still have some in the bank.'

Vance went to the cash register and extracted seven pounds and ten shillings, which he handed to TC. As an afterthought, he took another fifty from the till.

'Here, take this, too,' said Vance. 'This is the fifty that was bet on the horses. Put it in the bank, there's a good girl. Who knows? I may need to borrow it back one day.'

'I wish I had money to help you, Boss,' replied TC sincerely.

'I know,' nodded Vance as he glanced at the clock on the wall. I have to see Jake; Yappy wants him to place a bet tomorrow.'

Talk about revolving doors, thought TC as Vance departed via the back door and Lou arrived at the front door.

'I got a letter,' said Lou excitedly waving an envelope in her hand. 'I got a letter from Colin!'

'That's a surprise' replied TC with a smile. 'How is Colin?'

'I'm surprised, all right, TC! Wait 'til I read it to you!' said Lou while jumping up and down on the spot, clutching the letter to her chest with both hands.

'Must be a pretty good letter,' replied a smiling TC. 'Come on, read it to me.' With sparkling eyes and trembling hands, Lou opened the envelope, unfolded the letter, then began to read slowly with a slightly shaky voice.

Dear Lynette,

I do hope this letter reaches you. Should it one day come back to me I'll know I'm out of luck.

If it does not come back, I'll be happy with the knowledge that you have received it and look forward to (hopefully) sometime in the future receiving a reply. I am sorry not to have said much of a goodbye to you when you left. One moment you were here, the next moment you were gone.

I wish we could have spent time alone together when you were in Sydney. My parents' rule on my not being able to date staff members prevented it. As you are no longer employed by my parents, that rule no longer applies. Whatever you are doing back in your home town, I hope you are happy.

I have been thinking about you quite a lot since you left. I find myself bored with my lifestyle. Too much of the same old things. I have had more than enough of the Rock, footy, and party scene. Now I am aiming for a sane, quiet life. I believe I'm looking for a girl just like you.

You are intelligent and pretty; you also have a sense of humour. You are worldly insomuch as nobody could successfully dupe you, while on the other hand, in many ways you are as innocent as a little girl.

I am hopeful we can develop a closer relationship than we shared when you were here. If you are reading this, we are heading in the right direction. Only time will tell where we go in the future.

I find you refreshingly different from all the other girls I know. Impossible to compare. I'll wait impatiently for a reply. I love your name, Lynette. Lou sounds more appropriate for a French truck driver.

Take care of yourself,
Colin.

'Read it again, Lou,' said TC with tears of happiness for her friend glistening in the corners of her eyes.

'Isn't it a lovely letter, TC?' said Lou, whose tears were actually running down her cheeks. 'I don't want to read it again. If I do, I'll cry even more.'

'I understand, Lou,' replied TC as she leaned forward to hug her friend. 'It is a lovely letter written to a lovely girl.'

'TC, Colin is twenty-four years old,' said Lou as she wiped her wet cheeks with her hands. 'He's six years older than I am.'

'Lou, six years is only three hundred and twelve weeks,' replied TC softly. 'Look how quickly a week passes. Blink and it's gone.'

Lou began laughing.

'So if I blink three hundred and twelve times, I'll be the same age as Colin?' TC joined Lou in laughter.

¶

Vance and Jake were sitting in Jake's car parked in front of Jake's shop.

'Yappy wants you to put this on a winner or two for him, Jake,' said Vance as he handed over Yappy's hundred pounds.

'Happy to try for him,' replied Jake.

'Jake, why did you tell Lou and TC to get stuffed? That it would do them good?'

'Listen, mate, you don't know what precious little TC said about us,' replied Jake defensively.

'I do know. Quite frankly, Jake, I couldn't agree with her more,' said Vance. 'She described us for what we are.'

'Maybe you think that, mate. I disagree,' replied Jake angrily.

'All right, Jake, put your head in the sand,' said Vance seriously. 'I'm telling you if you talk to either of those girls like that again, we will no longer be mates, even if I do owe you money. You're a gambling man, Jake. Time to call a spade a spade.' Jake sat in silence as Vance got out of the car and said, 'See you later, Jake,' and walked away.

'You can get stuffed, too Vance,' said Jake aloud to himself as he watched Vance cross the street.

Trust Jake to get the sulks because someone tells him the truth about himself, thought Vance as he walked towards the pharmacy.

'Hello, little ladies,' said Vance when he walked into the dispensary where Lou and TC were talking while TC was busily tidying the prescription medicine shelves. The girls were surprised to hear him say, 'You can go home early, TC. I'll be here until closing time, and I have to make a call to Delores. I don't think it will be a call that needs an audience. Apart from that, I hear the town will be very busy next week, so I'm sure you'll make up the time then. I'll call you tonight. Now, go on, get out of here.'

'Thank you, Boss,' said TC. 'Thank you, thank you, thank you! I'll talk to you tonight.'

'See you when I see you,' said Lou. Both girls pecked Vance on the cheek, then they were gone.

§

The girls went to Con's Café to buy Cokes for later.

'I was about to come across to see you, TC,' greeted Lisa. 'I've got a little surprise for you girls. Come, follow me into the kitchen.' Once in the kitchen, Lisa uncovered a pretty plate on which there were a dozen little heart-shaped, home-made, cream cakes.

'I made them especially for you girls and Constable Graham to enjoy at your Scrabble party tonight,' said Lisa with a proud smile.

'Thank you, Lisa,' said TC and Lou in unison before giving Lisa a three-way hug.

'They look lovely, Lisa,' said TC, who was deeply touched by Lisa's thoughtfulness. 'You are spoiling us.'

'I got a letter from a guy in Sydney, Lisa,' said Lou. 'Is it okay if I bring it for you to read tomorrow? I would like your opinion. Just in case TC and I have interpreted it incorrectly.'

'Lou, I'm flattered. Of course, luv, I'll have a look at it and tell you honestly what I think,' replied Lisa before handing the covered plate of cakes to Lou.

§

'Isn't it strange, TC,' said Lou as they walked home. 'Last night Graham kissed you on the forehead and today I received a letter from Colin.'

'Coincidental, Lou,' replied TC. 'At least we know that we aren't total rejects. You have Colin after you, and I'm pretty certain Constable Graham really likes me.'

⁋

Come six-thirty, the girls were on the stairs with the King singing, Love me Tender, in the background. They had cleared away all remnants of last night's sewing binge, showered, and prettied themselves in preparation for Graham's pending visit.

⁋

'There's your welcoming committee, mate,' said the sergeant as he drove the police car around the corner. 'If I was thirty years younger and fancy free, I would hide this bloody car somewhere and go in there with you.'

'If you were thirty years younger, Sarge, I think you might be a bit wild for Lou and TC,' replied Graham with a laugh as the sergeant braked to an idling stop outside the girls' house. As Graham got of the car, the sergeant called to the girls.

'I'm officially warning you two. Be gentle with him. I need him in one piece for work tomorrow.' Graham was embarrassed as he closed the door. The sergeant drove off laughing.

'Come here, gorgeous! We want to smash your pretty face,' laughed Lou as Graham reached the bottom of the stairs.

'Come inside, Graham,' invited TC as she got to her feet.

'What about me, TC?' said Lou in a feigned, little-girl voice. They all laughed.

'Here, Lou, this is some Coke,' said Graham as he passed a bag to Lou and placed three on the table. 'Lisa sent us some dinner, compliments of Con's Café. She had Con make us steak sandwiches with the lot on toast. She's concerned we don't eat enough.'

'God bless her,' said TC. 'She's already given us cakes. I'll get some plates and knives.'

As they ate, they discussed the vast differences in personality and character of Brolgaites.

'I must admit, I sometimes feel more than a little out of place here,' said Graham seriously. 'I come from a fairly conservative family, I don't drink, and I wear a police uniform. I have to learn not to judge people's character by their façade. I have begun to realise that a lot of people who talk and appear rough externally are, in reality, kind, honest, and God-fearing. The opposite is often there as well.'

'My dad says you can never judge a book by its cover,' interjected Lou. 'You have to read the words inside to get to the heart of it.'

'I agree with your dad,' said Graham.

'Me, too,' said TC. 'Now, let's clear up and get down to business. In a couple of hours, we'll know which one of us has the best word power.' Graham laughed.

'It depends on which letters we draw,' he said flashing a smile.

'Well, I'll be okay,' quipped Lou. 'If anyone can draw, it's me. I can sketch anything.'

'Lou, please be serious,' said TC with a giggle.

'Certainly,' replied Lou lightly. 'I'll put on a record. You get the game and Graham can set it up while he contemplates our slaughter.'

Within minutes Graham was seated at one end of the table, Lou was on the right side and TC on the left. Each had a little letter rack, a tiny notepad, and a pencil in front of them. The Scrabble board was open in the middle along with a cotton bag containing the letters.

'This sure is exciting, isn't it, TC?' said Lou sarcastically.

'Lou, let's consider this an adventure,' replied TC. 'Something we have never experienced before. Who knows, Lou, we might enjoy it.'

While Graham endeavoured to refrain from laughing, his mind was racing. 'Never heard of a game of Scrabble being portrayed that way. Sure can think of something else that would be appropriate. If only!'

'Sorry, I drifted away there for a moment,' said Graham. 'Each of us has a pad and a pencil and in order to keep each other honest, we do not record our own scores. I'll keep Lou's, TC will keep mine, and Lou will keep TC's.'

'Once a cop, always a cop,' said Lou.

'Yes, Graham, I thought you were off-duty,' said TC.

'Are we playing for money?' asked Lou, feigning innocence.

'That would be illegal. Now, let's get started. Lou, you go first,' replied Graham as he handed Lou the bag from which to choose her letters.

'I think we like you better when you are smiling,' said TC with a pout. 'Tell bossy-boots to go outside.' To the girls' surprise, Graham stood up, walked through the house, down the stairs, and opened the gate.

'You've upset him, TC,' said Lou with concern. 'He's gone.'

'I was joking, Lou,' said TC as she pushed back her chair and ran through the hallway where she literally fell into Graham's arms.

'That was quick. I've got you in my arms already,' whispered Graham with a smile. TC smiled back as she stepped away from him.

'I thought you had gone home. I was coming after you to apologise.'

'No, I'm still here,' replied Graham softly. 'Bossy-boots has been sent on his way. He won't be back tonight. I promise.'

'Never seen you move so quickly, TC' said Lou. 'You sure are a lucky man, Graham, to have TC run after you. Let's play this game.'

They laughed a lot as Graham won two games in a row.

'We'll have to practice on the quiet behind closed doors, Lou,' said TC as they packed up the game.

'It's way after ten. I'll switch on 2UE,' said Lou.

'Let's have coffee with Lisa's pretty cakes,' said TC, who went to the kitchen to boil water in the electric kettle. Graham followed TC into the kitchen. She had her back to him as she was filling the kettle at the kitchen sink. He desperately wanted to put his arms around her waist and pull her close. Instead he tapped her on the shoulder.

'What's the matter?' asked TC in alarm as she turned to face him.

Graham gave his disarming wink and smile, then leaned down, and whispered in TC's ear, 'Someone told me to give this to you,' as he placed a folded piece of score-sheet paper into her hand. Graham quickly left the kitchen to join Lou. TC curiously unfolded the piece of paper. Her heart began racing when she read, I don't mean to rush things, but I think I'm in love with you.

How beautiful, thought TC. She read it over and over as she struggled to hold back her tears. I thought this kind of thing was reserved for the movies.

The phone rang, then Lou called. 'It's Vance, TC.'

'What's wrong? Are you crying?' asked Lou as TC took the phone while shaking her head.

'I'm going to camp early tomorrow, TC,' said Vance.

'You told me to remind you about the laundry,' replied TC.

'I forgot about that. I'll go collect it when we have finished talking,' said Vance. 'Delores is coming back, probably mid- to late next week. I want you and Lou to clean the house one night early in the week. Tell Lou I'll pay her. I ate with the Doctor tonight. He's happy with our arrangement. See you when I get back.' Vance hung up.

¶

Vance collected his clean laundry from Neil's mother, who had waited up for him. When he pulled the ute into his yard, he noticed there was a light on in the kitchen. He was confused.

'Delores couldn't possibly be back by now. I must have left it on this morning.' Vance walked through the house towards the kitchen. He was shocked when he heard Claudia's voice.

'About time you came home. I've been waiting here for hours.' Claudia was sitting on a chair naked except for a gold neck chain.

'What the hell are you doing here?' snapped Vance angrily. 'What if my wife and kids arrived home unexpectedly. Are you crazy? Get some clothes on and get out of here.' Claudia got off the chair where she had been sitting.

'What's wrong with what I'm wearing?' said Claudia seductively as she walked slowly towards Vance rubbing a finger backwards and forwards on her gold chain.

'Stop it, Claudia. I told you, get dressed and get out.'

'You don't really mean that, Vance, darling,' murmured Claudia as she began slowly unbuttoning his shirt. 'Give me what I want, then I'll go home. I'll even let you drive me. Come on, darling, you know you want it as much as I do. There's no one here except us. Please, Vance, darling. Please.' With his shirt buttons all undone, Claudia began to undo his belt.

Bugger it, thought Vance. She's right; there's nobody here but us. Make hay while the sun shines.

'Come on, Claudia. Let's find a bed. Will have to be more comfortable than the dispensary floor and desk.' Claudia giggled.

'I knew I'd convince you!'

'Don't be sure of yourself. I can still throw you out,' laughed Vance.

'Not yet, you won't,' replied Claudia confidently.

⁋

Jake was parked down by the creek. He was with one of the local girls he had dated for a while a couple of years back. He had decided to give the nurses a rest for a while.

'Gee, Jakie it's nice to be with you again,' said the girl as she redressed herself in the back seat of Jake's car. 'That was just great, Jakie.'

Jake was sitting in the front seat with a cigarette in one hand and fiddling with the car radio with the other. He was hoping to hear the late-night racing tips for the next day's races.

'Why don't you come back here with me, Jakie?' asked the girl in her ridiculous sing-song voice. 'We can do it again.'

No wonder I got rid of her before. She's a bloody airhead, thought Jake as he continued to play with the radio.

'Come on, Jakie,' persisted the girl.

'I'm coming, but only if you stop calling me Jakie. My name is Jake, not bloody Jakie.'

⁋

Graham and the girls had finished their coffee and Lisa's cream hearts. They were sitting in the lounge room talking while Buddy Holly sang, Maybe Baby, on the radio.

That's it, that's the song I'm going to sing for TC when the time is right, thought Graham. The overhead light was off in order not to attract insects from outside. There was a small table light in one corner. Graham and TC sat comfortably on the big chair. Lou was curled up on the armchair opposite them.

'Why don't you let Graham hold your hand, TC?' asked Lou seriously. 'Poor Graham has attempted to hold your hand at least a dozen times. You keep pulling away. Don't you like him?'

Graham was surprised by the open, straightforward manner in which Lou had questioned TC. He was also relieved because he had wanted to ask the exact same question. TC hesitated before replying. Vance's words of warning were ringing in her ears. She looked directly into Graham's eyes.

'Of course, I like you,' she said softly. 'I much more than like you. That is the problem. I like you too much.'

'Well, if you like him that much, why can't he hold your hand?' persisted Lou.

'The Boss said holding hands and kissing leads to other things,' replied TC.

Graham took both of TC's hands in his softly and sincerely said, 'TC, other things happen only if you want them to happen. I'm not going to hurt you. All I want to do is hold your hand. I want to feel close to you.'

'Let's sit on the steps,' suggested TC. 'The insects are after the little light now.'

As they stood up to move to the stairs, Lou said, 'I didn't notice before. We are all dressed the same. Black jeans and white tee-shirts.'

'Yes, but I'm not wearing cute girlie slippers,' said Graham.

'I think I'll let you lovers sit on the stairs by yourselves tonight,' said Lou flippantly. 'I'm going to compose a rough draft of a letter I might send.'

'We are not lovers, Lou,' said TC.

'Not yet,' said Lou. 'I'll be busy, so please don't disturb me.'

⁊

'Can I stay tonight?' said Claudia as she lay cuddled up to Vance in his bed.

'I'm leaving for camp early in the morning,' replied Vance as he blew smoke at the ceiling.

'You can drop me off at the quarters before you leave,' said Claudia pleadingly.

'Claudia, my wife and kids are coming back this week,' said Vance matter-of-factly. 'Under no circumstances are you to come near this house or the pharmacy. Don't even call the pharmacy. I'll contact you when I get back from the bush.'

'What if I want to buy a lipstick?' asked Claudia coyly.

'Wait until I get back,' replied Vance.

'Can I stay with you tonight, darling?' persisted Claudia as she began gently rubbing her hand up and down Vance's inner thigh.

'Sure, you can stay,' said Vance with a sigh. 'You're a hot bitch, aren't you?'

'I certainly hope so,' replied Claudia softly as she positioned herself astride Vance's stomach.

⁊

Down by the creek, Jake was worn out by the local girl. Apart from being exhausted, he was furious. He swore to himself that he would strangle her if she called him Jakie one more time. I'll commit bloody suicide or become a bloody monk before I'll ask this bitch out again, he thought as he started his car.

'Time to take you home,' he said to the girl. 'I've had a great time.'

'You lying bastard,' he said to himself as he drove towards town.

⁊

Graham and TC sat on the stairs in silence. Graham held one of TC's hands in both of his. TC was trembling.

'Why are you shaking,' whispered Graham as he put the back of her hand to his lips and kissed it as he looked into her eyes and said softly. 'I meant what I wrote in that note. I won't hurt you.' He then kissed the back of her hand again. TC's body was experiencing sensations she had never felt before. 'I think about you all of the time,' continued Graham. 'I can't sleep because I'm thinking about you. When I do manage to get to sleep, I dream about you. I'm in love with you, TC.' TC desperately wanted to hug him and kiss him. He was so beautiful in every way. She longed to feel Graham's arms around her, holding her close to him. She wished Vance's words would disappear from her mind.

'You have lovely eyes,' she said softly as she looked into them. 'I don't know what to say. I feel as if I'm in a dream. I never thought anyone like you would tell me they love me.'

'Well, I just did,' said Graham as he held her hands tightly to him and leaned across and kissed her on the cheek, then stood up.

'I'm going home now. I'm in a rush to get to bed so I can think or dream about you.' He winked and smiled at TC as he patted the top of her head. After closing the gate behind him, he turned to blow TC a kiss. Then he was gone.

One more minute and I would not have been able to control myself, thought Graham as he walked slowly down the street. I wonder how she would react if I put my arms around her and kissed her. Just do it without warning. Catch her off guard. No, I'd most likely scare her away. I told her I wouldn't rush her. I'd best keep my word. 'This is going to be one hell of a sleepless night,' he said aloud to himself as he reached the police station gate.

¶

'How is your "perhaps" letter coming along Lou?' said TC after she had closed the front door and joined Lou in the dining room.

'Take a wild guess,' replied Lou as she gestured towards screwed-up writing pad pages strewn all over the floor. 'I suppose gorgeous Graham has gone home. Have you let him kiss you yet?'

'Mind your own business,' replied TC with a smile. 'I'm going to bed, Lou. As soon as I brush my teeth, that is.'

'I had best go to bed, too,' said Lou. 'I can finish this tomorrow instead of illegally listening to other people's personal business.'

¶

Come the early hours of the morning, the bank staff, stock agents, and station agents' staff, and the hierarchy of Brolga's younger members of society were still partying as was the norm for Friday nights. They could party until dawn if they wished. They had weekends off. As long as they didn't keep the cops awake with their noise, everything was fine.

Jake was in his bed smoking while wondering how much money he would win on the horses tomorrow.

At camp, Yappy was wide awake wondering the same thing.

Graham couldn't sleep. No matter how hard he tried, he just couldn't stop thinking about TC.

Lou couldn't sleep because she was thinking about the letter she wanted to write to Colin.

Vance and Claudia were in the throes of passion again! This bloody woman is sexually insatiable, thought Vance. 'I'll be well and truly buggered tomorrow. Already am, for that matter.

TC was wide awake while she wondered what the future held in store for her. Would it include Graham? She hoped so.

Delores was in her bed in Brisbane. She couldn't sleep. She was too excited by the fact that she was going back to Vance. She so desperately wanted to see her husband.

¶

Daylight at camp found the men eating breakfast. While not looking forward to another day at the hill, they were in high spirits. Apart from going on strike, they had no option. Even if they did pull the pin, they had no means of transport to get them to town.

'Cross off another day on that bloody calendar of yours, Yappy,' said Neil.

'Cross off half a dozen while you're at it, Yappy,' added Faith. Little Joe said nothing.

'Don't know why you mongrels are in such a hurry to get out of here,' said Yappy. 'You'll all be drunk within an hour of hitting town. Not only that, you'll be broke in less than a week. I guarantee that.'

'Then we'll bite you, Yappy mate,' said Faith.

'Not bloody likely,' replied Yappy. 'I'm not giving you bastards money to piss up a bloody wall. 'I'll buy you a feed if you need one but I draw the line at giving you money for bloody grog.' Nobody said a word. They knew Yappy was serious as well as correct in what he had said.

¶

'I'll probably fall asleep at the wheel on the way to camp,' said Vance before yawning as he dropped Claudia off behind the Empire.

'Don't tell me you didn't enjoy our night together,' said Claudia demurely.

'I'm out of here,' said Vance. 'I'll see you when I get back to town. Claudia smiled as she watched the ute turn onto the back street.

Your wife will have to be pretty good to match me, she thought before stepping onto the verandah of the quarters.

Vance went to the dispensary to call TC.

'What's wrong, Boss? It's early,' said TC when she heard his voice.

'When you clean the house, change the sheets on my bed,' said Vance. 'Better wash them too. See you later.'

TC turned on the radio. Elvis was singing, That's All Right, Mama.

'Sounds as if 4CL is lifting its act,' said Lou from the dining room where she was finally satisfied with the 'maybe' letter to Colin.

'I think I'm happy with this, at last. I don't want it to sound as if I'm desperate, which I am. I have left the door wide open for him to call me or come for a visit.' Lou handed TC her finished letter.

'Here, read it while I get ready for the gossip pit.' TC read as she followed Lou into her bedroom.

'Well, what do you think?' enquired Lou.

'It's you,' replied TC. 'Straight to the point with a touch of your dry humour.'

'Good,' replied Lou.

'I'll run his letter and my reply by Lisa, listen to what she has to say, then either post it or tear it up. Read it out aloud to me, TC. While you are reading, I'll pretend to be Colin.'

TC nodded, then began to read the letter aloud.

Dear Colin,

Obviously, your letter has found me. To say I was surprised to receive it would be an understatement. Yes, I'm happy to be home. Sydney is not the place for a girl from the bush, especially not one like me. I got my old job back at the telephone exchange. Sometimes I do a bit of work for TC's boss.

I have a house with TC. Most nights find us sitting on the front steps listening to records until ten. After ten, we usually get 2UE.

I hope your parents are well and happy. I doubt very much you'll be telling them we are in contact. Should you wish to call me, you will need to dial operator connect. When you get through to Brolga exchange, simply ask to be connected to me. Chances are I'll be at work and you'll be talking to me before you ask for me.

Sorry to hear you are bored with your lifestyle. Perhaps you should visit Brolga, Colin. Our little town is perfect for someone like yourself who is seeking a quieter, sane life.

Take care of yourself,

Lynette.

'Lou, I think Colin's letter has had more effect on you than you realise,' said TC laughing.

'What do you mean?' replied a confused Lou.

'It's Saturday, Lou. You don't have to go to the gossip pit today. You are off today and tomorrow,' said TC shaking her head while gesturing, 'I don't know what to do with you,' with her outward and upwards-posed hands.

¶

'Stupid me!' laughed Lou. 'I may as well stay dressed. Let's go to Con's before you go to work. I want to show Lisa my letters.'

¶

En route to camp, Vance's mind was racing hither, thither, all over the place.

I hope the girls remember to change the sheets. Hope Claudia doesn't show up at the house when Delores is there. Wonder if the men have found more boulders? Christmas is coming. Don't know where I'll get the money to pay them. Hope that opal cutting gear arrives soon. Wonder what my kids look like. I feel sorry for Louise, having to work with Claudia. Wonder where my Anna is? I hope TC calls the sergeant if Claudia gives her trouble. I'll never get over Anna. Oh, dear Lord, I wish I knew where she is. My life where women are concerned is a diabolical bloody mess. At least, I'm off the grog! I suppose that's something I've got going for me.

¶

Over the border, Old Bert Black was in bed with his young lover, Leanne.

'Leanne, my dear girl, we are going to take a trip to Brolga. I hear that mad bloody chemist has found good colour. I want to get my hands on some of it. We'll leave tomorrow. If we leave early, we'll be there late the day after tomorrow. I want to try to strike some sort of deal with him.'

'What about your wife, sweetie?' purred Leanne.

'I'll give her bloody sister twenty quid to look after her while we're gone. That bitch will do anything for a quid.'

§

Jake was lying awake in his bed listening to the racing tips for Sydney and Melbourne as he made notes on a pad. He heard the tipster say, 'And for the fifth race at Randwick, I'd be putting my money on Cook's choice.'

That's it, thought Jake. I'll put half of Yappy's hundred quid on that one. He continued listening and taking notes until the tipster session concluded. Better get myself ready for the day. I think it will be a good one. I'll win a few quid.

§

A little after seven, Lisa, Lou, and TC were seated at a table in Con's Café. Lisa had just read Colin's letter, then Lou's proposed reply.

'Fine, Lou,' said Lisa with a kind smile. 'Send it, Lou. I think Brolga will be getting a visit from this Colin. I also think he'll be here in the very near future.'

§

That'll be Vance, thought Yappy when he heard a car turn off the main road. Noise travels out here. It's so bloody quiet. Apart from the sound of the loader in the distance and my little companion, the radio, the only bloody thing a man hears is the occasional crow squawking. Don't know how I survived all that time without the company of that wireless. A wonder a bloody man didn't go stark raving bloody mad.

Sure enough, within a few minutes, Vance was there.

'You look like bloody shit, Vance, mate,' said Yappy after Vance got out of the ute.

'Feel like it, Yappy,' replied Vance with an attempt at a smile.

'What have you been up to?' laughed Yappy. 'As if I didn't know. Some bloody woman, I reckon.'

'As usual, you are right on the mark,' replied Vance. 'The mail truck will bring most of your order tomorrow. What's not coming tomorrow is in the back of the ute. How are all the men?'

'They are counting the days until we go on break,' replied Yappy with a grin. 'I told the bastards they will all be broke within a week.'

'I think you are right on that one, too, Yappy,' laughed Vance. 'Speak of the devils, here they come. Must be smoko time.'

'Look at your bloody watch, Vance,' said Yappy. 'Of course, it's bloody smoko time.'

'You look like shit, Boss,' said Neil when he, Faith, and Little Joe were just a few feet away from Vance.

'Yappy already told me,' replied Vance before yawning, then reaching to his pocket for his packet of Craven A.

'How's town, Boss?' asked Faith.

'Brolga is Brolga,' replied Vance.

'How is the Little Flower?' asked Little Joe.

'I think she's sweet on some young cop,' replied Vance with a hint of concern. 'Don't worry, I've given her a lecture and the cop a veiled warning. How's everything going here?'

'We've got more rocks for you,' replied Neil. 'That's the good side. Bad side is I think we're going to have transmission problems with the machine.' Suddenly Vance was no longer tired.

'How bad is it, Neil?'

'Not that bad yet,' replied Neil. 'I thought I'd warn you so you are forewarned. I could be wrong but I doubt it.'

'Well, we'll have to face it if and when it breaks down,' replied Vance seriously. 'Let's hope it's not too soon.'

'Check the heap out,' said Faith, pointing to the huge pile of boulders near the marquee.

'Holy hell,' laughed Vance. 'It's hard to believe after all that time with virtually nothing. I still can't get over it. Good on you, men. You've done well.'

They enjoyed their smoko break as usual. When the men had returned to the hill, Yappy turned to Vance, who was looking even more tired than when he arrived.

'Why don't you have a sleep for a while, Vance? Would do you good, mate'.

'Too much on my mind, Yappy,' replied Vance with a frown. 'I'll just sit outside and smoke a few cigarettes while I sort things out in my head. Jake is going to place a couple of bets for you, Yappy. He said he'll try his best to pick winners. Knowing Jake, he'll probably do just that.'

Just what we need, thought Vance as he went outside and lit a cigarette. Where the hell am I going to pluck money from for a new transmission? Maybe I've bitten off more than I can chew with this opal thing. Time will tell. It always does.

⁋

Bert Black and Leanne were well on their way driving towards Brolga.

'What sort of deal are you intending to strike with the mad chemist, sweetie,' asked Leanne as she lay back in the passenger seat in her short shorts and low-cut slinky top with her bare feet propped against the dashboard.

'Don't know yet,' replied Bert. 'First I have to find out how much and what, if anything, he needs from me.'

'You'll handle him, sweetie,' said Leanne confidently as she leaned forward and across to stroke Bert's wrinkled whisker-bearing chin.

'Hard to say, Leanne, my lovely,' replied Bert slowly. 'The man can't be a complete idiot. He is a chemist, after all. Apart from that, he's got the bloody opal. Not us!'

⁋

In the pharmacy, it was quiet again for a mail-order day, probably because of the looming cattle-sale day when anyone and everyone from far and near would be in town. Almost all the incoming calls had been from opal people in South Australia and New South Wales. The attitude of people who called ranged from, 'Never mind, luv,' to, 'Where the hell is the bastard?' when told Vance was not available. The phone rang again just as TC was about to close at one. It was Graham calling from the telephone booth outside the post office.

'What time are you closing?' he asked.

'Now! For once, I'm getting away on mail day before dark,' replied TC happily.

'Good! See you at Con's in two minutes.' TC's heart was rushing at the thought of seeing him.

They arrived at Con's door simultaneously. Graham leaned down and whispered, 'I'd like to kiss you right here in the street.' TC giggled.

'Stop that now, you two,' came Lisa's voice from inside the café. 'You'll give the town gossip feed. They've already got more than they can handle.'

'Full marks for subtly, Lisa,' said Graham with a smile.

'I can but try, darling,' replied Lisa, smiling demurely. 'Please enjoy.'

❡

Jake, as usual on Saturday, was sitting in the ladies' lounge of the Empire. He was alone with a glass of beer on the table in front of him. He was in a bad mood. None of his selected horses had won so far. This next bastard better win, he thought while scowling at the notes which he held in one hand and inhaling deeply on the cigarette he held in the other. I'm already down eight hundred quid plus thirty quid of poor bloody Yappy's money. Can't do a bloody thing right today. Hope Cook's Choice romps in for him. Think I'll put a few quid on it for myself. If I don't, I'll be pissed off if it wins.

❡

'Come sit with me,' continued Lisa. 'Oh, you two darlings look wonderful together. Did you enjoy your evening with the girls, Constable Graham?'

'Very much so. Thanks again for the food,' said Graham. 'We especially liked the heart-shaped cream cakes. I think you are up to something romantic,' he concluded with his wink and smile.

'Not me,' said Lisa feigning innocence. 'Where's Lou?'

'She's visiting her parents. She hasn't seen them all week. She wants to show her mother Colin's letter. It's my turn to shout, Graham. What will we have?'

'Let me make you ice cream sundaes,' said Lisa.

'Only if we pay you for them,' replied Graham and TC in unison.

When Lisa presented the finished sundaes, both Graham and TC burst into laughter. Everything was heart-shaped—the scoops of nuts and the strawberries.

In Brisbane, Delores was packing in preparation for her drive back to Brolga. She had decided to get on her way a few days earlier than planned. She wanted to surprise Vance by being settled back at home when he arrived home from camp.

Come lunchtime at camp, Vance was still sitting outside the kitchen, staring into space, chain-smoking and deeply engulfed in silent thought. His mind was plagued with worry as to where and how he could come up with quick money when the transmission on the machine became defunct. He couldn't bite Jake again. He already owed him ten thousand. Vance's thoughts were interrupted when he felt Neil touch him on the shoulder.

'Are you all right, mate?' asked Neil in concern as he leaned down to look directly into Vance face. Vance shook himself back into reality, rubbed his forehead, then his eyes.

'Yes, Neil, I'm just a bit tired,' he replied while thinking to himself, If only it was that bloody simple.

'You need to get some beauty sleep, Boss. You look like some bloody thing the cat dragged it,' said Faith with a laugh.

'Sure you are okay, Boss?' asked Little Joe softly and seriously. Vance nodded as Yappy called from the kitchen door.

'Come on, you mongrels, your bloody tucker is ready. A man hasn't got all bloody day.'

'Don't think we need a feed, Yappy,' replied Neil.

'Too bloody hot, mate,' added Faith. 'We'll eat lunch tonight when we feel a bit cooler.'

'I'm taking a shower,' said Little Joe.

'Must be bloody hot to get to you, Little Joe,' said Neil. 'You are without a doubt the toughest bastard I know.' Little Joe shrugged as he removed his work boots and socks before pulling his towel off the clothesline and walking to the shower.

'Think you're bloody right,' said Yappy. 'Must be a hundred and ten.'

'Yeah, that would be in the bloody shade, Yappy,' said Faith matter-of-factly.

'Dry as buggery, too,' said Neil. 'Faith lit a smoke on the way back from the hill. Nearly had a fire on our hands.'

'The match must have still been alight when I threw it near the pile of chopped-down trees between the hill and here,' said Faith. 'Some leaves started burning straight away. Just as well Little Joe was behind me to stamp it out.'

'Is that so,' said Vance who was instantly wide-awake and ultra-alert. After a few moments of thought, he added, 'You'll have to be more careful, Faith! We'll load the ute with some of the boulders. I'm going back to town. I have to see someone about something important. I'll probably be back out here tomorrow. By the way, it is bloody hot. Too hot to work out in the sun. Have the rest of the day off.'

'Does that include me, Vance?' asked Yappy while knowing it did, apart from cleaning up after dinner. 'Not fair if these bloody mongrels get the afternoon off while I have to keep working as usual.'

Vance laughed as he replied, 'Yappy, mate, the men are going to eat lunch for dinner. Surely that gives you a break.'

'Oh, a man bloody forgot about that,' said Yappy feigning innocence.

Vance arrived back in town as the sun was setting behind him. He drove directly to his backyard in order to unload the boulders. When he got out of the ute to unlock the fowl-yard gate, he noticed the back door of his house was wide open. He could hear his favourite Ray Charles song sounding from within.

'Bloody hell,' he said aloud. 'Surely Claudia hasn't had the gall to come to the house when, as far as she knows, I'm at camp.' TC appeared in the doorway.

'That was a quick trip, Boss,' she called in surprise. 'Is there a problem?'

'No problem. Help me unload these boulders,' replied Vance.

'Lou and I have just finished cleaning the house,' said TC as she approached the ute.

'Hope you remembered to wash those sheets,' replied Vance. TC nodded.

'Also remade your bed.'

'Good girls,' said Vance. 'Now get Lou; she can help us unload, too. I'm in a hurry. I need to track down Jake before he gets too drunk or hits the creek bank with one of his floosies.'

§

Jake was in the bar of the Empire. He was drinking alone and indecisive as to how and with whom he would spend his time tonight. Jake was disappointed with his day's gambling results. While he was relieved that he had broken even, his mind was telling him he should have won a heap. He should have stuck to his instincts instead of placing his bets all over the place like a bloody novice punter. Thank God, Cook's Choice had bolted in at twelve to one. He had put a hundred on it for himself after backing losers all day. Yappy's seventy on Cook's Choice would make the little man happy as he was in front by over eight hundred quid after allowing for the thirty Jake had wagered for him on a loser. At least on the bright side, Yappy was ahead even if Jake was not.

As Vance drove the girls home after finishing at his house, he noticed Jake's car parked outside the Empire. Through the open pub doorway he could see Claudia was on duty behind the bar. No way am I going into the bar with her on duty, thought Vance. If she knows I'm in town, it will be a repetition of last night. I can hardly ask the girls to wash the sheets again tomorrow. He began laughing loudly as he stopped the ute outside the girls' house.

'Why are you laughing, Boss?' asked TC.

'Nothing you little girls need to know,' replied Vance. 'I'm going back to camp in the morning. See you later in the week.'

'Vance seems a little strange,' remarked Lou as Vance drove off up the street.

'He's got something on his mind for sure,' replied TC. 'Who knows? Where the Boss is concerned, he could be thinking anything. Nothing would surprise me.'

¶

Vance went home and immediately phoned the Empire. Jack Romeo answered. Vance asked him to bring Jake to the phone.

'On the quiet, please, Jack. I don't want a certain member of your staff to know that I am back in town.'

'I understand, Pill-Pusher,' replied Jack Romeo. 'Please wait. I'll go fetch young Jake.'

¶

Jake met Vance in the dispensary a little later. He immediately gave Yappy's winnings to Vance. They talked for a long time. At the end of the conversation, they shook hands as Jake said seriously, 'Deal, mate, just let me know when you are ready.'

They left the dispensary to go their separate ways. Vance went home to his bed, where he immediately fell into a peaceful, sound sleep. Jake went to his mother's house from where he phoned the nurses' quarters.

I'm so bloody excited, I need to get laid! he thought as he waited for one of the nurses to pick up the phone.

§

Bert Black and his Leanne were on their swag alongside Bert's car, which was parked in the bush about sixty miles east of Brolga.

'Hope there are no snakes around here, sweetie,' said Leanne.

'I'll kill the bastards if there are,' replied Bert as he ran his fingers through Leanne's hair.

'I know you would, sweetie,' purred Leanne. 'You are the bravest man in the world. That's why I love you,' she continued before beginning to gently nibble on Bert's hairy ear.

'Lovely Leanne, I know what's on your mind. Not now. Let's get some sleep. I'm not as young as or as randy as I used to be. If you insist on loving a worn-out old bastard like me, you'll have to come to terms with my sexual limitations. Otherwise, find yourself some young stallion to fulfil your needs. 'Must be a million horny young shit-heads looking for a girl like you. I'm certain they would love to point their stiff pricks in your direction. Now, please stop trying to eat my ear. Come here, I'll hold you close to me while we drift off into the land of nod.' Leanne cuddled close to Bert.

'I love you, Bert Black,' she whispered. Bert did not reply. He was asleep.

§

Old Jock and his Seat of Knowledge regulars decided to quit their Saturday night vigil after the last movie patron had returned to the theatre after interval.

'Sweet bugger, nothing's happening tonight,' complained Jack.

'Yeah, mate, it's bloody dead all right,' agreed a crony.

'S'pose we might as well go home,' suggested another.

'Let's go,' replied Jock as he, along with his mates, reluctantly got to their feet. All mumbled disappointment regarding the lack of bloody action downtown. On a bloody Saturday night, at that! What was Brolga becoming!

'Perhaps something of interest will occur next week,' said Jock as they dispersed in different directions. They all nodded.

'Bloody hope so,' replied one of them.

§

Doctor Jackson was sitting in the lounge room of his residence. He was attempting to read a book, which, quite frankly, he found boring. On the coffee table in front of his chair was a brandy glass half-filled with cognac from which he sipped every time he turned a page. A couple of houses away some locals were enjoying what sounded like a pretty happy gathering. Everyone was laughing, with great jazz music playing in the background.

Wish I possessed the intestinal fortitude to crash their party, he thought to himself somewhat sadly. What a miserable way to spend a Saturday night. Really do not know how I shall manage to retain my sanity in this town. I wish I had not signed that damned contract. Doctor Jackson threw his book on the coffee table before picking up his glass of imported brandy and telling himself not to be impatient. He was bound to make at least a couple of friends sooner or later. He desperately hoped it would be sooner rather than the alternative.

§

TC and Lou were busy sewing. Their aim was four new outfits each before Christmas.

'Don't know why we bother,' said Lou casually. 'Nothing will change much for us. Christmas is just another excuse for people like my dad to get drunk, pass out, wake up with a hangover, and be in a bad mood for the next few days.' TC laughed before replying.

'At least your dad will have a good time before pass-out time. As for us, Lou, if nothing else, it will give us an excuse to look pretty in our new clothes.'

'At least you'll have Graham to tell you how beautiful you look,' said Lou.

'He might go home to his parents for Christmas,' replied TC softly.

'What? Leave the poor old sergeant here by himself to handle all the mad drunks? I don't think so, my friend,' said Lou with a smile. Bill Haley was singing his old Rock Around the Clock song on the radio. 'That's it, Bill. Pity I don't have anybody to rock with,' continued Lou wistfully.

'You will hear from Colin,' said TC confidently. 'I know it! You'll probably marry him!'

'Only if you will be my bridesmaid,' laughed Lou.

'Of course, I will,' replied TC with a smile. 'Let's tidy up this sewing mess. Graham is coming to finish after his patrol.'

'You've fallen for him, haven't you, TC?' said Lou seriously. TC nodded slowly with sadness in her eyes and facial expression.

'I doubt you will ever be my bridesmaid, Lou. In my heart I know I'll never be a normal housewife and mother. I'll be different! It will break my heart to hurt Graham; yet, I know I will. I'll never meet anyone like him again. I know that, too.'

'Let's tidy up before he gets here,' said Lou, as she quickly began neatly piling this and that while thinking how sincerely saddened her friend was obviously feeling regarding her self-inflicted, pre-ordained future.

¶

A little later Jake drove around the corner from the nurses' quarters as Graham arrived at the gate to the girls' house and greeted Lou and TC, who were sitting on the stairs waiting for him.

¶

What's that bastard cop doing visiting those little bitches this time of the bloody night? thought Jake as he sped past. If he's after a screw from either of them, he's barking up the wrong tree. Shit, what a crappy, bloody day. I didn't win any money, the bloody nurse I took to the creek is menstruating, and now I see that prick calling on them at my own bloody Aunt's house, to boot. Oh, stuff it!

¶

Come daylight, Vance was well on his way back to the opal mine. He was on a bad stretch of the dirt road, concentrating on avoiding the numerous potholes and the ute sliding while negotiating the patches of heavy bulldust when suddenly Claudia popped into his mind.

I should have left her a note or sent her a message via Jake, he thought. Some busybody is bound to tell her I was in town. Half the population would have spotted the ute. Bugger it!

When Vance arrived at camp, he was surprised to find Yappy in camp alone. He had expected to find Neil, Faith, and Little Joe there, as well.

'Thought the men started late today, Yappy?'

'Thanks for the "Hello, Yappy, how are you mate?"' replied Yappy sarcastically. 'They went to the hill the moment the sun peeped its bloody eye from the sky. They skipped breakfast, and they told me they don't want smoko. They'll take a long break at lunch time; too bloody hot for them on the hill in the middle of the day. Weak bloody mongrels.' Vance laughed.

'Come on, Yappy, you know that's not true.'

'I can say any bloody thing about them I want,' replied Yappy. 'No other bastard can, or they'll have me to deal with. That goes for you, too, Vance.'

'I'll consider that a warning,' replied Vance with a broad smile as he reached for his cigarette packet. 'Jake gave me your winnings, Yappy. He backed a horse called Cooks Choice. It romped in at twelve to one. Unfortunately, he lost thirty quid of yours on a loser; so, you had only seventy on the winner.'

'That's bloody great, Vance!' said an elated Yappy. 'Rate I'm winning on the bloody horses, I'll be richer than you.'

Vance wanted to say, you already are; instead, he went to retrieve Yappy's winnings from the ute's glove box.

'You look a lot bloody better than you did yesterday, Vance,' said a smiling Yappy when Vance handed him the money.

'Had a lot on my mind, Yappy,' replied Vance. 'Today I'm just fine. I'm going to load the rest of the boulders into the ute. I might go back to town this afternoon. Some saws and other gear are due to arrive on the goods train tomorrow morning.'

¶

Bert Black and his Leanne were finishing a meal in Con's Café.

Don't like the look of that bloke, thought Con as he observed from behind the counter. Stupid, old bugger with that young tart. If her shorts were any shorter, her tits would be on show.

'You don't happen to know where I would find the chemist?' asked Bert.

'No,' replied Con shortly.

'Is he in town?' asked Bert

'I don't know,' replied Con.

'Who would know?' asked Bert.

'I don't know,' lied Con.

'I thought in a tiny town like Brolga, everyone would know everything,' said Bert Black with as much civility as he could muster.

'Not me. I'm just a Greek,' replied Con. 'I know nothing.'

'Let's go, Leanne, my love,' said Bert as he stood to pay Con. 'Thank you for being a Greek know-nothing,' he continued as he paid Con.

'My pleasure,' replied Con with a false smile.

Bert Black and Leanne paused on the footpath outside the café. Con wanted to vault the counter and punch Bert when he heard him say loudly, 'I hear the chemist is a drunk as well as mad. We'll ask at the pubs when they open. Some bastard is sure to know where we can find him.'

'All right, sweetie,' agreed Leanne as she took Bert's hand in hers and they strolled off across the street to peer through the pharmacy door on the off-chance that Vance would be there.

TC and Lou were in the newsagency/plus-anything-else-you-need-to-buy, next door to the pharmacy. They were negotiating a deal on a second-hand washing machine. Since Jake had told Lou they should both get stuffed, they had not felt comfortable about doing their laundry at Jake's mother's house.

Deal done and delivery pending, they quickly left the newsagency in order to get home before the store owner arrived with the somewhat used but still-in-good-working-order machine.

They were in such a hurry that they almost bumped into Bert Black and Leanne who were looking through the closed pharmacy door.

'Did you need something?' asked TC politely as she paused briefly.

'Looking for Mr Callahan,' replied Bert Black.

'He's out of town. Not sure when he'll be back. Sorry, I have to go,' said TC as she ran to catch up with Lou, who had kept walking.

'I think everybody in this one-horse town must be rude, sweetie,' remarked Leanne.

'She wasn't rude, Leanne. It's obvious she and her friend are in a hurry,' replied Bert slowly.

'I don't like her. I don't like the redhead, either,' pouted Leanne. Bert laughed as he squeezed Leanne's hand tightly.

'You don't like them, little Leanne, because without a doubt they are both prettier than you.'

'Thanks a lot,' snapped Leanne as she pulled her hand away from Bert's. 'Screw you and screw them.' Bert Black laughed again.

'I doubt very much that will happen, my dear, jealous little offended one,' he said as he took Leanne's hand back in his. 'The chemist is out of town; so, we may as well find somewhere to camp.'

'I don't want to camp, sweetie. I want to stay at one of the pubs,' replied Leanne in her impersonation of a spoiled, hurt little girl.

'All right, you win,' agreed Bert Black with a smile. 'You always do!'

❡

Vance left the camp after attempting to chat with the men over lunch. He was relieved when he drove away. Yappy was the only happy one amongst them. It was obvious the other three were totally despondent for one reason or another. Of course, the heat was getting to them.

Never mind, thought Vance, they'll cheer up! Pretty soon they'll be in town drinking themselves into oblivion and worrying me witless once they've run out of money.

As the men heard Vance's ute turn onto the main road, Yappy broke the silence.

'What the bloody hell is wrong with you bastards? Vance just about turned himself inside out trying to get you mongrels to talk. I'm not referring to you, Little Joe, because you rarely have much to say even at the best of times.'

'Put a sock in it, Yappy,' interrupted Faith. 'We're sick of being isolated out here in the middle of bloody nowhere. All right for the boss; he comes and goes when and if it suits him. We're stuck in this God-forsaken bloody place!'

'Yes, Yappy, mind your own bloody business,' said Neil. 'Otherwise, we won't talk to you, either.'

'Pull that bloody shit on me and I promise you'll all bloody starve,' replied Yappy seriously. 'Now, get the hell out of my bloody kitchen. If you want to be miserable, be bloody miserable somewhere else.'

'Consider us gone, Yappy,' said Little Joe as he, Faith, and Neil left the kitchen.

¶

Vance arrived back in town around four. He unloaded the boulders, hosed down the ute took a shower, then went to find Claudia. He found her sitting on the steps to the Empire staff quarters. She was painting her long, tapered fingernails with bright, dark-red, glossy nail varnish. Claudia was so engrossed in her task that she was unaware of Vance's presence until he spoke.

'How appropriate; scarlet talons for a scarlet woman,' he smirked. Claudia looked up at Vance.

'Piss off and mind your own damned business,' she said icily. 'You were in town last night, you bastard. Suppose you thought I wouldn't find out.'

'I needed a sleep!' replied Vance. 'I spent the night before with a sexually insatiable tart named Claudia. I wonder where she is now that I am here.' Claudia jumped up and threw her arms around Vance's neck while making sure not to smudge her freshly-painted nails.

'She's right here, Mr Callahan,' she whispered. 'Your place or the dispensary?'

'Better be the dispensary. My wife might drive home unexpectedly,' whispered Vance in reply as he hugged her tightly. 'I'll leave the back door open for you.'

'See you in five minutes,' said Claudia still whispering. She reluctantly pulled her arms away from Vance's neck as he released her, then turned towards the street and his ute.

Vance parked at the rear of the dispensary. Once inside, he phoned Doctor Jackson to invite him to eat with him later at Con's Café.

'I'd like that very much,' was Doctor Jackson's reply. 'What time?' Vance glanced at his wristwatch. It was a little after five.

'I'll meet you there at eight,' he replied.

As Vance put the phone down, Claudia walked in.

'Whom are you meeting at eight and where are you meeting whom?' she demanded.

'Don't be like that!' replied Vance with a smile. 'I'm going to have a meal at Con's with the doctor. Now be a good girl, get your gear off, and get over here.'

'Bet Doctor Jackson can't give you what I can,' said Claudia with a shrug as she began to unbutton her blouse.

¶

Jake was at the Sunday afternoon session at the Empire. He looked at his Rum and Coke on the bar in front of him, lit a cigarette, then glanced around the bar in search of a likely drinking buddy. When he didn't spot anyone of interest, he wished Vance were there with him. Why did the bastard have to give up the grog? he thought. Not only that, he's hardly been in town these days, so not only am I without a drinking mate, Con and I don't have a third for poker, and I sure as hell miss his company on Saturdays when I'm playing the horses! I even miss the two little bitches. Fancy Vance taking Miss Goody Two-Shoes' side.

'Oh, stuff it,' he muttered, as he stubbed out his cigarette in an ash tray, threw down his drink in one gulp, then left the bar.

¶

Bert Black and Leanne had rented a room at the rear of the Empire. The room was, as Bert Romeo had described it, 'Sparse, cheap and clean.'

'It's sparse, all right, sweetie,' complained Leanne when they entered the room, furnished with a double bed, one side of which was pushed up against the wall, a bedside table, and a small, old-fashioned, dark-stained matching wooden wardrobe.

'It's also cheap, Leanne,' replied Bert Black. 'As we do not know how long we will be in Brolga, we need to be careful with our money.'

'Okay! Okay! I don't know why you're so bloody tight with money, Bert,' whinged Leanne. 'Everyone knows you have plenty of it.'

'The reason I have a lot of money, Leanne, is because I don't throw it around. I respect it,' replied Bert Black with a smile. 'Now, let's make use of this bed. Later, I'll take you to the Greek's café for dinner.'

'At least the Greeks serve a good meal,' said Leanne softly as she got onto the bed and into Bert Black's open arms.

¶

Lou and TC were in their dining room finishing off their day's work of house-cleaning, washing, ironing, sewing, shampooing, and rolling their hair as well as making their first joint purchase of the new second-hand washing machine.

'I'm tired, TC,' said Lou as she dramatically slumped forward onto the dining room table. 'It's been a long, busy day. I wonder how normal girls our age have spent their day?'

'I suppose that depends on how we interpret the word "normal,"' replied TC as she folded the ironing board.

'I wonder if Colin will reply to my letter,' murmured Lou.

'He will,' replied TC confidently. 'I told you Lou, Colin and you will get married someday. I know it. I also know I'll be your bridesmaid. Come on, Lou, try not to be miserable. Your parents love you, I love you, and I do believe Colin loves you.' Lou jumped to her feet and hugged TC.

'TC, I hope you are right,' said Lou excitedly. 'By the way, TC, I love you too. You are the best friend I ever could have wished for.'

'That swings two ways, Lou,' replied TC with a smile. 'Now, I suggest we take our showers before the snake brigade hits the path. The sergeant gave Graham the night off. He'll meet us at Con's after the movies start!'

❡

Lisa beckoned to Graham, Lou, and TC when they arrived simultaneously.

'Come and sit here, my darlings. Talk with me while my Con cooks your dinner.'

❡

In the dispensary Vance glanced at his watch repeatedly.

'Claudia, you'll have to go,' he said firmly. 'I'm meeting Doctor Jackson at Con's at eight.'

'I want to come with you, darling,' replied Claudia softly while stroking Vance's cheeks as she looked pleadingly into his eyes.

'Well, you can't!' said Vance as he removed her hands from his face.

'Screw you, Vance!' replied Claudia angrily.

'Claudia we've been screwing for the past two-and-a-half hours,' said Vance matter-of-factly, while endeavouring to conceal his annoyance. 'Now, please leave!'

'I am not bloody well leaving,' screamed Claudia. 'I am coming with you!'

'That's it! Out you go,' ordered Vance as he picked up Claudia's blouse and jeans, which he threw out the back door before firmly guiding Claudia through the door after them. He then firmly closed the door and locked it.

'Mad bloody bitch,' he mumbled to himself as Claudia began bashing on the door while screaming obscenely.

Vance quickly washed his face, redressed himself, turned off the dispensary light, then left the shop via the front door.

When he walked into the café a couple of minutes later, Lisa called to him.

'I have a message for you, Vance. The doctor had to go to the hospital, so he probably won't make it. Come join us.'

'That was quick, Boss!' said a surprised TC.

'The men were in a pretty down state of mind, so I decided to come back to town,' replied Vance before acknowledging Graham and Lou.

'You're back already, mate,' came Jake's voice from the doorway as he arrived with two nurses. 'Come and have a feed with us.'

'See you later,' said Vance as he turned to join Jake and the nurses at a table flush with the side wall.

§

Bert Black and Leanne entered the café a couple of minutes later. It was a luxury for them to eat a little later because back home Bert's wife insisted on eating the evening meal at five-thirty in the afternoon.

'This is an unexpected rush, darlings,' said Lisa. 'I had better take their orders.'

Con partially opened one-half of the kitchen swinging doors, which had porthole-sized, clear-glass windows at Con's eye level. He beckoned to TC, who got up and went into the kitchen.

'Your food is ready, TC. One half-size each for you and Lou, one regular for young Constable Graham. That man who just walked in with that young girl was asking about Vance this morning. I don't like him, TC. I don't like the girl either.' TC stood on her tip-toes to look through the porthole window.

133

'He asked me, too, Con. I'll tell the boss.'

'Make sure you tell Vance I don't like him.' TC nodded as she returned inside, where she beckoned to Vance, who was laughing with Jake and the nurses. Vance immediately stood up and walked to the rear of the café.

'What's the problem, TC?' asked Vance.

'That man and girl were asking about you this morning,' replied TC softly. 'Con said he does not like them.' Vance took a cursory glance at Bert Black and Leanne.

'They can wait until tomorrow. They are probably opal people,' said Vance as he turned to re-join Jake and the nurses.

As Lisa took the food orders into the kitchen to Con, Claudia charged through the front door of the café. She stood stationary for a moment as she looked around for Vance. Her clothes and hair were in disarray. She had obviously been crying. She was barefooted, with her arms by her sides. She clenched, then unclenched, her fists repeatedly as she absorbed the scene of Vance obviously enjoying himself with Jake and two young women.

'You lying bastard, Callahan,' she screamed. 'Which one of these sluts is supposed to be the doctor? You threw me out for them!'

Everyone seated in the café was silent. Con and Lisa were silent as they peered through the kitchen door portholes.

Oh, shit, thought Vance. Thank God, the doctor isn't here!

'Wonder which one of them is Callahan,' thought Bert Black and Leanne as they stared at Jake and Vance with great interest.

Graham and the girls looked over their shoulders at the scene behind them.

Jake thought he should say something in defence of the two nurses.

'Now, come on, Claudia, you shouldn't call these ladies names. They are respectable nurses.'

'Respectable, my arse,' yelled Claudia. 'They are about as respectable as you are, Jake! Everyone in this shithouse town knows about you and the nurses, so shut your smart mouth and mind you own effing business.'

Vance stood up as he said, 'Claudia, you are making a spectacle of yourself. I think you should leave before this goes any further.'

'Don't you dare pull that shit on me again, you bastard! You already threw me out once today!' retaliated Claudia, still screaming as her body shook with anger.

Lou was thinking, Once word gets out, the Seat of Knowledge group will have a hell of a time with this.

Graham was thinking, I'm not quite sure what to do about this. Pity I'm not in uniform. Wish the sergeant would appear.

TC was thinking, Poor Boss, he must feel terribly embarrassed.

Claudia picked up a silver-topped, glass pepper shaker from the table nearest to her. She threw the shaker at Vance. It missed, hit the wall, and on impact smashed into small pieces, causing a cloud of glass and pepper to envelop the nurses and Jake, who were still seated.

'You stupid bloody moll, Claudia,' yelled Jake as he jumped to his feet while attempting to brush glass and pepper off his clothes. 'You should choke the bitch, Vance!' Both nurses got to their feet while sneezing uncontrollably. They also were attempting to shake the glass and pepper from their clothes.

'Come on, ladies. I'll take you home,' said Jake.

Con and Lisa hurried from the kitchen, Con with a broom and dustpan; Lisa had a bucket of water and cloths.

'Sorry, mate,' said Con as Jake escorted the sneezing nurses out of the door.

'Not your fault, mate. I'll see you later,' replied Jake. Con turned to Vance.

'Get this mad woman out of here, mate. She's costing me business. Take her out the back way.'

Claudia began crying hysterically as she attempted to put her arms around Vance, who responded by saying, 'Get the hell out of here, Claudia. I hope you're happy now! You have just succeeded in creating enough gossip to keep the town talking for weeks. Well done!'

'I'm sorry, darling,' said Claudia between sobs as she started towards the back door of the café.

'Best entertainment I've seen in a long time,' said Bert Black out loud and on purpose. 'Not only that, it was free.'

'I suggest you shut your mouth,' said Con angrily. 'I warn you, one more word and you won't eat your meal when it's ready. You'll wear the bloody thing!'

Vance ignored Bert Black's comments. He joined Graham and the girls.

'Sorry about that, kids,' he said with a sigh. 'Think I should let you choose my women, TC.'

'The only woman I would select for you, Boss, is Mrs Callahan,' replied TC. 'She is your wife.'

'Finish your meals,' said Vance.

'Not hungry anymore' replied Lou.

'The excitement has filled me up,' said TC. 'We're going home now.'

'I'm finished, too. Nice to see you again, Mr Callahan,' said Graham as he and the girls stood up and walked to the counter.

'Pay us tomorrow, darlings,' said Lisa as she busily wiped down the affected table and chairs.

'Vance, come in the kitchen with me while I cook,' invited Con.

Once in the kitchen, Con threw three steaks on the griller. As he did so, he spoke to Vance.

'Mate! I don't care about the smashed glass and pepper. That's happened before! I don't care what Jake, the nurses, that old bloke, and his young tart think about what just happened inside. Doesn't bother me what the young cop thinks. I do care about my wife, who happens to adore Lou and TC. She calls them her darlings to their faces. Behind their backs, she refers to them as her sweethearts. She even serves them heart-shaped bloody eggs amongst other things! 'I will not have my wife nor these girls subjected to that language again. Tell that putana Claudia to stay away from here. The likes of her are not welcome in my café.'

Vance lit a Craven A. After exhaling he replied.

'I understand, Con. All I can say is that I'm sorry. As well as being sorry, I'm embarrassed to buggery. I don't know why I get mixed up with these crazy women! Perhaps it's me who sends them crazy.'

'Perhaps you do, mate,' agreed Con. 'Maybe you should have quit women instead of the booze. Here, sit in here and eat this,' continued

Con as he handed Vance a large plate on which were steak and eggs and chips. 'You look as if you need a decent feed.'

Con picked up two more plates of steak, eggs, and chips for Bert Black and Leanne.

'I'll come and sit with you after I serve these to the cradle-robber and his girlfriend.'

Vance finished his cigarette while deep in thought as he stared at the ceiling. 'Why am I so damned weak where women are concerned?' he asked himself repeatedly. 'Could it be I'm hoping to find a replacement for Anna? Every time one of the mad bitches pulls something, I ask myself the same questions. What a mess! Delores and the kids will be back in a couple of days.'

'Come on, mate, eat up,' said Con as he re-entered the kitchen.

'Thanks, Con, but I'm not hungry. I'm going home to bed,' replied Vance as he stood up and patted Con on the shoulder. 'Thank you for being a good friend,' he added before leaving the kitchen. Vance paused when he reached Bert Black's table.

'I believe you've been asking about me. I'll see you at the shop in the morning.' Bert Black nodded as Vance moved on.

Lisa was behind the counter with her back to the eating area when Vance left. She immediately went to the kitchen to speak to Con.

'I hope you told Vance I never want that woman in this café again?'

'Of course, I did,' replied Con defensively. 'It was not Vance's fault. We will not discuss it again, Lisa.' Saved by the bell, thought Con as he glanced through one of the kitchen door portholes.

'It's interval time,' he said. 'Come, my beautiful wife, help me make some money.' Lisa rolled her eyes and sighed as she followed Con into the café, where the movie goers where eagerly waiting to be served.

In the dispensary Vance called TC.

'I'm at the shop,' he said. 'I wanted to tell you and Lou that I'm sorry about the drama with Claudia.'

'You already apologised, Boss,' replied TC. 'You sure know how to pick your women.'

'I'm going home to bed, TC,' said Vance.

'Make sure you go alone, Boss,' replied TC. 'Mrs Callahan will be home soon.'

'Nobody is more aware of that than I am,' concluded Vance. After he put the phone down, he noticed Claudia's shoes on the floor. As he picked them up, he thought, Don't want to give her an excuse to come to the shop. After a moment's hesitation, Vance scribbled a note— Claudia, Con does not want you in his café ever again!' He then wrapped Claudia's shoes and the note into a brown-paper parcel on which he printed Claudia. En route to his home, Vance placed the parcel on the steps of the Empire staff quarters.

¶

After leaving Con's Café, Jake had driven the nurses to their quarters, then gone directly to his mother's house, called, 'Good night, Mum, I'm home,' before flopping fully clothed onto his bed. His clothes and hair reeked of pepper. Jake didn't care. He was sulking. He had been secretly relieved when Claudia bunged on her performance. She had unknowingly given him a perfect excuse to escape the café. He had wanted to leave the moment he saw TC and Lou with the cop. Why does the bastard have to be so bloody good-looking? thought Jake. Bloody prick should be in bloody acting school instead of a bloody cop's uniform in Brolga. Every bloody girl's dream. Even the nurses think he's just lovely. Pity he wouldn't zero in on them instead of TC and Lou. Suppose I'll have to tell them I'm sorry. Won't be bloody easy. Sorry is not a word that comes easy to me. Bloody little bitches! I can imagine them sitting on the stairs, listening to bloody 2UE while they drink Cokes. I heard that bloody cop bastard doesn't even have a beer.

'Oh, stuff it!' said Jake aloud as he threw one of his pillows at the wall.

¶

Graham left the girls' house at exactly midnight. The girls and he had played two games of Scrabble, both of which were won by TC.

'It's not fair,' he joked as he closed the gate behind him. 'I get whipped by a girl novice two games in a row. Now, I'm going home to dream about the same girl.'

'My dad says there's a fool born every minute,' said Lou with a laugh.

'That's comforting, Lou,' replied Graham. 'Consider me gone!' Lou and TC waited until Graham was out of sight before closing the front door.

'I'm on night shift for the next week,' said Lou. 'Will you miss me?'

'Of course, I will,' replied TC sincerely. 'Let's go to bed.'

¶

Vance went to the railway station early. Sure enough, the station master's paperwork indicated the shipment of gear Vance had anticipated arriving on the goods train was indeed there.

'We'll unload it as soon as possible, mate,' promised the station master. 'As soon as we locate it, I'll give you a call.' Vance then went to the dispensary, where he chain-smoked and drank one cup of coffee after another until TC arrived. When he heard her unlock the front door, he looked at his watch. She was early as usual. TC was only a few feet into the shop when Bert Black and Leanne stepped in behind her.

They are eager, thought Vance as he stood up to greet them.

'TC, make some coffee,' directed Vance as he reached out to shake Bert Black's hand, then acknowledge Leanne.

'White with two sugars for both of us,' ordered Leanne in a holier-than-thou, condescending tone of voice.

'Certainly,' replied TC with a forced smile while thinking, Perhaps I'll lace the sugar with some laxatives. Sure is tempting!

'I shan't be long. I'll go buy some milk.'

Once TC was out of earshot, Vance turned to Bert Black and Leanne, whom he looked directly in the eyes.

'I'm not certain why you have been asking about me. I imagine it's something to do with the opal I am supposed to have found. Leanne, I heard you speak to TC as if she is a servant. She is no one's servant! If your man, Bert, and I are to do business of any description, either now or in the future, I suggest you don't speak down to her again,' finished Vance with a nod of his head and a mock smile. Bert Black looked at Leanne. His mouth was open before she spoke.

'You didn't mean to come across that way, did you, Leanne?' Leanne did not reply. As she glared at Bert, she was thinking, You old bastard, of course I did!

'Good. Now what is it you want with me?' asked Vance as TC returned with the milk. Bert Black hesitated as he and Leanne looked in the direction of the medication shelves behind which TC was preparing their coffees.

'I see,' said Vance loudly. 'You don't want TC to be privy to our conversation. That's all right, isn't it, TC? I'll fill you in word for word later,' continued Vance as he walked behind the shelves and winked at TC with a broad smile.

'The coffees are ready, Mr Callahan,' replied TC formally while desperately suppressing looming laughter. 'I'll go fetch the mail.'

Although outwardly smiling, Bert Black was inwardly fuming as he thought, Smart bastard, I should deck him.

I hate him as much as I hate her, thought Leanne.

'Your coffees are on the sink,' said TC with a smile as she took the mail box key from its wall hook before leaving for the post office.

'Now, what can I do for you?' asked Vance after he was seated at his desk with a lit cigarette in his hand.

'Rumour has it you've found opal,' replied Bert Black.

'If I have?' questioned Vance.

'I thought perhaps we could help each other,' said Bert Black. Vance did not reply; instead, he took a drag on his cigarette. 'Do you know how to process your opal?' asked Bert Black. 'That is, if you have found any,' he added.

'Please continue,' replied Vance with interest.

'I thought Leanne and I might cut it for you for a percentage of the finished stones,' Bert Black said enthusiastically. Vance shook his head slowly, took another drag of his cigarette, then replied.

'No, Bert, I intend to do the whole deal here in Brolga. Don't quite know how as yet, but that is my plan. Apart from that, Bert, I believe it would be a huge mistake to pass over to outsiders the opal we have now or will have in the future. Nothing personal towards you and Leanne. I strongly feel if I lose sight of my opal, I shall also lose control of it.'

Oh, shit, thought Bert Black, he might be labelled the mad chemist, but he sure as hell isn't a fool.

'Who will cut it for you, Vance?' asked Leanne, who sensed Bert's disappointment.

'Don't know,' replied Vance. 'All I know is that it will be done here.' Bert Black stood up as did Leanne.

'Well, Vance, I really wanted to get my hands of some of this opal,' said Bert honestly. 'I saw some of it years back. It's very beautiful. Not only is it beautiful, it's also stable. Nice meeting you, Vance. We'll pop in to say goodbye before we leave town.'

'All right, Bert. Sorry your proposition isn't for me,' replied Vance courteously. 'The door is open should you come up with a plan I can live with.' As Vance watched Bert Black and Leanne leave, he thought, Nice try, Bert. You must think I came down in the last shower, old man.

Once outside the pharmacy, Leanne said, 'Bloody arsehole!'

'No, he's not, Leanne,' replied Bert Black seriously. 'He's a smart man. We'll have to come up with another plan. Let's go back to our room. I suddenly feel energetic,' he suggested as he took Leanne's hand and squeezed it tightly.

Vance phoned Con's Café and asked Con to tell TC the coast was clear for her to come back to the shop. As he put down the telephone, it rang.

'Your gear is on the platform, mate,' advised the station master.

'Will it fit in the ute or will I need a truck?' enquired Vance.

'I'd say one-and-a-half loads in the ute,' replied the station master.

'See you soon!' said Vance. 'I'm going to find Lou's dad,' he advised TC as she entered the dispensary with the mail. TC nodded.

The telephone rang as Vance drove off. TC picked it up. She didn't have the chance to speak before she heard Claudia's voice on the other end.

'Where the effing hell is he?' demanded Claudia. 'Don't effing tell me he's not here, you little bitch. I checked. His ute is out the back.' TC didn't say a word; she simply placed the telephone in its cradle.

'Just another day at the Brolga Pharmacy,' she muttered to herself as the phone rang again. TC reluctantly picked it up. She was almost certain it would be Claudia. Still, there was a chance it could be Mrs Callahan or a customer. It was Claudia.

'Don't you effing hang up on me. I'll have you fired!' TC placed the telephone on the bench, clicked the handset buttons with her fingers, then began opening the mail as she thought, Poor Boss. Finished with the mail TC placed the phone back in its cradle. It immediately rang. TC gingerly put it to her ear and answered.

'TC, is Vance in town? If so, is he there?' asked Delores.

'Yes, Mrs Callahan, he is in town,' replied TC. 'Sorry, he's not here at the moment.'

'Tell him the kids and I are back in Brolga, please.'

When Vance returned a few minutes later, Lou's father was with him. They chatted as to the possibility of this or that being positioned here or there until it was decided that Vance would take the new equipment to Jordan's place, where Jordan would construct appropriate shelves, stands, etc., before permanently fitting out the rear of the dispensary. TC had never seen Vance so excited. He seemed an entirely different man to the one she knew. Immediately there was a pause in Vance's conversation with Jordan Blake, TC spoke.

'Mrs Callahan called, Boss. She said to tell you she and the kids are home.'

'I see,' responded Vance as he reached for a cigarette and turned to

Lou's dad. 'Jordan, I'll meet you at the railway station in five minutes. Then we'll load the gear and take it to your place.'

'Sure, no problem, mate,' replied Jordan, who immediately exited via the back door.

'When did Delores call?' asked Vance.

'Just before you and Mr Blake arrived,' replied TC.

'Any other calls?' enquired Vance.

'Claudia called twice,' replied TC, 'I took the phone off the cradle.'

'She abused you again?' said Vance angrily.

'She wanted you. She thought you were here,' replied TC. 'Please don't worry about it. You have enough on your mind, Boss.'

'I'd like to strangle the bitch,' said Vance softly as he picked up the telephone.

'Please connect me with my house,' he instructed the telephonist. TC busied herself in the far front of the shop as Vance spoke with Delores. The conversation finished, Vance told TC he would see her next morning. He said he would take the stuff from the railway station to Jordan's, then go home.

Come siren time, TC closed the pharmacy, then went across to meet Lou at Con's Café. Lou was seated with Lisa at Lisa's table in the rear of the café.

'I got a letter from Colin,' announced Lou excitedly as she waved the unopened letter in her hand.

'Why haven't you opened it?' asked TC with a huge smile.

'Because I want you to read it to me,' replied Lou. 'That way if he's written anything I don't like or don't need to hear, you can change it by making up something nice.'

'You are incredible, Lou,' laughed TC.

'She's one of a kind, all right,' said Lisa.

'Here, TC, read it to Lisa and me,' said Lou as she thrust the unopened letter towards TC.

'Calm down, Lou,' laughed TC as she carefully opened the envelope.

'Read it through silently first,' insisted Lou. 'That way you can change the words where necessary.' TC did as instructed, smiled, then with eyes sparkling began to read aloud—

My Dear Lynette,

I was both thrilled and relieved to get your letter. Your handwriting is lovely. I expected no less as everything about you is lovely in my opinion.

I am glad you are happy now that you are back with the familiarity of your hometown. I always listen to 2UE. You can guarantee I shall be picturing you on the steps every time I have the radio on at and after midnight, Sydney time.

I have read your letter repeatedly since I received it. I keep it under my pillow. I have researched Brolga on a map of Queensland. I see it is the end of the railway line. When I visit you, I'll probably fly to Brisbane, then drive to Brolga. Then again, maybe I'll take the train. I imagine that would be an interesting trip.

I shall call you very soon, Lynette. I have repeatedly picked up the telephone to do so but decided to give you time to receive this first.

You are one in a million, Lynette. I wish you lived closer but you probably would not be the special girl you are if you had grown up around here. Where you are concerned, I say full marks to your parents and small bush town environment.

I'll call you real soon, Lynette.

Can't get you out of my mind.

Colin.

Lou was shedding silent tears of disbelief and happiness as she took the letter from TC. The moment was lost when they heard Sam yelling frantically from the front doorway.

'TC, come with me now! Hurry up! Run!'

'Oh, no! What's wrong with Sam this time,' said TC as she pushed back her chair, then ran after Sam through the Empire's gate and into the staff quarters verandah. Lou was but a couple of feet behind her.

'I'm here!' said Sam anxiously as she pointed through an open bedroom door. Both TC and Lou were in shock as they entered the bedroom.

Claudia was sitting on the floor while staring into space. She was propped against her bed with her skirt scrunched up around her hips. On the top section of both legs were numerous shallow cuts not much more than an inch long. From each cut ran a river of blood. Jess was sitting on the bed holding one of Claudia's hands; in her other hand, Claudia held a razor blade firmly between two fingers.

'Thank you for coming, luv,' said Jess. 'I found her like this when I came on break.'

'Should I get Doctor Jackson?' asked TC.

'No!' replied Jess firmly. 'She hasn't cut any main veins, luv. I'd say this is just a case of attention-seeking. This is about Vance, luv. Get him!' TC took a deep breath before replying.

'Jess, he's at his house. Mrs Callahan came back this morning.'

'All the more reason to get him, not anyone else,' said Jess seriously. 'Those nurses have big traps. The town is already buzzing about Claudia's effort in the café.'

'I'll go call him now,' said TC.

'I'll come with you,' said Lou.

As they rushed across to the dispensary, Lou said, 'TC don't tell him why you need him over the phone. If the gossip pit gets hold of it, everyone in the district will know before sundown.'

What am I going to say without saying anything, thought TC as she picked up the telephone. I hope it's the Boss who answers, not Mrs Callahan. She was in luck. Vance answered.

'Mr Callahan, I need you to come to the shop,' said TC seriously.

'TC, I told you I will see you tomorrow morning,' replied Vance with a tinge of anger in his tone.

'Mr Callahan, Doctor Jackson has written a prescription for a mixed ointment. I need you here now,' persisted TC. Vance picked up on the urgency in her voice as he glanced at his watch.

'I'll be right there,' replied Vance, who put down the telephone, then turned to Delores. 'I'll be back soon.'

What on earth can be wrong, he thought as he drove off in the ute. TC only calls me Mr Callahan when she's angry with me. I doubt she is at the moment. Jackson said he would avoid scripts for mixed ointments. Lunch hour is not over; so, the shop shouldn't be open.

'What on earth is so urgent it can't wait until tomorrow?' demanded

Vance on his arrival in the dispensary. TC told him quickly as Lou nodded her head in agreement. Vance thought for a moment before speaking.

'Lou, I saw Jake's car outside the Empire. Do me a favour. Please go get him. TC, you go tell Jess "thank you" from me. Also tell her Claudia will be collected soon.'

As the girls rushed off, Vance said aloud to himself, 'This shit could only happen to me!'

'She's cut herself a few more times,' said Jess when TC got back to the quarters. 'I have asked her to put the blade down or give it to me. She won't, luv.'

'She's bloody mad,' said Sam, who was observing from the bedroom doorway.

'I have to go back to the bar,' said Jess, who reluctantly got to her feet. 'Keep this to yourselves; I'm not telling anyone who does not already know, not even Jack or Bert.'

'My Boss said to thank you, Jess,' said TC. 'Claudia will be picked up soon.'

Jake and Lou arrived in Jake's car a few minutes after Jess had returned to the bar.

'Put the razor blade down, Claudia,' commanded Jake once he'd summed up the situation.

'Get effed, Jake,' said Claudia while continuing to stare directly ahead with the blade still firmly between her fingers.

'Claudia, I told you to put the razor blade down,' said Jake with impatient anger. 'If you don't put the bastard down, I promise you, I'll borrow a carving knife from the kitchen. With it I'll cut your effing throat.'

'Won't give you the effing satisfaction, Jake,' mumbled Claudia as she placed the razor blade on the floor.

Jake leaned down, put his hands under Claudia's armpits, and pulled her to her feet. As he removed his hands from her body, Jake said in obvious disgust, 'Pull your skirt down, you mad, foul-mouthed bitch. Find me a towel, please, Sam,' he requested. 'I don't want Claudia's blood on my car seat.' Sam quickly located a towel, which she spread across the back seat in Jake's car. Jake glared at Claudia.

'You get in the car and put your head down until I tell you to sit up. If you pull any crap, Claudia, I'll take you to the creek, strangle you, then throw you in.'

'Eff you, Jake,' snarled Claudia as she begrudgingly began walking out of the bedroom.

'Everyone knows I'm not fussy, Claudia, but I'd draw the line at you,' replied Jake. 'I wouldn't eff you with a forty-foot barge pole! Now get in the bloody car!' Jake turned to Sam.

'Keep your mouth shut about this, please, Sam.'

'Sure,' Sam nodded.

'You two go to the café,' he instructed Lou and TC. 'I'll come and get you when Vance gives me the okay.' As Jake drove away in the direction of the back street, Lou and TC returned to the café.

'Is Sam all right?' asked Lisa.

'She's fine, Lisa,' replied TC.

'You know, Sam; she's dramatic,' added Lou with a laugh.

'We have to pay you for our dinners last night,' said TC in order to change the subject.

'You don't have to, darlings,' replied Lisa with a smile. 'Constable Graham paid Con this morning.'

'He's naughty for doing that,' said TC.

'He's also lovely,' said Lisa.

'Are you talking about me, darling wife?' enquired Con from behind the counter. They all laughed at the questioning, innocent expression on Con's face.

In the dispensary, Vance was silent as he went about cleaning the blood off Claudia's legs with Dettol-soaked gauze. Claudia was sitting on the front of the desk in her briefs and blouse. Her blood-stained skirt was thrown over a stool. Jake was sitting in Vance's chair behind the desk.

'Should let her clean herself up, mate,' he said as he was about to light a cigarette.

'Shut up, Jake,' said Claudia.

'You're not as mad as I thought,' replied Jake. 'You wanted my mate's attention, and you sure have got it.'

'I told you to shut up, Jake,' said Claudia.

'Both of you, be quiet!' said Vance, who was obviously on short fuse. He went inside the shop and returned with a bag of cotton balls and a bottle of iodine, which he handed to Claudia.

'Here, dab this on your cuts. It will sting. I'll give you a tetanus shot after I smoke a cigarette.'

'Jake, will you go outside? I want to talk to Vance,' said Claudia.

'Stay where you are, please, Jake,' said Vance.

'I want to talk with you alone, darling,' insisted Claudia in what she considered to be her most seductive 'he won't be able to resist me' tone of voice.

'Claudia, don't call me darling and Jake stays where he is,' replied Vance coldly.

'Why don't you screw each other!' retaliated Claudia. Vance stubbed out his cigarette in the ash tray.

'I'll give you the tetanus shot now, Claudia, then Jake will drive you back to your quarters,' he said as he opened the refrigerator. 'Take the iodine and cotton balls with you. You can finish after Jake drops you off.' Vance swabbed, then injected Claudia's upper arm. As he stepped away, he said, 'Put your skirt on, Claudia.' Vance then turned to Jake.

'Thanks for bailing me out again, Jake.'

'When will I see you again, darling?' asked Claudia pleadingly as tears began to trickle down her cheeks.

'I urge you not to hold your breath, Claudia,' responded Vance indifferently.

'I'll be back soon, mate,' said Jake as he followed Claudia out the back door.

Vance slumped down in his chair behind the dispensary desk. As he lit a cigarette, he thought, Oh, Lord, how I would love a drink.

¶

When Jake returned, he seated himself on a stool opposite Vance.

'You feel like a drink, don't you, mate?' said Jake. Vance nodded,

'Yes, Jake, but I'm not having one. Delores is back. She'll be wondering where I am.'

'You go, mate,' suggested Jake. 'I'll go tell TC she can come back. I told her and Lou to wait in the café.'

'Thanks, Jake. Tell her I'll see her in the morning,' said Vance as he slowly got to his feet. 'She'll have locked the front door, so you'll need to release it by hand. I'm out of here.'

Jake walked across to the café door, beckoned to TC and Lou, then turned back towards the pharmacy. He was standing in the dispensary when the girls walked in. Without looking them in the eyes, Jake spoke quietly. 'I'm sorry for what I said,' turned his back on them, and walked out.

'Never thought I'd hear Jake Carmichael say sorry to anyone,' remarked Lou.

'It was a feeble apology, Lou.'

'Feeble it may have been, TC. Nevertheless, for Jake that was difficult and definitely out of character,' replied Lou. 'I'm going home to take a shower, then I'll probably read Colin's letter ten or twenty times before I go to work. I'll see you shortly after midnight. You and Graham will be alone for a change,' finished Lou with a smile.

TC shook her head as she replied, 'No, Graham is going to play tennis. He doesn't frequent the pub because he's not a drinker. So, he's joined the tennis club in order to give himself at least some social activity.' Lou laughed.

'Does he realise all the tennis players are women?'

'I don't think do,' replied TC.

'Those Brolga society girls are going to love him,' said Lou, who continued laughing as she left the shop.

You're not wrong there, Lou, thought TC as she looked around the shop, deciding what needed doing most. Vance phoned a few minutes before closing time.

'TC, Delores has gone grocery-shopping. I want you to quickly go to the Empire quarters, check that Claudia is all right, then call me back.'

'No, I'm not doing it, Mr Callahan!' replied TC adamantly.

'TC, do it now!' demanded Vance.

'No! You do it yourself, Mr Callahan!' replied TC stubbornly.

'Don't be so bloody ridiculous, TC,' snapped Vance in angry frustration. 'Do as I say and do it now!' TC slammed down the telephone, then ran out of the shop and across to the quarters, where she found Claudia reclined on her back on her bed while blowing smoke rings into the air.

'What do you want?' snarled Claudia venomously.

'Mr Callahan told me to check on you,' replied TC calmly.

'Piss off, you little bitch,' said Claudia indifferently. 'Don't come here again!' TC ran back to the dispensary to phone Vance.

'Just as well I'm on duty,' said Lou before connecting TC to Vance's house number.

'Well?' asked Vance.

'She's all right, she's Claudia!' replied TC before once again slamming down the phone.

When Vance heard the thump of the receiver on the other end, he smiled as he thought, One thing I know for certain is that tomorrow the kid will be calling me Mr Callahan, not Boss. Can't say I blame her!

TC felt miserable. As she locked the shop door, Lisa called to her from across the street. 'Come with me, darling. What's wrong?' asked Lisa as they walked inside the café.

'Why do you ask?' replied TC.

'Darling, please don't pull Con's tricks on me,' said Lisa with a half-hearted smile. 'Whenever Con does not want to answer my questions, he always replies with a question.'

'Perhaps it's life, Lisa,' said TC softly as they sat down at Lisa's table. 'Perhaps I'm finally growing up.' Lisa reached across the table and patted on one of her hands.

'You and Lou were born grown up, darling. That is one of the reasons you are both so special. You are wise far beyond your years. I tell my Con that I deeply believe you have been here in a former life.'

TC laughed, then replied somewhat wistfully, 'Perhaps that is why some people don't like me. They might remember me from when I was here before, so they are mean to me. Maybe I was not a nice person!' Lisa hesitated as she searched for the right words to subdue TC's obviously troubled state of mind.

'My darling TC,' she said. 'People are mean for many reasons. Not necessarily because they do not like you. Sometimes people don't like themselves, so they are mean to others. Could be insecurity, could be jealousy, perhaps anger or frustration with their lives in general. Some people hate the whole world! If you allow these folks to get you down, you will be a sorry fool. Ignore their most likely self-inflicted misery, TC. Pity them if you must. You be what you are; a lovely, intelligent, happy, open young woman. Happiness brings laughter, and laughter is infectious. It attracts other happy, laughing people.'

'I understand, Lisa,' replied TC with a smile. 'I shall ignore the people who are mean to me. I won't waste my time worrying about them. I shall slot them into my memory bank and always be on guard.'

'Good girl,' beamed Lisa. 'Smart girl, too.'

'I'll go home now,' said a relieved TC. 'Lou is at work, so I want to take my shower before it gets dark.'

'Still frightened of those snakes, are you, luv?' came Con's voice from the kitchen doorway.

'Always, Con,' said TC seriously. 'Thank you,' TC said as she hugged Lisa prior to leaving for home. Neither of them realised the advice Lisa had given TC would be a decisive factor in all of TC's future people relationships, both personal and business.

Lou came home from work to find TC asleep on the couch in the lounge room. The house was silent but for the crackling noise made by the stereo needle on the trackless section of an Elvis LP record which was turning relentlessly around and around. Lou removed the needle arm from the record, then shook TC gently on the shoulder.

'Unlike you to be sleeping so early,' she said when TC opened her eyes.

TC slowly sat upright, blinked a few times, then shook herself awake.

'Have you heard from Graham tonight?' asked Lou.

'No, he went to tennis,' replied TC drowsily.

'I know, TC,' said Lou. 'I also know he was a star with the girls. In more ways than one, I might add.'

'Please enlighten me, Lou,' said TC softly.

'He won the games he played, and the girls are wondering which one of them he will ask out first. Their phones have been running hot since they got home from tennis.'

'I don't blame them, Lou; he is gorgeous,' replied TC. 'How many times did we hear those guys in Sydney say that they had to go where the action was. Graham is young, extremely handsome, and he's a male. He knows he won't get what he needs from me, so who could blame him if he goes elsewhere. I have to go to bed, Lou. See you in the morning.' A little while later, when Lou went to bed, she heard TC crying.

I shouldn't have told her, thought Lou. 'Still, being forewarned is better than blind innocence. My dad says that!'

❡

Vance was in his bed puffing on a cigarette. Delores was sound asleep beside him. Hope Jordan hurries that job along, he thought as his mind raced here, there, and back again. I'm getting impatient to see what is hidden inside those boulders!

Bert Black and Leanne were both asleep in their room behind the Empire. Bert had come up with a proposition he planned to put to Vance next morning. Bert Black was very confident that Vance would grab it with both hands.

Jordan Blake was hammering and sawing his way through the night. Of course, he'd had a few and, of course, Slim Dusty was singing along keeping Jordan company.

Thel Carmichael was in her bed in her home opposite. She was trying desperately to go to sleep but couldn't because of Jordan's noisemaking. As she tossed and turned, she was endeavouring to figure out why Jordan would be making a coffin. She had not heard about any poor soul passing away. She would have to ask Jake in the morning.

Jake was sleeping peacefully. He had gone to bed early, steeped in self-gratification due to the fact that he was man enough to have said sorry to Lou and TC.

Louise was sitting up in her bed. On the bedside table near to her was a stiff Rum and Coke. She was also smoking a cigarette. She knew some drama with Claudia had occurred in the quarters during the day, but she was buggered if she could figure out what it was. No way would Jess crack a word about it. 'I hope Vance has given Claudia the arse," she said to herself, as she reached for her drink.

Graham was sitting in the chair in his room. He was deep in thought. He had enjoyed playing tennis. He had always loved the game. While he was glad he had won, he had a nagging feeling that all the female opposing players possibly had let him win. A few of the girls were very pretty and had openly flirted with him. Of course, he was flattered. Still, they weren't TC. He had five-night shifts in front of him. From all reports, Brolga would be more than a little chaotic towards the end of the week. Graham looked at his bed and thought, I hope I can sleep tonight. If I can't have TC, at least I can dream about her.

Claudia was tossing and turning in her bed. She was plagued by the thought of Vance being in bed with his wife. She questioned herself for what seemed the millionth time, 'How am I going to get him alone again?'

TC was making her bed the next morning when Lou called from the other bedroom.

'I'm hungry, TC.'

'So am I,' replied TC. We haven't eaten anything since Claudia interrupted our meal the other night.'

'There's nothing here. I'll shop today. Let's go to Con's for breakfast,' said Lou.

'Sounds good. We'll get there at seven when Con opens,' replied TC.

'What a lovely way to start the day,' greeted Con when he opened the door and saw the girls outside.

'We are hungry, Con,' said Lou.

'You have come to the right place,' laughed Con. 'What would you like? No, don't tell me. Let me guess. Two poached eggs, one strip of bacon, and one slice of toast each.' Both girls smiled at Con and nodded.

'Also, a glass of orange juice each,' said Con. 'Take a seat at Lisa's, darlings. It won't be long.' Con disappeared into the kitchen.

TC told Lou about the advice Lisa had given her.

'Sounds good,' said Lou. 'I can't understand why Vance made you check on Claudia. He knows how she treats you. All his women treat you like dirt. Perhaps he's fallen for her!'

'I don't know, Lou,' replied TC sadly while shaking her head from side to side. 'Every new woman he gets seems to be worse than the previous one. By the way, Lou, I didn't tell Lisa about anything that happened yesterday.'

'Of course not!' replied Lou. 'We say nothing to nobody.'

'Sorry about the eggs. I forgot to use Lisa's heart-shaped cake rings,' said Con with a giggle when he gave the girls their breakfast.

'We won't dob you in, Con,' laughed Lou.

Bert Black and Leanne came into the café for breakfast. After ordering, Bert walked up behind TC and tapped her on the shoulder. TC was startled. She quickly turned to see who it was.

'Good morning, Mr Black. You gave me a fright,' said TC with a smile.

'Sorry to frighten you. If you sat facing the door, you would have seen me coming,' said Bert Black in almost chastisement. 'What time are you expecting Mr Callahan to be at the pharmacy?' asked Bert Black.

'I really don't know, Mr Black,' replied TC, truthfully. 'Mr Callahan doesn't keep a fixed schedule.'

'I understand,' said Bert Black, as he turned and walked back to Leanne who spoke softly and maliciously the moment he sat down.

'That smart little bitch thinks she knows every bloody thing.' Bert Black looked directly at Leanne.

'Stop being so catty towards that girl,' he said seriously. 'She has done nothing to you. I strongly suggest you change your attitude towards her. The proposition I'm going to put to Vance Callahan revolves around her.' Leanne began to speak. Bert did not give her the opportunity. Instead, he took one of her hands, squeezed it, and said ever so quietly 'Please, little Leanne, be a good girl, be quiet, and, most of all, be nice.' Leanne pulled her hand away from Bert, shrugged, and pouted while looking anywhere except at Bert. Bert sighed while thinking, Women! Now she's sulking. Well, let her sulk. I'm going to get my hands on some of Callahan's opal. If it means I'll have to put up with her sulking for a while, so be it.

'I'm not looking forward to work today, Lou,' said TC, when the girls were in Con's kitchen, washing their breakfast dishes. 'The boss will be in a foul mood because, now that Mrs Callahan is back, he'll be feeling guilty.'

'There's not much happening at work, so I'll come home at lunch time,' said TC as they were waiting at the counter to pay Con.

'We'll come over in a little while to see Vance if he's there,' called Bert Black from his table. TC was surprised when Leanne gave her a smile.

'I'll tell him, Mr Black,' replied TC while returning Leanne's smile.

¶

The telephone was ringing when TC opened the shop. She rushed to answer it.

'Is the chemist there?' asked an abrupt male voice.

'No, sir, I'm sorry. Would you care to leave a message?'

'Bugger it! Has he found bloody opal or not?' asked the man.

'If you care to leave your number, sir, Mr Callahan will return your call,' replied TC.

'Bugger you, too!' was the reply.

Great start to the day, thought TC, as she picked up the broom.

155

Bert Black and Leanne came to the front door when TC was almost through mopping the floor, most of which was still wet when Bert and Leanne came in in hope of catching Vance. Bert Black stopped Leanne when she was about to walk on the wet floor.

'If he's not here yet, we'll come back later.'

'Mr Black, I'll find you when he comes in,' offered TC.

'Thank you. We'll wait in the beer garden at the middle hotel,' replied Bert Black.

§

Vance had not phoned or arrived at the dispensary by siren time. TC closed the shop, then walked across to the beer garden to tell Bert Black and Leanne that Vance had not come in. She need not have bothered. When she got there, Vance was sitting at a table with them. He was in deep conversation with Bert Black. TC did not interrupt. She backed off and walked home, where Lou was sitting on the steps waiting for her.

'Let's go inside, Lou,' said TC. 'Too hot out here. I'll get us a Coke.'

'What is wrong?' asked Lou as she followed TC through the hallway.

'I've had a lousy morning,' replied TC. 'Ever since word got out about the opal, phone calls are coming in from nameless, no-return-number, usually rude people. I have hardly been off the phone all morning. Only two people were polite enough to leave their names and numbers. Seems to me that the opal industry must be like some secret society. I hope the boss knows what he's got himself into.'

They sat down in the dining room to drink their Cokes. The phone rang almost immediately.

'You answer it, will you, Lou?' said TC. 'I have had enough of the phone today.' A moment later, Lou called.

'It's Vance, TC.' TC slowly got up and took the phone from Lou.

'What is it, Mr Callahan?'

'I expected you to be here at the shop.'

'It is lunch time, Mr Callahan,' said TC. 'That is why I'm not there at the shop.'

'When will you be here?'

'In time to re-open the shop on time, Mr Callahan,' replied TC.

Something is wrong, she thought as she heard the phone click. I'd best go find out what it is. I hope he's not drinking again.

'I'm going back to work, Lou,' announced TC.

'Something wrong?' enquired Lou with concern.

'Probably,' replied TC as she recapped her Coke bottle and replaced it in the refrigerator.

'Why doesn't Vance lay his problems on his wife like normal husbands do?' asked Lou.

'I think it's called guilt, Lou. I'll see you later,' replied TC.

§

Vance was sitting at his desk, smoking and deep in thought when TC walked into the dispensary.

'What is wrong this time, Mr Callahan?'

Vance gave TC a cursory glance, squashed his cigarette in the ash tray, then reached for his cigarette packet. After lighting a fresh one and exhaling after the first drag, Vance replied softly with sadness in his voice.

'Everything is wrong, as usual, Little Flower. Probably worse than usual because I am denying myself access to my old faithful rum-and-Coke escape route. Believe me, it's not easy! The only person I trust is you. That is why I lay all my crap at your feet. I know you won't betray me. Delores is jealous of you, my slutty girlfriends loathe you; and you know it, yet you tolerate it. After all this time, the strength of your loyalty still surprises me. On a lighter note, TC, I hate it when you call me Mr Callahan.'

'I know,' replied TC. 'Obviously, there's something you want me to do. Reading between the lines is something I won't want to do.' Vance laughed as he stretched back in his chair with both hands behind his head.

'My God, am I that transparent?'

'Yes,' replied TC, bluntly. Vance became serious, sat straight in his chair, lit a cigarette, then directed his attention towards TC.

'I need you to learn opal-cutting. Delores wants to do it, but that won't last long. She's got the kids and other things to deal with.'

Wonderful, thought TC. That will give Mrs Callahan another reason to resent me. Just what I don't need.

'Who will teach me?' she asked, hesitantly.

'Bert Black,' replied Vance as hesitantly. 'Of course, you would have to go away for a few weeks or so. You'll stay in a motel.'

'Go where?' questioned TC.

'Over the border where he comes from,' replied Vance enthusiastically. 'I would drive you there and come bring you back when you were finished.'

'I don't want to do it,' said TC while shaking her head from side to side.

'I didn't ask you if you want to do it. I told you I need you to do it,' replied Vance with a trace of angry frustration.

TC was silent for a moment before replying, 'Appears as if I have no choice. I shall resign myself to the fact that I am going away.'

'Thank you, TC,' said Vance as he quickly stood up. 'I'm going to see Bert Black, then Lou's father. I'll be back in an hour; then you can go home.'

§

Vance went to his house, where he collected two medium-sized boulders at random from the heap in the old fowl house. He then drove to the rear of the Empire, where he handed over the two boulders to Bert Black.

'Leanne and I are leaving early in the morning,' said Bert as he anxiously took the rocks from Vance. 'Give me a few days before you call me.'

'I'll give you a week, Bert' replied Vance. 'That will give you plenty of time to get home.' Bert Black smiled broadly.

'Also give me time to see what opal cuts out of these,' he said while indicating the two boulders he had placed on the path in front of him.

'Good luck. Talk to you next week,' farewelled Vance.

With Vance gone, Leanne emerged from the bedroom to join Bert.

'You should have hit him for more than two, Bert,' she said as she kneeled down to examine the rocks.

'Be fair, Leanne. He's given us pretty good-sized ones.'

'Yes, Bert, and you are going to teach Little Miss Bitch-Face how to cut and polish,' snapped Leanne. 'The chemist is getting off cheaply, if you ask me.'

'I didn't ask you, Leanne,' replied Bert Black calmly. 'Apart from that, I have no intentions of teaching her much. We'll just show her the basics. Bottom line is, where this type of opal is concerned, I'm not absolutely certain myself as yet how to process it for maximum yield and best colour. We'll soon find out.' Leanne was determined to have the last word.

'Well, Bert, don't expect me to be nice to her when she's down home.'

'We will put her in the little shed. The toilet is outside, so you won't even have to see the girl, okay?' reasoned Bert Black.

Leanne turned her back on Bert and rushed into the bedroom while muttering to herself, 'Up yours, Bert, you old bastard.' Bert Black shrugged as he observed Leanne's theatrics.

Women, he thought. Whoever coined that old saying, "We can't live with them, and we can't live without them," sure hit the nail on the bloody head.'

When Vance returned to the dispensary, he was accompanied by Lou's dad.

'You can go now, TC.' said Vance excitedly. 'Jordan and I will be here for as long as it takes to change things around.' TC hesitated.

'Are you sure you want me to go?'

'Yes! I'll watch the shop,' replied Vance. 'Now, go! I'll see you tomorrow.'

TC went outside. She stood on the footpath indecisive as to whether to go home or go to Con's. The street was deserted, apart from two men talking loudly on the footpath out front of the Majestic, herself, and Carmel, who was waving. TC waved back, then walked up the footpath to join Carmel.

'Hello, TC. I haven't seen you for a while, luv,' said Carmel with a welcoming smile.

'No, I don't get out of the shop much of late,' replied TC. 'My boss has been spending a lot of time at the mine.'

'So I heard, luv. Great that he's found opal. Should do big things for our town. Good, too, he's off the grog at last,' said Carmel.

'He's excited. He has told me today that he's sending me away to learn opal-cutting,' replied TC.

'Thel told me Jake hasn't been seeing much of you and Lou,' said Carmel. 'We hope he didn't upset you, luv.'

'Jake is Jake!' replied TC with a smile. 'I must call his mum to thank her and tell her Lou and I bought a washing machine of our own.'

'You do that, luv. Thel would like to hear from you,' said Carmel before turning back into her shop to answer her ringing telephone.

TC decided to buy a loaf of bread in case she and Lou were hungry later. They couldn't afford to go to Con's very often. When TC left the bakery, Jess called from the Empire window, so TC went across the street to her.

'Sorry about sending for you yesterday, TC,' said Jess softly. 'It's just that I know you'll keep your lips zipped. That Claudia is one troubled young woman. God only knows what has happened to her in the past to make her the way she is.'

'It's all right, Jess. You know I will do anything I can for you,' replied TC in almost a whisper. 'After all, it was you who told the boss to hire me.'

'How is he? Apart from getting himself involved with mad barmaids, that is,' asked Jess with a smile.

'He's happy he's found opal. He's doing really well regarding not hitting the drink. Mrs Callahan is back. He's a good person overall,' replied TC.

'He is a good man, TC. His only weakness now is mad women,' laughed Jess. 'I'll see you soon, luv. Thanks again.' TC turned away from the window to see Lou walking towards her from the other end of the street.

Good, thought TC. We can talk with Lisa for a little while before Lou starts work. I hate it when Lou is on the night shift! TC waited outside Con's until Lou got there.

'Why aren't you at work?' asked Lou in surprise.

'Your dad is doing some work over there, so the boss told me to go,' replied TC with a smile.

'I was hoping you'd get some bread,' said Lou eyeing off the loaf TC held.

'Have you heard from Graham today?' whispered Lou.

'No. Let's go inside to see Lisa and Con,' replied TC.

'Hello, Lisa's darlings,' said Con from behind the counter.

'Hello, darlings,' called Lisa from her table. 'Come have a look at my new magazine.'

'Save me some money and tell her everything in it is ugly,' said Con while rolling his eyes. The girls joined Lisa at her table.

'I wish I was young like you, darlings,' beamed Lisa. 'There is so much I would buy.'

'If you were as young as the girls, you wouldn't be able to afford to buy the magazine,' interjected Con.

'Dear husband, please be quiet. Let us girls have some fun in this dreary place,' pleaded Lisa softly as she flicked through the pages.

After discussing their likes and dislikes of the fashions in Lisa's magazine, Lou went off to work.

'How was your day, darling?' asked Lisa.

'The boss is sending me away to learn how to cut opals,' replied TC. 'Well, he's not really sending me, he'll be driving me there; then he'll come back there to bring me home.'

'You don't seem to thrilled about it,' said Lisa.

'I'm not, Lisa. He said he needs me to do it, so I'll do it,' replied TC.

'You haven't heard from Graham today, have you?' said Lisa.

'No, he's probably busy,' replied TC.

'Did you have an argument?' enquired Lisa.

'Not at all,' TC replied. 'He was happy and laughing last time I saw him. Why did you ask me that, Lisa?'

'Because he left a note for you with Con. He dropped it in about an hour ago. He's on duty tonight. Con and I were worried you'd had a run-in about something.'

'Not that I know of, Lisa,' said TC. 'I'd best go home now, take my shower, and wash my hair. All the exciting things we girls do.'

'All right, darling, I'll see you tomorrow,' said Lisa before calling to Con. 'Con, don't forget to give TC her note from Constable Graham.'

On her way out of the café, TC took the envelope from Con. She desperately wanted to run home so she could read it sooner. Instead, she strolled home at the normal after-work pace, took her shower, and washed her hair. After doing so, she wound her hair in rollers while listening to Elvis songs playing on the stereo.

'You can't stall it any longer,' she told herself as she sat down by the table lamp in the lounge room and opened Graham's note, letter, whatever it was. She took a deep breath before she began reading.

"Dear TC,

As I write this, it is only thirty-two hours since I last saw your smiling face. To me it seems like an eternity. Beginning tonight I shall be on duty for five consecutive nights. I believe this is the perfect opportunity for us to slow things down. At least until I come off night shift.

Look forward to seeing you when I do.

Graham."

Lou was right, thought TC, after reading it twice. I was worried that I would hurt him. Guess I don't have to worry about that anymore.

With tears streaming from her eyes, TC went downstairs to turn the sprinklers on the front lawn, which would be desperate for a drink after the hot day. She then threw herself on her bed, where she cried herself to sleep.

❦

TC woke when Lou arrived home from work and shook her.

'What's wrong, TC?' said Lou. 'The front yard is flooded, both back and front doors are wide open, and all the lights are on.' TC jumped off her bed.

'I must have fallen asleep.'

'That's obvious,' laughed Lou. 'You sure must miss me. That's two nights in a row I've found you asleep when I got home. Have you had anything to eat?'

'Not since breakfast,' replied TC, who didn't feel at all hungry.

'Good. Let's have a sandwich while we listen to 2UE. I had a call from Colin. He told me to be listening to 2UE at 2.30 a.m., Sydney time. That's almost fifteen minutes away. I told him we'd be sitting on the steps with a Coke while we listened.'

Ten minutes later the girls were sitting on the steps. Each had a cheese and vegemite sandwich on a plate balanced on their laps and a bottle of Coke on the step beside them. The radio was turned up a little louder than usual.

They listened carefully as the DJ gave the time. Then they heard him say—

'I have a special request coming up from my mate, Colin, who is sitting in his hotel room on the north shore thinking about a lovely girl named Lynette, who is sitting on the steps of her house in a little town called Brolga in south-western Queensland. Here we go, Lynette. My mate, Colin, wants you to pretend he is singing this to you instead of the great Buddy Holly. Tell you what, Lynette, I think my mate must really have the hots for you. Here's Buddy.

"Maybe baby I'll have you,

Maybe baby you'll have me."

Although Lou sat in silence while listening to Buddy Holly's song, she was so excited she was beside herself. She was shaking and covered in goose bumps. Inwardly, she was laughing and crying simultaneously.

When the song was finished playing, the DJ said—

'Hope you received that loud and clear, Lynette, on the steps way out there in the Wild West of Queensland.'

¶

'We are cry-babies! Look at us; we are both crying!' said Lou.

'I'll get some tissues,' said TC. As she got up, the telephone rang. 'That will be for you, Lou. I bet it's Colin.' Lou jumped up and ran to the phone while almost knocking TC over in the process. TC went back to the steps. She could hear Lou laughing a lot.

I'm so happy for you, Lou, thought TC. Could not happen to a better person. I think Colin loves her. I'm going to be a bridesmaid for those two.

When Lou returned to the steps, she was quiet.

'What's the problem, Lou?' asked TC. Lou didn't answer.

'Lou, that was so romantic,' said TC. 'You away out here in the wild west, as the DJ said, and Colin in Sydney. Lovely, Lou, really lovely.'

'TC, stop,' said Lou seriously as she produced Graham's note. 'When I was talking to Colin, I spotted this on the table under the lamp in the lounge room. Why didn't you tell me?' TC shook her head.

'Nothing to tell, Lou. This is your night. Let's talk about you and Colin.'

¶

When Graham had finished for the night, he had turned the radio on when he got to his room. He turned it to 2UE because he knew the girls would be listening to it if they were awake and on the stairs. He was surprised when he heard the DJ dedicate the song to Lynette on the steps in Brolga. He realised it must be Lou. He was dumbfounded when the song was Maybe Baby.

'Well, Colin, mate,' he said. 'You beat me to the punch. That's the song I was going to sing to TC. She doesn't even know that I sing and play guitar.'

Now Graham was on his bed, hoping he could sleep. His body sought sleep desperately while his mind wouldn't turn off. Where was she tonight, he thought. The door was open, the water was spraying the lawn, the lights were on, but she wasn't on the stairs. I shouldn't have written that note. I thought it would make it easier for me if I don't see her. It's not easier; it's worse. I laid down the rules; now I have to stick to them. What a mess!

§

After Lou and TC finally got around to going to their beds, Lou could faintly hear the sound of TC crying.

§

TC was early to work in the morning. The dispensary was a mess with bits of wood and pipe scattered all over the place. The back door was wide open, and Vance's ute was parked out behind the fence. She was wondering where Vance was when he called to her from the front door.

'Don't touch anything. Take twenty from the till and come over to Con's.' TC got the money, then went to the café. Vance and Jordan were seated at a table while Con was in the kitchen cooking their breakfast. TC placed the twenty-pound note on the table in front of Vance, said 'Hello' to Lou's father, then turned to leave.

'Are you sick, TC?' asked Vance.

'No, I'm fine,' replied TC with a smile.

'Well, you don't look it. You look terrible. Go put some make-up on,' said Vance.

'You told me not to wear make-up,' replied TC.

'That's because usually you don't need it. Today is different; you need it,' replied Vance matter-of-factly. 'Don't argue with me. Go put some colour on your face, then come back.' TC was gone in a second. Jordan Blake looked at Vance as if seeing him for the first time.

'You are a bit hard on the kid, mate. Lou is my daughter. If I spoke to her like that, my old girl would throttle me.' Vance laughed.

'TC is all right, Jordan. She's probably upset because I told her she has to go away to learn to cut opals.'

Con brought their food to their table.

'Looks great, as usual, Con,' said Vance. 'Would you mind throwing something together for TC? I told her to come back.'

'No problem, mate,' replied Con as he returned to his kitchen.

'You look like a painted doll,' complained Vance with a sarcastic smile when TC returned and sat down. Jordan Blake could sense TC was on the verge of tears as he noticed her discomfort.

'A beautiful doll, he means, luv. Don't you, Vance?'

'Anything you say, Jordan,' replied Vance off-handedly. TC longed to disappear. She would have if Con had not placed a plate in front of her.

'I remembered today, TC,' he said with a smile.

'God strike me bloody pink,' said Jordan Blake when he glanced at TC's breakfast. 'Lou told me about the heart-shaped eggs. I thought she was pulling my leg. I've seen the bloody lot now.'

'Lisa's idea,' said Con as he placed a glass of orange juice near TC's plate. Vance said nothing; instead, he grimaced.

'Come on, luv, eat up,' said Jordan. 'Take no notice of your boss. If he says or does one more thing to upset you in front of me, I'll botch his bloody gob; then I'll wring his scrawny neck.'

Vance laughed before saying, 'You mean that, don't you, Jordan?'

'You better bloody believe it. mate,' replied Jordan seriously.

'In that case, I'm sorry, TC,' said Vance with a sincere smile. 'Come on, Jordan, let's go,' said Vance when he and Jordan had finished their breakfast. He left the money on the table. 'You pay Con when you are finished, TC.' TC breathed a sigh of relief when they walked out of the café.

'You aren't hungry, are you, TC?' said Con from behind his counter.

'Sorry, Con. I did eat one egg,' replied TC.

'Give the plates here, luv,' said Con as TC stacked them. TC did so and paid him.

'I had best go, Con. I'll see you later.' She walked slowly across to the pharmacy.

I hope the boss' mood changes for the better, she thought as she went inside. He's got a lot on his mind. So he doesn't need any hassles from me.

'Keep yourself busy in the front of the shop,' instructed Vance.

'There are some names and numbers here from opal people who would like you to return their calls,' said TC. 'A lot more people have called but they didn't want to leave their details.'

'Not now, TC. I told you to keep yourself busy,' replied Vance angrily. 'Are you deaf!?'

'I'll check the mail,' said TC.

'Good idea,' snapped Vance.

TC was closing the mailbox when Jake pulled up in front of the post office.

'How's Miss Goody Two-Shoes?' asked Jake. 'Got your war paint on, I see. Feel sorry for the poor bloody cowboys.'

'Jake, be quiet, please,' replied TC calmly.

'That's not very nice,' said Jake feigning hurt.

'Jake, your smart mouth bores me,' replied TC still calmly. 'I suggest you save it for someone who finds it impressing.'

'I'd like to bore you all right,' said Jake. TC rolled her eyes and shook her head in disgust.

'Grow up, Jake,' she said as she walked past him.

'Get off your bloody high horse,' muttered Jake as he unlocked his mailbox.

Why do I always have to come across like an arsehole, thought Jake, when he got back into his car. God, that girl frustrates me. Little bitch, that's what she is. Jake drove off as if he was in a race-car rally and he owned the track.

¶

Around midday Jordan announced that he was finished.

'Contact me when those few parts arrive, Vance,' said Jordan.

'How much do I owe you, Jordan?' asked Vance.

'A couple of hundred should be fine, if you clean up the mess, that is,' replied Jordon.

'Suits me,' said Vance as he extracted two hundred pounds from the till.

'I bet I know who'll be cleaning it up, TC, luv,' called Jordan.

'That's all right, Mr Blake,' replied TC as she thought, Thank heavens, it's finished. It's cattle-sale day tomorrow.

'I'm taking Jordan and his gear to his place, then I'm going home,' said Vance. 'I'll be back when I'm back.'

TC looked around at the mess, wondering where to startI'm glad Lou's dad did most of it at his house, she thought as she began collecting the smaller bits and pieces and throwing them into the large outside bin.

Lou phoned.

'Are you coming home at siren time?'

'No! I have work to do, Lou.'

'Good. I'll come to the shop.'

Jake phoned.

'Will you and Lou come to the movies with me?' asked Jake casually.

'I told you to grow up, Jake,' replied TC.

'Why not?' persisted Jake.

'Jake, I'm very busy at the moment.'

Jake hung up saying under his breath, 'Get stuffed, bitch.'

Vance phoned.

'Are you all right to clean up that mess?'

'Lou's coming to help me,' replied TC.

'Good.' Vance hung up.

§

'I think there's a dust storm heading our way,' said Lou when she arrived. 'Like your make-up, by the way. We had best get this cleaned up, otherwise we will have a mess on top of a mess. It's hot as Hades out there, and there's wind coming from the west. Not strong yet, but it's building up.'

Lou left to go to the exchange before four. TC quickly went home to close up the house in preparation for the dust storm if, indeed, it did eventuate.

The wind was becoming stronger as TC made her way back to the shop. Just as well I have my war paint on, she thought. Need it to protect my face from this hot wind.

Come six o'clock, the dispensary was in order. Everything was in its place, so TC relaxed and took her first real look at the new equipment for the opal cutting. It was surprising to TC how everything had fitted into the area behind the dispensary wall of the shelves.

'Compact and neat,' she decided. The regular sink had been replaced by a newer, half-sized one alongside which extended a long, narrow stainless-steel trough with several plug holes. Suspended over this was a series of some sort of wheels of various sizes. Above that there were shelves to the ceiling. Opposite was a series of circular sails of different sizes which protruded from metal housings mounted on the strong timber bases with underneath storage space.

In a small room off the side of the dispensary, there were many shelves on the walls, and in the middle, screwed to the concrete floor, was a round, three-foot metal pole on top of which was a small motor.

※

Looks impressive, thought TC. Still, it's all double-Dutch to me. Suppose I'll understand more about it after I've been to Mr Black's.

TC was surprised by the number of people in the street when she closed the shop. Then she remembered it was Flea and Movie night. She had intended to visit Lisa. It was too busy, so she decided to go home. 'No doubt about it,' she mused, the wind is blowing wild; there's probably a dust storm heading our way; yet, because the Flea is arriving, which means the movies are on, most of the population are out in force. Must be something to it.

TC heard the train whistle, which meant the Flea was about to cross the bridge. On impulse, she turned onto the path that led to the railway station. The platform was crowded as it had been both times that she had arrived on the Flea.

TC stood behind the crowd as the Flea pulled to a halt alongside the platform. The wind was blocked by the railway station building. A few locals stepped down from the one small passenger carriage. There was a lot of hugging and laughter. An outsider would have thought the arriving loved ones had been absent for an eternity instead of a couple or three weeks, holidaying in the Big Smoke.

TC turned to continue home. Standing close and directly behind her was Milt Elliot, the American who had helped Vance with the hill. TC smiled as he said in his broad American accent, 'I wondered when you would turn around, TC. I saw you leave the chemist shop and followed you.'

'I'm sorry, Milt. I didn't see you,' replied TC.

'I've been standing so close to you it's a wonder you couldn't feel me.'

TC laughed, then said, 'Sorry, again. I didn't.'

'Has Vance found opal yet?' asked Milt.

'Yes, as a matter of fact,' replied TC.

'That is good news, TC.' said Milt with a smile to die for. That means I get to take you on a date. That was the deal! He found opal. I get to date you.' TC smiled.

'I wish someone had cleared it with me.' Milt looked hurt.

'Don't you want to go on a date with me, TC?'

'I didn't say that, Milt,' TC replied with a laugh.

'I'd ask you to the movies tonight but I've got a bunch of guys waiting for me in the Empire,' said Milt disappointedly. 'I have to get them out to camp tonight before this wind blows us all to the coast.'

'Yes, I know. I have to get home before it does the same to me,' said TC.

Milt walked TC to the street, looked down at her, and said seriously, 'I like you better with just lipstick.'

'It's a long story,' replied TC with a smile.

Milt touched TC on the arm as he said, 'See you soon, TC.' They went off in different directions.

¶

Jake was at the railway station with a couple of his mates. When he saw TC talking with Milt, he said to his mates, 'That Yank bastard is back.

Not bad enough he scores with the nurses. Now he's zeroing in on TC.'
Jake's mates laughed.

One of them said, 'Jake, everyone in town knows nobody zeroes in on TC or Lou.'

'Bloody little bitches,' said Jake.

'Give it a break, Jake,' said another of his friends. 'You are pissed off because they are awake to you.'

'Oh, shut up, all of you. Let's go to the pub,' said Jake angrily.

¶

Graham did not see TC at the station because he was on the platform and she was behind the building. When he drove down the street after leaving the railway station, he saw her walking home. She looked so small and defenceless as she was wind-blown along the footpath. She also looked cute as usual in her pink uniform and pony tail tied back with pink ribbon. He wondered if she was missing him even half as much as he was missing her. Impossible, he thought. You are all I think about all of the time, TC. When I manage to sleep, I dream about you. Wish this dust storm would hurry up and get over with. Can't possibly be as bad as the Sarge reckons. Better park and parade my presence on foot for a while. Not much happens around here, but when it does, everything comes at once.

Graham parked the police car opposite the Empire. He noticed the Seat of Knowledge was vacant. That says it all, he thought. Those old boys are too wise to be caught in a dust storm. Has to be a sure sign we are in for one. Graham looked through the Empire window and door in passing. He heard an American voice say, 'Come on, you guys, we leave now or I leave without you.' He saw a totally different Claudia to the one who had stormed into the café. This Claudia was laughing girlishly as she flirted with a man Graham had not seen before while Louise was wiping the far counter where Jake and his mates were drinking. The movies must have started because the street was deserted. As usual he dropped into the cafe to say hello to Con and Lisa. He was surprised to see Con sitting with Lisa at her table at the rear of the café.

'This is the first time I have seen you sitting down, Con,' said Graham with a smile.

'Even Greek café owners must rest now and then, Constable Graham,' replied Con with his usual shrug and smile.

'You look handsome in your uniform as usual, young man,' said Lisa, also smiling.

'Does that mean I'm ugly when I'm out of uniform?' replied Graham with a laugh.

'I'll ignore that,' said Lisa still smiling.

'I'll come back later,' said Graham. 'Have to check no crime is in progress between here and the end of the block.'

After Graham was gone, Lisa said, 'I wanted to tell him TC is going away to learn about opals.'

'Mind your own business, my wife,' replied Con.

'It's not easy,' pouted Lisa.

¶

Vance and Delores were entertaining Doctor Jackson over dinner. Vance was happy because Delores and the young doctor communicated well from the first hello. As the evening progressed, it became apparent via the conversation that they shared common interests in art, literature, and music. So much so, in fact, that Vance found himself feeling as if his presence was superfluous. He would prefer to be yarning with the men, discussing race horses with Jake, or reading his books on opals. He had to admit to himself that he missed the "say anything, do anything, get away with anything" part of his drinking career. He missed the fun.

Between main course and dessert, Vance excused himself to make a phone call.

'Did you get the mess cleaned up?' he asked TC when she answered.

'Yes, everything looks good,' replied TC. 'It's cattle-sale day tomorrow. Should I ask Lou to help me, or will you be there?'

'I'll go to the mine in the morning, so, ask Lou,' said Vance. 'I can't use those saws yet because we are a few parts short. There's a dust storm coming. When you are busy tomorrow, don't forget to charge the customers a bit extra for the dust.'

'You sound as if you are in a better mood, Boss,' replied TC.

'Don't be fooled by the way I sound,' said Vance. 'By the way, I am sorry about this morning. You know by now I always take my crap out on you. I'll see you when I see you.' He hung up. Within an instant, Lou rang.

'What's wrong?'

'Nothing, Lou! The Boss is going to the mine in the morning. The shop will be busy. I'm hoping you'll help me,' replied TC.

'Of course. I bet it's hot inside the house,' said Lou.

'I tried the steps. I don't know which is worse; stifling inside or the hot wind outside. The louvres are rattling, so the storm can't be too far away.' Lou laughed.

'You are beginning to sound like a native Brolgaite, TC. You talk about the dust storm in the same way you say you are going to take a shower or have a glass of water.'

'I won't feel that way tomorrow when there's red dust on everything,' replied TC matter-of-factly.

'I have to go now. I hope the storm has come and gone before I finish work,' said Lou before clicking off.

¶

TC had been listening to a country-and-western record they had bought in Sydney. She loved the words in the songs. She turned on the radio. Fats Domino was singing, 'I want to walk you home'.

'Well, Fats Domino, if you were here, you could walk me home as long as you sang as we walked,' said TC to the radio as she covered the stack of records and radiogram with an old sheet.

Suddenly the house was shaking. The louvres on the front, back, and even the eastern side of the house were rattling like crazy. The roof was making changing noises, and there was a repetitive crashing sound, which seemed to be coming from the house next door on the creek side. TC was sitting in the lounge room. Every door in the house was closed with dust stoppers where the door met the floor.

Never ceases to amaze me, thought TC. Every door, window, and louvre is closed; yet, I can smell the dust and actually see it permeating the air.

After what seemed forever, there was a moment's silence, then the sound of heavy rain beating on the roof along with more wind.

At least the roof and outside will be dust-free, thought TC.

The rain lasted ten minutes, if that. TC went to the front steps. There was a tiny pool of water on each one. She stretched and took a deep breath. It was now humid and hot instead of dry. Everything outside smelt clean. She wanted to clean the house, yet knew there was no point until the dust had settled. She decided to take a gamble that the storm had frightened away any snakes, so she bravely went downstairs to take a shower, searching everywhere under, over and inside, before closing the bathroom door and turning on the water.

After her shower, TC sat on the steps with a Coke and the radio for company. She was wrapped in a towel and was brushing her wet hair.

No rollers tonight, she thought. I'll have to wash it again tomorrow night because it will be full of dust after the shop.

Jake's car came hurtling around the corner and screeched to stop in the middle of the street in front of the gate. Jake jumped out of his car, wolf whistled and yelled, 'God, you look beautiful,' then got back into his car, and drove off.

Fool! He must be drunk, thought TC, shaking her head from side to side. A few minutes later the police car came around the same corner. The lights blinked as it went past.

'Goodnight to you, too, Graham,' said TC under her breath.

As Graham drove by, a voice inside his head asked, Why did you write her that damned note? Another voice inside replied, Could it be because you want to see how things pan out with the girls at the tennis club who are hot for you?

Stop it, both of you, thought Graham as he continued driving towards the end of town.

§

Doctor Jackson was saying goodnight to Vance and Delores.

'Two firsts for you tonight, Doctor Jackson,' said Vance. 'You have experienced your first of our dust storms and you have met Delores.'

'Both interesting,' replied Doctor Jackson with his polite smile.

'You won't have to be lonely anymore,' said Vance. 'I'll be out of town quite frequently. You and Delores have a lot in common. You'll be able to keep each other company from time to time.'

'That would be nice, Vance,' replied Doctor Jackson while looking at Delores for confirmation of Vance's invitation.

'Of course, Jackson,' said Delores with a smile and a nod of her head.

'I'm going to the mine tomorrow morning,' announced Vance as Doctor Jackson drove away. 'I'm going to get fuel now if I can find the garage owner.'

'Fine,' replied Delores as she began clearing the table.

Vance took the back street in the direction of the garage. Instead of finding the garage owner, he drove to his favourite spot down by the creek, opened the doors of the ute, then lit the first of many cigarettes he would smoke while he was steeped in silent analysis of his life, the mess it was in, and how to fix it.

§

TC decided to hose down the veranda, louvres, walls, and floor before Lou came home from work; less to do in the morning. She saw the police car go by a couple of times while she was hosing.

Poor Graham, she thought, driving up and down and around all by himself.

§

Lou came home a little early. The woman doing the midnight shift had gone to work early because she'd had a fight with her husband.

'Must have been a long movie,' said Lou. 'Just finishing when I walked past the theatre. Didn't take Claudia long to get over Vance. I saw her get into a car with some man. I don't know who he is. Must be from out of town.'

'Nice to see you, too, Lou,' interrupted TC as Lou prattled on twenty to a dozen.

'Yes, I see you have started cleaning up the dust,' replied Lou. 'Colin rang again. I'll tell you about that later. Con and Lisa must be tired. They were still open. Waiting for the after-movie rush, I suppose. I saw Graham outside the theatre. He was laughing with a girl from the tennis club. One of the three who are hoping he'll ask them out. She's nowhere near as pretty as you are, TC.'

'Lou, stop, please,' said TC. 'It's none of my business who Graham talks to or asks out. It's none of your business, either. Graham has given me the flick, Lou. I don't blame him! I'm hurting pretty bad, Lou. I think Graham is, too. If he's not, he's a great actor.'

'Big deal, TC! I'm beginning to believe the only difference between guys like Graham and those we had the misfortune to meet in Sydney is that the ones in Sydney come right out and say it. "If you won't come across, don't waste my time".'

'How is Colin, Lou?' asked TC.

'He's all right. He thinks I'm wonderful. I wonder if he'll still think that when I don't come across on the first date,' replied Lou coldly.

'Lou, that's not fair to Colin,' defended TC. 'He's tired of those girls. That is why he wants you. He said it in his letter. He'll be patient. He'll wait until you are ready, Lou. Now, let's just sit for a while and listen to 2UE while he thinks about you. He'll know you are hearing the same songs he is at the same time he is.'

'You are a romantic, TC,' laughed Lou.

'I'll get us a Coke,' replied TC. 'We'll go to bed after we drink it. Big day tomorrow.'

'I'll get into my baby dolls,' said Lou.

A few minutes later, they were seated on the steps when the police car appeared from around the corner.

'If he makes the lights wink, he's thinking of you,' said Lou.

Please let them wink, thought TC. They did and she smiled.

❦

When Graham got home to his room, he turned on the radio, hung up his uniform, then sat down with his bedtime Coke. The little voices in his head started again.

Why didn't you stop and say hello instead of just blinking the car lights? from voice number one.

Because you are playing two sides against the middle, from the second voice. You blinked the lights to let her know you still care.

You expect her to hang around while you have some fun with the tennis girls. You want to get laid. You know you will. Go for it! You are young but once.

Be quiet! I'm going to bed. Please let me get some sleep, said Graham silently.

❦

Vance arrived home from the creek in the early hours of the morning.

Won't get much sleep, he thought as he got into bed beside Delores. I'll leave for the mine at six. I'm looking forward to seeing the men. He was asleep almost as soon as his head was on the pillow.

❦

Ninety percent of Brolga's population was up and at it before Vance started out for the mine at six. The single working people were busy cleaning their dust-infested accommodations before heading off for work. Housewives were nagging their husbands and children to get out of bed so they could finish their dusting before the heat of the day.

Lou and TC were up at five; swept, dusted, and mopped the inner rooms of the house by six; showered, dressed and at the shop by half past.

'We'll do the counters, floors, and cosmetic section, Lou,' said TC. 'The rest will have to wait.'

Come eight o'clock the street was full of cars with groups of people, both men and women, catching up with each other on the footpaths.

'I'll go to Con's and get us a toasted sandwich,' said Lou. 'My shout! I'm going to earn a lot of money today,' she continued while rubbing her hands together in anticipation.

'How about collecting the mail while you are out?' asked TC as she placed the mail key next to Lou's purse.

It was the beginning of the busiest face-to-face day with the customers TC had as yet experienced in the pharmacy. She was glad to see Lou return twenty minutes later. People were patiently waiting all over the place.

No time to eat. We'll save it for lunch, thought Lou as she threw the food, mail, and her purse on the dispensary table before rushing to help TC in the shop.

⁋

Ten minutes after the siren sounded TC closed the door behind a lady who had brought in one of many prescriptions which would be collected after lunch. Lou opened the toasted sandwiches, looked at them, then threw them in the bin. TC was looking through a pile of prescriptions. She said casually, 'Open a packet of jelly beans. They are loaded with glucose. Good for you!'

Lou went into the shop and pulled a packet of jelly beans off a stand, then came back into the dispensary where she dramatically fell onto Vance's chair behind the desk.

'I saw Graham when I was at the post office,' announced Lou as she opened the packet of jelly beans. 'He's working long hours for the next few days. He said to say hello to you. I told him to say it himself.' TC laughed as she began counting tablets.

'Looks like Doctor Jackson had a busy morning,' said Lou with a mouthful of lollies.

'Lou, will you go fill some of the gaps on the shelves while I concentrate on these scripts?' said TC. Lou jumped to her feet.

'Only if I can have some more jelly beans.'

'Have as many as you want,' replied TC. 'Just please leave me alone to do these.'

With time to spare, the prescriptions were done and lined up like soldiers in alphabetical order on the dispensary bench.

'You can come back in now, Lou,' called TC. 'You can also talk as much as you like. We have a little while to spare before the shop is re-opened.'

'At last, I have your attention,' said Lou as she skipped like a little girl into the dispensary.

'I think those jelly beans have done something to you, Lou,' laughed TC.

Vance had not yet arrived at camp. He was asleep in the ute, which was parked off the road under a large gum tree thirty miles from the mine. Only when he began falling asleep at the wheel did he realise that he had been asleep for only a few hours in the past forty-eight plus.

I'm buggered, he'd thought. I'd best pull over and have a sleep before I run off the road and kill myself.

So there he was, stretched out across the seat of the ute with his legs dangling out through the driver's side door. He was in a deep, peaceful sleep. For once his mind was switched to off.

¶

The bar at the Empire was full. Jess, Louise, and Claudia were raced off their feet as the patrons ordered their last drinks before the sale at the cattle yards resumed.

Con's Café was also full. As the first patrons to leave began lining up at the counter to pay, Con's personal adding machine in his head began calculating the take.

Wish I could hide some from Lisa, he thought momentarily. She'll probably have another shopping spree. Poor darling has nothing else exciting to do. So as long as it makes her happy, let her buy whatever she wants.

In fact, every business owner in Brolga was happy with the money spent by the cow cockies so far, and the day was not over yet. Their willingness to spend was obviously due to anticipated high prices being paid for their cattle.

Good, thought almost everyone. If the property owners do well, so does the town.

‡

It was back to business at the pharmacy. TC opened the door at two. By five-past there were half a dozen or so ladies in the shop. Apart from a lull in mid-afternoon, probably for afternoon tea at the café, the entire day was busy. It was great. Dust-covered stock and all.

The boss will be happy, thought TC.

'I feel guilty leaving you,' whispered Lou at five minutes to four.

'You can't help it, Lou. Off you go,' replied TC also in a whisper.

Doctor Jackson phoned to tell TC there may be some late scripts again. She assured him there was no problem.

When TC put the phone down, she thought briefly, Doctor Jackson is a nice man. He's so well mannered and considerate. I hope he stays here for a while. He makes me feel as if we are doing him a favour instead of the other way around.

‡

When Vance drove into camp, he was still tired, hot, sweaty, and thirsty. His back was aching, and he was irritable.

'This is late for you, mate,' greeted Yappy. 'You look as if you are buggered again.'

'I need some water, Yappy,' said Vance. 'Hope you've got some.'

'I'll get it for you. You sit down,' replied Yappy as he produced a large bottle of water from the refrigerator. 'What's wrong, Vance?' asked Yappy, who was obviously concerned.

'Everything, Yappy. Just everything!' replied Vance as he poured himself a large glass of the cold water, which he quickly drank before refilling.

'Anything I can do, Vance?'

Vance shook his head before replying, 'The only one who can fix things is me, Yappy. Thanks, anyway.' He then drank three more glasses of water before lighting a cigarette.

'Want something to eat?' asked Yappy.

'No, I'll wait until the men eat,' replied Vance. 'How are the men, Yappy?' enquired Vance seriously. 'Has their morale improved since I was last here? If it hasn't, you can write a list of anything you need and I'll go back to town now.'

'Vance, mate, it's stinking hot out here,' began Yappy. 'They are counting down towards their break, which they well and truly deserve, by the way. One minute they are happy and on a high; next minute they are so far down I feel like digging the bastards a bloody hole. They can already taste the grog. Mark my words, Vance, when they leave on break, they'll be drunk by the thought of getting bloody drunk before they hit the main bloody road. God only knows what the bastards will be like once they get to town.'

'I know, Yappy; I'm a drunk myself, remember?' said Vance.

'Not like this lot, Vance,' replied Yappy. 'I have seen you drunk, Vance. Compared to these boys, you are a bloody novice.'

'Well, Yappy, there is no point in us worrying about it now,' said Vance. 'Get your list together, Yappy. I'll probably go back to town in the morning. If you want to place any bets, write them down, too. I'm going outside now. I'll signal the men to wind it up for the day.'

When Vance went outside, he saw a dozen or so more boulders heaped alongside the marquee.

Won't be long now, he told himself. We'll be sawing them up and producing stones soon. Like with everything else, we have to be patient.

We've waited this long; we can wait a little longer. As long as when we do it, we do it properly.

Vance walked down to where the men were working. Neil stopped the loader and climbed down while Little Joe and Faith joined Vance.

'I came out to see how you are going,' greeted Vance. 'Why don't you pack it in for the day.'

'Sounds good,' said Neil.

'Sure does,' said Faith.

'Thanks, Boss,' said Little Joe.

Vance went to the kitchen, armed himself with a mug of coffee, then sat outside to wait for the men. He had to admit, they looked tired. Although they were healthy and tanned, the tiredness showed in their faces.

When the men joined him, Vance decided to let them go on leave a week earlier than previously agreed. He decided not to say anything yet. He would spring it on them as a surprise.

'I see you've uncovered a few more boulders,' he said once they were all seated with a coffee and a rollie. The men all smiled and nodded.

'Yappy, you should join us,' said Vance. Yappy was standing at the kitchen window. He quickly joined the others. He was elated that Vance had included him.

'How's the machine holding out, Neil?' asked Vance.

'It's holding. Just,' replied Neil. 'It will need some major work done on it soon.'

'Hopefully, it will hold out until you men take your break,' said Vance. 'We'll get someone out to do whatever has to be done.'

'How is Little Flower?' asked Little Joe.

'She's fine. I'm taking her down south to learn about opal cutting,' replied Vance. 'You usually always ask about her, Little Joe. I must remember to tell her.'

'Neil, his brother and I named her that,' said Little Joe.

'Everyone was calling her Little Miss Dynamite because she was always yelling at you through the pub window. We decided Little Flower is more suited to her,' said Neil. They all laughed.

'We'll be able to saw the boulders soon,' said Vance. 'Jordan Blake finished installing the gear yesterday. By the way, Yappy, you'll have your toilet door and seat soon.'

'Where did Jordan put the saws and stuff?' asked Faith.

'At the back of the dispensary,' replied Vance.

'I hope you remembered to tell Jordan we want that bloody toilet door painted pink,' said Yappy.

'I'll let you tell him that, Yappy,' replied Vance seriously. 'He'll take more notice of a big bloke like you.'

Everyone laughed except Yappy, who snapped, 'Think you're a smart bastard, don't you, Callahan. You are all bastards for laughing at a man's bloody height.'

'Or lack of it,' teased Neil. More laughter.

'That's it, you can all bloody starve tonight,' retaliated Yappy with a sombre expression on his face and his head held high.

'Oh, come on, Yappy, mate. We didn't mean anything,' said Neil.

'Not everyone can do what you can, Yappy. You were a jockey,' said Faith. 'Bet John Wayne couldn't be a jockey.'

'No, but he rides a lot of horses,' said Neil. Everyone except Yappy laughed again. Little Joe tried not to laugh but did.

'That's it, you bloody mongrels,' whined Yappy. 'I thought you were more intelligent, Vance. You are a bloody chemist!'

'We were only having some fun, Yappy, mate,' apologised Vance.

'Yes, at my bloody expense, as usual,' complained Yappy. 'I'm going inside to do something.'

'What are you going to do, Yappy?' asked Vance.

'Yes, Yappy, what are you going to do?' mimicked Neil.

'Cook your bloody dinner, of course. You bastards would starve if I went on strike,' said Yappy, who was at the end of his tether with the lot of them. They all wanted to laugh but didn't dare.

'Little Joe, did we actually see you laugh?' said Faith.

'I'm going to take a shower,' replied Little Joe.

Vance was relieved the men were in a good frame of mind. Knowing they were okay removed more than a little pressure from his overall concerns. They were good men. Real men. He was blessed to have them with him. Honest as the day is long. Each and every one of them.

§

Jack and Bert Romeo were happier than bugs in a rug. Their pubs hadn't been this busy at the same time since either of them could remember.

'Perhaps when the floods were here a while back,' wondered Bert Romeo.

'Yes, Bert. The difference is these people are sane. At the moment, that is,' replied Jack. 'They were all mad then because they were drinking our privately stilled supply.'

'Yes, Jack, those floods were kind to us,' reflected Bert Romeo. 'We got rid of almost all of our home-made grog and made a lot of money on it, to boot.'

'Yes, yes, yes, Bert, that was then, this is now,' said Jack Romeo impatiently.

§

Most of the property gentry had left town by five, all by six. Some of them had a long way to travel. Most of the drivers would be women because the majority of their menfolk would have enjoyed a couple or three more drinks than they should have.

Two shearing teams were now in town from two sheds in different directions, which had cut out that day. One shed had cut out a day earlier than expected, the other on schedule.

§

The shearers were happy. They had money in their pockets, three pubs to choose from, and a room with a proper bed to sleep in when they got too drunk to drink anymore. Both teams were starting new sheds on Monday, so, they would be in Brolga until Sunday. Most of them were gambling men who were enthusiastic about having the opportunity to have a few bets on Saturday.

Word was out that another team of shearers would be in town tomorrow, and the fettlers on break would arrive in town later in the evening

In the café, Con was worried he would run out of steaks. Almost all his lunchtime patrons had eaten steak, and he knew that shearers always wanted steaks. Probably because they were tired of looking at sheep. Naturally, he had known about the cattle sale. The shearers had caught him off guard. Now the latest news was the fettlers were going to be in town for the weekend as well.

'You should give the butcher a call, Con,' suggested Lisa. 'Come closing time at the hotels, all those people will be hungry.'

'And drunk,' replied Con.

'Con, my husband, it is not our business if they all get drunk. It is our business to have enough steaks to feed them.'

'All right, I'll phone the butcher,' conceded Con. Within an hour he had enough prime steaks to feed an army.

'One thing I like about living in a small town,' said Con. 'Everyone knows everyone. If we need anything anytime, we simply make a call.'

❡

TC was tired for one so young. She typed the label for the last prescription at a quarter to six as the customer waited. I'll total the takings in the morning, she thought. I know it's a lot. The ladies bought everything today! She picked up the phone.

'Number please, madam,' said a British aristocratic-type voice. TC giggled.

'Nice try, Lou!' she said. 'I have just finished. I must be getting lazy because I'm tired.'

'I'm tired, too, TC. I'm also hungry,' replied Lou. 'Maybe we are tired because we rarely eat.'

'I'll ask the boss about some vitamin pills,' said TC. 'What would you like to eat, Lou? I'll get it and fetch it to you.'

'Bring a packet of jelly beans as well. Vance can take the money out of my pay. I'll have a hamburger on toast.' TC collected a packet of jelly beans, then locked the shop.

§

'Looks as if we are all feeling tired tonight, darling,' said Lisa when TC walked into the café. TC joined Lisa at her table.

'Lou is hungry. I'll take her a hamburger. I thought you'd be busy with the shearers in town,' said TC.

'We will be busy after ten when the hotels close, darling,' replied Lisa.

'I'll go order Lou's hamburger,' said TC.

'Con's in the kitchen talking to Jake,' said Lisa. TC pushed open one side of the kitchen door.

'Excuse me, Con, would you make a hamburger on toast for Lou, please?'

'What about you?' asked Jake. 'You're getting too bloody thin.'

'Leave her alone, mate,' said Con. 'You are tired, aren't you, TC? All right, come with me, Jake. I'll see what you owe me.' Con left the kitchen, followed by Jake. They talked at the cash register as Jake paid his café account.

'I'll see you later, mate. You, too, Lisa. Oh, I forgot you, Miss Goody Two-Shoes.' Jake was laughing as he walked through the café door. He almost bumped into Graham, who was about to walk in.

'Have you seen Graham, darling?' asked Lisa. TC shook her head.

'No.'

'He's just walked in,' whispered Lisa.

'A wonder that bloody cop didn't knock me over,' mumbled Jake as he walked into the Empire. 'I'll have to tell Con to ban that bastard from the café.'

Lisa called, 'Hello, Constable Graham. Working again tonight, I see.' Graham finished talking with Con, then walked towards Lisa's table.

'Hello, Lisa. Who is your friend?' he said as he tugged TC's pony tail from behind. TC turned her head around and upwards to look at him. He was in uniform. He looked wonderful. He smiled and gave her a wink.

'Lou told me I have to say my own hello to you.' TC smiled.

'So I heard.'

'Are you here for dinner?' asked Lisa.

'No,' replied Graham. 'The sergeant's wife fed me tonight. There's a lot of shearers in town and the fettlers arriving soon for their long weekend. The sergeant asked me to find out what time you are closing.'

Con went past them to the kitchen. 'Lou's hamburger will be a few minutes.'

'I thought Lou was on night duty,' said Graham.

'She is. She is also hungry, so I'm taking her some food,' replied TC.

'All right if I walk with you?' asked Graham.

'Sure,' replied TC with a faraway smile.

'I'm thinking of bringing my car out here,' said Graham.

'Good idea,' said TC. 'What sort of car do you have, Graham?' enquired TC with interest.

'A new Ford Falcon,' replied Graham with pride.

'The girls will love that,' said TC, who wanted to kill herself for saying it. Graham touched TC on the shoulder.

'You think so, do you, TC?' he said while looking her directly in the eyes with the hint of a smile.

'Here you go, TC,' said Con from the kitchen door. 'Lou's burger.'

'I'll take it to her, then come back,' said TC. 'I'll pay you before I go home.'

'I'll see you later, Con, Lisa,' said Graham before accompanying TC to the door and along the footpath.

'I've missed seeing you, TC' he said. 'I hope you have missed me, too.' TC did not reply. Instead, she looked up at him and smiled.

'I want to hold your hand, TC,' said Graham quietly. 'I can't. I'm in uniform.'

'How was tennis?' asked TC.

'Good. I won.'

'Could be a few drunken brawls in the next few days,' said TC. 'Be careful.'

'TC, I shouldn't have written that note.'

'That's all right. I understand,' replied TC. They were at the post office.

'Be a good girl. I'll see you,' said Graham.

'I'll try,' replied TC as she began walking up the post office steps.

TC knocked on the small wooden change window. Lou opened it. 'Yes!'

'Here's your dinner, Lou. I'll see you at home.'

'Where's my bag of jelly beans?' asked Lou, imitating a small, disappointed child.

'Sorry, I left it in the café,' replied TC. 'You can have them when you go home.'

As TC headed back to Con's, Jock and one of his mates were in the process of positioning themselves on the Seat of Knowledge.

'Hello, luv,' said Jock. 'Bet you enjoyed the bloody dust storm.' TC laughed.

'Not really.'

'Come and talk to us for a minute,' invited Jock. 'Can't do our reputation any harm to be seen with a pretty young thing like you.'

'Might get us smacked over the head with a bloody saucepan if our old girls hear about it,' said Jock's friend.

'Should be some action tonight, luv,' said Jock. 'The Greeks will be rubbing their bloody hands together. The bloody pubs are full.' TC laughed. She loved to listen to Jock talking.

'Where's your pill-pushing boss?' asked Jock's mate.

'He's at the opal mine,' replied TC with a smile.

'You go home early tonight, luv,' said Jock. 'These bloody shearers will be brawling later. I'd lay a hundred to one on a bet about that.'

'I'll be going now, gentlemen,' said TC. 'Nice to see you again.'

As TC walked away, she smiled when she heard Jock say, 'Good kid, that one. My wife likes her! That means a lot!'

¶

TC went back to the café.

'You look sad, TC,' said Con. 'Lisa has gone to freshen up. She said she will see you tomorrow.'

'No, I'm just tired, Con,' replied TC as she paid him. 'I'm going to bed. Enjoy the action later.'

'I hope there is none,' said Con. 'Have a good sleep, TC.'

The fettlers have obviously arrived, thought TC as she passed by the Majestic Bar. It was full to the rafters with loud, happy men of various ages.

'Now, calm down, boys. It's early yet,' she heard Bert Romeo command.

'Good luck, Mr Romeo,' she said silently. No wonder those men are happy. I can't imagine how terrible it must be for them to work out in the open on the railway lines in the heat.

In the Empire, Jess, Louise, and Claudia were flat-out. It appeared as if one team of shearers drinking on the southern side of the bar was trying to outdrink the other team drinking on the northern side. Appropriately, the shearers on the southern side came out of New South Wales while the shearers on the northern side were Queenslanders.

'Bloody mongrels are having a drinking competition,' complained Jess. 'We fill their glasses, take their money; when we return with their change, the mongrels' glasses are empty again. Need twenty barmaids here, not three. I'm getting too bloody old for this. Mark my words, they'll be brawling by the end of the night.'

The sergeant was in the police car with Graham driving. One thing to let the kid go on patrol by himself driving during normal times in Brolga. No way is he leaving my side with this crowd in town. The kid is still on probation. Oh, well, perhaps I can teach him a few tricks of the trade over the next few days. We'll see how quickly he learns.

'Park up, Graham,' said the sergeant. 'We'll take a stroll down the street. Might give us a clue as to what to expect later.' Graham did as instructed. He parked in front of the bakery opposite the Empire as usual.

'Come on, we'll go say hello to Jack Romeo,' said the sergeant.

'They look like a ripe mob,' said Graham as they entered. The sergeant led the way to Jack Romeo's office.

'How's it going Jack? Any problems?'

'The three hotels are busy,' replied Jack Romeo with a smile. 'Most of the rooms are taken and the bars are full. Bert said the drinkers at the Majestic are a rowdy lot.'

'Suppose I'd be rowdy myself if I hadn't seen a town for months, Jack,' said the sergeant. 'Come on, Constable, we'll leave Jack to get back to counting his money. Be back later, Jack.'

'Aren't you talking to us tonight?' called Jock from the Seat of Knowledge when the sergeant and Graham came out of the Empire.

'Why's that, Jock, mate?' asked the sergeant.

'Well, you parked your bloody car a few feet behind us, then walked past us without so much as a bloody nod of the head.'

'Sorry, mate, got a lot on my mind,' replied the sergeant.

'Yeah, well, don't let it happen again. Consider yourself told,' joked Jock. Jock's mates laughed as did the sergeant and Graham, who moved towards the far end of the street.

They waved to Con and Lisa as they passed the café. At the Brick Hotel, the Railway, the drinkers appeared to be the usual in-town railway and council workers enjoying their regular nightly routine.

In the beer garden were locals who normally drank at the Empire. Tonight they had been crowded out by the shearers. Jake was there drinking with a couple of his truckie mates.

'Think I'll go get a woman for the night,' said Jake casually. 'It's a bit hot for sex but it's something to do other than sit here and get pissed with you buggers.'

'Get us a woman, too, will you, Jake?' said one of his mates. 'It's never too hot for me to have sex.'

'That's because you never get any,' said the third young man.

'You must be desperate, you poor bugger,' said Jake. 'Desperate. That's a great name. From now on you answer to Desperate. 'All right, you two, go get cleaned up while I get the women. I'll tell them we are having a small party down at the creek. Just remember, I get the best-looking one and it's up to you whether or not you score. I'll find out what they want to drink. Meet you in half an hour outside the Empire. We'll buy some grog, pick up the girls, and who knows?' Jake's mates were gone in a flash while Jake finished his drink before going to his shop to call some girls. This is the perfect opportunity to get rid of that "Jakie" bird, he thought. She drives me mad with her bloody baby talk. No, I couldn't wish her on anyone, let alone one of my mates. He picked up the phone and asked Lou to connect him with the nurses' quarters.

'Some things never change, Jakie,' said Lou.

'What did you call me?' demanded Jake.

'I heard somewhere that Jakie is your new name,' teased Lou.

'That's your problem, Lou. You hear too bloody much,' replied Jake. He was livid. 'Be careful, Lou. Someone might report you.'

'You be careful, Jake. Tell your tarts not to gossip about you to their friends,' replied Lou. 'Connecting you now, sir!'

❡

Jake met his mates at the Empire, where they purchased beer, gin, rum, tonic water and Coke.

'How many girls are going?' asked Desperate. 'We've got enough grog to last us a week.'

'One regular nurse and two relieving nurses who arrived last night. I'm taking the regular one. As for the grog, it's not my fault if two drink gin and tonic and one drinks Rum and Coke.'

'That's why he never gets a woman, Jake. He asks too many damned questions. What about glasses for their drinks?'

'Everything we need is in the boot of my car,' replied Jake. 'I'm always prepared. I'll pick up the girls and meet you down at the creek. Park your cars at that spot where we used to go swimming as kids.'

Less than fifteen minutes later, Desperate was watching the love of

191

his life stepping out of Jake's car down by the creek. They were married after a few years. Jake was best man.

¶

The sergeant and Graham had been patrolling both in the car and on foot up and down the main street, keeping an eye out for potential trouble all evening. So far, there was no trouble except for the noise, which nobody in Brolga, including the sergeant, considered a problem, especially when the noise was prior to the pubs closing at ten. The sergeant had arranged with Jack and Bert Romeo that the Brick Hotel be closed first because the locals had all gone home. The bar was empty, which rendered the close nothing more than a formality. They would, as usual, leave the Empire until last, so they moved to the Majestic. Although it was still noisy with the stayers still drinking, the crowd was less than half the numbers prior. The sane members of the crowd had pulled the pin and gone to Con's for a meal much earlier. Some of them were already in bed asleep. The sergeant and Graham showed their presence by standing stern-faced at the hallway door while Bert Romeo closed the front door of the bar, then said, 'Come on, boys, drink up. It's closing time.'

There was silence momentarily before one voice, then another, and another, and another said with slurred broken speech, 'One more, just one more, give us another bloody drink.'

'In the morning, boys. Ten o'clock in the morning you can get another drink.' More than a few garbled expletives were mumbled in chorus throughout the bar. Nobody moved. It was as if they thought if they stayed put for long enough, they would get another drink. The sergeant coughed loudly in order to get their attention.

'Come on, men, you heard the publican. It's closing time. Come on. Clear the bar. The café is still open if you are hungry.' One by one, they filed past the sergeant and Graham. Bert Romeo stood behind the bar, fiddling with his worry beads.

'I want another bloody drink,' yelled one man, who was almost incapable of standing, let alone walking. Two of his mates helped him by positioning themselves one each side of him and guiding him while holding him up on his feet.

'Gotta be the blind leading the bloody blind,' muttered one of them.

'Good men, put him to bed,' said the sergeant.

'All clear,' said Bert Romeo before turning to the barmaid, who was busily clearing and cleaning the counters.

'I'll be back to do the final lock-up soon. I'm going to the Empire to help my brother get the drunken shearers out of there.'

The sergeant and Graham were halfway up the block towards the Empire. In front of them were a dozen or so drinkers who had been at the Majestic. Obviously, they were heading to Con's for some food.

'That was painless,' said the sergeant. 'Let's see how we go at the Empire.'

They entered the Empire. This time they stood in the smoking room where everyone could see them. Bert Romeo stood behind them. Same as at the Majestic, the numbers were fewer than previously. Jack Romeo repeated word for word what his brother had told the patrons at the Majestic. He also received the identical reaction of the expletives and staying put. Wearing faces of stone, the sergeant and Graham stepped inside the bar room. The sergeant coughed for attention, then began, 'Please, gentlemen, you heard the publican. The bar is closed. Time to leave.'

A loud voice from the southern side of the bar interjected, 'You can't effing tell us to leave. Cops, you think you rule the whole effing world. Mole of bastards. I hate bloody cops.' The voice came from a man perhaps thirty-five years of age, a little over six feet, with shoulders the width of the Harbour Bridge and a mouth like a sewer.

Jess was silently saying, 'Arrest the mongrel, sergeant. He's been a rat since his second beer.'

'As I said,' resumed the sergeant, 'the bar is closed.'

'Oh, shut your effing cop mouth,' from the voice. 'I hate effing cops!'

'You'll hate us more if we lock you up,' said the sergeant loudly. 'Everyone except staff and publicans, leave now!' commanded the sergeant. 'If the gentleman with the mouth has any friends, I suggest they get him out of here before we do. If you are tired, go to bed. If you are hungry, the café is open.'

¶

Everyone filed out quietly except for "BIG Mouth", who was swearing loudly as three men who were obviously embarrassed by his behaviour literally dragged him out of the bar and into the street.

A few minutes later one of the three men returned to the bar door.

'Excuse me, Sergeant,' he said. 'I'm sorry about that.'

'Not your problem, mate,' replied Sergeant. 'Thanks, anyway. How long are you men going to be in town?'

'Until Sunday,' replied the man.

'Try to get your friend to tone it down,' said the sergeant.

'We all will try,' agreed the man sincerely. He was gone in less than a second.

Jess, Louise and Claudia were cleaning. Bert Romeo went back to do the final lock-up at the Majestic.

Jack Romeo said, 'Thank you, Sergeant. Thank you, Constable. Would you like a drink, Sergeant?'

'Not tonight, Jack,' replied the sergeant. 'We are still on duty.'

That never used to stop you in the past, thought Jack Romeo. Must be something to do with the young constable being in Brolga.

'All right, maybe next time,' said Jack Romeo with the typical Greek shrug.

'Come on, Graham, we'll see what's happening at Con's,' said the sergeant. 'Goodnight, Jess, Louise, Claudia. Goodnight, Jack. See you tomorrow.'

The street was deserted when the sergeant and Graham went outside.

'We haven't seen nor heard the last of that one with the grudge against cops and that mouth,' said the sergeant. 'Seen his kind too many times before, Graham. He's looking for trouble. I have a feeling he'll find it, too. I'll walk down to the café; you drive the car down to the corner and bring it back to Con's.'

Con's doing all right. That's good, thought the sergeant when he walked into the café. Must be twenty-five or thirty customers here. Lisa was behind the counter, making coffees.

'He's out back cooking, Sergeant.' The sergeant walked through to the kitchen, where Con was frantically preparing meals.

'You'll be here for a while, Con?' asked the sergeant.

'At least an hour, mate,' replied Con. 'Depends how quickly they eat. So far, no trouble.'

'Graham and I will drive around for a while. We'll be back,' said the sergeant. 'It's been a long, hot day, Con. I'm getting too bloody old for this.'

'Drive to the western end of town, then back to the bridge, Graham. Then we'll do a couple of laps around the back streets before we go back to Con's. If I fall asleep, don't wake me until we are almost back at Con's.'

'Sounds good, Sarge,' replied Graham as he started the car.

'I've heard you in your room after work all this week. Aren't you visiting Lou and TC anymore?' said the sergeant.

'No. Not this week,' replied Graham.

'They are nice girls and hard workers, too,' said the sergeant. 'Most of the young studs around here would love to be their friend. Maybe they are too nice, eh?' concluded the sergeant with a smile. Graham said nothing.

Down by the creek, Jake and his mates had parked their cars in a row. All had the doors open, the same radio station blasting the airwaves. The three nurses and Desperate were all quite drunk. Jake's other mate had played barman from drink one, so he was happy, not drunk. Jake was bored. Everything was taking too long. He was accustomed to driving to the creek, engaging in minimal conversation, having sex, then going back to town when he was ready. Tonight, his date was too busy mucking around with the others. Jake felt left out.

I'm never doing this as a crowd again, he thought to himself. Stuff it! He sat in silence for a little longer. He then announced, 'I have a terrible bloody headache. I'll have to go home.'

'Poor Jake,' said the nurse who was supposed to be his date. She turned to the others. 'Can I get a lift with you guys when we go?'

'Yes, sure,' replied two male voices.

'Sorry, Jake. I'm having fun, so I'd like to stay. I'll get a lift home with the others. You go home. Take a couple of aspirin before you go to bed.' Jake stood up abruptly.

'Hope you all get stuffed. Don't forget to return my rugs and drink tumblers. Continue having a good time. I'm going!' Jake threw himself into his car, turned off the radio, slammed both car doors, then reversed and drove off down the track in his angry, faster-than-usual, break-neck speed.

'Jake hasn't got a bloody headache,' slurred Desperate.

'No, Jake's sulking because we are all enjoying ourselves,' giggled Jake's date. She held up her drink tumbler. 'Fill me up again.'

'Delighted,' replied the acting barman.

¶

The police car was approaching the bridge when Jake's car left the creek track, slammed onto the bitumen, spun sideways, straightened, and passed the police car at lightning speed as Jake drove towards town.

'Bloody young Jake Carmichael,' said the sergeant drowsily. 'He drives like a lunatic.'

Should be arrested, thought Graham. The sergeant guessed Graham's thought.

'Jake's harmless, Graham. He's his own worst enemy. Been spoiled since birth. I knew his dad. He was a good man. I can't wait to put the town to sleep. I'm buggered!'

¶

When Jake hit the bitumen, he was travelling so fast he almost lost control of his car. As he struggled to right it, he saw the police car slowly approaching. Oh, shit, just my bloody luck, he thought. That young prick cop would love to book me. Stuff it! I'm not stopping! He quickly gained control of his car, pointed it in the direction of town, and slammed his foot on the accelerator. As his car literally flew past the police vehicle, Jake said to himself, 'Hope the sergeant is on board. He was mates with my dad.'

He drove directly home. Headache or no headache, he took two aspirins, then went to bed, wondering how the night would end up for his ex-friends down by the creek.

§

It was almost midnight. The drunks were asleep, apart from a few fettlers who possessed the foresight to have purchased a carton of beer before the pubs closed. They were drinking quietly and harmlessly behind the Majestic. They could sleep in the next morning.

The café was closed. The main block was devoid of people and cars, and the back streets were in slumber. The sergeant declared Brolga asleep, which he almost was himself. He was out of the police car and inside his house immediately Graham parked the car in the police station yard. Graham was locking the gate when he saw Lou at the post office corner. She looked towards him and waved before starting across the street. Graham quickly caught up with her.

'If I had my own car, I would drive you home, Lou,' he said with a smile. 'Is TC all right, Lou? She hasn't been on the steps tonight. 'I looked for her every time I drove past.'

'She's probably asleep, Graham,' replied Lou. 'She'll wake up when I get home. All this week, she's been crying herself to sleep. I wake her when I go home from work.'

'Why is she crying herself to sleep, Lou?' Lou looked at Graham in surprise.

'Take a wild guess, Graham. I'm going home to sit on the steps with my friend while we listen to 2UE. Do you want to come with me?' Graham hesitated. He was still in uniform. 'No, I didn't think so,' said Lou as she resumed walking. 'Good luck with the tennis players.' Graham ran after Lou.

'Tell TC I'm thinking about her, Lou. Please!'

Lou shook her head while replying with a smile, 'Tell her yourself, Graham.' Lou continued on her way home while Graham walked back to the police station.

'Going to be a bloody scorcher today, Vance,' said Yappy. It was five o'clock in the morning. Vance was drinking coffee and enjoying a smoke in the camp kitchen while Yappy put the final touches to breakfast.

'Looks like it, Yappy,' replied Vance.

'Bloody feels like it, too,' said Yappy. He handed Vance two fifty-pound notes. 'Here's another hundred to bet for me again, Vance.' Vance didn't reply. Neil, Faith, and Little Joe came in, helped themselves to scrambled eggs and toast, then sat down.

'Remember to knock off work when it gets too hot, men,' said Vance.

'You can dock our pays,' said Neil.

'Don't be so ridiculous, Neil,' replied Vance. 'You men can't help it if it gets too bloody hot to work. Anyone want anything in particular from town apart from your tobacco, razor blades, and stuff?'

'That's a dangerous question to ask these mongrels, Vance,' said Yappy.

'Yes, Boss, you can bring us a few fast women and a truckload of grog,' said Faith.

'Bugger the bloody women! Just bring the grog,' said Neil. Little Joe said nothing. He continued eating his breakfast.

'It's almost Christmas, men,' said Vance. 'You'll have all the grog you want for a month or more.'

'What? Are you going to buy it for them, Vance?' asked Yappy.

'No, Yappy, they'll have money, they can buy their own,' replied Vance with a laugh. 'Won't you, men?' No one replied. Vance got to his feet.

'Okay, everyone, I'll see you soon. I enjoyed our yarns this time. Yappy I'll have your order sent on the mail truck Sunday.'

'Are the rocks in the ute, Boss?' asked Faith.

'Yes, Faith. There's also fuel in it, mate,' replied Vance, who went outside, got into the ute, and slowly drove away from camp. As he did so, he was feeling bad about leaving the men behind. Not long now and he would be taking them into town with him. He laughed as he thought, God help us then.

§

TC left for work at six. She expected a busy day with all the people in town. The shelves were still loaded with dust, and there were gaps everywhere. She noticed Con had already opened the café, probably to accommodate the early risers. They were men accustomed to being on their jobs by six.

By regular opening time, TC had filled the gaps and had the shop looking presentable. The dust would have to wait. She was unlocking the front door when the telephone rang. It was Bert Black, advising that he and Leanne had arrived back home and he looked forward to hearing from Vance as to when he would be bringing TC for her opal-cutting lessons.

I don't want to go! thought TC when she put the phone down.

There was a rush of shearers purchasing personal essentials. Once again, she reached the conclusion that most shearers presented themselves very well. Always clean and properly dressed, just like Yappy.

I'm proud that my dad is a shearer, thought TC. I wonder if any of his mates are in town this time?

§

Vance called late in the morning.

'How're things, TC?' he asked.

'Busy. I'm afraid we'll run out of aftershave and deodorant. You are back from camp sooner than I expected. Mr Black wants you to call him. I have to go. I have customers waiting.'

The shearers and a few fettlers kept TC busy until siren time. All of them were lovely to TC. Most of them didn't rush in, make their purchase, then rush out. They chatted amongst themselves and with TC, as well. She felt good about herself. They treated her as an intelligent adult, not a subordinate kid.

Vance came through the back door as Lou walked through the front.

'Close the door behind you, please, Lou,' said TC.

'Been busy,' said Vance.

'Yesterday was the busiest day I can remember with non-phone-order customers, and today so far has been very busy,' replied TC.

'Good. How much money have you taken?' asked Vance.

'I don't know, Boss,' replied TC. 'I was going to do it this morning, but I've been too busy. It must be a lot.'

'Surely you've had time to total the takings!' snapped Vance.

'I'll do it now, Mr Callahan,' said TC shortly.

'Don't bother! I'll do it myself,' replied Vance angrily. 'I'd hate to intrude on your lunch break,' he continued sarcastically.

'I'm out of here,' said Lou. 'I'll be at Con's if you are looking for me.'

'I don't blame you, Lou,' said TC before turning on Vance.

'Mr Callahan, I work like a drover's dog for you. A few days ago you told me how you trust me and appreciate my loyalty. Today you abused me in front of Lou. The other day you did it in front of her father. I think it's time you abuse the people who deserve it. If you are angry with Claudia, go abuse her. If it's Mrs Callahan, abuse her. If it's yourself you are angry with, go out in the bush and scream on down to the creek and drown yourself.

'Quite frankly, Mr Callahan, I believe I preferred you when you were a drunk. At least I knew what to expect. I realise you are worried about money. There's nothing I can do about that except what I do now— the best I can. I'm going to find Lou! You owe her eighteen pounds; she owes you for a packet of jelly beans. I gave her another packet because she was hungry and the café was too busy to bother Con. Here is the money.' TC extracted two shillings from her purse and put it on the bench, then walked out, closing the door behind her.

Vance lit a cigarette, squashed it out because he'd lit the filter, and cursed, then lit another one. Smart move, Vance, he scolded himself. *We're on the verge of making history in the opal industry and I piss off one of the key players.* He went to the cash register, hit a few buttons, and waited for the tape to print out. 'No wonder she wasn't in a hurry to total up. Yesterday was all on accounts except for forty-three quid. Big deal! I went off at her over forty-three quid.'

Lou was seated at Lisa's table. Lisa was busy behind the counter.

'I'm earning my keep, for a change, darling,' she said as TC made her way to Lou.

'I don't know how you tolerate Vance, TC.'

'Let us not talk about it, Lou,' replied TC quietly. 'He's got a lot on his mind.'

'Yes, and you are the doormat he dumps it on,' said Lou. 'Lisa is going to make us a sundae when she gets the chance.'

TC had not taken much notice of the crowd in the café when she came in. Now, after a quick look around, she observed it was almost full.

❡

'These men are the smart ones,' said Lou. 'They'll have a good feed now before they hit the pubs. Then they'll have another meal after the pubs close. My dad says that gives them staying power.'

Lisa beckoned to Lou, who was sitting in Lisa's usual chair facing the counter. Lou went to collect the sundaes.

'Enjoy, darlings. No charge today. Con is making tons of money,' said Lisa.

'Lisa and Con shouted,' said Lou when she re-joined TC at the table and placed the ice cream and goodies-filled dishes on the table.

'Lou, if you aren't doing anything after I go back to the shop, you should ask Con and Lisa if you can help them in some way. They are very busy. Perhaps you can wash the dishes or clean the tables after this crowd goes. I can help them tonight if they need me.'

'Super idea, my friend,' replied Lou with a smile. 'Wish I had thought of it myself.'

So, it was arranged. When TC went back to the shop, Lou began helping Con in the kitchen by clearing tables, washing dishes, and delivering meals. The time came for Lou to go to her job at the exchange. Con tried to give Lou a ten-pound note. She refused it.

'Take it, darling,' said Lisa. 'Your help means my Con can have a couple of hours rest instead of cleaning up in the kitchen.'

'No,' refused Lou adamantly. 'TC and I are forever parking ourselves here without spending a penny, and we get more than our share of complimentary shakes and sundaes. I have a day off tomorrow. I'll come by to help you then if you are busy. TC will help you tonight if you need her. I must go.' Con and Lisa looked at each other. Con shrugged and threw his arms up and out as usual.

Lisa smiled and said, 'Now you understand why I like those two girls so much, my husband.'

'I have to call the butcher,' said Con. 'We need more meat. Then I'm going to have a rest while it's quiet.'

¶

There was a note from Vance on the desk. It was in large block letters on a page from a lined writing pad.

"AGAIN I FIND I MUST SAY SORRY."

TC looked at it, tore it up into tiny pieces, then discarded it while thinking, Notes! I hate notes!

Jake pulled up at the truck depot where his ex-mates were doing some work on one of the trucks in the repair shed. Desperate looked like hell. The would-be barman was in far better condition.

'I came to get my gear,' said Jake gruffly. 'I might need it.'

'It's in my car, Jake. How's the headache?' replied the barman with a smirk.

'Get stuffed,' said Jake. 'Hope you all had a bloody good time.'

'Can't remember,' said Desperate while rubbing his head. 'Thank God, we are working undercover. I'd be a goner if we were in the sun.'

'We slept at the creek,' said Barman. 'Desperate and I slept in the back of my ute, and the three girls slept in the back of Desperate's.'

'Sounds like you didn't get a screw,' said Jake. 'That makes three of us.' Jake took his neatly folded rug and leather tumbler container from Barman. 'See you tonight at the beer garden. The Empire will be full of bloody shearers.'

The shearing contractor for the third team of shearers was in Jack Romeo's office. He was trying to arrange accommodation for his men.

'Best we can do is make up some stretchers on the verandah of the Brick and here at the Empire for the men who have missed out on a room,' said Jake Romeo. 'We'll charge you full price for the four rooms and ten bob a night for each stretcher.'

'Don't see we have much choice, Jack,' replied the shearing contractor. 'The poor buggers sleep on stretchers at the sheds all the time. I think I'll have them draw straws for the rooms. Let Lady Luck take control. I'll take one of the stretchers upstairs here for myself. Let one more of my men have the luxury of a real bed for a couple of nights.'

'Bad timing, my friend,' said Jack Romeo. 'If a flea needed space, we'd have to turn it away.'

Vance did not return to the shop that afternoon. After writing the note for TC, he went down to the creek, where he sat smoking and thinking for a couple of hours.

I might as well pitch a tent down here, he thought, when he realised how long he had been there.

He went to see Jake, gave him Yappy's punting money, had a short conversation, then went home to have a look at his boulder heap. Vance desperately wanted to get started. He was frustrated time was passing as he waited on a few parts which he had overlooked ordering with the other gear. He decided to select some boulders to take to the dispensary, where he could examine them carefully and mark where he thought would be the appropriate spot to put the saw through.

Business was steady during the afternoon. A few phone calls from opal people. Vance had not yet bothered to return their calls. TC was embarrassed. She implied that Vance was still out of town. These people were amongst the half dozen who had actually left their names and return numbers.

TC totalled the day's takings, then wrote a note for Vance.

Today's takings are all cash, Mr Callahan. One thousand, three hundred and ten pounds plus change. One gentleman told me they are all spending here because they don't know when they'll next hit a town with a chemist shop.

Please consider returning the calls from the opal people. Alternatively, advise me what I should tell them when and if they call again.

TC then locked the shop and went home. While she was walking to the house, she realised she had not turned the radio on all day. Perhaps she had caught the depression disease from the boss!

TC picked up the telephone as soon as she was in the house.

'Yes?' answered Lou.

'Con's Café please,' said TC.

'How was work and how was Vance?' asked Lou.

'A few customers. I have not seen Mr Callahan,' replied TC.

'I'll connect you to Con's,' said Lou. 'Let me know what you'll be doing.'

§

'Do you need some help tonight, Lisa?' asked TC.

'Not busy at the moment, darling,' replied Lisa, who sounded tired. 'It will be busy after Jack and Bert close. Is that too late for you?'

'Not at all, Lisa. I'll be there at nine-thirty,' said TC. 'See you then.'

Vance phoned while TC was drying her hair.

'Yes, TC, I thought I'd let you know we are leaving for Bert Black's early on Sunday morning.'

'What time is early?' asked TC.

'Five,' replied Vance. 'I got your note. Did you see mine?'

'Yes,' replied TC.

Vance hung up.

I should have told him to go by himself, thought TC. Lou is right; the boss treats me like a doormat. Why do I tolerate it? I don't know!

¶

The action at the pubs was very much the same as the previous night except that the Railway Hotel was also full of shearers. The newly-arrived team had chosen it as their watering hole, as they referred to it.

'They seem like pretty good blokes,' said one of the locals when asked by Bert Romeo if the shearers were behaving themselves. The beer garden was full of regular local drinkers because the shearers had taken over the bar.

'We'll end up drinking on the bloody footpath if any more bloody tourists arrive,' complained Jake to his reinstated truckie friends.

'Can't do that, Jake. The cops would arrest us. We'd have to go to the creek,' said Desperate.

'Stuff the bloody creek!' countered Jake. 'I hate the bastard of a place!' His mates laughed. They knew Jake was still cheesed off about the night before.

The Seat of Knowledge patrons were geared up, waiting for something exciting to happen tonight. Last night had been a disappointment.

The sergeant and Graham were on the job.

Jess, Louise, and Claudia were run off their feet more so than the previous night because a combined group of stock and station agents and bank employees were partying on the back verandah of the Empire. Big Mouth from the night before was becoming loud again.

'He's got the foulest mouth I have ever heard,' complained Jess. 'That's saying something after all the years I have been here listening to mongrel drunks. This one also has one of the loudest voices it has ever been my misfortune to tolerate.'

Big Mouth persisted in attempting to bait the Queensland shearers on the other side of the bar. The more his mates told him to give it a rest, the more aggressive he became. In particular, he had it in for a younger man who was drinking light shandy. It was obvious the Queensland shearers, who were minding their own business, were finding it extremely difficult to ignore him; however, they managed to do so.

'There'll be a brawl here before the end of the night, Jack,' said Jess when Jack Romeo paid one of his many brief visits to the smoking room to observe how things were going. 'That creature with the loud, filthy mouth is a fight waiting to happen.'

'Now, Jess,' began Jack Romeo.

'Don't now Jess me, Jack. That creature is trouble. If I had a gun, I'd shoot the mongrel.'

'I'll ask the sergeant to keep an eye on him,' agreed Jack Romeo.

'Keep an eye on him yourself, Jack. The sergeant isn't here all the time,' said Jess before hurrying off to refill empty glasses.

¶

TC left home a few minutes before nine-thirty. She was wearing her white pedal-pushers with a gold belt, yellow, sleeveless blouse with a Peter Pan collar, matching yellow bow securing her pony tail, and gold flatties with the usual bow on the front. As she walked past the Majestic, one of her customers during the day called out to her.

'TC, I'm wearing my new aftershave. Does it smell good, luv?' TC smiled and waved. When she passed the Railway Hotel, another customer was standing at the window. He was a nice man around her father's age.

'Where are you going so late, luv?' She stopped briefly as she told him she was going to help Con and Lisa.

'My mate and I will be there for a meal later, luv, so we'll see you there. You look very pretty, by the way.'

TC smiled. 'Thank you.'

The sergeant and Graham were talking to a couple of the men on the footpath outside the bank on the other side of Con's. They were facing her. Graham felt a pang of jealousy when he spotted her talking to someone at the Brick's window. Why does she have to look so damned cute? he thought while trying to listen to the sergeant's conversation as well as keep as eye on TC. He couldn't fathom what she was doing out by herself this time of night, especially with so many strangers in town.

TC entered the café. Lisa was sitting at her table while Con was talking to a party of four men seated at one of the tables.

'Give me a hug, darling,' said Lisa. 'You look like one of those young girls in the magazine.'

'The boss rang me tonight. I'm going away on Sunday at five o'clock in the morning. I don't want to go but I have to,' said TC anxiously.

'You are upset, aren't you, darling?' said Lisa.

'Yes, Lisa, I am,' replied TC. 'Lisa, I'm sorry I blurted that out the way I did. Please forget I said it.' TC smiled but Lisa was not fooled.

'We are going to be very busy later, TC,' said Lisa. 'I shall stay behind the counter and do drinks, teas, and coffees. Con will be in the kitchen cooking. When you take the orders, make sure to put the table number on the docket.'

'I didn't know you have table numbers,' said TC in surprise.

'We don't put them out except at times like this when the town is full of passers-through. Usually we know everyone, so we simply put their names on the dockets. You'd best sit on my side of the table so you can see the door.' TC quickly moved to sit down beside Lisa.

A few minutes later, the sergeant and Graham paused outside the doorway. The sergeant waved, then they moved on.

'I bet you are wondering what TC is doing out this time of night,' said the sergeant as he and Graham slowly walked along the footpath.

'Yes, Sarge, as a matter of fact I did wonder about that,' replied Graham.

'She's going to help Con and Lisa with the rush after we close the pubs,' said the sergeant. 'Lou helped them this afternoon. If you are curious as to how I know, Con told me a while ago when you were moving the car. If you've got any brains, you'll pursue this girl, Constable. Then, again, when we are young, we don't always think with our brains, do we?' The sergeant laughed. Graham said nothing. 'We'll close the Majestic first tonight,' said the sergeant as he checked the time on his watch. Less than ten minutes later, the Majestic bar was empty.

¶

Jake, Desperate, and Barman were happily drunk. They had spent the evening in reminiscence of past experiences.

'This joint's about to close,' said Jake. 'Let's go to Con's and order a feed before the bloody tourists grab all the bloody tables.'

¶

'I told you bastards!' said Jake to his mates when they walked into the café. Half a dozen tables were already occupied by fettlers who had been drinking at the Majestic. Jake led the way to a table at the rear of the café. He wanted to be located in the best vantage point to view anything and everything should anything or everything come to fruition. In Brolga, one never knew!

'Has TC left the chemist shop?' asked Barman, who was seated next to Jake.

'No way,' replied Jake. 'She wouldn't leave there. Why?'

'Because, unless I've lost my bloody marbles, she is down the front taking orders from those blokes at the third table,' replied Barman.

'Well, bugger me dead,' said Jake as he observed TC, who was laughing as she wrote on one of Con's order pads. 'Bloody little bitch!'

'Sure, Jake,' said Desperate and Barman in unison while both rolling their eyes.

I hope Jake doesn't give me a hard time, thought TC when she noticed him and his friends. Can't worry about that now. I'm too busy. She was still laughing as she rushed to the kitchen with orders.

'Those are ready, TC,' said Con, pointing to the plates of food on the huge centre stainless steel bench table. 'What are you laughing about?' asked Con as TC loaded the plates onto a large tray.

'So far, I've had three orders for me on a platter,' laughed TC. 'The last one was for one TC rare, please, no trimmings necessary.'

'Mad mongrels!' said Con with his smile and shrug. 'Come straight back, TC. There's more almost ready.'

At that moment in the gents' toilet block at the Empire, Big Mouth was bashing the young Queensland shearer he had been targeting all night. When Big Mouth had seen the Queenslander leave the bar a little earlier, he had followed him, gone up behind him while he was concentrating at the urinal, pulled him around by the shoulders, then king-hit him. The young man's head hit the concrete floor with a thud. Not satisfied, Big Mouth leaned over, pulled his victim up by the neck of his shirt, and punched him twice more in the face before two pairs of hands from behind pulled him away. Big Mouth let go and the young shearer's head once more hit the concrete floor.

There was blood everywhere. One of the two New South Wales shearers who had walked in on the scene ran to get help.

'Oh, shit!' said the second newcomer, who was kneeling beside the bleeding body on the floor. 'You've really done it now! This young bloke's been ignoring you all bloody night. You couldn't let it go! Shit!'

'Up the bastard,' yelled Big Mouth. 'He looks like the effing arsehole who was effing my effing slut wife when I was away working last year. He was an effing Queenslander, too.'

'Not this bloke's fault,' replied the man as he adjusted the Queenslander's shirt and the underpants, then zipped up the jeans. 'Leave you with your dignity,' he said silently.

Big Mouth was punching the wall and yelling at it as if it was still the young man he was hitting. 'I'll kill you, you Queensland effing trash!'

'Looks as if you've done that already,' said the sergeant from the doorway. 'Sit there in the corner. Don't move and don't open your mouth. We should have locked you up last night.' The sergeant turned to Jack and Bert Romeo, who were directly behind him and Graham.

'The doctor is on his way,' said Jack Romeo.

'I hope he's quick,' said the sergeant. 'Bert, go finish closing the Brick. Jack, go close up inside. Find this young man's boss. If anyone gives you any trouble at all, tell them we'll arrest them later.' Jack and Bert went off as instructed. The sergeant turned his attention to the man still kneeling on the floor.

'You and your mate came in here when this was happening? Is that right?'

'Yes, Sergeant,' replied the man as he stood up.

'Give the constable your name and any other details he needs; then you can go. We'll want to talk to you and your mate later. If there's a crowd outside, please tell them to go about their business. There is nothing they can do here.'

Doctor Jackson arrived. He knew at a glance that the shearer's nose was broken. There was also a deep gash on one of his cheeks and possibly a broken jaw, judging by the slackness on one side of the face. Doctor Jackson felt for a pulse, raised the young man's eyelids to expose his eyes, then gently lifted his head to find the source of the blood spread.

'What is wrong with him, Doctor?' demanded the injured shearer's boss as he arrived, panic stricken.

'Are you his boss?' asked the sergeant.

'Yes. I'm also his father,' replied the shearing contractor near to tears at the sight of his son lying helplessly on the floor.

Doctor Jackson cleared his throat.

'Your son's nose is broken, deep facial laceration, possible broken jaw. He is comatose with possible concussion, which in layman's language means your son is unconscious with possible brain damage. I shall contact the Flying Doctor. Your son will have to be taken to Curloo. I'm sorry. I'll call the hospital here and tell them he's coming. Then we'll get him moved. Please don't touch him.'

'He's only twenty-five years old,' said his father, who was in shock and had tears streaming from his eyes. 'He's got a wife and a baby. How will I tell his mother and his wife?'

'You stay here with your son. The constable and I will get Big Shot there in the corner locked up, then we'll come back,' said the sergeant.

'You effing bastards aren't taking me anywhere,' yelled Loud Mouth.

'I told you before, Big Shot, don't open your mouth. Now get up.'

'Eff you,' snarled Loud Mouth with absolute hatred in his eyes and facial expression.

'All right, Constable,' bluffed the sergeant. 'Go fetch that blood-stained length of four-by-four hardwood from the station. We'll use it to do to him what he did to this kid on the floor.' Graham made as if to go as instructed. Loud Mouth belligerently got to his feet, cursing and cussing.

'Put the cuffs on him, Constable,' directed the sergeant.

'I hate you effing cops,' yelled Loud Mouth. 'Especially you Queensland bastards.'

'That's good. The feeling is mutual,' said the sergeant calmly. 'Come on, let's go.'

Members of the shearing team were gathered on the back verandah of the Empire when the sergeant and Graham escorted Loud Mouth from the toilet block and onto the verandah.

'Is he going to be all right, Sergeant?' asked one of them with obvious concern.

'Someone should go give the kid's father support,' suggested the sergeant.

'I'm the kid's uncle,' said the most senior-looking man of the group, who immediately separated from the others and quickly went inside the toilet block.

'We'll be back soon,' said the sergeant as he and Graham continued with Loud Mouth along the verandah. When they reached the doorway to the footpath, Loud Mouth suddenly yelled, 'Effing Queenslanders! I hope you all effing die!'

The sergeant sensed how the shearers behind them would react, so he called over his shoulder, 'Let it go, men. He's not worth dirtying your hands on,' as he gave Loud Mouth an "accidental" shove off the verandah onto the footpath.

Once across the road at the police station, Graham asked Loud

Mouth to give his personal details. Loud Mouth ignored the request. He was yelling abuse.

'I hate you mother-effers. I hate your effing uniforms.'

'Empty your pockets and take off your belt,' instructed the sergeant. 'Put everything on the desk.' Loud Mouth did as directed. He then calmly dropped his trousers and underpants, squatted on the wooden floor, and took a dump. Both the sergeant and Graham were speechless. Loud Mouth stood upright, slowly pulled up his underpants and trousers, looked at the wet mess on the floor, then the sergeant, then Graham.

'That is what I think of the Queensland Police Force! You are shit!'

'Is that so?' said the sergeant calmly while seething with disgust. 'We have a strict rule around here, Big Shot. Whoever makes the mess cleans it up. Unfortunately, we don't have a mop, but I think I know something you can use.' Without warning, the sergeant up-ended Loud Mouth, grabbed him by the head, and pushed his face into the wet excrement. The sergeant moved Loud Mouth's head from side to side several times. He told Graham to fetch the hose.

'Now you know what the Queensland Police Force thinks of you, Big Shot. You can hose what's left of your mess off the floor. Better be careful of the bore water, Big Shot. While it's great for hosing shit off wooden floors, it's far too hot to wash anything off your face. Your skin would probably peel off. Constable, give Big Shot that hose, then make a list of whatever he took out of his pockets. He can sign it when he's finished hosing.'

Loud Mouth was finally quieted. He hosed the wooden floor in silence. He was also silent when he was locked in his cell.

'Perhaps you'll be ready to give us your personal details in the morning, Big Shot,' said the sergeant as he and Graham walked away. Once out of earshot of Loud Mouth, the sergeant continued.

'Come on, Constable, let us go find out how things are going with the kid and his father.

¶

'They have taken the injured young man to the hospital,' said Jack Romeo when the sergeant and Graham returned to the Empire. 'His father and another man went as well. He's in a bad way. The doctor has gone to the hospital. The Flying Doctor or probably Flying Surgeon will be here early in the morning.

'Any trouble, Jack?' asked the sergeant.

'No,' replied Jack. 'Bert had none, either. I think everyone who was here at the Empire are upset.'

'All right, Jack, we'll go by the hospital later, and we'll see you tomorrow,' replied the sergeant.

Every table at Con's was occupied. There were a few men sitting on the grassy median strip across from the café. They were waiting for some people to leave before they could sit inside.

'That is it, Con,' said TC as she entered the kitchen with a tray of dirty dishes. 'Everyone has a meal, and the first people to arrive are beginning to leave. There are a few more people waiting outside.' TC scraped the soiled plates, then piled them in the sink. 'I'll go wipe down the tables before others come in.'

As she hurried past Jake and his mates, Jake said, 'Look at the little bitch. Vance's men call her Little Flower. She looks like a bloody sunflower to me. Yellow top and ribbon and stupid bows on her shoes.'

'Give her a break, Jake,' said Desperate with a cunning smile. 'She's working her butt off. You've got a burr up your butt because she doesn't fall all over you.'

'That's right, Jake Burry Butt,' laughed Barman. 'Very clever, Desperate.'

'I thought so!' replied Desperate, who was also laughing. Jake was spitting chips. He couldn't bear humour at his expense.

'You can both get stuffed,' he snapped as he got to his feet. 'I'm going. If you two smart bastards are coming with me, let's go.'

When they stopped by the counter to pay Lisa, Jake called to TC, who was clearing their table. 'See you at the creek later, sweetheart.' TC was furious and embarrassed. Every eye in the café was on her. She was shaking with anger. She had to think quickly.

'It must be my common face. You have me mistaken for one of the nurses from the hospital. Sorry to shatter your dream!'

'You tell him, luv,' called one man. Disaster and Barman burst into laughter and were joined by the rest of the crowd. Jake disappeared faster than he drove his car.

By half past eleven only the people who had waited to get in were still in the café. They were enjoying their meal. In the kitchen Con was cleaning up in general while TC was washing up when the sergeant came in.

¶

'Hello, Con. Still busy I see, mate,' said the sergeant. 'I suppose this Greek has been working you hard, TC?

'I'm enjoying it, Sergeant,' replied TC. 'Breaks the monotony of step-sitting.'

'Hello, mate,' replied Con. 'I'm too old for these long hours.'

'Join the club,' said the sergeant. 'TC, give me a minute with Con, luv.' TC dried her hands, then left the kitchen. Graham was at the counter talking to Lisa.

'TC, come here, darling, please,' called Lisa. 'Give these coffees to those gentlemen at table five.'

'Hello, TC. I have been thinking about you,' said Graham. He was smiling. He was also sincere.

'Isn't that lovely, TC,' beamed Lisa. 'He said it in front of me, too. That means you really have been thinking about her, Constable Graham. You had to get it out, no matter who was listening.' TC was bubbling with happiness as she delivered the coffees to table five. Graham's mind was racing.

'I can't believe I said that. I mean, I wanted to say it but not like that. It simply came out.' He snapped out of thought when he heard

Lisa whisper, 'TC's going away on Sunday morning, Constable Graham. Don't tell her I told you.' TC was laughing. She was talking with the men at table five and six who had finished their meals.

'Two strawberry milkshakes for these gentlemen, please, Lisa,' said TC.

'We wanted her for dessert, but she wouldn't be in it,' laughed the man who had been in the shop during the day and had spoken to TC at the Brick's window.

'They settled for strawberry milkshakes,' laughed TC as she waited in front of the counter.

Poor substitute, thought Graham.

The sergeant came from the kitchen.

'We'll drive around for a while, Constable'.

TC delivered the strawberry milkshakes and began gathering the dishes off the two tables.

'This is for you, luv, from the eight of us,' said the Brick's window gentleman as he pushed a five-pound note across the table.

'I can't take that,' replied TC in surprise.

'Yes, you can. It's a tip for good service and your smile. It's from all of us.'

TC shook her head while smiling, 'No.'

The man looked across to Lisa. 'She can take the tip, can't she, Boss?' he asked.

'Of course, she can. Look at this,' replied Lisa as she held up a glass filled with notes of different denominations. 'This money is yours, darling. With the exception of Jake and his friends, everyone has left you a tip tonight.' TC burst into laughter as tears began welling up in her eyes.

'Now will you take the five quid, luv?' said the man. 'I'll give it to your boss when we go.'

¶

'That's it for the kitchen, Con,' said TC as she put the last dishes in the sink.

'I'm finished here. I'll do these last few dishes, TC.'

'Would you like me to sweep the floors?' enquired TC. Con was more than a little surprised.

'No, thank you, TC. You might ruin my routine. I always do the floors before I open in the mornings. You go see if Lisa needs any help. By the way, TC, thank you.'

'I've enjoyed myself Con,' replied TC happily. 'I should be thanking you and Lisa. I got out of the house for a few hours. I'll go clean the last couple of tables.'

Lisa was all smiles. The late comers were leaving.

'See you tomorrow night, luv,' called the man who had insisted on the tip. The others all waved.

'Have something to eat, TC,' suggested Lisa. TC thought for a moment, looked at the clock, then replied.

'No, thank you, Lisa. I'll go home. I'll have a Coke with Lou. She should be leaving the exchange now. It's right on midnight. I'll go now to meet her.'

'I'll close the doors behind you, darling,' said Lisa, who looked as if she was asleep on her feet.

Sure enough, Lou was crossing the road between the post office and the Empire. TC ran to meet her friend.

'I had a great night, Lou,' she said excitedly. 'I was so busy. Graham told me he's been thinking of me, and I got some tips.'

'Slow down, TC. Tell me as it happened,' said Lou. 'You know I like to hear about everything blow by blow.' After relaying to Lou every detail regarding her evening in the café, TC finished by telling Lou that Vance wanted her to leave on Sunday morning.

'How long will you be away?' asked Lou.' How much did you get tipped?'

'I don't know to both questions, Lou,' replied TC with a sigh. 'I'll know tomorrow.'

'There was a fight in the Empire toilet,' stated Lou matter-of-factly.

'Some young guy was beaten up by some big guy. The young guy might have brain damage. The big guy is in the lock-up. That's all I know,' concluded Lou.

'They must have been drunk,' speculated TC.

'Probably,' replied Lou. 'My dad says booze turns some people into animals.'

Graham walked into his room, looked around, then checked his watch for the time. The sergeant had gone to bed, and Loud Mouth was asleep in the lock-up.

What a night! He briefly thought about the twenty-five-year-old, then the incident on the police station floor with the sergeant and Loud Mouth. He told himself to leave work at work. If he stayed with the police force and the police force stayed with him, who was to know what he would see in the future.

The voices started in his head. He ignored them as he hung up his uniform. A few minutes later, Graham was on his way to see TC. She was going away and he wasn't going to have the opportunity to see her again before she left. Not without the entire population looking on. He had to see her alone. He didn't know where she was going or for how long.

Lou was on the stairs by herself when Graham reached the house. The radio was playing. As usual, it was tuned to 2UE.

'What a surprise, Constable Graham,' said Lou softly with a broad smile while pointing to inside the house. No guy on earth does blue jeans more justice than Graham, except Elvis, of course, thought Lou as she watched Graham walk quickly through the back of the house. TC was removing the cap off a Coke bottle when Graham entered the kitchen.

'Got an extra one of those, please, waitress?' said Graham with his to-die-for smile as he leaned against the kitchen door frame. TC was flustered, surprised, and excited simultaneously.

'I'm surprised to see you here,' she said shakily. She took another Coke from the refrigerator, then opened it.

'So is Lou. So am I. Come here. I want to hug you,' replied Graham. He stepped forward, put his arms around her, and held her closely to him. He looked down at her upturned face.

'I love you, TC. Every time I see you, my gut tightens. It was torturing me to come here, ruffle your hair, hold your hand, kiss you on the cheek or forehead, and not be able to have you. It's bad, or even worse, not seeing you at all. That note was a mistake. Now you are going away, I'm scared witless you won't come back. I'm going to kiss you now.' He took TC's face in his hands, then leaned down and kissed her on the forehead, on each cheek, then again on the forehead.

'Now we should go and join Lou before I get carried away.'

'Who told you I was going away?' asked TC as they sat down with Lou.

'It sure is hot this time of year,' said Graham avoiding TC's question.

'It gets worse,' said Lou. 'When does your car get here?'

'On the next goods train,' replied Graham. Del Shannon was singing 'My Little Runaway' on 2UE.

'That'll be you, Graham,' teased Lou. 'You'll be walking along thinking about TC next week and the week after and the week after.'

'Stop now, Lou! Listen to the music,' laughed Graham, who lifted his Coke bottle to his mouth with one hand and squeezed TC's hand with the other. They listened to music and talked until after three in the morning, when Graham said, 'Go inside, Lou. I want to say goodnight to TC.'

'Not until you promise me you'll come visit me while she's away. I'll be lonely,' replied Lou in little-girl mode.

'Okay, I promise. Now go,' replied Graham as he stood up, pulling TC to her feet with him. He hugged TC, then ruffled her hair.

'I have missed you all week, and I'll miss you when you aren't here. I'll keep in contact via Lou. I love you!'

'Thank you,' replied TC softly. 'I love you, too.' Graham kissed her on the forehead, then was gone.

¶

A cloud of solemnity blanketed Brolga's main block about Loud Mouth and the young man in the hospital. There was a long queue outside the red phone box at the post office.

The shearers all identified with the situation. What had happened to the young man could have happened to any one of them. Those who had family felt an urgent necessity to call them and hear their loved ones' voices because who knew when or if they would have the opportunity again.

Everyone in Brolga had heard the flying doctor's plane arrive and leave early in the morning. Those who were unaware of the reason why the flying doctor had paid the fleeting visit would make it their business to find out.

¶

Doctor Jackson, the matron, and the sergeant had been at the airstrip to see the young man placed on the plane.

'It's good the kid's father was here to go with him,' said the sergeant as the plane started down the runway. 'How is the kid, Doc?'

'We'll have to wait and see, sergeant,' replied Doctor Jackson with a heavy sigh.

'You need some sleep, Doctor,' said the matron. 'You've been with the patient all night.'

'I'll give you a lift back to the hospital,' said the sergeant. Both Doctor Jackson and the matron nodded, 'Thank you.' The matron told the driver of the ancient ambulance van to go ahead.

¶

On arrival back at the police station, the sergeant had been greeted by Loud Mouth's boss, who was the same man who had apologised for Loud Mouth's behaviour a couple of nights previously.

'You couldn't control him, eh?' said the sergeant.

'No, unfortunately,' replied the man seriously. 'How is the bloke he belted up?'

'Not good, poor bugger,' said the sergeant. 'Your man is in a whole lot of trouble. We'll let him have a shower in a little while when the constable comes on duty. He will need to talk to the two men who walked in on the incident; also your man in the lock-up will need fresh clothes.'

'All right, I'll round up the two blokes you want to see and I'll bring Slugger's gear,' replied Big Mouth's boss.

'You call him Slugger. How appropriate,' mused the sergeant. 'Bring Slugger's gear at eight or a little before. Ask the two men to come to the station around nine. Thanks, mate.'

The sergeant went to check on his prisoner, who was lying on the bunk with his hands behind his head. The sergeant eyed him with contempt.

'You can have a shower in a little while. Your boss is bringing fresh clothes for you. If you would like some breakfast, we'll order some in for you from the café.'

'Get effed,' replied Slugger without looking at the sergeant.

'Suit yourself.' The sergeant turned towards the residence, where he knew a hearty breakfast awaited him.

¶

'It's great to be young,' announced Lou when she returned from the bathroom after taking a shower. 'We can stay up all hours and bounce back after just a couple of hours' sleep.'

'Speak for yourself, Lou,' replied TC, who was carefully folding clothes into a suitcase.

'TC, you feel miserable because you have to go away and you don't know what sort of mood Vance will be in today,' said Lou flippantly. 'And, of course, you don't want to leave me. Oh, I forgot about Graham!'

'Lou, please be quiet,' replied TC. 'Let me be miserable in peace.'

The telephone rang. Lou ran to answer it, thinking it might be Colin, who was now calling regularly. It was Vance for TC. Lou called to TC, then said, 'Vance, I'll come to collect my pay this morning if that's okay with you.'

'I'll see you then,' replied Vance. TC took the telephone.

'We are leaving at eleven o'clock tonight,' said Vance off-handedly. 'I have to be back here by noon on Tuesday.'

'Why don't we leave after the shop is closed at one today?' asked TC.

'Because that doesn't suit me. Don't ask questions!'

'Mr Callahan, if you don't show me a little courtesy, you can go by yourself. You have been treating me like a mongrel dog lately. I've had enough!' TC placed the phone down. It rang again in seconds.

'Point taken, TC. I'll watch my attitude,' said Vance.

'Thank you!' TC firmly placed the handset in its cradle.

'What is wrong now?' asked Lou.

'It's a pity the shearers and fettlers aren't in town all of the time,' replied TC. 'If they were, I would ask Con and Lisa for a job. I'm going for a shower.' Lou knew her friend meant what she had said about a job with Con and Lisa.

§

Jake had a feeling he was going to back winners that day. He intended to wage a thousand. He remembered the hundred quid Yappy had sent with Vance.

You are one lucky little man, Yappy, thought Jake. You have sent your loot to the right person, mate. Today I'm going to win a lot of money. Every horse I back will romp home. I know it!

§

TC was surprised to see Vance smile when she arrived at the shop.

'You had a good day yesterday, I see,' said Vance.

'Yes, it was busy all day,' replied TC.

'TC, I haven't bothered to return the calls from those opal people because all they will want to do is pick my brain. Sooner or later they'll be up here chasing opal themselves. If they ring again, ask them what they want. Con told me you helped out at the café last night. He also said you seemed to enjoy it.'

'I did,' replied TC. 'Nice to see you smile again. When will I be coming home?'

'I'm not sure,' replied Vance.

⁋

The morning went quickly in the chemist shop. Lou collected her money, making certain she paid for the packet of jelly beans. Vance paid TC her wages.

'I remembered, for a change,' he said.

There were quite a few customers, both visitors and locals. Doctor Jackson came to familiarise himself with the layout of the dispensary. He was going to fill any prescriptions he wrote in Vance's absence. TC heard Doctor Jackson tell Vance that the young man the Flying Doctor had collected that morning was being operated on in Curloo Hospital as he spoke.

'I'll pick you up at eleven tonight,' said Vance at one o'clock. It was closing time, and TC was happy to leave. 'I'm taking the station wagon,' said Vance. 'It will be more comfortable than the ute. It's a long trip.'

TC said goodbye to Doctor Jackson, told Vance she would be ready at eleven, then went to the café.

⁋

It had been a busy morning at the police station. Slugger was cooperating regarding taking a shower. That was as far as it went. He swung into his 'I hate the effing Queensland Police Force' routine when Graham requested once again his personal details. He showed no remorse whatever regarding what he had done. He didn't enquire about the condition of the young man he had victimised. He either didn't realise or didn't care how much trouble he was in.

Slugger's boss furnished the sergeant and Graham with the details they required. The witnesses to the tail-end of the attack gave their statements. The sergeant got Jess to give a statement as to what had gone on in the bar prior to the event. Calls were back and forth to the police in Curloo and the Curloo Hospital.

The sergeant put the telephone down, then said to Graham, 'They are operating on that kid. Apparently it will be risky. Something to do with pressure on his brain. You go grab something to eat. It's going to be another long day. Tell Jack Romeo about the kid's operation on your way to Con's. If you are lucky, you might run into TC. She should be finishing work about now.' Graham smiled.

'Thanks, Sarge.'

No doubt about it, thought Graham as he crossed the street to the Empire. Nothing gets past the sergeant. He doesn't miss a trick.

Graham spoke briefly to Jack Romeo, who appeared genuinely concerned when he heard the news. The Empire bar was full with race results blasting from the radio. As Graham passed the ladies' lounge, he saw Jake sitting alone writing something on a piece of paper.

To Graham's surprise, the café was almost empty. Only one table was occupied by customers eating their meals. Lisa, Lou and TC were seated at Lisa's table. Lisa and Lou were facing the door; TC, as usual, was facing the kitchen. They were engrossed in conversation. Lou and Lisa saw him but continued talking. Graham walked up behind TC and put his hands over her eyes. TC was startled until she realised who it was.

'What are you doing here?' she laughed.

'The sergeant told me I might be lucky and find you here,' replied a smiling Graham. 'I also came to get some food.'

'Con is in the kitchen, Graham,' said Lisa. 'He's listening to the races.' Graham went to the kitchen to order, then returned to join Lisa and the girls.

'Who's rich?' he asked when he spotted a pile of notes on the table in front of TC.

'I am,' replied TC while smiling.

'She robbed the bank,' said Lou.

'That money is TC's tips from last night,' said Lisa.

'I got fifty-nine pounds and ten shillings,' said TC proudly. 'That is the equivalent of almost twenty-four weeks' wages. I'm going to buy a fan for my bedroom, pay some off our washing machine, and bank the rest.'

'I'm going to do the same with what I supposedly earned at the chemist shop,' said Lou.

'My boss says we are leaving at eleven tonight, Graham,' said TC matter-off-factly. 'I think it's a strange time to leave but he said he has his reasons. I hope he doesn't hit any roos.'

'TC, put your hand on your knee. I want to hold it,' said Graham ever so softly.

'You are in uniform,' whispered TC as she placed her hand on her knee closest to him.

'Lisa and Lou won't dob me in,' he whispered back.

'Anyway, darling, the sergeant knows he's here,' smiled Lisa. Graham squeezed TC's hand tightly. She squeezed his back. Her heart was beating wildly.

¶

In the ladies' lounge at the Empire, Jake was over the moon. His first three horses had bolted in. One had been a favourite, so the odds had been short. It didn't matter as the other two paid big money.

When my other two win, I'll have won big-time, thought Jake as he went to the bar for a beer refill. I'll work it out at the end of the day. I know these other two will win. They are certainties.

'How are you going, Jake?' asked one of the handful of locals in the bar. 'Are you winning?'

'I'm a couple of quid ahead, mate,' replied Jake as he placed money on the bar to pay for his beer.

Bet the young prick is winning a bloody fortune, thought the local as Jake picked up his drink.

'See you later, mate,' said Jake. 'I have to get back to my office.' Jake pointed to the ladies' lounge.

¶

In the café, Graham was telling Lisa and the girls the same.

'Well, my TC, you be a good girl and think of me a lot while you are away,' said Graham with a half-hearted smile.

'Your sandwich is on the house today, young Graham,' said Lisa. 'Con doesn't need the money.' Graham reluctantly stood up to go.

'Thank you, Lisa. See you later. You, too, Lou.' He touched TC on the cheek, ruffled her hair, then hurried towards the door.

TC was on the verge of tears. She said, 'Come on, Lou. We'll go buy a couple of fans, pay some money on our washing machine, then go home so I can have a cry.'

'Not again,' said Lou. 'We'll both be back to help you tonight, Lisa.'

§

'The kid died,' announced the sergeant the moment Graham returned to the police station. 'Poor young bugger died while the surgeon was operating. That makes Slugger a murderer.'

'Does he know yet?' asked Graham.

'Haven't told him yet,' replied the sergeant. 'Doubt the bastard will care! Last night I heard a bloke say he was the kid's uncle. Please find him. I need to see him. Round up Slugger's boss while you are at it. Tell Jack Romeo, too. After all, the kid was murdered in his pub. I have calls to make.'

§

Jake was jubilant. He jumped up and threw his hands in the air, yelling, 'Yes! Yes! Yes!' when his last horse came home. His mind was calculating his winnings.

'Are you all right, Jake?' came Jack Romeo's voice from the hallway.

'I'm fine, Jack,' replied Jake. 'I've backed five winners today.'

'Good boy,' smiled Jack Romeo before moving on.

Jake quickly sat down to calculate his winnings while thinking, Am I good or what? After a couple of minutes, Jake sighed heavily. Silently, he said, Well, Yappy, mate, you are fourteen hundred and twenty quid richer. Well, Jake, you genius! You are fourteen thousand two hundred quid richer. Bloody hell! Wish my mate, Vance, was here. Oh, stuff it! I'll go and see how Con went with his bets.

¶

When the sergeant told Slugger that the young man had died, the instant reply was, 'Good! One less effing Queenslander to pollute the earth.' The sergeant was overcome with disbelief and disgust that anyone could be so cold and unrepentant after killing an innocent twenty-five-year-old who had a young wife and baby.

Graham returned with the uncle and Slugger's boss. When told the news, they both stood silent with shock and sorrow combined. After a minute or so, Slugger's boss turned to the uncle.

'My men and I are deeply sorry that one of ours could do this. I can't find the words to suffice. I'm truly sorry, mate. If there's anything I can do, please tell me.'

'It's not your fault, mate,' replied the uncle. 'Thank you for offering to help. There's nothing, Sergeant, I'll need to contact my brother at Curloo Hospital. He'll be a mess. His only child has gone. If there's an Anglican Church in town, I'd like to see the minister.'

'Use the telephone in there,' said the sergeant, pointing to a small room behind the desk. 'Call your brother. Then the constable will drive you to the church. The minister will be there. I know his schedule.'

'I'll go now,' said the shearing contractor. 'I'll phone Slugger's wife. Then I'll tell my men what has happened. Thank you, Sergeant. Thank you, Constable.'

¶

After being dropped off at the Church of England, the uncle and the minister had a long conversation. The uncle had gone to the church to ask the minister to say a prayer for his nephew's soul as their family were

226

staunch Anglicans. The minister said he would be happy to dedicate the service to the man's nephew the next morning, it being Sunday. All he needed were details of the nephew's life.

When finished, the Minister of the Bush Brotherhood said, 'I'll see you in the morning at seven.'

'Thank you, Brother. I guarantee all my men will attend your service in the morning,' said the uncle, who was desperately restraining himself to break the news to the other members of the team of shearers, all of whom were devastated to hear of the loss of one of their own. They all vowed to be at the service next morning.

❡

The New South Wales team offered sincere condolences. They were obviously upset, to say the least. Every one of them felt heavy guilt for not having seen it coming and preventing it. They also would attend the service for the deceased shearer.

Jess told Jack Romeo about the service. Jack told Bert Romeo, who told the shearer who drank at the Brick. They too would attend the service for the shearer whom they did not know had died until Bert told them. The contractor for the team went directly to offer his sympathy to the uncle and his men.

❡

Lou and TC were en route to the café when they heard the whistle of the Flea.

'Let's go meet it,' said Lou. 'You met it by yourself when I was at work. I want to meet it tonight.'

The train was about to pull in when Lou said, 'Look to the left, TC. That girl talking to Graham is the one I was telling you about. She won the toss. Jake used to take her out a while back.'

TC looked left. She saw Graham about ten yards away, talking to and laughing with a pretty, blonde girl who came to the shop occasionally.

TC turned away quickly 'Let's go, Lou, before he sees us.'

'Too late, I'm afraid, TC' said Lou. 'He already has. He's got panic written all over his face.'

'It's a free country, Lou,' said TC over her shoulder as she walked towards the street. Lou hurried after TC.

'She probably started flirting with him, TC. Everyone in town knows the police meet the Flea.'

'Lou, I don't own Graham,' said TC. 'He is human, after all.'

'And you aren't?' argued Lou.

'That's different, Lou. I'm female,' replied TC.

¶

Graham was stuck. He wanted to tell the girl to take a hike. He wanted to run after TC but couldn't because the train had arrived.

Foul timing, he thought as the girl from tennis hung around while the train and platform emptied. Only the workers remained.

'I have to go now,' said Graham.

'Will you be at tennis tomorrow afternoon?' asked the girl.

'That depends on how busy we are,' replied Graham. 'Now, I really do have to go.'

'I'm going to the movies. I'll see you after they finish,' the girl persisted.

'You had better hurry or you'll miss the start,' said Graham as he got into the police car. Subtlety is definitely not that girl's strong point, thought Graham as he drove away from the railway station.

¶

Saturday night at Con's was much the same as the night before except for the rush of locals at movie interval time. TC left when the café was full at a quarter to eleven. She quickly hugged Lou, Lisa, and even Con before making her getaway. Best to make it quick; there was less chance of her crying.

The movie crowd was leaving as TC approached the theatre. Most were walking to their cars; a few were heading towards Con's, as usual. The crowd cleared quickly. Directly ahead, Graham and the blonde girl were standing on the footpath in front of the theatre. Once again, they were laughing as they were talking. Neither of them saw TC approaching. As she walked past them, she looked at Graham and said, 'Good evening, Constable,' then smiled at the girl.

TC felt sick! She wished Lou was with her because she would have to put on a brave front. She wanted to cry. She wouldn't because Vance was picking her up in a few minutes. The last thing she needed was the boss asking questions.

¶

She was at the front of the gate waiting when Vance's car came around the corner from the back streets. Vance didn't speak when he got out of the station wagon. He opened the rear window through which he put TC's case. TC was carrying a pillow. She reached to open the door to the back seat to place the pillow inside.

'No! Leave that for a while, TC.' said Vance. 'Sit in the front and nurse your pillow.' TC did as she was told.

'How far is it to Mr Black's place?' asked TC.

'About a thousand miles,' replied Vance as he started the car.

'How is Mrs Callahan?' asked TC as he drove along the street to go around the median strip.

'Delores is Delores!' replied Vance curtly. 'Stop asking questions, TC!'

'Mr Callahan, please stop the car. You are doing the mongrel dog thing again. I'm going to Mr Black's because you need me to go. Do you remember telling me that? Leanne will treat me like dirt when I get there. You know that. You are angry with the world, Mr Callahan. You vent all of that anger on me. Why me?'

'Be quiet, please, TC,' said Vance calmly as he reached for his cigarette packet. TC clicked on the car radio, then fiddled with the dial until she heard the 2UE disc jockey's voice. She was thinking, If I have to be silent for a thousand miles, at least I'll have the radio.

About five miles past the end of the bitumen, Vance stopped the car. He got out and opened the back door.

'Come on. Time for you to get out from under that blanket,' said Vance as he lifted a rug off the seat. 'Poor girl, you must be dehydrated under there,' he laughed.

'You are not wrong, darling,' replied Claudia sweetly. 'I hate that station, darling. We'll have to change it. I need some water, darling.'

TC was in absolute shock. She could not believe her ears. Now she understood why they had left Brolga at eleven. Vance had to wait for Claudia to finish her shift at the Empire. She wanted to scream. She wanted to jump out of the car and run back to town. TC would have done just that except for her fear of snakes. They were in the bush. The only sound was that of the radio and Claudia drinking her water. TC felt old and lonely as she stared out into the night. The moon was glowing in the cloudless sky; everything was still, even the leaves on the trees. The air was hot and dry. TC closed her eyes and remembered her childhood near the beautiful, blue Pacific Ocean with the cool sea breeze and baby waves gently lapping the white sand.

Vance said, 'You and your pillow can get in the back, TC.' TC did so as if she were a robot. Vance and Claudia kissed passionately before getting into the car. They were underway again in seconds.

Claudia said loudly, 'I hate this music, darling. Would you mind terribly much if I change the station. I'm sure I can find something more tasteful.'

'Go ahead, Claudia. Whatever makes you happy,' replied Vance as he laughed.

'Thank you, darling,' said Claudia, who kissed Vance on his arm.

'No wonder he didn't want to talk about Mrs Callahan,' thought TC, who curled up on the back seat with her pillow before making herself oblivious to the conversation and goings-on in the front seat.

She didn't care! TC was crying inside as she hugged her pillow. She couldn't pin-point any particular reason for her state of mind. Was it self-pity? No, she didn't think so. It was a combination of everything. The injustices of life, like the young man being bashed to death, leaving behind a wife and child; Mrs Callahan leaving the boss so much and that she kept coming back to him; Claudia slicing her legs to gain attention; most people considering Lou's dad a fool when, in fact, he was an extremely intelligent, principled man; Louise endeavouring to drink herself into the grave because she couldn't have the man she loved; Graham flirting with other girls because of his sexual needs; Jake, who was capable of being a nice person, yet usually played the part of a spoiled, self-centred arrogant brat; Jess working at the Empire all those years because of her love for a man she knew she could never have; the dear Seat of Knowledge patrons who sat on the seat night after night in anticipation of something happening; Brad Lester attempting to commit suicide because of his love for Sam.

The list could go on forever, so TC ceased thinking sad thoughts and concentrated on getting some sleep. Doing so would not be easy due to the bumpy road over which the station wagon was travelling at high speed.

⁋

In Brolga, Jake was reclining on his bed, pondering the thought of one day becoming a bookmaker. Jake was sober, especially for a Saturday night. He hadn't felt like doing the same old thing.

'Bugger the nurse and creek routine tonight,' he told himself after visiting Con for a yarn in the afternoon. Jake decided he would go to the movies. He would go alone. He liked the thought of his own company for a change. At interval, he had one beer at the Majestic, which was full of fettlers. When the second movie finished, Jake joined the crowd to exit the theatre. You could have blown Jake over with a feather when he saw Graham talking with "Miss Jakie". As Jake walked to his car he thought, 'Constable Dickless Tracey! You poor bastard! I feel sorry for you, mate.' Jake laughed all the way home. He still found it amusing and that had been over an hour ago.

⁋

Lou was sitting on the top step, missing TC's company. Even 2UE wasn't helping her. Loneliness sucks! she said to herself. Now I know how TC feels when I work night shift. Lou thought she was seeing things when Graham appeared at the gate a few seconds later.

'Can I come in?' asked Graham.

'She's gone!' replied Lou.

'I know!' said Graham.

'Get yourself a Coke before you sit down,' said Lou, 'if you want one, that is.'

Graham returned from the kitchen and settled himself on the step next to Lou.

'I thought you'd be with Miss High Society,' said Lou flatly. 'Or does that happen after your car arrives?'

'Lou, I feel so bad,' replied Graham sincerely. 'I truly do. That girl is after me all the time, Lou. She had me bailed up outside the theatre when TC was on her way home.'

Lou wanted to tell him, That is because she won the toss, you idiot. Instead, she spoke with all the control she could muster. 'That is great, Graham. Last night you were here declaring your love to TC. Tonight she sees you twice within a few hours flirting with another girl. Exceptional farewell for TC, Graham. You deserve to go to the top of the class. Class of crap-heads, that is! To quote my dad, 'All you guys think with your penis instead of your brain. A stiff one has no conscience.'

'Please, Lou, don't be like that,' replied Graham. 'I didn't plan it! That girl is determined. She corners me!'

'Graham, do the girl and yourself a favour,' said Lou matter-of-factly. 'If you don't enjoy talking and laughing with her, do as my dad would. Tell her to piss off. It's that simple. If you do enjoy her fawning over you, leave things as they are. Now drink your Coke before it gets warm!' Lou laughed before adding, 'With a little luck you'll choke on it.'

'I probably deserve it,' laughed Graham.

¶

Vance woke TC when they arrived in Curloo.

'You drive for a while,' he said. 'There's around three hundred miles of paved road ahead before we hit dirt again. If I'm asleep when we hit the dirt, wake me.' TC yawned and rubbed her eyes.

'Are you sure?' Vance poured water into a mug, which he passed to TC.

'Here you go. Get out of the car and splash some of this on your face. Drink what's left. Chew some gum. That will keep you awake.'

Claudia was slumped sideways and asleep on the front passenger seat. Vance shook her awake, then guided her out of the front and into the back seat, where she immediately went back to sleep.

'I have topped up the fuel. Sit on fifty,' said Vance once he was settled beside Claudia.

TC tuned the radio to 2UE before driving off in a south-easterly direction. TC was on alert for roos. She didn't have a clue what she would do if one or two or even three suddenly jumped in front of the car. She was scared, which kept her wide awake.

'Thank you, Lord, for this being the only car on this road while I am driving.'

§

TC came to a tiny township. It was so small that, in comparison, Brolga was a city. It was almost eight o'clock in the morning. She pulled off to the side of the road. Vance woke when TC opened the car door. TC turned away while he disentangled himself from Claudia.

'I think this is where the dirt road starts, Mr Callahan,' said TC. 'There is a sign fifty yards back that points south. I need a toilet.'

'Go behind a tree,' replied Vance. 'I'll go behind the car.'

'What if someone sees me?' asked TC.

'Just go,' said Vance with a half-smile, a sigh, and rolling eyes.

After urinating behind the car, Vance woke Claudia, who wanted him to climb back into the car with her. Initially, Vance laughed but soon became impatient when Claudia insisted.

'For heaven's sake, Claudia, there's time for that when we get where we are going. Get out of the damned car.'

'Doesn't little bitch-face want to drive anymore?' snapped Claudia. 'Tell her to turn off that shit music. It gives me a headache.'

'I warned you, Claudia. Don't pick on TC. She's done nothing to you except put up with the crap you lay on her every chance you get. By the way, I happen to like that music. Now sit up and move yourself into the front seat.'

'Screw you, Vance,' snapped Claudia. 'Screw you, too, you little bitch,' added Claudia as she turned her attention to TC, who was standing outside the driver's door.

'Stay there, you moron,' commanded Vance. 'TC, get in the front. I'll drive.' Vance slammed the back door.

Claudia screamed, 'You mad bastard!' Vance got into the driver's seat. He drove into the township. There was not a soul to be seen. There were eight houses that could be seen, a tiny pub, which was built flat on the ground, a tiny hall with the CWA insignia on the front, and a general store with a single petrol bowser out the front. On the door to the general store was a handwritten sign which read—

It is Sunday. If you want fuel, push the bell. Don't push it before eight. If you are here before eight, you will have to wait.

Vance laughed. He pushed the bell. A young man opened the door. He looked hung-over and dishevelled.

'Fill it up, please,' said Vance. 'You look as if you had a good night.'

'I sure as bloody hell did, mate,' replied the young man. 'I'll pay for it today when my mum sees me. She hates it when I hit the piss.' Vance laughed.

'My mother was the same when I was your age. It's because they love us.'

'Sometimes too bloody much,' was the reply.

'Wait until you get a wife,' laughed Vance.

'Bugger that! I'm having too much fun being single. That's it, mate, you'll be full,' said the young man as he hung up the bowser hose, then locked it. Vance followed him inside to pay for the fuel. He returned a few minutes later, smiling from ear to ear.

'That kid offered me fifty quid to leave you here for a few days, TC,' laughed Vance. 'He said I could collect you on my way back to Brolga.'

'Don't worry about the fifty quid, darling. Tell him you'll leave the little bitch here for free,' said Claudia spitefully. 'Then I can sit in the front with you.'

'Claudia, you had your chance to sit in the front. You are the one I would like to leave behind. If you call TC a bitch again, I will throw you out of the car. There is a bitch in this car; her name is Claudia.'

Vance turned the car onto the dirt road.

TC sat in silence. She still couldn't believe Vance had brought Claudia with them. Why? she kept asking herself.

Claudia has to be the craziest woman I have ever hooked up with, thought Vance. She's a stunner to look at. She's also mad. I would probably have been better off if I had let her carry through with her threat to blab to poor bloody Delores. TC must be feeling miserable being stuck in the car with Claudia. It's hell for me; must be worse for her.

They had travelled only a few miles along the dirt road when Claudia screamed.

'Stop this effing car! I need to pee.' Her scream was so sudden and piercing that it startled Vance. He braked hard and the car swerved off the road, coming within inches of crashing into a tree. Claudia opened the car door, jumped out of the car, hiked up her skirt, pulled down her pants, then squatted beside the car.

'Mad moll! Could have got us killed,' said Vance in disgust. TC couldn't hold her tongue a second longer.

'Why did you bring her, Mr Callahan?'

'She blackmailed me, TC,' replied Vance while holding his head in his hands as he leaned against the steering wheel. 'I'll tell you the full story when I get the chance. You look whacked, kid. Get in the back. Try to get some sleep.'

Claudia's "butter wouldn't melt in her mouth" personality took over when she heard TC get out of the front and into the back seat of the car.

She was smiling as she stood and fixed her clothing. She had managed to get her own way.

'Okay, darling, that was the longest wee. It took forever,' she said sweetly as she positioned herself in the front passenger seat.

'Right. Let's get going,' said Vance as he started the car. Claudia sat close to Vance with adoration in her eyes. With her right hand, she began moving it gently up and down his upper inner thigh.

'Yeah,' said Vance while wriggling in his seat.

'When, darling?' murmured Claudia longingly as her left hand reached over to the knob on the radio.

'Never if you fiddle with the radio!' replied Vance. Vance drove back onto the road. Claudia rested her head on his shoulder. She continued rubbing his jean-clad leg. She didn't touch the radio. TC was already asleep on the back seat.

¶

Back in Brolga, the Bush Brother was feeling exhilarated as he stood with a large group of shearers outside the church. The dedication service for the deceased shearer had been a marvellous success. The church was filled to capacity plus. Those people who could not be accommodated in the process stood shoulder to shoulder, chest to back. One of the handful of loyal locals who attended most Sundays commented, 'It's a wonder the bloody floor didn't collapse under the weight.' Those who couldn't fit inside the church had patiently stood outside for the duration. They couldn't hear much, if anything. Their presence was the important factor. The shearers went to farewell a fellow shearer. The fettlers who attended were there out of respect to a fellow, hard-working Australian. Doctor Jackson and the sergeant attended, as did Jack and Bert Romeo.

It was unbelievably hot in the church with only half a dozen small wall fans to cool the mass of bodies. With the exception of Jack and Bert, everyone wore short-sleeved shirts. The Romeo Brothers were attired in formal, imported, designer, made-to-order black, fine-woollen suits.

Brother had kept the heat in mind when preparing the service, which was over in thirty minutes. He was relieved he had spent many hours the previous night researching and comparing appropriate passages from the Bible that would identify with the details he possessed on the young man's short life. After everyone had gone, he was astonished when he opened the contribution box. It was jam-packed with money. All notes!

Saturday night, when the bars were full, Slugger's boss had taken the hat around for donations to help the dead man's wife and baby. He raised over five hundred pounds, which he gave to the sergeant to send to the young widow. Along with the money was a letter of condolence signed by every shearer in town.

Two Curloo detectives came to town to collect Slugger. They stayed long enough to refuel their car, have a meal at Con's, and have a talk with the sergeant before starting back to Curloo with Slugger as their passenger. A murder charge was far too big a deal to be handled in Brolga.

By mid-day the only transients still in town were the shearers who had arrived last and the fettlers. The men who had been sleeping on the verandah stretchers were happy. They would have a real bed for the night.

¶

At the camp, Yappy was wondering if he was any wealthier after yesterday's races. He had a feeling Jake had backed winners.

Lou was missing TC. Nothing seemed the same without her in the house. She decided to visit her mum.

Graham was deliberating over whether or not to join the females for tennis that night. So what if he was the only male player? He enjoyed playing. He was excited because his car would be on the next morning's goods train. He was disappointed TC had gone away. He would have liked her to be the first female apart from his mother and sisters to take for a drive in his new car, which he had bought only days before being told he was going to be stationed in Brolga, which seemed like a million miles away from his family and home town.

¶

South of the border, Bert Black and his Leanne were discussing what they would and would not teach TC during her pending stay in their town. After just a couple of minor initial mistakes while processing his two boulders into stones, Bert was confident he knew the shortcuts. His years of experience cutting Lightening Ridge black opal had been no hindrance. While this new boulder opal was an entirely different composition, the cutting method was the same once the opal seam was exposed. Bert Black was happy with the yield of stones from the two boulders. Only he and Leanne would see them until one day he found a buyer who would appreciate them enough to pay top dollar. That would be a long time off. Callahan didn't even know how to saw the bloody stuff as yet.

'She's not staying long, Bert,' stated Leanne. 'I can't stand her.'

'Yes, Leanne, I'm well aware of that,' replied Bert.

'She has to go in the little shed down the backyard, Bert,' continued Leanne. 'You said you'd put her there.'

'Yes, Leanne, I remember,' replied Bert. 'I suppose you expect me to give her a couple of pieces of bloody agate to lean on.'

'Good idea, Bert,' agreed Leanne happily. 'You are not going to teach her much. You promised me that, remember?'

'Yes, Leanne. I'll give her two pieces of tough agate. Bloody stuff's as hard as the hole of hell. Will take the poor bugger a week to shape it, let alone polish it.'

'Bert, promise me we are not putting up with her longer than a week,' insisted Leanne.

'Anything for peace, Leanne,' replied Bert. He knew who was boss. It certainly was not him. He could not understand why Leanne was so concerned. He had no intention of teaching TC anything but basics. Basic basics, at that. He had what he wanted—the opal!

§

Vance drove into Bert Black's hometown just on dark. It appeared to be perhaps double the size of Brolga. Only once since the morning had they stopped briefly for fuel and drinks in a town not far from where the dirt road merged with a paved highway.

Three blocks into town they saw a motel sign.

'That must be it,' said Vance. 'Bert Black told me to book you in here, TC. You'll only have a four-block walk to his place.'

'Let's check in, darling. I can't wait to get you to myself,' said Claudia between kisses she was depositing on Vance's left arm.

'We'll find somewhere to eat first, Claudia,' replied Vance. 'I also need a cigarette. We need fuel, as well.'

'I'm not eating with her,' complained Claudia.

TC wanted to yell, the feeling is mutual. Instead, she kept her lips clenched.

'All right, we'll get a pie or a hamburger to take to the motel,' placated Vance. 'Anything for peace!'

¶

The town was a bigger version of Brolga. Being Sunday night, there were few people to be seen. Everything was closed except for two cafés, one either end on opposite sides of what appeared to be the main block, and a service station. After refuelling the car, Vance parked outside the nearest café. He went inside while Claudia and TC remained in the car.

Claudia was stretched out on the front seat with her head against the driver's side window. She was observing Vance through the wide café doorway. He was in the process of lighting a cigarette while sitting at a table waiting for the food. Claudia's manipulative mind was riffling through ideas on how she might successfully eliminate his wife. She was unaware of the fact that many of her predecessors had schemed to achieve the same. They had all failed! The only one who could have pulled it off was Anna, who was too principled to wreck a marriage. She simply disappeared.

Another one who definitely has to go is bitch-face here in the back seat, thought Claudia. I'd like to strangle her. She knows too bloody much, and Vance thinks the sun shines out of her arse! Claudia would have been surprised to know that, where TC was concerned, she and Delores shared identical sentiments.

TC sat in the back seat. She was also watching Vance. Her thoughts were in contradiction to Claudia's.

Why does the boss get involved with women like Claudia. Mrs Callahan is attractive. She is the mother of his children. I think one of the reasons the boss gets so angry is because he hates himself for getting involved with the Claudias of the world while knowing Mrs Callahan loves him more than he deserves. I can't wait to get out of this car. I can feel Claudia's hatred. She was relieved when she saw Vance go to the café counter to collect his order.

Vance checked them into the motel, which was new. It was the first and only motel in the area. Judging by the lack of cars in the bays, it appeared they were the only guests in the motel for the night. Their allocated rooms were alongside each other.

Claudia was out of the car in a flash. She threw her arms around Vance, who was annoyed because he was trying to concentrate on taking their luggage out of the rear of the station wagon.

'Darling, if she wasn't here, we could pretend we are on our honeymoon,' gushed Claudia.

Consider me gone, thought TC, who quickly picked up her case and went into her room, which she had already unlocked. She closed the door behind her, then placed her case on a low, broad shelf against one wall of the room. She began to unpack while wishing she was back in Brolga sitting on the steps with Lou.

A few minutes later Vance knocked on the door.

'It's me, TC.' he said before opening the door. He was carrying a couple of sandwich bags and Cokes, which he placed on a small table alongside the suitcase bench. 'I'll eat with you if you don't mind. I told Claudia if she didn't want to eat with you in the café, then she can eat by herself in the motel room.'

'You don't have to do that,' replied TC softly.

'I want to, TC,' said Vance, taking a deep breath. 'This has been a lousy trip. I need to explain to you why Claudia is with us.' Vance sat down on one of the two chairs at the small table. He reached for a cigarette, then changed his mind.

'Come on, we'll eat. I'll tell you between mouthfuls.'

It evolved that Claudia had telephoned Vance's house. It was fortunate that Delores had been in the shower and Vance had answered the phone. Claudia told Vance that, if he didn't meet her, she would come over to his house. She didn't care if Delores was there. It was about time Delores knew he had another woman in his life. Vance had met Claudia in the back street behind the pub quarters and driven to the creek. He told Claudia it was over between them. Claudia's reply was, while it may be over for him, it was far from over for her. If Vance did not agree to continue their relationship, Claudia would call on Delores when he was out of town. She had no intentions of allowing the love of her life to slip through her fingers simply because he had a wife.

'She's off the planet, TC,' concluded Vance. 'Poor bloody Delores has tolerated enough of my shit. She doesn't need this mad woman throwing it at her.'

'I agree, Boss,' nodded TC, who sensed she now knew one of the reasons, if indeed not "the" reason, for Vance's foul moods of late.

'How do you feel about being left behind when I leave in the morning?' enquired Vance.

'Not good,' replied TC.

'I want you to ignore Bert's girlfriend,' urged Vance. 'She's his toy. What I want you to do is look, listen, and learn. I don't think the old bugger has any intentions of showing you too much. From where I sit, anything you learn is a bonus. I noticed a phone box across the street. I want you to call me at the shop, reverse charges, every night at seven o'clock. I'll be back in town when you call. I have paid two weeks in advance for your room and breakfast. I told the woman you probably won't want breakfast, so she agreed to give you a piece of fruit to take with you for lunch. I paid a little extra so they'll give you an evening meal instead of breakfast.'

Vance put his hand in his pocket. He fished out a couple of fifty-pound notes, which he pushed across the table to TC.

'Hang onto this,' he said. 'You should always have some money on you in case you need it.'

'I have some money of my own,' said TC.

'Keep this anyway. If you don't have to use it, you can give it back,' replied Vance. 'You are far away from your comfort zone, TC. Best to be prepared.'

TC put the money in her pocket. A loud cough came from the open doorway and gained the instant attention of both Vance and TC. It was Claudia. She was naked except for a sexy come-to-bed look in her eyes and a matching smile directed at Vance, whose chair faced the door. Vance was instantly on his feet. He grabbed Claudia by both shoulders and half-pushed, half-guided her backwards into their next-door unit, where he slammed the door behind them.

TC mumbled to herself, 'I've said it before and I'll probably say it a million times more; you sure can pick them, Boss.'

TC unpacked the rest of her clothes, then showered. She could still hear muffled raised voices coming from Vance and Claudia's room.

'Give it a break, Boss,' she thought. I have to stay here. I'm happy our rooms are not close to the owner's residence. Wait until Lou hears I have air conditioning. I wish there was a radio. I should have borrowed the one from the dispensary. She sat at the table to towel-dry her hair before rolling it. Like clockwork, the moment she fixed the last roller in her hair, the voices next door went silent. TC breathed a deep sigh of relief.

I'll go crazy if I have to endure silent solitude every night I'm here, thought TC. TC went outside to check if the motel reception was still open. She looked towards the end of the long verandah. Lights were still on; a woman around fifty years of age was sorting through paper work at a desk behind the counter. The woman had her hair in rollers with a scarf tied around her head to camouflage them.

'Hello, luv,' she smiled when TC approached the counter. 'We must be going to the same function tomorrow,' she laughed as she patted her head.' TC smiled.

'I always wanted curly hair! I'm TC. I'll be staying here for a while.'

'Me, too,' was the smiley, happy reply. 'My name is Maggie. I'm the owner's sister. I'm here most nights. What can I do for you, TC?'

'I was hoping I could borrow a radio, Maggie. Just for tonight. Hopefully, I'll have time to buy one tomorrow.'

Maggie got up from the desk. She was petite, shorter than TC by a couple of inches. She was wearing a smart shorts suit and lots of gold jewellery. She had a ring on three fingers of each hand, gold dangly earrings, gold bangles, and a heavy gold chain around her neck.

'I had a rich boyfriend once, TC,' she laughed. 'He loved to buy me eighteen-carat gold jewellery. Naturally, I let him! When I get rid of this,' pointed to her scarf, 'I'm a blonde like you, TC.' TC felt good. She liked Maggie very much.

'There's a radio in the room, luv. It's also a clock. It's in the top drawer of the right bedside table. You push the button on the side of the bedside table and the drawer with the radio in it will pop out. Latest stuff, TC. Gotta move with the times, luv.' TC was relieved and happy.

'Thank you, Maggie. My boss is going back to Brolga in the morning, so I'll be here by myself. Is it all right if I come to see you some nights?'

'Come every night if you want, luv,' replied Maggie. 'I'll look forward to seeing you.'

TC went back to her room, located the button, pushed it, and out popped the drawer with the radio compactly fitted inside. She turned it on and tuned it to 2UE. She was delighted with the fact that it was only nine o'clock and she could hear it clear as a bell. A male voice was singing about a little, white cloud that cried. TC involuntarily thought of Graham with the pretty blonde. She spoke to the radio. 'I can identify with you, little, white cloud.' She switched off the light then curled up on the bed.

Bert Black and Leanne were in their bed. Leanne was nestled in Bert's arms. They lay side by side, gazing into each other's eyes. Leanne was looking ever so innocent while running her fingers through Bert's thinning hair. Bert was thinking, What is she up to now? I know that look!

'Bert, what time is bitch-face coming in the morning?' asked Leanne in a voice to match her innocent facial expression.

'We'll pick her up at the motel at seven. Callahan will be long gone.'

'Let her walk, Bert! You can phone the motel and give her directions,' was the curt reply as Leanne pulled away from Bert's arms. Bert surrendered; he had no option.

'All right, my lovely Leanne. I'll call her with directions. Now come back here; I haven't finished with you yet.' Leanne's pout instantly became an alluring smile.

'How would you like it tonight, sweetie?'

'You know,' replied Bert softly in anticipation of his Leanne's next move.

⁋

TC was awakened by the sound of a car starting. She looked at the clock radio. It was four in the morning. She hugged her pillow and went back to sleep.

⁋

Vance felt like a real mongrel, leaving without telling TC. He had to get out of the motel room and on the road back to Brolga. He wanted to rid himself of Claudia's company as soon as possible. The earlier they left, the better. He reasoned that TC would understand. He scribbled a short note, which he slid under her door.

⁋

TC was up at six. She made her bed and was deciding what to wear when she spotted the note on the floor near the door. Curiously, she opened it, never dreaming it was from Vance.

'Oh, no! He's gone!' she cringed when she read it.

"Good morning, TC. By the time you read this, I'll be well on my way back to Brolga. I'm sorry to leave without saying goodbye.

"Bert Black is going to come for you at seven. I called him last night to tell him I was leaving early. Your light was out, so I didn't disturb you. Remember everything I told you last night. Look, listen, and learn. Don't forget to call me tomorrow night at seven.

"P.S. I'll be relieved when I dump my cargo named Claudia back behind the Empire."

TC felt abandoned as she dressed herself in jeans and a shirt-style blouse.

'I'll phone Lou,' she decided as she secured her pony tail with a blue ribbon to match her blouse. In minutes she was in the phone box across the street talking with Lou.

'How was the trip?' asked Lou.

'I don't want to talk about it,' replied TC. Lou told TC about the church service for the shearer and the detectives taking Slugger to Curloo. She didn't bother to mention her talk with Graham. This isn't achieving much, thought TC as she listened to Lou, so she ended the call by saying, 'I miss you, Lou. I'll call you again soon.'

¶

To enable her to see Bert Black arrive, TC left the door to her room open. She checked the clock at ten past seven, then pushed a chair to the doorway. She assumed he had been delayed. A few minutes later, a lady, who looked like a carbon copy of Maggie minus the gold jewellery, came to the door.

'Hello. I'm Nancy and you are TC,' said the smiling woman. 'My sister, Maggie, told me about you. I have a message for you from Bert Black, luv. Everyone around here calls him Black Bert or Bert Black the Bastard. My husband and I own this place. My husband is away a lot. He's a shearing contractor; that's how we got the money to build this place. My sister is the glamorous one; I'm the worker.' Nancy pointed to her denim shorts and cotton blouse. 'That's why I'm dressed like this. Maggie and I are twins. Anyway, TC, follow me up to the office, luv, and I'll give you a couple of apples for your lunch. Black Bert asked me to give you directions to his place. He was supposed to pick you up but he's busy. I'd bet my half of this motel that his "busy" has something to do with his little harlot, Leanne.' TC followed Nancy to the office.

'You go two blocks that way, turn right for another two blocks, turn left, and Black Bert's house is the third one on your right. You can't miss it. There's a huge tree stump in his front yard. It's painted black.'

'Why do people call him Black Bert?' asked TC, who was quite confused. 'He's white!'

'Because of all the dark deals the bastard has done, luv.'

TC nodded. 'I see.' Nancy handed TC a small, brown paper bag.

'Here's your lunch, luv. I'll tell you now, you'll be lucky to get so much as a drink of water out of Black Bert. He's as tight as a fish's arse. You can tell me tonight why you are going to his place. You can eat with me in the kitchen. Off you go now, TC. I'll see you when you come back.'

TC was filled with trepidation as she set out for Bert Black's. From what Nancy had said, it sounded as if he was not a nice man, nor was he well-liked or respected. 'Never mind! What he did to others is none of my business,' she told herself as she walked along the street. She decided not to worry about anything until it happened.

¶

TC was relieved that the temperature was much lower than in Brolga. She noticed the houses were mostly constructed of weather-board and sat flat on the ground. All the roofs were corrugated iron. Some were painted green, which matched the green lawns. Must be great soil here, thought TC as she mentally compared the barren, apart from grass, yards in Brolga to the masses of coloured flowering bushes and shrubs on show in the gardens she passed en route to Bert Black's house, which she recognised immediately she saw the black stump. His house was similar to all the others except the grass in his yard was overgrown. There was a concrete slab the length of the house on one side. On the tin fence dividing his yard from his neighbour's was a large arrow painted in black pointing to the back of the house. TC walked on the concrete slab to the rear of the house, where she heard Bert Black's voice coming from behind the open door of a large, tin shed.

'She's not a bloody bird, Leanne. She can't fly here. I didn't leave the message until a quarter past seven.'

TC steeled herself, then smiled as she arrived at the shed doorway where she came face-to-face with Bert Black and Leanne, who were both stern-faced. They were sitting at an old, wooden table facing the door. When they saw TC, they quickly got to their feet and literally rushed to her before she stepped inside the shed.

'Good, you are here at last,' said Bert Black abruptly. 'Come with us. We'll show you where you'll be working. I'll get you started straightaway.' TC followed Bert and Leanne to another very small tin shed located at the rear of the backyard. It was perhaps six feet wide and nine feet deep. It had no windows; one light globe dangled from a beam which ran from one side of the shed to the other. There was a free-standing, bare, wooden bench against the near wall. On one side of the shed was a grinding well mounted over a tin tray with a hole in one corner of the base from which ran a piece of plastic hosing into a bucket below. On the other side was a motor mounted on a wooden upright approximately three feet high; from the motor protruded a shaft with a circular disc attached.

At least the boss is on the right track, thought TC. That is the same sort of machine he has in the little room off the dispensary.

'This is where you will start,' directed Bert as he indicated the grinding wheel. He pointed to a tiny tap on the wheel hood. 'You turn this on when you are grinding. You have to keep an eye on the bucket underneath. When it is almost full, throw the water outside on the grass.' Bert placed three pieces of what he called agate (to TC it looked like marble) in the grinding tray. The pieces were jagged with rough ridges, bumps, and sharp points. Bert told TC to sit on the stool in front of the grinder.

'There you go. Make them smooth. It doesn't matter at this stage what shape they are as long as you get rid of all the rough bits.' TC looked at the wheel. It was revolving very fast. She was frightened she would cut her fingers.

'How do I do it, Mr Black?' she asked.

'Pick up a piece of agate and start grinding it,' snapped Leanne, who had neither spoken nor smiled since TC's arrival. 'Come on, Bert. We have things to do. If you need to use the toilet, TC, it's on the right of the big shed. Use the wash tub outside the back door of the house to wash your hands. Come on, Bert!'

Bert Black almost felt sorry for TC as he said, 'We'll check on you in a couple of hours.'

TC knew she had two options. She could either storm out of the place, which would let Vance down, or stay and have a go. She knew Leanne wanted her to leave. No, I won't give her the satisfaction, thought TC determinedly. She turned on the tiny tap on the grinder hood, then picked up the least daunting piece of agate. She located the roughest point and decided to start there. She gingerly held it to the wheel. It instantly flew out of her hands and out through the open door onto the grass. TC quickly retrieved it as she realised she must not have held it firmly enough. She tried again.

¶

Vance was a few miles onto the first stretch of dirt road. Claudia was asleep on the back seat. From the second he had pulled out from the motel parking lot, he had driven, Jake style, as fast as the car could handle. Apart from a couple of trucks, he had not encountered any other traffic. I hope Claudia stays asleep until we get to Brolga, he thought while fully aware that she would wake up long before then. His mind wandered to TC. He wondered how she was going with Bert and his girlfriend. TC will handle it, he concluded with a smile. His thoughts switched to the men at the mine. 'They'll be crossing off every second of every hour of every day. Lord only knows how

I'll handle them when they're on break.'

Graham was at the Brolga railway station waiting to collect his car. The station master had instructed his people to give top priority to getting it unloaded ASAP. Help the cops whenever you can was his motto. Never know when you might need them to help you. Patiently watching and waiting, Graham sat on one of the platform's bench seats. He had enjoyed tennis the night before. Once again, he had won every game in which he participated. He was now certain the females purposely allowed him to win. If it made them happy, who was he to complain? The pretty, blonde stalker had not let a chance go by when it came to flirting with him at tennis. She appeared to be showing off for her friends, who kept urging her on. She caught him off guard when, in earshot of everyone present, she asked him, 'When are you going to ask me out on a date?' Silence reigned as she along with the other girls waited to hear his reply. Graham smiled. He was lost for words, so did not say anything. He just continued smiling.

'Am I ugly?' asked the girl.

'Not at all,' replied Graham. 'I have to work most nights.'

'Are you working tomorrow night?' she enquired.

'No, my car will be here tomorrow, so the sergeant gave me the day and night off,' replied Graham honestly.

'Good! You know where I live. I'll be ready at seven-thirty,' said the girl with a satisfied smile.

'She's got you, Graham!' called one girl. Everyone laughed except Graham.

That morning as he sat on the platform he was filled with anticipation of the coming night. It was a different feeling to the one he experienced when he thought of or saw TC. This feeling was one of cold-blooded, sexual need. He was going to get laid that night. He knew it! Graham didn't dare think about TC. If he did, he would call off the date. Lou already knew about Graham's plans for the evening. The phone had been running hot with the tennis group's gossip from the moment she had donned her head phones at eight.

¶

The third team of shearers were loaded and ready to leave. The contractor was settling up with Jack Romeo.

'We'll see you next time, Jack,' said the contractor.

'Look forward to it,' replied Jack Romeo. 'You have a good lot of men! No trouble at all with your team. Wish they were all like yours.'

'Luck of the draw, Jack,' replied the contractor. 'See you!'

'Only the fettlers left, and they'll be gone at five tomorrow morning,' commented Jack Romeo to his wife, who was in the money-counting room, as the locals called it, or inner office, as the Romeos referred to it.

'What a week!' continued Jack as he sat down with a sigh.

'What a lot of money!' added his wife seriously.

¶

TC was persevering in the tin shed. She now knew not to use the same section of the grinding wheel consistently because it caused a groove to appear. She concentrated on using the wheel either side of the groove until the surface was once again even. Bert Black and Leanne returned to check on TC early afternoon.

So much for Mr Black's couple of hours, thought TC.

'How are you going?' asked Bert Black.

'Slowly, Mr Black,' replied TC with a half-smile. 'I have smoothed one and half-finished the second one.'

'You're slow, all right,' said Leanne. 'I would have had a couple of dozen done by now.'

TC switched off the grinding machine in order to empty the bucket again. She had already emptied it three times. When done with the bucket, she excused herself to use the toilet. When TC left the shed, Leanne glared at Bert.

'At this rate, bitch-face will be here for a month. Give her a course in grinding wheel, Bert. You'd take forever yourself on this one.'

'Not in front of her, Leanne,' replied Bert in a whisper. 'We'll change it tonight after she's gone. It's my fault. I should have changed it before she came.'

TC returned. 'I'm happy it's not as hot here as it is in Brolga, Mr Black. I don't mean to complain, but it is really hot in here. I don't know how you cope with it.'

'Easy! You have to be a real woman!' snapped Leanne. 'Come on, Bert!'

'I'll finish this second piece; then I'll go back to the motel,' said TC. 'I shall be here at seven tomorrow.'

'Make sure you close the door when you leave this afternoon, and don't make a noise when you get here tomorrow,' commanded Leanne. 'Come on, Bert!'

TC finished smoothing the second piece of agate, emptied the bucket, turned off the light, and securely closed the shed door before leaving. She could hear Bert Black's voice from inside the house. She could also hear the sound of cutlery on plates.

They eat early, thought TC as she made her way to the grassy footpath. I would love to put Leanne in her place. I wonder if she would fit in a rubbish bin. I hate being here! It's one thing the boss talking to me as if I'm a mongrel dog. Leanne doing it is a totally different deal.

TC turned on the radio the minute she was in the motel room. A glance at the clock told her it was almost six. She took a bite from one of her apples, stretched, then undressed for a shower. 'Sweet Little Sixteen' was playing on the radio. 'Sorry. I'm about a hundred years too old,' said TC. After her shower, TC went to the office to find out what time Nancy wanted her to come for dinner.

'I'm running a bit late, luv,' said Nancy. 'About seven-thirty.'

'I see you have a few more guests tonight,' said TC, referring to the cars parked outside the units.

'That's why I'm running late, luv,' replied Nancy. 'Nine rooms full plus you.'

TC walked across to phone Lou. She desperately needed to hear a familiar voice, preferably Lou's. She felt lonelier than she had when she had been in the car with Vance and Claudia. TC wanted to jump through the phone and hug her when she heard Lou's voice.

'I had to call you, Lou! I had a lousy day,' said TC emotionally. 'Mr Black didn't show me how to do anything. He told me what to do but didn't show me. His girlfriend treats me like dirt. I don't want to be here, Lou.'

'I know you don't, TC,' replied Lou sympathetically. 'I hope Vance realises what you go through for him.'

'The boss has enough problems, Lou,' replied TC.

'He creates most of them himself, TC,' said Lou matter-of-factly. 'I'm going to tell you something else you don't want to hear, TC. I figure since you are already upset and miserable, what I tell you can't make you feel any worse.'

'I'm listening,' replied TC with a sigh.

'Graham has got his car, TC. It came on the goods train this morning. Tonight he's got a date with the blonde.' TC took a deep breath before replying.

'I expected that, Lou. I have told you heaps of times, I can't and don't blame him. I'll call tomorrow night. I miss you.'

'The steps and I miss you, too,' said Lou sincerely. They hung up simultaneously.

Lou got a Coke from the refrigerator, put Elvis on the stereo, then sat on the steps to watch the sprinkler. TC went back to her room to watch the clock until it was seven-thirty. The Delltones were singing, 'Blue Moon, You Saw Me Standing Alone.' 'You are not wrong, boys,' said TC.

¶

Vance and Claudia were almost in Curloo. Claudia was in sweet mode. She was begging Vance to spend the night in Curloo. Not likely, thought Vance. Everyone and their dog in Curloo know me.

'Why can't we stay over, darling?' asked Claudia, who was cuddled up close to him as he drove. 'You look tired, darling. A sleep is what you need.'

'Yes, Claudia, I am tired,' replied Vance. 'Even if I did agree to spend the night in Curloo, which I won't, you know very well that I wouldn't get any sleep. You would keep me awake because you'd want to screw all night. We'll get fuel in Curloo. I promise you that is all we'll be doing there. Now be a good girl and be quiet.'

❡

TC was relieved when it was time to join Nancy. She didn't feel like eating. It was the company she needed to take her mind off other things. Maggie was in the office and all smiles when TC walked in.

'We are much prettier without our rollers, aren't we, luv? Sit down here and talk to me, luv. Nancy will call us when the food is ready. How was your day at Bert Black's?'

'It was okay,' replied TC.

'Diplomatic little fibber!' laughed Maggie. 'What do you think of his slut?'

'It's not my place to think anything, Maggie. I would like to cram her into a rubbish bin, if that answers your question,' replied TC.

'A shithouse would be more appropriate place for her,' said Nancy, who had been listening from the kitchen next door.

'Watch your language, Nancy,' chastised Maggie.

'Well, it's the bloody truth,' insisted Nancy. 'Come and eat. I hope you are both hungry. If you don't eat it, you'll wear it. That's a bloody promise.'

Dinner was roast beef and baked vegetables. TC couldn't remember when she had last been treated to such a meal.

'Tomorrow night you'll get cold roast and salad,' said Nancy. 'Come on, eat your bloody tucker.'

'Don't take any notice of my sister's bossy nature, TC.' said Maggie with a laugh. 'She's been bossy and foul-mouthed since we were born.'

'What are you doing with the likes of Black Bert and his harlot?' asked

Nancy. Both Maggie and Nancy were interested when TC told them about Vance and the opal.

'I hope your Boss hasn't paid Black Bert for your lessons yet, luv,' said Nancy. 'If he has, he'll get short- changed.'

After dinner, TC helped Nancy with the dishes, then with the preparation of the breakfast trays for the other guests. TC thought the Irwin sisters were lovely. They were down-to-earth, real people. She could tell they liked her, too. Time passed quickly in their company. It was almost eleven when TC returned to her room.

¶

Graham had spent most of the day, after he finally took possession of it, detailing his car. He had gone to Con's earlier than usual for his dinner. He had difficulty making eye contact with Lisa when she told him it was a pity TC was away because he looked extremely handsome tonight. He picked up his date at exactly seven-thirty.

'Where would you like to go?' he asked.

She giggled, then said, 'You must be kidding. There's only one place I want to go—the creek. I'll show you where it should be quiet.'

'You've been to the creek a lot?' asked Graham. Except for a giggle, there was no reply. His date was too busy undoing his shirt buttons. By the time they got to the end of the bitumen, she had one hand on his crotch and was trying to undo his belt with the other. Graham had difficulty concentrating on driving. I'm not quite sure about this, thought Graham. I would have liked a bit of a challenge. Too late now. I'm past the point of no return. His date pointed him in the direction of Jake's usual parking spot, where she was naked and on the back seat of his car before he had switched the ignition key to off. By eight o'clock it was over.

That was terrible, thought Graham as he buttoned his shirt, then zipped up his fly. She's a pretty girl, got a beautiful body but no brains. All that squealing and giggling!

'Can we do it again, Graham?' she giggled.

'You had better get your clothes on,' replied Graham.

'Why? Then I'll have to take them off again,' she argued.

'Let's go for a drive,' suggested Graham, being polite.

'No. I want to stay here so we can do it again,' she replied.

'To be quite honest, I don't think I can handle that,' said Graham with a laugh. 'Early old age must have a grip on me. Come on, get yourself dressed, then I'll take you home.'

'All right, Graham, but promise me we can do it again on our next date.' Graham didn't reply. He wanted to take this girl home, then go to his room for a shower before going for a drive in his own car rather than the patrol car. He wished tonight had not happened.

That was quick, thought Lou when Graham drove past and blinked his lights. She had seen him drive towards the creek not that long ago. As far as Lou knew, Graham had been without the real thing since he had arrived in Brolga. She thought he would have been at the creek all night making up for lost time. Hardly any time had passed when Lou was surprised to see Graham's car come around the corner and stop outside the gate. Graham got out of the car and joined Lou on the steps.

'Nice car, Graham,' said Lou. 'The tennis set will love you even more in that.'

'Please don't be sarcastic, Lou. Have you heard from TC?'

'Yes, she called tonight,' replied Lou. 'I told her about your date, which, by the way, must not have been too exciting. It didn't last long.'

'I don't want to talk about it, Lou,' said Graham. 'I wish you hadn't told TC. It could hardly be called a date.'

'Graham, this is Brolga,' replied Lou defensively. 'Better me tell her than she hears it elsewhere. Apart from that, I guarantee you, within the hour, every girl in the tennis club will know how hot you are, or are not, in the back of your red-and-white fancy Ford. Your date would have been on the phone spreading the word within a minute of you taking her home.'

'Would you like to go for a drive, Lou?' asked Graham. He did not wish to dwell on what she just said.

'Yes! I would love to go for a drive,' replied Lou. 'I thought you would never ask. Would you like a Coke, Graham?'

'Yes! I thought you'd never ask,' he laughed. A few minutes later they were settled in the car.

'Anywhere but the creek, driver,' directed Lou, feigning aristocracy. 'I believe you have already done that route tonight.'

Unfortunately, you are right, thought Graham as he drove towards the eastern end of town.

'Take me on your patrol route, Graham,' requested Lou. 'Then I can tell TC I've been where the cops go.'

Graham laughed. 'My pleasure, Miss Lynette.'

¶

Brolga was asleep when Vance drove into town. Vance felt relieved to be back, while Claudia was not at all happy.

'When will I see you, darling?' she whinged.

'I'll have a busy week, Claudia,' replied Vance, who was exhausted by the lack of sleep and driving. 'Under no circumstances do you call my house. If my car is not behind the shop, you'll know I'm at the mine or busy doing something else.' Claudia insisted on giving Vance a long, lingering kiss when he pulled up outside the Empire quarters. Vance pulled away from her. He leaned across to retrieve her overnight bag from the back seat, then pushed it towards the passenger-side door.

'Off you go, Claudia. I want to go home to bed.'

'Yes! Go home with your effing wife,' snarled Claudia. Vance got out of the car, rushed around to the passenger side, threw Claudia's bag onto the quarters' verandah, then pulled Claudia out of the car and slammed the door.

'That's it, Claudia! I'm going! Tell my wife if you must! Please remember if you do, you will never see me again.'

¶

At exactly seven the next morning, TC turned on the tiny tap and switched on the grinding wheel. Leanne had told her not to make a noise. TC assumed that did not include the sound of the grinder. She knew something was different as soon as she put the third piece of agate to the wheel. The points and ridges were disappearing much faster. She didn't need to apply nearly as much pressure to the wheel as yesterday.

Bert Black and Leanne showed up at the shed door at eight. TC was sitting in silence waiting for further instructions.

'I thought I told you not to make a noise', snapped Leanne. TC wasn't going to take any more of Leanne's "crap", as Lou's dad would say.

'Yes, Leanne, you did!' retaliated TC. 'I didn't think that meant not turning on the grinding machine. Did you expect me to sit here staring at the tin walls until you and Mr Black decided to get out of bed? I know you hate me, and quite frankly, I think you should be flushed down the toilet. You don't want me here, and I hate being here. I don't know what you did to this wheel last night, but I do know you added a day to my stay by not doing it yesterday morning. Mr Callahan and I are fast learners. We will know all the tricks of the trade in the not-too-distant future. I suggest, Leanne, you speak to me in a civil manner. Otherwise, don't speak to me at all. As a matter of fact, I would prefer the latter.' TC turned to Bert Black.

'Mr Black, I believe Mr Callahan has an arrangement with you that you will teach me the basics of cutting and polishing opals. He is not a fool, Mr Black. He is well aware of the fact that you will show me as little as possible. I will only take direction from you and you only, Mr Black. Please, sir, I would appreciate it very much if you would keep your pet, Leanne, on a short leash during the remainder of my stay.' TC could see that Bert Black and Leanne were caught off guard by her outburst.

'You can't speak to me like that, you ugly, little moll!' snarled Leanne.

'Leanne, shut up!' snapped Bert Black before calmly speaking to TC. 'Point taken, TC. Let me have a look at how you have done so far.' He examined the three pieces, which were all high-domed, odd shapes approximately four inches in length at their longest point.

'I suggest you shape two to template regular shapes and sizes and leave the other one the shape it is. I'll go to the big shed and find a template. Leanne, you come with me.' Bert Black returned without Leanne in tow a few minutes later. He passed a rectangular piece of hard plastic with different shaped and sized cut-outs.

'Using this same grinding wheel, shape your pieces to fit whichever cut-outs you select. I'll be back to see how you are going in an hour.'

'Thank you, Mr Black,' said TC as Bert left the shed.

Bert Black was in to see TC periodically all day until three o'clock, by when she had shaped and domed her pieces to both Bert's and her own satisfaction.

TC was feeling both hot and tired. She had forgotten to bring her apple, which didn't concern her so much as being thirsty. She had considered getting a drink in her hands at the wash tubs but decided against it. She told herself to remember to bring her own water the next day.

'You go back to the motel now, TC. Leanne and I have to go out,' said Bert Black. 'Don't come until eight tomorrow morning.' TC heard their car leave as she secured the shed door. As she walked past the rear of the house, she saw the laundry tubs and couldn't restrain herself from hurrying to the first tap and splashing water on her face, then cupping her hands and drinking the water she caught. It felt and tasted so good.

No wonder people hallucinate in the desert, thought TC as she turned off the tap. TC thought she heard a female voice calling from inside the house, 'No!' Leanne and Bert Black had both gone out. She told herself she must be imagining things or perhaps she was hallucinating without being in the desert.

Nancy had given TC permission to use the motel washing machine. So, as soon as TC had filled herself up with water and taken a shower, she went to see Nancy to find out where the washing machine was located.

'Hello, Nancy', smiled TC. 'How are you today?'

'I'm over the bloody moon, luv,' replied Nancy, who looked tired yet happy at the same time. 'First time since we opened a couple of months ago, luv, we've got a full bloody house! About time this joint started to pay for itself. Here's the key to the laundry, luv. It's round behind the office. You'll find everything you need in there. You can tell Maggie and me about your day tonight over our cold roast beef and salad. See you about seven, luv.'

'I have to call my boss at seven, Nancy', replied TC apologetically. 'I'll be about five minutes late.'

Nancy laughed. 'God, you are bloody gorgeous. Looks like I'll see you at five-past-seven instead of seven. Now, get out of here and do your washing before I hug you.'

TC called Lou at five. Lou gave TC the rundown on Brolga's gossip for the day, and TC told Lou about her day. Lou, being Lou, left the part about Graham taking her on the patrol route until last.

'Poor Constable Graham must get bored driving around by himself,' said Lou.

'I thought he had a date, Lou,' replied TC while secretly hoping he hadn't.

'Yes, I don't know what happened there. Call me tomorrow afternoon.'

You are not a good liar, Lou, thought TC when she hung up.

❡

'How's it going?' called Vance when he answered TC's seven o'clock call.

'Better today than yesterday,' replied TC. 'I'll tell you blow by blow when I see you. The motel owner and her sister are lovely. What time did you get home last night?'

'I'm not sure. I was very tired. Probably around midnight,' replied Vance. 'Madam started with one of her deals when we got back. I told her to tell Delores if she never wanted to see me again. So far, Delores hasn't mentioned anything, so Claudia was perhaps bluffing.'

'Or perhaps you bluffed her, Boss,' surmised TC. 'I'll be finished here on Friday, so you had best make a plan regarding when you'll be coming to get me.'

'How do you know you'll be finished Friday, TC?' questioned Vance.

'Because I know, Boss. They want to get me out of here as soon as possible. By Friday, I will have learned as much as Mr Black is prepared to tell me.'

'That's as I expected,' agreed Vance. 'I'll talk to you tomorrow night.'

Vance was furious with himself. His mind was racing as he put down the telephone.

'TC's not telling me everything. I know her too well. I'd lay money Bert's girlfriend has been throwing shit at TC. I shouldn't have given the old bastard the boulders until I was satisfied with the results. I hope TC stands up to them.'

TC joined Maggie and Nancy in the motel kitchen.

'How did you go today, luv?' asked Maggie.

'All right, thank you, Maggie. Better than yesterday,' replied TC.

'She's being honest, I can tell!' said Nancy. 'I suppose any improvement is better than none. Have you met Black Bert's poor wife yet, TC?'

'I didn't think Mr Black had a wife,' replied TC while thinking, That must be the voice I heard today.

'Don't bother telling TC about how the poor woman lies sick and bed-ridden in one room while Black Bert, the bastard, and his slut are at it in the room next door,' said Maggie with disgust.

'It's really none of my business, Maggie,' said TC. 'I won't be going to their place after Friday.'

'TC's right, Maggie. It's none of our bloody business, either,' said Nancy. 'Have you got a boyfriend, TC?'

'Not really,' replied TC shaking her head with a wistful smile.

'Trust me, boyfriends suck,' said Maggie.

'You should know, you've had enough of the bastards,' laughed Nancy. 'I've had one boyfriend and I married him.'

After helping Nancy and Maggie finish in the kitchen, TC returned to her room, then remembered her washing was still on the clothes line. As she walked along the verandah, a white Mercedes Benz sedan pulled into one of the car bays in front of her. Three men got out of the Mercedes. They were in serious conversation about an oil exploration project. They were obviously Americans because they spoke with broad

American accents. They wore jeans and short-sleeved shirts with driller's boots and large, oval buckles on their belts. They appeared to be waiting for someone because they looked over their shoulders every time a vehicle drove by.

One of the men said, 'Good evening, young lady,' as she passed them. TC smiled at him. When she was returning with her dry laundry, a large, white Ford ute with a cover on the back pulled into the car bay beside the Mercedes. The driver quickly got out. TC recognised him immediately. It was Milt Elliot. He spotted her when she was but a couple of yards away. He looked, then looked again.

'TC, darlin', what are you doing here?' he asked in surprise. TC smiled. She was also surprised.

'My boss brought me here to learn how to cut opals.'

'I'm sure happy Vance did that, TC. After a day on the road, seeing your pretty face makes all that drivin' worthwhile.' TC laughed. Milt was a real charmer. She felt as if she were in a movie.

'It's nice to see you, too, Milt.'

'We have to pick up our room keys, then go find something to eat.' He looked at his watch. 'I hope we'll find somewhere open. Which room are you in? If your light is still on when we get back, I'll come see you—if that's okay with you.'

'That would be nice, Milt. I'm second from the end,' replied TC with a smile. 'I think your keys are coming to you.' TC saw Maggie come out of the office and walk towards them. TC smiled at Milt, then continued on to her room. A few minutes later, TC heard the Mercedes drive off, then a knock on her door. It was Maggie.

'I love Yanks, TC. I saw you talking to that real good-looking one. I didn't picture you for being a girl like me. You are really quick, luv. I was watching through the office window. You were on him the second his feet hit the ground.' TC burst into laughter.

'Maggie, I know him from Brolga.' Maggie patted TC on the shoulder as she burst into laughter herself.

'I'm sorry for jumping to conclusions, luv. I must admit I was feeling pretty jealous of your super-fast pick-up ability. Did he tell you where they were going? I might follow them.' TC was still laughing.

'They have gone to have something to eat, Maggie.'

'The timing was great, TC,' said Maggie. 'I'm over the moon that my poor twin sister is buggered and rushed us through our dinner. If she hadn't, you wouldn't have run into Mr Good-Looking and I wouldn't be sitting here with you waiting for them to come back so you can introduce me to him and he can introduce me to his friends.' TC couldn't stop laughing.

'As my girlfriend's dad would say, Maggie, you are about as subtle as a sledge hammer.'

Maggie became serious as she said, 'TC, always remember it's who we know, not what we know, and if we have connections, use them.' Maggie then relaxed and smiled. 'That is what I'm doing now, TC. You know Mr Good-Looking, and he knows the others, so I'm using you as my connection.'

'I must remember that, Maggie,' said TC seriously. 'What about the office?'

'Bugger the office, luv,' replied Maggie. 'The joint is full and Nancy is asleep. The only reason I waited was to give the Yanks their keys. I'm going to pile on my make-up. I'll also re-do my hair. I'll be back before they are, luv, then we can be casually sitting on the verandah, gazing at the stars, when our unwary prey wander innocently into our trap.'

'Speak for yourself, Maggie,' laughed TC. Maggie hurried out of TC's room. She quickly returned.

'I didn't mean to paint you scarlet like me, luv. I'm a desperate, old woman. Think of yourself as my young friend and helper.' Maggie smiled and was gone again. TC smiled as she talked to herself.

'I believe I'm learning a lot more than grinding agate while I'm in this place. I find it incredible that Milt Elliot is in the same town, staying at the same motel at the same time as I am.' TC looked at the clock radio. She was surprised to see it was not quite nine-thirty. It felt as if it was much later. 'Oh, Donna' was playing on the radio. Wish my name was Donna, she thought. No one ever sings a song about TC.

TC was folding her freshly laundered clothes when Maggie bounced in. She was all smiles.

'What do you think, luv? Do you think the Yanks will find me irresistible?'

TC laughed. 'Of course they will, Maggie, because you are irresistible.' Maggie's perfect make-up job was highlighted by her gold jewellery. She had piled her blonde, curled hair to one side of her head with lots of fine strands framing both sides of her face and her neck. She was wearing a very expensive designer-label, cream pants suit with matching strappy sandals.

'You changed your clothes as well as your hair and make-up, Maggie,' remarked TC admiringly. 'I love your outfit, Maggie. You'll blow them away.'

'I always keep a couple of sets of clothes here, luv,' replied Maggie with a wink. 'Always come in handy for unexpected occasions such as now. Come on, luv, time to stop star-gazing,' laughed Maggie. 'We'll sit on the verandah near the office. We can talk there without disturbing the other guests. The Yanks will be back soon. Won't matter which one of the cafés they choose to eat in, they'll be thrown out at five-to-ten whether they have finished eating or not. Bloody Greeks aren't too hot on customer consideration.'

'My friends in Brolga are Greek,' said TC defensively. 'They own the café! They stay open until the last customer leaves.'

'Sorry, luv, I wasn't talking about all Greeks. I was referring to the two here.'

Maggie and TC had been sitting outside the office for only a few minutes when the white Mercedes turned into the motel parking lot.

'Remember, luv, you introduce the one you know; I'll do the rest,' whispered Maggie. They watched the four men get out of the Mercedes. Three of them retrieved their luggage from the boot of the Mercedes while Milt Elliot took his bag from the front of the Ford F100 ute.

As the men walked across the verandah to their rooms, Maggie looked at TC and laughed for no reason at all other than to get their attention. She was successful. The four men looked towards the office, Maggie, and TC. Milt waved to TC. Maggie waved back.

'Come on, guys. We'll dump our gear in our rooms; then I'll introduce you to TC.'

Maggie poked TC in the ribs while whispering, 'I told you.'

Milt was the first out of his room.

'TC, darlin', I didn't expect you to wait outside for me,' he laughed as he dramatically leaned forward, picked up one of TC's hands, and kissed it. TC pulled her hand away. She was laughing again.

'I didn't tell you that you could do that, Milt.'

'I was overcome by your beauty, darlin'. I was wishin' it was your lips instead of your hand,' replied Milt innocently. TC composed herself. She knew Maggie was waiting with bated breath for the first introduction.

'Milt, this is Maggie. Maggie, this is Milt. Maggie is the motel owner's twin sister, Milt. Milt is Brolga's transient Casanova extraordinaire, Maggie.'

'That cap fits you nicely, Milt,' laughed Maggie. Milt got down on his knees in front of TC. He looked longingly into her eyes.

'TC's mean to me, Maggie. I can't help it if other girls want me. My little darlin' TC here is the only girl I want.'

'Come on, lover boy, hit your pins and introduce us to these young ladies,' said the more senior of Milt's companions, who was looking Maggie up and down, over and across. Milt sprang to his feet.

'Yes, sir! This beautiful lady here is Maggie, whose sister owns this fine establishment. This little, plain- Jane here is TC. Maggie and TC, allow me to introduce my boss, the president of our company, Mr Mitchell Hargreaves.' Milt then introduced the other two men whom, he made a point of telling Maggie and TC, were happily-married, familied men who needed a good night's sleep. One of the men was the manager of the Australian branch company office based in Sydney. His name was Pete. The other man was Pete's assistant. On this trip, he was also the driver. His name was Rob. Pete and Rob said, 'Hello', followed by 'Goodnight' as they went back to their rooms. Mitchell Hargreaves looked directly at Maggie.

'It sure is a nice night. I suspect you gals will be sittin' out here for a while longer.'

'Oh, yes, Mitchell, we sit out here every night until at least midnight,' lied Maggie.

'Good, Maggie. I'll go and get freshened up. I'll be back, so don't you go anywhere.'

'I'll do the same, so don't you go anywhere either,' added Milt, who touched the tip of TC's nose with his finger.

'What age do you think Mitchell is, TC?' asked Maggie quietly.

'Probably mid-fifties,' replied TC just as quietly.

'He's perfect, TC,' said Maggie, whose excitement sparkled in her eyes. 'He's everything I ever wanted, luv! He's tall; his eyes are blue; his hair is thick and sandy-coloured; he has fair skin and white teeth; and he's an unmarried Yank. If he lacks a sense of humour, I'll kill myself. Milt is gorgeous, too, TC. Tall, dark, and handsome; he's got one hell of a sense of humour; and he's quick-witted, to boot. You are a lucky girl, TC. He's crazy about you.'

'No, Maggie; Milt Elliot isn't crazy about me. You heard him; he gets any girl he wants.'

'Are you talking about me, darling?' interrupted Milt, who placed one of the chairs from his room opposite TC.

'I told TC you are crazy about her,' said Maggie.

'You are not wrong, Maggie,' agreed Milt as he reached unsuccessfully for one of TC's hands, which she pulled away when she realised his intention.

'Don't be like that, darlin'. All I want to do is hold your hand,' pleaded Milt.

'Watch him. He's pretty smooth,' said Mitchell Hargreaves as he joined them. 'The chair is a good idea, Milt. I'll fetch one from my room, too.'

'Only if you don't feel like coming inside, Mitchell,' said Maggie. 'Perhaps you'd like a beer. We'll leave the kids alone to talk out here. You and I can talk inside.'

'That sounds great, Maggie,' replied Mitchell with a gleaming, surprised smile. Maggie stood up. 'Come on, Mitchell, let's leave the kids alone.' Maggie hesitated at the office door.

'Milt, come here, please, wait for me a minute. Mitchell, I'll show you to the lounge.' Milt re-joined TC with a beer in one hand and a Coke in the other.

'Do you want to come inside with me, TC?' asked Milt hopefully. He gave her the Coke. 'In my room, I mean.'

'No!' replied TC while shaking her head from side to side.

'Please, TC,' said Milt sincerely. 'It's more private in there. I promise I won't come on to you, darlin.' I treasure you too much to upset you.'

'We'll go to my room, Milt,' replied TC. 'We can listen to 2UE until you finish your beer. Then you have to leave. If you try and come on to me, I'll shoot you. My boss bought me a handgun to keep people like you at bay.' Milt was speechless. She had to be having him on. No! She wasn't! She said it too seriously and with too much confidence to be kidding.

'Let's go, darlin'. I've always like gun-toting women. I'll put this chair back in my room on my way.' TC was smiling on the outside but buckling up with laughter on the inside as they got to her room. Milt believed her about her gun. Once inside, TC closed the door behind them and turned on the radio.

'Can we sit on your bed, darlin'?' asked Milt childishly.

'No!' replied TC firmly. 'We'll sit at the table. What brings you here, Milt?' asked TC.

'You,' replied Milt seriously.

'Not into this room, Milt. You know very well I meant this town.'

'Oh, sorry, darlin', my mistake,' was the innocent reply. 'We have to have a look around some places for a few days. On Saturday we'll leave for Brolga. Mitchell wants to see what we are doing out there. How long will you be here, darlin'?'

'I'll be finished on Friday,' replied TC happily. 'My boss is coming to collect me. I'm not sure when as yet.' TC sipped her Coke. She noticed Milt had not started on his beer. 'Why aren't you drinking your beer, Milt?' Milt laughed.

'Come on, darlin'. I thought you were smarter than that. I'm not drinkin' it because you told me I have to leave when it's finished.' TC laughed.

'Come on, Milt, I thought you were smarter than that. I thought you would drink most of it and leave a couple of mouthfuls in the bottom of the bottle.'

'Very good, TC,' Milt put the beer to his lips. He took a swig.

'How old are you, darlin'? You look young but think old.'

TC smiled. She thought of what Lisa had said. 'A friend of mine told me she thinks I've been here before.'

'I think I would have to agree with your friend,' replied Milt with a far-away look in his eyes. 'How old do you think I am, darlin'?' TC thought for a moment before answering.

'Hard to say, Milt. I don't know you very well. You look around twenty-three or perhaps twenty-four. You must be older than that because you are in charge of a lot of people.'

'I have recently turned thirty,' admitted Milt. 'Now please tell me your age, darlin'.'

'I'm too young for you, Milt. In years, that is. You do make me laugh, which is something I don't do too often. Maggie makes me laugh, too. I have known her only two days but I feel as if I have known her all my life.'

'How long has your life been, TC?' persisted Milt. TC laughed again.

'Very tricky, Milt. Nice try! It doesn't matter how old I am, Milt.' She became serious. 'Please don't ask me again.' TC didn't want to tell him her age because she would have to tell him she had lied about it when she worked for the Romeos. She didn't want him to think she was a liar. Only Sam, Vance, and Lou knew her real age.

'Crazy' was playing on 2UE.

'Do you like this song, Milt?' asked TC in an effort to change the subject.

'If you like it, darlin', I like it,' replied Milt indifferently. His mind was elsewhere. 'Look at me, darlin'.' He took TC's hands in his. 'I'm thirty years of age. I've had so many women in so many places that I have lost count. They are mostly nothing but blurs in my memory. The ones I remember were either great sex, great lookers, or both. None of them meant nor mean anything to me.'

TC couldn't understand why she hadn't pulled her hands away nor why she was looking into his eyes as intensely as he was into hers. She hung on every word he said as he continued talking to her.

'I'm tired of the so-called good times, TC. I have been thinking about you since the first moment I laid eyes on you. So damned young and innocent, yet fiery as they come. The way you hollered at Vance through the pub window.' TC was certain Milt was going to say something that she wasn't ready to hear. She interrupted him.

'Milt, please don't say anymore. Not now! We hardly know each other. I'll be nineteen next birthday, next year.

Milt pulled her hands to his mouth and kissed first one, then the other.

'I scared you, didn't I, darlin'! I'm sorry! I wouldn't hurt you for the world, TC.' He kissed her hands again. 'Tell Vance you can ride back to Brolga with me if you want. That'll save him the trip. I must go to my room now, darlin'. I look at you and see the bed out of the corner of my eye. I desperately want to make love with you.'

Silence as TC thought of what to say. She decided on the truth.

'I don't know how.' Milt kissed her hands once more.

'I know that, darlin'.' He let go of TC's hands, threw down the rest of his beer, then quickly got off his chair.

'Make sure you lock the door behind me, darlin'.' He was gone. TC was confused. She thought of Graham. She was more confused.

⁋

Milt took a long shower after he left TC. He realised there was no point in being angry with himself for saying too much too soon. He prayed he hadn't scared TC away for keeps. He thanked the Lord that she was wise beyond her years and stopped him before he actually proposed. Why did he have to be twelve years older than she? With just a couple or three more, he'd be old enough to be her daddy.

⁋

Next morning TC called by the office to collect a bottle of water Nancy had offered the previous night. The car park was empty apart from Maggie's car, which was parked in front of the office. Nancy housed her car in the garage at the rear of the motel. Maggie was helping her sister in the kitchen washing up the guests' breakfast dishes.

¶

'Come in, luv,' called Nancy. 'I got you a bag of lollies to take with you today. They are in the bag with your water, a mug, and an orange.' Nancy pointed to a striped cotton bag with handles on the kitchen bench.

'Did you hear about Maggie and the Yank?' Maggie was standing behind her sister. She was drying dishes. Maggie shook her head vigorously at TC.

'What did Maggie do, Nancy?' asked TC.

'She picked up one of the bloody Yanks, that's what she did. She can't help her bloody self, TC. She got the bastard drunk; that's another thing she did. I got up at five, walked through the lounge, and there they were. Him asleep on the couch and Maggie sitting on the floor leaning against the couch. She was asleep. She was also snoring. Empty beer bottles all over the bloody coffee table and floor. She'll get the motel a bad name.'

'Okay, shut up, Nancy,' said Maggie in good humour. 'You are jealous because he's so good-looking and the president of an oil company.'

'I have to leave for Black Bert's, ladies. I'll see you tonight.' Maggie caught up with TC at the office door.

'Guess what, luv, Mitchell has got a great sense of humour,' she whispered. 'I think I'm in love.'

TC replied, 'Good on you, Maggie. I hope you were a good girl!'

TC laughed when Maggie replied with a naughty look in her eyes and a smile, 'Not for long, if I have my way, TC.'

¶

At exactly 8 a.m., TC met Bert Black at the shed. Leanne was there. She didn't acknowledge TC except for glaring at her with loathing plastered all over her face. TC ignored Leanne.

'We'll get you started on sanding your pieces now, TC,' said Bert Black. 'Sit over here in front of this disc. Do the same thing you did on the grinding wheel. This time you need to secure the stones to these sticks. To do that, you use sealing wax.' He pointed to three pieces of round pine an inch in diameter and a couple of sticks of red sealing wax which were on the bench along with a box of matches, a floor tile, and a small glass spirits-burner. Bert showed TC how to heat the wax over the lighted burner, dob it onto the stick, then roll it along the tile to smooth it.

'There you go,' said Bert Black. 'You prepare the dop sticks for your stones.'

'Mr Black, how do I put the stones on the sticks?'

'Easy. You heat the stones and heat the waxed dop sticks, then press them together. I've put a piece of sandpaper on your disc. We'll be back in a while.'

'Bert, I want to talk to you, please,' said Leanne coldly. 'Outside, please! Why the hell don't you put the effing agate on the sticks for the bitch? While you're at it, give her some more effing sandpaper. While you are at it, Bert, show her how to use the effing sander. I'm warning you, Bert Black; if that bitch is here past Friday, it will cost you another one of these.' Leanne pointed to a new diamond pendant she had flung around her neck. The pendant had been a bribe to ensure Leanne didn't harass TC during the remainder of her stay.

⁋

TC was surprised, to say the least, when Bert Black returned to the shed. His attitude, under Leanne's surveillance, was courteous and very helpful. He fixed the pieces to the dop sticks, showed TC how to move them from the edge to edge on the sanding disc and how to change the sandpaper when the piece on the disc was worn shiny.

'Thank you, Mr Black,' said a grateful TC. 'If you had not shown me, I would have been forever trying to figure it out.' Leanne coughed loudly.

§

Vance was with Yappy in the camp kitchen. He had arrived feeling tired. He didn't know why. He put it down to all the driving he'd been doing of late, in and out to camp, the trip over the border and back; now out to camp with the prospect of returning to town almost straight away.

'How was your trip, Vance?' asked Yappy.

'Terrible, to put it bluntly,' replied Vance. 'Looks as if I'll have to repeat it in a couple of days. We're not into the opal game properly yet, Yappy. I'm already aware that there are bastards in it. I've thought of backing off a few times. Unfortunately, I'm in too far to do that. I finally got to put a saw through a few of the boulders yesterday. The opal runs all over the place inside them. I can see a lot of trial and error in front of us.'

'How is town, Vance?' asked Yappy casually.

'A shearer killed another shearer at the Empire the other night,' replied Vance. 'The sergeant told me the killer was a ripe bastard. He crapped on the police station floor in front of the sergeant and the young cop. The sergeant rubbed the bastard's face in it, then made him clean it up.'

'Shit!' exclaimed Yappy.

'Exactly!' replied Vance. 'Jake won over twelve thousand quid on Saturday, which reminds me, Yappy, I have to give you your winnings. I forgot to give it to you.' Yappy smiled from ear to ear.

'I thought I must have lost, Vance. That's why I didn't say anything.'

'Here you go, Yappy.' Vance passed an envelope to Yappy. 'Jake said to tell you he backed the same horses for you that he backed for himself.'

'Jake's bloody phenomenal when it comes to picking winners,' remarked Yappy as he counted his winnings. 'If that keeps up, you'll be looking for a new bloody cook, Vance!'

'Come on, Yappy. Don't say that, mate! I've got enough problems! I'll have to tell Jake not to bet for you!'

'Don't bloody do that to a man, Vance. I'm not going anywhere. Look around here, will you? How could a man leave this bloody place?' Vance smiled.

'I'm not staying long, Yappy. I can't expect the doctor to keep filling his own prescriptions.'

'He must be a dinkum sort of bloke. You were lucky you landed him and not some bloody uptight arsehole.' Vance nodded.

'Indeed, I am lucky, Yappy. I'll go see the other men. You have your list ready, Yappy.'

¶

Bert Black checked on TC's progress after lunch. Leanne was with him. This time she didn't look at TC. She stood impatiently in the doorway while Bert Black examined TC's effort.

'Good. Now turn them over and do the backs. Tomorrow you'll have to work on the tops again.' Leanne stepped forward and picked up the three stones atop the dop sticks.

'I'll get them off the sticks, Bert,' she snarled. 'Your student can do the dobbing herself for the backs. Come with me, Bert.' Five minutes later they came back.

'There you are. Fix them on the dop sticks upside down, then sand the backs. When you are finished, go back to the motel. We have to go out.'

'Thank you, Mr Black. What time tomorrow?'

'Nine will be fine.'

¶

TC drank the last of her water. She giggled when she thought about Nancy giving her the lollies. There was no way she could eat anything in the confines of the shed. It was stifling. She decided Bert Black and Leanne must do their work day after day in the windowless, tiny workplace she had been allocated.

It was after five when TC was satisfied she had done the best she

272

could with the back surface of the agates. She was hoping opal-cutting would prove to be more exciting than this was.

¶

Maggie was sitting outside the office when TC reached the motel.

'Hello, darlin',' said Maggie imitating Milt. TC smiled and with a sigh slumped onto the chair next to Maggie's.

'The shed I work in is like what I imagine a steam bath to be, Maggie. I'm saturated in perspiration. Only two more days, though. I'm counting the minutes.'

'Do you think Mitchell will like my strapless dress, luv?' asked Maggie, who was smiling with eyes once again twinkling.

'He'll love it, Maggie,' replied TC. 'Stand up and let me see.' Wearing high-heeled gold shoes, Maggie stood up and slowly turned around in her flaming-red, strapless, tight-fitting dress that accentuated her curves, with a wide, sash-type belt and lashings of gold jewellery.

'He won't be able to resist you, Maggie,' reassured TC. 'Is it okay if I refill my bottle and put it in the fridge for tomorrow?'

'Go ahead, luv. I think Nancy is in the shower. She's buggered again. She thought motel work would be a piece of cake instead of a lot of bloody hard work. She misses her husband, too, luv.'

TC went to the kitchen to fill her water bottle. When she came back outside, she told Maggie she was going to take a shower.

'Hurry, TC. They'll be back soon. Mitchell is taking me to one of the pubs tonight.' TC laughed. She was amused by Maggie's rationale.

'That doesn't mean I have to hurry, Maggie. You have fun if I don't see you before you leave.'

'You can count on that, TC,' said Maggie. As far as she was concerned, her having a good time was a foregone conclusion.

¶

After her shower, TC donned her pink pedal-pusher outfit she had bought in Sydney. She had not worn it before because her work uniform was pink. She got bored with the colour. Now, after wearing jeans and a shirt to work for a few days, she decided she did like pink, after all. She tied her wet hair back with a matching pink ribbon and slipped on her also new pink jiffies with a bow on the front, then applied pale pink lipstick.

It was only twenty-to-seven, too early to call Vance. She went outside to see if Maggie was still sitting outside the office. She was, so TC joined her.

'Has he stood you up, Maggie?' said TC lightly.

'Are you blind, luv? You just walked past their cars.' TC looked around and, sure enough, the Mercedes and F100 were parked in their bays.

'You look cute, luv,' said Maggie. 'Like a pink doll! Nancy isn't feeling too well, luv. How about making yourself a sandwich for dinner?'

'I'm all right, Maggie. I've got my lollies, an orange, and a couple of apples. I'm sure that will fill me up if I'm hungry. My girlfriend and I drink Coke every night. We eat only when we are hungry.'

'Go get yourself a Coke out of the fridge, luv. It will make up for the dinner you are not going to get,' suggested Maggie.

'I'll phone my boss first, Maggie, then I'll take you up on it.'

❡

Vance was slumped at his dispensary desk. He was chain-smoking, as usual. In front of him on the desk was a steaming cup of black coffee. Vance desperately wished it was a double Rum and Coke. He longed for the oblivion of reality which his drinking had temporarily afforded him during his many years on the booze, "carefree, live for the moment, stuff tomorrow" attitude of his past. Now he had to face facts full on. The loader would break down any day because the transmission was on the way out. Miracle it hadn't gone already. The men were on break real soon. That meant money. He had a wife and kids to think about! Claudia was being an absolute bitch. He was tired.

Vance abruptly stood up, threw his chair at the wall, picked up his cup of coffee, which smashed when he threw it into the sink. There were pieces all over the floor. Vance didn't care.

The telephone rang. It was TC.

'You are late!' he snapped.

'I'm sorry, Boss. Sounds like you're in a great mood.'

'I'm tired and I have to leave to pick you up in a couple of hours. Book me a room for tomorrow night. I don't know what time I'll get there. I'll wake you up to get my key if it's late.'

'All right, I'll tell you when I see you,' replied TC before hanging up.

¶

Nancy insisted on cooking breakfast for TC because it was her last day.

'Come on, eat up,' directed Maggie.

'It's my last day at Mr Black's,' said TC. 'Why do you refer to him as Black Bert?'

'The old bastard is as rich as Midas, TC. People around here say he made his mystery money on the black market. That's why we call him Black Bert. But I don't think that's the truth. I heard on the quiet that he was involved with some high-flying opal miner in South Australia who got into a fight with Bert. A week later the opal miner's body was found rotting in a black blanket. Bert had flown the coop and so had all the miner's opal and money. That's why they call him Black Bert. It's because of the black blanket. His poor bloody wife knows the truth; that is why she is delusional. Bert leaves her in her room day after day, week after week, year after year. Her sister knows the truth, but she's too scared to say anything. Bert's been banging that slut, Leanne, since she was nothing more than a kid. That was about the time his wife went out of her mind.'

'Something similar happened at Lightning Ridge, luv,' said Maggie. 'You go there today, do what you have to do, then get the hell out of Texas. No pun intended!'

'I understand, Maggie,' said TC while thinking, I hope the boss knows what he has gotten himself into.

¶

Maggie dropped off TC at Bert Black's at exactly 8 a.m. Bert and Leanne were both waiting in the tiny shed.

'I hope I'm not late, Mr Black,' said TC.

'Not at all,' replied Bert Black with a smile. 'Little Leanne and I are early.'

'That's probably because we want you out of here as soon as possible,' said Leanne with a fake smile. TC ignored Leanne. What was the point in snapping at Leanne's bait.

Where the sanding disc had been yesterday was a white-coloured, covered disc with tiny ridges in it.

'Now, TC, using the same technique as with the sanding, you are going to put the final shine on your stones.' Bert Black switched on the motor, and the disc began whirling. He took a jar of white-coloured mixture that resembled moist cornflour from the bench. With a small paint brush, he wiped some of the mixture across the disc.

'Start, TC. We will be back soon.'

Don't know what this stuff is, thought TC. All I do know is that it works. The rocks are shining!

Bert Black and Leanne returned. Bert inspected the polished agates, still attached to the sticks with sealing wax, and handed them to Leanne, who disappeared towards the house.

'You have done well, TC.' TC nodded and smiled before replying.

'I'll do better, Mr Black. What was the white mixture I put on that polishing disc?'

'That is my secret recipe, TC,' replied Black Bert. 'Tell Vance it will cost him a few more boulders if he wants that.'

'I'll tell him, Mr Black,' replied TC with a smile.

'I'm sure you will,' agreed Bert Black. Leanne returned with TC's agates.

'I've cleaned the wax off them. Please leave now!' TC smiled. 'Thank you. I shall tell Mr Callahan how kind you have been to me.' Bert Black and Leanne left the shed after Leanne instructed TC to lock up before she left. Although TC desperately wanted to look at her finished pieces, she quickly placed them in her bag, locked up, and left. Plenty of time to look at them at the motel.

As TC walked back to the motel, she thought about Bert Black and Leanne. If she had not learned very much about opal-cutting, she had certainly learned how not to treat others, especially outsiders who were alone in a strange town. She silently thanked God for the welcome extended to her by Maggie and Nancy.

By the time TC reached the motel, she had made herself a promise to always treat others the way she would like to be treated herself. Her mind harked back to her childhood Bible lessons—"Do unto others as you would have others do unto you." Now she knew first-hand the true meaning of those words.

Once back in her room, TC decided to examine her polished agates. She took them outside so she could see them in the sun after looking at them under the bedside lamp. She couldn't see any scratches. The boss would be happy.

I wish these were beautiful opals, she thought as she put the agates in her bag. I'll be happy to get back to Brolga. I wonder what's happening there, she said to herself as she prepared to shower.

*

At camp Yappy was preparing the evening meal.

Bloody Vance, he thought. The bastard said he'd be back. I won't have any money riding on bets tomorrow. I'd kill for a bloody telephone.

Neil, Faith and Little Joe were happy that another day in the worsening heat was coming to an end. That made them one more day closer to going on break.

*

Jake was on a high as he contemplated winning more money next day. He didn't care too much about the family business of late. The staff could handle that more than adequately. It never dawned on Jake that he took advantage of the staff. He was Jake Carmichael after all. He was doing fine! He was winning money hand over first on the horses. He could get any girl he wanted in Brolga with the exception of bitch-face TC. Stuff her! His mother was happy because three of her other kids would be home for school holidays next week. Jake was not quite sure how he would handle that. His mother would be gushing over them. Never mind that! He knew he was on a roll. In his mind, he was already listening to the broadcast tips late that night and next morning.

Graham Sandler was in his room strumming his guitar as he contemplated night shift. He wished the tennis girls would leave him alone. Of late he could hardly turn around without bumping into one of them. Something inside his head told him he had lost TC. He had no chance! That didn't mean he would quit trying. He loved her!

Nancy was not well, so went to bed early after saying goodbye to TC, who was sitting in the motel office when Vance pulled into the motel courtyard just on dark.

Oh, no! thought TC. He's got Claudia with him. Regardless, she ran outside to greet him with her usual kiss on his cheek the moment he was out of the station wagon.

'Don't you effing kiss him, you little bitch,' yelled Claudia from inside the car.

'Claudia, keep your foul mouth closed,' commanded Vance angrily.

'Claudia, go jump off a cliff,' added TC defiantly before smiling broadly at Vance.

'Sounds like you've grown up a lot since you've been here, Butterball,' said Vance. 'I'm impressed.'

'It's only been a week, Boss,' replied TC.

'I'm still impressed,' said Vance. 'Claudia and I need a shower, then I'll take her downtown for a meal. I don't suppose you want to come with us?' TC shook her head vigorously.

'No, thank you.'

'I didn't think so,' said Vance, who was obviously amused.

Vance collected his room key from Maggie, who gave him a refund of the extra week he had paid for TC less the charge for his room for the night.

'She's a good kid you've got here, Mr Callahan,' said Maggie. Vance laughed.

'Most of the time; she gets upset with me on occasions.'

'I don't blame her if you pull tricks on her like sending her to Black Bert's,' said Maggie seriously.

'Yes, TC will talk about that experience on our way back to Brolga,' said Vance over his shoulder as he left the office to join Claudia, who was waiting by the car.

'Maggie, I'll never forget you and Nancy,' said TC sincerely. 'I would have hated being here if it wasn't for you ladies. One day I hope I have lovely jewellery and clothes like yours.'

'You will, love!' said Maggie convincingly.

Vance returned to tell TC that he and Claudia were leaving.

'I want to get away around four, so get your gear ready tonight.'

'I'd best go pack, then. Go to bed, Maggie,' said TC. 'I love the present, whatever it is. Thank you and please thank Nancy for everything. I hope she feels better soon.'

'Give me a hug and get out of here, luv,' said Maggie. 'I don't want tears ruining my make-up.'

❡

As planned, they were on the road at four. They drove in silence for what seemed an eternity to TC. She correctly guessed Vance and Claudia had been fighting, about what she neither knew nor cared. She simply wanted the trip over as soon as possible. After the first fuel stop, located halfway along the dirt stretch, TC curled up on the back seat and tried to sleep. Suddenly, Claudia screamed.

'Stop the effing car now! I want to walk!'

Vance slammed on the brakes, and the car swerved off the road. Luckily, there were no trees close to the road on that stretch. TC sat bolt upright. Claudia jumped out of the car and ran off towards the bush. Vance jumped out and ran after her.

I can't believe this! thought TC. The Boss should wake up to himself. If he must have a woman on the side, he could at least find a sane one.

After several minutes of Claudia screaming and Vance quietly reasoning with her, they returned to the car and were once again underway.

'Can we have the radio on, Boss?' asked TC when they were almost at the end of the dirt road. 'This silence deal is getting to me.'

'Put that effing thing on and I'll jump out,' shrieked Claudia.

'TC, lean over and open the door for the mad bitch, please,' said Vance casually as he leaned forward and switched on the car radio. 'I must admit the silence has been annoying me, too.' Claudia turned and spat at TC.

'You effing little slut! Don't you come anywhere near me!'

TC reached for a tissue, then slowly wiped Claudia's ejected saliva off her face and neck.

'You no longer intimidate me, Claudia,' said TC calmly. 'I could spit back at you; however, doing so would bring me down to your repugnant level. I strongly suggest you wash your filthy mouth out with soap next time the Boss stops for fuel.' Vance burst into gales of laughter, and Claudia burst into tears.

When Vance's laughter declined, he said, 'What type of music would you like to hear, Miss TC?'

'Probably country or rock music, please, sir. I know Miss Claudia would love either,' replied TC with a mischievous smile.

Claudia's ridiculous, fabricated tantrum continued until she realised it wasn't getting her the attention from Vance she had reckoned for. She suddenly sat upright, then with all the force she could muster punched

Vance on the left side of his face. The punch caught Vance off-guard, and he momentarily lost control of the car, which swerved, slid, and slithered all over the dirt road until he managed to right it and brought it to a halt on the side of the road.

Breathing quickly and deeply, Vance turned to TC, who was clutching the back of his seat with her hands. Her body was shaking, her eyes the size of saucers, and she wore an unmistakable, much-warranted expression of terror on her face. TC's heart was racing. She nodded and put her head in her hands.

'Breathe deeply and slowly, Little One,' directed Vance.

Claudia sat quietly and innocently, looking directly ahead through the car's windscreen. She had achieved her goal. She had Vance's attention regardless of Miss Bitch-Face TC sitting in the back.

Vance switched off the crackling radio, then lit a cigarette. He calmly got out of the car against which he leaned while he smoked it. His mind was racing with "what ifs". He threw his finished cigarette on the dirt, then stepped on it before calmly walking around to the passenger-side door, opening it, and roughly dragging Claudia outside. Claudia's smile turned to shock as Vance shook her by her shoulders.

'You crazy moll! You could have killed us all,' he said quietly and slowly. His face was red with anger. Claudia started to cry as Vance stopped shaking her and put his hands around her throat.

'Oh, please, Claudia, save the waterworks. If you want to die, I'll help you out. I'll effing choke you here and now. You and I are both worthless pieces of shit. We'd be no loss to the world, but that girl sitting in the car hasn't begun to live yet.'

Claudia began gagging for air as Vance's hands tightened around her throat. TC had never seen Vance like this before. She was terrified he was actually going to continue choking Claudia until she was dead.

'Stop now, Boss. Please stop now,' she pleaded as she got out of the car. 'Please, Boss, don't do it,' she continued as she attempted to pull one of Vance's hands away from Claudia's throat.

Vance did not respond apart from briefly glancing at TC, who was shocked to realise Vance was as if in a trance. To no avail, TC continued to tug at his hand before looking directly into his face and firmly, in a loud voice, commanding, 'Stop NOW, Boss. She's not worth it! Please, Mr Callahan, STOP NOW! This is selfish, Mr Callahan! Think of your kids, Mrs Callahan, the men, me, the opal ...'

Claudia's face appeared to have no colour whatsoever and her frantic eyes were bulging. TC removed her hand from Vance's and began crying. She put her arms tightly around Vance from the side and begged, 'Please, Boss, leave her alone! Don't kill her.'

Vance's body stiffened as he realised what he was doing. He quickly pulled his hands away from Claudia's throat, moaned, 'Oh, no!' pulled away from TC, and disappeared to behind the car, where he sat down in the dirt, put his head in his hands, and silently cried.

Claudia was coughing and rubbing her throat as colour gradually returned to her face. TC poured some water into a mug. She offered it to Claudia, who snatched it from her, gulped it down, then thrust it back towards TC for a refill.

'The bastard nearly killed me,' complained Claudia after her third mug of water.

'You nearly killed all of us, Claudia,' TC countered. 'You pushed the Boss past his limits.'

'I'll report him to that cop you and your friend hang around with.'

'No, you won't, Claudia!'

'He deserves to be in prison. I'm going to make sure he goes there,' persisted Claudia.

'Who will take notice of a delusional psychopath such as yourself, Claudia?' said TC. 'I suggest you sit in the car. I'm going to talk to the boss.'

'Come on, best boss in the world,' said TC lightly as she rounded the rear of the station wagon. Her tone of voice went into speedy reverse when Vance lifted his head out of his hands to look at her. She was immediately consumed by compassion for Vance, who sat on the dirt with tears streaming down and the defeated look of helplessness on his face.

'I'll be back in a minute, Boss.' TC gathered Vance's cigarettes and lighter from the driver's seat along with tissues and the water bottle.

'That's right, run after the bastard,' jeered Claudia.

'I suggest you keep quiet, Claudia, before I choke you myself,' warned TC before returning to Vance.

'Wash your face and have a smoke, Boss,' suggested TC gently.

'She shoved me over the edge, TC,' admitted Vance while splashing water on his face.

'I know!' said TC as she handed Vance the box of tissues.

'I'm sorry you had to see me like this, TC.'

'See you like what, Boss?' replied TC with a shrug. 'Here're your smokes. I'll sit here with you while you have one.'

'I can't remember when I last cried, TC. I have wanted to many times, especially over Anna. I suppose in the past I always found refuge in the bottom of a rum bottle.'

'My lips are sealed about everything that's happened this morning. I'm going to consider it a bad dream,' assured TC.

'Is that a deal, TC?' asked Vance seriously.

'It's a deal!' confirmed TC with a nod and a smile. They sat in silence until Vance finished his cigarette; then Vance stood up and brushed himself off.

'Come on, TC, let's get going. The sooner we get back to Brolga, the sooner I'll see the last of Claudia.'

I hope you mean that, thought TC as she picked up the water bottle and tissue box. Both were covered in road dirt. She didn't care. Vance was okay and that was all that mattered.

¶

Apart from Vance ordering fuel at the bitumen road turn-off and Curloo service stations, nobody spoke a word until they reached Brolga. The radio was broken. Probably had a loose wire. The only sound in the car was the engine and the occasional whimper from Claudia when she gingerly rubbed her throat.

It was almost midnight when Vance pulled to a stop in front of TC's house.

'There you go, TC, home safely,' said Vance. 'I'll talk to you tomorrow. Here comes your reception committee!'

TC grabbed her bag. She was hugged by Lou the second her feet hit the ground.

'Seems like you've been gone for a year,' said Lou excitedly.

'Feels like it, too, Lou,' replied TC. 'Have we got anything in the house to eat? I forgot how hot it is here. I need a shower.'

'I haven't spotted any snakes, so it's probably pretty safe,' comforted Lou confidently.

'I feel filthy, so I'll have to brave it,' said TC before yawning. 'The condition I'm in at the moment, even the snakes would turn their noses up at me.'

'I didn't know snakes had noses,' said Lou seriously.

'I don't know, either, Lou, but they must have some sort of breathing mechanism,' replied TC matter-of-factly.

¶

After TC had showered and washed her hair, they sat on the stairs to eat vegemite and cheese sandwiches and talk.

'Colin wants me to go to Sydney,' said Lou casually. 'I told him I'm not going without you.'

'You shouldn't mould your life around me, Lou,' replied TC. 'You have to do what's right for you. Don't worry about me!'

'But you are my best friend, TC. You are my only friend, if the truth be known,' reasoned Lou.

'Same goes for me, Lou. That's why I won't hold you back,' replied TC. Lou was confused.

'You have changed, TC.'

'The Boss said I have grown up,' replied TC. 'It's about time, as far as I'm concerned.'

'Vance has a heap of mail orders to do before morning,' said Lou as they watched and heard the truckies loading across the street. 'I took them for him all day yesterday at the exchange. I slid them under the shop door this evening. He'll have to fling the other girl a couple of quid.'

TC was instantly on her feet.

'Come on, Lou, let's go help him. I can't understand why he didn't tell me.'

Of course, I can, thought TC as she hurried to her room to change from pyjamas to pedal pushers.

When they arrived at the shop, Vance was not there, and Lou's notes were still on the floor behind the door.

He must have forgotten, thought TC.

'Not like him to forget,' said Lou.

'He's got a lot on his mind, Lou,' replied TC. 'Let's get started!'

A couple of hours later, the girls were still at it when they were distracted by a knock on the front door. It was Jake, who was obviously blind drunk. Lou let him in.

'Hello, ladies. You are working early,' muttered Jake. He was experiencing difficulty holding his head up straight. It appeared to be on a swivel from side to side.

'You are very drunk, Jake,' observed TC.

'I know that, TC.'

'You shouldn't be driving,' said Lou.

'Are you worried your boyfriend will catch me?' replied Jake. 'Which one of you is he after? Poor bastard's got no hope.'

'You should walk home, Jake,' advised TC.

'And leave my lovely chariot outside for some prick to steal? I don't think so!'

'Make yourself a coffee, Jake,' said TC.

'What if I don't want to?' replied Jake still mumbling. 'I won a lot of money again today, ladies. Been winning for weeks. I'm riding on a bloody rainbow.'

'Good for you, Jake,' chorused the girls.

'Sit at the desk, Jake. I'll make you some coffee,' said TC. 'Looks as if you intend hanging around, so you may as well try to sober up a bit before you speed off.'

'I think TC's worried about me, Lou. Do you think she is, Lou?'

'Go sit at Vance's desk, Jake. We are busy,' replied Lou while rolling her eyes.

TC poured Jake a coffee and put it on the desk before calling, 'Come on, Jake. Please drink this.' Jake with his out-of-control head winked at Lou before staggering into the dispensary.

'I won a lot of money today, TC,' he repeated as he sat down.

'I know. You already told us,' replied TC.

'Don't you want to know how much I won?'

'Not really, none of our business,' replied TC. 'Lou and I are busy, Jake. Please be a good boy and drink your coffee.'

'Boy! I'm no boy! I'm a man! Have you missed me, TC?'

'No!' replied TC from the counter where she was wrapping a parcel.

Jake began talking incoherently to himself. He continued so doing until the girls had finished the last of the orders at a quarter-past-four. The mail trucks left at five.

'Jake, I need to borrow your car to take the parcels to the truckies,' pleaded TC. Jake was oblivious as he prattled on to himself.

'Lou, I'm going to run down to the truck yard and ask the guys to pick the parcels up from here,' called TC as she flung open the front door and hurried out.

TC arrived at the yard puffing. She quickly explained the situation to Jake's mates.

'No problem, TC.' said Barman. 'Calm down. I'll drive you back to the chemist shop and pick them up in my car.'

'Thank you, thank you, thank you,' said a relieved and grateful TC.

'Where's Vance?' enquired Barman as they got into his ute. TC didn't reply. Instead, she commented on the heat.

¶

When all the parcels were in the back of Barman's ute, TC thanked him again.

'I'll tell my boss he owes you a carton.'

'That would be nice,' replied Barman. 'What's Jake's car doing out the front?'

'He's out the back, drunk,' said Lou.

'I better take him home,' said Barman with concern. 'He's my mate!' It took some persuasion before Barman managed to convince Jake to leave his car. With them gone, TC locked the shop and the girls walked home. It was daylight.

'Looks like dry vegemite and cheese sandwiches for breakfast, TC,' laughed Lou as they approached their front gate.

'I'm worried about the boss, Lou,' said TC seriously. 'No matter how tired he is, it's not like him to forget something as important as the mail orders.'

'No need to worry any longer, TC' said Lou. 'Unless I'm hallucinating, that's the rear end of his station wagon I can see in the driveway.'

'I'm here, girls,' came Vance's voice from his car. 'I'll meet you on the back landing.'

Lou and TC quickly went to open the back door. They were both speechless when they saw Claudia standing alongside Vance.

'TC, Lou, I need a favour,' said Vance. 'Claudia is leaving on the Flea in a couple of hours. She needs to get cleaned up.'

'No problem!' replied TC. 'Come in.'

'I'll get Claudia's gear from the car,' said Vance. 'Hope you've got some coffee.'

'I'll turn on the kettle,' said Lou.

TC pointed to the dining table and chairs.

'Please sit down if you wish, Claudia.' TC felt a rush of pity for Claudia, who looked forlorn, lost, and lonely.

'Thank you, TC' replied Claudia as she pulled out a chair.

'Sorry we don't have milk,' called Lou from the kitchen.

'Black will be fine, thank you,' replied Claudia politely.

This has got to be a different woman from the Claudia I have come to know, thought TC, who was confused to say the least.

Vance returned with two suitcases.

'Where do you want them, TC?'

'You can use my room, Claudia,' offered TC.

'Thank you, TC,' replied Claudia demurely.

'Good!' said Vance before heading towards the front of the house.

'You look terrible, Claudia,' said Lou bluntly when she fetched the coffees from the kitchen.

'She's had a rough day,' said Vance as he re-joined them.

Claudia had a scarf wound around her throat. It looked out of place with the square-necked, short-sleeved blouse she had worn leaving the motel.

'You must be hot with that scarf around your neck,' said Lou unknowingly.

'I have a heat rash on my throat,' lied Claudia with a smile.

'You poor thing!' said Lou in sympathy. 'I got a heat rash on my legs once. It nearly drove me around the bend.'

'Thank you for helping us out, girls,' said Vance in order to change the subject.

'What were you two doing out until daylight?' asked Vance curiously. TC smiled before replying.

'What we were doing is on those mail trucks we heard pull out of the trucking yard a while go.' Vance's mouth flew open.

'We also entertained your drunk mate, Jake,' said Lou.

'What was Jake doing at the shop?' asked Vance.

'He was drunk. He pulled up out the front and knocked on the door, so we let him in,' replied TC.

'You've lost me,' said Vance before he apologised. 'I forgot about the mail orders. Totally slipped my mind. Thank you both. Claudia, you should start to get ready. The girls will give you a towel and show you the bathroom.'

'I'll take you to my room and get you towels, Claudia,' said TC.

'Thank you, TC. By the way, I'm sorry for treating you as I did.'

'It's forgotten, Claudia,' replied TC softly. 'If you need anything ironed, let me know. I'll put a couple of clean towels in the bathroom for you.'

'TC, I need to talk to you while Claudia is having her shower,' whispered Vance when TC passed through the dining room.

'That means you want me to make myself scarce while you talk to TC,' whispered Lou. 'By the way, you owe my workmate two quid for taking yesterday morning's orders,' she added in normal voice tone. 'You don't have to worry about paying me for Friday or helping TC this morning. Everyone knows you are broke.' Vance could not help but to laugh.

'Is that so, Lou? I had no idea everyone knew. For what it's worth, thank you for helping TC and for taking the orders and doing it free, to boot.'

'That's all right, Vance,' said Lou flippantly. 'You can make it up to me when you are a wealthy opal tycoon. My dad says we should never kick a man when he's down.'

❡

Claudia went to shower, and Lou perched herself on the steps while Vance and TC talked.

'I've got a lot to tell you later. I have to give Claudia some money. The Romeos don't know she's leaving town yet. She didn't tell them she would be away before we left on Thursday night. It was a spur-of-the-moment thing. We had a long talk, and she sneaked into her room to pack while you and Lou were doing the mail orders.'

'I have the money you left with me at the motel,' said TC. 'I also have most of the tip money the shearers gave me. The rest of it is in the bank.'

'That won't be enough, TC,' said Vance, shaking his head.

'You are paying Claudia to leave town, aren't you?' Vance nodded slightly.

'Something like that, TC.' TC frowned.

'How much are you paying her, Boss?'

'A lot! I need to see Jake. You said he was blind drunk a couple of hours ago?'

'Drunker than I've ever seen you and Jake combined,' replied TC matter-of-factly. 'He was too drunk to drive. His car is parked in front of the shop. How do you know Claudia won't come back?'

Vance immediately replied, 'Where would she get a job? Let me think, TC. I have to figure out a way to see Jake. I have to borrow some money before the Flea goes.'

'I'll leave you to it,' replied TC. She went to her room and took her purse from her still-unpacked bag on the floor.

Claudia has got lovely clothes, she thought as she glanced at the open suitcase on her bed.

'Here's your money, Boss. I'll sit with Lou.'

'No, it's all right, TC. I have a plan. When Claudia is ready, I'll take her to the dispensary. I want you to sit on the railway station until they open the ticket window. Buy a ticket. Make sure to get a sleeper cabin for the Curloo to Brisbane part of the trip, then bring it to the dispensary. I'll find Jake and meet you there before the Flea leaves.'

⁋

Claudia was ready to go. She came up the back stairs from the bathroom. She looked lovely in a cream silk blouse with a Peter Pan collar and cropped-cuff sleeves, black fitted skirt, wide cream leather belt with gold buckle, and matching high heeled sandals. No tell-tale marks were visible on her throat. Her hair was piled on top of her head and her make-up perfectly applied. She twirled around for Vance's benefit.

'I bet you'll miss me, darling,' she said coyly.

'Probably, Claudia,' replied Vance. 'I'll put your stuff in the car.

'Come on, Lou, let's go see the Flea,' said TC.

'What for?' asked Lou. 'Are we leaving?'

'No, the Boss wants me to buy Claudia's ticket! Another day in the unpredictable, sometimes exciting, rarely boring life of a Vance Callahan employee.'

'You mean slave!' quipped Lou adamantly. 'An underpaid slave, at that!'

'Lou, stop harping!'

'Like to see Claudia step out of our bathroom looking the way she did an hour from now,' said Lou. 'Hopefully, she'd drown in perspiration. She can't fool me with all her plastic niceness.'

'There's no such word as niceness, Lou,' corrected TC. Lou shrugged.

'If it's good enough for my dad, it's good enough for me.'

The tiny Brolga Railway Station was scrupulously clean and ready for Sunday morning's action. The Flea was packed, with the engine facing east. Obviously, it had been hosed down during the past half hour. Water was still dripping off the lower body. Apart from an old, blue cattle dog drowsing on the platform near the goods carriage, the station was devoid of life.

'Looks like we sit and wait for someone to appear,' said Lou.

'Looks like it! That old bluey's got a great life, Lou,' replied TC between yawns. 'Wouldn't it be great to sleep when we want?'

'Sure! Unless some dog-hating mongrel came along and kicked us,' said Lou with a grimace. They both stretched and yawned.

'Looks like you had a late night, girls,' said a railway worker who appeared from around the corner of the station.

'More like an all-nighter,' smiled Lou.

'Now, now, young Lou, don't talk like that. People might get the wrong impression,' chastised the man. 'I drink with your dad. He's proud of you. Why are you sitting here? The Flea doesn't pull out for another hour.'

'TC wants to buy a ticket,' replied Lou sweetly.

'Don't tell me one of you is leaving without the other! I don't believe it!' said the surprised gent.

'I'm buying the ticket for a friend,' explained TC.

'Come on. I'll sell you a ticket, luv. Come inside with me.'

§

Vance was talking to Jake across the road from the Catholic Church where Jake had arrived with his mother and siblings a few minutes prior. When Jake spotted Vance standing beside his station wagon, he told his mother he'd see her in church later.

'You look like hell, Jake!' laughed Vance.

'Feel like it, too! What brings you here, Pill-Pusher? I know it's not because you are going to church.'

'I need to bite you again, Jake. I need a couple of thousand, and I need it now,' replied an embarrassed Vance. He already owed Jake a fortune.

'No problem, mate,' agreed Jake without hesitation. 'I haven't got it on me. I keep my money at work.' Silence as Jake thought. All right, mate. I'll tell Mum something's come up. She'll be pissed off as buggery. It's the first family mass since the kids came home from school. But can't be helped. I'll be back in a minute.

I wonder if I used to look that stuffed after a night on the piss, thought Vance as he watched Jake enter the church. Who are you kidding, Callahan? You probably looked worse because you are a lot older.

§

'How did you know where to find me?' said Jake a few minutes later, en route to his mother's house to collect keys.

'Because I've listened to you complain about your mother dragging you out of bed, rain, hail, or shine, ever since I met you, Jake,' replied Vance.

'Poor Mum's not happy. Can't say I blame her. Never mind!' said Jake, who now suffered guilt along with his hangover. 'Is your business in trouble again, mate?' asked Jake as Vance drove from the house to the main street.

'No, it's worse than that, Jake! What say we have a yarn after the train leaves. You deserve to know why I've put the bite on you again,' replied Vance seriously.

¶

Claudia's train ticket in hand, TC entered the dispensary, closely followed by Lou. On the floor, both Claudia's suitcases were open. On top of her clothes in both were scattered bottles of perfume, lipsticks, face creams, and every other beauty product stocked in the shop. TC and Claudia all but collided as Claudia rushed towards the dispensary from the shop with her hands and arms full.

'So, you are robbing the boss as well as everything else, Claudia,' said TC, shaking her head in disgust and disappointment. She felt like a fool.

'Get out of my way, you effing moll,' snarled Claudia. 'I pulled the wool over your effing eyes for as long as it took to use your effing ugly bathroom. You are stupid! I sucked you right in!'

'You didn't fool me!' said Lou defiantly. 'Heat rash, my foot! If you had heat rash in this weather, you wouldn't wear a silk scarf around it.'

'Leave it, Lou!' commanded TC. Vance spoke from the rear of the dispensary.

'You heard TC, leave it alone, Lou. Do me another favour. Go out the front. Jake's there. Ask him not to leave until I come out. You stay with him.'

'Put that stuff in your bags with the rest of your loot, Claudia. You are one piece of work. TC, you stay here while I pay this mad bitch.' Vance counted the two thousand, then put it on the desk. 'You recount it, Claudia. I'd hate you to be able to say I stiffed you, at least not where money is concerned.'

'Eff you, Vance,' snarled Claudia as she began counting the money. When finished, she slowly arranged the notes in her handbag.

'It's been a pleasure doing business with you, Mr Callahan,' she purred. 'Where's my ticket?' Vance pointed to the desk.

'There! TC, I'm going to ask Jake to drive this piece of garbage to the station. If she moves or opens her mouth, hit her over the head with this piece of rock.' Vance handed TC a jagged piece of boulder about ten inches long and eight inches wide.

'You wouldn't have the guts, you stupid moll,' sneered Claudia when

Vance was out of earshot.

'Try me, Claudia!' bluffed TC. She lifted the rock into a threatening position. She was relieved when she realised her false threat had been successful.

'Jake's bringing his car around the back,' advised Vance when he returned to the dispensary. 'Come on, Claudia. I want you and Lou to go with Jake. You, too, TC. Don't let this creature out of your sight until the train goes.' Vance literally threw Claudia's cases into the boot of Jake's car.

'There, Claudia. I'm thrilled to see the last of you.'

'Don't count on it, darling!' whispered Claudia seductively before leaning forward with the smile of an angel and kissing Vance on the cheek.

Vance said, 'Thanks, Jake and the girls,' before almost running inside to wash his face. He made himself a coffee, then sat at his desk to drink it and smoke while his mind ticked off every second until he heard the train whistle. 'One obstacle out of the way,' he told himself in contradiction to a nagging premonition within telling him he had neither heard nor seen the last of Claudia.

Jake came back. He was alone.

'The ladies have gone to Con's for a feed. They are both starving,' said Jake as he positioned himself on a stool opposite Vance. 'I'm bloody starving, too—not for food though. I need a hair of the dog. What the bloody hell's going on, mate? Looks to me like you borrowed money from me to give to Claudia. Please don't tell me she's pregnant.'

'I'll lock the door, Jake. After I call Delores to let her know I'm back, I tell you everything.'

¶

Jake listened intently until Vance concluded his story with, 'Thanks for taking her to the station, Jake. I couldn't take her myself with half the town there. Someone was bound to tell Delores.'

'You and I are stars when it comes to women, mate,' said Jake as he stood up. 'I'd best get home. I'm certain my darling mother has a tongue-lashing waiting for me because I missed church. I need a drink. Can't wait for session time!'

'How did you go with the horses yesterday, Jake?' asked Vance.

'I won a few bob. I won a few for Yappy, too. Tell the little mongrel he owes me when he comes to town. Let me know when you are going to camp. I'll give you his money to take with you. I've got to go, mate, I'm crook.'

Vance followed Jake, locking the back door behind him. Halfway home he remembered the front door of the shop. It wasn't locked.

Stuff it, he thought. Not much left there to steal except the opal. No other bastard in town knows what to do with that, so why would they steal it?

The girls ate every crumb of food Con cooked for them before going home to sleep. They hoped to get a few hours' sleep before the heat of the day made sleep all but impossible. Both girls fell onto their beds fully clothed.

'Glad we only reckoned on a few hours, TC. We got two!' said a groggy Lou while gently shaking TC awake. 'Come on, TC. Wake up. Vance is on the phone.'

'Leave me alone, Lou. I'm tired. Tell him to call back later.'

'All right.'

TC was sound asleep again before Lou got to the telephone. Vance was angry when Lou asked him to call later.

'Get her out of bed, Lou. I'm coming to get her. Tell her I want to get started on the opal.'

'That's it!' thought Lou. Wish I didn't help him with his orders or any other bloody thing. He can wake TC himself! Lou opened the back door before going back to bed. She heard Vance's car pull into the driveway. He got out and bounded up the back stairs before yelling at TC from her bedroom doorway.

'TC, wake up! Surely you didn't expect to sleep all day! I didn't drive all that way so you can sleep for the rest of your life. Get up now!'

TC yelled back at him, 'I'm not a machine like you, Mr Callahan! Get out of my bloody way so I can clean my teeth.' Vance was really angry now.

'Don't swear, TC. Do you want to end up sounding like my girlfriends?'

'Bloody is not swearing!'

'It's a beginning! Clean your teeth. Do whatever you have to do. Hurry up about it! I want to get started on the opal.'

At least I'm already dressed, thought TC as she ran downstairs to the bathroom.

Lou was relieved when she heard the car doors slam and Vance reverse out of the driveway. Now she could go back to sleep.

¶

Vance and TC drove in silence to the rear of the dispensary. Once inside, Vance said, 'I've bought you a raincoat and a shower cap to wear while you grind the rock off the top of the opal seams. Water combined with the rock becomes mud splatters. It will splash all over you.'

'Good,' replied TC coldly. 'Don't know where you learned that, Boss. Anyway, give me the raincoat and shower cap.'

'Don't be smart!' snapped Vance. 'Perhaps I plucked it out of the air, read it in a book, or Delores made a feeble attempt at opal-cutting and I learned it then.'

'Who's being smart now!' retaliated TC. Vance lit a cigarette. He could say nothing.

'Give me bits to grind,' said TC calmly.

'Good! Let us see what Bert Black taught you,' replied Vance impatiently. TC sighed.

'All about how not to treat others and never to pay up-front. I learned that!' TC remembered the three pieces of agate in her bag. She gave them to Vance. 'This is what your boulders bought you. Let's get started!'

Vance produced a bucket filled with sawn pieces of various-sized boulders soaking in water. Some of the seams of opal were all thick. The colours highlighted by the water were beautiful.

'You've obviously been a busy man,' said TC. Vance smiled proudly.

'Look under the saw bench, TC.' TC laughed when she saw more buckets lined up like soldiers on parade.

'Looks like I'm going to be a busy girl.'

'The course wheel is on the left, so start with that one,' instructed Vance. TC suddenly realised she had learned something at Bert Black's.

'Okay, I'll take the rock off with that until I get close to the opal, then I'll move to the fine one. Do you want me to grind them all on the course wheel, then move, or do one at a time?'

'No! I'll go off my head waiting,' replied Vance seriously. 'Pick ten pieces. Work on facing those, then I'll decide.'

Goodbye to what's left of my fingernails, thought TC. She put the raincoat on back to front. As she fixed the shower cap over her hair, Vance handed her a pair of rubber thongs.

'Take your shoes off and wear these. Can't have your bows getting ruined.'

Minutes into grinding rock, TC began to wonder which she preferred; the solitude of the tiny shed in Bert Black's backyard or Vance looking impatiently over her shoulder.

'Boss, please leave me alone. I can't concentrate with you hanging over my shoulder. Why don't you go and clean the shop?' Vance laughed.

'Point taken, Butterball. I'll make myself a coffee while I think about which one of our creditors to call first.'

¶

Later TC switched off the course grinder and moved to the fence wheel. Vance rushed to stand beside her.

'Go away, Boss! I'll call you when I have something to show you.'

'Please hurry, TC,' said Vance anxiously before retreating.

TC picked up one of the ten pieces at random and gingerly began grinding the thin layer of iron stone still covering the opal seam. The more opal exposed, the faster her heart raced. She was shaking. Finally, she understood the reason for the numerous anxious calls from opal people in other states. No wonder Bert Black had been desperate to acquire his couple of boulders. Nature is magnificent! thought TC. She gingerly put the piece to the grindstone and held her breath. Seconds later, she jumped up excitedly and called to Vance.

'The first piece is done, Boss. It's beautiful! It's thick and green and orange.' TC held the piece of matchbox-sized opal and gazed at it in awe. Vance had it out of her hand instantly.

'Go on, keep working!' he commanded before sitting down at his desk to examine the opal. TC turned back to the grinding wheel. She felt extremely sad. The boss could have let me hold it for at least a little while. We could have talked about it, she thought as she reached for the second of the future thousands of pieces of boulder opal she would cut and polish into stones of such incredible beauty that many experienced gem dealers throughout the world would consider fakes. Too beautiful to be the real thing!

TC made a silent promise to herself there and then. She would never again permit herself to become openly emotional about the opal she worked on. She was simply a small cog in the production process. She was there to work, and work she did until every piece in the first bucket had been faced.

Vance hardly noticed when TC told him she was leaving. He was engrossed by the pieces of opal spread on the desk and in the bucket in front of him. It was two in the morning. TC was wrecked. She felt filthy, and her back was aching from leaning forward. TC walked home wondering how Vance managed to survive without sleep.

'How was your day, TC?' called Lou from her bedroom. 'I got tired of waiting for you.'

'The opal is beautiful, Lou,' replied TC. 'I'm about to pretend I'm that cattle dog. I'm going to sleep because I feel like it,' replied TC. 'No shower, not even a lick and a promise.'

'My dad calls it "the mongrel-dog act",' called Lou. 'Looks like Vance is going to work you till you drop, TC. I suggest you put your foot down straightaway. Do it tomorrow before he starts to take you for granted the way he did with the shop when he was on the booze.'

TC didn't hear Lou. She was asleep with the fan blowing cool air onto her face and still fully-clothed, perspiration-drenched body.

¶

Vance was at his office desk deliberating over which of the pieces of opal should first be cut into the stones. Everything he'd seen in the gem feature were oval or round shapes, which was a shame because obviously, if the pieces TC had faced were to be uniform template shapes, there would be an extraordinary waste of opal. He reluctantly concluded if there had to be wastage to furnish the markets requirements, so be it! After all, other opal miners and cutters must face the same problem. Countless carats of colour must be ground off on wheels and flung down drainpipes every day. Vance selected ten pieces for TC to shape and polish next day before lighting his last cigarette for the night while wondering how and where he would get the money to carry on. He yawned, realised he was exhausted, and fell asleep at his desk holding the cigarette in his hand.

¶

Vance was asleep with his head cushioned by his left arm on the desk and the burned-out cigarette between two fingers of his outstretched right hand when TC arrived for work at seven. She was early. TC filled the kettle and switched it on before patting Vance on the shoulder.

'Come on, Boss, it's time to wake up,' said TC softly so as not to startle him. Vance raised his head slightly while blinking his half-closed eyes before sitting upright and shaking himself awake. 'It's a wonder you didn't burn your fingers with this thing,' said TC as she took the cigarette butt and threw it in the bin.

'TC, stop fussing and make me some coffee. The way I feel, I wouldn't care if the whole place burned down and took me with it,' replied Vance despondently.

'I'll get your coffee. I know you are depressed because of money problems,' replied TC matter-of-factly. 'Unfortunately, I can't help you much in that area. Why don't you wash your face? That is always the first thing you do when you wake up here because of booze.'

'Good idea. Why didn't I think of that?' replied Vance with a half-hearted smile. 'I'll wash my face if you stop nagging me.'

'Deal,' replied TC while pouring his coffee. 'Would you like me to get you something to eat from Con's?'

'No! I'll smoke a cigarette or ten instead,' replied Vance with a smirk. TC rolled her eyes and sighed as she placed Vance's coffee on the desk next to the ten pieces of opal. 'I assume you want me to start with these?'

'Yes! Shape them into the largest ovals you can manage,' replied Vance flatly. 'Don't waste any more opal than absolutely necessary.'

'I'll do my best,' promised TC as she collected and placed the pieces into an empty ice-cream container.

'The shop looks a mess, Boss.'

'I know!' agreed Vance. 'It'll be all right. You concentrate on the opal.'

TC switched on the fine grinding wheel and began shaping the first stone. Shortly afterwards, she decided it was too slow, so moved to the course grinder, which was much quicker. She would use it until she had almost the perfect shape, then switch back to the other one to round off the domes.

When Vance finished his coffee, he left via the back door after advising TC he would be back soon.

Good! I won't have him looking over my shoulder, thought TC with relief. Vance returned to the dispensary, soon to be referred to as the cutting room, in time to open the shop.

'Have you finished yet, Butterball?' he asked with sarcasm.

'I suggest you do this, Boss, while I clean the shop and answer the phone,' replied TC seriously.

'Sorry, I'll leave you alone!' said Vance, who quickly moved away towards the shop to open the front door.

¶

Come siren time, Vance was happy to be carefully examining his ten oval-shaped, smooth-surfaced, high-domed, magnificent-coloured opals, which were ready to be disc-sanded prior to polishing.

'I'm going to meet Lou at Con's. I haven't eaten since forever. 'I'm not sure whether to do the backs or the faces next. You might want to think about it.'

'You and Lou enjoy yourselves,' snapped Vance.

'I told you yesterday, I'm not a machine. Mr Callahan,' retorted TC. 'I'll be back soon!' The forlorn look on Vance's face made TC reconsider. 'Would you please go to Con's and tell Lou I'll see her tonight? I'll start sanding the stones.' Vance was suddenly a happy man.

'Thank you, Little One. I'll go now and you start. I'll be back soon.'

He didn't tell me to do the top or back first, thought TC. 'I'll flip the coin like they do in "two up".' She went to the cash register and selected a penny. She flicked it with her thumb as she had seen Jake and his mates do at Lou's dad's house.

'Heads I start on the opal face and tails I do the back first.' The penny landed heads up. TC's decision was made on the toss of a coin. A penny.

¶

Vance returned with food for TC. She was not interested in anything other than the opal.

'Go away, Boss!' she told him when he attempted to interrupt her. 'I'll finish these. If you are not happy with them, sack me!'

With tremendous self-restraint Vance left TC alone in the sanding/polishing room. He pretended to be content answering the telephone and tidying the shop, checking on her progress only occasionally. He knew he would have to go to the mine. The poor men probably thought he had deserted them.

§

Finally, he decided to see how TC was faring with the first ten. If they turned out all right, and he had no doubt they would, she could carry on without him. He had sawed enough to keep her going for weeks. He needed to establish a buzzer or bell system she could hear out back when customers came through the front door of the shop.

§

TC was confused after course- and fine-sanding the stones to her satisfaction.

'The next step is polishing. What are we going to use?' she asked Vance. 'Mr Black uses his secret concoction. All I know is that it is white. Mr Black said it would cost you more boulders to get his recipe.'

'Old bastard, he's trying to scam us. Can't say I'm surprised. We'll use tin oxide.' Tin oxide worked perfectly.

Although TC was astounded by its beauty, she remembered her promise to herself. When the first stone was finished, she took it to Vance. Without uttering a word, she returned to the polishing buff and started on the second.

§

'We're done, TC!' said Vance when she presented him with the tenth stone. 'What do you think of them?'

'They are beautiful, Boss,' replied TC as she looked down at the stones Vance had displayed atop a towel on his desk. Every colour of the sunrise, sunset and rainbow was looking back at her.

'I'm going now.'

'Start as early as you can tomorrow,' said Vance without lifting his head. He was absorbed by the stones. TC walked across to the café. It was almost after nine o'clock. She looked like hell and felt like it, too. Jake was at the counter talking with Con.

'You look bloody terrible, TC' said Jake who, as always, including the occasions when he was wearing the wobbly head, was meticulously attired and groomed.

'Take a hike, Jake!' responded TC with a sugar-sweet fake smile. 'A chocolate thick-shake, please, Con.'

'Darling, I missed you this morning. I was sleeping in,' called Lisa from her usual table.

'She missed you when you were away, TC,' said Con as he scooped chocolate ice cream into a milkshake container.

'Don't charge TC for that,' called Lisa.

'That's not fair, I don't get any freebies,' complained Jake.

'Not here, anyway, mate,' said Con with a wink. TC picked up her shake and joined Lisa while Jake and Con laughed.

'Give me a hug, darling,' said Lisa. 'Have you seen Graham? He missed you, too.'

'That's not what I heard, Lisa,' replied TC flatly.

'Those girls don't mean anything to him, TC.'

'That's Graham's business, Lisa. I wish Lou wasn't on late shift. I'll have to snake-scout by myself tonight,' said TC with a smile. Lisa laughed.

'You changed the Graham subject quickly, darling.' TC laughed.

'That was my intention, Lisa.' They chatted until TC finished her drink. Jake and Con were still yarning at the counter.

'I'll give you a lift home, TC,' offered Jake.

'I can walk,' replied TC.

'I know you can bloody well walk. I said I'd give you a lift. I didn't ask if you could walk.'

'I'm sorry, Jake. No, thank you. I'll walk.' Jake turned his back on TC.

'Suit your bloody self.'

'Thank you, Jake, I will,' replied TC sweetly. She was more than a little surprised to find Jake perched on the stairs when she got home.

'Hello, darling,' he said superciliously. 'What took you so long? I took the back street. I know it well.'

'What do you want, Jake?' asked TC shortly.

'I know I won't get what I want. I'll tell you why I'm here instead.'

'Why are you here, Jake?' demanded TC as she unlocked the door. Jake followed TC inside, took a deep breath and stuck out his chest.

'Lisa told me Lou's at work and you are still frightened of snakes. I came to protect you.' TC laughed. She couldn't help it.

'I'll always be frightened of snakes, Jake.'

'Not with me around, you won't. Don't tell me you have forgotten how I slaughtered that poor thing on the path?'

'I'll never forget it, Jake. Every time I have to go to the bathroom after dark, I'm terrified. Lou is, too!'

'Have you got any beer?' asked Jake casually.

'Your beer from forever ago is there,' replied TC. 'It's not cold. We took it out of the fridge and put it in the cupboard.'

'That's all right. I've got rum in the car. I'm certain you have some Coke,' said Jake confidently as he ran downstairs to his car in the driveway. He was back in seconds.

'Go on, hurry up, TC. I'll check for snakes, get myself a drink, and sit guard on the landing. Don't be too long. I've got a date at ten o'clock.'

'Of course, Jake,' said TC as she rushed to her room to get her pyjamas and gown.

⁋

TC quickly showered, dressed, and wrapped a towel around her wet hair.

'I knew you'd come out of there wearing a pink turban,' said Jake.

'You can go now, Jake,' said TC. Jake checked his watch, then sighed.

'No, I don't have to go yet. I've got time for another drink.'

'Suit yourself, Jake,' said TC. 'I'm sitting on the front steps. Out here reminds me too much of reptiles.'

Jake poured his drink while TC sat down and began towel-drying her hair.

'Don't you listen to the radio these days?' called Jake.

'Please turn it on, Jake,' replied TC while thinking, I can't believe I didn't turn on the radio. I must be getting old.

Jake plonked himself down on the top step next to TC, put his drink between them, then lit a cigarette.

'Vance told me what happened with Claudia, TC,' he said seriously after exhaling the first puff. TC said nothing, so Jake continued.

'TC, I'm frightened I'm going to end up like Vance, at his age and still screwing anything and everything that comes my way. I hope my upbringing would restrict me if I was married with a wife and kids.' TC thought before replying.

'Jake, not many men are like the boss.'

'Bullshit, TC! Most men play around, given the right opportunity and circumstances,' interrupted Jake.

'You didn't let me finish, Jake. The boss has a weakness for women of a certain kind. The opposite to Mrs Callahan and a woman he loves.'

'Her name is Anna! He told me about her!'

'That's right! I don't know what attracts the boss to his girlfriends. I don't think he knows himself. I do know he's forever telling me not to be like them.'

'Hopefully, after Claudia's performance, there won't be another one, TC,' said Jake.

'We can hope all we want, Jake, but we both know the boss. Consequently, we know there'll be another woman on his scene very soon.'

Jake checked his watch.

'I have to go, TC. I don't want to. I'd like to stay here talking to you. This is the first time you and I have had a conversation without someone else being around.'

'Off you go, Jake. You'll get a bad reputation if you start standing up your dates,' laughed TC. Jake smiled, then sighed.

'My reputation already sucks, TC. I'll see you soon. I'll leave my rum here. Put some beer in the fridge, will you? I like it cold!'

TC waved as Jake reversed onto the street. Not five minutes later, she saw his car come off the back street and turn towards the creek.

Jake is a lot like the boss, thought TC. The difference is Jake has half a dozen girlfriends who obviously don't mind sharing him whereas the women the boss attracts wouldn't share him in a fit, except with Mrs Callahan, that is.

TC was deliberating over whether to go to bed or wait up until Lou came home when the police car came around the corner. The lights twice blinked as it slowly cruised past. Her heart skipped a couple of beats.

'Graham has that effect on you,' she said aloud as she quickly stood up, closed the doors, and went to bed.

Lou came home from work to find TC asleep. She did not disturb her. She told herself TC needed the sleep to get rid of the dark circles under her eyes.

❡

Vance left the dispensary at midnight. He drove past the post office as Lou was leaving the exchange. He had spent the last hour wondering over where and how he would market his opal once TC had cut enough stones to give him credibility. He figured he needed at least a hundred. It had taken TC two long days to cut ten stones. Vance reckoned on her getting faster as she gained experience. Apart from that, the ten stones she had done were all large. Smaller stones would surely take less time from start to finish. He had selected ten pieces approximately half the size to get her started next morning before deciding it was time to go home. He needed sleep. Once again Vance locked the back door but forgot the front.

❡

TC switched on the course grinder at exactly 6 a.m. By the time Vance showed a couple of hours later, she was shaping the fourth of her ten stones. Again, all the opal faces were beautiful.

'Did you wet the bed, TC?' joked Vance. He was happy to see she was already shaping so early in the day.

'No, you told me to be here early. I was here at six.'

'Good girl! Make me a cup of coffee,' replied Vance.

'No, Boss, you can make your own coffee if you don't mind,' replied TC. 'I'm busy. By the way, you left the front door unlocked last night.'

'I did yesterday morning, too, TC.'

'If that's the case, I'd best lock it behind me when I leave in the future. You've got too much on your mind. Please make your coffee and leave me alone. I'm timing myself today.'

TC heard the phone ring several times and Vance answer it before she finished shaping her stones.

'I'm going to do the backs first today, Boss. I want to find out which process I prefer.'

'Do whatever you want, TC,' replied Vance. He was at his desk smoking and looking desolate.

'What's happened now?' asked TC with concern.

'The rush is on, TC. There'll be three opal miners from South Australia here next week. Going to try their luck!'

'You knew that would happen,' replied TC. 'We are way ahead of them! You already have a huge pile of boulders, and, judging by these stones, it's beautiful opal. Don't worry about it, Boss. They'll probably come and go like the gold rushes in the movies.' Vance cracked up.

'Maybe some Hollywood producer will make a movie about Brolga's opal rush. I wish they'd make one now; they might pay me enough money to keep mining.'

'You'll keep mining, Boss. It's in your blood now,' said TC seriously as she lit the wick to melt the wax for dopping.

'I'm going to camp, TC. You'll hear the phone from the polishing room. Keep an eye on the counter through the one-way mirror.'

'That kisses my timing goodbye.' Vance shrugged.

'I have to see the men. Do the best you can. Come early again tomorrow.'

'Sure, but don't complain if the stones aren't finished because I'm leaving at eight, finished or not.'

'Try to finish them before you go, TC.'

'I can walk on water, too, Boss,' mumbled TC. She continued fixing the stones face down to the dop-sticks.

¶

Vance refuelled his ute and started for camp. He was at the end of the bitumen when he remembered Yappy's money. He turned around and drove back to town.

Jake was talking with a Stock and Station Agent on the footpath in front of Carmichael and Carmichael. Vance sat in his ute and waited until the agent left. Jake leaned and spoke to Vance through the ute window. 'How you going, mate?'

'I'm heading to camp, Jake. You asked me to collect Yappy's winnings. On second thought Jake, how about coming with me and paying the little prick yourself. It will be a flying visit. We'll get there, have a yarn with Yappy and the others, turn around, and come back to town.'

'Sounds good to me, mate. I'll tell my people to grab the little mongrel's money and be back in a minute.'

They chatted about this, that, and everything else en route to camp. They also laughed a lot about past shared experiences, local characters, and the wiles of women.

¶

Yappy was finishing washing up the men's lunch dishes when he heard the ute approaching.

'Vance has come at bloody last,' he said to the dish in his hand. 'About bloody time!' He bustled outside to greet Vance with a tongue-lashing for not having come to see them for a whole week. His mood changed to happy when he saw Jake was there.

'You young bastard, hope you brought me more winnings.'

'As a matter of fact, I did Yappy,' replied Jake.

'What about me, Yappy?' said Vance pretending to be hurt.

'Stuff you, Callahan, you bastard. You haven't been here for bloody ever. Suppose you are bloody hungry.'

'Suppose you're bloody right, Yappy,' replied Vance, who was subconsciously comforted by the sound of the loader operating a few hundred yards away.

'No need for sarcasm, Vance! I get enough of that shit from Neil and Faith,' responded Yappy seriously. 'There's another ute-load of boulders there for you. The men and the machine have been working hard. I don't know how the poor bastards keep going in this heat, Vance. They're knackered at the end of every day. They don't complain, though. As a matter of fact, the poor bastards are knackered before they even start in the morning.'

'You and Jake do your business, Yappy. I'm going to talk to the men,' said Vance.

'So, I'm not a bloody man?' came back Yappy.

'Of course, you are, Yappy,' placated Jake. 'We'll discuss our business while Vance talks to Neil, Faith, and Little Joe about their business.'

'All right if I go, Yappy?' asked Vance imitating a small child seeking his mother's permission to leave the room.

'Get out of here, Callahan. Jake and I have serious business to discuss,' replied Yappy as only Yappy could do.

Vance walked towards the sound of the loader, wondering where on earth he was going to get the money to pay Yappy and the others when they went on break.

§

'Here's your winnings, Yappy,' said Jake in the camp kitchen. He handed over five hundred quid. 'We had two bets, Yappy. One paid four, the second horse, six.'

'Shit, Jake, you're making me a rich man.' Jake smiled.

'On a roll, Yappy, mate. It won't last forever. Let's enjoy the ride.'

'You must have won a lot, Jake?' said Yappy while depositing his five hundred in an empty powdered-milk container on a shelf above the bench.

'I won a few quid, mate,' replied Jake lightly. He had bet two thousand pounds on each of the two horses and won twenty all up.

'You already always look like a bloody millionaire, Jake,' said Yappy. 'Soon you'll be one.'

'Time will tell, Yappy, time will tell!'

¶

Vance was welcomed by Faith and Little Joe. Neil stopped the loader and jumped down.

'Thought we'd been abandoned, Boss!'

'I wouldn't do that, mate!' laughed Vance.

'Not when there's more boulders waiting for you to take back to town,' said Faith with a smile. Vance laughed.

'You could be right, Faith. Who knows? Jake's with me. We're not staying long. I have to get back to town. TC's started cutting stones. They're pretty good.'

'You should have brought some stones to show us,' said Neil. 'We bust our guts finding the bloody stuff. I think we deserve to see the finished product.'

'Me, too,' muttered Faith. Little Joe nodded in agreement.

'You are right, I should have,' apologised Vance. 'Next time, I promise. Come on, call it a day. I've got Jake with me. We can't stay long.'

'We'll be saying that when we get to town on break,' quipped Faith.

'That's right mate. We'll be no sooner in Brolga than we'll be on the Flea and heading towards Sydney,' said Neil. Vance laughed and looked skywards.

'Poor Sydney.'

'I think we should go to Brisbane. It's closer to home,' said Faith.

'Me, too,' said Little Joe.

'We'll see,' said Neil.

¶

Vance, Jake, Yappy, Neil, and Faith talked and laughed outside the kitchen while Little Joe suggested it was time to load the boulders into the back of the ute. He was tired of listening to the never-ending bullshit being parleyed by all but himself.

'Vance and Jake haven't eaten any of my bloody tucker yet,' complained Yappy.

'Lucky them!' said Faith.

'Go screw yourself, mate,' from Yappy.

'Calm down, all of you,' said Neil. 'Let's get these bloody boulders into the back on the ute before I jump into the bastard myself. I've had a gutful of this joint.'

Both Vance and Jake recognised Neil's mood. He'd had enough! Obviously they all had. Everyone, including Yappy, quickly loaded the boulders into the ute.

After numerous 'Good to see you, mates,' from Jake and the men, Vance said, 'I'll be back as soon as I can,' before driving away with relief that he was leaving a somewhat volatile situation behind him.

'Can't blame the poor bastards,' said Jake. 'They've been out here forever and a day.'

'How much money do I owe you, Jake?' asked Vance seriously.

'I don't know, mate, ten, maybe twelve,' replied Jake.

'It's twelve, Jake. The men are all going on break. I think it's time to put the plan we talked about a while back into action.'

'I've got plenty of money at the moment, mate,' replied Jake matter-of-factly. 'I'll find you whatever you need.'

'No! I can't bludge off you forever, Jake. I'll cause a drama with Delores. She'll piss off with the kids. Then we'll do it.'

'Whatever is right for you, mate,' agreed Jake. 'By the way, I think I'm in love with TC'

Vance was momentarily silent.

'She's too good for the likes of you! Concentrate on your tarts.'

'You do the same, mate!' replied Jake. He was not happy.

❡

Jake and Vance didn't exchange many more words during their return journey to Brolga. Both were deep in their own thoughts. Vance was conjuring methods to evoke Delores to a state of mind where she would pack herself and the kids up and leave.

Jake was relieved when Vance finally dropped him off. He was going to jump in his car, go home, tell his mother he loved her, get cleaned up, then go to the Empire.

❡

TC was in the process of writing a note to Vance when he arrived in the dispensary via the rear door.

'Did you finish the stones, TC?'

'Yes!' replied TC shortly. 'Claudia sliced her wrists. The train cleaners found her in Brisbane. She was rushed to the hospital by an ambulance. They asked her what happened to her throat. She's going to tell them you tried to kill her.' Vance's face went white.

'Who contacted you?'

'She did! She wants another thousand!' 'I reminded her I was there, too. I don't recall seeing anything unwarranted occur. Claudia told me to get stuffed. I told her to do the same. I'm going home.'

'Thank you, TC. You have grown up, that's for bloody sure.' TC shook her head.

'How could I help but do so? I'll see you tomorrow.'

'What would you do, TC?' called Vance as she opened the front door.

'I already told you, Boss. I told her to get stuffed.'

'I don't want you talking like that, TC,' replied Vance curtly.

'We don't always get what we want, Boss,' replied TC with a shrug before locking the door behind her.

Vance made himself a coffee and sat at his desk to peruse the stones. They were beautiful.

TC's right about Claudia, he thought. Stuff Claudia! If I give her another thousand. The bitch will blackmail me till Doomsday.

¶

TC went home and showered. She didn't give a tinker about the snakes. If one bit her and caused her to die, so what!

¶

Vance tossed up options of actions which would cause Delores to leave him. He wished he was drunk! He was not! He'd have to do this one stone-cold sober!

After hours of contemplation, he cleared the cash register. Delores would need some money. Vance drove home and created a scene over sweet bugger-all, the kids crying, he couldn't sleep, et cetera.

Delores and the children left Brolga in the station wagon early next morning.

'We'll be back when you wake up to yourself, Vance,' said Delores unemotionally before driving away.

'I know!' replied Vance confidently while feeling devoured by guilt. He'd hit rock bottom. He checked his cigarette packet before driving to the creek where he sat in deep meditation until it was time to open the shop.

¶

TC was shaping stones when Vance walked in. He was all smiles.

'How long have you been here, TC?'

'Since five. You didn't leave anything for me to cut, so I grabbed ten pieces from the top of what's left in the bucket. There's an opal man from Coober Pedy sitting in his car out front of the shop. He's been there since before I came in at five. Leave me alone, please, Boss. I want to concentrate.'

TC paid little attention a few minutes later when Vance made coffee for two. By the time she had finished shaping her ten stones, the Coober Pedy miner had gone.

'What are you going to do about Claudia, Boss?'

'Nothing!' replied Vance.

'Good! There're a couple of mail orders beside the phone.'

TC met Lou at Con's a little after siren time. They sat with Lisa at her table as usual.

'Mrs Callahan has gone away again. The boss said we can borrow any of his records we fancy. He said we can borrow the lot if we like.'

'I wonder why he's so thoughtful all of a sudden?' said Lisa. TC shrugged.

'I don't know. He told me out of the blue.'

'I'll go to his house and grab a few before I start work,' said Lou.

'TC, don't look around, darling. Constable Graham is in the doorway. Looks like he's been caught off-guard by one of the giggling tennis girls,' said Lisa with contempt. He looks adorable in his uniform, as always,' she added matter-of-factly.

'Graham looks adorable in anything, Lisa,' said TC wistfully. Her heart was racing. She couldn't help but feel more than a little jealous when she heard the girl flirting with Graham laughing loudly.

Vance was in the Empire with Jake. Jess placed a beer on the bar in front of Jake and a Coke in front of Vance.

'Bet you wish there was a glass of rum and ice to go with the Coke, Mr Callahan,' said Jess with a forced smile. Vance laughed.

'I think you'd win the wager, Jess!'

'What are you babies whispering about?' asked Louise when it came time for refills. 'Don't tell me you are planning to knock over one of the banks!'

'Mind your own business, Louise,' said Vance. 'Do your job. Jake wants a beer. I'll have another Coke.'

Louise laughed. While drawing Jake's beer, she wondered what on earth they were up to.

'See you then, Jake,' said Vance after they finished their second drink.

'I'll be there, mate,' replied Jake while collecting his change from the bar.

¶

TC noticed Vance was agitated. All afternoon he sat at his desk, chain-smoking with one hand while he tapped the fingers on his other hand. Even when she presented him with ten perfectly shaped and polished, magnificent opals, his spirits didn't lift.

'I'm going home now, Boss. I'll see you tomorrow,' said TC.

'I hope so, TC,' replied Vance off-handedly. It was as if he was in another world.

The Boss is probably worried about Mrs Callahan leaving, thought TC as she locked the front door.

Come five-past-midnight, TC was sitting on the stairs, waiting for Lou to come home from the telephone exchange.

¶

Jake and Vance were splashing kerosene over the floorboards and furniture in Vance's house. They worked quickly in the silent darkness. Most of Brolga's inhabitants were in their beds asleep. The sergeant had finished his rounds. He'd gone home earlier after seeing the pubs close. Graham was in his red-and-white Ford with one of the tennis girls. They were parked at the creek. Vance worked on the front section of the house while Jake doused the rear rooms.

Shit! Why the hell didn't those stupid girls borrow more records? thought Vance while pouring kerosene over two high piles of LPs.

'Are you ready?' called Jake from the back doorway.

'Yes, light up now,' replied Vance from the front verandah.

Simultaneously, they struck matches and threw them onto the kerosene-soaked floorboards before running to their cars parked two blocks away in different directions.

Jake drove home to his mother's house. As quietly as possible, he crept to his bed. For once Thel Carmichael didn't hear her eldest son come home!

❡

Vance quickly drove via the back streets to his cutting room, made a cup of coffee, and smoked a couple of Craven As before laughing as he fed a boulder to the razor blade.

Jake and I have burned down the house, he thought. The insurance will pay ten thousand more than what I need to pay the men! Pity about the bloody records!

❡

Vance's house was the last one on the western end of Brolga's main street, apart from his neighbours. No one was aware of the tragic fire until it was too late to do anything.

'Looks like it's too late to save the Pill-Pusher's Joint. Might as well watch the bastard burn,' said the husband to his wife as they observed the yellow flames rising skywards.

'Someone should find Vance,' said the wife.

'Don't worry about it, darls,' replied the husband casually. 'The poor bugger will know when he gets home and finds he has no bed.'

'Fair enough!' agreed the wife. 'We better call the cops.'

❡

'Your house has burnt down, mate,' said the sergeant when he located Vance sawing through boulders in the rear of the cutting room. Vance pretended shock.

316

'Don't eff with me, mate!'

'I'm not, Vance. Your house went up in flames. I had to get out of bed, mate. Looks like you'll be sleeping in one of the pubs for a while. I'm going home. I'm getting old, I need my sleep.'

Vance lifted another boulder onto the cutting bench. He smiled as he pushed it towards the saw blade. He realised Jake and he had successfully burned down his house without anyone having a clue it was purposefully orchestrated.

'I'll borrow the money from Jake to pay the men. When the insurance company comes good, I'll repay him. Easy! Piece of cake!'

❡

Brolga buzzed as the locals pondered on the cause of the fire.

Jock and his Seat of Knowledge mates weren't fooled. The night after fire had destroyed Vance's house, they had a lengthy discussion.

'Callahan's place looks funny from the road,' said Jock. 'I drove past there this afternoon on my way to the dump. Black ash is still smouldering. All that's left standing is the fence, shithouse, clothesline, and a few stubborn house stumps.'

'Don't forget the chook-yard full of rocks,' said one of Jock's cronies.

By closing time at the Empire, they had agreed on a name for the fire. Future Brolga generations would need a substantial title of reference.

'Don't know how the smart bastard did it, but he did do it,' said Jock. 'In the future, we'll refer to last night's occurrence as "The Pill-Pusher's Funds Fire".'

They all nodded in agreement, laughed, and headed towards their homes.

❡

Life went on in Brolga.

TC continued producing ten cut and polished, magnificently-coloured opal gemstones per day. Vance took up residence in the rear of the Majestic. Ironically, he was housed in the same room Bert Black and Leanne had shared previously.

Jake dropped in on the girls whenever he came up with a pleasurable excuse. Usually it was to do a search for snakes prior to the girls showering.

Whenever Graham was on patrol and the girls happened to be perched on the stairs, he would blink the police car lights as he passed by. He was too embarrassed by his new-found popularity with the tennis club girls to face TC.

Vance travelled to camp to collect the men. At last they were going on break. Prior to leaving the camp, Neil drove the loader to within feet of the kitchen, where he lovingly parked it before jumping to the ground, kissing his hands before slamming them against the loader door, saying, 'See you after the break, baby.'

The men folded their wire bunks and swags. They placed them securely under the flap at the western end of the marquee before throwing their gear into the back of the ute.

Yappy happily got in the front of the ute with Vance while Neil, Faith, and Little Joe climbed into the back.

'At last, we are free men!' declared Neil.

'This time next week, we'll be in Sydney,' said Neil.

'Or Brisbane!' said Faith hopefully.

'At least, we'll be away from camp,' said Little Joe.

'Where are you off to, Yappy?' asked Vance while driving over the dirt road. He didn't care where Yappy was going nor what Yappy planned on doing. He asked the question as a means of conversation, not interest.

'Don't know, Vance. Got a sister who lives in the central west. I'll probably pay her a visit. What are you going to do for Christmas, Vance?'

Vance laughed loudly before replying.

'I've got a wife and kids in Brisbane, mate. I'll probably pay them a visit.'

'Smart bastard!' laughed Yappy.

Faith, Neil, and Little Joe were drunk by thinking about getting to the Majestic and hitting the grog. Every mile they travelled in the back of Vance's ute, the more plastered they became, if not in body, they sure as buggery were in mind.

On reaching town, Vance parked behind the pharmacy. In the dispensary, he paid each of the men thirteen hundred quid before ushering them out through the front while telling them, tongue-in-cheek, to behave themselves, have a great break, and he'd be waiting to hear from them when they got into trouble or ran out of money.

'I'm going to see my Mum and give her a few quid. I'll meet you bastards in the Majestic in an hour,' said Neil.

'The Flea goes in the morning, Neil,' reminded Faith. 'Doesn't go again till Sunday. If we miss it tomorrow, mate, we'll be too pissed to catch the bastard on Sunday.'

'I know. We'll be on it. If Jake's at the pub, tell him he's coming with us.' Little Joe took a deep breath. He followed Faith to the Majestic.

Yappy confidently strode across the street to the Empire, where he hoped he would find his gambling mate, Jake.

Vance remained confidently in the dispensary. The Romeo Brothers had replaced Claudia with a very nice woman. Her name was Coral. She had purchased lipstick from him earlier in the week when TC was busy in the polishing room. He was due to meet Coral outside the Empire staff quarters in an hour. They would park by the creek, hopefully have sex, and cement a relationship. Coral drank gin and tonic. So what! She could buy her own. If nothing else, Coral would help him fill in time until summer passed. He would have to find another house for his family, route a marketing avenue for his opal, and keep the shop going.

Vance had resigned himself to the fact of work experience and would-be, "let's have a go" people flocking to the Brolga area. In the meantime, it was as hot as Hades! No one in their right mind would be mining now. Surely not!

❡

Unbeknown to Vance, a Greek had secured an opal mining lease ten miles down a beaten track off the main road between Brolga and Vance's mine. He was known to his ex-girlfriends in the Northern Territory as Greg the Greek. He was movie-star handsome, and his eyes were as deep as the blue Pacific. He was a loner. He had to be!

A few months previously, Greg had heard about Vance's find over a few beers in a Darwin pub. Late that night, he had knifed the publican to death during a fight over the publican's wife with whom the deceased had discovered Greg having wild, no-holds-barred sex in an upstairs bedroom.

Greg immediately gathered together his sparse worldly goods. He hitched a ride with an interstate truck driver to Curloo, where he spent a week-and-a-half mucking around waiting for a "miner's right" to come through from the Mines Department in Brisbane. He bought a ute in Curloo and managed to slip in and out of Brolga like a midnight shadow.

As yet, to his knowledge, apart from two feral cats he had found along the way, no Brolgaites were aware of his pitched tent and himself smack bang in the middle of his claim, which he had hopefully named "The Small Miracle".

To Greg the Greek's thinking, it would be a huge miracle if he found opal. He didn't have so much as a shovel. He did have a tent and at least a supply of canned food.

¶

Two Croatian brothers were parked on their lease not more than twenty miles from Greg's Small Miracle. They too had managed to slip through Brolga's gossip net undetected. They were better equipped than Greg. They had a truck and a loader. They had constructed a tin shed in which to sleep, cook, and dine. The brothers had enough Scotch whisky to sink a ship. They drank the Scotch straight every night as they played poker by campsite light.

While the Croatian Brothers had ways and means to occasionally go shopping for essentials in Brolga, Greg the Greek was hoping his ferals would produce offspring soon. He was hungry! The canned food wouldn't last forever.

❡

In Andamooka, Coober Pedy, and Lightening Ridge, future Brolga opal miners were relaxing. They would wait for Christmas and the summer to be over before making their moves on Brolga and the smart-arse chemist who had accidentally found the best bloody opal they would ever see.

❡

Neil, Faith, and Little Joe drank as much grog as they could handle at the Majestic before camping on the railway station platform. No way were they going to miss the Flea next morning.

❡

Vance had a good time with Coral.

At least this one is sane, he thought. Absolute opposite of Claudia. I don't care how much gin and tonic she drinks; I'll have fun watching her.

❡

Graham was going east to spend Christmas with his much-loved family. Lou and TC were perched on the stairs when Graham screeched his red-and-white Ford to stop opposite them.

'I love you, TC,' he yelled before taking off.

'I love you, too, Graham. Happy Christmas,' mouthed TC.

'What are you doing Christmas Day, TC?' asked Lou.

'I don't know!' replied TC bluntly.

'My Mum would invite you to our place except Dad always gets pissed, bungs on a turn, and they have a fight,' replied Lou matter-of-factly.

Yappy didn't last very long with his sister and family in Central Western Queensland. He missed the men.

The mongrels piss me off a lot, he thought lovingly. I'm going back to Brolga. Jake and I can keep each other company. Hopefully, we'll win money on the nags while I wait for the men to come back.

Yappy's mind was made up. He purchased lavish Christmas gifts for his sister, her kids and husband before heading back to Brolga by the same means he had left. He thumbed a ride from town to town with the first truckie who needed company.

¶

'Jake, I want you to invite TC for Christmas,' said Jake's mother, Thel. 'I know Lou will be going to her parents. I don't want to have to think about TC being by herself at Doug and Flo's. She's a nice girl, Jake. It's about time you settled down.'

'Yeh, Mum, yes, yes, yes,' complied Jake. 'I'll ask her!'

'Thank you, Jake,' smiled Thel Carmichael as Jake scowled and left the family lunch table.

Women! thought Jake. I've got stupid bloody TC nagging on my mind twenty-four bloody hours a day. Now it's Mum's turn.

'I'll see you later, Mum,' said Jake. He kissed his mother on the cheek before acknowledging his brothers and sisters who were sitting at the table thinking, What about us, Jake?

'See you later, too.'

Everyone smiled. Jake jumped in his car and drove away. He was nervous. What if TC knocked back his mother's invitation? Anyway, he decided to throw caution to the wind. Whatever his mother desired, he would get it for her—if he could, that was! Jake swallowed his pride. He parked behind the chemist shop, strode inside, and said to TC, 'My mother expects you to be at our house for Christmas.'

TC was caught off-guard. She was in the process of polishing an opal. She nodded at Jake.

'Your mother is a nice lady. Please thank her. I'll be there.'

'Good!' said Jake.

TC resumed swiping the opal up and down, over and across the polishing buff.

Jake was cheesed off as he did a wheelie before driving at breakneck speed to park his car on the street directly in front of Carmichael and Carmichael. He had hired a new girl a few weeks previously. She kept giving him an inviting eye while laughing at every joke he cracked. Her name was Madison. She was the daughter of a Brolga Council worker who periodically scrounged the dump in search of Brolgaite's discarded possessions. Madison was also a virgin! Jake intended to deflower her, come hell or high water.

Madison was a petite, sixteen-and-a-bit-year-old with short, blonde hair. She was not pretty; neither was she plain. She had a squeaky, screechy voice and eyes that lit up like twinkling stars on a clear night sky whenever Jake was in proximity.

Madison was Jake's younger sister's school friend. When college in Brisbane broke up for the year, Madison's parents gave her the news she would have to leave school. They could no longer afford to pay her tuition at the fancy Brisbane ladies college. They had Madison's younger sister to consider. Everyone in their family had to get the same breaks!

After continuous badgering by her daughter, Thel Carmichael insisted Jake employ Madison in the family business. Thel felt sorry for Madison having to leave school. As always, Jake fulfilled his mum's request.

¶

Christmas Eve was hot. Very hot!

Many Brolgaites had left town to visit relatives or friends, mostly in the east. Of those who remained, the drinkers stocked up with grog. The pubs were closed on Christmas Day. The women cooked. Some men did too.

'Don't know why mad bloody women cook so bloody much,' said Jock to the sacred-seat gentry.

'Be too bloody hot to eat! Christmas is just another bloody day as far as I'm concerned.'

'We'll have to fight the bloody blowflies off before we get a mouthful of tucker, anyway,' added one of Jock's mates.

With eyes glued to the Empire's open windows for any sign of action within, everyone on the Seat of Knowledge laughed in agreement.

¶

Jake was in the Empire bar with a few mates. Not one of their mothers permitted alcohol in their homes.

'Be a dry argument tomorrow,' predicted Jake. 'Better get a gutful tonight. It will give us an excuse to sleep in.'

'In your bloody dreams, Jake. You know very well our mums will insist on us fronting up to bloody mass,' laughed one of Jake's drinking mates.

'Oh, shit! I forgot about that, mate,' complained Jake as he placed his empty beer glass on the bar.

'I'll switch to Rum and Coke, Jess. That way I'll be plastered faster.'

'You are all mad!' declared Jess with a scowl. 'Young mongrels should cherish your mothers for the pain they went through giving birth to you.'

Jess dumped their empty glasses in the sink to rinse before gathering fresh ones and pouring more drinks.

'Come on, Jess, you know we all love you,' said Jake suavely. His head was already showing signs of wobbling, and there were still a few hours till closing time.

¶

'I'm not working Christmas Day, Boss,' announced TC after her ten stones for the day were neatly displayed on Vance's desk. 'I'm going to Jake's mum's house.'

'Be careful of Jake,' advised Vance.

'I am,' replied TC bluntly. 'Happy Christmas, Boss. All your money problems will be history this time next year.' TC smiled, then kissed Vance on the cheek before leaving.

I hope you're right, Little One, thought Vance as he watched TC lock the front door. Sometimes of late I think you are a thousand years old instead of not nineteen yet. He went to switch off the sanding/polishing room light. On TC's stool was a neatly gift-wrapped package and a card which read, 'Best worst boss in the world. Happy Christmas! TC.

Vance was not the sentimental type. He felt embarrassed as he tore the wrapping from his gift. He hadn't so much as wished TC a Happy Christmas. He laughed when he saw the carton of Craven As and a note.

'Know you'll need these, Boss. Enjoy! I'll be at work at five on Boxing Day. Please leave pieces for me.'

TC met Lou at Con's. They wished Lisa and Con Happy Christmas before consuming heart-shaped scoops of chocolate ice cream, compliments of Con's Café, of course. Con and Lisa were joining the Romeo Brothers and their wives for Christmas Day lunch in the dining room of the Empire.

Yappy hadn't made it back to Brolga for Christmas. He became morose on hearing the 'Up on the Roof' song on the truck radio a few minutes before the obliging, "I'll give you a lift, mate" truckie hauled his loaded truck into a one pub-cum-service-station-post-office-boarding-house-and-general-store stop called Wingtree. Yappy was loaded with cash.

Stuff it! he thought. That bitch broke my bloody heart. A man might as well stay here and piss it up against the pub wall. He jumped down from the truck, dragging his gear behind him.

'Thanks for the lift, mate. I'll buy you the best feed this joint's got to offer, then I'm going to drink the dump out of grog or myself out of dough, whichever comes first.'

Come pub closing time at ten, Lou and TC were seated on the stairs, waiting to hear Colin's request for Lou hitting the airwaves of 2UE. It was midnight in Sydney. Christmas Day!

"This is a special request from my mate, Colin, on Sydney's North Shore, for his lovely Lou in outback Queensland," announced the DJ. "Happy Christmas, Lou. Here we go. It's the King singing, 'Loving You'."

Lou immediately jumped to her feet and bounced around the verandah.

'I love him, TC,' she squealed while tears flowed from her eyes. TC began crying herself. She got to her feet and hugged her friend.

'I think you should go to Sydney, Lou. The sooner, the better.' They cried in each other's arms.

There was a screech of tyres and dirt flying all over the place when Jake whirled his car into the driveway. Jake was drunker then fifteen bastards on a good night out.

'Sounds as if Jake has passed his wobbly-head stage,' said Lou matter-of-factly while wiping evidence of tears from her cheeks and leading the way to the back landing. TC looked towards the ceiling and shrugged.

'What else can we expect from Jake?'

'I couldn't wait until tomorrow to see you,' mumbled Jake as he slowly negotiated the back stairs. His arms were laden with booze.

'I've got Coke in the car. Go get it,' he slurred as he plonked six bottles of Bundaberg rum and a carton of beer on the kitchen table.

'Go to buggery, Jake,' responded Lou curtly.

'Get it yourself, Jake!' said TC. 'We didn't invite you here. Six bottles of rum is ridiculous, Jake.'

'Yes, Jake, I agree with TC,' said Lou.

Little Richard was screaming from 2UE in the background. Jake turned on the girls and mumbled.

'I've had enough of whinging bloody women.' He lurched towards the landing and stairs.

'I'm going to get the bloody Coke myself. By the way, I'm going to marry you, TC.'

'In your dreams, Jake,' said TC so softly she didn't think Jake would hear her.

'What are you going to do with him!' whispered Lou, who also underestimated Jake's hearing range.

'Throw me in the bloody creek, that's what you can do with me,' called Jake over his shoulder while endeavouring to retrieve a carton of Coke from the boot of his car.

'Having trouble there, Jake?' said Lou while running downstairs to assist. 'You're so drunk, you might drop the damned thing. Give it here.'

Bossy bitch, thought Jake as he slammed his car boot closed before staggering in Lou's path up the stairs and into the house. He settled himself on the front verandah squatter's chair before falling asleep within seconds.

⁊

Neil, Faith, Little Joe, and newcomer Jakkie were in a pub in Brisbane. That's as far as they got! The hotel was located in the heart of the city and had everything the men required, including three bars, great rooms, a publican who was hungry for their money, and a juke box that lit up with bright colours flittering all over the place every time a coin was deposited.

⁊

Brad once again proposed marriage to Sam.

'Why not,' agreed Sam. 'After all, you did try to do away with yourself over me.' Brad was elated. The girl he loved would soon be his wife.

⁊

Graham was at his parents' home a short distance inland from the coast. While he enjoyed being the shining star and centre of attention, his mind persistently wandered to Brolga and TC.

⁊

The sun blazing through his aunt and uncle's louvered verandah windows woke Jake early.

'I hate these rotten windows,' he said to himself as he sat up and looked at his watch. 'Better make mum happy. I'll go home, take a shower, and go to mass.' Jake paused at TC's bedroom door. She was sound asleep while curled up hugging her pillow.

Little bitch, he thought before taking a leak over the back landing, grabbing a beer from the fridge, and driving home, deep in thought regarding the debacle ahead of him later in the day.

Mass for his mother's sake was simple. He was worried about TC and Madison. They were going to be in his mother's house simultaneously—TC because his mother had chosen her as the perfect prospective wife for him, and Madison because his young sister had invited her, after lunch, of course. Still, it was going to be a bloody fiasco, conceded Jake as he walked through his mother's front door.

¶

Vance and Coral were in the dispensary. They'd been there since last night's closing of the Empire. Vance would prefer to be in his room behind the Majestic, but Coral was afraid of the consequences should Jack and or Bert Romeo see or hear she was there. Vance had compromised by fetching the pillow and bed linen from the room and placing same on the dispensary floor.

Neither Vance nor Coral had enjoyed so much as a wink of sleep since retiring to the dispensary. Coral had knocked off a bottle-and-a-half of gin while Vance drank coffee after coffee and smoked countless cigarettes. They shared very little conversation. When either of them felt boredom closing, they would provoke prolonged sexual activity.

Any thoughts of Delores and his children were fleeting for Vance. Too much guilt!

Apart from coffee, gin, tonic water, and cigarettes, the only source of sustenance available to Vance and Coral that Christmas Day were jelly beans, dry biscuits, and multitudes of vitamins, neatly arranged on the chemist shop shelves.

¶

After Jake's and his friends' hypocritical "please our mums" attendance at the church service, they shook hands, wished each other Happy Christmas, and parted company by saying, 'See ya at the pub tomorrow morning, mate.'

Jake avoided the traditional Carmichael family Christmas breakfast by telling his mother he had to take care of something at their shop. In fact, he was hanging out for a reviver in the form of Rum and Coke. He invited himself back to the girls' house, where he enjoyed three drinks in thoughtful solitude before Lou and TC emerged from their bedrooms to join him at the dining room table.

'You're on the turps early, Jake,' said Lou imitating her dad. Jake looked at Lou, took a long drag on his cigarette, then a sip of his drink.

'I needed a heart-starter. As far as I know, there's no law against that.'

'Go to buggery, Jake,' said Lou. 'I'm going to take a shower, TC.'

After Lou went downstairs to the bathroom, Jake turned his attention to TC and warned her.

'I don't want to hang around forever after lunch at my mum's. So, don't go offering to wash the dishes. We leave as soon as we've eaten.'

'No problem, Jake,' replied TC. 'You sit there and get plastered. I'm going to make my bed. By the way, Happy Christmas.' Seconds later, TC heard Jake's car door slam and the car screech out of the driveway.

Bloody bitch, she's always right, thought Jake as he jammed his foot on the accelerator.

Lou and TC finally had an occasion to wear one of their new dresses.

'I hope I look as good as I feel,' said Lou when they were ready to their satisfaction. 'My dad probably won't notice, but my mum will appreciate my effort.'

Jake collected the girls at exactly noon. His face was like stone when they got into his car.

'You're in a foul mood, Jake,' said Lou. 'What's the problem?'

'Mind your own business, Lou,' snarled Jake. 'Both of you be quiet while you're in my car; otherwise, you'll have to walk.'

'I can see you're going to have a great time, TC,' said Lou. 'I'm glad I'm going to my parents' place.'

Jake turned to glare at Lou, and the car mounted the median strip for a few yards.

'Shut up, Lou,' yelled Jake. 'Your yapping will get us killed.'

'You're the driver, Jake!' responded Lou sweetly. TC remained silent. She wished she was going with Lou instead of to Mrs Carmichael's. She had no idea why Jake was in such a foul mood. She didn't care. Being nobody's fool, she was soon to find out.

Jake wanted to be going anywhere except his mother's. His young sister had insisted on Madison joining them for lunch. She would go to Madison's for dinner. Jake knew Madison would be all over him like a bloody rash. He also knew TC would zero in on the situation the second Madison started squealing and throwing herself at him. Sometimes he wished his mother was more streetwise and didn't always look at the world through rose-coloured glasses.

Mum can't see the bloody forest for the trees, he thought as he braked his car to a stop on his mother's drive. Carla came running to greet them. She was excited.

'TC, Mummy told me you were coming. I haven't seen you for a long time. I got lots of toys from Santa. I want to show you every one of them.'

'You've got plenty of time for that, Carla,' said Jake abruptly.

'Thanks for the lift, Jake. Wouldn't have missed it for the world,' said Lou with rampant sarcasm. 'Come across to see my mum and dad later, TC.'

TC nodded, 'I will,' as Carla thrust a door at her.

'She's beautiful, isn't she? She's got hair like yours, TC.'

'Jake's here!' announced a high-pitched screech from the front door, followed by Madison bounding towards Jake and throwing her arms around him.

Not here, Madison, he thought. 'Happy Christmas, Madison,' he said politely. 'This is TC, who works in the chemist shop.' Madison looked at TC, then turned back to Jake and shrugged.

'I know. Come on, Jake, let's go inside.'

'If your shorts were any shorter, they'd choke you, Madison,' remarked Jake with distaste.

Madison giggled. 'You told me I had good legs, Jake.'

Jake spoke hardly another word throughout lunch. He spoke only when absolutely necessary.

If it hadn't been for little Carla and Jake's brother, Duke, welcoming TC openly, she would have gladly run across the street to Lou and her parents. Of course, Thel Carmichael was as lovely as always. Under the circumstances, she was very busy. It was Christmas Day, her kids were home, and she had to give them her undivided attention. She did intend to have words with Jake. She hoped he hadn't been encouraging Madison to behave the way she was.

Madison's persistent and open flirting with Jake was embarrassing and quite unacceptable. TC was both relieved and surprised when, off the cuff, Jake spoke on her behalf.

'No dessert for TC and me, thanks, Mum. We promised Lou we'd meet her at the Shack.' He immediately stood up and pointed to his watch.

'Come on, TC. We're running late.'

'She can go by herself, Jake,' pleaded Madison.

'Off you go, both of you,' said Thel Carmichael sternly. 'Thank you for coming, TC,' she said with a smile.

'Get in the car, TC,' said Jake. 'I want to get as far away from this place as possible.'

As Jake started the car, Madison appeared at the front doorway and screeched, 'I thought you were going across the road, Jake.'

'Get effed, Madison,' said Jake almost inaudibly.

'I think she already has, Jake,' said TC with a shrug and knowing smile.

'We'll go by your place. I'll collect some grog. Then we'll come back to Jordan's,' said Jake. 'No one goes to the Shack without booze.'

'Especially when they haven't been invited,' agreed TC.

¶

'Some Christmas Day,' remarked Lou eight hours later when they left the Shack to walk home. 'My mum, you, and I watching my dad and Jake get smashed and bullshit to each other. I hope Colin's not a drunk!'

'Don't think so, Lou,' replied TC. 'His parents own a hotel. He's probably seen too many drunks to become one himself.'

'Did Jake get too drunk to drive you girls home?' called the sergeant from the police patrol car, which pulled alongside them.

'Something like that,' replied Lou with a smile.

'Come on, I'll give you a lift,' offered the sergeant.

'How did you know Jake was supposed to take us home, Sergeant?' asked TC curiously as she and Lou climbed into the back seat.

'I'm paid to know everything, young lady,' replied the sergeant with a smile. 'Constable Sandler is due back tomorrow night. Seeing he's not here to tell you, I'll tell you on his behalf. You both look very pretty. It's a shame more girls don't dress like you two.' Both Lou and TC smiled and were on the verge of tears.

'Wish my dad would say that,' said Lou.

'Thank you, Sergeant,' said TC. 'Thank you very much. It's nice to have someone say we look pretty.'

'Here we are, young ladies, home safe and sound,' said the sergeant before driving off.

'Your dad might not compliment you too often, but everyone he's ever shared a drink with knows he's proud of you.'

'Wish my parents had a phone,' said Lou. 'I'd call my dad and tell him I love him.'

'He knows that, Lou!' replied TC.

¶

The sergeant drove towards the police station thinking, Jordan, you should tell your daughter what you tell your mates about her. Constable Sandler, if you let TC slip through your fingers, you're a bloody fool.'

¶

At five sharp, TC unlocked the pharmacy door. She found Vance and Coral asleep on the floor. They each had a pillow. Both of them were naked. Cigarette butts were everywhere, two empty gin bottles on Vance's desk along with a few empty jelly bean packets. The dispensary smelt revolting.

TC threw Vance's jeans over his exposed private parts, then Coral's discarded skirt over hers before writing a note, which she left on the desk next to the gin bottles.

Grow up, Boss! I've had enough! You knew I'd be here at five. Getting off the booze has made you worse instead of better. Call me after you are clothed and have sterilised the dispensary. It stinks!

When TC left the shop, she deliberately slammed the door and left it unlocked.

'What's wrong, TC?' enquired Lou when TC stormed back into the house.

'Nothing! Everything, Lou,' replied TC, who at last felt hopeless to help Vance. 'Let's go and sit in the gutter outside Con's until he opens. I'm hungry.'

'And angry!' said Lou. 'I'll get dressed, TC. Perhaps we can sit on the sacred seat instead of in the gutter.'

'Everyone in Brolga knows I have done more than my share of that,' replied TC.

¶

Vance's eyes had sprung open when he heard the door to the shop slam. He sat up, absorbed the scene, and started shaking Coral.

'Eff it, Coral, wake up. Look at this joint. TC has been here! We haven't got any effing clothes on. Oh, shit, what an effing mess. Wake up, Coral! Put your clothes on and get out of here. Take your effing gin bottles with you!' Vance was beside himself as he quickly dressed and ran to the front door. What a surprise, he thought when he found it was not locked. Can't say I blame her. He frantically looked down the street. TC was nowhere in sight. She must have run home. Can't say I blame the poor little bugger for that, either. Fancy walking in and finding Coral and me stark naked. Shit!

Vance raced back to the dispensary. Coral was still on the floor with her skirt covering her bottom half. TC obviously put the skirt there. Coral had been too bloody drunk to do it. 'Coral, stand up and get your clothes on,' he yelled as he pulled her to her feet and shook her.

❡

Later, Lou and TC were seated on the Seat of Knowledge, hoping Con would soon appear to hose down the footpath in front of his establishment, when Coral staggered across the road towards the Empire staff quarters' gate. She was clutching a bottle of gin with both hands.

'Eff you, TC,' said Coral out of the corner of her mouth.

'All Vance's sluts tell her that,' stated Lou matter-of-factly.

❡

Vance bundled bedclothes from his Majestic room, then threw them into the front seat of his ute. Make it more discreet in order to smuggle the bloody stuff back, he thought. It was not until he'd cleared the dispensary floor and dumped the cigarette butts in the bin that he directed his attention to his desk and saw TC's note. He read it once, then quickly scrunched it before throwing it in the bin with the butts. He quickly retrieved it and re-read it over and over again.

'She's right,' Vance told himself. He flung open the back door and all the back windows, including the steel-barred one in the polishing room, before detailing, sterilizing, and whatever else he thought needed attention until the place was scrupulously clean and smelled of nothing but germ-killing antiseptic he had splashed and poured all over the place. After two cups of coffee and no cigarettes—he'd run out—Vance could still detect a "not too pleasant" odour. He sniffed his armpits and shirt collar before admitting the smell emanated from himself.

Of course, you dumb bastard, he told himself. What do you expect! You've been wearing the same bloody clothes since you and Jake burned down the house. A smart man would have stashed a few things away before doing the job. As soon as Con opens the café, I'll buy cigarettes, then contact Jake. I need fresh clothes. In the meantime, I'll fish through all the buckets. I'll find the best pieces I can for TC to cut and polish. Don't know what the eff I'll do if she tells me to get stuffed. No, she won't say that, he reasoned. All she will do is tell me to grow up. Hopefully, she'll start on more stones immediately.

¶

Con finally showed, hose in hand, ready to clean the footpath. He was surprised to see Lou and TC perched on the Seat of Knowledge.

'Pete from the pub has done his half an hour ago, Con,' called Lou.

'What are you doing here this early? It's supposed to be a holiday,' replied a laughing Con.

'Waiting for you, Con. We are hungry,' replied TC. Both girls were smiling with relief to see Con appear. By now the girls were on the footpath.

'Lou and I will hose off the footpath for you while you go inside and cook us breakfast. Could that be a plan?'

'Sounds like a good deal to me,' laughed Con as he dropped the hose before warning them. 'Make sure you roll it up neatly before you bring it inside to me.'

'Of course, we will,' chorused TC and Lou seriously.

After hosing, they went to great measures to present Con with the most perfectly coiled and knotted flexible water conveying tube he could ever see.

'I'll have to show my Lisa. You girls are clever,' said Con. 'No wonder she calls you her darlings.' Con then indicated to the girls' breakfasts, which came complete with heart-shaped, poached eggs. Both girls laughed and hugged Con, who shrugged, then threw his hands out and up.

'It's Christmas time!'

While TC and Lou were enjoying their breakfast and chatting with Con, Vance was driving to wake Jake. He needed new clothes and didn't dare wake Jake's mother by phoning so early.

Luckily, Vance spotted Jake's car parked in Jordan Blake's yard. He had no hesitation in knocking loudly on Jordan's door. The door was open. Jake was asleep on one chair and Jordan on the other. A couple of overflowing ashtrays, an almost empty rum bottle, and a couple of half-full glasses adorned the wooden table between the chairs. Neither man stirred. Vance put his face close to Jake's ear and yelled, 'Wake up, you drunken bastard! There's a fire!'

Jake was instantly awake. 'Oh shit, not another bloody one!'

Jordan remained asleep while Lou's mum jumped out of her bed and rushed into the room.

'Where's the fire!!' she asked frantic with panic.

'Sorry, Mrs Blake. I was playing a joke on Jake,' apologised Vance.

'Mad mongrels!' said lovely Mrs Blake. 'Get out of here. Take Jordan with you, as far as I'm concerned.'

'Come on, Jake. I need some new clothes,' said Vance. 'I've got what I'm wearing. Everything else was burned in the fire.'

'Poor man,' said Mrs Blake from her bed. 'Jordan and I are sad about that. Could happen to any of us.'

Jake jumped up and almost ran out the door. He was drowning in guilt, wide awake and alert. 'Follow me to my shop, you mad bastard,' he told Vance. 'Maybe I should give you a key to the dump so you can help yourself instead of waking me or catching me outside mass every bloody time you need something.' Vance laughed, so did Jake.

¶

Lou and TC were walking home from Con's. Vance's ute and Jake's car were parked out front of Jake's shop.

'Wonder what those two are up to,' pondered Lou casually.

'I don't know and I don't care,' was the indifferent reply.

What Vance and Jake were doing in Carmichael's store was talking. Vance had selected a few new sets of clothing. Now they were discussing their problems regarding women, mostly TC. Vance told Jake about TC finding Coral and himself stark bollocks in the dispensary, leaving the note, and slamming the door. Jake told Vance about Madison's performance at his mum's place and lying to get TC out of there quickly.

'I've told you before, Jake, leave TC alone!' said Vance. 'Stick with the sluts like I do, Jake! My problem is I need TC to cut the effing opal. After what she's seen this morning, who knows if she'll come back to me.'

'After what she saw yesterday, who knows if she'll come back to me,' retorted Jake.

'She's never been with you, Jake. I'm talking about working for me, cutting opals.' Jake pondered momentarily.

'I see what you mean, mate. I'm going home to get cleaned up. I suggest you do the same. You stink, mate!' Vance laughed.

'I haven't got a home anymore, Jake. We burned the bastard down!' Jake laughed, too, and they left the store.

¶

Attired in their two-piece bathing suits they had purchased on sale while in Sydney, Lou and TC decided to sit on the steps and play records as loud as they wished. Both neighbours were away, and there was no one working at the truck depot. They literally had the creek and main street of Brolga to themselves. It was as hot as buggery. They decided to

337

turn on the sprinkler, run through it, cool off, and sit back on the steps until they felt like running and standing under it again.

A song came on the country L.P. they had bought in Sydney. It was called, 'Let's Think About Living.'

'About time we did that, TC,' said Lou. 'What did you get for Christmas?' TC thought before replying.

'I got a card from you, a thick-shake from Con and Lisa, and a meal and Christmas wishes from Jake's mum. Also Happy Christmas and welcome from your mum and dad.'

'That's what I mean,' said Lou with a sigh. 'Colin said he sent me a present. I haven't got it yet! I'm in love, I think!'

TC could see Lou was heartbroken. She'd not seen her friend like this before. She didn't know what to say. She put her arm around Lou's shoulders and gently patted her. This was the closest TC had ever felt to Lou. Real nitty-gritty stuff. They had always breezed over everything without totally opening their innermost thoughts and/or feelings.

'Lou, if Colin said he sent you a Christmas present, I'm certain he did. He has all those songs played for you. Every one of them tells you he loves you.'

'Do you really think so, TC?'

'I know so Lou,' comforted TC with blind hope, before adding, 'Let's run under the sprinkler again. You are the one who said we have to think about living.'

Both girls were dripping wet and laughing when they heard the phone ring.

'Ignore it,' said TC. 'It's probably the boss.'

'I can't ignore it, TC. It might be Colin,' said Lou as she ran up the stairs. She was laughing and her heart was pounding in expectation of hearing Colin's voice. Lou's face dropped when she answered the telephone. It was Vance.

'Is TC there, please, Lou?'

'No, Vance. A handsome stranger on a white stallion rode off with her a half hour ago,' was Lou's dry reply.

'Don't be clever, Lou. Tell TC I want to talk to her,' from Vance. He was obviously desperate to speak with TC.

Lou hung up. She wasn't in the mood to play message girl. Apart from that, she wanted TC to herself today. TC was the only person in the world who understood how she felt about Colin—and every other thing for that matter.

Vance was angry and frustrated. How dare Lou hang up on him? He needed TC cutting stones. The opal sharks would swarm to Brolga in probably less than a month. If need be, he'll have to swallow his pride and beg the girl to come to work. He needed those stones cut! Vance threw his cigarette at the wall, kicked the counter, then picked up the telephone.

TC happened to be in the kitchen when the telephone rang. She knew it was Vance. Should it be Colin, she could apologise for the abrupt manner in which she answered.

'Yes! TC speaking.'

'TC, it's Vance. I need you to come to work. We need to get this opal cut.'

'You are the one who needs the stones cut, Mr Callahan. Not me! I told you I'd be there at five. I was! I'm off men forever if they look like you when they are naked. Pathetic!' Vance burst into laughter; he couldn't help it. TC was disgusted. He was laughing.

'This is not a laughing matter, Mr Callahan,' she snapped before slamming the phone into its cradle. Vance continued laughing. He sat down at his desk. He lit a Craven A, fiddled with the uncut pieces of boulder in front of him, then phoned Jake. He needed help to get TC back to cutting opal.

Jake was not very sympathetic.

'She doesn't have to be at work today. She was there at five; you and Coral were buck naked on the bloody floor, mate. What did you expect her to do, take no notice? I don't think so! Miss Bloody Prim and Proper has a right to be pissed off. I wouldn't mind walking in on Coral under those circumstances. I'd draw a bloody line at looking at your naked arse and whatever else you've got.'

'Give it a break, Jake. Be a mate! Get TC back to work today. I need those bloody stones.'

'I'll come up with something,' promised Jake. 'Any bloody thing is better than hanging around here with the family and Miss Madison, who just happened to arrive an hour ago. Apart from that, mate, I'm hanging out to go to the pub. I need a drink.' Short silence. 'Okay, I've got an idea. I'll talk to you later. Don't leave the bloody chemist shop for any bloody thing.'

Jake hurried to the bathroom and removed his deceased dad's cut-throat razor from the cabinet, then fervently took a half-empty bottle of tomato sauce off the kitchen bench, told his mum he'd see her later, and headed for his car and a drink at the pub.

Giggling, Madison pursued him to his car.

'Why and where are you going, Jake?'

'Out!' said Jake abruptly. 'Go back inside the house and play dolls with my little sister.' Jake drove to the rear of the cutting room, cut-throat razor and tomato sauce bottle in hand. He told Vance, 'Here, mate, pour tomato sauce on your wrist and open the cut-throat. When you hear me come back, I'll have TC with me. That's when you pick up the cut-throat and make out like you'll slit your bloody throat.

Vance laughed. 'She won't be fooled!'

'Trust me, mate, she'll be bloody fooled all right. I'll make the bitch believe you are going to do away with yourself. You keep up your end of the deal, mate. I guarantee she'll be at your effing cutting wheel or whatever you call the bloody thing the second she sees the tomato bloody sauce on your wrist and the cut-throat in your hand.' Vance said nothing.

Jake jumped in his car and sped via the back streets. He was going to make TC feel as guilty as buggery for letting Vance down. So what if it wasn't her fault? Nothing ever was! Screw her! He wished he could. The second he told the little bitch Vance was about to commit bloody suicide, he knew she'd be full of concern and climb bloody mountains if she had to in order to prevent it.

Blind bloody loyalty, thought Jake as his car hurtled into their drive way. The sprinkler was still twirling. Lou and TC were sitting on the stairs.

'Jake's got a burr up his butt over something,' said Lou matter-of-factly.

'Looks like it!' agreed TC.

Jake bounded the back stairs. He yelled as he ran through the hallway.

'Vance is going to slit his effing throat, TC! Poor bastard needs you to cut his opals! He's already done in one of his wrists.'

'Sure!' said TC shaking her head in disbelief.

'Bullshit!' said Lou also shaking her head.

'Come on, come on, we can't let the poor bastard do away with himself,' persisted Jake.

'You are a great actor, Jake,' said Lou. TC laughed.

'The boss must be desperate to pull this scam. Tell him I'll be there soon, Jake.' Jake relaxed.

'All right if I use your phone? I want to call Vance and tell him to wipe the blood off his wrist.'

TC felt trapped. She took a deep breath and sighed. 'Tell the boss I'll be there soon Jake.' Jake made the call to Vance, advising him all was clear, TC had surrendered.

'Forget the tomato sauce deal, mate. Keep the cut-throat handy. If she bungs on a turn, you can threaten her with it.' Vance laughed, relaxed, and lit a cigarette. Brolga Opals was about to be back in production.

§

Little Joe, Faith, Neil, and Jakkie had not ventured outside the confines of their Brisbane hotel since checking in. The way they saw it was, why bother to go anywhere else when their needs were fulfilled where they already were. The publican catered to their every whim! To his way of thinking, they were harmless bush bums with a seemingly bottomless pit of money to spend in his establishment. Only time they caused a problem was when one of the four got down on his knees and played in front of the juke box. The changing dazzling lights appeared to have an effect on the man when he was pissed to the stage of passing out. In the meantime, as long as the money kept flowing out of the men's pockets and into his cash register, the publican didn't give a stuff. When one of the staff complained about Jakkie praying to the juke box, he told them to be tolerant.

'The man's harmless. He's got money to spend. So have his mates. Money is what pays your wages, in case you've forgotten.' The staff member did not complain again. Neither did her fellow-workers.

§

Yappy was in Wingtree drinking, drinking, drinking while reminiscing about his past lost love. He was throwing money around like confetti at a wedding. Other patrons of Wingtree Pub that time of year were stranded by choice—drovers, shearers, and transients like Yappy, who didn't care where the eff they were as long as this bullshit time of year passed quickly. Brought back too many memories for all of them. Some sad, some happy. Whatever! These memories were best forgotten. Left in the past where they belonged. The way to do that was to drink themselves into oblivion.

§

Come midnight, TC finished cutting and polishing ten of the most beautiful boulder opal stones the world would ever see. Coral was sitting on Vance's lap near the dispensary desk, full glass of gin and tonic, half-empty gin bottle, and overflowing ash tray. TC carefully spread the stones on a towel next to the ashtray.

'I'm going home now, Boss. I'll see you tomorrow. I'll be here at five. If you are here, please don't be naked.'

'I can guarantee that, TC,' said Vance seriously.

'Get stuffed,' said Coral.

'I'll leave that to you,' replied TC sweetly.

'Please lock the door behind you,' said Vance.

Looks like this is the way it will forever be, thought TC as she walked the block and a half home. The boss working me like a drover's dog and his girlfriends telling me to get stuffed. I'm a victim by choice! Have no one to blame but myself! The sergeant said Graham would be back tonight. I hope he tires of those tennis club girls soon.

¶

Colin called Lou. He asked her to marry him. Lou said yes on the proviso they lived together for a minimum period of six months prior to taking the plunge. She wanted to see how Colin's parents would treat her.

Lou was on the next Flea out of Brolga after a tearful farewell to her parents and TC.

The sergeant told Con and Lisa that Constable Graham would not be returning to Brolga, after all. He would be working in and around Curloo. Con and Lisa told TC and anyone else who was interested. When the news filtered through to the Brolga Tennis Club members, more than a few faces dropped and shoulders slumped.

'Bloody hell,' said one of the girls. 'He was the best bloody screw I've ever had.' She was bewildered as to why everyone in earshot laughed.

¶

Jake deflowered Madison, who found a reason five-and-a-half days a week to hang back in the Carmichael's store after all other staff had gone home. Jake and she would partake in fast, "get your gear off, stick it in and pull it out" sexual activity before Jake went to the Empire and Madison went home, pretending to her parents she was a virgin.

¶

TC missed Lou something terrible. She began working longer hours. She told Vance, 'Keep yourself and your women away from me, Boss, and I'll work twenty hours a day. Lou's gone, Graham's not coming back. I don't need more than four hours sleep.'

Vance had a lot of stones he was relentlessly searching for a market for. Delores was still away. The kids were in school. The poor thing was forever phoning Vance as to see if he had found a place for them to live after the disaster of losing their home to fire.

§

Vance's research came up with a company in Germany. Oblivious to him, it was the mob the other opal miners he had heard about dealt with.

'No! I'll do it myself,' he declared. He did not come up with a plan. It struck Vance one day in late January.

'The bloody men will be back soon! Oh, shit! I need that damned loader ready.'

Vance now owed Jake twenty-five thousand. The insurance money for the house had not yet come through. The loader needed fixing. Hopefully, the men would come back soon. Apart from that, he had to find a house for Delores, the children, and himself.

Sometimes he needed a Rum and Coke so much he felt capable of killing to acquire it. With a wish and a prayer, an insurance cheque would soon arrive. Vance phoned the loader manufacturer's representative company in Brisbane and requested they send a maintenance engineer to Brolga. Jake was a mate; he would wait. After all, first things first.

§

Vance was at camp with the said engineer when a call came from a police officer in Brisbane. TC answered the telephone, wondering if it was some creditor chasing payment of an outstanding account or Mrs Callahan wanting to speak to Vance.

'Good morning, Brolga Pharmacy,' she said.

'Yes, good morning,' came the official reply. 'Do you have four maniacal juke-box lovers in your employ?' TC hesitated before replying. The police officer had to be referring to Neil, Faith, Little Joe, and Jakkie.

'Neil, Faith, and Little Joe are employed by us, sir. Jakkie is a friend of Neil's.'

'That's him!' confirmed the police officer. 'I'm glad I don't live in Brolga. Would hate the thought of this drunken lot filling my prescriptions.' TC laughed uncontrollably. 'How old are you?' demanded the police officer's voice on the other end of the line.

I'm almost nineteen, sir,' replied TC seriously. 'Neil, Faith, Little Joe, and Jakkie don't work in the pharmacy. Three of them work at Mr Callahan's opal mine. Jakkie is their friend.'

'That's a relief!' said the police officer. 'Appears they have run out of money. They bunged on a turn when the publican wouldn't give them a grog on credit. Jakkie threw a beer bottle at the Juke box. Now we have all of them in the lock-up. They said Mr Callahan would post their bail.'

'Mr Callahan isn't here, sir. He's at the opal mine. I can probably get one of his friends to help get the men out of jail.'

'Good. We can't wait to get rid of them. Tell Mr Callahan's friend to give me a call. See what we can do.'

TC phoned Jake; Jake called the Brisbane police officer, then an old friend who lived there. That night the men were on the train Brolga-bound.

'Up the Big Smoke. Never going back there again,' declared Faith.

'That goes for me, too, mate,' said Neil.

'I liked the lights on that Juke box,' said Jakkie. Little Joe said nothing.

§

Yappy was stranded in Wingtree. He was broke, having drunk or given away all his money.

'I like you, Yappy,' said the publican-cum-store-owner-postmaster-and-everything-in-Wingtree. 'You can pay me when some money comes through to you.'

'Why the bloody hell wouldn't you like me, you bastard,' replied Yappy. 'I've spent a bloody fortune in your shithouse pub.'

'Now, now, Yappy, mate. No need to be like that,' said the jovial publican. 'I'll give Vance Callahan a call and you can talk to him. I'm sure he'll send you a few quid.'

'Bastard better or he'll be without a cook,' said Yappy as he grabbed the phone.

'What are you up to, Yappy?' asked Vance while knowing full well Yappy was short of a few quid.

'I'm up to shit, Vance. I need you to wire me some money so I can pay this bastard publican what I owe him. Then I'll hitch a ride back to Brolga.' Vance laughed.

'What if I haven't got any money to send you, Yappy?' he teased.

'Come on, Callahan. You can't leave a man broke in a joint like bloody Wingtree,' pleaded Yappy.

'Okay, Yappy. How much do you need, mate?' said Vance.

'A hundred quid should do, Vance,' replied Yappy with relief. 'That should be enough to see me through.'

'All right, Yappy. I'll send TC to the post office now. Your hundred quid should be there in an hour.' Vance laughed as he extracted a hundred from the cash register, then scribbled on a piece of paper, which he gave to TC.

'TC, Yappy needs some money. Go to the post office and send him the hundred to the address on the paper.' TC discarded her raincoat and shower cap, wiped her face, and set out for the post office. She literally cracked up with laughter when she read Yappy's address, as did the post office clerk when she handed it across the counter with the hundred pounds plus telegraphic fees.

'You've got to be bloody joking, TC,' said the clerk. TC shrugged.

'That's the address Mr Callahan gave me.' The clerk beckoned to the post master.

'Is this okay? Can we wire money to Yappy at this address?' The post master laughed as he nodded.

'Give it a try.'

Less than an hour later, an irate Yappy phoned the pharmacy. TC answered the telephone.

'Where's Callahan, TC?' demanded Yappy, who was obviously angry.

'He's not a happy Yappy, Boss,' whispered TC as she passed the phone to Vance. Vance held the telephone receiver away from his ear as Yappy yelled.

'Smart bastard, Callahan! Fancy sending a man money care-of outside the bloody pub!' Vance was doubled over in laughter. With great difficulty he managed to speak seriously to Yappy, who was seething while awaiting a reply.

'Where were you, Yappy?' he asked innocently.

'Smart bastard,' yelled Yappy. 'I was outside the bloody pub. Where the eff else would a man be?'

'I have to go now, Yappy, mate,' said Vance while restraining more laughter.

'That wasn't fair, Boss,' said TC.

'Go cut some more opal, TC,' replied Vance.

THE BUSINESS

Doctor Jackson kept in touch. He visited with Vance regularly. The men came back. Yappy helped them through the drying-out process. Vance's relationship with gin-drinking Coral continued. TC cut opal from 3 a.m. until 8 p.m. Jake won more and more money on the horses, and opal miners from other states flocked to the Brolga area. Some were up-front and announced their presence and intentions to Vance. Most were like the snakes in TC's yard. They slithered quietly through.

¶

Jake became obsessed by TC. He began pursuing her like a rat up a rope. He was bored with the nurses and Madison. They were too easy. Apart from that, his mum, Thel, had her heart set on TC as the perfect daughter-in-law. Didn't matter what time TC finished work, somehow or another Jake always managed to be there waiting to drive her home, buy her thick-shakes or hamburgers at Con's. Whatever! It doesn't appear to impress TC too much, thought Jake. Anyway, I'll persevere. Got sweet eff to lose.

¶

Vance was by now way ahead of the other miners who flocked to the area. He knew how to turn the boulders into stones. A lot of people smashed the boulders with heavy hammers because they could not deal with the suspense. They wanted, needed to see, the colour within, immediately. By breaking the boulders in that manner, most veins of opal were cracked, thus rendering their precious finds specimen-material only. On the other hand, the smart, more patient miners waited to see what Vance would do next. They would follow his lead, if, indeed, they had the opportunity to find out just what his lead was.

⁋

Delores returned to Brolga. As far as she was concerned, her reunion with Vance was one made in heaven. She was enthralled to be back in the arms of the man she loved. She didn't care if their new residence was not her dream home and the furniture was not to her taste; she loved Vance, was back with him and that was all that mattered.

On the other hand, Vance embraced Delores, told her he loved her, did what husbands and wives do, then checked on how TC's production of stones was going before Coral arrived in the dispensary.

TC missed Lou. She also thought about Graham frequently. Couldn't understand why he hadn't so much as sent her a card, or message via the sergeant, or even called her. Obviously, he had not loved her, after all.

Vance was understandably engrossed by the stone production, visiting the mine, sawing through boulders, and Coral. With Delores back in town, Vance sometimes felt as guilty as buggery about his situation with Coral. Never mind. 'Still! Delores doesn't seem to mind the doctor's company,' he reasoned whenever he felt guilty.

⁋

The pharmacy business was thriving. The income was just enough to keep things going. Vance still owed Jake a lot of money. Didn't matter. Jake didn't seem to be worried. He continued to back winners week after week.

Decimal currency was introduced. A shilling became ten cents; one pound became two dollars and so on. No problem!

By now Vance had accumulated more than a thousand stones, all beautiful. One day he got a call from a man in Melbourne who was keen to enter the opal retail world. He'd heard about Vance via the opal grapevine. He sounded more than keen to purchase opals from Vance.

'Okay, TC,' said Vance. 'Off you go. This guy sounds a bit slimy to me. Nevertheless, take what we've got and show it to him. He'll probably try to beat you down. I've heard that's what they do. Give him forty percent off, not a cent more. If he asks for any more than that, tell the prick to come mine it himself.'

Despite Vance's assurances she would do fine. TC was frightened; so nervous she shook. Armed with a briefcase filled to the hilt with opals, she took the Flea to Brisbane, a taxi to the airport, then a plane to Melbourne. She'd never flown before, terrified the plane would crash. Once in Melbourne, she phoned the would-be boulder-opal buyer. It was almost midday. After a brief conversation with the man, who offhandedly told her he was busy, couldn't see her until later, which was two days away, TC phoned Vance reverse charges.

'Boss, I don't like this man. Shouldn't he see me today? He's the one who wants the opal. He contacted us. What do I do? Where do I stay?'

'Phone me back in ten minutes, TC,' said Vance. 'I'll sort this bastard out. He was frantic to get his mitts on our opal; now he's having second thoughts. He's playing games. If he can't see you today, he can get effed.'

TC marked time outside a telephone booth at Melbourne airport for ten minutes. She kept looking at the terminal clock. Perhaps one day she'd have a watch of her own. She hated being in this situation. Didn't even know where she'd be sleeping that night. TC was distraught.

I know I've made a lot of vows to myself before, she said to herself. I mean this one! I'm never getting myself into this situation again. A bagful of opal, know no one, nowhere to stay, and sweet bugger-all in my pocket.

'He's obviously up himself, TC,' said Vance when he answered TC's call. 'Here's his address. It's a suite on the fourth floor of a ritzy Melbourne hotel. He is expecting you in an hour. Go there, do a deal if there's any deal to be done, then take a plane back to Sydney. When you have a flight number, phone Lou and make arrangements to stay at her boyfriend's hotel. If the bastard you are seeing today buys any opal, make sure he pays you up-front in cash.'

With the pretence of more confidence than she felt, TC agreed. What she really wanted to do was stroll onto a runway at the Melbourne airport and have a plane run over her in take-off or landing, opals and all; she couldn't care less.

Instead, she took a cab to the prospective opal buyer's hotel, found his suite, and introduced herself to a woman typing. TC noted an ornate coffee table which had obviously been hauled from some other location within the suite to within a few feet of the door.

Probably to impress others, thought TC. On the other hand, maybe to intimidate the bush girl from Brolga. That's me!

'I'll tell Mr Cowlegg you are here,' said the typist. 'Please take a seat.'

That's a strange name, thought TC, suppressing a giggle and clutching the opal-filled briefcase. The typist returned and informed TC, 'Mr Cowlegg is busy on the telephone. He'll see you soon.'

TC wanted to escape. The typist woman spoke to her as if she were an unwanted intruder on her day. It didn't dawn on TC the typist was Mr Cowlegg's "on the side" girlfriend who longed to spend uninterrupted time with him, especially when they were working out of a hotel suite.

After what seemed forever to TC, for she was tired, hungry, and fed up with waiting for Mr Cowlegg, whom she was not sure would buy any, all, or none of Vance's opals, she decided to bite the bullet.

'How much longer will I have to wait?' she asked the typist lady. 'I have to be in Sydney by seven tonight. I have an appointment with Australia's leading opal dealer. He wants to see Mr Callahan's stones. If Mr Cowlegg can't see me now, I'll have to go!'

'I'll ask him,' replied the typist confidently as she knocked on an adjacent door. It was opened and she disappeared inside. TC waited as long as she thought was necessary, picked up her bag, and headed for the door.

'Sorry to keep you waiting. Please come in now,' said a voice from the adjoining room doorway as the typist lady hurried back to her typewriter. TC turned towards the voice and took a deep breath. In front of her was her impression of a humanised cane toad; bloated body plus frog face. TC composed herself.

'Yes, Mr Cowlegg. My name is TC. Mr Callahan sent me to see you. I have to be in Sydney tonight, so I can't sit here all day waiting for you.'

Pompously, Mr Cowlegg sat at a desk and falsely apologised to TC for keeping her waiting. He made a few complimentary remarks regarding TC's appearance. She wasn't fooled! She got straight down to business. She started hauling stones clad in 4x2-inch plastic packets from her brief case and placing them on the desk for his perusal.

'Mr Cowlegg, I have a schedule. Any stones you like, please put to one side. I'll pack the rest back in my bag.' An hour later, Mr Cowlegg had selected a hundred or more stones. TC ignored his countless sexually suggestive remarks. She had reached the end of her tether. He kept mucking around, wasting time.

'Mr Cowlegg, I have to take a plane to Sydney,' persisted TC. 'Please make up your mind about these stones.' Frog face smiled.

'How much for these,' he said as he pushed the packeted stones towards TC. Painstakingly, she wrote the price of each stone, calculated the total twice to make certain it was correct, before telling Mr Cowlegg.

Cowlegg leaned back in his chair, watching TC. He was conjuring methods to get the opal for the lowest price possible. This girl was green, straight from the bush; she was a push-over with any luck! He'd get Callahan's stones for almost nothing.

TC handed her sheet of paper to Cowlegg.

'That's the total, Mr Cowlegg.' Cowlegg checked the stones off one at a time against TC's list. He paused periodically to give TC one of his cane-toadlike smiles.

'How much discount for cash, TC?' he asked while leaning back in his chair with his hands clasped behind his head.

'Mr Cowlegg, everything is cash. Mr Callahan told me bottom line is forty percent off.' Cowlegg sighed, leaned forward, and pushed the stones slowly towards TC.

'Can't afford them. I wanted ninety percent off. I know Callahan's struggling. Anything is better than nothing.'

TC opened the brief case, held the mouth against Cowlegg's desk, and whisked his chosen stones into it. She snap-locked the briefcase, got to her feet, and smiled.

'Mr Cowlegg, my boss may be struggling, but, unlike you, he'd never kick a man when he was down. Sorry I can't say it's been nice meeting you, Mr Cowlegg.' TC nodded to Mr Cowlegg's typist as she exited the hotel suite.

TC was waiting for the elevator to reach the fourth floor when Cowlegg's typist, secretary, lover, whatever she was, ran from Cowlegg's suite, calling, 'Please don't go. Mr Cowlegg will take the stones at forty percent off.'

TC wanted to tell the woman to get stuffed as she had been told to do by Vance's girlfriends. Instead, she grimaced, thought of Vance, how much he needed the money, smiled, and followed Cowlegg's typist into his suite.

'I'll take those stones at forty percent off,' said Cowlegg. 'Give them to me now. I'll pay you cash.'

TC wanted to slit her wrists; she'd willy-nilly flung Cowlegg's chosen stones into the briefcase with all the others. That meant she had to go through the entire procedure again, which, in turn, meant she had to spend another "as long as it took" with the cane-toad look-alike.

I learned a lesson today, thought TC after Cowlegg's cash was in the briefcase and she was once again waiting for the hotel lift door to open on the fourth floor. The deal is never over until the deal is done. If someone is interested in stock, put it aside for a day or so. They'll either call and say they want it or forget it forever.

¶

Brolga Opals' first-ever sale of stones was a done deal. Mr Cowlegg had spent twenty-two thousand, three hundred and twenty dollars. TC called Vance after buying a plane ticket to Sydney. She had an hour up her sleeve before leaving.

'How did you go, Butterball?' asked Vance anxiously.

'Twenty-two thousand, three hundred and twenty,' replied TC flatly. 'I never want to see Mr Cowlegg again, Boss. He wanted the three hundred and twenty off. I didn't give it to him; you need the money. I wanted to tell him and his so-called secretary to get stuffed.'

'TC, I don't want you talking like that!' replied Vance. He was angry.

'Don't worry, Boss. I won't become a slut. I hope I never have to see Mr Cowlegg again. I have to phone Lou. I'll call you from Sydney. Decide what you want me to do there.'

Vance put down the telephone. 'So there is a market,' he assured himself. What on earth have I done to TC? She sounds as hard as nails, he thought fleetingly before lighting a cigarette and sitting at his desk to ponder his next move; where and how to spend Cowlegg's money to the best advantage of Brolga Opals.

¶

Lou and Colin met TC at Sydney airport. Lou was ecstatic. She was jumping up and down and squealed, 'I love you, TC,' when TC emerged from the arrival hall.

'I love you, too, Lou,' said TC as they hugged each other after TC handed the opal-and-cash-filled briefcase to Colin for safekeeping.

'Brolga's not the same without you in it,' said TC.

'Sydney's not the same without you in it,' replied Lou.

¶

Tall, blonde, handsome, green-eyed Colin, attired like his rock-star mates, clutched the brief case and observed the girls. He was happy because his Lynette was happy. Both girls were crying. He felt tears welling in his own eyes.

'Come on, girls, we'll collect your luggage. TC, go to my parents' pub, then you can talk and hug all night if you want.'

'Not much luggage, Colin,' said TC while wiping tears from her cheeks. 'One small case, that's all.'

'You are staying in my room, TC,' said Lou. 'Colin put a bed in there for you. we can talk all night, just like we did in Brolga. How long are you staying? Wish it was forever. I've missed you, and missed my mum and dad. What's been happening in Brolga? I can't wait for you to tell me everything!'

TC smiled. She felt secure in the knowledge Lou was her friend for life. She realised they were heading down different paths in different directions. No matter what, they were closer than most sisters. They were friends forever.

❡

Jake was in Brolga having sex against the wall in the rear of his store. Madison was declaring her never-ending love for him. Jake hoped it would be over and done with as soon as possible. His mind was on TC. In fact he was imagining Madison was TC.

No, TC would be better than this stupid, young, screeching bitch, he thought as he pulled out and his ejaculated sperm splattered on the floor and Madison's legs. A stiff prick has no conscience, he thought as Madison adjusted her clothing, told Jake she'd love him forever and left the store, smiling innocently as she greeted her mother, who was waiting outside to drive her daughter home.

❡

Yappy, Neil, Faith, Little Joe, and Jakkie were at camp. Over dinner, Yappy earwigged as the other four relived for the umpteenth time their escapades during their break.

As always, Little Joe said sweet bugger-all unless he felt it pertinent to intervene when the bullshit being bandied around by his mates became too outlandish.

❡

In the dispensary, Vance had come up with a plan. TC was in Sydney, after all. May as well test the market there. He watched and listened for the phone to ring. Come ten o'clock and no call, he said to the dispensary walls, 'Screw the little bitch! If she doesn't call me tomorrow, I'll fire her.' Vance would have sworn he heard the dispensary walls reply, 'You can't do that, mate. TC's got your stones and money.'

Lou, Colin, TC and her briefcase spent hours in Colin's apartment.

'Lynette and I are getting married,' announced Colin.

'I haven't asked my parents' permission yet,' added Lou. 'I want you to be my bridesmaid, TC.'

'More like witness, Lynette,' said Colin matter-of-factly. 'Don't think we will be having a white wedding. My parents don't even know there's going to be one.'

'Whatever it is, I'll be there,' said TC. The deal was sealed by a three-way hug amidst laughter from all and tears shed by Lou and TC. Both Lou and TC cracked up laughing at midnight when Colin's DJ mate said, 'We don't usually play country music on this station. Tonight we are making an exception. This song is for my mate Colin's sweetheart, Lynette, and her best friend, TC, who's come from the end of the line in south-western Queensland. I understand the girls had a tearful reunion earlier this evening. Here we go with 'I Fall to Pieces'.

'Look in the phone booth,' directed Vance when TC phoned him next morning. 'You are there. I expect you to work, not have fun with Lou and her boyfriend.' TC was on the verge of tears when she put down the phone. Never once could she recall Vance thanking or praising her for her efforts. No matter how hard she tried, how much she achieved, she got no recognition whatsoever from Vance.

I'm nothing but a machine to you, Boss, she thought as she flicked the pages of the telephone directory to Gem Dealers. Cold turkey, she rocked up at all the addresses.

'Yes, I've heard about it. Don't want to see it,' said some while others looked at the stones out of curiosity. Most were negative and found some reason to knock the beauty. Too beautiful, they look like fakes, you're pushing it uphill, et cetera, et cetera.

TC was too young and inexperienced to realise the negative remarks were brought about by fear that Vance's boulder opal would take over the market. With trepidation, TC walked into the reception room of Australia's most famous black opal dealer, renowned for quality, value, and service. TC knew they wouldn't buy anything. Still, it didn't hurt to say hello. From what she'd heard from other Sydney opal dealers she had visited, these people had beautiful black opal protruding from their ears, so to speak.

'The boss isn't here,' said the receptionist politely. 'One of his sons is, though; I'll ask if he'll see you.' Almost immediately, a handsome, young man appeared in the reception area, introduced himself, and ushered TC into his office, which had huge windows overlooking the Sydney Harbour Bridge. While impressed by the view, TC was surprised to see Bert Black's lovely Leanne sitting in a chair close to the young man's desk. Leanne was all smiles; the young man was friendly. Obviously something was going on between them. If it wasn't already, it would be pretty soon.

After a few minutes of chatting about anything and nothing, TC excused herself, said, 'Nice to see you again, Leanne; nice to meet you,' to the young man and she was gone. TC found a park bench. She sat on it and scribbled names and comments on a small notepad while her ankles hugged the briefcase below her knees.

I'm a failure, she thought as she despondently picked up the briefcase and headed off to find a train, bus, taxi, or any other means of conveyance which would take her to the North Shore. A few blocks along from the park bench, TC noticed a tiny shop with its front sign boasting 'Opals and Gems'.

Nothing to lose, she thought, so she went inside. The elderly couple who owned the business welcomed her with open arms. It turned out they had a granddaughter TC's age who was also blonde, five-feet-two with green eyes. They loved TC on sight, as she did them. After purchasing three thousand dollars in opals for which TC felt guilty for taking their money, the gentleman took TC aside.

'Go to America, luv. Tell your boss to go to America. That's where things are happening.'

'The Yanks bailed us out in the war. They love us. They love everything Australian. Go to America, luv.'

TC phoned Vance from a telephone booth fifty feet from the front of Colin's parents' pub. 'I sold another three thousand, Boss. The people are lovely. I didn't want to take their money. They told me we should go to America because Americans love us.'

'Slow down, TC,' said Vance. 'What did everyone else say?' Silence, before TC replied. 'Nothing, Boss. I think most of them are scared our opal will take over their markets.'

'Get a plane to Brisbane in the morning. TC. I'll meet the Flea Saturday night. I expect you to be on it.' The phone went dead.

Looks like I'm out of here, thought TC as she entered the foyer of Colin's parents' hotel.

❡

Lou and TC talked forever. Colin hardly got a word in. Promising she'd be back to be witness, bridesmaid, or whatever when Lou and Colin got married, TC was out of Sydney next morning.

Vance met the Flea Saturday night.

'Where's the money, TC?' he asked.

'No hello or how are you or anything else,' thought TC as she handed over the briefcase.

'It's in there with the opals,' she replied coldly. 'I'm going home.'

'I'll drive you,' said Jake, who appeared from nowhere.

TC looked at Jake's smiling face. She had not seen anyone better dressed than Jake in her travels. If nothing else, Jake sure knew how to present himself.

'Why not, Jake,' responded TC. 'I want to sit on the stairs and listen to 2UE.'

'Consider it done,' said Jake with enthusiasm as he strode towards his car with TC's suitcase.

'Be careful of Jake, TC,' warned Vance. 'I'll see you in the morning.' TC shook her head in disbelief.

'No, you won't, Boss. I'll be busy doing other things. I'll be at work when I'm ready. Leave some pieces for me to cut.'

'What will you be busy doing, TC?' demanded Vance.

'Sleeping in, washing, ironing, cleaning, and wondering why on earth I bust my gut working for you,' said TC before following Jake to his car.

❡

'I'm going to the pub to get some beer, TC. I'll get Con to make a couple of hamburgers,' said Jake after dumping TC's suitcase on the landing. 'I'll be back soon. Got something on my mind I want to ask you.' Jake wanted to ask TC to marry him. He wasn't quite sure how to go about it. Far out, he thought. She's the only girl I've ever met who hasn't fallen for my bullshit.

TC showered, washed her hair, which she brushed and rubber-banded into a pony tail before putting the King's record on the radiogram. Dressed in her baby-doll pyjamas, short, cotton housecoat and pink-bowed slippers, she sat on the stairs thinking about Lou and days gone by. She had a nagging at the back of her mind. She asked herself what Jake was going to ask her.

Jake returned with a hiss and a roar of his car's motor.

'What do you want, TC?' he called from the dining room seconds later.

'Come here and I'll tell you what I want. Probably a bit of recognition from your mate, my boss, wouldn't go astray. I saw Lou in Sydney. She's getting married. At the moment, I'm the loneliest person I know.'

'I got you a Coke,' said Jake as he plonked himself down on the top stair beside TC and handed her the bottle. 'You are rude, TC. I shouted out and asked you what you wanted. You didn't bother to reply. I want you to marry me. There's a hamburger in the kitchen. I suggest you eat it. You are getting too thin.' TC was speechless, stared at Jake's mates loading their trucks across the road, and sipped from her Coke bottle.

'I don't know what to say, Jake. You've got girls eating out of your hands. Why me?'

'Because you don't eat out of my hands, TC. The others are push-overs. Not you. You are nobody's fool. Apart from that, my mother loves you.' Didn't dawn on Jake to tell TC he loved her, too. Other than his mother, the only person Jake loved was himself. He wanted to marry TC because she was hard to get. Some said she was the prettiest girl in the district. She didn't play around, and she sure as buggery would be a great trophy if and whenever he needed to show her off.

TC knew she didn't love Jake. Wasn't love supposed to be like it was in the movies? Like it could have been with Graham? What was love, anyway? Nothing but a state of mind, she recalled hearing someone somewhere saying.

'I'll think about marrying you, Jake.'

Jake couldn't believe his ears. In a rare show of true emotion, he put his arms around TC and pulled her close to him. 'I'll treat you good, luv. I promise you that.' TC felt safe and secure. In Jake's arms, her feelings of being lost and lonely disappeared temporarily.

'I didn't say I would marry you, Jake Carmichael. I said I'd think about it.'

Jake desperately wanted to drop the weight on TC. He didn't dare. She'd most likely push him down the stairs.

'I'm going home now, TC. You think about marrying me while you eat your hamburger.'

Yes, Jake, I'll marry you, thought TC as she watched his car disappear up the street.

I think she'll say yes, thought Jake as he jumped out of his car outside the post office and walked towards the red phone box. 'I know she'll marry me,' he told himself before asking the on-duty telephone operator to connect him to the nurses' quarters.

❡

TC did all and everything she had to do around the house next morning before going to the dispensary/cutting room to turn some ironstone-encased seams of opal into stones. Vance was not there; neither had he left any pieces to be processed on his desk. TC selected ten bits from a bucket and began working on them. During the following hours, as she sanded and polished the stones, TC's mind wandered all over the place. Should she marry Jake? She probably would. Lou was in Sydney. The boss didn't care what she did as long as she kept the stones rolling in. Graham was gone; hadn't so much as sent her a message.

She lined up the finished stones on Vance's desk before plastering a fake smile on her face and going across the road to visit with Lisa and Con. Lisa was happy, to say the least, when TC walked into the café.

'Hello, darling, did you see Lou? How is she? Did you have a good trip? I'm so pleased to see you are home safely and in one piece. Come sit with me and tell me everything.'

A chocolate thick-shake and much discussion later, Lisa asked, 'Have you heard from Constable Graham?'

'No, have you?' replied TC despondently. 'Jake wants me to marry him.' Lisa collected her thoughts.

'Don't do it, darling. Jake is nice, sometimes too nice. He'll never be faithful to you, darling. Run like the wind from him.'

'I'll see, Lisa, I'll see. I have to go home now.'

❡

It was interval time at the picture theatre when TC left Con's Café. In order to avoid the crowd rushing towards Con's, TC crossed to the other side of the street. She passed by Jake's car opposite the picture show. Jake was in it and so was Madison. They were in a clinch.

I'd like to open the car door and announce to Madison that Jake proposed to me last night, thought TC. Instead, she kept walking. Out of the corner of his eye, Jake glimpsed TC walk past his car.

Eff it, he thought as he propped Madison's breasts and nibbled on one of her ears. His erect appendage became limp, and he pushed Madison away.

'Time to tidy yourself up, Madison. The second movie will start soon. I'll see you at work tomorrow. Off you go.'

'But, Jake, I want to stay with you,' squealed Madison in a whisper.

Shit! thought Jake. Even when she's whispering, she sounds like a bloody screeching bird.

'You can't stay with me, Madison. I told you, I'll see you tomorrow. Now piss off.' The instant Madison closed his car door, Jake drove off. He turned his car around the corner towards the back street. If he drove directly to TC's house, it would be too obvious. Madison would know where he was going. He knew she'd be watching.

§

TC was in the shower when he arrived, so he took a beer from the fridge and sat on the landing to wait for her.

'Aren't you frightened of Joe Blakes anymore,' he laughed when she opened the bathroom door.

'If a snake bites me, it bites me, Jake,' replied TC matter-of-factly. She was not at all surprised to see Jake sitting on the landing waiting for her.

'Are you going to marry me or what?' asked Jake. TC smiled.

'Probably, Jake. Haven't exactly been flooded with offers. If I do marry you, Jake, I would expect you to be discreet concerning your goings-on with your girlfriends. Don't think I'd care too much to be walking down the street and see my husband sitting in his car mauling a moll.' Jake burst into laughter.

'No wonder I'm crazy about you, TC. You sure as buggery don't muck around with words. When are we getting married?' asked Jake anxiously. He couldn't believe his luck. Neither could he wait to get TC in the cot. Almost every other bloke wanted her. He was going to get her!

TC shrugged as a far-away look appeared in her eyes.

'I don't know, Jake. I'm under twenty-one. I'll have to get written permission from someone. I'm going to bed now, Jake. You should go back to doing what you were doing before you came here.'

'No!' replied Jake. 'I'm going home to tell my mother you and I are getting married.'

⁋

Jake's early, thought Thel Carmichael when she heard his car whirl into her drive. Jake paused at his mother's bedroom door.

'Are you still awake, Mum?' he asked quietly.

'Yes, Jake, I'm awake,' came his mother's reply.

'TC and I are getting married, Mum,' said Jake casually before going to his room. Thel Carmichael got out of her bed and followed him.

'I'm happy you and TC are getting married, Jake. When and where is all I want to know.'

'I don't know, Mum,' replied Jake. 'All I know is she's marrying me.'

Thel Carmichael smiled and returned to her bed, safe in the knowledge she would soon not have only a daughter-in-law but more likely another daughter. She loved TC and knew TC loved her.

⁋

TC was in bed tossing and turning. Even with the fan blowing on her, it was still hot as Hades.

I must be crazy, she thought. I've all but agreed to marry Jake. Jake's about as loving and emotional as a dry piece of grass. Still, he's got a nice mother, she reasoned on the positive side.

⁋

The men were back at the mine. Jakkie was one of them now.

'Hard worker he is, too,' said Vance to Neil on one of his visits to the mine.

The boulders kept emerging from the ground. Every time Vance went to the mine, he dropped off care packages of food to Greg the Greek on his way.

Can't believe any poor bastard is waiting for the kittens to grow so he can eat the poor little things, thought Vance. If I call in and leave Greg some food, hopefully it will prolong the cats' lives.

¶

The insurance company finally came through with the payout. Vance asked Jake if he could hold out for his money a bit longer. There was a house coming up for sale because a family was leaving Brolga due to personal reasons. The bonus was the house was fully furnished.

'Delores has been nagging me, mate,' said Vance. 'Can I keep you hanging for your money a bit longer.'

'No problem, mate,' replied Jake. 'Get your family back together. That's the main thing.'

¶

Occasionally TC would think about Graham and what could have been. Lou was almost happy, it seemed. Colin's parents were trying hard to accept her. They had given her a room two floors beneath Colin's and did their best to monitor movements between Colin's apartment and Lou's room.

It's not easy, wrote Lou in one of her numerous letters to TC. To quote dad, TC, "Don't know where the bloody hell this is going." Anyway, I love Colin and he loves me. I've just got a job as a receptionist at another pub. Colin's parents' opposition. Bet that cheeses them off. TC, ain't life funny?

The Coratian brothers were finding boulders faster than they could stack them. They had no idea what to do with what they found. The more boulders they accumulated, the more Scotch whiskey they consumed. To add excitement to their poker games, they began playing for rocks. Two matchsticks represented two boulders, et cetera. On a night they were both blind drunk, one brother won all the boulders. His sibling was so pissed off, he casually picked up his 303 and shot his brother in the head, right between the eyes. Feeling no remorse whatsoever, he dug a hole, threw the body in, then covered it with dirt.

I'll be a bit lonely, he thought fleetingly. Nobody will miss the bastard but me. Nobody knows we are here. He resumed drinking whiskey and wondered where, how, and when he would sell his boulders, now that they were all his.

⁋

Jake saw very little of TC prior to Vance's return to Brolga, apart from dropping by his aunt and uncle's house a few minutes before siren time to tell TC he loved her before going to the Empire, having a few beers, then home to eat lunch with his mum and little sister.

At closing time at Carmichaels and Carmichaels, Jake would tell all staff, apart from Madison, he would see them the next day. He and Madison would share abandoned sexual activity in the office before she joined her mother to get a ride home and Jake went to the Empire, bullshitted to anyone who would listen for a while before calling the nurses' quarters and arranging a date for later.

As far as Jake was concerned, he was going to get laid as often as he could before he made the final commitment by saying 'I do' to his soon-to-be-wife and trophy, TC.

⁋

TC displayed little interest when Vance showed up in the dispensary next morning. She was concentrating on shaping a stone. Vance switched off the motor, causing the grinding wheel to stop turning.

'I'm going to America.'

'Where have you been and when are you going?' questioned TC in alarm.

'None of your business where I've been, TC. I'm going to the US as soon as I can make arrangements. I've heard about a man in California who apparently loves opals. As soon as I can set something up, I'm going to see him.'

'Good!' said TC indifferently before turning on her grinding wheel and resuming stone shaping.

Vance made numerous phone calls at all times of the day and night. Finally, he tracked down and spoke to the jeweller in Carmel, California.

'I'm leaving on Friday, TC,' he said. 'The men will probably go on strike once I'm out of town. They have been threatening it. I know they'll do it. I've told them they are not to hassle you. Definitely not to come into the shop. If they come near the place, pay the bastards off. You know how to sign my name. We both know I've made you practice enough. Don't know how the pricks will get to town. Knowing them, they'll find a way. Probably on the mail truck. I know Yappy will stay at camp. He's saner than the others. I'll be gone two weeks. Turn out as many stones as you can. You can take as much money in the shop as you can. If you need help, ask Jake.'

To date neither Jake nor TC had told Vance they intended to get married. Thel Carmichael had told her sister, Carmel, and that was that.

¶

Armed with one briefcase filled with cut stones and another containing sliced slabs of boulder opal, Vance drove to Brisbane from where he caught a Qantas flight to Los Angeles via Honolulu.

It was the end of March. The men had been back on the job only six weeks. Already they were bored with it and the mundane, day-after-day routine of camp life.

'Stuff it,' said Neil. 'Vance has gone to the bloody USA and we are stuck here.'

'Yeah, let's go to town,' said Faith.

'I'm coming, too,' agreed Jakkie.

'You are all bloody mad,' said Yappy.

'I'll stay with you, Yappy,' said Little Joe.

'Thanks, mate,' said Yappy. 'These bastards think they are back in Brisbane playing to be a bloody juke box.'

¶

Vance left on a Sunday. On Tuesday morning, Neil, Jakkie, Faith, and Neil's recruited younger brother were sitting in the gutter out in front of the Brolga pharmacy. TC ignored them when she opened the door at nine. She had been cutting opals since three. She suppressed a giggle when they all called, 'Little Flower, we love you,' simultaneously. She ignored their repeated calls of pledged love until the Greek newsagency owner from next door barged through the back door of the pharmacy, threatening death if she didn't get rid of those mad bastards soon.

TC apologised. Hands on hips, she strode to confront the men.

'You know the boss is away! Why are you doing this to me?' she demanded.

'We want our money, Little Flower,' said Neil.

'Yeah, we want to get on the grog,' said Faith.

'Give the bastards their money and get them out of your hair, Little Flower,' urged Neil's young brother.

'Come on, luv, give us a break,' pleaded Jakkie while Neil and Faith held their heads in their hands suppressing laughter. TC looked at them all. Her heart melted. They were good men. They were also mongrels.

'All right,' she said. 'The boss told me you would do this. I'll pay you as soon as the bank opens.' TC didn't have a clue as to how much money the boss owed the men. She'd long since forgotten what he owed her. Her savings were dwindling. As radio station 4CL announced it was ten o'clock and the Commonwealth Bank was open for business, the Romeo brothers, as usual, opened the bar doors to their pubs and TC wrote a cheque for five hundred dollars and told the men to watch the shop as she strode across the road to the Bank.

The bank manager took the cheque, glanced at it, and began taking money out of the drawer.

'I thought Vance was away, TC,' he said casually.

'Yes, he's in America,' replied TC. 'Then men have gone on strike and I have to pay them.'

'So, Vance left signed cheques for you, TC?' persisted the bank manager. TC smiled and shrugged.

'Mr Callahan warned the men would strike. He told me to pay them when they did. I'm following his instructions.'

'I see,' said the bank manager as he pushed five hundred dollars across the counter to TC, who smiled, said thank you and left the bank. TC hurried across the street to pay the men.

'Go,' she said as she handed the five hundred to Neil. 'Don't spend it all at once and please don't bother me again.' They all laughed.

'You've got to be joking, Little Flower,' said Faith. 'If Vance isn't back before the Romeos get all this loot, of course we'll bother you again.'

'Whatever,' replied TC before rushing into the shop to answer the ringing telephone. It was mail-order day after all.

§

The bank manager told one of his underlings to check the balance on TC's savings account. Something wasn't quite right as far as he was concerned. Vance was in the US and the girl was cashing a cheque for five hundred dollars.

I'll have to tell Delores, he thought. She plays golf with my wife. She deserves to know TC is ripping Vance off.

§

TC didn't cut very many opals that day. She concentrated on mail orders and filling prescriptions. Doctor Jackson was obviously busy.

Around midnight, Vance called her at home from Carmel, California. She had just walked in the door. TC told him about the men and the bank manager's attitude and everything he and she had said.

'Don't worry about it, Butterball. None of his business. Don't put up with shit from anyone. Do as I say, not do as I do.'

'I'm not going to work until eight tomorrow, Boss. Today's been a long one. I'm tired.'

'Whatever, TC,' agreed Vance. 'I'm a million miles away. Do the best you can.'

§

TC was shocked when she arrived for work next morning. Delores was seated at Vance's desk. Doctor Jackson was standing beside her.

'I want your shop key, TC,' demanded Delores. 'Consider yourself fired.'

Mrs Callahan may as well be speaking to a bit of steel dirt, thought TC.

'Why, Mrs Callahan?' asked TC in dismay as she placed her shop key on the desk.

'You forged Vance's signature, TC,' replied Delores in a frigid voice with a satisfied "at last I'm getting rid of you" confident, superior expression on her face.

'The boss told me to do that, Mrs Callahan,' replied TC defensively. 'He knew the men would go on strike. Who will do the prescriptions?' Delores smiled and nodded towards a somewhat embarrassed Doctor Jackson.

'Okay,' acknowledged TC before turning and leaving the shop.

Thanks, Boss, she thought as she walked towards home. The bank manager, your wife, and Doctor Jackson all think I'm a thieving cheque-forger. Pretty soon the whole town will think the same.

TC felt desolate. She wished Vance would suddenly appear so she could strangle him. She desperately needed a shoulder to cry on. Someone who understood she had done nothing but follow Vance's instructions.

Suddenly, Jake pulled his car to a halt beside her.

'Hello, my future wife. You look like shit. What's on your mind?' he asked as he jumped out of his car, perfectly attired and smelling like fifteen or twenty brands of expensive after-shave lotions.

'The boss' wife fired me, Jake,' replied TC. 'The men went on strike; I wrote a cheque for five hundred so they could have some money. Looks like the bank manager told Mrs Callahan. She obviously thinks I took the money for myself.' Jake was outraged, pissed off beyond belief.

'You've go to be effing joking, TC!' Silently, he thought to himself, I helped Vance burn down his effing house. Apart from that, he owes me a bloody fortune. To TC, he replied, 'He's complained forever about Delores' "born to shop" habits. Now she fired you for doing exactly what Vance told you to do?! I know I've been there when you've been practising writing his bloody signature.'

'I'm really upset, Jake,' exploded TC. 'Right is right, and wrong is wrong! This is wrong, Jake!'

Jake grabbed TC by her shoulders and looked into her eyes.

'When are you going to marry me, TC?' TC shook her head slowly.

'Whenever you want, Jake. I already have my sister's letter of consent.'

'Come on, luv! We'll tell Mum. She'll be over the bloody moon.' TC hesitated.

'Get in the bloody car, will you, TC!' said Jake. 'We'll go and tell Mum we're getting bloody married.' Thel Carmichael was thrilled.

'When?' she asked repeatedly.

'Soon, Mum,' said Jake.

'Soon, Mrs Carmichael,' said TC.

Jake and TC spent all day with Thel Carmichael and Carla. They talked about everything, including what had happened with Delores Callahan that morning.

¶

'Don't worry, TC. The truth always comes out in the end,' comforted Thel. TC knew in her heart Mrs Carmichael was right. While pretending to be bright and happy, TC felt anything but. Her heart was broken. She wouldn't steal a cent from anyone, especially not Vance. Poor man had sweet bugger-all, anyway.

After observing TC's interaction with his mother, Jake decided he really was in love with TC or, at least, in love as much as he was capable of being with anyone other than himself.

'I have to find another job. I've got less than a couple of hundred dollars in my bank account,' said TC as Jake drove her home. 'Thanks to your Auntie Flo and Uncle Doug, I don't have to pay rent.'

'TC, I've got more than a hundred thousand dollars plus what Vance and a few others owe me,' said Jake when he pulled into her driveway.

'That's good, Jake,' said TC as he got out of his car. 'Can't say money impresses me much.'

Bitch, thought Jake as he followed her up the stairs.

'Get yourself a beer if you want, Jake,' said TC.

'Skip the bloody bullshit, TC. We are getting married. I want to try before I buy. Eff the beer, we are going to bed.'

'As you wish, Jake,' said TC calmly. 'If you want to make your soon-to-be wife like all your other girlfriends, let's go to bed and do it now.'

'Get stuffed, you smart bitch,' said Jake.

'Been told to do that lots of times before, Jake,' replied TC. She didn't give a tinkers what Jake or any other person on earth thought of her.

'I'm going!' snapped Jake.

'Good!' replied TC. TC turned on the radio as Jake gunned his car out of the driveway.

'I wish Lou was here,' said TC aloud to herself before throwing herself on her bed and bursting into tears.

¶

Hours later she was woken by the persistent sound of the telephone ringing.

'TC, it's me,' said Vance. Why wasn't TC surprised?

'You really played a number on me this time, Boss.'

'I'm sorry, TC. Delores had no right to do what she did. As for the bank manager I'd like to shoot the bastard.'

'That's okay for you, Boss. I'm the one who'll end up with the reputation of being a thief. I expect the sergeant to knock on my door any moment. If he throws me in the slammer, I hope you'll bail me out.'

'Don't be ridiculous, TC,' said Vance impatiently. He felt as guilty as buggery for instigating TC's predicament and helpless to do one iota of anything to support. He was on the other side of the world, after all.

'I'll have to find another job,' said TC. 'Don't know who will hire me once word gets out that I'm a thieving forger. I'm also going to marry Jake.'

Silence reigned as Vance searched for something to say. Not only did he feel like shooting the effing bank manager, he also wanted to throttle Delores for not minding her own bloody business, and do away with Jake because he owed the bastard money, and was a shithead, just like a bitter man. Vance struggled to compose himself.

¶

'TC, please don't look for another job,. I'll be back in Brolga soon.'

'Sure, Boss, whatever you say,' replied TC. She carefully placed the telephone handset in the cradle and returned to her bed.

Should take a shower, she thought. What for, TC? You've got all day tomorrow to do that and the next and the next and the next, said a little voice from within.

With 2UE broadcasting in the background, TC went back to sleep feeling alone and lonelier than she ever had before.

¶

In his motel room in Carmel, California, Vance sat on the edge of his bed looking at the telephone.

I'm going home, he thought. Everything is falling to pieces without me there. The jeweller guy is okay. He obviously loves my opal; the problem is all he wants to do is trade my opal for his jewellery. I think I'll do a deal and haul my butt back to Brolga before every effing thing goes to the shithouse.

Vance met with the jeweller, traded a dozen or so stones for some jewellery, booked a flight, and high-tailed it back to Australia. He was anxious to be in Brolga so he could hopefully fix the situation created by the effing busybody bank manager and interfering Delores, who did nothing but spend money he didn't have.

¶

The Romeo Brothers were happy at the end of each trading day. Callahan's men had boosted takings at the Majestic by one hundred percent.

'Don't know how long it will last,' said Bert Romeo.

'Don't care, Bert. We'll grab the stupid bastards' money while it's there,' replied Jack.

¶

Little Joe and Yappy were at camp tidying everything up.

'Hope young TC comes here soon. I want to hear her comments on our illustrious shithouse,' said Yappy.

'I hope Little Flower comes here soon, too, Yappy. I've got a daughter her age back where I came from.'

'I think I heard something about that, Little Joe,' said Yappy. 'Must be bloody hard, mate.'

¶

It was early morning when Vance and his opal-laden briefcase returned to Brolga. He pulled his car to an abrupt halt when he saw TC sitting on the stairs. Vance laughed as he walked to her gate.

'Waiting up for me, are you, Little One?' TC remained calm. As far as she was concerned, Vance had some major sucking-up to do.

'Not really, Boss,' she replied calmly. 'You had better be careful about wrecking your reputation. If anyone sees you talking to a scheming, forging thief, you'd be up the creek without a rudder.'

'Don't be ridiculous, TC,' said Vance as he quickly returned to his car to collect his cigarette packet and lighter before joining TC on the stairs.

'You and your wife are the ridiculous ones, Mr Callahan. All I was doing was following your instructions. Perhaps you should have told your wife, the bank manager and the doctor what was going on. Maybe you should have told them to pay off the men. Jess told me the men are cheesed off with what happened to me. They have drunk the five hundred dollars. They are shacked up at the rear of the Majestic waiting for you to come back.'

'TC, you are talking like a bitter, old woman,' said Vance. He was steeped in concern and riddled with guilt. What the eff have I done to her? he asked himself silently while waiting for her reply.

'You and Lisa Kara have always told me I'm old beyond my years. Probably I am,' said TC with a shrug.

'Are you really going to marry Jake?' asked Vance between inhales and exhales of his cigarette smoke.

'Looks like it, Boss. I've got no one else who gives a tinkers about me,' replied TC flippantly. 'Apart from that, I like, perhaps love, his mother. I have not had one, so to say, of my own.'

'Don't marry Jake, TC. He's too much like me,' said Vance.

'So you've told me a million or so times, ex-Boss,' replied TC with no interest whatsoever.

'I'll see you in the morning?' said Vance hopefully.

'Better sort things out with Mrs Callahan first, ex-Boss,' replied TC 'By the way, you might want to mention to Mrs Callahan, her bank manager and doctor-protector that you owe me at least three months wages. That's why I've been living on my savings.'

Vance tossed his cigarette onto the concrete path and squashed it out with his booted foot. 'I'm sorry, TC. I'll sort things out and come and see you tomorrow.'

Yes, that's the least you can do, thought TC as she watched Vance drive away.

'Working for the Man' began playing on the radio.

That's me, thought TC. I'll be back working for the boss tomorrow.

She felt lost and lonely. Depressed and trapped.

¶

Vance banged on TC's front door early next morning. He'd had whatever he had to have out with Delores. He told her to mind her own business and keep her boyfriend, the doctor, under wraps.

'As for the effing bank manager, when I'm worth money, I'm changing banks. Come on, TC, time to cut opals. Get your act together. I'll see you in the cutting room half an hour from now.'

'Sure, sure, sure,' replied TC with no enthusiasm whatsoever.

¶

Vance rounded up the men. Heads down and feeling second-hand, they were sitting while leaning against the outside rear wall of the cutting room waiting for TC to come to work before Vance drove them back to camp.

'A few mongrels out the back, TC,' said Vance. 'Trouble-makers, they are. Want to tell you something before I take them back to the bush.'

'Sorry, Little Flower' said Neil without lifting his head.

'Me, too, luv,' said Faith.

'Me, too, Little Flower,' said Jakkie.

'I'm the trouble-maker. I'm sorry, too, Little Flower,' said Neil's younger brother, Michael, who was obviously a newly recruited member of Vance's mining team.

Everyone including Vance and TC laughed when Neil looked pleadingly at TC and begged, 'Please forgive us, Little Flower; we didn't know what we were doing.'

'Come on, you mad bastards,' said Vance. 'You can finish drying out at camp. I feel sorry for poor bloody Yappy and Little Joe. They have to put up with you until you become sane again.'

¶

Cutting and polishing along with Vance sawing through boulders resumed in the dispensary's opal cutting-room of Brolga's chemist shop. Coral was a frequent visitor and always happy when TC called it a day and left.

Stone production went on day after day, night after night. Vance did deals here and there. Managed to keep the pharmacy afloat. He gradually repaid Jake what he owed him.

More hopeful, would-be miners filed claims and arrived in Brolga. Some were good, honest people hoping to realise their dreams. Others were crapheads who would rip off their own grandmothers for ten cents.

Every time Vance went to the mine, he dropped in on Greg the Greek's claim. It was obvious to Vance Greg was into consuming cats due to the evidence of cat skins spread on a wire fence surrounding Greg's feeble abode.

§

Jake and TC got married in a Registry Office in Sydney. Lou and Colin were their witnesses. Half an hour later, Colin and Lou made their vows in the same Registry Office. Jake and TC were their witnesses.

After dinner at a flash restaurant, Colin and Lou went to Colin's apartment. They made love while TC screamed at Jake to stop the car straightaway as he drove a rental car across the Harbour Bridge. She knew she'd made a huge mistake.

Jake stopped the car long enough for TC to get out before continuing over the bridge and to a motel a couple of miles further on. It was windy on the bridge. TC considered climbing over the rail and hurling herself into the water below.

Too easy, she thought.

A couple of minutes before taking their vows, Jake casually mentioned that Madison had told him she was pregnant. Jake did not appear at all concerned. On the other hand, TC was beside herself. It was too late to turn back. Lou, Colin, and the registrar were there!

Shit. Shit. Shit. Shit. Shit. Shit.

Jake was asleep when TC finally made her way to the motel. Along the way, she'd been subjected to enticement, then abuse by several carloads of Sydney youths, cruising the streets looking for whatever female they could convince to jump in their cars.

Eventually Jake opened the door in reply to TC's relentless knocking.

'Where the hell have you been?' he asked while still half-asleep.

'As if you care!' replied TC acidly.

'You're pissed, aren't you,' said Jake as he staggered, still half-asleep, back to the bed.

'Who wouldn't be, Jake!' yelled TC. 'You must be the rat of the world! Sure picked the right time to tell me Madison is pregnant!'

Jake lit a cigarette. While holding it in his right hand, he folded his left arm behind his head and looked at TC innocently.

'She sent us a telegram, too. It's on the table.' TC glanced at the table, saw the open telegram, and snatched it to read.

"Thinking of you both, Love, Madison."

TC screwed the telegram in her hand before throwing it at Jake. He laughed when it hit him between the eyes, took a drag on his cigarette, then spoke matter-of-factly.

'Too bloody late now, TC. We are married.'

TC flung herself into a couch opposite the bed, wanted to cry but didn't.

What a mess, she thought. I'm legally married to Jake, I can't stand him, Madison is pregnant with his child, and I want to kill myself.

Jake switched off the bedside light and thought, Eff it, I'm a prick. Madison's not pregnant. I pulled out every effing time I effed her.

§

Pretending nothing was wrong, Jake and TC bid farewell to Lou and Colin at Sydney's Kingsford Smith Airport. Lou cried. So did TC.

'Colin and I haven't told his parents we are married,' whispered Lou tearfully while hugging TC. 'I want you to be godmother to our children, TC. I love you.'

'No problem, Lou. I love you, too,' whispered TC in reply.

Jake and TC spoke very little to each other during their flight to Brisbane and road trip to Brolga.

Jakes thoughts were consumed by what the buggery he would do if Madison wasn't bluffing about being pregnant. He now had a wife he hadn't so much as laid a finger on and a possibly-pregnant, years-younger-than-he girlfriend declaring she was carrying his baby.

¶

Jake and TC's marriage was consummated the night they arrived back in Brolga. It was over quickly. Physically painful for TC, Jake didn't care. It was over and done with. TC felt terrible. If this was what sex was all about, she was off it forever.

Jake was happy. He'd had sex with his forever-trophy, new wife, TC. He was anxious for morning to come so he could come face-to-face with Madison and see for himself whether or not she was pregnant or had been bullshitting.

TC and Jake had been away from Brolga a week.

Vance was brassed off that he no longer had control of TC. She had been stupid enough to marry Jake, who was an arsehole where women were concerned, just like himself. What could he say? Never dawned on Vance that TC was lonely and needed some company. Didn't matter who it was, at least she'd have someone.

Jake went to face Madison. He didn't know how he'd handle things. It was more than a worry, especially as others, all long-time, loyal staff, would be present at the family store. If Madison threw a fit, he was buggered. The others would probably quit. Who could blame them?

¶

TC went to the pharmacy to resume work. A tall, scantily-clad version of Madison greeted TC. Tight, short, white, revealing blouse. Same screechy voice but with a foreign accent.

'My name is Almut,' announced the girl. 'You must be TC. Vance, Vance,' she squealed anxiously while blocking TC from entering the cutting room.

Wearing a guilty, caught-out expression, Vance appeared at the dispensary doorway.

'You are early, TC. I didn't expect you until tomorrow.'

'That's not true, Boss. You knew I'd be here this morning.'

'TC, I have employed Almut to work in the shop while you cut the opal.'

'Fine, Boss!' replied TC. 'Is it okay if I start doing that now or would you prefer I come back tomorrow?'

'Of course, start now, TC,' replied Vance before addressing Almut.

'You begin work in the shop tomorrow at nine, Almut. I suggest you wear more appropriate clothing. This is a pharmacy, not a sex shop.' Almut smiled at Vance alluringly before replying.

'I'll see you tomorrow morning, Mr Callahan.'

Vance's eyes were focused on Almut's swaying hips, long legs, and shapely butt as she exited via the front door.

'Where are the pieces you want me to cut today, Boss?' demanded TC. 'You make me sick, Boss. You already have Mrs Callahan and Coral; now you're doing Almut.'

'Don't be bloody ridiculous, TC,' replied Vance.

'Give me the pieces, Mr Callahan. Otherwise, I'm going home to lure a snake from under the house, get bitten, and die.' Vance laughed lightly as he handed her a bucket filled to the top with pieces.

'Choose whatever you want to cut, TC. As of tomorrow, you'll be working from 3 am. until 6 pm. I want Almut to learn how to cut opal. I'll teach her. She can do the shop from nine till six when you leave. I'll take over from there.'

I bet you'll teach Almut more than opal-cutting, thought TC as she switched on the grinding machine wheel.

'When will you grow up, Boss?' she asked as she began grinding ironstone in order to expose the face of the opal seam.

¶

Winter came. It was cold. Daylight hours were shorter. Nights were black and long.

Madison turned out not to be pregnant.

The bitch was bluffing all the bloody time, thought Jake repeatedly as he spent more and more time at the pub, drinking with his mates. He resumed visiting the creek with nurses. Every Saturday, he gambled on the horses. Usually, he won. The money he wagered was his. The staff didn't know that. They thought Jake was gambling away Carmichael and Carmichael's assets. One by one they resigned. A few left Brolga to search for a new life in the east. Others found employment within town. Madison, of course, stayed on. Jake employed another young girl. Day by day, they lost business as Jake lost interest.

Jake's mother decided to leave Brolga. She didn't want to have to send Carla away to school. She had done that with her other children. Carla was the last one. Thel Carmichael hoped to bond with Carla better than she had with the others.

Jake purchased his mother's house and cashed in an insurance policy his father had taken out for him when he was born. Combined with the money he'd won on race horses, he had more than enough to qualify for a bookmaker's license. Some said he was the youngest bookmaker in Queensland. Seat of Knowledge elders agreed Jake was too bloody smart for his own good.

TC continued cutting opals while making occasional trips to Sydney and Melbourne, where a few jewellers were becoming converts to boulder opal. Every trip she made, she managed to sell a few more stones by referrals. Word was spreading.

As a bookie, Jake was winning money hand over fist, getting drunk and screwing anything and everything he could. He still had Madison any time he felt the urge.

TC saw very little of Jake. That suited TC fine. A week after they were married, Jake came home drunk on rum. They had an argument about Madison and Jake hit TC hard at least a dozen times. She didn't tell anyone although Jake's mother and aunt were suspicious because TC's face would twinge with pain every time she moved. Her body was black and blue. Nobody knew that but herself.

When Vance wasn't sawing or going to the mine, he was busy with Delores and his girlfriends, so TC and he didn't get the opportunity to talk too often. Apart from Lisa Kara, TC felt she didn't have another friend in Brolga, especially since Jake's mother was gone.

⁋

Lou was pregnant. She and Colin had moved into a flat in Sydney. Colin's parents didn't approve of their marriage.

'We love each other, TC. That's the main thing,' said Lou every time they spoke. 'Hopefully they'll change after the baby comes.'

⁋

It was the race day in Brolga's mid-winter. A couple of weeks prior, Jake told TC to make a new dress. He expected her to look better than any other woman at the Race Ball.

'I'll do my best,' replied TC subserviently.

Next night she visited Lisa, who offered to lend TC a dress she had ordered out of one of her magazines.

'No, Lisa, all I need is some ideas,' replied TC. 'I have lovely, black, silky fabric I bought when Lou and I were in Sydney. Better sew it before it falls to pieces.'

'All right, darling,' agreed Lisa with a loving smile. 'Borrow my books for as long as you need them. I want you to promise me you'll let me see your dress before you go to the ball.'

TC searched through Lisa's fashion books. A bit out of this one and a bit out of that one in mind, she began cutting, pinning, and sewing. It was not easy to get the right fit without Lou there to help her. Eventually, TC felt confident she had made the best dress anyone and everyone would see at the Race Ball. She paraded it in front of Lisa after work two nights prior to the event.

'What do you think, Lisa?' asked TC outside the café kitchen.

'You need long, black gloves, something silver or gold around your throat, and high-heeled gold or silver shoes. Then, TC, you'll be perfect! I'll lend you the gloves, pendant, and shoes, TC,' said Lisa, who was excited as a hatful of bunnies. 'I hope my shoes fit you, darling!'

On Race Day, Jake won a lot of money at Brolga's bus race track. In the Empire after the races, he paid some punters who had placed on-the-nod bets and from others he collected money. Plastered beyond walking straight, he drove home to collect TC

'Come on, luv. We're going to the ball,' he announced as he threw his bookie's bag filled with cash into the top of their bedroom wardrobe.

TC stood nervously waiting for Jake's comments on her black, strapless, empire-line gown, complemented by Lisa's long, black gloves, sliver stilettos, and white-gold pendant.

Nothing!

Jake looked TC up and down, over and across, before stumbling to the bathroom. She sat in the lounge room waiting for him until he joined her. He was dressed like a movie star. He grabbed TC's hand and said, 'Come on, we're running late,' and they were off to the Brolga Race Ball.

Jake abandoned TC when they entered the Brolga Town Hall. He joined his mates, who had all either lost or won money at the races. They drank until they dropped while discussing "what ifs" regarding their day's bets.

TC felt like a lost soul. Jake's aunt was at the Race Ball, spotted TC, and fussed over her briefly until businessman friends of her husband joined them. TC went outside to breathe fresh air. As far as she was concerned, the air within the hall was infected with bullshit. Everyone sucking up to each other for one objective or another to their mutual benefit. She was standing outside the hall wondering what to do when the police patrol car pulled up. Her heart raced when Graham got out of the car and smiled down at her.

'Enjoy yourself, Constable,' said the sergeant before driving away.

'You look beautiful, TC,' said Graham. Love was shining from his eyes.

TC was thrilled to see Graham. He looked wonderful in his dinner suit. 'So do you, Constable Graham. I'm a married woman now,' she said sadly.

'I know, TC. I've thought about you all the time,' replied Graham. 'My heart broke when the sergeant told me you married Jake.'

'Why didn't you contact me if you were thinking about me?' asked TC.

'I didn't know what sort of reception I'd get, TC,' replied Graham, sincerely.

'Too late now! Why are you back in town? How long are you staying?' asked TC. She desperately wanted to throw her arms around Graham and beg him to run away with her.

'There's been some sheep-stealing going on. I'm here with the stock squad. There's four of us. We've come to guard a couple of thousand sheep on a property twenty Ks out of town.'

TC shivered. She was cold. 'I'd best go back inside, Graham. Jake was drunk before we got here. His head's probably wobbling all over the place by now.'

'Are you happy with Jake, TC?' asked Graham seriously.

'No,' replied TC. 'Not at all. I'm the most miserable person I know. The tennis club girls will be happy to see you. They are all here looking lovely.'

'TC, they meant nothing to me. I came to the ball because I knew you'd be here. Jake wouldn't miss an opportunity like this to show you off.'

TC shrugged. 'That's about all I am to Jake, something to show off. A possession.'

'Will you dance with me, TC?' asked Graham when they entered the hall. I want to hold you in my arms, he thought.

'Of course,' replied TC while thinking, I want to feel your arms around me. The imported-for-the-occasion band began playing a jazz waltz.

'Hey, Jake, that bloody cop's back, and he's trying to steal your old woman,' mumbled one of Jake's drunk mates.

'Where?' asked Jake in alarm.

'He's dancing with her on the other side of the hall,' pointed another mate.

'Bloody bastard,' said Jake as he lifted his glass of Rum and Coke to his mouth.

'Let TC have a dance, Jake. It is a ball, after all, mate.'

'More like a piss-up,' added someone else.

The tennis club girls were beside themselves with jealously.

'What's that bitch dancing with Graham for?' snapped one.

'She's a married woman!' snarled another.

Madison was keeping an eye on Jake. She didn't care who TC was dancing with as long as it wasn't Jake.

'I love you, TC,' whispered Graham.

'I love you, too,' whispered TC in reply before pulling away from him. 'The tongues are wagging. Can't say I blame them. We better nip this in the bud, Graham.' The music stopped.

'Thank you for the dance. I'll never forget,' said Graham.

'Me, neither,' replied TC with a sad smile. 'I'm going home. I'm sure just about every girl in the hall wants to dance with you.'

'I'm going to the station to change into my uniform. I have to start guarding sheep at midnight,' replied Graham also with a sad smile. To the dismay of the tennis girls, he left the hall.

'I'm going home, Jake,' announced TC.

'I'm not ready to leave yet,' slurred Jake with his body all over the place and his head way out of control.

'I didn't say anything about you leaving, Jake. Why should tonight be any different to every other one?' TC collected her coat and purse. Outside the hall, she took off Lisa's shoes so the heels wouldn't be ruined by her walking on the road. TC wasn't tired, so she sat in the dark on the glass-enclosed verandah. Her mind was out of control with thoughts of Graham and the mess she'd made of her life by marrying Jake. She was lonelier married to Jake than she'd been before. Jake's car pulled into the drive a few minutes later. He barged past her into the house. He didn't see her because she was sitting in the dark.

'I'll kill the effing slut,' he yelled. 'I'll kill that effing bastard of a cop, too.' TC stood up and walked inside.

'Which one of your sluts are you talking about, Jake?' she asked calmly.

'Don't be effing smart with me, TC,' yelled Jake.

'You smell like a rum distillery, Jake,' said TC.

'Don't be smart, TC. That's your bloody problem. You're too effing smart,' Jake yelled as he began shaking TC by her shoulders.

'Go to bed, Jake,' said TC.

'I'll go to effing bed, all right,' screamed Jake. 'After I've effing killed you.'

With that, Jake hurled TC against the wall and began punching her in the body where it wouldn't show. Rum had that effect on him. She had long since refrained from talking back to him when he'd been on rum. Tonight she slipped up because her mind was on other things.

TC was crying hysterically. She tried to pull away so Jake couldn't keep bashing her. He was so drunk he missed his aim and one of his fists caught her in the face.

'You've done it this time, Jake,' sobbed TC as she fell to the floor and curled herself into a ball. while her body was hurting something terrible, her head was spinning and her face throbbing.

¶

'Okay, eff it,' he yelled before rushing to his car and driving back to the town hall to re-join his mates.

'You were wrong,' he said to no one in particular but loud enough for all of them to hear. 'TC wasn't with the cop. She was at home. In the future, mind your own business.'

'Here, have another drink, Jake,' offered the young man who had half-jokingly suggested TC had left the ball with Graham.

¶

TC cried herself to sleep while still curled up on the lounge room floor. She didn't go to work next morning. She wasn't up to it. Come six o'clock, she phoned Vance and asked him to come and see her. She needed to talk to someone.

As always after bashing TC, Jake didn't come home. He'd do that when he needed a shower and a change of clothes.

The thought fleetingly crossed her mind to take some cash from the bookie's bag and catch the Flea. She was too frightened. Jake would come after her and kill her. Anyway, in the past, she had concealed her bruises caused by Jake's bad temper by wearing long-sleeved, buttoned-to-the-neck blouses. This time he'd hit her in the face. She felt ashamed knowing this time she wouldn't be able to hide it. The entire population of Brolga and district would know Jake was a wife-basher if Vance couldn't come up with a solution.

Vance was ropable when he saw the condition of TC's face. He was so furious he kicked the door of his ute.

'How effing long has this been going on TC?' he demanded.

'Since a week after we got married. It's only when he hits the rum and if I stand up to him. Unfortunately, last night I did.'

'Why on earth didn't you tell me, TC?' asked Vance while shaking his head in disbelief as he took a close look at TC's face.

'How bad is it, Boss?' asked TC. 'I haven't been game to look in the mirror. The bruises on my body are bad enough, but my face hurts much more.'

'It's ten times worse than Carla's throat was, TC. Don't look in a mirror, Butterball. We'll go to the shop the back way. We don't want anyone else to see you like this. I'll do what I can to clean it up, give you some painkillers and anti-inflammatory tablets.'

Jake's a gutless prick doing this to TC, thought Vance as he slammed the ute door, once again kicking it.

'We're lucky it's Sunday. Almut won't be in today.'

'You are playing with fire there, Boss. I've seen the way she looks at you. She's forever flirting with you. Instead of ignoring her, you laugh. That encourages her more.'

'There's nothing going on there, TC,' denied Vance. He was a little too emphatic. He was lying.

'I know you too well, Boss,' said TC. 'If there's nothing happening with her yet, there will be soon.' Vance changed the subject.

'We are almost there. I'll see what I can do to fix your eye and cheek. Lucky the bastard didn't break your nose.'

'I had a dance with Graham at the ball, Boss. I think Jake thought I left with him.'

'Pity you hadn't got more serious with him, TC. Can't see him bashing you.'

'You are the one who told me not to get serious with him,' reminded TC. 'You told me nobody wants used goods, so I wouldn't ever get a husband. I'd be used goods.'

'Perhaps you should ignore what I tell you sometimes, TC.' said Vance.

'I did when I married Jake.'

They were in the dispensary. Vance told TC to sit on the stool and pull back her hair.

'You've got a gash on your left temple. It will probably leave a scar unless it's stitched. There's also a smaller one running from the outer edge of your eye downwards towards your cheek. That one probably won't scar. I'll put some iodine on them. It will sting.'

'Don't tell me anymore, Boss,' instructed TC. She is surprisingly calm, thought Vance.

'I'll call the doctor and ask him to do the stitches for you,' said Vance.

'No, Boss! I don't want him to see me. I'm sure you can do it for me. I don't want anyone else to see me.' The only time TC had seen Vance so emotional was after the Claudia incident when he sat behind the station wagon crying.

'All right, Butterball, I'll do the best I can,' he agreed. As Vance removed the pain-killer injection from the refrigerator, he wished he had a gun he could use to shoot Jake. 'I should take TC to the hospital and show the bastard's girlfriends what he's done.' Six stitches in TC's temple later, Vance gave TC some tablets and eye drops. He took her home before driving around town and to the creek in search of Jake, who was nowhere to be found.

Vance sliced boulders for a couple of hours before going back to Jake's house to check on TC.

'I want to go to work, Boss,' she told him. 'I don't want to stay here all day feeling sorry for myself; I need to get my mind off the pain.'

'You're a tough one, TC. I don't think you can sand or polish, though. The dust from the powder might infect your eye and cuts.'

'Okay, I'll face and shape all day,' she said before bursting into tears when she realised the inappropriate words she had spoken.

'Come on. I'll drive you to work. I couldn't find Jake. If he's still on the rum, he might come home and lay into you again.'

¶

TC began immediately after Vance insisted that she pull the shower cap well down over the left side of her face and wear an eye-patch. Vance was like a concerned father all day, asking TC was she feeling all right and making sure she took her pills and put drops in her eye. Mid-afternoon he went to Con's and returned with a chocolate thick-shake for her.

'Don't fuss over me so much, Boss,' she said lightly as she switched off the grinding wheel. 'I'll be all right. How long do you think before my face will be normal.'

Vance felt TC needed to see what Jake had done to her. He quickly got a mirror from the cosmetic counter and placed it in front of her.

'You tell me how long you think it will be,' he said angrily. 'Go on, pull off your shower cap and eye-patch and tell me. Sit at my desk and take a good look. You should go to the sergeant and have Jake locked up.'

TC's left eye was red. There appeared to be small floaters of blood in it. Both top and lower eyelids were swollen and badly bruised a purple/black. Her left cheek and forehead were swollen beyond belief and also very bruised. The cut from the corner of her eye to her cheek was encased by bruising and covered with iodine yellow. Vance had stuck a gauze square over her stitches with surgical tape.

'That's your face, TC. I shudder to think what you're hiding under your jeans and blouse.'

'Black and blue, Boss,' replied TC softly as she recalled Graham telling her she looked beautiful the night before. She was glad he couldn't see her now.

'How many times has Jake belted you?' asked Vance seriously.

'This is the seventeenth time. I learned a while back not to talk back to him when he's been drinking rum. Last night I forgot.'

'Come on, I'll take you home,' said Vance. 'I'll tell Almut not to come until four tomorrow. You can come at six and leave at half-past-three. Here, wear these on your way to and from work. They might conceal a bit of damage.' Vance handed TC the largest framed pair of sunglasses they had in stock.

⸿

TC took a bath as hot as she could bear. It would bring out the bruising on her body. After drying herself, she looked at her reflection in the mirror.

'You've really done a number on me this time, Jake,' she said aloud. 'I should wait until you are passed out in a drunken stupor, then bash you so you know what it feels like. I'd have to use a shovel or a big piece of wood. Might be simpler to stab you with a carving knife.'

⸿

Graham was sitting in his old room behind the station. He was glad when he'd been allocated it as his accommodation during the sheep-stealing case. He was fiddling with his guitar and thinking about TC just like he had when he'd been stationed in Brolga before.

I love her, he thought. I should have been patient instead of messing around with the others. Now she's married to Jake Carmichael. Knowing TC, she'll stick with him come hell or high water.

Thoughts of TC had helped him through his first night guarding sheep. The night had been cold, so cold, and as black as pitch. He couldn't see his hand before his face. It was a somewhat daunting experience. There was no means of escape. The officers he had relieved at midnight drove the vehicle back to Brolga as Graham had done that morning.

Graham desperately wished he had TC in his room with him. He could sing her the song he had never gotten around to doing in the past. She still didn't know he played the guitar. He thought of the dance they'd shared and doubted he would ever find another girl who felt like TC did when he held her in his arms. Graham knew TC felt the same way about him. He just knew it!

Armed with her eye drops, pills, alarm clock, glass of water and long-bladed knife, TC locked herself in one of the bedrooms and tried to sleep. She jumped nervously every time she heard a car. At one stage, she thought of using the knife on herself. She finally knew for sure that Jake was home after session time when she heard his car pull into the yard. She took a deep breath and sighed with relief when she heard another car stop outside, then voices.

Good. He'll leave me alone, she thought. He won't touch me in front of them. He'll be too busy drinking booze and bullshitting. TC set her alarm for five and went to sleep, thinking of what could have been with Graham.

A gem dealer from Los Angeles contacted Vance that week. The dealer had seen the stones Vance traded with the jeweller in Carmel. An arrangement was made and the dealer was flying to Brolga. Vance would take him to the mine, then they would do some business. The dealer was keen to be the first in the States to have "rock opal", as he referred to it.

Vance heard on the grapevine a few other miners had found opal.

He also heard more than a few had run out of friends and/or patience, had thrown in the towel, and returned to wherever they had come from.

It didn't bother Vance what others were doing. Unless they approached him, he kept to himself. He was hopeful the American dealer would spend up big. If so, Vance would begin mining one of his other leases. One US dollar was two Aussie dollars. He would lease another machine, keep Neil, Yappy, Little Joe, and Faith where they were and move Michael and Jakkie to the new lease. He would need to find a machine operator and a cook.

¶

Jake and TC rarely saw each other. He was still sleeping in his room when she went to work. She was asleep in her room when Jake came home from wherever, whenever.

It seemed to take forever for her face to heal enough to resume sanding and polishing. Vance was secretive about the stones Almut produced. Never showed TC one. For that matter, Almut was never mentioned. TC was appreciative of Vance's consideration while her face was in the process of mending.

He did the shop himself on Saturday mornings and drove to camp in the afternoon, giving TC the weekends to work by herself. Every day he went to Con's and returned with a chocolate thick-shake. Lisa asked him every day, 'Tell TC to come and see me.' On more than one occasion, Vance was tempted to tell her why TC hadn't visited. He didn't. TC never betrayed him, How could he do it to her.?

¶

'How many have you got shaped?' he asked the morning he gave her the go-ahead for the polishing room.

'I haven't counted them. There's a lot,' she replied, nodding to a bucket under his bench saw.

'Bloody hell!' said Vance. 'I should have kept count of them myself!'

TC smiled.

'Perhaps you and Almut have been too busy doing other things between four and when Coral finishes work, Boss.'

'Don't start, TC,' retaliated Vance. 'Get on with those stones. We've got gem dealers from California coming in a couple of weeks. I want to be able to floor them with colour and numbers.'

'I'll do my best, Boss,' promised TC.

'You always do, Butterball,' smiled Vance.

At camp, the men were working all day every day, happy when they found boulders and miserable when they didn't. Yappy was content to be at camp. After drinking away, giving away, or gambling away his thousands over Christmas break, he was content to stay in the bush forever. The only thing he felt miserable about was the fact that Jake told him he would never place a bet for him again.

'What the buggery did you find to bet on in Wingtree, Yappy?' asked Jake when they met in the street after Yappy returned to town.

'You know me, Jake. I'm a gambler. Nothing to do in bloody Wingtree except get on the piss. Get me drunk enough, I'll gamble on any bloody thing. Even flies, cockroaches, or grasshoppers crawling up the wall.'

Jake replied, 'In that case, mate, I'm not wasting any more of my time making you money to gamble on bugs. See you later, Yappy.'

That was that!

Little Joe, after the fiasco in Brisbane, decided he was better off in the bush. 'Fancy getting arrested because Jakkie insisted on praying to a juke box, not to mention us running out of money before having the sense to ask Vance for more.'

Neil, Faith, Jakkie, and Michael were still ashamed and angry with themselves for what they did to TC when they went on strike.

'We're a menace to society, all of us,' said Faith one night over the kitchen table.

'Don't include me, you mongrel,' came from Yappy.

'Come on, Yappy,' said Neil. 'At least we enjoy ourselves, mate. We drink our money, not throw it away betting on vermin.'

'I didn't bet on bloody vermin, Neil,' snapped Yappy. 'Vermin are parasites. I bet it on bugs.' Everyone laughed. Yappy spat the dummy and began crashing pots onto the bench.

'Poor Yappy,' said Little Joe.

'We're bastards, all right,' laughed Neil. Jakkie, Faith, and Michael nodded in agreement.

❡

Graham was on the sheep-guard shift. He didn't bother going back to the tennis club. It wasn't that he didn't want to play, he didn't want the bother of those girls again. He had his car there, so he worked on it a lot. Every time he drove it or walked to Con's to eat, he hoped to catch a glimpse of TC. He was surprised neither Con nor Lisa had seen her since the day of the race ball.

'She's working hard, Constable Graham. Vance buys her a thick-shake every day,' advised Con.

'Something is wrong, my darling husband,' said Lisa with a concerned expression on her lovely face.

'I agree with Lisa,' thought Graham. It's weeks since the ball. I need to see her.

'I'm going to the chemist shop to see her now,' said Lisa with determination. 'I want to ask her if I have upset her in some way. She's been a different girl since marrying Jake Callahan. Darling girl should have waited for you, young Graham.'

I should have waited for her, too, Lisa, thought Graham as he and Con watched Lisa cross the street.

❡

'Hello, Vance,' said Lisa sweetly. 'I'd like to talk to TC, if possible. I won't take up too much of her time.'

'She is in the polishing room, Lisa. She's pretty busy,' replied Vance.

'One minute is all I need, Vance. One minute,' pleaded Lisa.

'I'll get her, Lisa,' replied Vance while breathing a sigh of relief he'd removed the stitches from TC's temple just that morning. He paused in the dispensary to grab TC's sunglasses, a pen, and a slip of paper on which he scribbled, 'Pull down your hair over your face and put on the glasses.'

'Lisa is here to see you, TC,' Vance announced loud enough for Lisa to hear. TC quickly loosened her pony tail and pulled her hair so it was hanging over the left side of her face and jammed on the sunglasses. Mustering confidence and hopefully a convincing smile, TC hurried into the shop.

'Darling, I've been worried about you,' said Lisa, hugging TC. 'Why haven't you been to see me? I thought you would come back and tell me about the ball.'

'I've been busy cutting opals, Lisa,' replied TC honestly. 'The Boss has a customer coming from America, so I have to get as many finished as I can.'

'Yes, darling, I understand,' said Lisa. 'But it doesn't take very long to say hello. What happened to your pony tail? It suits you.'

Vance was watching via the one-way mirrored dispensary wall as Lisa pulled TC's hair back from her face to expose the healed but still red scratch below her eye.

'Why are you wearing those huge glasses, darling?' asked Lisa tenderly.

'I've got a sore eye,' replied TC. Vance showed from the dispensary.

'TC fell over after the ball, didn't you, TC?' said Vance.

'How did you fall over, darling? I know you don't drink. Must have been my high-heeled shoes.'

'No, your shoes are fine, Lisa. I really need to get back to work.'

'Not before you show me your eye, darling,' persisted Lisa with concern.

I've had enough of this, thought Vance. Lisa's the only friend apart from me TC's got in this town now Lou's gone. It's about time people knew how Jake treats her.

'Take your glasses off, TC,' commanded Vance. 'Show her what Jake did to you.'

'It's almost better now, Boss,' started TC.

'I don't care. Show Lisa. She's also bruised all over her body, Lisa. That's where he usually belts her so there's no visible evidence. This time he made a mistake and punched her in the head, as well.' TC didn't move as Vance snatched the glasses from her face. She felt ashamed. She was ashamed of allowing herself to be Jake's victim.

'You poor darling,' said Lisa, who began weeping with shock. 'Why didn't you come to me? I'm your friend. Con and I love you.' TC mustered a smile.

'It's nearly better now,' she replied confidently. 'I'll be able to cover it with make-up soon.'

'You go back to work, TC,' directed Vance with a resigned smile of satisfaction for what he had done. Now TC would have someone else to confide in. Vance and Lisa talked at the front door of the pharmacy.

'I didn't have a clue, Vance,' said a distraught Lisa. 'Con heard a rumour from one of their neighbours a while back. We didn't believe it.'

'It's been going on since a week after they got married,' said Vance matter-of-factly. 'This is the seventeenth time he's done it.'

'She's never said a word to me,' said Lisa, shaking her head in disbelief.

'Me, neither. She wouldn't have told me this time, except the bastard jabbed her in the face. She doesn't want everyone to know...'

'I'm telling Con,' said Lisa adamantly. 'I'd like to tell young Constable Graham, too. I'm certain he's in love with TC.'

'Please don't, Lisa. If she wants Graham to know, she'll tell him herself.'

'All right,' agreed Lisa with reluctance. 'Tell her to pull her hair over her face, wear her glasses, and come see me when she finishes work. Not everyone is as curious as I am.'

'Not everyone cares about her the way you do, either,' replied Vance.

§

'You shouldn't have done that, Boss,' said TC when Vance came to the polishing room door.

Poor TC looks so sad, thought Vance. Wish I'd spent more time paying attention to her. I would have talked her out of it instead of not caring enough to ask her where she was going when she asked for a week off. I abused her for wanting time. I didn't so much as ask her why. I wish I had a way to turn back time. I would have talked her out of it.

'You need someone else you can turn to. I won't always be here,' he said matter-of-factly before answering the ringing telephone.

¶

'I'll go now, Boss,' said TC at three-thirty. 'Almut will be here soon.'

'No, not today. I'll send her home at five. She can tidy the shop for an hour. She won't be working on opal until you finish those stones. Keep the polishing room door closed until she goes.'

Every time TC turned the motor to change a disc or buff until five o'clock, she could hear Almut and Vance arguing in the dispensary. TC got the impression from the bits and pieces she heard that Almut wanted to stay back with Vance as usual. Why was the bitch staying instead of her? She could cut opals better than TC, and she wanted to spend time with Vance alone.

I knew it, thought TC. That's girlfriend talk. I've heard it too many times before to be fooled. Poor Boss, he can't help himself. Poor Mrs Callahan, she wouldn't have a clue. She thinks I'm the threat. It's a joke! If only she knew! One thing I'm sure of; I won't be the one telling her. She can think whatever she wants about me; I know I'm innocent and so does the boss.

Vance opened the polishing-room door. He was not happy. 'I suppose you heard a lot of that?'

'Enough!' replied TC without looking at him.

'I don't know what to say, TC,' from Vance.

'Then say nothing, Boss,' replied TC. 'I'm like the three wise monkeys, Boss. I see nothing, speak nothing, and hear nothing.'

'I know that, Butterball. I'm going home for a while. Before I go, would you like me to tell Lisa you'll be working late, so you won't be over to see her tonight?'

'That would be nice. She's worried about me. She's a lovely lady.'

¶

Vance returned a little later carrying a napkin-covered plate.

'Con and Lisa sent you a hamburger and a chocolate. Lisa said she's worried about how thin you are. She's right. Your bones are sticking out everywhere. I'll be back to drive you home before Coral gets here.'

¶

And so the new routine continued until the gem dealer from Los Angeles hit town. Coral had long since volunteered to do all night shifts at the Empire so she could be with Vance after pub closing time. Vance went to the mine Saturday afternoons and returned Sunday. TC began at 6 a.m. and finished 9.30 pm. Almut worked in the shop from nine 'til five. She loathed TC. They had no reason to see each other. TC kept the polishing-room door closed. Every day Con or Lisa delivered something for TC to eat with a note of love and encouragement under the napkin. They always gave it to Vance, never to Almut. They would call prior to coming to make sure he was there.

Jake was Jake! Occasionally book-making, always gambling, drinking, fornicating, and neglecting the business more and more.

Graham knew something was wrong with TC even though Lisa assured him TC was working long hours. He would see her soon and hopefully they could and would have a long talk. Not seeing TC when she was so close made him love her more.

TC cut a long fringe so her hair would cover the scar on her temple. When her facial bruises became pale yellow, she began wearing powder base-cream to cover them. One night she found a note from Jake on the lounge-room table.

'When are you going to do some laundry? I'm running out of white shirts.' TC ignored it. Next night there was another note from Jake. 'I asked you about my shirts.' TC wrote a quick reply. "Get one of your girlfriends to iron them, Jake! You don't bash them!'

TC was now accustomed to taking the carving knife to bed with her. She slept with it under her pillow.

A couple of days later, Jake was drinking with a couple of mates in the Empire.

'How's TC? Haven't seen her around,' enquired one of the men.

'How would I know? I never see her myself, mate. She's a lazy bitch. Won't do any ironing.'

'I won't have that, Jake. She works her guts out at the pill-pusher's.'

'Maybe so, but she still should do my bloody ironing,' defended Jake.

Jess was on duty. Naturally she overheard the conversation. She saw red and couldn't hold her tongue.

'I won't have you say one bad word about TC, Jake Carmichael. I know who the lazy one is! It's you! Why don't you get Neil's mother to do your laundry like you have since you took over running your father's shop? If you can't afford to pay her because you've drunk and gambled everything away, I suggest you have your plaything, Madison, do it. She can do your ironing in the back of the shop where she does every other bloody thing for you! Now get out of here! Go drink at one of the other pubs. I can't stand to look at you.'

Jake and his mates threw down their drinks, collected their change, and left without a word. All of them including Jake knew Jess was right.

¶

The American gem dealer's visit was looming. A couple of days away. Vance was at his desk busy sorting his bagged stones into price ranges. He wanted to concentrate. Almut was supposed to be stocking shelves in the shop. Instead, she was hanging around Vance, flirting. She repeatedly asked him to get rid of TC early so she could stay back with him. Vance lost his cool. He really did his block. He threw his chair back, picked up his cigarettes, and threw them at the wall.

'Get out now, you stupid effing moron,' he yelled. 'You haven't got an effing brain in your head. This man is almost on the doorstep, and you want to eff around. Go on! Go away now! I'll tell you when you can come back.'

'You can't do this to me. I'm underage. I can get you in trouble, Vance,' was Almut's screeching, threatening reply. Vance was trapped. He knew Almut was capable of carrying out her threat.

'Get in the shop now, Almut. Do what you were employed to do,' he said in a controlled, flat tone of voice. 'You leave at five.'

Almut threw her head in the air and returned to stacking shelves. She was angry. She made a point of smashing things around.

'I should have cut my effing dick off,' mumbled Vance. 'I should cut the bastard off myself.' He flung open the polishing-room door. 'I suppose you heard that?' TC rolled her eyes.

'How could I help it?! Lucky there were no customers in the shop. You've got yourself in deep water now, Boss.'

'How are you going with the stones? Will you have them finished before the Yank gets here?'

'Perhaps you and Coral should hit the creek tonight. I want to work later than nine-thirty.'

'I'll cancel Coral for tonight and tomorrow night, TC. I want this man to buy some stones, but we don't want to give them away. I've done too much of that already. I want the prices to be not only fair to him, but to us as well.'

Vance's cancellation with Coral didn't work. As usual, she rocked up at the back door a bit after ten. For a while now, she'd suspected Vance had another woman besides her and his wife. He wasn't as sexually active as he used to be.

TC was working with the polishing-room door open. Vance was checking his pieces of stone, comparing one stone with another when Coral burst into the dispensary and confronted him.

'I knew you had someone else, you bastard! Where is she? I'll kill the effing moll!'

Here we go again, thought TC as she pushed the sliding door closed and continued working.

Vance looked at Coral innocently.

'Don't be silly. I told you I'm working.'

'I don't believe you, Vance,' snapped Coral as she slammed open the sliding door to the polishing-room. TC glanced at Coral indifferently.

'Leave me alone, Coral. I'm busy.'

'I bet you effing are!' screamed Coral as she moved threateningly towards TC. Vance grabbed Coral from behind and pulled her away from TC.

I've had it, thought TC. She switched off the motor and placed the stone she'd been working on the shelf.

'I've had enough, Mr Callahan,' she calmly stated. 'No more abuse for me from anyone. It's high time I stand up for myself.'

'That's good, slut,' spat Coral, who was still being restrained by Vance. TC smiled and shook her head in disbelief, then walked slowly towards the front door. No surprise, it wasn't locked. She heard the back door slam shut.

Bet the boss has thrown Coral out, she thought as she stepped onto the footpath.

'TC, don't go!' called Vance behind her. 'I understand! At least, let us talk about it. Come back inside before that mad bitch comes around the corner and sees us.'

'All right,' agreed TC. 'I've had my share of abuse today.' Vance click-locked the pharmacy door behind them. Once in the dispensary, he sat at his desk and lit a cigarette.

'TC, I need you to finish those stones before the Californian gets here.'

'Almut can do them. I heard her say she's a better opal-cutter than I am. I didn't hear you say any different.' Vance was silent. He was guilty as charged.

'Please, TC, we'll talk after this man has been and gone.' TC wanted to say, 'No,' then remembered how caring he had been when he fixed her eye.

'All right! Keep your girlfriends away from here and me. I'll have the stones finished. Then I won't be back until after we have the talk. I'm tired, tired of everything.'

¶

The California gem dealer, first name Patrick, flew into Brolga in a chartered plane out of Sydney. Vance waited at the airstrip to meet him. It was nine o'clock on Saturday morning and windy as buggery, as the locals would say.

The night before, the Seat of Knowledge gents had predicted a dust storm.

The poor bastard is in for a shock if it starts blowing dust, thought Vance as he watched the flight land into the wind. 'Fancy coming from Los Angeles to be greeted by a dust storm.' Vance smiled to himself when the visitor stepped from the plane attired in a business suit, white shirt, and tie. He was wearing a smart city-style hat, which was ripped off his head by the wind and carried into the air to land who knew where. Along with his travel bag, he carried a briefcase. Vance hoped it was filled with money.

As always when a plane was heard landing in Brolga, the owner of the fuel depot would immediately drive to the airstrip with a tank full of aviation fuel on the back of a truck. The wind got stronger. The concerned pilot spoke with the fuel depot owner while he fuelled the plane. After a brief conversation, the pilot approached his passengers.

'Patrick I've just been told Brolga is going to be hit by a raging dust storm. I'm getting off the ground as soon as the plane is fuelled. If you are still staying two days, I'll be here at nine on Monday morning. It's a small plane. I'd hate to see it up-sided. I'll fly to Curloo and come back for you.'

'Should be a quick flight. You'll have a strong tail-wind,' laughed Vance.

'I'm excited about being in the middle of a dust storm in Australia,' said Patrick.

Vance smiled inwardly as he started the car. The plane flew over them when they were halfway to town. Vance explained to Patrick it was a bit early in the year for dust storms, but it had been very dry for a couple of years.

'None of us can control nature,' remarked Patrick.

Vance drove Patrick to the Empire, introduced him to Jack Romeo, then went to the dispensary to collect a few stones to show Patrick when they were at the mine. He wanted to display the comparison between rough and finished product.

'When will you be back, Vance?' whined Almut.

'I don't know, Almut,' replied Vance.

'Will you be back tonight, Vance?' she persisted.

'I don't know, and if I am, I don't want you here,' replied Vance impatiently. 'I'll be busy with the American.'

'I hope she's not coming here today, Vance,' said Almut.

'If you mean TC, no, she's not. She didn't finish the stones until two o'clock this morning. She's having a couple of days off.'

'Where are the stones? I want to see them.'

'The stones are in a safe place, and, no, you can't see them. Close the shop at one o'clock and don't come back until Monday morning. I'm going.' Almut stamped her foot.

'Don't treat me like a child, Vance!' Vance raised his eyebrows.

'Why not? That's what you are. See you Monday.'

¶

As if synchronised, the wall of red dust hit the western end of town as Jack and Bert Romeo opened the pub doors and the warning siren sounded. They quickly closed them again. Patrick was now more suitably dressed for the locality. He wore jeans, denim jacket, and boots. Briefcase in hand, he was waiting for Vance to pick him up for their trip to the mine. Vance drove around the corner when the siren sounded and laughed to himself.

'Well, Patrick, you are about to experience your dust storm in Australia.'

Patrick was sitting in the hallway a few feet from the Empire's main entrance. It was too windy on the footpath.

'What was the siren all about?' he asked when Jack Romeo rushed to close the door.

'The dust storm will hit any second,' replied Jack. 'I hate the mongrel things.'

Patrick jumped to his feet as Vance appeared via the rear entrance.

'Come quickly, Patrick. Follow me. If we're quick, you'll see what a Brolga dust storm looks like. It's almost on top of us.' Jack Romeo pointed to the base of the door.

'You're too late Vance. It's here.' Red dust was billowing through the tiny gap between the door base and the floor. Outside, the wind was raging.

'Sounds like a tornado,' exclaimed Patrick in disbelief. 'Will this go on all day or be here and gone like a tornado?'

'Here and gone. We'll be on our way to camp before you know it,' replied Vance matter-of-factly.

'Say hello to the boys from Bert and me. Bert misses them at the Majestic.'

Vance laughed. 'Misses their money, you mean, don't you, Jack?' Jack Romeo laughed while walking towards the office.

❡

The storm soon passed and Vance and Patrick were on their way. It was after lunch and the men were back working when Vance pulled up at camp. Vance introduced Patrick to Yappy, who had never met anyone from Los Angeles before. The only Americans he'd met were Milt Elliott and his crew, who had blown the cap-rock off the hill. They were all from Texas.

'So is Los Angeles a big bloody city or not?' asked Yappy, who didn't have a clue where Los Angeles was. Sounded more Mexican or Spanish to him. Patrick laughed.

'Yes, Yappy, it's big.' Vance interrupted any further conversation between Yappy and Patrick.

'Yappy, how about making us some sandwiches or something else to eat. I'll take Patrick to the hill and introduce him to the men. We'll be back soon.'

'You're in a great bloody hurry today, Vance,' mumbled Yappy to himself as he began preparing lunch for two. He'd make sandwiches for the bastards. Seeing as Vance was in such a bloody hurry, he could take them with him if need be.

Vance introduced Patrick to the men. They exchanged first names and handshakes. That was about it. Vance is in one hell of a hurry, thought all five men as they resumed working.

Vance was, indeed, in a hurry. He wanted the mine visit over as quickly as possible, without appearing rude, of course. He was eager to get back to town and down to business.

After coffee and sandwiches, interrupted by Yappy's usual chatter, Vance produced the cut stones, showed Patrick some rough boulders while explaining the process of extracting the stones from the rocks. Patrick was impressed, to say the least. He asked multitudes of questions, all of which Vance answered off- the-cuff while going to great lengths to explain every one of them.

By the time Vance and Patrick got back to town, Vance knew a great deal about Patrick while all Patrick knew about Vance was he was a pharmacist-cum-opal-miner. Patrick was Vance's age and lived in an inner-city Los Angeles apartment. He was not married. He had decided not to marry years ago because he loved women too much. Wouldn't be fair to take a wife because he'd be one shit of a husband. He had been in the gem business since leaving college to learn and eventually take over his father's business, which he had done ten years prior.

Vance dropped Patrick off at the Empire to get cleaned up while Vance went home to do the same. They agreed to meet at Con's for a meal an hour later.

Wonder if Patrick's ever been a pisshead, thought Vance as he drove home, feeling guilty as buggery because he was married to Delores but had never given up other women. Oh, well, he told himself as he pulled up outside his house, Nobody's perfect! I don't care how good a man

Patrick is, all I care about is how deep he digs into his briefcase.

¶

That morning TC was woken by the sound of the wild wind banging the shutters on the windows and the corrugated roof at Jordan's shack across the street.

'This house needs a good clean,' she reasoned. 'Better the dust comes now than tomorrow after I've cleaned it today.' She stayed in bed, waiting for the storm to pass. Mentally she planned her day. Being Saturday, she knew she didn't need to worry about Jake bothering her. He'd be backing horses, getting drunk, then hopefully heading for the creek with one of his floosies. She decided to do the washing, clean the house, wash her hair, put it in rollers, take a bubble bath, put on one of her long-ago-made-but-as-yet-not-christened dresses, visit Lisa and Con, then go to the movies. She didn't care which movies were showing, she wanted to see them.

After much deliberation, TC chose a cream, shift-style dress with rolled, high-neck collar and cuffed three-quarter length sleeves. The bruising on her face had faded and her fringe covered the scar where the stitches had been. For good measure, she patted a little foundation make-up over it, brushed mascara on her lashes, applied lipstick to her lips, and she was ready to go.

Come six o'clock, TC was on her way. She felt good. This must be the way prisoners feel when they are released from prison, she thought. Thinking of prisoners caused her to think more of Graham. It made her feel sad. Memories of him playing Scrabble with Lou and her at Auntie Flo and Uncle Doug's house popped into her head. She remembered a word Graham had used to win a game. Lou hadn't believed it was a word. She had insisted on looking it up in the dictionary in the hope of proving Graham wrong. The word was "I".

That's what I'm in now, thought TC, who was suddenly overcome by a feeling of hopelessness.

Apart from Con, Lisa, and three men TC had not seen before, the café was empty. The men watched with interest as Con and Lisa welcomed TC with open arms. Even Con came from behind the counter to hug TC. TC handed Lisa a string-handled, paper bag.

'I finally brought your shoes, gloves, and necklace back, Lisa,' said TC apologetically in a soft voice so the strangers could not hear. 'Sorry it's taken so long. I'm taking myself to the movies. There's a pair of my own high heels in the bag. I'll leave my little-girl, bowed flatties here and collect them after the movies for the walk home, if that's okay.'

'Of course, it is, darling,' whispered Lisa. 'Go in the kitchen and change them now. Then come and sit with me. You look lovely, by the way.'

'Who is that young woman, Lisa?' enquired one of the three men.

'That's TC, Sergeant. She works for the chemist,' replied Lisa. The three men were members of the police stock squad out of Curloo.

TC joined Lisa at her table, as usual with her back to the door. Con surprised her by placing an ice cream sundae in front of her.

'See, TC. I remember,' he said. TC looked at the dish. The ice cream scoops were heart-shaped.

'I remember, too, Con,' replied TC with a wistful smile. 'Thank you.'

'Go on, darling, enjoy your hearts,' urged Lisa. 'Con and I have been so worried about you. So has young Graham.'

'Lisa, I hope you didn't tell him what Jake does to me.'

'No, darling, we didn't. Both Con and I have wanted to tell him since the second Vance told me, and I told Con. Every time he comes here, he asks about you. He loves you, darling.' TC toyed with her ice cream.

'I love him, too, Lisa, but I'm married to Jake. I don't love Jake. I never did. Jake doesn't love me. He loves no one apart from himself, except perhaps his mother. To Jake, I am nothing but a trophy.'

'Everyone knows that, darling,' comforted Lisa. 'What are we going to do!' TC shook her head and sighed.

'Nothing! Nothing I can do. I married Jake because I was lonely, Lisa. Now I'm even lonelier! I sleep with a carving knife under my pillow!' Lisa didn't look at all shocked.

'I don't blame you, darling,' she whispered seriously before looking up over TC's head and smiling.

'Hello, Vance.'

'Hello, Lisa. Good to see our girl taking time off and looking pretty,' said Vance. TC turned around in her chair. She was all smiles.

'Hello, Boss. I'm going to the movies.' Vance laughed in surprise.

'You are what? Carmel will faint from shock when she sees you roll up.'

Patrick was standing silently beside Vance, who first introduced him to Lisa, then TC.

'This is TC, Patrick. She's been working day in and night out cutting opals since you told me you were coming.' Lisa had to bite her tongue. She wanted to say, 'TC's been working day in and night out since the day she went to work for you. That's three years ago.'

TC stood up and reached out her hand. Patrick was surprised by the firmness of the handshake. Vance had made her practice shaking hands until he was satisfied before he sent her off to Melbourne to sell opal to Cane Toad Face.

'You'll be dealing with men, TC, so don't shake hands like a limp-wrist. The bastards will think you are weak, a pushover, and they'll try to beat you down,' Vance had told her.

'Some handshake you've got there,' said Patrick. 'Pretty strong for such a small, young lady.'

'That means she's nobody's fool,' said a smiling Vance.

The Flea whistle sounded, which meant the movies would be starting soon.

'I hope you like the opals, sir. They are all very beautiful,' said TC sincerely. 'Sorry I didn't finish the ice cream, Lisa. I'll see you at interval. I'll see you later, Boss.'

Vance, Lisa, Patrick, and the three police officers, who were still seated at their table, watched TC pause at the counter, speak to Con, then walk out. Vance and Lisa shared a feeling of pride. Patrick thought, That young woman will go places! The police officers were thinking, So, she's the one breaking young Sandler's heart.

¶

'Hello, luv. What are you doing here?' asked Carmel at the door after TC had purchased her movie ticket.

'Don't know, Carmel. Suddenly I got the urge to come to the pictures,' replied a smiling TC.

'You picked a good night, luv,' said Carmel. 'We've got two old Elvis films—'Jailhouse Rock' and 'Love me Tender'.

'That's probably why I got the urge, Carmel.' Carmel watched TC take the first chair she saw.

'Poor little bugger, she should never have married Jake. He might be Thel's son, but he's not good enough for TC. I bet those rumours I heard about him bashing her are true. Thel believed they were.'

Suddenly the small theatre was almost full. The usual movie crowd who followed the projectionist and his reels of film from the Flea to the theatre all appeared to know exactly where they were going to sit. It was as if the chairs had names on them. The lights went out, the King's voice was singing 'Warden Threw a Party ...', and TC's eyes were glued to the screen for Lou's idol's face to appear.

Out of the corner of her eye, she saw Carmel's torch direct someone to the seat beside her. Seconds later, she felt a finger rubbing over and across her wrist. Electric shock! She knew who it was before turning her head. It was Graham. TC's heart raced out of control. She quickly looked back at the screen. Graham squeezed her hand. TC squeezed his back. Both of them wanted to get out of there and run as far away from Brolga as possible.

Although Graham and TC sat with their eyes glued to the screen, neither of them had a clue as to what the movie was about other than the King singing lots of songs. They heard but at the same time did not hear. Their minds were racing around in circles with what ifs, what to dos, and what could have been. The movie was coming to an end. Graham squeezed TC's hand tightly, then left before the theatre lights came on.

Carmel saw Graham leave. She smiled to herself, then sighed, hoping neither the young constable nor TC realised she had purposely directed him to the chair she had chosen for him. If ever she'd seen a couple made for each other, it had to be them, especially after watching them dancing together at the recent Race Ball.

TC waited for the stampede through the door to subside before standing up.

'Did you enjoy the film, luv?' asked Carmel.

'Elvis is Lou's favourite, Carmel,' replied TC. 'Lou's going to have a baby, so I guess her dreams of going to Memphis and marrying Elvis are long gone.'

'You say hello to Lou for me, luv. Wish her all the best,' said Carmel.

The rush was almost over by the time TC got to Con's. She was surprised to see Vance and Patrick were still there. They were seated at a side table towards the rear of the café.

'Enjoy the movie, TC?' called Vance.

'Yes, Boss,' nodded TC as she approached his table. 'Lou would have loved it. It was Elvis.'

'Do you love Elvis, too?' enquired Patrick. TC smiled.

'Everyone loves Elvis, sir, but I don't dream about him. Guess I'm a realist.' Vance laughed.

'That's for sure.'

It suddenly struck TC how similar Vance and Patrick were in appearance. Both very Steve McQueenish.

'You and this gentleman could pass for brothers, Boss.'

'Please call me Patrick, TC.'

'TC won't do that, Patrick,' laughed Vance. 'She doesn't call me Vance. It's either Boss or Mr Callahan, depending on what mood I've put her in.' Patrick laughed.

'Okay. What say you call me Mr Patrick?'

'That sounds fine, Mr Patrick,' smiled TC. 'I'd best say hello to Lisa now the crowds have gone. If I don't see you again before you go, Mr Patrick, I hope you enjoy your visit to Brolga, and I hope you love our opals even half as much as we do.'

'I'm sure I will,' replied Patrick, who stood up and held out his hand. 'I'd like to shake your hand again, TC. It's one in a million.' TC smiled.

'Thank you, Mr Patrick. I must confess, I had to practice a lot to get it right.'

'Would you like something to drink, darling?' enquired Lisa when TC went to the counter.

'No, thank you, Lisa. The second movie has probably started,' replied TC before lowering her voice to almost a whisper. 'If you get an opportunity, please tell the Boss I need to talk to him.' TC hurried back to the picture show. The film had just started. To her surprise and relief, Graham was there.

Graham was also surprised and relieved. He didn't think TC was coming back. He took her hand in his, held it to his lips for a second, then put it down, holding it tightly until almost the end of the film, when he kissed it again before leaving.

Once more TC waited for the rush to be over before leaving. The sergeant was outside on duty and in uniform. Graham was standing a couple of feet away, endeavouring to be polite to one of the tennis club girls who had obviously caught him off-guard.

The sergeant smiled at TC.

'I don't believe I've seen you walk through that door very many times.'

'No, you haven't,' replied TC matter-of-factly.

'That's right, luv. You and young Lou used to prefer sitting on those stairs listening to rock 'n' roll.' TC smiled and nodded.

'I enjoyed those times.'

I bet you did, thought the sergeant as he watched TC walk away. He too had heard rumours about Jake abusing her.

Graham felt like throttling the persistent tennis club girl. He had intentionally stood with the sergeant waiting for the movie crowd to leave the theatre. That way he would have had an opportunity to speak to TC. He wanted to hear her voice. He wanted to hear her speak. Now he was stuck with this giggling girl who, by the looks of things, would never grow up. She was no different now than she had been when he was stationed in Brolga last time.

The sergeant sized up the situation.

'Excuse me, Constable Sandler. Don't you have to see Con before the café closes?'

'That's right, Sergeant, I do. Thank you for reminding me,' replied

Graham. 'I have to go,' he said to the tennis girl.

'Hope you play tennis soon,' said the girl. Graham ignored her.

Con's after-movie rush was all but over. TC was about to sit down at Lisa's table when Graham walked in.

'Sit at my table, Constable Graham,' said Lisa from behind the counter. 'I'll join you soon.' Graham pulled out the chair beside TC.

'Is this chair taken, sweetheart?'

TC smiled and said, 'It is now.'

Con closed the café door immediately after the last customer left. Lisa suggested they leave the kids alone for as long as possible. Con told Lisa he couldn't agree more, and they would dawdle in the cleaning-up process.

Graham held his hand over hers on the table.

'Please look at me, TC,' he said ever so softly and gently. TC turned her head to look into his eyes.

'What, Graham?' she murmured.

'I love you, TC. I think about you all the time. I think of you when I'm guarding the sheep, working on my car, walking down the street, eating a meal, driving. Even when I'm conversing with my workmates, Con and Lisa, anyone. You are always in the back of my mind. When I go to sleep, I dream about you. I love you. I'm desperately in love with you. I don't care about Jake. We can handle that. I don't know how, sweetheart, but we can.' Tears were streaming from TC's wide-open eyes. Graham continued to hold his right hand on hers while he gently wiped the tears away with his left.

'I love you, too, my beautiful Graham. But I'm used goods now. You deserve better than that.'

'Listen to me. That's unimportant. I love you.'

Con and Lisa could stall no longer. Con paused to speak to Graham and TC as he passed by to the kitchen. On seeing their hands on the table, the look of boundless love in Graham's eyes, and the hopeless defeat in TC's, he said nothing. What could he say? Lisa stood beside the table feeling exactly the same.

Graham squeezed TC's hand.

'Come on, sweetheart. We better go so Con and Lisa can go to bed.'

'Sorry, Lisa,' apologised TC. 'I was in another world.'

'Vance said he wants to see you, TC,' said Lisa. 'He's left the door unlocked. I suggest you go the back way to the station, Graham. Heaven forbid anyone see you leaving together.' Graham nodded in agreement.

'Thank you, Lisa. Good idea. I'm not worried about me. It's TC's reputation I'm concerned about.'

Or Jake killing her, thought Lisa.

Graham patted TC on the shoulder, smiled his wonderful smile, and was gone.

'You poor darling. Let me hug you before I let you out,' said Lisa.

'Thank you for being you, Lisa,' said TC as they hugged.

'Promise I'll see you soon, darling,' said Lisa as she watched TC cross the road to the pharmacy.

¶

'Here she is,' said Vance when TC entered the dispensary.

'I'm still here, TC,' said Mr Patrick with a beaming smile. 'You were right, these opals are beautiful.' TC smiled.

'I'm glad you like them.'

'Like them! I love them! So will my clients in the States.'

That's wonderful, thought TC. That means he'll buy some.

'Make us a couple of fresh coffees, please, TC,' said Vance.

TC was more than a little amused when she placed the coffees on the table. Not only did Mr Patrick and the Boss look alike. Mr Patrick was also a smoker. 'I wonder if he's a womaniser, as well?'

'I want you to work tomorrow, TC,' said Vance. 'Patrick wants to see how you cut the stones.'

'No problem. What time?' replied TC. Vance looked at Patrick.

'Nine o'clock, okay?' said Patrick.

TC smiled. 'Sure,' then looked at Vance. 'I'll be here at seven, Boss. I need to talk to you about something before nine if possible.'

Vance looked at TC curiously. Surely Jake hadn't laid into her again.

If he had, he'd kill the bastard. TC read his mind and shook her head slightly. Vance sighed in relief.

'I'll be here not later than eight.'

'I'm going home now,' said TC.

'You can't walk home in those heels,' said Vance. 'We'll drive you.' TC looked at her feet and remembered her flatties. They were still in Con's kitchen. Five minutes later, Vance and Mr Patrick said goodnight to TC out the front of her house. To her relief Jake's car was not there. After brushing her teeth, she locked herself in her bedroom, checked to make sure the knife was under her pillow, then laid on her bed. She decided she would have to hide it under her mattress in the future and put it under her pillow when she went to bed.

'I can't live like this much longer,' she told herself before torturing herself by thinking about Graham and how wonderful it would be if she were safe in his arms.

§

Graham was in his bed thinking virtually the same. He couldn't go on much longer like this. He didn't know which was worse, not seeing TC at all or seeing her and not being able to hold her.

§

TC heard Jake come home. She glanced at the clock. It was almost five. As soon as she thought he was asleep, she got out of bed.

He'll be asleep until session time, she thought as she dressed for work. When she left the house, she looked across at the Shack and thought of Lou. She owed Lou a call, and a letter was overdue.

Never thought I'd have a better friend than Sam, she thought. Not so! Sam lives in Brolga, she's got two kids, and I never see her. Lou's a million miles away in Sydney and I hear from her all the time.'

§

TC switched on the course grinder a little after six and began facing one of twenty pieces she had collected from a bucket under the saw bench.

'How did I know you'd be here early, Butterball?' said Vance when he arrived a little while later.

'Perhaps you've got a crystal ball you haven't told me about, Boss,' replied TC lightly.

'Or perhaps I know you as well as you know me,' replied Vance. 'Turn that thing off and make me a coffee. Then tell me what you want to talk about.'

With coffee on the desk and cigarette in his hand, Vance leaned back in his chair, took a draw on the cigarette, then exhaled.

'What's your problem, Little One? I'm all ears.' TC looked at Vance. He could tell she was in the depths of despair.

'I don't want to be married to Jake. It's terrible! I'm frightened of him. I lock myself in my bedroom, and I sleep with a carving knife under my pillow. I swear if he bashes me again, I'll stab him with it. I can't stand anything about him. Everything about Jake makes me feel bilious. The way he speaks, the way he eats, the way he bullshits to everyone. There's nothing about Jake I like. Nothing at all! He dresses well. That's it!'

Vance stood up, went to the shop, and returned with a box of tissues, which he opened and placed on the bench beside where TC was sitting on the stool. TC wiped her face but the tears kept flowing. Vance opened his mouth to speak.

'Please don't say anything yet, Boss,' pleaded TC. 'I haven't told you everything. There's more! I'm in love with Graham Sandler. He loves me and I love him. I know we were meant for each other. He doesn't care about me being used goods. He said it's unimportant.'

'I never should have said that to you, TC,' said Vance softly while shaking his head slowly from side to side. I should have minded my own business. I said it because I didn't want you to wind up like the women I have had—and still have, for that matter. Anna was the only special one. I should have trusted your judgment. I should have paid you more attention after Lou went to Sydney. I know you wouldn't have married

Jake if I had. I would have talked you out of it. I was so busy doing whatever I do, I didn't listen to you.'

TC's tears were out of control.

'I wish you had, Boss.'

Vance grabbed a handful of tissues and wiped TC's eyes. He then put his arms around her, and she sobbed against his shoulder with her arms dangling by her sides.

'I'm sorry, Little One,' soothed Vance. 'I'm so, so sorry.'

TC forced herself to stop sobbing. She sat up straight, pulled tissues from the box, and blew her nose.

'I'll be all right, Boss,' she said feebly. 'I'll be strong. Along with everything else I have learned from you, I've learned the weak crumble while the strong carry on. I'd best wash my face and get back to work.'

Vance looked at TC in amazement. It suddenly dawned on him that he respected TC more than anyone else on earth. He'd have to tell her one day.

'That's a good girl,' he said.

'I gave up being a girl long time ago, Boss. It was the first day I came to work for you.'

¶

Vance and Patrick went to the dispensary to talk and do business. TC finished shaping, then dopped all the stones except the big one. She would do that by hand.

Patrick took great interest in watching the procedure.

'This is great,' he said. 'I'll be able to explain everything about the opal when I'm selling it.'

I hope you sell it all, Mr Patrick, thought TC. Then you'll come back and buy some more.

'I'm going to Con's,' announced TC. 'I won't be long, Boss.' Patrick looked at TC in alarm. TC smiled.

'Don't worry; I'll have the stones finished before you go.'

'TC reads minds as well as cuts opals,' said Vance.

'You're kidding!' said Patrick in amazement. Vance did not reply. He lit a cigarette instead.

§

'Hello, darling. You left your shoes here,' greeted Lisa.

'I know. The boss drove me home,' laughed TC. 'Wouldn't have bothered me walking barefooted. I did it from the ball.'

'You must have something to eat,' insisted Lisa. 'What do you weigh, darling? Con and I are worried about you.' TC sighed.

'So am I, Lisa. I have no idea what to do. I'd run away except that wouldn't change a thing. I truly don't want to talk about it. If I do, I'll start to cry. Crying is a sign of weakness. I have to be strong.'

Con appeared from the kitchen. 'I saw you come in. Eat it! You're too thin,' he said as he plonked a plate in front of TC. On the plate was a toasted ham, cheese and tomato sandwich on top of which thin strips of cheese formed the letters TC.

'Isn't my Con a darling?' said Lisa.

TC smiled at Con. 'You sure are.' Con shrugged and threw his arms upwards and outwards.

'Graham hasn't been in today. He must be guarding sheep,' said Lisa.

Wish he was guarding me, thought TC wistfully. She ate her sandwich, most of it anyway.

§

TC was concentrating on shaping a large and extremely beautiful piece of opal when she felt a presence behind her. She looked up over her shoulder and smiled.

'Hello, Mr Patrick, how long have you been standing there?'

'Long enough to know I want you to finish turning that into a stone before I go. I want to take it with me,' replied Patrick eagerly. TC switched off the grinder.

'Good. In that case, you can tell me something?'

'What's that, TC?'

'This is a very beautiful piece. To shape it to a perfect oval, I'll have to waste a lot of the opal. Would you mind if I cut it to save the colour?'

'Without a doubt!' agreed Patrick without hesitation. 'Taken millions of years for that beauty to form; don't want to waste any of it.' TC smiled.

'Thank you, Mr Patrick, that's exactly how I feel. You can sit and watch if you'd like, but please don't talk to me.' Patrick sat on a stool beside TC and watched in silence until she had finished shaping the soon-to-be-his-piece of opal, which was probably the first odd-shaped boulder opal stone cut and sold. It was an inch-and-a-half wide and squared at the base, three-and-a-quarter inches deep flared out to three inches on one side and two on the other. The only colour wasted was the tiniest amount where the outer top sharp corners were rounded. It was high-domed with broad orange rolling flashes all over it. When polished, it would be magnificent.

'Did my boss say where he was going?' enquired TC. She thought it was strange Vance wasn't hanging around, seeing as Mr Patrick was there.

'He's on the telephone; that's why I came back to watch you. I thought I'd give him some privacy. Don't waste any colour on those, either,' added Patrick, indicating to the half dozen or so stones TC had not yet shaped.

'Fine,' smiled TC. More colour, more weight, more money, she thought as she started on the next piece. Be a lot faster, too; won't have to waste time shaping the perfect oval.

Vance joined Patrick and TC.

'Sorry, Patrick. That was an important call; otherwise, I would have ended it sooner.' Patrick laughed.

'Not to worry, I've got TC customising stones for me.'

'I'm shaping them to save the colour, Boss,' said TC. She switched off the machine, picked up the large red-orange-flashes piece and gave it to Vance. 'Mr Patrick is buying this if I have finished it before he goes.'

Vance was visibly relieved when TC returned to polish the stones. Patrick must have checked his watch a thousand times during the short time TC had been at Con's. Vance looked at TC and rolled his eyes while Patrick's head was turned.

'Suppose I'd best get started,' said TC.

'Would you please polish the big one first?' requested Patrick. TC smiled sweetly.

'I could and I would, but only if you insist. Mr Callahan often insists that I finish the most beautiful stones first. I prefer to leave them till last. I like the thought of revealing their mystery slowly. If I have all the other stones finished, I can take as long as I like on the last one. Something very beautiful deserves time and patience.' Vance was speechless. Didn't TC know Patrick was about to spend a small fortune with him? Patrick too was stuck for words as he digested what TC had said. 'Good. We'll leave it till last,' said TC demurely.

TC finished the backs of the other nineteen stones. To speed the process, she asked Vance to take them off the sticks and re-dop them face-up while she worked on the back of the big one. She didn't want to cause Mr Patrick to suffer apoplexy brought on by suspense.

'Would you like to watch me do the back of your stone, Mr Patrick?' she asked.

'I sure would,' replied Patrick. He was on his feet in an instant, then stood silently in the polishing-room doorway until the ironstone back of the stone was silky smooth and shiny. TC felt sorry for Patrick as he was anxious to see the colour. So was she.

'The boss is taking a long time dopping those stones, Mr Patrick. What say I give the stone its first sanding?'

'Please do that, TC!'

Poor man, thought TC. If the Boss asked a million dollars for this stone, Mr Patrick would probably pay it.

'There you go. It has one more sanding, then we'll polish it.'

'It's magnificent already!' said Patrick, who was obviously awestruck. 'Can I hold it?' TC passed him the piece.

'Of course, it's going to be yours soon.' TC was awake to Vance. He was dawdling with the re-dopping of the other stones. Given enough time, he thought she wouldn't be able to resist finishing the big one. He was wrong. But a deal was a deal.

Vance and Patrick went out for a few hours. Vance took Patrick for a drive around town, showed him the creek, even took him to the cemetery, which brought back a few memories to Vance of his long-ago escapades with Louise, who, in retrospect, was the most amusing and by far the most principled and sincere of the girlfriends he'd had in Brolga. He wondered where Louise was now. Tour over.

Patrick and Vance went to the café, where they drank coffee and had a long chat with Con. Patrick found the experience not only interesting, but it was also extremely amusing. One thing was for sure. Patrick would never forget his trip to Brolga.

TC was back at the course grinder facing pieces when they returned to the shop. Nineteen lovely stones of various sizes and shapes were lined up on Vance's desk. The big one was in the polishing room. She wanted to see Vance's face when she gave it to him. It was magnificent—colour-wise possibly the most beautiful stone she had yet cut. She had no idea what a jeweller would do with it. It was huge, as were the brilliant red and orange flashes.

'You've finished,' said Vance. 'That's good!'

'They are on the desk,' replied TC as she switched off the grinding wheel. Vance, followed closely by Patrick, all but ran past her.

'Where is the big one, TC?' shouted Vance angrily. He was tired.

'I threw it out of the window because I knew you'd use that tone of voice,' replied TC facetiously. Vance glared at TC. Patrick didn't know whether TC had or had not thrown the stone out the window. He certainly hoped she hadn't.

'It's in the polishing room, Mr Callahan. I'll get it immediately. Trust me for being sentimental about a stone. I should have remembered the promise I made myself when I first started cutting,' mumbled TC to herself. 'Here it is. It's quite good. I'm out of here. Once again it's been nice meeting you, Mr Patrick. Looks like you have to suffer another one of my handshakes.'

'My pleasure, TC,' smiled Patrick. 'Thank you for coming in today.'

TC replied, 'No problem,' and was gone.

Vance didn't notice. He was too engrossed in the stone while mentally calculating what it weighed and how many dollars per carat he should ask. He passed the stone to Patrick, then looked in the polishing room. He wanted to ask TC which bucket the stone came from. He hoped there'd be more from the same boulder in it.

'Did you see where TC went?' he asked Patrick.

'She left, Vance. Can't say I blame her. This stone is wonderful.'

TC started across to the café. She quickly changed her mind when she saw Jake's car parked in front.

'TC, wait for me,' came a female voice from behind her. TC turned around. It was one of her neighbours; an Italian girl married to a young drover. They lived in the corner house a hundred yards or more from what used to be Jake's mother's house, but was now Jake's and supposedly TC's. The block on which Jake's home was located was vast. Beside the house was located a huge tin shed, then an old, neglected-for-many-years tennis court, which was overgrown and an eyesore. Next to the tennis court was a vacant half-acre lot, then the drover's house.

The girl's name was Angelina. She preferred to be called Lena. TC knew her from the pharmacy, where she bought baby formula. She was eighteen, pretty, with black hair and huge, brown eyes. Lena's thick, long, almost-black lashes would never need the enhancement of mascara. Lena was an inch or so taller than TC. Their builds were similar. Lena was pushing her nine-month-old boy in a stroller.

'I'm taking the baby for a walk, TC. We get bored at home. Jack's away droving most of the time, so I get lonely.'

I know the feeling, thought TC. She said, 'Yes, Lena, it must be hard.' They chatted all the way to Jake's house and parted with Lena inviting TC to visit her.

'Come anytime, anytime at all! Jack's usually away for months!'

¶

TC phoned Lou. They talked about anything and everything for ages. Lou and Colin's baby was due any day. They lived in a flat now, and Colin's mother was lovely to Lou.

When TC put down the telephone, she realised she hadn't listened to the radio or played a record for a long time. Probably since she had married Jake. She decided to buy herself a little radio she could listen to in both the polishing room and her bedroom. She would get one next day. It would drown out Almut's ridiculous chit-chat with Vance. A sudden fleeting gust of pity for Delores burst into TC's mind. Poor woman was firing her bullets of jealousy and insecurity at the wrong target.

I wonder if she'll apologise if she ever finds out the truth? thought TC. I doubt it!

TC placed the L.P. of assorted rock 'n' roll artists on the stereo. She listened to it and a couple of others while she did her ironing, then took a shower and washed her hair.

¶

At camp, the men were finishing their evening meal.

'Wonder how Vance went with the Yank,' said Yappy.

'We'll never know, Yappy,' said Neil. 'You should know he never talks money to us.'

'He's probably frightened we'll ask him for a raise,' said Faith.

'Wouldn't hurt! We've been on the same bloody money ever since we came here,' said Neil.

'More money wouldn't be any good to you mongrels,' said Yappy. 'Wouldn't matter how much money you mob have, you'd still piss it up against a wall.'

'Look who's talking,' said Jakkie.

'Think I'll join you in the future, Little Joe,' said Yappy. 'I'll say nothing.' They all laughed, including Little Joe.

¶

Vance was in the dispensary closing the deal with Patrick for two hundred and eleven thousand dollars. Patrick had brought only two hundred thousand with him, so gave Vance an I.O.U for eleven, which he would have his staff in Los Angeles wire first thing Monday morning

Los Angeles' time.

The big red-orange stone weighed two hundred and forty point six carats. Patrick purchased it for a hundred dollars a carat. It came to twenty-four thousand and sixty dollars. Vance discounted the sixty dollars. Vance took the cash after they both counted it twice and Patrick bundled the stones into his briefcase. They shook hands then went to Con's for a meal.

¶

TC was locked in her bedroom and in bed by eight o'clock. She fell asleep immediately. She was exhausted in both mind and body. She woke with fright when she heard Jake yelling, then bashing on her door. Obviously he'd been on the rum again.

'TC, open this Effing door or I'll kick the bastard in,' he threatened repeatedly. She was terrified. Her heart was thumping and her body was shaking.

If Jake kicks the door in, one of us is going to die, she thought. The bashing and threatening abuse continued for what seemed an eternity, then there was silence. TC knew he was still there. She could sense it. She didn't move.

'TC, come out here or let me in!' said Jake in his normal, sober voice. 'I'm your husband. I have rights.' More silence. 'You effing bitch, open the door now,' then two kicks followed immediately by a loud crashing noise and a heavy thump.

He must have fallen over on the wood floor, thought TC. I hope he knocked himself out. Thank heavens for heavy doors and old-fashioned key locks. I must remember to keep that key with me at all times so he can't take it. If I don't have the key, I can't lock myself in.

After a few minutes of nothing, TC removed the key from the lock and went back to bed. She looked at the clock. It was almost midnight. If Jake kicked the door again, the noise would alert her. With one hand under the pillow, she held the knife handle. Her mind was blank as was her life.

¶

At 2 a.m. TC dressed for work. With her heart in her mouth, she unlocked her bedroom door. Knife in hand, she slowly and timidly opened it. The coffee table lay on its side on the lounge room floor. Fully clothed, mouth open and snoring, Jake lay spread-eagle on his back beside it.

TC placed the knife under her mattress, then tip-toed over Jake's legs and hurried out of the house as quietly as she could. She was anxious to reach the dispensary, which she had come to regard as her sanctuary. She wished she could live there.

After brushing her teeth with a new toothbrush she took from the shop and Vance's toothpaste, which he kept on a shelf above the sink, TC resumed course-grinding the rock off the pieces she had started on while waiting for Vance and Patrick the afternoon before. She was happy but not surprised when thirteen of the twenty looked as if they'd been left out to be smaller versions of the yesterday's big stone. Didn't look like the flashes would be quite as striking. That was probably because they were much smaller stones. All would have medium to high domes. The boss likes that, thought TC. She decided by her own volition to save the colour and make them all odd shapes. The other seven could be ovals.

¶

Vance saw Patrick off at the airport. He went directly to the dispensary. He wanted to count his money one more time before he started parting with it. In his mind it was already spent.

¶

TC was in the polishing room. She was in the process of sanding. In the dispensary, Almut was leaning back on her chair with her legs crossed and feet on his desk. She was wearing short shorts and a low-cut sleeveless T-shirt-material top.

'What are you doing here?' asked Vance abruptly. 'Isn't it still a bit cool for that outfit?'

'I came to find out how much money the American spent,' was Almut's reply.

'That's my business! Now, get out of here and don't come back until one, when you start work. By the way, Almut, work means keeping the shop clean, the shelves stacked, and serving the customers, not hanging around me all the time.'

Then it started. Almut began her screeching. TC turned off the sanding disc, calmly walked past Almut and Vance, went the back way to the newsagent's, purchased a small battery-operated radio, then returned to the polishing room. She closed the door behind her, switched on the radio, placed it on the sill, turned up the volume, and resumed sanding.

Almost immediately over 4CL's airwaves, she heard Faron Young's 'Hello Walls'. TC felt as much like smiling as a thirsty barefoot man with no hat would feel about trudging a desert in the middle of summer. Still, she couldn't help herself. How appropriate, she thought. Suddenly the door slid open.

'Sorry about that, TC.' said Vance.

'Sure, Mr Callahan,' replied TC nonchalantly.

'I'm sorry about the way I spoke to you yesterday,' said Vance. TC shrugged as she continued sanding. Calmly she spoke.

'You shouldn't have done it at all. If you are cheesed off with Coral, Almut, or Mrs Callahan, or yourself, don't take it out on me. I know you were tired. That's still no excuse.'

'Turn that thing off. I want you to help me count the money. Patrick spent two hundred thousand, plus another eleven we'll get tomorrow. He bought all those odd shapes. We'll have to start cutting more like that.'

I have already started, thought TC.

'I got a hundred dollars a carat for the big stone. The most money per carat we've got so far.'

'He would have paid more,' said TC matter-of-factly. 'Somewhere down the track, it will be a thousand per carat or more. How can a stone like that ever be repeated? Impossible!'

'I know that,' replied Vance as he pulled out the bottom drawer of the filing cabinet and reached for the bag of notes underneath.

'But we need the money now. I've got plans. Now help me count this money. Repeat to me what I've told you about dealing in cash.'

'If I'm paying cash, I count it out to them, then make certain they count it themselves in front of me. If someone is paying me cash, I watch them count it, then count it myself in front of them,' said TC as if reciting a poem. 'That prevents come-back from either party at a later date.'

Vance counted the notes. As he finished with each bundle, he passed it to TC. At the end of the exercise, they both agreed on the amount. It was exactly two hundred thousand.

¶

'How're things on the home front?' asked Vance seriously.

'Jake was on rum again last night. He tried to kick in my bedroom door. He fell over. He was passed out on the lounge room floor when I left this morning. He said I'm his wife. He has rights. I've decided to stab him if he kicks in my bedroom door,' continued TC despondently. 'As for his marital rights, my skin crawls at the thought of it.'

'I see,' said Vance, who had been listening intently. 'Have you had sex with Graham Sandler?' TC shook her head and smiled wistfully.

'No. I wish I had. I'd love to but it would be adultery. Apart from that, he's never asked me. He's a gentleman, Boss. He's lovely.'

'I've spoken to an old friend of mine,' said Vance. 'He's a solicitor in Brisbane. That's who I was talking to on the phone yesterday when Patrick was here. He told me domestic violence is insufficient grounds for a respectable divorce. It's been going on forever and somewhat acceptable to society. Things may change in the future but at the moment that's the way things stand. On the other hand, adultery is instant grounds. The spouse of the adulterer is considered the victim of a heinous crime. Only problem is the adulterer has to be caught "in the act" and there has to be an impartial witness.

'Jake commits adultery every day of the week, Boss. Everybody knows that!' said TC. 'Not that I care!'

'Yes, but where is your witness?' replied Vance.

'I'd best finish my stones,' said TC. 'You'll like them. Thirteen of them are odd-shaped with red-orange flashes like the big one Mr Patrick bought. I've cut them all for colour, so they are odd shapes.' Vance's eyes lit up.

'They're out of the same boulder. I was hoping there'd be more. Show me!'

'Better put your cash away first, Boss,' advised TC. 'Knowing you, it's already spent.'

'You know me too well!' laughed Vance. 'I'm going to pay the last of my debts, which is five thousand to the doctor. The rest I'm going to spend on finding and mining more opal. We are just beginning, TC! We are just beginning!'

And so, it was! Just the beginning!

¶

It was early spring. Lou gave birth to a baby boy. On the rare occasions Graham and TC happened to see each other, both their hearts would skip a few beats just as they would both cry inside for what they could have been. TC didn't go to the movies again. She knew if there was a repetition of the last time, things would get out of hand with Graham and her. Graham continued guarding sheep, working on his car, and playing his guitar in his room. Occasionally, he played a game of tennis, only because he loved the game, definitely not because of the girls. He wasn't interested. There was only one girl for him. Her name was TC. If he couldn't have her, he'd have no one.

¶

Vance made a point of seeking out Jake. They had a discussion down by the creek. Vance told Jake if he ever heard of him bashing TC again, he should consider himself a dead man.

'If I don't do it myself, Jake,' warned Vance, 'I'll have some other bastard do it. There's a man in the area who's murdered before. He's desperate for money. For a few hundred, he'd bump you off without hesitation. As for your conjugal rights—bullshit! You forfeited those the first time you bashed her, which, I'm told, was a week after she was lonely enough to marry you.'

Jake's face drained of colour. He got out of the car and threw up. Vance was serious, and Jake knew it. From that day on, Jake's attitude towards TC changed. He encouraged her to drive the car and was always polite. He avoided rum like the plague and quit referring to TC as a bitch when yarning with his mates. In turn, TC cooked him an evening meal when and if he was home and resumed doing his laundry. She still locked herself in her bedroom every night, and the knife was there just in case.

¶

Vance went to Brisbane and acquired a machine. He had intended to lease, but he bought one instead. He also organised everything required to set up a second camp. He employed a local couple who were down on their luck. They were good people and hard workers; had a rough trot, that's all. The wife's name was Alison. She preferred to be called Ali. She was going to be the cook. Her husband, Ted, would operate the machine. Michael and Jakkie would transfer from the original mine site.

¶

Six weeks after the deal with Patrick, the gem dealer from Los Angeles, Vance had two mines operating. To speed the cutting process in town, he hired a fourteen-year-old girl who came from a somewhat troubled family. She soon learned to do the course grinding and face the pieces. This meant TC had to shape, sand, and polish only. Production of finished stones increased almost immediately.

The fourteen-year-old's name was Marla. TC liked her on sight. Almut couldn't stand her. As far as Marla was concerned, the feeling was mutual. Marla may have been only fourteen but, like TC, she was old beyond her years. She woke up to what was going on between Vance and Almut within a week of observing their interaction.

'What's the deal with Almut and Mr Callahan?' she asked. TC played dumb.

'I don't understand what you're talking about, Marla.'

'You know, TC. Are they doing it?' said Marla with a cheeky grin.

'Pass me those pieces, please, Marla. I'm in a hurry,' was TC's reply.

¶

Vance was like a machine that was never switched off. In and out to the mines, the second one of which was a half-day drive from town, sawing boulders, taking load after load of discarded, colour-not-good-enough rock to the dump, mail days in the shop, running around getting this and that, juggling accounts ... He seemed never to stop.

On top of his workload, he had two demanding women and a demanding girl to keep happy. His only form of sustenance appeared to be cigarettes and vitamin pills.

'You look bloody terrible, Vance', commented Yappy one day when Vance arrived at mine number one. 'I'm worried about you, mate. You're burning the bloody candle at both ends. Want to watch out you don't burn the bloody thing all together.'

'Yes, Yappy, I'm a bit worn out, mate,' admitted Vance, who didn't have time for so much as a coffee. He loaded the ute with boulders, said hello to Neil, Faith, and Little Joe, made sure they had no problems, collected Yappy's order for the mail, and was off.

It was no surprise to anyone, including Vance, when he suffered a warning heart tremor. The cigarettes disappeared, all but essential-to-be-kept-cold pharmaceutical goods were removed from the dispensary refrigerator and replaced with carton after carton of chocolate bars. Whenever Vance sat at his desk or on the telephone, there were a couple of chocolate bars ready just as a packet of cigarettes and his lighter had been in the past.

TC cut opals from 3 am. till 5pm. when Vance was in town, from 3 am till 5 pm when he wasn't. She had to be there to fill prescriptions in Vance's absence.

As for the doctor, he rarely if ever visited the dispensary. TC had not seen him since the day Delores fired her, and Vance no longer mentioned him.

§

The horse-racing circuit was about to begin, which meant Jake would be away many weekends Friday to Sunday during the coming months. His brother, Duke, had married Seat of Knowledge elder Jock's daughter. She was a lovely girl, both personality- and beauty-wise. Duke and she complemented each other. They had a marriage made in heaven, and everyone agreed it would last forever. Duke worked at the local council office. He was fortunate insomuch as he could get a day off here and there whenever he wanted and deduct it from his annual leave. He was Jake's penciller at the race meetings. 'I demand a good penciller, too,' said Jake, often with pride, regarding his younger brother.

TC paid little attention to Jake's bookmaking. She knew very little, if anything, about it. All she knew was if he won, he was in a good mood and celebrated by getting drunk. If he lost, he was in a downer mood and drowned his disappointment by getting drunk.

The first race meeting on the circuit was two weeks away. It was going to take place at a tiny settlement in the middle of vast cattle territory situated in the far south-western corner of the state. The population of the area was sparse, but they always managed to get a good turnout of people at their once-yearly race meeting. People came from everywhere, mostly by light plane while others drove long distances over red-dirt roads to attend the verging-famous race meeting in the middle of nowhere. Hopeful owners and/or trainers brought their horses from here, there, and everywhere to have a go at winning the coveted cup.

¶

TC was in bed when she heard Jake come home. She knew he had three men with him because she heard three different voices. All were strange to her. It was early for Jake to be home. It had just gone on eight o'clock. She was glad she hadn't dallied before going to bed. TC couldn't help but overhear their conversation as they sat in the lounge room to drink a few beers and discuss the forthcoming race meeting. It soon became obvious to TC the three men were cattle property owners from the way-out west area and they all had horses entered in the race for the cup. This was the first inkling TC ever had about rigged races.

Amidst much laughter and somewhat lengthy discussion, she heard them reach an agreement on whose turn it was to win the cup that year.

'We'll all shake on that,' said one voice. After a few seconds, another voice, 'Come on, Jake. Now that that's settled, take us back downtown. We'll have a feed at the café.'

TC was not sure what advantage it was to a bookie to know the winning horse in a race before the race was run. She put it out of her mind. She didn't know, didn't care, didn't ask.

¶

'TC, I want you to go to Melbourne. Cowlegg wants to buy more opal,' announced Vance a few days later.

'No, Boss! I don't want to go!' replied TC. 'I don't like Mr Cowlegg. I don't like the way he looks at me. It's as if he's undressing me.' Vance laughed.

'The bastard probably is, in his mind, TC. You have to go. You can try your luck in Sydney on the way back. Just think about it. You can see Lou and her baby, become a godmother, and sell opals all at the same time.' TC frowned and pouted.

'That's bribery and you know it, Boss,' she replied. 'If cane toad's hand accidently touches me this time, I'll chop the ugly thing off!' Vance laughed again as he imagined the look on Cowlegg's face if TC produced a hatchet.

'You're leaving in the morning. I've arranged a lift for you on a light plane to Curloo. You can catch a regular flight to Brisbane, hook up with a flight to Melbourne, spend tomorrow night in Melbourne, see Cowlegg next morning, pick up whatever else you can all day, then catch a plane back to Sydney and ...'

'Boss, you don't have to spell it out for me,' interrupted TC. 'I know what I have to do. You get the opals ready. I'm going to Con's for a thick-shake. I want to sulk for a little while.' TC was halfway to the door when she turned back to the dispensary.

'Tell Cowlegg I'll see him at 8 a.m. sharp, not to keep me waiting because I have other people to see. If he wants first pick of the stones, he'll have to see me then or wait till last.' Vance laughed as he picked up the telephone.

No flies on TC, he thought. I think I've created a monster.

§

It was eight-thirty in the morning. Probably a bit early for Lisa, thought TC as she crossed the street.

'You're early, TC. Did you go on strike, luv?' asked Con.

'Something like that, Con,' replied TC lightly as Con grabbed a milkshake container. He knew without asking what she'd have. Chocolate thick-shakes were probably what kept the kid alive. At least they were loaded with calcium. Con nodded towards the side on the café behind her. TC turned quickly. Her heart told her who was there.

'Hello, pretty lady. I'm surprised to see you here at this time of day,' said Graham, smiling his wonderful smile.

Why did you have to be here, my lovely? thought TC as she took her drink from the counter. 'An angel told me you'd be here so I thought I'd come check for myself,' said TC as she sat down opposite him.

'You've been avoiding me, sweetheart,' said Graham softly. TC stared at the wall behind him momentarily, then took a deep breath and sighed.

'I'd say we've been avoiding each other.'

'I'd say you are right,' agreed Graham. 'It's too painful for me to see you knowing I can't hold you.'

'I know. It's like that for me, too. You are always with me, even though you're not.'

'What are we going to do, TC?' asked Graham. He was sad. TC could hear it as well as see it just as Graham heard and saw the same in her.

I don't know, my beautiful, darling man. I just don't know! said TC to herself. Then, 'This is getting nowhere, Graham,' said TC half-seriously. 'You eat your breakfast while I drink mine.' Graham laughed and shook his head.

'No wonder I love you, TC Carmichael.' TC shrugged and smiled.

'Let's face it, I'm hard not to love,' she said flippantly. 'The boss is making me go to Melbourne tomorrow; I'll see Lou's baby at last when I stay in Sydney.' Graham looked at TC in alarm.

'How long will you be away?'

'Should be back on Saturday's Flea or perhaps by plane. Depends what the boss decides. That reminds me, I have to go back to work. I told the boss I was coming here to sulk because he's making me go to Melbourne.' Graham smiled and winked.

'I'm glad you did.'

TC winked back. 'So am I, Constable. See you in my dreams.'

§

'Why are you all smiles? I thought you are supposed to be sulking,' said Vance when TC walked into the dispensary and the giggling Almut hurried past her into the shop.

'I'm still sulking, Boss. I'm temporarily smiling, as well. I've been talking to Graham.'

'I see! Cowlegg will be happy to see you at eight sharp Wednesday morning. He promised he won't keep you waiting.'

'Surprise,' said TC. 'I knew he wouldn't be able to resist first look at the stones.'

'Come on, let's check out the stack ourselves,' said Vance.

Vance and TC disagreed about the pricing on some of the stones, particularly the thirteen red-orange odd shapes. TC thought Vance priced them too low.

In the end they decided not to put prices on the stones in question. TC would play it by ear. She would take only four of the red-orange stones with her. If her customers saw too many of them, they might think red-orange was common, which it definitely was not.

'I made your bookings while you were sulking at Con's,' said Vance tongue-in-cheek. 'Make your own arrangements between Sydney, Wednesday night, and catching the plane from Brisbane to here on Saturday.' As usual, Vance was in a hurry.

'Come on, get on the phone to Lou now! I don't want you going away without a plan.'

'That's what I was trying to do when you interrupted me,' said TC defensively as she picked up the telephone.

One of Vance's many counterfeit friends entered unannounced via the rear door while TC was talking to Lou and Vance was piling bundles of bagged stones into the briefcase.

To qualify as a counterfeit friend of Callahan's, one had to be an opal miner who was trying but had not found any as yet, or be a miner who had been lucky enough to find boulders but had neither the equipment nor the facilities to turn them into stones.

Frequently one of them would interrupt Vance's hectic schedule by rocking up as if they owned the place, checking out what was going on, asking Vance how things were for him, drink free coffee, then leave, seething with hatred brought about by undiluted jealously.

Vance had a stock-in-trade reply for the 'How are things going?' question. No matter what his current situation was, he would always answer, 'Not too bad; getting there.'

Today's counterfeit plonked himself on the stool as Vance quickly scooped the remaining bundles of the stones off his desk and into the briefcase, which he then placed under his desk.

'See you at the airport, Lou,' said TC, then put the phone down.

'Going on a trip, TC?' asked the man.

'TC's going to be a godmother in Sydney, aren't you, TC?' said Vance.

'Sure am, Boss,' replied TC with a fake smile. Vance and she had a lot to talk about. It was bad enough having Almut interrupting them every time she thought of something ridiculous to tell Vance.

Awkward silence!

'Don't I get a cup of coffee today?' said the counterfeit man. Vance looked at TC. He, too, wanted the man out of there. TC smiled sweetly.

'Not today. I have urgent personal business I need to discuss with Mr Callahan. How about next time?'

'I know when I'm not wanted,' said the man, who quickly left in a huff.

Vance opened the Sydney telephone directory business section to O for Opals.

'No point in seeing the big shots,' he said. They are armpit-deep in Lightening Ridge Black or Coober Pedy opal.'

The siren sounded. It was one o'clock. Suddenly, TC wondered why Vance had Almut start work at one. The shops were closed from one till two. She didn't have to wait long for the answer.

Marla switched off the grinding wheel and was out the door in seconds. Almut closed the door and came into the dispensary. She stood impatiently by the desk listening while Vance and TC continued talking.

'It's lunch time, Vance,' said Almut. Vance ignored her and kept talking.

'It's lunch time, Vance,' repeated Almut impatiently. 'Vance, I said it's lunch time,' she screeched.

'I'm out of here, Boss,' said TC. 'I'll see you at two.' Vance was furious.

'TC and I were talking business, Almut. You do know what business is, don't you? Or are you too effing dense?'

As TC closed the door behind her she heard Almut wail, 'You told me lunch time is our time, Vance!'

So that's why Almut started at one when I had the smashed head, thought TC as she crossed the street. Poor Boss!

TC knocked on the door of Charles Cowlegg's hotel suite on Wednesday morning spot-on at eight. She was ushered in by his secretary and asked to wait.

'Please remind Mr Cowlegg I shan't wait long. I have other appointments,' said TC matter-of-factly. The secretary returned almost immediately, followed by Charles Cowlegg. He was smiling profusely.

'TC, how lovely to see you,' he gushed.

Wish I could say the same, thought TC. 'Hello, Mr Cowlegg. It's a long trip from Brolga. I'm a little tired but here I am.' TC began placing stones on Cowlegg's desk the moment they were seated. She wanted him to concentrate on the stones, not on her.

'There's no discount this time, Mr Cowlegg. Mr Callahan has already taken that into consideration when pricing them.' Cowlegg looked at TC with a sickening smile.

'Not even ten percent, TC?'

'That's correct, Mr Cowlegg,' replied TC seriously.

After being there almost two hours by his desk clock, TC felt as if she'd been there ten. Cowlegg kept deciding on stones, then changing his mind, then changing his mind again. Come a quarter-to-eleven, TC's patience expired. Charles Cowlegg had chosen the stones he wanted to buy ages ago. Now he was just messing around while making an occasional feeble attempt at flirting with TC.

'Mr Cowlegg, I'm sorry,' lied TC. She wasn't sorry. She was fed up with Cowlegg's fiddling. 'I have to go. I have other people to see. Would you like me to begin listing those stones?'

'Go ahead, TC. I think I'm satisfied with these.' TC tallied up the stones and prices. She pushed the list across the desk for him to check.

'I'm surprised you didn't choose one of the red-orange stones, Mr Cowlegg.'

'Odd shapes won't sell.'

※

With Cowlegg's twenty-four thousand cash and the opal in her brief case, TC decided to hit the streets of Melbourne and try her luck anywhere she saw an opal sign. She walked into four shops cold turkey and sold opal in three. The owner of the fourth was away on business.

She boarded the plane to Sydney that evening with thirty-nine thousand, three hundred dollars.

The boss will be happy, she thought. He's obviously right; the opal shops are the way to go. The people who bought from her during the afternoon were all happy to be dealing directly with the miners.

¶

Colin met TC at Sydney airport. Lou was at home with the baby. He drove TC to his parents' hotel and showed her to her room. He was very quiet.

'Is everything all right, Colin?' asked TC.

'Yes, TC, everything is fine! Lynette and I are tired, that's all. The little fellow cries a lot. That's what babies do, I guess. Lynette wants you to have dinner with us tomorrow night at our flat, and she's organised with the priest for the baby to be baptised Friday afternoon.'

'Sounds good, Colin. Give Lou my love. I can't wait to see her, and I can't wait to see the baby.'

'Lynette's excited about seeing you, too, TC,' said Colin. 'I'll pick you up downstairs tomorrow night at seven.'

TC hung her few clothes in the wardrobe, then went downstairs to call Vance. She knew he'd be waiting for her call.

'How did you go?' were Vance's first words. Not 'How was your trip?' or 'How are you?' Just 'How did it go?' In other words, 'I'm not interested in anything else, only the money.'

'Mr Cane Toad spent twenty-three, and three from opal shops combined.

'Where are you, TC?' asked Vance.

'In the phone box out the front of Colin's parents' hotel.'

'Where's the opal and money?'

'In the briefcase between my ankles.'

'Good. Don't let it out of your sight. Call me tomorrow night.'

'Did TC sell anything, Vance?' asked Almut the moment Vance was finished speaking to TC.

'That's between TC and me, Almut,' replied Vance before biting into a chocolate bar.

⁊

Later, TC lay in bed listening to 2UE.

I wonder if Lou and Colin still listen to the radio, thought TC. Maybe, maybe not. How quickly we change! She thought about the day ahead of her tomorrow, the hopeless situation with Graham, cleared her mind, then went to sleep with the radio still playing softly on the table beside her bed.

⁊

TC sold to five shops next day and had two appointments for Friday morning. It was six o'clock in Sydney and four in Brolga when she phoned Vance. Almut answered the dispensary telephone.

'Vance isn't here. He's taken some rock to the dump. I'll give him a message. Have you sold anything?'

'Tell him I'll call again later, please, Almut,' replied TC. 'As if I'd tell you what I've sold,' mumbled TC as she picked up the briefcase from the phone booth floor.

⁊

Colin collected TC at seven as arranged and stopped to pick up pizzas on the way to their flat. Lou was much thinner and looked very tired, just as did Colin. After a hug, Lou said, 'We mustn't talk too loud, TC, it might wake the baby.'

'Is there something wrong with the baby?' asked TC.

'No, he's fine. The doctors say some babies are criers. He's one,' replied

440

Lou. 'Little darling's asleep now, but he'll probably cry all night after he wakes up.'

'Looks like I'll have to wait till tomorrow to see him,' said TC.

Colin drove TC back to the hotel as soon as they finished eating. She made the excuse she needed an early night to prepare herself for the next day. In reality she wanted to leave because she could see both Lou and Colin desperately needed sleep.

TC called Vance before going to her room.

'How did you go?' he asked,

'Twenty-one thousand, two hundred,' replied TC. 'That's five shops. I sold two of the red-orange odd shapes to a gentleman who is a jeweller himself, and I have two appointments in the morning. People know our opal now, Boss. They love it!'

'That's good! When are you going to Brisbane?' enquired Vance.

'Tomorrow night. I'll stay at a motel close to the airport.'

'Okay, call me when you get there,' said Vance.

TC sold again Friday morning. In the afternoon Lou's beautiful baby was baptised. Throughout the ceremony, he didn't so much as whimper. His large, blue eyes were wide open. TC held him in her arms and marvelled at his perfection. Tiny little hands and fingers, flawless white, soft skin, and silky, reddish-blonde hair.

'He's worth the sleepless nights, Lou,' she said when she handed the little darling back to his mother.

A few hours later, TC was in a motel room in Brisbane talking to Vance on the telephone. She didn't give him the chance to ask his, 'How did you go' question. She spoke the second he picked up the phone.

'Twelve today, Boss. It was twelve and one, but I felt generous. I like the people, so I knocked off the hundred.' Vance laughed.

'You're beginning to sound like a numbers runner.' TC was confused.

'What's a numbers runner?'

'Never mind,' replied Vance. 'How are you TC?'

'I can't be hearing right, Boss. Did you just ask me how I am?'

'Don't be clever,' said Vance. 'I'll meet the plane tomorrow.' Vance put down the telephone, tore the wrapper of a chocolate bar, and sat down at his desk.

'Not bad at all, TC,' he said to himself. 'Seventy-two-and-a-half thousand in three days. Two-and-a-half days actually. She would have been playing godmother the rest of the time.'

Chocolate in one hand and pen in the other, Vance began making notes on how to spend the money to improve his mining operation.

9

'I need a thick-shake and a new pair of stilettos, Boss,' said TC when Vance met her at the airstrip.

'Don't I get a kiss on the cheek?' said Vance feigning disappointment.

'Sure,' replied TC. She pecked him on the cheek, handed him the briefcase, then sat in the ute while Vance collected her case.

'This is a good time of year to sell,' said TC as they drove towards town. 'Apparently the international tourists start coming soon. Everyone loved the opal. I feel confident they'll become regular customers.'

'How was your mate, Cowlegg?' laughed Vance. TC ignored the question.

'I made notes and got a card from everyone.'

'How much discount did you give, TC?' asked Vance.

'None except the hundred dollars I told you about when I was feeling generous.' Vance laughed.

'You're joking.'

'I'm not! The only one who asked for a discount was Mr Cane Toad. I explained to him you had taken into consideration when pricing.'

'I do owe you a new pair of heels and a thick-shake,' laughed Vance.

'Good. I saw a pair in a store window in Sydney but I didn't have any money to buy them.' Vance cracked up with laughter.

'What's so funny?' asked TC. She was confused.

'You, TC. That's what's funny. You had a bag full of cash, but you didn't have enough to buy a pair of shoes.'

'I don't think it's funny,' said TC seriously. 'That is, unless you want me to be a thief as well as a forger.' Vance stopped laughing.

'Point taken, TC, point taken.'

⁋

'Where have you been?' screeched Almut when Vance and TC arrived in the dispensary. Marla stopped grinding, stood up, and kissed TC on the cheek.

'I want to hug you but you'll get wet and muddy. I'm so glad you're back.'

'You and TC can talk later,' said Vance. 'She's only been gone a few days.'

'I asked you where you've been, Vance,' demanded Almut.

'Take a wild guess. I'm sure you've got something to do in the shop,' replied Vance bluntly. 'It is mail-order day, after all.'

'Gives me the bloody horrors, that girl,' mumbled Vance.

Too late now, Boss, said TC silently. You should have thought of that before you got yourself involved with her.

'Come on, TC. I'll buy you that thick-shake. At least we can talk without interruption at Con's,' said Vance. His voice was so loud it drowned out the noise created by the grinding wheel. Briefcase in hand, Vance stormed past Almut with TC following.

'I heard you, Vance,' said Almut.

'Good! You were meant to hear me,' snapped Vance.

The café was empty apart from Con. TC and Vance sat at the rear side table next to Lisa's.

'Now tell me about your trip,' said Vance. 'Leave nothing out. I want to hear every detail.'

'Even about the baptism?' enquired TC facetiously. Vance laughed.

'Not necessarily that.'

⁋

Forever later, after countless questions and answers, Vance was satisfied he knew everything of any importance he needed to know about TC's excursion to the Big Smoke. They were about to leave.

'How much were those shoes you didn't have the money to buy?' enquired Vance.

'Forty-nine, ninety-nine,' replied TC. Vance pushed two fifty-dollar notes across the table.

'Here. Buy two pairs. I bet they've got bows on them.' TC smiled.

'Of course. Twirly ones. Thank you, Boss! I'll buy the same shoes in two colours. Thank you, thank you, thank you!' Vance laughed again.

'Surely two pairs of shoes deserve another kiss on the cheek, Butterball.'

'No! You'll get spoiled. You've already had one today.'

'Come on!' said Vance. 'Come on. I'll drive you home. You can have this afternoon off. Marla's got a lot of pieces ready for you. Start those tomorrow.'

¶

Vance had promised Delores and himself he would slow down a bit after his heart scare. Not so! He kept on driving himself to the limit day in, day out, week after week. Boulders kept coming out of the hill at mine number one. The men were happy. They were unearthing boulders at the second mine site. The colour in those was nowhere near as beautiful or thick as the opal from number one.

Jake won money at the first race meeting on the circuit. He also won at the second and third while breaking even on the fourth. All in all, he was having a pretty good trot. The next meeting on Saturday on the agenda was in Curloo for the Melbourne Cup Carnival. Jake would leave Brolga on Friday afternoon after Duke finished work and stand up at the meeting on Saturday, Monday, and Cup Day Tuesday.

When the big weekend arrived, Jake left as scheduled on Friday. TC was happy. It meant four nights of sleep with an open door. Even though Jake had treated her okay for a long time, she still couldn't be sure when and if he'd come home drunk on rum.

On the Saturday night, TC was sitting in the café talking with Lisa when Vance called to her from the doorway.

'I want to see you, TC.' TC was immediately on her feet and at the door.

'What's wrong, Boss?'

'I want to talk to you. Come to the shop,' replied Vance with some urgency.

'What's wrong?' asked TC.

'Nothing! I want to talk to you. That's all.'

TC laughed when she spotted a chocolate bar carton on the desk with chocolate wrappers scattered around it as well as on the floor.

'No doubt about you, Boss. You take everything to the limit. Even eating chocolate.'

'TC, have you seen Graham lately?'

'No. We try to avoid each other. It's less painful,' replied TC with a heavy sigh.

'Do you remember our discussion about a shameless divorce?' asked Vance ever so seriously.

'How could I forget it?' replied TC.

'This could be your chance to catch Jake at it, TC. The bastard's got Madison with him in Curloo. I got a call a while ago from the owner of the Curloo Hotel. He asked me what's going on with you and Jake.'

'I see,' said TC.

'I suggest you go to Curloo on the Flea tomorrow morning. With a bit of luck, you'll catch Jake and his tart in the middle of things and you'll have the publican as your witness.' TC was confused. How did the publican know her? Vance saw the expression on her face.

'You'll know George when you see him. He used to frequent my parties when I was a wild boozer.'

'Okay, Boss. I'm doing it!' said TC with determination in her voice. 'If I don't, I'll never forgive myself.'

'Are you sure?'

'I'm positive! I feel nothing for Jake! Never did!'

'All right. I'll ring George back and ask him to meet the Flea,' said Vance.

TC nodded, 'Good. Thank you, Boss. Are you going to the mines tomorrow?'

'I am, but I'll pick you up and see you on the Flea first.'

Vance was right. TC did recognise George when she saw him standing on the Curloo Station Platform.

'Are you ready, TC?' he asked.

'Sure am! If I can catch Jake and Madison, my life of misery will be over.'

They were at the Hotel in minutes, and George led the way to Jake's unit. Without knocking he unlocked and opened the door. TC's heart sank. She was too late. Looked as if Jake and Madison had just completed their act of copulation. They were on a single bed by the window of the room. Jake was attired in underpants only while Madison wore her bikini briefs and a T-shirt. Jake had one hand behind his head and a cigarette in the other. Madison was half on top of Jake, toying with the hairs on his chest.

TC said nothing while Madison began screaming abuse at her. George raced off to turn the air conditioning on, hoping the drone of the motor would drown out the noise.

Poor little bugger, he thought. Ten minutes earlier and she would have the bastards in the act.

'Madison, stop screaming,' yelled Jake. 'Get your clothes on and get the eff out of here.' Madison continued screaming.

'But, Jake, you promised me. But, Jake, I love you. But, Jake, I want to be with you.' The 'but Jake's' continued for minutes until Jake grabbed Madison by the shoulders.

'Madison, I told you to stop screaming. Get dressed and leave.'

'Madison doesn't have to leave, Jake. I am,' said TC. 'I'm going to ask in the bar if anyone is going to Brolga today. If I have no luck, I'm taking the car.'

'TC, don't do that,' said Jake.

'Let her go,' said Madison. Jake lost it.

'Madison, get the eff out of here now!' he yelled. 'If you don't, I'll throw you out.'

TC left the room and went to the bar where George called out for anyone going to Brolga. She was lucky. A couple of oil company people were about to leave.

The two men who gave TC a lift knew TC and she knew them from the pharmacy. TC found chatting with them very interesting, which made the trip seem shorter and kept her mind off other things. They dropped her off at the café. She needed to talk to Vance. He had gone to the mines.

The Boss must still be in town, she thought with relief as she looked across the road to the chemist shop. The front door was slightly open. Surely he wouldn't forget to close it before leaving if he went bush.

TC could hear Vance talking when she opened the door. He was obviously angry with someone or about something. TC decided to announce her presence by calling out before entering the dispensary. Never knew what she'd find.

'It's me, Boss. I'm back.' TC thought she was hallucinating when Claudia appeared in the dispensary doorway before Vance.

'Well, well, well, if it isn't Miss Perfect!' snapped Claudia. 'Vance's pet bitch.'

'Claudia, be quiet, please,' said Vance. 'Go now. Come back in an hour if you must. I need to talk to TC.'

'You're the boss,' said Claudia, oozing sarcasm. 'See you in an hour.'

'What is Claudia doing back in Brolga?' asked TC.

'She wants more money or she'll blow the whistle on me to Delores.' TC shook her head in shock and disgust.

'I don't believe it! What are you going to do?'

'Not much I can do. I'll give her the money. She wants three thousand.'

'That's blackmail!' said TC.

'I know, but I don't see I have much choice. How did you go in Curloo?'

'They were on the bed together but the action was over,' said TC in despair. 'Looks as if I am married to Jake forever. Of course, I could have an affair with Graham, who loves me enough not to care if I'm used goods. What would I be then, Boss?' Vance munched on a chocolate bar, screwed up the wrapper, and aimed it at the bin.

'Do you really love Graham?' asked Vance.

'Yes, I do. That's the problem,' replied TC without hesitation.

'You'll have to let him go, TC. You've got no option. If you start something with him, it won't end. You'll get a divorce, his family will most probably disown him, his friends will laugh at him, and chances of going far with the police will be stuffed. Don't get any closer to him than you are already. If you love him, you have to let him go.'

TC sat silently in deep thought as she analysed Vance's advice. He was right. She had to think of Graham and his future. She'd made a mess of her own life. She couldn't consciously wreck his.

¶

'I know how it feels to love someone and not be able to have them. That's precisely how I feel about Anna. Memories of her haunt me every day of my life. I think I'm subconsciously searching for another Anna. That could be the reason for my obsession with women.' TC smiled.

'I hope I don't get that way about men.' Vance smiled, too.

'Don't be ridiculous. It's not in you.'

'I'd best go before Claudia comes back,' said TC.

'No! I'm glad you're here. I want you to stay,' said Vance seriously. 'I need a witness. If the bitch comes back again, I'll nail her for bribery.' TC shrugged.

'I don't blame you. The three will make five thousand she's scammed from you.'

Vance placed a sheet of paper in the typewriter and began furiously typing. No sooner had he finished typing when Claudia reappeared.

'What's she still doing here?' snapped Claudia while indicating to TC with a venomous glance.

'TC is here because I asked her to be here, Claudia,' said Vance. His tone was icy.

'Come out the back with me while TC gets your money. TC please go to the safe, extract three thousand dollars. Call me after you've relocked the safe.'

TC switched on the radio. As quietly as possible she pulled out the bottom drawer of the filing cabinet. Within seconds, she had the bag of money. She carefully counted out three thousand dollars, replaced the bag, locked the drawer, turned the radio down, and called Vance.

'Your pet bitch knows everything, Vance. Even the combination to your safe,' snarled Claudia.

'Do you want this money or not, Claudia?' demanded Vance. Claudia smiled sweetly.

'That's why I'm here, darling.' Vance pushed the typewritten piece of paper across his desk.

'Good sign this and it's yours.' Claudia read it then read it again.

'I'm not signing this,' she said angrily as she threw the paper on the desk.

'Good! You don't get the money,' bluffed Vance. 'I happen to know Delores is at the house. Would you like me to call her and tell her you're coming to see her?' Claudia was furious!

'You rotten bastard!' she screamed. 'You can't do this to me!'

'You are doing it to me, Claudia,' replied Vance calmly. 'Not a nice feeling, is it?' Claudia grabbed the paper and pen from the desk, signed it, then thrust it at TC.

'Here, pet bitch, you're the witness.' TC signed where Vance had typed, 'Witness – TC Carmichael.'

'Here's your money, Claudia,' said Vance. 'Now get out of here and don't come back.' Claudia rushed form the shop. She quickly got into a car driven by a man waiting outside. The car sped off in the direction of Curloo.

'TC, did you read that before you signed it?' asked Vance.

'No!' replied TC.

'NEVER sign anything without reading it first!' said Vance seriously.

'But you wrote it, Boss,' reasoned TC.

'I don't care if the Pope wrote it. You shouldn't have signed before reading it,' continued Vance.

'What does it say?' asked TC.

'Read it.' As TC read, she was amused by Vance's cunning. 'I hereby confirm receipt of five thousand dollars from Vance Callahan. I have threatened to tell his wife details of an extra-marital affair in which I was a willing participant if he refused to pay me the money.'

'Very clever, Boss!' said TC. 'I have to go now. Need to do some deep thinking.'

While walking home, TC decided to leave Jake. Perhaps if she waited long enough, domestic violence would be recognised as grounds for a so-called "respectable" divorce. She also had to see Graham. She needed to tell him there was no hope of their relationship progressing any further. Not now, nor in the future. Tears welled. She restrained them. Crying changed nothing. All it did was leave her with red, puffy eyes.

As TC approached her front gate, she heard a piercing scream emanating from Lena and Jack's house on the corner. She stopped to listen. There was another scream. Then she saw Lena run out of her side yard, clutching her baby.

'Help me,' screamed Lena as she ran towards TC. 'Jack's drunk! He's pulled out my hair. He said he's going to kill me!'

TC couldn't turn Lena away. She remembered how she'd wished she had somewhere to run herself when Jake had laid into her.

'Come inside, Lena,' invited TC. 'I didn't know Jack was a drinker.' Lena was frantic. A look of terror was in her huge, bulging eyes. 'Sit down on the couch,' said TC. 'Would you like a glass of water?'

'No, thanks,' replied Lena as she laid her baby on the couch beside her. 'Jack doesn't drink very often. I went to the pub to tell him to come home. He came home and then started bashing me. I think he's pulled some of my hair out. When I tried to run away, he grabbed my hair.'

TC looked at the back of Lena's head. Sure enough, there was a bald patch the size of her palm. It was red with a few thin rivulets of blood where scalp as well as hair was missing.'

'Would you like me to call the doctor?' asked TC.

'No. I don't want anyone else to know,' replied Lena.

'I understand! I think you should at least have some iodine on it.'

'All right, if you think so,' agreed Lena. TC went to the bathroom for the iodine. She quickly returned to the lounge room when she heard a scream. Jack was in the process of pulling Lena to her feet. He was pulling her by her hair.

'Stop that NOW, Jack!' commanded TC loudly. 'She's already half bald.' Jack let go and stepped back. He looked at TC, who could see he was sad about the situation. 'Go home and sleep it off, Jack. Think of your baby,' said TC softly.

Jack was a larger-than-life, hard-working, extremely handsome man, the same age as Jake. They had been neighbours since birth. While Jake's parents were amongst the so-called upper crust of Brolga society, Jack's mother had died when he was a small child. He was raised by a caring aunt and an uncaring father, who was the most hopeless of the town drunks. Rumour had it Jack's dad had his first drink the day his wife was put in the ground and didn't stop until the day they buried him beside her.

TC felt helpless to say or do anything when broad-shouldered, six-feet-two, black-haired, blue-eyed Jack slumped to the floor in a corner of her lounge room and cried with remorse. Head in hands, every few seconds or so he would raise his head and look at Lena and his baby as if searching for reasons why and for her forgiveness. TC wet a towel which she handed to Jack.

'Come on, Jack. Wipe your face. Unfortunately, what's done is done.' Jack took the towel. As he wiped his face, he replied, 'That's the problem, ain't it?'

'Come on, Jack,' said Lena. 'Let's take our baby home now.' Jack slowly got to his feet.

'Sorry to barge in on you, TC. I hate grog. It killed my old man. Sometimes when I've been in the bush for months, I like to meet up with old mates. They all drink. Usually I drink lemonade. Today I drank rum.'

'You don't have to explain to me,' said TC. 'It appears rum does strange things to people.'

TC stood on her front doorstep and watched Jack, Lena, and baby walk to their house. I like Jack. He's a good man, thought TC. Can't imagine Jake crying after he's bashed me.

❡

While driving bush, Vance decided to buy a vehicle for camp number two. It was located so far away from town and the nearest property homestead was eighty miles away. Should an emergency arise, they needed a reliable means of transport in order to seek help or get to town, whereas Yappy and the men at the number one site were but a few miles from a homestead. The water truck would get them there. He knew it would cause flak and he'd more than likely be accused of favouritism. Nevertheless, he had to do it.

Even if I wanted to buy a vehicle for that mob, I couldn't, thought Vance as he wrestled with his conscience. 'The bastards would go on strike every week. Best thing I can do is keep my mouth shut. Hopefully, by the time they find out, they'll be on break and too drunk to worry about it.'

❡

In Curloo, Jake bore the brunt of joke after joke about being caught out by TC.

'I feel like crap,' he said to his brother Duke.

'Oh, well, Jake, if the cap fits, wear it,' replied Duke indifferently.

❡

Graham was arriving back in town after his sheep-guarding shift. He knew Jake would be in Curloo for the races and lived in hope he would get the opportunity to see TC in Jake's absence. Not that he cared if Jake was around or not. Graham simply figured TC would be more relaxed, knowing Jake was out of town.

❡

Yappy was cleaning the kitchen after the evening meal when Vance pulled in. Neil, Faith, and Little Joe were sitting outside smoking and drinking coffee while yarning about the day's production, past experiences, and what they planned to do next break, which was months away.

'What are you doing here?' asked Neil.

'Must be running early or late,' said Faith.

'Hello, Boss,' said Little Joe.

'Hello, Little Joe,' replied Vance. 'As for you other two, it's good to see you, too. I'm here because I need a bed for the night and, yes, I'm running late. I'm going to see if Yappy has anything to eat. Since I quit the fags, I'm hungry every minute of the bloody day.'

'What are you doing here, Vance?' greeted Yappy.

'Already been through that one, Yappy,' laughed Vance. 'I need something to eat.'

¶

With the radio blasting as in the old days with Lou, TC lay in the bath wondering where she would go and what she would do. Only thing she was sure about was she was leaving Jake and she was going to call the Sydney shoe store next morning and ask them to hold two pairs of stilettos. She would wire the money plus postage and ask they be sent by airmail.

I'll get one beige pair and one red pair, she thought while deliberately barring thoughts of Graham and the inevitable from her mind. She was successful at doing so until Patsy Cline came on the radio singing, 'Sweet Dreams of You'. Like a robot, TC got out of the bath, dressed, and walked to the café. Her heart told her Graham would be there. The darling is probably waiting there, hoping I'll show, she thought.

TC was right. Graham was sitting with Lisa at her table. His back was to the door.

'Here she is,' said Lisa. 'Hello, darling,' she called.

TC's heart began racing when Graham turned around. He was

smiling his beautiful smile. His expression was one of relief, and love shone from his eyes.

'I told him you'd be here,' said Lisa. Graham stood up and looked down at TC.

'I was about to give up. I thought you weren't coming.' TC smiled.

'How could I not come? I got a message from my heart. It told me you'd be here waiting for me.'

'I heard you left on the Flea this morning, darling,' said Lisa. 'Then I heard you came back with two men from the seismic crew.'

'News travels fast in Brolga,' smiled TC as Graham pulled a chair out for her.

'Pity nothing else does,' said Con from the kitchen doorway.

'Would you like a shake, TC?'

'No, thank you, Con,' replied TC, while thinking, I could do with a rope to hang myself or a razor blade to slit my wrists. Here I am sitting next to this darling young man whom I love desperately, knowing the closest physical contact we'll ever experience is in the past. The dance, his hand-holding, the few kisses on the cheek and forehead are gone.

'Why did you take the Flea this morning?' asked Lisa seriously.

'I had to see Jake about something,' replied TC. 'He's in Curloo for the races.'

'You must not have stayed long,' continued Lisa. TC smiled.

'About half an hour.'

Graham wanted to ask TC a million questions. He didn't. He was happy she was sitting beside him talking mostly to Lisa. He loved listening to TC speak, and her laugh made him want to hug her.

Interval at the movies brought the usual rush to the café. With Lisa leaving her table to help Con serve their customers, Graham looked adoringly at TC.

'I want to hold you, TC.'

'I know,' was the soft reply.

'Let's get out of here.'

'Good idea. I should go home,' replied TC, who wanted nothing more on earth than to get out of there with him.

'I'll drive you. You've never been in my car,' said Graham eagerly. TC was silent while weighing up possible consequences. What if Graham wanted to kiss her goodnight? She couldn't let that happen. If he held her or kissed her, it would be the end of her resolution to let him go for his own good.

The movie crowd gone, Lisa re-joined them.

'TC's going home, Lisa,' said Graham. 'Please tell her to let me drive her.'

'Of course, I will,' said Lisa. 'TC, let Constable Graham drive you home. You are safe with him, darling. He's a police officer.' TC laughed.

'Not fair! You are ganging up on me. All right, Constable Graham, let's go. Get more than a foot closer to me and I'll scream.'

'Thank you, Lisa,' beamed Graham.

'I'll see you tomorrow,' said a smiling Lisa, who watched them leave while thinking how wonderful they looked together.

'This isn't the way home,' said TC when Graham turned his car in the direction of Auntie Flo's house. 'I don't live there anymore.'

'I know that, sweetheart. I want to talk to you alone. Every time we've ever talked, we've had an audience or people close by.'

'Well, there's a first time for everything,' said TC lightly as Graham pulled up alongside the creek. 'Never thought of myself as the park-by-the-creek type.'

'You're not, TC, but there's nowhere else to go,' said Graham seriously.

TC was sitting as close to the passenger-side window as she possibly could while Graham leaned back in the driver's seat and looked at her. He didn't know what to say. He couldn't believe he was actually parked by the creek with TC in his car. He wanted to hold her, he wanted to kiss her, and he wanted to make love to her. His body was aching for her. A new song he'd heard a few times which reminded him of exactly the way he felt about TC began playing on the radio.

'Listen to this, sweetheart,' he said. 'This is how I feel about you.' TC listened to the words, 'When a man loves a woman, can't keep his mind on nothing else.' She wanted to slide across the car seat, throw her arms around Graham, and be with him for the rest of her life.

'I want to hold you, TC,' said Graham tenderly.

'I want to hold you, too, Graham. Unfortunately, I'm married to Jake,' replied TC sadly.

'I only want to hold you, sweetheart, that's all,' pleaded Graham. TC was on the verge of surrender when a ute filled with partying, part-Aboriginal locals pulled up twenty yards or so away.

'We must go,' said TC while thinking, I was on the verge of wrecking your life, darling Graham.

Graham wanted to get out of his car and tell the drunken lot to get the hell out of there. Instead, he started his car.

When he dropped TC home, he squeezed her hand and looked hopefully into her eyes. 'I'll see you soon?' TC shook her head and smiled.

'I don't think that's a good idea.'

¶

Although Jake won a heap of money in Curloo, he was miserable. He dreaded the thought of returning home to Brolga. The whole bloody town would know about TC's visit to Curloo. He knew TC was tight-lipped. She had probably told her protector, Vance. He was sure she wouldn't tell anyone else. The problem was there'd been quite a few Brolgaites in Curloo, and they'd be blabbering their guts out.

Didn't dawn on Jake to consider Madison's reputation. As always, he thought of Jake and Jake only. He came up with a plan as Duke drove past the 'Welcome to Brolga' sign.

'I'm going to burn the shop down, get the insurance, and piss off,' he told himself. 'Callahan got away with it. Why can't I? I'll do it tomorrow night. It's Wednesday. Everyone will be at the movies. No! Better leave it till early morning when everything's closed and the joint is dead.'

That's exactly what Jake did. At 3 a.m. Thursday morning, he flooded the rear of the shop with kerosene, torched it, jumped in his car, and sped home via the back streets, threw himself into his bed, and pretended to be asleep.

What Jake didn't count on was one of his truckie mates driving past on his way to the truck depot, spotting the fire, drove like a mad man to the power house to have the siren sounded, then raced to collect Duke Carmichael, who was in charge of Brolga's small but efficient fire-fighting team.

We missed out on the Callahan fire. We're not missing out on this one, thought the truckie as he told Duke his family store was ablaze.

The only person in Brolga under eighty and mobile who didn't get out of bed and wonder what the bloody hell was going on was Jake. He stayed in bed pretending to be asleep.

Even TC ventured from her locked bedroom. She had heard Jake come home not long before.

Strange, Jake's not up, she thought. Then she thought again. He's probably drunk and passed out.

A while later, Duke was there. TC was dressed for work. She didn't see any point in going back to bed,

'Where's Jake, TC?' asked Duke.

'He's in bed. He's probably drunk,' replied TC.

'I'll get him up,' said Duke. 'The shop almost burnt down. Luckily, we saved it in time.'

§

While the entire town, including the police sergeant, were suspicious Jake had started the fire, there was no proof. The racing circuit was completed. Jake had nothing to lose. He closed down the shop and arranged a job with his cousins in the Northern Territory. He was out of Brolga by the end of the week.

Word of Jake absconding travelled like lightning.

'Gutless young bastard,' agreed Seat of Knowledge patrons.

'Got too hot for the prick. He had to run away,' said Jock. They all laughed while concentrating on the goings-on in the Empire bar.

§

Graham left Brolga the following week. The sheep-stealing case had concluded and he was transferred to Brisbane. He stopped by the café before driving out of town.

'I came to say goodbye, Con and Lisa. Thank you for everything.' He passed Lisa a small package. 'Please give this to TC.'

'Of course, Graham. You take care of yourself,' smiled Lisa.

¶

Just as TC was relieved when Jake went away, she was devastated when Lisa told her Graham had gone. Deep down she knew it was for the best. It was the thought of never seeing him again that caused the pain.

'It's for the best, Lisa,' said TC after an eternity of silence. 'Had he stayed here, the temptation to wreck his life would always be present.'

'You wouldn't have wrecked his life, darling,' said Lisa softly.

'Yes, I would have, Lisa. The boss checked things out for me.'

'I see,' said Lisa. 'Graham left you a present,' she added as she gave TC a small package. TC opened the card first.

I always wanted to sing a song for you but never got the opportunity. I'm leaving you this record instead. I'll never forget you, TC. Love Graham. P.S. My phone number is ...

The record was Percy Sledge singing, 'When a man loves a woman'. TC knew it would be before she opened it. Although she desperately wanted to cry, she didn't.

'You poor darling,' said Lisa. 'I feel sad for both of you. You know, TC, love is a strange commodity. Often people fall in love, get married, and a few months after the wedding bells stop ringing, the thrill has gone and complacency sets in. Although they are content or pretend to be content, the mystery is lost forever, and their love runs hot and cold if, indeed, it runs at all. In the case of you and Graham, the mystery will remain with you for the rest of your lives. It will always be there.'

¶

Mr Patrick called Vance a couple of weeks later. He had a friend from New York who had seen the stones Patrick had bought. The New York gem dealer wanted to buy some himself. He couldn't come to Brolga, so he wanted to see Vance in Brisbane.

'I can't get away, Patrick,' said Vance. 'I'll send TC.' Patrick laughed.

'I'd love to be there when she shakes this guy's hand. It's a good thing she's nobody's fool. You need to be on the ball with New Yorkers.'

'I want to stay in Brisbane an extra day,' said TC when Vance told her she was doing the trip. 'I'd like to see Graham one last time.'

'TC, don't do anything silly,' warned Vance seriously.

'You know I won't, Boss. I love him too much. I need to see him one more time. That's all.'

TC saw the New York gem dealer in his Brisbane hotel room. Patrick was right. Her handshake was a surprise to the man.

'That's some handshake you've got there, TC.' TC laughed.

'So I've been told.'

The gentleman was understandably a discerning buyer. He asked multitudes of questions, which was fine. TC met him in his hotel room at nine. She left his room at five forty-five with eighty-five thousand in cash in the briefcase. She went to her hotel room near the airport and phoned Vance.

'Eighty-five, Boss. He is a nice man. No fiddling around, wasting time. I gave him two hundred and thirty discount.' Vance laughed.

'What are you laughing about?' asked TC.

'Just you, TC. You really must quit giving these huge discounts.'

'The man's happy, I'm happy, I hope you are,' replied TC, who chose not to comment on Vance's sarcasm. 'I'll see you at the plane on Saturday.'

¶

TC called the number Graham had written on her card. He wasn't there. He was working, so she left a message for him to call her next morning.

Graham collected TC at eleven. Although he smiled, he looked tired and sad. They drove around stopping here and there to look at buildings and other things of interest. They talked very little. TC knew this would be the last time she would see his beautiful eyes smile. She had a feeling he felt the same and that was the reason he looked so sad. When Graham dropped TC back at the hotel mid-afternoon, they looked at each other in silence before she stepped out of his car.

'Take care of yourself, Graham Sandler,' said TC softly and slowly. Graham forced a smile. His eyes were glistening with tears.

'You, too, TC Carmichael.' TC watched him drive away with sadness in her heart.

'Have a wonderful life, Graham,' she said aloud before going to her room, falling onto her bed, and crying until she fell asleep.

¶

Vance was happy with the eighty-five thousand.

There's a huge market in the US, he thought. All I have to do is find a way to tap it.

¶

Jake gave TC an obligatory phone call every now and again. She didn't care if he called or not. Jake was Jake. Nobody meant anything to him, and he meant nothing to TC, who had become skin and bone. One day Vance insisted she weigh herself in his presence.

'I thought so,' he said with concern. 'You weigh ninety-six pounds.'

'I eat when I'm hungry,' she said defensively.

'That's it? How often do you get hungry?' TC shrugged.

'I've got work to do.'

¶

The boulders kept coming, and the stone stock became massive. Christmas break time for the men rolled around again. This year the men stayed in Brolga.

'I'm staying in bloody Brolga,' said Yappy. 'Don't want Vance wiring me money care-of outside the pub in some bloody, tin-pot town ever again.'

'No more Big Smoke for me, mate,' declared Neil.

'I agree, mate. Stuff that,' said Faith.

Little Joe said nothing. He nodded and smiled. That's all.

Joined by Michael, Jakkie, Ali, and Ted, they took up residence in the rear of the Majestic. The Romeo Brothers were happy as pigs in muck.

⁊

Jake didn't come back to Brolga for Christmas. He stayed in a hotel in Darwin and gambled every chance he got.

⁊

TC spent Christmas day with Jack and Lena and their baby. After leaving their house on Christmas night, she went home and played Graham's record over and over and over again. She was miserable.

⁊

Christmas didn't mean a great deal to Vance. Even though his boys were home, he spent most of the day sawing rocks. A family man he definitely was not.

⁊

On Boxing Day, Vance visited TC.

'I want you to do a trip to Sydney and Melbourne first week in the New Year.'

'Sure,' replied TC.

'As soon as you come back, I want you to do another trip,' said Vance. He was ever so serious.

'Where?' asked TC.

'I want you to go to the US. You'll be away a long time. Maybe two or three years.' TC was speechless. 'There's a market over there, TC. I want you to find it.'

'Where in America do you want me to go?' enquired TC when she finally spoke.

'Start in the centre of the top end,' said Vance with great enthusiasm, 'Chicago, that's where you'll go first.' TC was dubious.

'I don't know, Boss. It's one thing going to Sydney and Melbourne, but it's an entirely different scenario going to Chicago.'

'Why is it different?' argued Vance. 'Americans speak English, they look the same as us. Only difference is the cities are bigger.'

'I'll think about it. There's nothing here for me, so it probably doesn't matter where I am. It's such a long way away. America is the other side of the world.'

'So!' said Vance impatiently. 'I went there myself, remember?'

'Yes, you did, Mr Callahan,' replied TC. 'You went to a smallish town in California for two weeks. I'm sure that's a lot different to going to a big city like Chicago for two or three years.'

TC did the Sydney–Melbourne trip. It was a raging success. Both cities were oozing with international tourists escaping the northern hemisphere's icy winter. Briefly she saw Lou, Colin, and their beautiful, not-crying-all-the time-as-he-got-older baby boy.

In Brisbane she applied for a passport and necessary visa application forms. She was tired and disgusted by the sexually suggestive remarks bestowed upon her by a few male clients. 'Must be because it's a new year,' she told herself.

Vance met her at the airstrip. He was angry.

'Why didn't you call me, TC? You've been gone a week!'

'I wanted to surprise you,' retaliated TC.

'How did you go?' asked Vance.

'That's the second reason why I didn't call you, Mr Callahan,' snapped TC. 'Never once do you ask me if I'm okay, how was my day, did I have any trouble with customers, or any other damned thing. It's always how did I go. I got a hundred and thirty thousand and I gave nobody a discount. Please take me home. I want to take a bath. Here's the briefcase. Please get my bag. We'll have to discuss the trip later.'

'I'm sorry, TC. I was worried about you,' said Vance seriously.

'No, you weren't. You were worried about your money,' replied TC. 'Perhaps you should send one of your girlfriends on these trips. They'd probably sell more opal than I do. I'm not prepared to throw in my body. I'm sure they wouldn't hesitate.'

＄

Apart from Yappy, the men were broke by mid-January. Ali and Ted still had a few dollars in their kit because Ali controlled their money and consequently Ted.

Vance put the men on a budget. They each got five dollars per day. Instead on drinking their beloved beer, they resorted to buying flagons of red wine, which they would consume day and night while congregating behind the Majestic in the dry heat of Brolga's summer.

Yappy was doing all right. He won a few dollars betting on the horses, so he moved to the Brick.

'Can't stand you drunken mongrels,' he told the others. 'I'm moving. Hate the bloody sight of the lot of you.'

＄

'I'm your husband. I should be going to America with you,' snapped Jake when TC asked him what he wanted done with the house.

'You are nothing to me, Jake,' replied TC, who couldn't care less about him or the house.

'Madison is working at the Empire, so perhaps you should come back here,' said TC indifferently. 'Let's face it, Jake, you'll have your girlfriend, your booze, and your gambling all combined at the same convenient location.' Jake slammed down the telephone. The truth always upset him.

¶

TC's passport and visa arrived by mail. Now it was becoming a frightening reality. She was terrified and wanted to back down.

'If I do that, I'll be a coward,' she reasoned. 'I'm going to the United States and that is that.'

Vance had earmarked his cash on hand to establish a third camp and buy machinery for his remaining lease. He gave TC a one-way ticket along with three thousand Australian dollars.

'When that runs out, you're on your own; you'll have to live out of what you sell. Keep your receipts; mail them to me every month. Withhold your float and wire me the rest. I'll bank your pay so you'll have money when you come back.' As an afterthought, Vance pushed four fifty-dollar notes across the desk along with an extra bundle of stones.

'Here's your shoe allowance for the first few months and some give-away stones. Only give them to people who help you.' TC smiled.

'I think you mean the shoe allowance is for the first few weeks, not months, and I'll be selective about who gets the stones.'

¶

The bank manager served TC when she withdrew all but a dollar from her savings account.

'I hear you're going to America.'

'Yes!' replied TC acidly. 'Mr Callahan is sending me there so I can learn to become a better forger.'

¶

Armed with two large briefcases filled to bursting with magnificently coloured boulder opal stones of all shapes and sizes, TC bid a tearful farewell to Lou, then boarded a Qantas flight from Sydney to Los Angeles via Honolulu. From Los Angeles she was booked on a flight to Chicago. With the briefcases safely stowed in the overhead locker, TC waited for the plane to take off. At one stage, she was tempted to grab the cases and run off the plane.

Eventually the plane was airborne and TC forced herself to go to sleep. She had a window seat, which made sleeping a lot easier. With her head on a cushion propped against the plane wall, she was out to it for hours.

TC was excited when the plane landed in Hawaii. She wished she had someone with whom to share the experience. The stopover time was four hours, three-and-a-bit of which she spent with a customs official. He was a nice man. He counted every bundle, made notes, and compared them to TC's detailed paperwork.

In Los Angeles, no sooner was TC off the plane from Hawaii than she was in the air en route to Chicago. She was overwhelmed by the size of the airport and thanked the helpful airport staff, without whose assistance she would have been wandering around forever.

Arrival time in Chicago was 9.15 pm. The airport seemed even larger than the Los Angeles one. TC waited for her suitcase. She had no idea how she was going to carry it as well as the opal. She noticed people with luggage racks on wheels, so she asked a lady how and where to get one.

After collecting her suitcase, TC wheeled the trolley through a door marked "Taxis" with an arrow, took her place at the end of what appeared to be a mile-long queue, and wondered where on earth she would spend the night. Apart from that, she was freezing. Eventually it was her turn to take the next cab. She was relieved. By now she was shaking from being cold.

'Where to, young lady?' asked the Hispanic cab driver.

'I don't know,' replied TC gingerly.

'You don't know?' said the cab driver in disbelief.

'I need a hotel somewhere in the heart of the city. I'm from Australia. I haven't been here before,' explained TC.

'An Aussie, huh?' laughed the driver. 'You're a long way from home.'

Eventually the cab pulled up at a very noisy hotel. A doorman opened the cab door for her while the cab driver delivered her suitcase onto the steps. TC paid him. She almost forgot the tipping part Vance had warned her about. Fortunately, she remembered in time not to appear a fool.

The cab took off, and the doorman asked if TC had a reservation. When she replied, 'No,' he told her there was a concert in progress and the hotel was booked out.

'So that's why it's so noisy?' asked TC. 'Is it always so cold and windy here? I feel as if the wind is blowing through me. I don't know where I'm going to stay tonight. I'm freezing and frightened.'

'That's understandable, Ma'am,' said the kindly, middle-aged doorman. 'Let me make a call. It's Friday night, so I might be out of luck.' Smiling profusely, he was back in less than a minute.

'Follow me, Ma'am. There's a vacancy across the street. It's an apartment building. Sometimes they take in casuals. At least you'll be out of the cold. You asked me if it is always so windy here, Ma'am. The answer is yes. That's why we are called "the windy city". And, no, it's not always this cold. It's still winter. Lucky it's not snowing tonight.'

TC sighed with relief the second they entered the heated building. She paid the doorman to whom she would be eternally grateful, then spoke with the desk man to whom the doorman had explained her situation. He suggested she check in for a week, which would give her time to research and find more permanent accommodation. He would help her should she need assistance. He too was a kind, middle-aged man.

While her home for the next week was tiny, it was beautifully appointed. Complete with stove, refrigerator, and, most importantly at that moment, a bathtub. She needed to thaw out, so she immediately turned on the taps.

¶

Her first day in Chicago, TC woke up hungry. She decided to get out of bed and look outside to see what the weather was like. To her great surprise when she drew back the curtains behind the bed, there was a blank wall. The compact apartment was windowless. Suddenly TC felt claustrophobic.

I hope there's not a fire, she thought. I'd have nowhere to throw the opal. It would have to burn with me.

Dressed in jeans and a long-sleeved cotton blouse, a briefcase filled with opals in each hand, she went downstairs to ask at the desk where she could buy a warm coat and some food.

'Two blocks down and one across, there's a department store,' directed the same friendly doorman from the previous night. 'You can buy everything there.' TC smiled gratefully.

'Thank you.'

'Do you want to leave your bags here?' offered the desk man.

'No, that's all right. Thank you, anyway,' replied TC. She would have loved to park the briefcases with him, but she couldn't. They could never be out of her sight.

TC hurried as fast as her legs would carry her to the department store. It was only two blocks down and one across, as the desk clerk had told her, but to TC it seemed a thousand miles.

Some store it was! It was huge. The ground floor must have been the length and breadth of Brolga's entire main block, and there were several same-sized levels above it. TC located the information counter and asked directions to women's winter clothing.

'There won't be much left,' said the lady. 'It's the end of season and the sales have been on.' TC couldn't believe her eyes when she saw how much equated to "not much left". Countless racks displayed multitudes of coats, jackets, and jumpers of all colours, shapes, and sizes. Huge "Sale" signs were prolific.

She purchased a fake-fur-lined, beige, ankle-length woollen overcoat, two thick, polo-necked pullovers, and a thigh-length, unlined woollen jacket. In the shoe section, she bought a pair of high, fleecy-lined beige suede boots with high heels. TC put on the boots and coat as soon as she paid for them. She ate a sandwich in the cafeteria before heading back to her room. On the way, she purchased a newspaper. She had to find a place to live.

'You look warmer, Ma'am,' greeted the desk clerk when she entered the lobby. TC smiled.

'Please call me TC. Ma'am makes me feel old.'

'In that case, TC, please call me James,' replied the clerk. 'See, it's written here,' he laughed while touching his gold-plated name badge. 'I see you bought a paper. No need to do that; there're always newspapers here.'

'Thank you, James. Guess I'll see you later,' said TC before taking the lift to the fifth floor.

TC scanned the accommodation section of the Tribune. After a couple of hours, she was hopelessly confused. She needed something close to the business sector, secure, clean, and reasonably priced. She decided she was getting nowhere, so she went downstairs to seek assistance from James. After explaining what she was hoping to find, James told TC he would be happy to help her.

'Give me an hour,' he said kindly. 'I'll circle the places I think might meet your needs. I've got a daughter your age or round about. I'd like to think if she was alone in Australia, some desk clerk would help her find somewhere to live.'

'I'm sure someone would,' smiled TC. 'I consider myself lucky. The hotel across the road was booked out last night. If it hadn't been, I wouldn't have met you.' James laughed as he wondered if all Australians were as friendly as TC.

'I'll see you in an hour, TC.'

Back in her room, TC began scanning the telephone directory for names and addresses of gem dealers. She was surprised when she realised most of them were located at the same street address. Oh, well, that's good, she thought. My heels will last longer.

¶

'This place is perfect for you,' said James, pointing to a circled-in-pencil, small advertisement in the newspaper. 'I know the building. It's on the lake, walking distance to State Street. It's secure, clean, and by the looks of this advert, cheap as chips. It says here the owner is leaving town for three months and wants a caretaker. That's obviously why the rent is so low.'

'Sounds great' agreed TC. 'I'd best make a call.'

'I'll dial the number for you,' offered James. 'I'm not supposed to use this phone for outside calls but who'll know?' TC smiled sweetly and shrugged.

'Only us, James.'

Minutes later, TC had an appointment to meet the male apartment owner at an address on Lake Shore Drive at 7 pm.

'Meeting the man at seven,' beamed TC when she handed the telephone back. 'I know I'll get it, James, and I'll have you to thank.'

As TC picked up the briefcases from the floor beside her, James' expression became quizzical.

'Why do you carry those bags with you all the time? Are they filled with money or gold bars?' TC laughed.

'No! Just some stuff to do with my work.' As she hurried towards the elevator, she pretended not to hear James ask her what type of work she did.

⁋

By 9 pm, TC had three months' accommodation on the fifteenth floor of a huge apartment building on Lake Shore. Directly opposite on the other side of the wide road was Lake Michigan. The apartment was a one-bedroom bachelor pad. It was tastefully decorated and fitted with all essentials plus T.V. and audio equipment. From the wide, living room window was a magnificent view of Chicago's city skyline and the right side of the lake. From the bedroom window was a perfect, broad view of Lake Michigan.

'On a clear day, you can see Canada from this window,' said the apartment owner. He was a geologist; a handsome man, perhaps in his mid-forties. He told TC he had half a dozen apartments scattered across the continent. He moved around a lot with his job, so he liked to have something he could call his own wherever he was located. He had been to Australia on several occasions. He said he loved it. He had found all Aussies friendly and straight shooters. He wanted five hundred dollars plus phone wage for thirteen weeks. 'Look after the place, keep it clean, forward my mail, and pay me the money up front.'

TC paid him the five hundred and the deal was done. The geologist introduced TC to the desk clerk from whom she would collect the keys next Saturday morning, then called her a cab on the call-for-free phone located in a corner of the lobby.

A little later that evening the geologist realised he hadn't asked TC what type of business she was in. He had been too engrossed by her accent. Never mind, he'd ask her some other time. She seemed like a decent young woman.

§

Vance was standing on the hill at his third claim. He was pondering where to locate the camp. The machine and everything else would soon arrive in Brolga.

Hope I haven't bitten off more than I can chew, he thought. 'Don't have a bloody clue whom I'll get to work this site. I'll have to be careful; hate to end up with Bert Black–type bastards. It'd be two boulders for them and one for me or, worse, three for them and none for me.' As he made his way down the hill, he thought of TC and wondered how she was coping in Chicago.

'I should have told her to call me as soon as she got there instead of telling her not to contact me until she was organised. Bloody hell, I'm a cold bastard. What on earth am I going to do about Almut? She's like a bloody leech the way she way she hangs around me all the time. I'm beginning to feel sorry for Coral. As for poor bloody Delores, well, that's an entirely different kettle of fish.'

Vance sat in his ute. Before turning the key, he unwrapped a half-melted chocolate bar.

¶

On Sunday morning TC dressed to go out. When she got downstairs, she saw through the glass inner-lobby door that it was snowing. She'd never seen snow before. It looked beautiful. It reminded her of Christmas cards she'd seen back home. James wasn't at the desk; another man was there. He appeared to be reading something, probably the newspaper. TC didn't want to disturb him. She was hungry but didn't care for the thought of going out in the snow, especially not with the bags of opal. She looked around the lobby and spotted a candy machine she hadn't noticed before. Luckily, she had enough change for two chocolate bars.

I'll wind up like the boss if it snows too long, she thought as she retreated to her room and turned on the television set she had located on a shelf behind a door opposite the bed. I'll have to find somewhere to leave the opal while I get to know my way around, she thought as she stared at the T.V. screen, absorbing nothing of the goings-on. I thought I was lonely in Brolga! This will be worse. At least I know people there.

TC sighed with relief when James was at the desk next morning when she ventured downstairs.

'I got the apartment, James. I move in on Saturday. So far, everything is going fine. Thanks to you, I'll have a home for three months.'

'Happy I was of help,' said James sincerely.

'I need to find a bank. Can you point me in the right direction?'

'You need State Street. It's still snowing outside. It's best if you take a cab,' replied James. 'I'll lend you an umbrella.' TC smiled and looked helpless.

'I'm afraid I can't carry an umbrella until after I've been to a bank. At the moment, my hands are full.'

¶

By midday, the opal, apart from a couple of "give-aways", was in a large, safety deposit box and TC had opened a bank account. She took a cab to the department store, where she bought a fake-fur cap she could pull down over her ears, an umbrella, a pair of flat, warm boots suitable for walking in snow, and a map of the city.

Happy everything's on sale, she thought. The added tax deal is misleading.

Once again, she ate in the department store cafeteria before returning to her accommodation.

'Where are your bags, TC?' enquired a smiling James.

'In the bank,' replied TC happily. 'My arms were growing longer due to carting them around.' James desperately wanted to ask TC again what was in her briefcases. He didn't dare. It was her business.

By the time Saturday rolled around, TC had familiarised herself with the downtown and commercial districts of Chicago. She temporarily felt like a tourist, a foot-sore one, at that. She thanked herself for having the intelligence to buy the flat boots.

'Sadly, it's time to say goodbye, James,' said TC. 'Now I'm going to tell you what I do.'

'What's that, TC? Can't say I haven't been curious,' replied James with his usual smile.

'I work for an opal miner in Australia. He's sent me over here to hopefully establish a US market for his stones.' James laughed.

'I wasn't far off with my money or gold theory, was I?'

'No, not far at all,' laughed TC. 'My boss gave me a few stones to give to deserving people. I have one here for you.' James was speechless as TC placed a stone on the counter. It was a medium, domed, green-orange stone around four carats. He picked it up and looked at it.

'I don't know what to say, TC. It's beautiful. My daughter will love it. It's her birthstone.'

'My cab's here,' said TC holding out her hand. 'Thank you for helping me.'

'It's been a pleasure,' said James as they shook hands.

§

TC settled into the geologist's apartment, used the laundry on the thirteenth floor, enquired at the desk, and was told there was a convenience store located one corner down. She went there and purchased essentials. That first night in the fifteenth floor apartment, TC pressed and ironed her clothes while looking up and out frequently to admire Chicago's city lights through the wide and high window. It sure was a wonderful view.

She spent all day Sunday planning Monday. Sunday night she phoned Vance. She had no idea what time it was in Brolga. She knew it would be Monday, nothing else.

'At last, Little One,' said Vance.

'You made the rules, Boss, not me,' replied TC.

'So, tell me everything, TC.'

Ten minutes later, TC put down the phone, then made a note of the time of the call. She would keep a record of her calls for the geologist to compare with his account.

Next morning was the beginning!

Immediately the bank opened, TC collected the opal, then went to the ten-story building housing Chicago gem dealers. She decided to start on the top floor and work her way to the bottom.

'No! I don't deal in opal; they're unlucky,' said the first gentleman.

'No, don't know enough about them,' said the second.

'Go away! I'm having a bad day,' said the third.

'I'd like to look and buy, but I'm having a rough time,' said the fourth.

And so it went.

TC pressed twenty-six buzzers that first day. In most cases, pushing the button caused the door to open while in others a rectangular peep-hole would slide open and a pair of eyes would speak to her.

They didn't even look, thought TC despondently as she made her way home. Never mind, that's their loss. I'll try again tomorrow.

Day after day was the same. It took TC twelve working days to cover those ten floors. Naturally, they were closed on weekends. Of that entire building filled with nothing but gem dealers, seven bothered to look. Five of those seven spent hours looking at the stones, only to decide they were too beautiful to be real. Must be fakes.

The remaining two gentlemen bought. She spent virtually an entire day with each of them while they looked at the stones between phone calls and other interruptions. The stones were marked in Australian dollars and converted to US dollars, depending on the exchange rate of the day. One man purchased all ovals. He wrote a cheque for eleven hundred dollars. The other man spent two thousand in cash after haggling with TC to round down the price.

Back in Brolga, Vance had employed a man who was great with machinery. Knew it backwards. He'd had a go at opal mining himself. Didn't do any good; went broke instead. While Vance had an adverse gut feeling about the man, he didn't see he had much choice. If he wanted to get the third mine operating, he needed people to work it.

Jake was back in Brolga. He got a job as bookkeeper at Brolga's garage.

'Jake might be the biggest bullshit artist on earth,' said the owner. 'All that aside, he's a bloody good bookkeeper. Neat as buggery, too.'

TC banked the thirty-one hundred dollars, then decided to try her luck with Chicago's jewellers. No luck! They all bought from the gem dealers. As had become her habit, she put the opal in the safety deposit over the weekend, then went home to make a decision as to what to do next.

She phoned Mr Patrick in Los Angeles.

'What do you think of my chances in Los Angeles?' asked TC.

'TC, I spent a lot of money with Vance. I don't want every gem dealer in L.A. competing with me,' was his curt reply. 'You owe me a favour— don't come here.'

TC then phoned Vance to bring him up-to-date. When she told him what Patrick's reaction was regarding her trying in L.A., Vance was initially angry.

'The bastard didn't buy our entire operation! So he spent a couple of hundred thousand, so what!'

'I don't know, Boss,' reasoned TC. 'He might come back and spend another couple of hundred.'

'All right, but stuff him, anyway,' said Vance.

'I think I might try New Orleans,' suggested TC. 'Perhaps people down there appreciate beauty more than here in Chicago. Apart from that, it won't be as cold.'

'Do whatever you want. Call me next week.'

¶

TC arrived in New Orleans early in the evening on Monday night. The desk clerk in her building had recommended a hotel on Bourbon Street, where she had booked a room. When her cab pulled up outside the hotel, TC was amazed by the multitudes of people on both sides of the narrow street.

'This place sure is alive,' she commented to the cab driver as he removed her suitcase from the boot of his cab.

'This is Bourbon Street, Ma'am. What do you expect?' replied the smiling cabbie.

TC was taken aback by the Old-World décor of her hotel room. It was beautiful. White doors with glass panels opened onto a small, curved, white balcony which overlooked the hustle and bustle of crowded Bourbon Street after dark. Fleetingly, she thought of Graham, wishing he was with her. It was expensive. Compared to the cost of her windowless-accommodation the first week in Chicago, it was cheap.

After showering, TC called upon room service and later ate a small portion of the biggest hamburger imaginable while perusing the telephone directory for names and addresses of gem dealers and jewellers. Although it was late when she closed the balcony doors, there were still people everywhere on the street with lots of laughter and music drifting from bars and clubs.

⁋

Next morning when TC opened the doors, Bourbon Street was deserted apart from street sweepers slowly going about their business. It was a beautiful day, the sky was blue, and the sun was shining. Made her feel good.

She decided to wear her red dress and red stilettos, neither of which she'd worn previously.

'I'm going to sell some opal today,' she told herself as she waited for her cab the doorman had ordered.

As the cab sped across the seemingly never-ending bridge spanning the Mississippi River, TC could see the skyline of a modern city, which was in stark contrast to Bourbon Street and its surroundings.

Incredible! she thought.

⁋

The first two gem dealers weren't interested. They sure were friendly, though. The third dealer asked her to come back tomorrow. She spent four hours with the fourth man. He spent six thousand cash. The fifth gentleman also asked her to come back tomorrow. The last man she saw that afternoon asked her to put aside eight thousand-plus worth of stones and come back first thing in the morning.

I knew it! thought TC. Another thing I do know is people in New Orleans are a lot friendlier than people in Chicago.

TC would have loved to walk along Bourbon Street that night. She couldn't; she had the opal. Instead, she ordered chicken and ate it while watching the action from her balcony. The chicken was great. Hot, she didn't mind. She enjoyed hot food almost as much as she enjoyed sitting on the balcony watching the action below. Reluctantly she went inside

476

to wash and roll her hair. She had another good feeling about tomorrow and wanted to look her best.

¶

The eight-thousand-put-aside-stones man spent twenty-one thousand dollars. He asked TC to stay away from the jewellers. She agreed and shook on it. One of the come-back-tomorrow men spent five and the second man spent nine after sounding off half-cash and half-cheque.

The boss will be happy, thought TC while crossing the bridge in the cab. I can't figure out why these New Orleans dealers are so keen on the stones when the people in Chicago shun them. I sold—that's the main thing and I've still got more people to see.

¶

During the four days TC worked New Orleans, she took eighty-three thousand dollars. The reason for the enthusiasm towards the stones was clarified by her second-last customers.

'I'd never seen this type of opal until a couple of weeks ago. There was a dealer from New York down here flashing some around at a meeting. He said he bought it from a girl in Brisbane, Australia.' TC smiled.

'I know the man. The girl was me! Small world!'

'Another thing, TC; why aren't you wearing opal yourself?'

'Too risky,' lied TC. She didn't want to admit she didn't own any.

Reluctantly, TC said goodbye to New Orleans. She would never forget the friendly people, Bourbon Street on one side of the mighty river, and the ultra-modern city on the other.

¶

The first thing TC did when she was safely locked in her apartment in Chicago was phone Vance. Hopefully she would catch him before he left Brolga for the mines.

How did you go, TC?' he asked as usual.

'Thanks, Mr Callahan. I'm well, too,' replied TC.

'I'm sorry, TC. How are you?' said Vance slowly while accentuating the sorry and you words.

'I'm tired, lonely, and happy. I sold some opal,' replied TC.

'Well?' from Vance.

'I loved New Orleans, the people were friendly, and the weather was great,' replied TC.

'TC, how much did you sell?' demanded Vance. 'I'm not interested in how lovely your holiday was.' TC was livid.

'Eighty-three thousand, Mr Callahan. If you think this is a holiday, I suggest you try it yourself. You'd last a week, if that!' Vance started to say something. TC put down the phone, then opened her suitcase to unpack.

The telephone rang.

'Yes!' said TC when she put it to her ear.

'TC, I'm sorry,' said Vance.

'No! You are not sorry. You have become as obsessed by money as you are by women,' replied TC matter-of-factly. 'You can't get enough of it. I liked you better when you were a drunk.'

'I'll call back later,' said Vance calmly. 'She's right,' he told himself as he reached for a chocolate bar. He wished he had a cigarette; a Rum and Coke to go with it wouldn't go astray.

¶

After spending the weekend sorting and re-bagging stones, doing her laundry, and thinking about what to do next, TC banked the cheques and cash from her New Orleans trip and caught a flight to San Francisco.

Unfortunately, the reaction was the same as in Chicago. After three days, she decided it was a waste of time and money to stay longer.

Best leave all of California to Mr Patrick, she thought. I do like the bridge, hilly streets, and trams. Talk about it! The people were nice; didn't they realise they were accusing her of fraud when they said the stones were fakes?

Withholding the float, TC had the bank transfer the cleared funds to the bank in Brolga. Vance still hadn't called her back. He would when he realised she'd sent the money. She knew that for sure.

He did.

⁋

TC wanted to get out of Chicago. She knew it was a lost cause. Problem was she couldn't let the geologist down. He had trusted her without so much as a signature. It was a matter of principle. She would stay till the three months were up.

During that time Martin Luther King was assassinated in Memphis. His assassination led to race riots in over sixty cities nationwide. On television news of these riots overshadowed the ongoing war in Vietnam. The weather became divine; the snow had gone, and the squirrels played in the park next to her building.

⁋

TC made a couple of repeat sales to the two Chicago gem dealers who had bought stones previously. One of them told her about a gem show coming up in New York later in the year.

'Everyone will be there. You should try your luck. Great place to make contacts.' The same man gave TC a list of independent jewellers in outer-Chicago areas.

'Go by train. You might be lucky. Lots of people are born in October.'

TC took the gentleman's advice. Initially, she was more than a little wary of travelling on the trains. She soon gained confidence. Overall, it was worth the effort. She sold a couple of stones here and there.

During her last week in Chicago, TC detailed the apartment, cancelled the safety deposit box, said goodbye to the two gem dealers who had supported her, and visited James to thank him once again for his help almost three months previously.

'Where are you going this time?' he enquired after expressing his surprise at seeing her again.

'Philadelphia. It's close to New York. I don't want to live in New York. I'm a small-town girl.' James laughed.

'Philadelphia is hardly a small town.'

'I imagine it's still smaller than New York. Did your daughter like her opal?'

'She hasn't gotten it yet,' smiled James. 'October third is her birthday. I'm having it made into a thing she can wear around her neck.' They shook hands, and TC went on her way thinking what a nice man James was.

The geologist phoned TC two days before she was leaving. He asked if she was on schedule. He was coming back a day early. It didn't matter, he'd stay with a friend, he said. They made arrangements regarding keys. The money TC owed for her phone calls would be left on the kitchen bench.

'What do you do?' he asked before concluding his call.

'I work for an opal miner. I'm in America testing the market.'

'I love opals! I wish I'd asked you before,' said the geologist. 'Have you got any with you now?' TC didn't know what to say.

'A few,' she replied.

'I'd like to buy one for my mother. Is it okay if I come and see you tomorrow?'

¶

At camp number one, Yappy was telling the men their meal was ready.

'Come on, you mongrels, it's tucker time. If you don't bloody come and eat it, you'll wear it!'

'Come on, Yappy don't be like that, you know we love you,' said Neil.

'You shut your smart mouth, you mad mongrel,' replied Yappy. 'That's the problem with you and Faith; you're too bloody clever with words.'

'Yappy, you are not a fair man,' said Faith pretending to be offended. 'Why is it you're always picking on Neil and me—never hear you going off at Little Joe.'

'Little Joe's different, that's why,' replied Yappy. 'He's a gentleman.'

'The gentleman is speaking,' said Little Joe to the others' surprise. 'When my mate, Yappy, says we eat, we eat.'

⁋

Meanwhile at camp number two, Ali was serving the evening meal to Ted, Michael, and Jakkie.

Both Michael and Jakkie missed Yappy's cooking. Ali was a nice woman. She wasn't much of a cook, that's all. They missed Yappy's scones. They also missed his whinges about them and anything else he could come up with. They were finding boulders that were good. Kept Vance happy even though the opal in the ones they unearthed at this mine weren't a patch on the opal coming out of mine number one.

⁋

Although mine number three was up and going, no opal had been found. Along with the expert-on-machinery-had-a-go-at-mining man, Vance had recruited two more of Brolga's so-called down-and-outers. Both were good, honest, hardworking men whose misfortunes in life had caused them to seek escape in the bottom of a bottle.

One of them was another of Neil's brothers. His name was Barry. The other man was Pete. He was Barry's best mate. Vance hadn't found a cook as yet, so Pete and Barry took turns at "knocking some tucker together", as they would say when referring to their culinary efforts.

⁋

The geologist visited TC. She showed him twenty stones. He was fascinated by them.

Imagine how he'd be if I produced the lot, thought TC.

He asked questions about where they were found, how deep in the ground, etcetera, while using several geological terms, none of which

TC understood. He bought two stones, one for his mother and one for his wife should he ever find one. TC added one of her give-aways to his purchase.

'That's for you. It would make a nice tie tack.' The nice geologist gentleman left after wishing TC good luck and telling her not to be surprised if he showed up in Brolga sometime in the future.

¶

TC asked the cabbie at Philadelphia's airport to suggest somewhere safe, clean, and not over the top cost-wise for her to stay.

'Holiday Inn is perfect for you, Ma'am,' replied the cab driver. He was right; it was perfect.

Philadelphia's gem dealers were mostly pessimistic. The few who weren't suggested TC call on them again closer to Christmas. She decided to try the independent jewellery stores. It was in the first of these TC visited that she met a woman wholesaling man-made, rough, semi-precious gem look-alike clusters. They struck up a conversation while waiting to see the owner-buyer. The woman, whose name was Valerie, was excited about her product, the end result of which had taken her years of trial and error to perfect. Valerie showed TC a few of her pieces—green clusters for emeralds, blue for sapphire, red for ruby, and so on.

TC listened but said very little. By the time the owner beckoned Valerie into his office, TC knew the names, ages, and occupations of the cluster-creator's husband, two sons, and daughters-in-law. Valerie eventually finished her business, and the jeweller beckoned TC to his office.

'See you around, TC,' Valerie said with a smile. TC smiled back.

'That would be nice, Valerie.'

'So, you're from Australia?' said the jeweller. TC was confused. How did he know! She hadn't yet opened her mouth. The jeweller saw the look on TC's face and laughed.

'Your talkative friend, Valerie, told me.' TC laughed.

'Yes, I've known the lady all of an hour.'

After fiddling through stones in packets for a while, the man told TC he thought the stones were beautiful, too beautiful.

'You should go to the Gem Fair in New York. Perfect opportunity to introduce these to every jeweller and jewellery house in the country.'

'I heard that from a few other people,' replied TC. 'Would you happen to know how I should go about being part of it.' The jeweller opened a desk drawer and extracted a small booklet.

'Here you are; all the details are in there. You can keep this one; I have a couple more.'

After purchasing two small stones from TC, he showed her to the door.

'See you in New York unless the crowd around your counter prevents it,' were his parting words.

TC was more than a little surprised to see Valerie waiting for her outside the store.

'Would you like to join me for a coffee?' asked Valerie.

'Why not?' smiled TC. There's a first time for everything, thought TC as Valerie led the way to a nearby coffee shop.

Two cups of coffee and a sandwich later, Valerie had invited TC to her home for dinner next weekend, wanted TC to meet her family. Not only that; she asked TC to consider sharing a space with her at the New York gem show as it was too expensive for her to go it alone. Valerie was just starting out and money was scarce. TC could identify with that.

The dinner invitation meant TC needed to find another safety deposit box. It was one thing keeping the opal with her at the Holiday Inn, but taking it with her to a stranger's home was an entirely different scenario. Once the box was arranged, she'd have to find a place to live; a base like the apartment on Lake Shore Drive had been.

Vance agreed to sharing with Valerie at the upcoming jewellery show in New York. TC visited Valerie's house and met her family, all of whom TC liked very much apart from one son who came across a bit too shifty for TC's liking.

Not for me to judge him, thought TC. Perhaps my intuition is off-track.

With Valerie's help, TC found a furnished, one-bedroom apartment in a new complex close to the Pennsylvania Turnpike bus route and train station. The apartment was very small, but that didn't matter; it was new, the furniture was new, and it was conveniently located. She signed a six-month lease. There was no television, which didn't bother TC. Brolga didn't have T.V. and she'd managed to survive without it there.

She bought cutlery and china and a tiny battery-operated radio. She also had a telephone installed. TC decided to try her luck in New York. She'd worked hard in Philadelphia, but barely sold enough to fill her float.

I'd best not contact the man I sold to in Brisbane, she thought. He might be like Mr Patrick, won't want me in his territory.

Valerie told her about a street in New York referred to as Jewellers Row.

'It's in the upper forties,' said Valerie. 'Not sure which street; never been there myself. It's an entire block of jewellers and gem merchants. Mostly Jews, I think. Smart people.'

TC's first visit to New York City was an eye-opener.

Can't believe I came from Brolga to this! she thought as she took in the size and height of the buildings. Of course, she'd seen Hancock Building in Chicago. It stood up into the clouds. In New York there were so many of them. Probably not as tall, but tall just the same. TC eventually found Jewellers Row. She saw four gem merchants that day. They all told her they would see her at the Gem Fair.

TC had travelled to New York that morning by bus. The traffic was unbelievably heavy, and it seemed to take forever to get to the bus station. It was no better on the return trip. At least not until the bus cleared the city limits. In the future, she'd take the train. Not that she saw any point in going back to New York until the Gem Fair.

If it hadn't been for her radio and Valerie's daily telephone call, TC was certain she would have lost her sanity. Although she was unfamiliar with most music she heard on the radio, it was company. There were neighbours surrounding her, but she had seen none of them. Occasionally, she heard a door open or close. Every night, the car park was full apart from her allocated bay, so she knew people were there.

Leading up to the Gem Fair, she became a prisoner in her base. She numbered and listed a hundred stones before fitting them into gem boxes. The other stones, she left in the briefcases. The stones she had chosen represented a cross-section of her stock in size, colour, and price. As TC fixed a price sticker on the back of the last stone box, she decided if the New York show didn't result in customers, she was going back to Brolga. She was tired of feeling insecure and juggling the float to get through while hanging out for her next sale.

TC travelled to New York with Valerie, her shifty-looking son, and his wife. Valerie had booked them into a hotel in Manhattan. When checking in, TC presented her passport as ID. The young man at reception opened it backwards, causing one of TC's Australian business cards to fall out of the passport cover. He looked at the card, then at TC, before replacing the card and turning the passport the right way around.

Valerie became vocal when the clerk gave TC her key and room number.

'I requested adjacent or connecting rooms,' she complained. 'Not only is Mrs Carmichael's room not near ours, it's on a different floor.'

'Sorry, Ma'am,' apologised the clerk. Valerie was intent on arguing. TC didn't care for a scene.

'It's okay, Valerie. It's no great problem. I'm only one floor above yours,' interrupted TC quietly, anything to avoid the attention.

The duration of the fair was three days, beginning Friday and winding down late afternoon on Sunday. TC was overwhelmed by the interest in the opal. Although she didn't see it herself, many people told her they saw her and the opals on Friday night's T.V. news report. In Sunday's newspaper appeared a photograph of Valerie beside TC, who was holding a 200-carat oval, high-domed stone. Beneath the photograph was a one-and-a-half-column editorial.

No opal sales were made during the fair. TC did get three bundles of cards from interested people who requested she contact or call them in the future, and she had two appointments for the following day, one of which was with a young man representing the Smithsonian Institute in Washington.

After the show, TC went to her hotel room to re-bag the display stones, sort her potential clients' business cards, shower, and go to bed. Valerie, her son, and his wife set out for home.

Come three-thirty in the morning, TC woke with a start. Someone was trying to open her door. She froze with fright as she heard muffled voices, then a loud crashing, splinting sound. TC frantically looked around the room; there was no way out except via the window or door. TC rushed to the window. It wasn't an option. The fire escape was about twenty yards away, and she was ten floors above an alley. She picked up the phone and hit the security button.

The would-be intruders were now pushing on the inner laundry-return door, which looked as if it would give in at any second.

'Hotel security,' said a serious male voice on the other end of the telephone.

'At least two people are bashing in my door,' said TC urgently. 'Please hurry. I'm by myself and frightened out of my wits.' TC then stood within three feet of the door and screamed, 'Go away. Leave me alone.' The banging stopped, then silence. TC stood fixed to the floor. Her heart was pounding and her eyes wide with terror. She stayed put for several minutes before sitting on the edge of her bed and crying in relief.

Later it was explained a hole had been smashed in the outer door to her room, presumably with a hammer. The paintwork on the inner door was mutilated by chip marks probably caused by the hammer handle. A hotel guest in the room opposite was alerted by the noise. He opened his door to investigate and saw two young men run towards the fire escape exit. The guest described one of the young men as the desk clerk who had checked him into the hotel. The other one fitted the description of Valerie's shifty son.

Obviously, the clerk is the one who saw my business card. As for Valerie's son, I wouldn't be surprised, thought TC. I'll have to be more careful in the future. I also have to cut all ties with Valerie. She told me they were going home to Philadelphia.

TC found alternative accommodation in the nearest Holiday Inn. She would feel safe there. Even so, she triple-checked to make certain the door to her room was securely locked before phoning Vance. She knew she'd made a mistake when his first words were, 'How did the show go?' In other words, how much did you sell? Money had become Vance's obsession. The more he had, the more he could spend on opal mining.

'I made a lot of contacts, Mr Callahan,' replied TC coldly. 'Sold nothing! I need a car if you want me to call on everyone who left their cards. I have appointments today. Your opals are safe. I'll call you soon.'

❡

In Brolga Vance put down the telephone.

Something is wrong with TC, he thought fleetingly as he surrendered to his sexual urges brought about by Coral's pernicious, persistent stroking of his upper inner thigh and nibbling on his neck.

❡

Jake was back on with Madison like a rat up a rope. Seat of Knowledge gentry agreed they deserved one another.

'Birds of a feather, peas in a pod, just rewards would be they're stuck together for life. After a month under the same roof, they'd hate each other's guts. That is, if they've got any.'

❡

TC kept her appointments. One took place in a coffee shop on Broadway.

It was with the Smithsonian representative. He asked for twenty stones to show his superiors in Washington. He was well-dressed, late twenties with honest, piercing-blue, trust-me eyes.

'I'll have to ask Mr Callahan,' replied TC to the young man's request.

'I'll contact you for Mr Callahan's answer next week,' he suggested. TC agreed and gave him her Philadelphia phone number.

Next, she met with a gem dealer, on the twelfth floor of a building on Jewellers Row. TC recognised the short, stout, middle-aged Jewish man on seeing him again after the gem fair, where he had caused her to laugh a lot. His name was Sammy L.

'Come in, my lovely, young, blonde, Australian beauty,' greeted Sammy L with outspread arms and a gushing smile. 'What can I rip you for?' Sammy L reminded TC of Con in his café back in Brolga. Not in build and looks. Yes, in welcoming gestures. TC laughed.

'Nothing, Mr L! You could buy a few stones. If I don't sell something soon, my boss will fire me and I'll be stranded, lost, and alone.' Sammy L gestured to a chair in front of his huge desk.

'Sit down there, TC. Show me your stones. Perhaps I'll buy two or three. Before we begin, I must warn you I'm tough when it comes to business.' TC smiled.

'So am I, Mr L.' Sammy L laughed.

'Is that a challenge, young lady?'

'No, not at all,' replied TC. 'I wouldn't dare compete with you. I come from a tiny, bush town in outback Australia; you're a New Yorker.'

'What does "bush town" mean?' asked Sammy L with interest.

'It means isolated, far away from a city.' Sammy L sighed and smiled.

'That's the kind of place I wish I was in ten times a day. Let's do business.'

Their first of many business transactions concluded hours later after TC threatened to jump out the open twelfth-story office window if Sammy L continued to plead for a cent more than the twenty percent discount she had already afforded him.

'Would you really have jumped?' asked Sammy as he slid a pile of cash across the desk. TC took a deep breath, then sighed before beginning to count the money.

'Not unless you pushed me.'

'Smart girl,' cackled Sammy L. 'You are recounting. I'll write you a cheque for the balance.'

'Don't be a stranger,' said Sammy L minutes later as he held his office door open for TC to leave.

'Thank you. I won't' replied TC. 'You've saved my job!'

'And from being lost and alone, I hope,' laughed Sammy L. 'How much money did I spend? No, don't tell me. Yes, tell me.' TC left giggling. He liked Sammy L. He had a sense of humour.

⁋

Vance gave TC the go-ahead with the sample stones for the Smithsonian representative, told her to lease a car if she thought necessary, and find more people like Sammy L, who had spent twenty-eight thousand. He also agreed to have a full-page colour advertisement placed in a famous U.S. jewellery magazine.

⁋

The young man with the trust-me eyes was an artist. When he didn't show for a New York meeting with TC a week after she parted with the twenty stones, she called the number on his card and was told she was speaking to an employer of a Washington laundry. TC felt desolate. She had entrusted him with twenty of the most beautiful stones she had. One of them was the 200-carat stone she was holding in the newspaper photograph.

Panic stricken she phoned Sammy L, to whom she quickly explained the predicament.

'Come to my office now,' suggested Sammy. 'I'll see if I can help you. Give me his name. I'll make some calls.'

'The institute has never heard of this guy,' advised Sammy when TC arrived at his office. 'Show me his card and tell me what he looks like.'

TC produced the card and gave it to Sammy as she quickly began describing the con man.

'I doubt this is his true identity,' said Sammy L seriously. 'This name is Jewish. It is highly unlikely the person you have described would have this name. He's probably an Irishman.'

'What on earth am I going to do?' asked TC hopelessly. 'I feel like a fool! How am I going to tell my boss?'

'Don't tell your boss yet,' replied Sammy. 'You work your way through the jewellery stores on the Row and I'll make some phone calls, one of which will be to a friend of mine in the police department.

It was almost a week before, with Sammy L's help, TC had retrieved all but the 200-carat oval and one other much smaller stone from various jewellers and gem dealers where the false Jewish-named-probably-Irish-tryster had left the pieces on consignment. The missing two were never located.

'Someone we've contacted has got them,' surmised Sammy L. 'Can't bring themselves to do the right thing. Unfortunately, not everyone is honest like me.'

TC didn't bother with leasing a car. The thought of driving in traffic on the opposite side of the road to back home didn't appeal to her. She might cause an accident. She would travel by plane, train, or bus.

§

'The colour advertisement in the jewellery magazine was a record-breaker,' explained the advertising agent. 'Earthfire from Down Under has resulted in more enquiries than all the other adverts in the edition combined. Sensational!'

While Vance was disappointed about the loss of the two stones, he didn't blame TC.

'I authorised you to let him have them. Guess we've both learned by our mistake. Trust no bastard in the future.'

§

With Christmas approaching, TC's sales improved. By request, she revisited New Orleans and for the first time went to Florida.

Christmas came. TC secured the opal in the bank's safety deposit vault and locked herself in her base for the duration. Lou and Jake phoned her on Christmas Eve.

'When are you coming home?' demanded Jake.

'Don't know if I ever will,' replied TC indifferently. 'Nothing to come back to.'

'What about me?!' asked Jake angrily.

'Exactly, Jake. Everything's about you,' replied TC. 'I have to go now.'

'I suppose you've got a boyfriend,' snarled Jake.

'Yes, and I'm certain you've got a girlfriend,' replied TC.

'Smart bitch!' retaliated Jake before slamming down his phone.

TC thought of Graham and wondered how he was spending his Christmas.

'I suppose he's found himself someone else to love by now,' she told herself sadly.

Lou talked mostly about her little boy, the number of toys he'd got from Santa, and how quickly he was growing.

That's what I need, thought TC when the call ended. I need a baby to love. I've got so much love to give. Unfortunately, I don't have a worthy recipient.

¶

In Brolga the men were on a break. As in previous years, they were living behind the Majestic. Yappy hated being there; he wanted to move to the Brick. He couldn't; he'd gamble most of his money away the first Saturday they were in town and Vance had him on an allowance.

'It's for your own good, Yappy,' Vance told him.

'What are you on about, Vance? I'll be the one who decides what the bloody hell is good for me,' retaliated Yappy.

'All right, tell me how clever it was to lose all your dough the first weekend away from camp?' laughed Vance.

'Smart bastard, aren't you, Callahan?' complained Yappy.

'No, I'm not smart at all. You are the one blessed with brilliance,' teased Vance. 'Here's fifty bucks; don't spend it all at once.'

'What's a bloody man supposed to do with a lousy fifty?' whined Yappy.

'That's up to you. You're the genius,' laughed Vance. Yappy left grumbling about his sad situation.

The know-machinery-backwards-operator, manager of mine number three was not invited to resume work after the break. Nothing was said, argued, or agreed. Vance's somewhat uneasy intuitive feelings had proven to be warranted. He had asked Barry and Pete to keep a mental record of the number of boulders unearthed at the site. Both concurred on thirty-one while Vance knew of only twenty six. Vance trusted Barry and Pete without reservation. They might borrow a loaf of bread if they were on the piss and hungry, but they would never lie about nor steal his boulders.

¶

Two days into the New Year, Coral left Brolga on the first available Flea. She vowed never to return. Her heart was broken and she felt inadequate as a woman.

In the morning of New Year's Day, she felt lonely. She decided to walk her usual back route to check if Vance's ute was behind the pharmacy. Although she'd been with him the previous night, she needed to see him again. Perhaps he was there, sawing through his beloved boulders. Coral sighed with relief when she saw his parked ute.

My darling will be surprised when I walk in behind him and tap him on the shoulder, she thought as she approached the open back door of the dispensary. There was no sound of sawing. No sound at all apart from a soft female moaning voice.

Coral stood in shocked silence as she observed Vance and Almut in the throes of passion. Coral had been with Vance the previous evening in exactly the same against-the-wall location.

'You effing bastard, Callahan,' she said loudly in the most dignified tone of voice she could muster. 'You disgust me! You are old enough to be her father!'

Vance instantly looked over his shoulder in alarm. Oh, shit, he thought, it's Coral. Could be worse, he reasoned, could have been Delores. Coral noted the gold chain and red opal pendant around Almut's neck.

'You bastard, Vance Callahan! You never so much as wished me a Merry Christmas. I'd wager my life that bauble is your young slut's Christmas present.' Coral turned and left while crying all the way to her room in the Empire's quarters where she immediately packed her belongings before going to Jack Romeo's office to advise him she was leaving.

'Why, Coral? Why are you going?' enquired Jack Romeo.

'It's a new year, Mr Romeo,' replied Coral. 'Time for a new start.'

I bet Callahan has done his dash with her, thought Jack Romeo as he told Coral to collect her pay in a couple of hours. Next morning she was on the Flea.

'I meant nothing to Vance,' she told herself. 'How can I compete with a girl? He didn't so much as track me down to apologise. Wish I'd never come to Brolga. Wish I'd never met Vance.'

¶

TC spent the next ten months living in planes, trains, hotel and motel rooms. She travelled all over the United States apart from the West Coast. Leave that to Mr Patrick. Sometimes she sold big time, often no sales for weeks on end.

On one occasion her float was depleted. She had to stay put in a hotel room in Atlanta, Georgia, for ten days because she didn't have money to pay her account. During this time she lived on crackers and boiled eggs purchased from a deli opposite the hotel.

She phoned Sammy L in desperation.

'This is my situation, Sammy. Do you have any contacts in Atlanta?'

'I'll send you money,' offered Sammy L without hesitation.

'No, you won't, Sammy,' replied TC adamantly. 'If I ask anyone for money, it will be my boss. I didn't ask you for money. I asked you for a contact.'

'I'll research and call you back soon, TC,' promised Sammy.

He did. Two hours later TC met with a jeweller; less than an hour after that she had eight thousand cash. Before checking out of the hotel, she called Vance and told him she was coming home.

'I've had enough, Boss. I've done what I came here to do. I'm coming back to Brolga.'

Vance said nothing. He simply replaced the phone in its cradle.

§

TC caught a plane to New York. She needed to see Sammy L before she left.

'What did you like about our United States?' asked Sammy seriously.

'You, Sammy,' smiled TC in response.

'Come on,' said Sammy with up-flung arms and a beseeching facial expression. TC frowned and remained silent while contemplating her reply. 'I'm waiting, TC,' insisted Sammy. TC looked at Sammy, shrugged, and smiled simultaneously before replying.

'My twenty months here have made me wise, Sammy. I've met wonderful you; a lot of other great, honest people scattered all over the country along with more than my share of would-be crooks. The blue-eyed trickster pretending to be a Smithsonian Institute representative taught me a lesson. Since him, I have encountered many such would-be artists. Thanks to my experience with him, I've not been fooled by them. I have come to the conclusion there are both good and bad people all over the world. I love America and its people, Sammy. My mother told my brothers and me since we were tiny children, "Always love America, always love Americans. They saved us during the war".'

'They saved us Jews, too,' nodded Sammy L before hugging TC and saying goodbye.

¶

TC caught a plane to Chicago. She reasoned she may as well end her adventure where it began. On arrival at O'Hare, TC booked and paid for her flight to Sydney. Although she was offered lower-priced fares, she insisted on flying Qantas out of Los Angeles.

'If the opal and I are going to drown, we'll go on the back of a Red Kangaroo,' she decided determinedly.

TC checked into a hotel joined by a footbridge to the airport, took a shower, then a train to downtown Chicago, where she terminated the bank account with the bank on State Street before deciding to go to the Loop. Not once had she been to the movies during her time in the U.S. She didn't care what it was. She just needed to be able to tell Lou, Lisa, or anyone else interested that she'd seen a movie while in America.

TC ate pancakes with maple syrup at a corner deli, then bought a movie ticket at the booth opposite. Briefcase filled with cash plus opal in one hand and opal to the brim in the other, TC was ushered into the movie theatre and seated three rows from the front.

The movie was about two Manhattan detectives who ventured into Harlem to solve a murder and arrest the perpetrators. Throughout the movie, patrons were yelling, 'Kill the white whatever! Rip his throat out! Stab him in the guts! Come on, White, show us what you're made of, gutless, white asshole,' and so on. The movie ended and the lights went on. TC looked around. She was the only white person in the theatre. She felt as if every eye was focused on her. A briefcase in each hand, she almost ran outside and hailed the first available cab. She was almost as frightened as she had been in the New York hotel when her door was being smashed with a hammer. Until then, the intensity of the racial situation in the U.S. had not hit home with TC. Sure, she'd heard about it and occasionally seen the riots on T.V.

'Why can't we all love each other,' she demanded out loud while flinging a shoe into her suitcase. 'What has the colour of our skin got to do with anything? I'm glad I'm going home. Life is less complicated in Brolga.'

I'll never need these in Brolga, thought TC when she came to condensing her possessions into the one-allowable-by-Qantas-suitcase-without-extra-charge for her international flight from Los Angeles to Sydney. She piled her fake-fur-lined coat and other keep-me-warm gear she'd bought twenty months previously onto a chair. While TC loved those things, especially the boots, common sense prevailed. 'I'll offer the lot to the next person I see.'

Packing done and paperwork for customs complete, TC phoned Lou.

'Guess what, my darling Lou, I'm coming home.'

'I'll meet you, TC,' replied Lou excitedly.

'No, I'll come to your flat. Please have at the ready at least four meat pies, a bottle of Vegemite, a pound of butter, and a fresh, crusty loaf of bread,' said TC quickly.

'You hate meat pies, Vegemite, and butter,' laughed Lou.

'Familiarity breeds contempt, Lou. Haven't been familiar with meat pies and Vegemite for far too long,' replied TC. 'Please have them waiting for me. Please! Please!'

'Of course, I bloody-well will!' laughed Lou, imitating her dad.

TC checked around her hotel room. The briefcases and her suitcase were ready, as was she. Can't wait to be on my way, she thought while responding to a knock on her door.

'Turn back your bed, Ma'am?' enquired a beautiful young woman with flawless ebony-coloured skin, snow-white teeth, and a smile that would melt a heart of steel.

'No, thank you,' replied TC. 'I'll be gone in an hour. I'm going home to Australia.'

'Have a nice trip, Ma'am,' smiled the young woman before moving to push her trolley forward.

'Just one moment,' said TC, scooping her coats, jumpers and boots off the corner chair. 'You look about my size. Would you like these? They'll be of no use to me. No snow where I come from.' The beautiful black girl looked at TC in disbelief.

'I can't take those, Ma'am.' TC laughed.

'Yes, you can. I insist. I'm going soon. I'll leave them in the room for you.'

'Bless you, Ma'am. I'll feel like a movie star in the coat and high-heeled boots.'

'You'll look like one, too,' assured TC with a smile.

¶

TC settled with customs in Los Angeles. That out of the way, the fact that she was going home became a reality. One opal-filled briefcase tucked under behind her legs and the other on her knees, TC sat and waited for the flight to be called. As she stared into space, she reminisced on experiences during her adventure in the USA. TC finally decided to file in her memory bank positive thoughts only. No space for negativity. She would always remember Sammy L, James, the geologist, Bourbon Street in New Orleans, the Boardwalk in Atlantic City, views from her apartment windows on Lake Shore Drive, the New York City skyline, San Francisco's Golden Gate Bridge and hilly streets and trams, orange-coloured autumn foliage in Pennsylvania, New England's huge, green, pine trees, and Florida's sunshine.

¶

In Brolga, Vance was chewing on a chocolate bar, wondering where he would put TC when she returned.

'Poor little bugger's going to feel like a third useless arm. Due to her nagging I-want-to-be-a-part-of-the-business persistence, Delores is now cutting opals. All day, everyday, she sits alongside Almut, the teenage sex maniac. Makes me sick to hear them laughing and chatting. Anyone would think they are the best friends in the bloody country. TC's the one who's put her life on the line! What the bloody hell am I going to do?'

¶

After surviving what seemed to take a million years with Australian Customs, TC phoned Lou from Sydney Airport.

'I'm home, Lou. Put those pies in the oven. I'll see you soon.'

'As my dad would say, you sound happy as a pig in muck, TC,' laughed Lou.

'Your dad would be right!' replied TC. 'I'm excited. Seems like forever since I've seen you and the baby. I'll call the boss, then catch a cab to your place.'

'The opal and I are safe, Boss,' announced TC happily when Vance answered the pharmacy phone. 'I'm going to see Lou; after that I'll book for Brolga.'

'TC, go to Melbourne and try your luck. I also want you to do Sydney before you worry about coming here,' instructed Vance. TC was devastated. Vance hadn't so much as asked her about her trip or told her he was happy she was safely back in Australia.

'You make me sick, Mr Callahan! I've been to hell and back for you. All you care about is money. The more you get, the more you want. You treat people like shit, Mr Callahan! I don't like you!' TC dropped the telephone and watched it dangle in mid-air while telling herself how big a fool she was. She moved herself and briefcases into the next phone booth, inserted a coin in the slot, then dialled Lou's number.

'Throw the pies in the bin, Lou. I'm going to Melbourne. No point in leaving the airport. I'll get the first flight I can. See you when I see you.'

¶

TC saw Cowlegg and other customers in Melbourne plus a few more on her return to Sydney. She was aware her heart was no longer in her job. No matter how hard she tried, Vance didn't appreciate her efforts. A voice within repeatedly told her she was nothing but a piece of money-generating machinery. Apart from remaining an admirer of slutty women, the person Vance used to be no longer existed. He was in love with money. That was that!

¶

While nursing her godson, TC once again decided she needed a baby to love.

'Don't know how I'll do it, Lou. I want a baby,' she told her friend. Lou laughed.

'As far as I know, you're still married to Jake.'

'That unfortunately is a fact,' agreed TC. 'Perhaps Madison will let me borrow him.'

§

'Here's your opal and money, Mr Callahan,' said TC as she presented Vance with his briefcases at Brolga's airstrip.

'Don't be like that, TC,' said Vance. TC shrugged and gave him a fake smile.

'Like what?'

'What on earth has happened to you?' asked Vance.

'Life has happened to me, that's all. Just life. I suppose Jake is on a race course somewhere, so a lift home would come in handy.'

'TC, Delores and Almut are cutting opal; so is Marla,' explained Vance hesitantly. 'I don't know what I'm going to do with you.'

'Do us both a favour! Kill me!' replied TC lightly.

'I'll see you Monday,' said Vance when he dropped TC and her suitcase off at her house.

'What for? You don't know what you are going to do with me,' replied TC. 'I worked like a drover's dog in America. Not once have you so much as said thank you.'

'I've bought Carmel's dress shop and the flat above it,' said Vance. 'Going to do the opal-cutting downstairs. Almut will live upstairs.'

'How convenient. Bet Mrs Callahan's crazy about that,' said TC with a shrug.

'Almut and Delores get along like a house on fire,' laughed Vance. 'No pun intended.'

'Guess you're a lucky man, Boss. Your wife and girlfriend like each other. That's good!'

'Don't be a bitch, TC. It doesn't suit you,' said Vance. 'The opal from the third mine runs all over the place in the boulders. Don't know what to do with it.'

'See you Monday,' said TC. 'Or should I look for a job somewhere else?'

§

TC cleaned the house. She knew Jake had been entertaining because she found a pair of female briefs in the bathroom. She didn't care. Jake was Jake!

All I want from Jake Carmichael is a baby, she thought as she went about her work. The idea of having sex with Jake was not at all appealing. She decided she would simply tell him she wanted to have a baby. If Jake loved the child as well, it would be a bonus. Knowing Jake, he loved himself too much; there'd be no surplus.

TC made a spur-of-the-moment decision. She would take the Flea to Curloo next morning, see a doctor, and either get a lift or Wednesday afternoon's Flea back to Brolga. She immediately phoned Vance.

'Don't worry about what you're going to do with me for a few days, Mr Callahan. I'm going to Curloo.'

'Why are you going to Curloo?' asked Vance.

'That's my business,' replied TC.

'No, I'm really curious,' laughed Vance. 'Call me when you get back.'

§

TC described her marriage to an elderly Curloo doctor a couple of days later.

'I'm stuck in a loveless marriage, doctor. I want a baby but I don't want to have sex with my husband a million times to get one.' The doctor smiled knowingly.

'I understand. With the right timing and a couple of injections, it's possible you could conceive without much fuss at all. I assume you are going to tell your husband of your intention to have a child?'

'Of course!' replied TC without hesitation.

The kindly doctor gave TC a prescription for a course of three injections with a letter to the matron at Brolga's hospital where TC would go to have them administered.

'Follow my instructions and come back to see me when you're pregnant,' said the doctor when it was time for TC to leave.

'Thank you, Doctor. I will,' agreed a smiling TC. All I have to do now is tell Jake, she thought. Don't know how he'll react or when I'll tell him. I'll handle that when the time comes.

TC called into the dispensary after she got off the Flea on the Wednesday night.

Vance was sawing through a boulder while Almut was in the polishing room. Vance switched off the saw and greeted TC by telling her she would be working in the big shed behind his house. He was sponsoring a professional terrazzo-polisher from Italy, and a terrazzo-polishing machine would arrive any day to make opal tabletops from the seams-running-all-over-the-place slabs from mine number three.

'What am I going to do in the shed?' enquired TC seriously.

'I don't know yet,' replied Vance. 'I'll want you to take a trip here and there.'

'Of course! When do you want me to start?'

'I don't know. I'll keep in touch.'

'All right, I'll see you when I see you,' said TC loudly as she nodded towards the polishing room. 'Be a good boy, Mr Callahan.' Vance burst into laughter.

'Do you want a lift home?'

'No, thank you, I'm going to visit Con and Lisa,' replied TC.

Jake's at the Empire, thought TC when she spotted his car parked in front of the hotel. Hope he's not on the rum. Think I'll ask him to drive me home. I can see Lisa and Con tomorrow. TC went to the Empire window. Jake saw her, gulped down his drink, collected his change, and joined her.

'What the buggery are you doing standing at the pub window?' he demanded impatiently.

'Yes, Jake, it's great to see you, too,' replied TC. 'I would like you to drive me home or give me the car key. I'm tired and don't feel like walking.'

'I'll drive you. I've got to be somewhere later.'

'Why, I didn't realise that, Jake,' replied TC, oozing sarcasm.

'Smart bitch!' from Jake.

'I know,' smiled TC.

'Come on, then,' snapped Jake.

Once in the car, TC made her announcement.

'I want to have a baby, Jake. I'm lonely and I need a baby to love.

Silence while Jake absorbed TC's words.

'Are you crazy?! You're not smart, you're stupid! Why the bloody hell do you want a baby?'

'I told you,' replied TC adamantly. 'I want a baby to love.'

'Go to buggery, TC!' snapped Jake. 'I don't want to hear the word baby again. No baby! No way!'

'We'll see,' said TC as Jake braked outside their gate.

'You're home. Now go inside before I choke you,' said Jake.

'Thanks for the ride, Jake,' said TC flippantly. 'By the way, I will have a baby.'

'Get stuffed,' snapped Jake as he slammed down his foot.

Yes, unfortunately, I'll have to do that, thought TC as he sped away.

¶

Three-and-a-half months later, after concluding her course of injections and seducing Jake on her perfect-for-pregnancy date, TC realised she was pregnant.

She told Jake. He didn't comment. Shrugged, glared at her, then headed for the pub.

She then told Vance, who fired her the next morning.

'Delores doesn't believe in pregnant women working,' he said matter-of-factly.

'I see. Mrs Callahan has wanted to get rid of me for years,' replied TC. 'Looks like she's finally found the perfect reason. See you around! By the way, until a few seconds ago I considered Jake to be the weakest bastard on earth. He's not. That badge is yours. You win it, hands down.'

TC cried all the way home, where she flopped onto her bed and cried until there were no more tears to shed. 'All those years, all those hours, all those miles, the insults and abuse from his girlfriends, my undying loyalty, and I get fired for being two weeks pregnant! Live and learn,' she told herself.

❡

A couple of hours later Vance arrived on her doorstep.

'I can't let you go like this,' he said seriously.

'Forget about it. You already have,' replied TC. 'I'd hate you, your wife, and girlfriend to be embarrassed by my two-weeks pregnancy.'

'Don't be like that. I've brought you some cutting gear. I want to put it in your shed. You can do opal-cutting for other miners and buyers.'

'Leave now, Vance. I'm pregnant. I can't work,' snapped TC. 'Save your guilt for someone who cares.'

Vance set the gear up in TC's shed before she heard him leave.

She's never called me Vance before, he thought as he drove away. 'She's right. I am a weak bastard.'

❡

TC received a phone call that night from a Sydney opal buyer. He'd bought rough opal from Vance late that afternoon and wanted her to begin cutting it for him next day.

'News travels fast in Brolga,' said TC. 'Who told you to contact me?'

'Callahan,' was the reply.

'I see,' said TC, who was not in the least bit surprised. 'Be here around seven tomorrow morning.'

¶

TC's freelance opal-cutting career was about to begin. During the following eight months, she cut opal for many people, most of whom were broke, so they paid her in stones. A few shady mongrels didn't pay her at all. They didn't consider she worked day and night. Sometimes the summer heat inside the tin shed was unbearable. On a few hundred-and-ten-degree days, she had to throw it in.

Every six weeks TC drove to and from Curloo over the red dirt road to see her doctor. Not once did Jake offer to drive her. Lena, her Italian neighbour, went with her to make sure TC was all right and didn't collapse at the wheel in the heat and dust.

Jake was living his usual carefree life of gambling, boozing, and bullshitting.

¶

TC was about seven months into her pregnancy. She was tired after working most of the day and trying desperately to sleep, which was all but impossible due to the noise from a party raging across the road at the Shack.

Jake came home rolling drunk. He went into her room and began teasing her about being fat. She wasn't. In fact, her doctor was concerned because she'd gained no more than a few pounds. Jake persisted, so calmly TC got off her bed and picked up a brick door stop.

'If you don't quit it, Jake, I'll throw this brick at you. I've had a rough day.'

'Poor, fat little thing,' he repeated in his ridiculous drunken voice. TC threw the brick at him. It hit Jake on the forehead before falling on one of his feet. Jake stood still in shock. So did TC as blood began trickling from a gash in his forehead, over his eyes, and down his cheek.

'You bloody bitch, you're bricked me,' mumbled Jake.

'I'm not the bloody one; you are,' replied TC. 'I strongly suggest you visit your old girlfriends at the hospital.'

Jake stumbled to the bathroom, yelled, 'You've bricked me,' grabbed a towel, and rushed to his car in which he quickly drove in the direction of the hospital.

¶

A while later TC was still trying to sleep when she heard Jake loudly sympathy-seeking at Jordan's party.

'TC bricked me. The bitch bricked me! I had to get four bloody stitches. Not only that, to add insult to bloody injury, the matron told me if she was married to a prick like me, she would have bricked me years ago.' Much laughter, then Jake repeated his story.

One thing for sure, thought TC as Jake's voice carried from across the street. When Jake Carmichael's got the limelight, he sure hogs it.

¶

TC rarely saw Vance. Sometimes he would drive past and sound his ute horn. Marla occasionally dropped in on TC and filled her in on unsought-after information as to who did what and so on.

Vance was doing well. Rumour had it his safe in the shed behind his house was stacked with row after row of bundled cash. His opal was now famous and sought-after. Apparently, he owned stud horses in New Zealand and had intentions of going retail sometime in the future.

TC also heard he had another girlfriend apart from Almut. Lisa told her she'd heard the girl raving about Vance in the café.

Looks like his search for another Anna will continue for the rest of his life, thought TC sadly.

505

⁋

TC forewarned customers she would soon have to quit. She now owned a couple of dozen opal specimens and over three hundred stones in lieu of cash payments for her cutting and polishing. Some of her stones were better than nice. All were commercial and saleable should she ever get the notion to sell.

A week before TC was due to go to Curloo for the coming birth of her baby, Jake came home reeking of rum. She could smell it the second he walked into the kitchen where she was slicing roast beef with her favourite under-the-pillow carving knife.

'Don't start on me, Jake. I can smell the rum on you. If you touch me. I swear I'll kill you. My baby is almost here. Leave me alone.'

'All you care about, TC, is your precious baby,' snapped Jake as he moved towards her.

'That's right, Jake, my baby is all I care about,' replied TC matter-of-factly. 'I'm telling you now,' continued TC, the knife raised in her hand. 'If you hit me now or after my baby is born, that will be it. On second thought, no, I won't kill you, you're not worth it. Neither will I care about the shame of divorce. The crappy life I've had with you will be over. Keep it in mind, Jake. I mean it.'

Jake backed off, went to the bathroom, and washed his face.

'What's to eat?' he enquired soberly when he returned to the kitchen.

⁋

TC caught the Flea to Curloo next week. Her doctor immediately ordered her to the hospital. The baby was due but nothing was happening. TC was told by the hospital matron they needed Jake to sign the paperwork before they operated. TC gave the matron Lena's number, knowing Lena's husband, Jack, was in Brolga and would find Jake wherever he was.

Jack found him. Jake was playing poker with Con and a couple of transient oil people behind the café.

'Jake, you need to get yourself to Curloo,' said Jack seriously. 'TC and the baby are in trouble. The mob at the hospital want you to sign papers.'

'Bugger her, Jack. She'll be all right, mate,' replied Jake indifferently as he got back to checking his hand of cards.

'Are you sure you're not going?' insisted Jack.

'Of course, I'm bloody-well sure, mate. I'm playing cards,' replied Jake, who was obviously irritated.

'All right, I'll leave you to your card game,' said Jack while shaking his head in disbelief.

Jack drove to his house, then returned to the rear of the café minutes later with his gun cocked and ready to fire. He pointed it at Jake's head.

'Get off your miserable, skinny arse, Jake. Drive to Curloo and sign those papers or I swear I'll blow your effing head off. TC and the baby could die and you're here playing poker. You sicken me, mate.'

Colour drained from Jake's face. He was instantly on his feet and on his way. He didn't so much as bother to collect his money off the table.

After regaining his composure, one of the oil men spoke.

'Incredible! Just like in the movies, man! If I didn't see it, I wouldn't believe it.'

'Welcome to the Wild West,' laughed Jack as he and his rifle turned to leave.

¶

Jake made the trip to Curloo in record-breaking time. He signed the necessary papers, refuelled his car, and drove back to Brolga.

TC's tiny baby boy came into the world by Caesarean section. He weighed three-and-a-half pounds. He could have fitted twice into a normal-sized shoe box and still have room to spare.

TC was very unwell; so was her baby. They were hospitalised in Curloo for four months and a bit before her now-friend, the elderly doctor, agreed to let TC take her baby home.

'The little fellow is still underweight, but I think you've had enough.'

During all the time, her baby, Robert John, and she were in hospital, they had only four visitors. Vance and Delores were the first. They came within days of the birth. TC was surprised, to say the least. TC almost choked on laughter a couple of years later when Vance told her Delores wanted to check out the baby to see if it resembled him.

Her other visitors were Jake's mother, who came through Curloo with her new husband. They were going to Brolga for the wedding of one of Thel's nieces. Baby Robert's adoring grandmother asked TC to consider moving to the coast so she could see him grow up.

Jake didn't visit once. TC and her baby flew from Curloo to Brolga, where Jake, the showman, had promised almost everyone in town and surrounding district the party of the century.

A month later, he gave it to them on the night after Robert was baptised. Lena and Jack were godparents.

'How could the little fellow have anyone else as godfather?' laughed TC on hearing about the deal with Jack and his loaded rifle.

❡

TC loved her baby boy more than life itself. She couldn't stand the thought of staying In Brolga and having to send him away to school a few years down the track. She'd had enough of the opal industry in which the sharks obviously outnumbered the honest people by at least ten-to-one.

'I want to leave Brolga, Jake,' said TC one afternoon when Jake came home to shower after a golf game. 'Opal has attracted too many crooks to the town. I want to move closer to your mother so Robert grows up closer to her.'

TC was more than surprised when Jake didn't hesitate before replying, 'Yes, good idea. Let's sell and go.' She never did find out why.

Within a month, the house was sold. They auctioned its contents and were on their way to the Gold Coast, where they bought a house. Jake soon found a job as a travelling shoe salesman, and TC took a casual position in a department store selling plated costume jewellery.

Jake loved his job. It represented freedom with no responsibility whatsoever other than selling his required quota of shoes to his drinking-mate clients. TC loathed her work. She knew after only a couple of days the counter manager was pocketing money and giving away stock to her friends and relatives.

Jake's mother sold her house. She, her husband and Carla moved into a caravan park where TC's many-years-since, hadn't-seen-for-years, sister, Maggie, and her husband, by pure coincidence, lived two vans away.

TC had no shortage of loving, doting babysitters for the couple of days she worked in the department store, where, one day her section manager approached with nose in the air and wearing a look of total disgust.

'One of your Bohemian friends is asking for you. He is filthy! I told him to wait at the haberdashery department.'

TC looked across to haberdashery and cracked up laughing. There stood Vance with his windblown hair off to one side. He hadn't smoked for years, but his shirt pocket was half hanging down as if damaged by frequent insertion and extraction of a cigarette packet. He was covered in red. Overall he looked like a derelict.

'That's my ex-boss,' said TC proudly. 'You shouldn't judge a book by its cover. He could buy this store ten or twenty times over and have change.' The section manager stood speechless as TC walked towards Vance, then kissed him on his dust-covered cheek.

'What brings you slumming, Mr Callahan?' asked TC. 'How did you find me?' Vance laughed.

'I have connections!' he replied before his expression turned to serious. 'I feel like crap, TC. Faith is dead. The men went back to camp after their break. Faith wasn't properly dried out. He pinched the lemon essence Yappy used for cooking and wandered off from camp. It was a stinking hot day and the men thought he'd gone to take a leak or get a drink of water. By the time they missed him, he was probably dead. They searched till dark. Next morning Neil drove the water truck to the property owner's homestead. The search began big time. Faith was eventually found dead under a tree in a fenced-off paddock near the mine. Silly poor bastard went over the fence. Probably because he didn't want Neil,

Little Joe, and Yappy to think he was a weakling.' Vance began shaking his head from side to side in denial. 'Poor bloody Faith, never should have crossed the fence.'

TC was speechless. She immediately remembered the Little Flower incident and the men's innocent faces as they apologised while slumped against the rear outside wall of the dispensary. 'Why is Faith's face standing out in my recollection?' she asked herself. 'Because he's the one who is dead,' she told herself.

Silence!

'What on earth are you doing selling junk in this joint' asked Vance with a smirk. TC sighed.

'I don't know. Gets me out of the house and gives Jake's mum and Maggie, my sister, an opportunity to spoil my little boy.'

'Go tell that stuck-up bitch you're leaving,' said Vance while looking over TC's head at the department manager, who was observing them from her vantage point near the costume jewellery counter. 'I want to talk to you!' TC smiled

'I don't like it here much, anyway, Ex-Boss. I'll tell her now. Meet me at the main door in ten minutes.'

'You can't just walk out, TC. You'll lose two days' pay,' exclaimed the department manager when TC told her she was leaving and needed permission to claim belongings from her locker.'

'Watch me!' replied TC as she turned towards the locker room.

'What do you want to talk about, Ex-Boss?' asked TC when she joined Vance outside.

'Let's find somewhere to sit. I wish I had a cigarette and a rum,' replied Vance.

'Sorry! You've got me instead.' TC led the way to a bench seat fifty or so yards away.

'What do you want to talk to me about?'

'I've got a lot of money,' replied Vance. 'It doesn't mean much. I thought being rich would be different. It's not! I'm not a happy man. Faith's death has made me remember the tough days when my career as an opal miner began. If I hadn't had people like you, Faith, Neil, and

Yappy, where the eff would I be?'

TC thought for a while before speaking.

'How are you're kids?'

'Andrew seems to be hooked on Marla. Little prick quit school early. If he didn't like the opal he was cutting, he'd turf it out the window into next door's backyard. If the woman who owned the dress shop hadn't come to me with the half-finished stones, I wouldn't have known.'

'How is Jonathon?' asked TC about Vance's oldest child, whom she always remembered as a boy clinging to his mother's skirt.

'He's all right,' replied Vance. 'I think he'll wind up being a mechanical engineer. Don't ask me more questions,' continued Vance after a short silence. 'What are you going to do?'

'Obviously, I won't be selling fake jewellery in a department store anymore,' laughed TC. Vance laughed too.

'One day I was so desperate for a smoke and a drink, I drove to the creek and ate a carton of chocolate bars. There are forty-eight in a carton. Delores and everyone were looking for me. I think they thought I'd done away with myself.' TC smiled and looked ahead at the blue water of the canal.

'They underestimated you, Ex-Boss. When you go, it won't be from over-indulgence in chocolate bars. It would be from over-indulgence in women if you haven't or don't change your ways.' Vance changed the subject as was his way.

'I want you to do sales trips to Sydney and Melbourne for me, TC. I can't stand the bullshit. I'll pay you twenty-five percent of the take. You'll save me that by not discounting. Find a business we can go partners in. You can run it plus take an occasional trip down south.'

'I haven't got any money. Jake controls it. Apart from that, what about my little boy?'

'As for Jake,' replied Vance. 'I know him; he'll go where the bucks are.'

'Just like you?' interrupted TC.

'Yes, unfortunately, just like me,' replied Vance matter-of-factly.

'I'm sure your sister and Jake's mother will help you out looking after your kid for a couple of days occasionally. Let's face it, TC, they've been doing it while you've been working in the job you just quit.'

⁋

Within months Jake and TC traded their house and everything in it for a half-share in a run-down motel on the Gold Coast Highway. Vance put in the other half. They renamed the motel "The Pink Brolga". With relentless hard work, dedicated determination, clean beds, great breakfasts, and low rates, TC soon had the enviable 'NO VACANCY' sign glowing seven nights a week.

Jake continued to enjoy his shoe salesman job and its unlimited freedom. He never so much as lifted a finger to help with the motel restoration. He would leave the Coast at four on Monday morning and return on Friday at lunchtime to his drinking spot a few kilometres south of the motel, drink and bullshit until the pub closed, drive to the motel, usually blind drunk, stagger inside, dump his bag of needed-to-be-done laundry on the floor, then fall into bed.

Jake's allocated time for his son was one hour on Saturday mornings before heading off to the pub for a day of S.P. bookmaking, drinking, and boasting to his mates about whatever or whomever he'd done during the week.

⁋

On Sundays Jake played golf, then took in a session at the pub before embarking on a cruise of the canals with mates and a copious supply of grog onboard his boat, which TC had not seen.

One such Sunday afternoon a well-spoken, prematurely grey-haired, fifty-year-old gentleman of presence showed up at the Pink Brolga. With a screeching hiss and roar, he whirled his vintage Chevrolet car into the courtyard, got out, and walked shakily to the motel office reception, where TC was absorbed in paper work.

'I'm Keith Dalton. I met your sister at a mutual friend's house,' he announced. 'I'm sick. I've got malaria. Here's my passport and bank book. I need a room.'

'Don't worry about your passport and bank book, sir,' replied TC with concern as she rejected his personal documents. She could see he was a sick man. 'I'll call a doctor.'

'No, you won't! Give me a bed and leave me alone until I get well,' commanded Mr Dalton with authority.

'Consider it done,' replied TC. 'You can have the unit right there opposite the office,' she continued as she selected a key and lead him to the door. 'If it's okay with you, I'd like to check on you occasionally.'

'How often is occasionally, girl?' he demanded.

TC grimaced and gingerly replied. 'Is a few times a day, okay?'

'All right! Don't fuss over me. If I'm sleeping, don't wake me,' said Mr Dalton condescendingly.

For three days Mr Dalton stayed in his unit. TC checked on him first thing each morning, twice through the day, and finally at night. She knew he was okay because he obviously ate and drank whatever she left as quietly as possible on his bedside table. At daylight on the fourth morning TC was surprised when she opened the office to see Keith Dalton large as life sitting on his doorstep polishing his boots.

'A man is judged by the condition of his boots,' he said matter-of-factly without so much as glancing at her. 'You're a good lass. Thank you for keeping your word, checking on me, the food, and all that stuff. I'm an engineer, got malaria. I stayed too long on a job in Papua. It comes and goes. Nothing to worry about.' TC smiled, then laughed.

'I like you, Mr Dalton. You are a man of character.'

'I like you, too, lass; you also have character. Not many of us left. Far too many mongrels in the world these days,' replied Keith Dalton as he continued shining his boots.

'Would you like breakfast, Mr Dalton?' asked TC.

'The powers that be are having a new airport runway constructed here,' replied Keith Dalton. 'I'm in charge of the project. I have to meet with some big shots this morning.'

'Does that mean yes or no to breakfast, Mr Dalton?' enquired TC with no confidence whatsoever.

'It means no, lass!' replied Mr Dalton. 'I've been here a few days and already you are sounding like my mother, whom I love dearly, by the way. Offer me dinner tonight if I don't drink too many bourbons in the meantime. Think I'll be staying at the Pink Brolga for a long time, so I suggest you drop the Mr Dalton crap and address me as Mr D, KD, or Keith.'

TC laughed nervously. 'I think I'll opt for the first one,' she replied timidly. The bond was forged. Mr D became TC's new mentor. Mr D reminded TC of Vance pre his obsession with opal and money days.

'What is your name, by the way?' asked Mr D.

'My name is TC Carmichael,' replied TC.

'Sounds good to me, Carmichael. I'll see you later,' said Mr D before closing his unit door, which he instantly re-opened.

'While we're on the subject of sound, Carmichael, that's what this joint needs! It's like a mortuary! No music! You need music, lass. It makes people feel happy. It shouldn't matter if it's opera, rock, or jazz, Carmichael. Get your act together.' Mr D closed his door again. TC left the office in the direction of the kitchen to cook breakfasts for other motel guests. Passing the radio, she turned it on and up loud. Gerry Lee was singing, 'You Shake My Nerves'.

I can identify with that, thought TC as she opened the refrigerator door and looked at the stacks of egg cartons, tomatoes, bacon, sausages, et cetera within. As soon as I've delivered breakfasts to the guests, I'll call Lou. Loud music reminds me of her, the stairs, Graham, and long ago.

¶

After Keith Dalton took up permanent residence at the Pink Brolga, things changed. TC had a second father figure and her little boy had another grandfather, whom he named Cranky Mr D because of Mr Dalton's HMS military, no-nonsense training attitude.

¶

The first time Vance met Mr D, the two men liked each other immediately.

'So, you're the famous opal miner,' said Mr D after TC introduced them. 'I feel I know you already. Carmichael never stops telling me what a great man you are.' Vance laughed.

'I feel the same, Keith. She's forever telling me how happy she is to have you here. I'm glad you're here, too. She needs someone to look out for her and her boy.' Vance turned to TC.

'Where is your pride and joy, by the way?'

'He's with Maggie and his grandmother,' replied TC.

'I see. How about making Keith and me some coffees before you start packing? I want you to do a trip down south; sell some opal.' TC looked at Vance in alarm. She had known this day would come. Still, she wasn't prepared for the sudden manner in which it was presented.

'TC, make the coffees, then start packing,' repeated Vance. 'We'll discuss the details after Keith and I have a talk.'

'Would you like a sandwich to go with the coffee?' she asked with a smile while telling herself a deal was a deal. She'd made the deal; now she had to adhere to it. Like it or lump it, she was doing the trip.

'A sandwich would be nice, thank you, TC,' replied Vance formally with the hint of a smile.

'All right, gentleman, please be seated in the dining room,' replied TC just as formally without the smile.

'TC tells me you're an engineer, Keith,' said Vance.

'Yes. Building a new airstrip. The old one can't cope with the increased traffic and heavier planes.'

'Interesting! That must mean more tourists are coming here,' remarked Vance with interest.

'That's the truth, Vance!' agreed Keith Dalton. They seated themselves at the dining room table.

'When does this all start?' enquired Vance.

'As soon as we get the right gear and crew here,' replied Keith Dalton. 'We have to bring in machinery and people from all over Australia. It's at least a month, maybe six weeks away.'

'Coffee and sandwiches for two,' interrupted TC as she placed a tray on the table. 'There's a coffee urn in the kitchen if you need more. I'm going to pack. How long will I be away, Mr Callahan?' Vance smiled at TC.

'That's entirely up to you. Depends on how fast you see your clients and sell the opal.' TC turned on her heel and stormed off to her bedroom.

'She's worried about her lad,' said Keith Dalton matter-of-factly. 'She lives for him.'

'I know that, Keith. He's all she's got,' replied Vance. 'I'll go see her sister, Maggie, later. I'm sure she'll come here while TC's away.'

'She will!' agreed KD. 'She'd do anything for TC.'

'How do you get along with Jake, Keith?' asked Vance.

'I see him at the pub sometimes. He's rarely here. He comes home drunk around midnight on Fridays, dumps his laundry, hits the pub at ten on Saturday morning, drinks, bullshits, and bets all day and night until the pub closes. On Sundays, he's off to golf at daybreak, sessions at the pub, then cruises with his mates on his boat. He leaves early Monday mornings, and I'm certain Carmichael is happy to see the last of him. Mind you, Vance,' added KD, 'I can't talk about Jake's boozing; I do a fair bit of it myself.' Vance laughed.

'I have to admit I've done more than my fair share of it, too, Keith.' He added seriously, 'If you see Jake on rum or he comes here reeking of it, keep an eye out for TC.'

'I'd like to ask you why, but I won't,' replied KD. 'Consider it done! I'll look out for the lass.' Vance smiled and changed the subject.

'Talking about airstrips, we've recently finished compacted-dirt runways at my mine sites. My oldest son, Jonathon, has his pilot's license. I bought a plane to fly the provisions out to the mines and the opal in to Brolga. It's made a huge difference to production. If machinery breaks down, Jonathon flies out and fixes it.'

'What do you mean? How does he fix it by flying to the mines?' enquired Mr D, who was a little confused. Vance smiled.

'Sorry, Keith. Not only is Jonathon a pilot, he's also a mechanical engineer,' he replied proudly.

'Is that so!' said KD, who was obviously impressed.

TC returned to the dining room and announced she had finished packing.

❡

Maggie happily agreed to take care of her nephew, the motel office, and breakfast cooking until TC returned.

'Anything to get out of this bloody caravan for a while,' she replied when Vance, in the company of Keith Dalton, made his request.

'I'll cook you a good meal every night, KD, if you promise to have a few drinks with me.'

'Does that go for me, too, Maggie?' asked Vance mischievously.

'What? Are you back on the booze again, Callahan?' asked Maggie seriously. 'TC told me you quit years ago!'

'I was talking about the good meal every night,' replied Vance innocently.

'Yes, sure, I'll cook you a great meal as long as you promise not to spoil Dalton's and my party time.'

❡

Vance and KD put TC on the six o'clock flight to Melbourne. The moment she was in her hotel room, she phoned the motel. She was amused to hear Vance's voice.

'Good evening, Pink Brolga Motel,' he said tongue-in-cheek.

'What are you doing answering the phone?' laughed TC.

'Maggie and Keith are on the piss, so someone has to be responsible,' replied Vance matter-of-factly. 'The little fellow is asleep. He cried a little while. I calmed him down by trying to dance to some stupid bloody rock 'n' roll songs on the stereo.' TC burst into uncontrollable laughter. The thought of Vance dancing to rock music was beyond her imagination.

'Stop laughing, TC. That's what your kid did!' commanded Vance. 'Laughing at me is what made the poor little bugger tired. I've decided to hang around here until you come back. I'll spend the days with Keith. He's going to show me where the new airstrip will be located and I want to have a good look around the place. Who knows? Maybe I'll open a shop here one day.'

§

At Vance's mines, the likes of Neil, Yappy, Little Joe, Michael, and company were doing the right thing while the outside manager Vance had brought in was robbing him blind. He wasn't there, so half the boulders were put on the pile and the other half were hidden for them to furtively place in their vehicles before going on leave.

'I know that bastard is robbing Vance,' said Yappy one night while the men were eating. 'Every afternoon he comes and fiddles with the boulders on the pile, then jumps in his ute and racks off to his caravan. Ten minutes later he drives past back to the hill.' The men nodded in agreement.

'How do we prove it, Yappy?' said Neil. Little Joe sighed heavily.

'Sad, but we can't.'

'Ask me, this industry is full of bloody thieves,' said Yappy.

'Don't count us in on that, Yappy,' said Neil.

'I didn't mean us, you silly mongrel,' replied Yappy indignantly as he slammed a saucepan onto the bench.

§

TC was gone four days. During that time, Vance and Keith Dalton bonded. They had mutual respect for each other's intelligence, humour, and protective attitude towards TC and her child. They also enjoyed Maggie's cooking. Vance couldn't recall having such a good time without booze or women for as long as he could remember. Vance especially enjoyed throwing his arms and feet around to the music on T.V. or the stereo and watching TC's two-year-old double up with laughter. Each night he went to bed asking himself why on earth he hadn't enjoyed such times with his own children. Each night a voice from within replied, 'Because you were too bloody busy boozing and screwing.' Vance felt guilt like never before.

§

KD and Vance met TC at the airport. She was surprised and tears welled when she entered the terminal and her baby came running towards her with his little arms spread wide, almost screaming, 'Mama, Mama!' He was closely followed by KD and Vance. Vance quickly relieved TC of the briefcase, and she scooped her reason for living into her arms. Both KD and Vance were starry-eyed as they silently observed the reunion. The tiny-for-his-age boy was clinging to TC as if he were part of her clothing.

'Don't you leave me again, Mama!' he scolded her loudly. Vance and KD laughed.

'Where does he get the "Mama" from?' asked Vance.

'Probably listening to too many Elvis records,' replied KD. 'Sometimes he calls her "Mother". Depends on what mood the little bugger is in.'

§

On arrival at the motel, TC put her already-sleeping child to bed before hugging Maggie, who had been drinking a scotch or two while waiting for them.

'Come on, Maggie,' said KD. 'We'll go to the pub for an hour so Vance and Carmichael can talk business.' Maggie laughed before replying.

'Are you asking me out on a date, KD?'

'Don't be so bloody ridiculous, woman,' replied KD. 'It's common sense. Your sister has been on a business trip for Vance. They need to discuss the outcome in private.'

'All right, you cranky, old bastard,' snapped Maggie. 'Can I finish my drink first?'

'No! We are leaving now!' was the curt reply. They were gone immediately.

'How did you go, TC?' asked Vance with urgency.

'How did I know those would be your first words?' laughed TC. 'Some things never change! I sold the lot. I could have sold more if I'd had it. Before you ask, I gave no discount. I did give a new customer two small stones as a bonus because he spent twenty thousand. There's sixteen thousand in cheques, the rest is cash. Have fun counting it! Now you can ask me if I'm tired, did I see Lou in Sydney, and how many offers for fun I rejected from offensive men. If you want a cup of coffee, you know where the kitchen is.'

Vance had worn a silly grin during TC's outburst. He began laughing.

'What are you laughing about?' demanded TC. Vance's laughter turned back into a grin as he shook his head from side to side.

'You! You just reminded me of the young spitfire who used to yell at me from the Empire window.'

'That's not funny! I could have killed some poor soul if I'd given them the wrong medication. Especially in the first month.'

'Yes, TC, but you didn't, did you?' replied Vance seriously. 'Now, be a good girl and make me a coffee. Something to eat would be nice, too. The only one who got fed tonight was the little guy.' TC glared at Vance.

'Sure!'

As she strode to the kitchen, fleeting thoughts ran through TC's head of sprinkling Vance's food with rat poison. Problem was she didn't have any.

On the kitchen bench alongside Mr D's bottle of Bourbon and Maggie's bottle of Scotch, the coffee percolator was full of freshly brewed coffee. She opened the refrigerator. To her relief, she saw four covered plates of corned beef and salad.

'Bless you, Maggie darlin',' she said aloud as she heard Louis Armstrong begin to play on the stereo. TC couldn't help but smile as she recalled how Vance had told her to borrow as many records as she liked before he and Jake had set his house ablaze. Silently she said, 'We sure go back a long time, Boss.'

'Did you find any shoes you liked in Sydney, Butterball?' asked Vance as she placed his food on the table.

'Didn't have time,' replied TC. 'Only saw Lou for an hour, and that was at the airport.'

'How is Lou?' enquired Vance with genuine interest.

'She's happy, very happy. Her little boy is gorgeous. Lou's the best friend I've ever had or ever will have.'

'What about me, TC?' said Vance ever so seriously. TC laughed.

'You are more like a dictatorial father figure than a friend. Eat your meal!'

'TC, look at me!' said Vance. 'I need to tell you something while I have the opportunity.'

'What would that be, Mr Callahan?' replied TC as she looked Vance in the eyes. Silence as Vance foraged for the right words.

'The first few years you worked for me, I found you precocious. Thank God you were. You are the most hardworking, loyal, honest, unpromiscuous woman I have ever known. I respect you more than any other female on earth, including Anna, Delores, and my daughter. I know you loved that young cop; yet, I lectured you on what would happen to him. I should have thought about you. He would have been all right. His family would have eventually accepted you, and once they met you, his superiors and colleagues in the police force would have understood.

TC was on the verge of tears. She held them back as she once more time recalled the vow she had made to herself years before.

'Stop, Boss! I feel like crying; I'm not going to. Yes, I loved Graham. Yes, you did talk me out of it because it would hurt him and his career. I've put him out of my mind for years. Wherever he is, I hope he's as happy as he could have been with me. My tears are now reserved for my son and my son alone. As for the way I am, you moulded me. I don't want to discuss this anymore! Let's eat!'

'Stop it, TC. We may never get an opportunity to have this conversation again.'

'I'm listening!' replied TC as she leaned back in her chair and resigned herself to the fact that she would have to hear Vance out. She had no option.

'I'm sorry, TC. I should have minded my own business. Selfishly, I manipulated you into letting go of the kid cop you loved and instead staying with a prick like Jake.'

'Your soul is cleansed, Mr Callahan. What's gone is gone,' said TC lightly. 'Mr D likes Tony Bennett. I'll play his record. When he sings, 'I left my heart in San Francisco', let's pretend he's singing, 'I left my heart with Graham in Brolga', and you sent yours with Anna when she absconded from Curloo.'

Vance smiled. 'Fair enough, Little One. Let's eat!'

As if on cue, Vance and TC heard KD's Chevrolet hurtle into the courtyard, two car doors slam, and footsteps on the stairs. The dining room screen was flung open by Mr D, who was closely followed by Maggie. Neither of them looked happy.

'Bloody hell, Carmichael,' said Mr D, whose disgruntled look turned to a smile. 'You are playing my favourite song—Tony left his heart in San Francisco. I left mine in some other place. I'm not telling you where!'

'Don't think you ever had a heart to leave anywhere, you old bastard,' snapped Maggie. KD turned to Maggie and scowled.

'Don't call me an old bastard; all I did was drag you away from the bloody poker machines.'

'Come on, kids, be nice,' laughed Vance.

'I'll get us a drink,' said Maggie.

'Good idea,' said KD. 'Carmichael, while she's gone, start 'San Francisco' again so we can listen to it in peace.'

Vance was amused by the scenario. He burst into laughter as memories of his drinking days flooded back. He would just about kill for a Rum and Coke. Instead, he began eating his meal and thinking of Anna.

❡

When TC entered the motel kitchen at 5.00 the next morning, the light was on and a note from Vance and twelve hundred dollars were on the kitchen bench. TC read the note—

"Butterball,

The two hundred is for a couple of pairs of new stilettos; the thousand is for your four days' work. I wanted to discuss other things with you. Never mind. I can do that on the phone. I'm hoping the shop opens Monday after next. I want you there! You'll receive an invitation. I want you to dress up. Want you to look the part. Wear stilettos!

Vance.

P.S. Ask your son if he thinks I'm a good dancer!"

Once again, the thought of Vance Callahan dancing made TC smile. 'I'll have to research how good a dancer Maggie and Mr D think the Boss is,' she told herself as she began perusing the breakfast orders, times requested, et cetera.

§

Keith Dalton and Jake had formed a half-hearted, hit-and-miss drinking-buddy friendship on the weekends because they both drank at the same pub and resided in the same motel.

It came about Friday night when they were both drunk, KD on Bourbon and Jake on beer, that an accommodation deal for a subcontracting company on the new airstrip job was cemented by a handshake between Jake and the general manager of the earth-moving group. TC was unaware of the agreement until she was told about it hours later by Jake with his wobbling head and KD, who tried to stand straight but could not. She was in disbelief.

'No! No! No! It can't happen! What do you expect me to tell my telephone company guests? The men from the electricity board? The regular weekenders?'

'Tell the bastards to get stuffed,' mumbled Jake with his forever-roaming head.

'TC Carmichael, wake up to yourself, lass,' commanded KD. 'This deal means a full house until the airstrip is completed. Could take years! Apart from that, if the bastards are housed here, I can make sure they front up for work every day and be on time. Come on, lass, be a clever girl.'

Jake began staggering towards his bed.

'By the way, TC, I forgot to mention, you'll have to cook them dinners at night instead of breakfasts in the morning. Poor bastards have to be on the job at five.'

'Won't worry you, Jake. You do bugger-all around here,' said KD. TC all but yelled.

'Both of you, leave me alone! I'll think about it!'

'Don't think too long, Carmichael. They arrive in two weeks and three days' time. Day before ANZAC Day.'

¶

Vance's first retail opal shop opened. After the opening. Vance phoned TC and demanded to know why she hadn't attended the celebration party.

'Why the bloody hell weren't you there, TC! I told you I wanted you there.'

'Because I didn't receive an invitation! That's why, Mr Callahan!' replied TC defensively. 'After all, I'm nothing but an ex-employee!'

'Get real, TC! If it wasn't for the men and you, I wouldn't be opening the effing shop!'

'Who sent the invitations, Mr Callahan?' enquired TC calmly. She knew Vance was extremely upset.

'The slimy, bullshitting bitch I was stupid enough to hire as manager, TC,' replied Vance. 'I'm pissed off you weren't here.'

'What's done is done, Boss. You are the one who has been preaching the reality of life to me for years. How did the opening go, anyway?'

'Let's see what happens,' replied Vance abruptly.

Vance put down the telephone and glanced at his female Japanese staff member, who smiled at him alluringly. Word had it Japanese tourists were everywhere; Vance intended to get his share of the supposedly lucrative market.

The woman's name was Chikako. She stood five feet, a nice person at heart, deep hard as the hobs of hell, was after money, and would endeavour to move mountains to acquire it. Vance was Chikako's target. She knew from the way he looked at her that he was a possibility. His wife had not shown her face apart from being at the opening. Piece of cake! Thought Chikako. In her eyes, Vance was the king of opals. She had her heart set on being his queen.

¶

At camp number one, Yappy, Neil and Little Joe were conversing about how bloody incredible it was.

'Can't bloody believe it!' said Yappy. 'The ex-drunk pill-pusher has hit the effing sky. He's opened a bloody high-falutin shop in the Big Smoke.'

'Good luck to him!' said Neil. Little Joe thought for a while before uttering rare few words.

'Wouldn't and couldn't have done it without us,' he said flatly before stabbing his fork into a piece of corned beef and slowly lifting it to his mouth.

¶

At 3 pm the day before ANZAC Day, a bus carrying the earth-moving group's personnel pulled into the Pink Brolga's courtyard. KD was standing at the office window. TC was beside him as the men disembarked.

'Look like a motley mob to me, Carmichael,' remarked KD.

'Me, too, Mr D,' replied TC despondently as reality struck home. She would have to clean their rooms and prepare their dinners for at least a year, perhaps two.

Under Mr D's instructions, TC had left all motel unit doors open in order to allow the workmen to choose their own roommates. He was right. Bonded-friend-with-friend they chose their rooms and disappeared inside to don their work clothes.

'These poor bastards have to go straight to work, TC,' said KD. 'It's called job orientation. No rest for the wicked, lass!'

'Why is the bus staying there with the motor running?' asked TC after a couple of minutes of no one leaving the vehicle.

'Perhaps there's some hung-over poor bastard sleeping off last night's binge in there,' replied KD with a smile. 'Who knows?'

Within seconds, Mr D was proven right. The bus driver ushered a well-dressed, had-been-sleeping, shorter version of Graham Sandler out of the bus. TC took a deep breath.

'Trouble just stepped out of that bus, didn't it, Carmichael?' said KD, whose observation was correct.

'I think so. I'll have to be on guard,' replied TC. Her heart was pounding as she watched the straggler approach the only still-open unit door in the motel.

'I have to go prepare tonight's dinner for this lot.'

¶

By the first weekend, mutual respect was established between TC and the earth-moving crew. They were all hard workers. The personnel carrier pulled into the motel's courtyard every morning at four-fifteen and left in the wake of KD's Chevrolet at exactly four-thirty. He had to be on the job at five.

TC heard them leave. She was awakened by the sound of the bus arriving and KD's revving of his Chevrolet's engine. When they had gone, she would drift back into slumberland, feeling relieved she had no breakfast orders to deliver at requested times. Instead of being up early to cook breakfast, she now was up late at night clearing and cleaning after the evening meal.

¶

The men's names ranged through the alphabet from A to Z. Initially TC was confused and addressed then by the wrong titles

'They're a motley mob, Carmichael,' said KD after Friday night's dinner. 'Hard-working poor buggers, though. You'll get used to them, lass. I strongly suggest you continue to ignore approaches by the last B off the bus. I've seen him winking at you over dinner.'

'Don't worry about him. I'm fine, Mr D,' replied TC. 'Only problem is he reminds me of a boy I fell in love with years ago. That went nowhere; so why should this?

¶

KD suggested TC consider a barbeque on Sunday nights. The earth-moving crew finished work at 3 pm on Sundays. If the weather was wonderful, they could come home to the motel, get cleaned up, go to a pub session, then come back to eat, and bring any friends if they wished.

'Sounds good,' agreed TC.

KD was right. The first Sunday night barbeque was a raging success. Maggie and Mr D drank countless Scotches and Bourbons. Most of the men brought a female companion they had met at the pub session. Those who didn't made a fuss of TC's little boy because he reminded them of children they had back home in various states of Australia.

Randall James, the last man off the bus, did his best to flirt with TC. His efforts were wasted. From overhearing conversations, she knew he came from Western Australia, the furthest state from Queensland. Sounded like it may as well be another country to her.

¶

It was after midnight. TC was washing dishes in the motel kitchen. Maggie had left an hour ago, the men who had met women were at the beach a block away, KD was in his unit, and TC's child was asleep. Everyone had gone to bed, for a walk, or whatever.

Jake came home. He'd been on his boat with mates. TC smelt rum the second he walked through the door.

'Got the people coming for a feed in an hour,' he mumbled.

'You have got to be joking, Jake,' replied TC. 'I suggest you look at your watch.'

'I promised my mates a feed. I can't let them down. I know you've been entertaining your so-called guests. Time to entertain my friends.'

TC lifted the lid of the freezer, looked at the contents, selected two six-packs of individually wrapped steaks, thought for a moment, then hurled one at Jake. It hit him in the chest. Both of them were in shock, TC because she couldn't believe what she had done, and Jake because he was caught off guard.

'You are a useless, bullshitting mongrel, Jake Carmichael,' said TC. 'I've had enough! You want to have your drinking mates here for dinner, give me warning. Do the right thing for once in your life. I loathe you!'

TC recognised the look in Jake's eyes. It had to come to this sooner or later, she thought as she attempted to walk past him to her son's room. Jake grabbed her by the shoulder with one hand and punched her in the stomach with the other.

'Brave, aren't you, Jake Carmichael,' taunted TC. 'Just like in the old days. Hit me where it doesn't show.'

'I don't give a stuff where I hit you,' yelled Jake, whose true colours emerged. He bashed TC's head against the wall. TC began screaming. Her child emerged from his bedroom and was clinging to her legs.

'Don't hit my mama, Daddy. I hate you. I hate you. I hate you! Leave my mama alone!'

'Piss off, you little shit,' snarled Jake as he kicked the little boy's legs. 'Mind your own effing business.' TC screamed even louder.

'Help me! He's hurt my baby! He's hurt my baby!' KD heard TC's screaming from his unit a few feet away. He smashed through the door, told Jake to piss off, collected TC's child from the floor, and held him up to his mother's arms as Jake cringed away.

'Here's your baby, Carmichael. You look like crap.'

'I know, Mr D. I feel like it, too,' sobbed TC as she hugged her son. 'I'm going to get a divorce. I told you years ago, Jake, if you ever hit me in front of my baby, I would leave you. I don't care about what people think regarding broken marriages. One of us is out of here! Either you go, or I do!'

'I've stuffed it now,' mumbled Jake as he staggered to his bedroom.

'You certainly have, Jake. You've lost your laundress,' responded KD with disgust. 'You'll have to find somewhere else to dump your washing

Friday nights.' Mr D then turned to TC, shook his head and sighed. 'Take the lad to his room and lock yourselves in, Carmichael. I'll have a man I know by six in the morning to repair the one I broke. Go on, now, lass, do as I said.'

T.C did as instructed. KD returned to his unit to find a group of the construction crew waiting outside his door.

'What was the commotion about, Keith?' enquired Randall James.

'Mind your own bloody business. That goes for all of you,' replied Keith Dalton. 'I suggest you men get some sleep. You have to be up for work in a few hours.'

As TC had followed his instructions without question, so did these tough, hardworking men. KD had an air of authority found in few. Consequently, rarely did anyone bother to differ with him.

§

Immediately TC heard everyone, including Jake, leave the following morning, she hurriedly showered. She had not slept a wink. Her mind had been racing every second as she laid on her restless, frightened, clinging, periodically crying little boy's bed.

'I got off lightly this time,' she told herself. 'One bruised shoulder, one very sore hip bone, couple of other extra-sore spots, and one egg-sized lump on the back of my head, which is aching beyond belief. I brought this one on myself,' she thought with guilt as she dressed. 'I shouldn't have thrown the steak at him.'

Why didn't Jake simply throw the steak back at you? reasoned a voice from within.

TC quickly located, then swallowed, a couple of painkillers before going to the office telephone to call Jake's mother, who had known for years about her son's wife-bashing, which TC until now had not mentioned to Maggie.

'It's early, luv. Is something wrong?' said Thel Carmichael with concern.

'Yes, Mum, it is,' replied TC, fighting back tears. 'Please come as soon as you can. Would you ask Maggie to come with you? I'd ask her myself except she doesn't have a telephone. I can't collect you because your grandson is sleeping and I'll have someone here soon to fix a door.'

'Jake's been at again, hasn't he, luv?' asked Thel Carmichael softly.

'It was probably my fault, Mum, but this is it!' replied TC also softly. 'I don't know how I'm going to tell Maggie.' TC heard her mother-in-law take a deep breath.

'Don't worry, luv. I told your sister long ago about my son's abusive habits. I'll talk to Maggie now. We'll be there soon. I apologise for my son, luv.'

'You don't have to, Mum, you don't have to,' whispered TC.

¶

Mr D's door-and-locks repair man arrived as promised. Thel Carmichael and Maggie were there only minutes behind him.

'Did some mad bastard kick in the door, mate?' asked Maggie as the two women walked up the stairs to the office next to where the men were working.

'Something like that, Maggie,' said TC while opening the office door. 'Please come through this way and leave the gentleman to get on with his work.'

'Where's Junior?' asked Maggie urgently.

'He's asleep in his room,' replied TC quietly.

'Mind if we check on him, luv?' said Thel Carmichael.

'Go ahead,' agreed TC.

After observing silently from his bedroom door for less than a minute, Thel and Maggie were satisfied the child was breathing while sleeping soundly.

'Tell us what happened and don't leave anything out while you make us a cup of tea,' said Maggie.

'Why would I leave anything out, Maggie?' replied TC as obediently she switched on the kettle and extracted cups from a kitchen cupboard.

'You'll need a new door with double locks, luv,' called the door repair man. 'This one's buggered. Whoever did it in did a bloody good job.' TC immediately went to the door to speak with the man.

'That will be fine. Thank you.'

'Okay, luv. I'll be back in less than it takes a cane toad to scare a cat at midnight.'

§

'No point in beating around the bush,' said TC as she placed cups of tea on the kitchen table. 'My marriage with Jake is finished! Not that it's ever been a marriage. I'll tell you what happened. Should I accidentally miss any detail, I'm certain Mr D will fill you in later. No matter what anyone says, I'm getting a divorce.'

Both Jake's mother and Maggie listened in silence as TC relayed to them what had taken place a little after midnight that morning.

'I shouldn't have thrown the frozen steaks. I was tired and not thinking,' she concluded.

'I would have hit the bastard with a sledge hammer,' stated Maggie seriously.

'Have to say I'd back you up on that,' said Thel Carmichael just as seriously.

'Mother, come here NOW. I told you NEVER to leave me again,' demanded TC's son from his bedroom door. His grandmother, aunt, and mother jumped to their feet immediately.

'Junior is calling,' said Maggie. 'Little shit has us all wrapped around his fingers. Too smart for his bloody age, if you ask me.'

'Didn't hear anyone ask you, Maggie,' replied TC defensively as she led the way to her child. 'Grandma and Auntie Maggie are here to see you, sweetheart,' she said as she hugged him. 'Mama wouldn't leave you for anything.'

'Why do you call him Junior, Maggie?' enquired Thel quietly.

'Because he's like his mother, he hates his name, that's why, Thel!' replied Maggie with a smile. 'We have to call him some bloody thing. Anyway, it works for me.'

'I never noticed because I always refer to him and my other grandchildren as "luv",' smiled Thel. 'Thank you, Maggie. We'll have to discuss it sometime in the near future, if you don't mind.'

The telephone rang.

'You answer that, TC. We'll look after him, won't we, Thel?' said Maggie.

TC answered the office telephone. She was shocked to hear Jake's voice. Jake did not make calls to her. She couldn't remember the last time she had spoken to Jake on the telephone. Didn't matter anyway, thought TC.

'What do you want, Jake?' she asked calmly.

'I want you to wake up to yourself. That is what I want,' commanded Jake. TC could tell Jake was furious. She forced herself to remain calm.

'I should have woken up to myself before I was stupid enough to marry you. I meant what I said, Jake; you go or I go. I'm divorcing you!'

'You know I can't run that effing joint!' yelled Jake.

'Good! Your clothes and golf gear will be packed and waiting for you in the motel laundry on Friday afternoon.'

'What are you going to tell my mother,' demanded Jake.

'I have already told her everything. She agrees with Maggie's suggestion that I should have hit you with a sledge hammer instead of a few pieces of frozen steak.' Jake began ranting. TC put the phone down.

❡

TC hadn't heard from Vance since he had called her after his shop opening when he'd chastised her for not attending. As yet he was unaware the motel was full of airport construction people. He hadn't given her a chance to tell him. TC wanted desperately to tell Vance about the latest episode with Jake and her final decision to divorce him. She knew Vance would understand; in fact, he would probably applaud it. She told herself he was busy with his shop. He would contact her when he was ready.

Vance was indeed busy with his shop. Seemed like a thousand times a day he would tell himself he wished he hadn't bothered. As far as he was concerned, it was a bloody nightmare.

⁊

Midweek, Maggie called TC from a public phone box.

'I want to move in with you for a while, TC. I'm a good cook! I can cook for that mob of bastards you've got in there in exchange for my room and board. I'm leaving your drunken, abusive brother-in-law. I've had a gutful. I'm already packed.'

'No problem, Maggie,' replied TC without hesitation. 'I was thinking of hiring someone to help me. I'm tired!'

Maggie was there within an hour.

⁊

That night Brolga's Seat of Knowledge elders gathered as always on Flea and movie nights. After observing the action of the train's arrival and locals flocking to the picture show, they sat in silence, gazing at almost nothing going on in the Empire's bar.

Jock broke that silence after a minute or so.

'It's true, you know!'

'What's true, Jock?' asked one of his mates.

'That rumour we heard about Callahan opening a bloody fancy opal shop in the city,' replied Josh matter-of-factly.

'Who told you?' asked another mate with interest.

'None of your bloody business; I have my sources,' replied Jock. 'Can't bloody believe it! Think the pill-pusher is going to put Brolga on the map. The bastard will probably become a bloody legend if he isn't already.' Josh's mates on the Sacred Seat all nodded in agreement.

⁊

While Jock and his cronies were discussing the probability of Vance becoming a Brolga legend, Vance was dialling the Pink Brolga. He intended leaving for Brolga next morning and needed to talk to TC before he left. Vance was surprised when Maggie answered the telephone in a somewhat hurried manner.

'What are you still doing there, Maggie? Have you moved in?' he laughed.

'As a matter of fact, I have, Callahan. We've got a dining room full of hungry men, TC is run off her feet serving dinner, and I'm the cook, so I have to piss off, mate. By the way, Jake bashed TC again last Sunday night, and she's kicked him out. Bye.'

Vance thought before putting down the phone, 'I'm not going to Brolga tomorrow. I've changed my mind. I'm leaving now to find out what on earth is happening with TC and the Pink Brolga.'

¶

When Vance entered the dining room unannounced, only KD, Randall James, and a couple of other men remained. KD and Randall James had a drink in front of them. Maggie was leaning on the serving counter, sipping a Scotch on ice, and TC was cleaning in the kitchen.

'Like the new door,' said Vance. 'Its green blends in well with everything else that is pink.'

'Sarcastic bastard, Callahan,' said Maggie.

'Carmichael insisted on it being painted dark green,' said KD. 'Who are we to differ?'

'Oh, well,' shrugged Vance. 'I suppose it will match her eyes.' Everyone laughed. The seated men, including KD, stood up.

'Let me introduce you, Vance. Of course, you know Maggie.'

'Of course, I do, Keith. So different to her little sister I sometimes wonder if they didn't come from different planets.' Maggie stood straight.

'Smart bastard, Callahan. I wonder if that could be because I didn't have someone like you telling me what I could and couldn't do since the ripe old age of sixteen-and-a-bit. Do you want a feed or not?'

'Thank you, Maggie. A coffee to go with it would be nice.'

'I'm Larry. Pleased to meet you, Vance,' said one of the men with some urgency. 'Excuse me if I leave now. I have a date.'

'I'm Norm. I also have to go for the same reason as Larry.' After shaking Vance's hand, he checked his watch.

'Wish I had the same problem,' laughed Vance. 'We'll probably meet again some time.'

KD turned to Randall James, who in his tight blue jeans, grey-and-white striped shirt, wide brown belt, and matching polished boots looked like a movie star.

'This is Randall James, Vance. Too good-looking for his own good. Works like a drover's dog, got a silver tongue, women love the bastard, and he drinks like a fish. He either has an eye affliction or he has the hots for TC.' Both Vance and Randall held out their hands.

'Pleased to meet you, Vance. I don't have an eye affliction. I'm trying with TC but making no ground.'

At least, the bastard's honest, thought Vance as they shook hands.

'Many men have tried and many have failed, Randall, so don't hold your breath.'

'Here's your bloody tucker, Callahan,' said Maggie as she approached the men. 'Now sit down and eat the bastard while I get back to my Scotch. Bloody ice is probably melted by now.'

'What about my coffee, Maggie?' teased Vance as he picked up his knife and fork and decided where to start on the enticing meal of roast beef, baked vegetables, and gravy.

'You can't bloody eat and drink at the same time, Callahan,' replied Maggie. 'Eat! Your coffee is coming.'

'You don't have much trouble eating and drinking at the same time, Maggie,' said KD.

'Oh, shut up, you old bastard,' snapped Maggie.

Randall James said nothing. He liked these people and the manner in which they interacted. He wished TC would hurry up in the kitchen. He wanted to know where Vance Callahan fitted into her life. He didn't have to wait more than a few seconds.

'Who wants the coffee, Maggie?' said TC. 'I've made a fresh pot.'

'Callahan does,' said Maggie, nodding towards Vance, who looked at TC and smiled.

'Maggie's a good cook, Butterball.' TC's face lit up.

'How long have you been here, ex-Boss? Why didn't you tell me, Maggie?' said TC as she quickly placed the coffee pot on the serving bench before kissing Vance on the cheek.

'Heard about your green door and needed to see it,' replied Vance. Everyone laughed except Randall James, who felt like a third arm. Ever so politely, he excused himself. Apart from that, he had a rendezvous with a nineteen-year-old stripper he and a few of his mates had met at a "club" they'd visited the previous week. He knew the others had not had her yet. Randall wanted to be the first cab off the rank, so to speak.

"Never let an opportunity go by" was his motto. Where women were concerned, Randall's appetite was insatiable. Fortunately, they usually pursued him, which made his life easier. He didn't have to buggerise around with bullshit preliminaries.

'Tell me what's been happening,' said Vance after Randall's departure.

'Maggie, get me another Bourbon,' said KD.

'I should tell you to get the bastard yourself,' snapped Maggie as she snatched his glass off the table.

'Mr D can tell you, ex-Boss,' said TC. 'I have to finish in the kitchen.'

'Don't take too long!' instructed Vance.

'I'll be as fast as I can,' promised TC.

§

'That's about it,' finished KD as TC returned to the dining room.

'That's about what, Mr D?' smiled TC.

'You,' replied KD, 'Jake, the motel full of men, and the new green door.' TC noticed the glass coffee pot was empty.

'Want more coffee, ex-Boss?' she enquired.

'I'll get it. You sit down,' from Maggie. 'Callahan drinks more coffee than KD, and I drink more booze combined.' Vance laughed.

'That's because I'm pretending it's Rum and Coke, Maggie. I used to throw those over pretty damned fast.'

'While you're at it, Maggie, I'll have another Bourbon,' said KD. 'I'm thirsty tonight.'

'Why aren't I surprised!' replied Maggie. 'I may as well pour myself another Scotch while I'm at it.'

'What about you, TC?' asked Vance with a smirk. 'Would you like a Bourbon or Scotch?'

'Not at this stage of my life, thank you. Who would look after Mr D and Maggie if they happened to get out of hand?' Vance leaned back in this chair, clasped his hands behind his head, and laughed.

'Like I used to, Butterball?' TC instantly recalled the "hide the money, no matter what, don't give me any" incident and a hundred or so others.

'No, I'd have to strangle them if they got that bad,' replied TC seriously.

'You'd have a tough time strangling me, Carmichael,' said KD. 'Look at you; you're not big enough to strangle a bloody flea.'

'I'd wait until you were asleep, Mr D,' replied TC

'Yes, you old bastard, and I'd bloody well help her,' said Maggie.

'That's enough, children,' laughed Vance. 'Talking about children, how is yours, Butterball?' KD laughed.

'He missed your dancing, Vance.'

'Junior is fine,' said Maggie. 'Too bloody old for his age.'

'Must take after his mother,' smiled Vance.

'That's because he is around adults all the time,' said KD seriously. 'Little lad needs to mix with his own age group.'

¶

Two Bourbons later KD announced he was going to bed. 'Great to see you again, Vance. Wish I could stay and talk, but I have to get up at four. Suggest you go to bed, as well, Maggie. You've had enough grog for tonight.'

'You mind your own bloody business, you bossy old bastard,' replied

Maggie. Vance laughed. Maggie reminded him very much of Louise Swagg, about whom he had not thought of for years.

'Yes, Maggie, you should call it a night. You are the cook. I'll expect breakfast before I leave at daybreak.' Maggie checked the wall clock.

'Tell you what, Callahan; you're a mercenary bastard. I'm out of here.' Vance once again clasped his hands behind his head, leaned back, and sighed.

'See you in the morning, Maggie.'

'Unfortunately, yes, Callahan!' replied Maggie as she stood up, swayed on her feet, and said, 'I'm telling you now, you bastard, if you don't eat every morsel I cook for you, I'll hold you down and SHOVE it in your mouth.'

'I look forward to that, Maggie,' laughed Vance as Maggie headed for her bedroom.

'How is the shop going, ex-Boss?' enquired TC.

'I hate the bloody thing, Butterball,' replied Vance abruptly. 'I'm a retired drunk and opal miner. Can't say I care too much for the plasticity, which obviously goes with retailing crap. I hate myself because I allowed a bastard named Fred to con me into giving him managerial rights. I've observed him in the shop. He's as smooth as silk with the few customers who have so far darkened the doorstep. Tells them his name is Fred Brolga. People believe him! When not in the shop, he parades around in the shortest shorts imaginable; cheeks of his arse are visible beneath the hemline. I know the prick is going to rob me. Problem is I don't when or how. Not only that, there's a Japanese woman there; her name is Chikako. She's driving me crazy. As if I haven't got my hands full enough, TC.'

TC said nothing. After a minute or so of deep thinking, she slowly shook her head, then sighed.

'You have always thought with your appendage, ex-Boss. I suggest you tuck it in and keep it under control where Chikako is concerned. If you have to give Fred Brolga a few thousand to rid yourself of him, so what! By the way, I'm at a crucial stage in my life, too. Wouldn't hurt you to ask how I am.'

Vance folded his arms and looked at TC.

'I'm sorry, Little One, I'm sorry.'

TC shook her head. 'No, you're not, ex-Boss. Doesn't matter, anyway. What will be will be.'

'I don't like Randall James, TC,' said Vance.

'Neither do I,' replied TC.

'Be careful of him,' instructed Vance.

'Just like I suggested you tuck it in where Chikako is concerned,' replied TC.

'It's do as I say, not do as I do, Butterball.'

'I know!' replied TC. 'One set of rules for you, the opposite for me.'

Vance cupped his forehead in his hands. 'I want you to be perfect, TC.'

'No one is perfect, ex-Boss!' replied TC softly. 'You expect too much. I'm scared witless by Jake. His drinking buddies range from politicians to thugs. He's capable of anything.'

'I know he is, TC,' agreed Vance. 'Don't be here when he comes back. Take your kid and get to buggery out. Maggie can handle Jake.'

'It's not easy, ex-Boss' replied TC despondently.

'Nothing in life is easy, Little One,' from Vance. 'We have to take each day as it comes.'

'You said you needed to talk with me about some things? What is it? What are they?' replied TC.

'Marla and Andrew are dead set on getting married,' replied Vance. 'I think it's wrong, but who am I to talk? Haven't exactly led the perfect life. I'm going now. I'm going to Brolga.'

Vance got to his feet, reached into his pocket, counted three ten-dollar notes and one twenty-dollar note, placed them on the table, smiled, and said, 'Give these to your sister, Maggie, for getting up early to cook me breakfast. See you when I see you.' A kiss on the cheek and he was gone.

⁋

Maggie, who was not yet asleep, heard Vance reverse out of the motel courtyard and drive north on the highway, got out of bed, and joined

TC in the dining room.

'Callahan tricked and stiffed me, TC. Bastard has gone. I heard his car leave.' TC laughed and shook her head.

'He left you fifty dollars for getting up early, Maggie.'

'Mad bastard,' said Maggie as she went to the kitchen to pour a whisky on ice.

As always, TC followed Vance's instructions. When Jake came to the motel on Friday, neither her son nor herself were anywhere to be seen. Maggie met Jake on the verandah outside the laundry.

'Where the hell is TC?' demanded Jake.

'She's not here, Jake,' replied Maggie. 'Take your gear and go, Jake. Nobody here wants any more trouble.' Jake packed his car, told Maggie to get stuffed, and sped off. Occasionally, I wish I could just do that,' thought Maggie.

A couple of weeks later, TC returned to the Pink Brolga after a trip to the bank. She was white and trembling from shock and disbelief.

'TC, what on earth is wrong with you?' enquired a concerned Maggie. TC sat down at the kitchen table and cupped her face in her hands.

'Jake has cleaned me out, Maggie. I went to the bank to cash a cheque for five thousand dollars. The young teller looked at me, then went to get the accountant. He invited me into his office and told me I had only one dollar in each of the five accounts.'

'You have to be bloody joking,' said Maggie.

'I'm not joking, Maggie! Jake took the lot!'

'How much is "the lot", TC?' demanded Maggie. TC hadn't asked the bank accountant how much was involved. She had been in too much shock, so didn't have a clue.

'How on earth would I know, Maggie? A lot! He's taken it all. I now have a five-thousand-dollar overdraft, whatever the hell an overdraft is. If I didn't have my son, I'd find Jake, bash him to death with a rum bottle, then do myself in.'

'Don't be so bloody ridiculous,' snapped Maggie. 'Wake up to yourself, TC, the bastard isn't worth it.'

'I have to call the boss,' replied TC.

After what seemed an eternity, TC was relieved to hear Vance's voice.

'What's the problem, TC?'

'The problem is Jake has taken all the money,' replied TC. 'Has left one dollar in every account, including that of the motel, of which he owns only a quarter. I've taken an overdraft for five thousand to keep the place going.'

'So, Jake hasn't only ripped you off, he's ripped me, too,' replied Vance.

'Looks like it!' agreed TC. Vance began laughing.

'I suppose I do owe the bastard for helping me burn down my house. I'll send you some opal. Sell it, TC. This time you'll get your twenty-five percent.'

'How are you going to send it, ex-Boss?' enquired TC.

'I beg your pardon. Think you should refer to me as "Boss" again,' laughed Vance. 'Don't worry how I get it there. It will be there.'

❡

Three days later, Vance delivered the stones himself. As usual, he looked like a refugee from red-dust hell.

'Here you go, Little One, take these wherever and sell them,' he said casually as if he'd driven only one mile instead of a thousand to deliver them. 'You go on your way tomorrow; I'll stay here nights until you come back. Days I'll go and see Fred, Chikako, and company.'

'Tell me you are staying here nights because you love my bloody cooking, Callahan,' said Maggie from the kitchen door.

'Something like that, Maggie,' laughed Vance. 'Where's your kid, TC?'

'I took Mr D's advice,' replied TC. 'Two days a week he's with children his own age in a kindergarten a couple of blocks away.'

541

'Sounds great to me. Go on, make your arrangements,' said Vance. 'Maggie, how about a coffee?'

TC thought, then looked at the clock, went to the office, and dialled Sammy L's New York number.

'Hello, Sammy L,' said TC.

'TC, where have you been all this time?' replied Sammy L.

'How did you know it was me, Sammy?' laughed TC.

'I'd know your voice anywhere. You could never rob a bank,' replied Sammy L.

'I'm down on my luck again, Sammy. Any chance you need some boulder opal?'

'I sure do, TC. There's been a rush on it. I lost contact with you. When are you coming?' said Sammy L.

'I won't come to see you this time, Sammy. Perhaps I can send the opal to you. You select what you want and return the rest,' replied TC.

'I'll take a hundred thousand, TC. Send the stones you like. If you like them, I'll like them. List them at a quarter of the real cost, save me money on import fees.' TC laughed.

'Whatever you say, Sammy. I'll call you when I've mailed the parcel.' Sammy L laughed, too.

'Write me a letter, TC. Tell me what's been happening.'

'Consider it done, Sammy,' replied TC. 'Thank you, Sammy! I hope I sound grateful enough.'

'Anytime, TC. Apart from that, I need opal. I'll make money, you'll make money, and everyone is happy.'

TC breathed a sigh of relief as she put down the telephone. She knew she would soon have twenty-five thousand, in U.S. dollars, at that. Didn't have a clue what the exchange rate was. Didn't care.

I hope the boss has brought enough stones, she thought as she returned to the dining room, where Vance was drinking coffee and chatting with Maggie.

'Sammy L will take a hundred thousand, Boss. He asked me to select the stones for him and we have to list them at quarter price.'

Vance's mouth fell open as he placed his coffee cup on the table and looked at TC in disbelief. 'How much discount did you offer him?'

'None. He knows we'll do the right thing,' replied TC. Vance smiled.

'You mean he knows *you* will do the right thing. The man has never met me.'

'Get the stones on the table, Boss. On behalf of Sammy L in New York I need to buy some.'

'In-bloody-credible!' said Maggie. 'I'll leave you to it.'

'I warn you, I'm going to be a discerning buyer, Boss,' warned TC as Vance spilled stones onto the table.

⁋

By the end of the next week, TC had done a trip south and Sammy had received, loved, and paid for his shipment. Vance surrendered to Chikako's relentless pursuit, then hightailed it for Brolga due to self-disgust. After confessing to TC per telephone how hopelessly weak he still was where women were concerned, he asked the inevitable question.

'How did you go, TC?' asked Vance with little, if any, interest.

'Sold everything except four stones, all cash. Sammy's money came in four lots. What do you want me to do?' replied TC.

'Take your twenty-five percent, shove the rest in a sugar bag, and throw it under your bed,' instructed Vance. 'I couldn't care less about anything other than a means of controlling my dick at the moment. Well done. I'll see you when I see you.'

'Why the bloody hell can't you use a bloody pillowcase?' demanded Maggie when TC went in search of a sugar bag.

'Because the boss told me to put it in a sugar bag, Maggie,' replied TC. Maggie threw arms into the air and rolled her eyes.

'That's it! Do as you are told. Callahan snaps his fingers and TC jumps to attention.'

'Maggie, go cook dinner and mind your own damned business,' suggested TC firmly.

⁋

By dinner rush time Vance's four stones and money were safely stashed under TC's bed in a washed and dried bag acquired from a greengrocer's a block away. TC now had over fifty thousand dollars of her own, which she had hidden in a pillowcase under Junior's bed. Along with the money, she also had her opals and specimens kept in the lounge room.

The Pink Brolga and its inhabitants kept Maggie, TC, and a housemaid busy, busy, busy. Junior became more and more a "star" with the crew members. Mr D doted on him. He would pull Junior into line when necessary. That wasn't too often because the kid was afraid of Cranky Mr D.

Apart from one young man, the crew were all married. Randall James and one other were in the process of divorce.

At mine number one Neil, Little Joe, and Yappy continued on. They had lost more than a little heart since Faith had gone. Only reason they continued was for Vance.

'Vance rescued us from shitsville,' said Neil. 'Think we should stick with the bastard.'

'I bloody agree with that,' said Yappy.

'Me, too,' said Little Jo.

At mines two and three, Vance's other rescuees felt the same. They loathed the so-called managers but stuck there for Vance.

TC heard nothing from Vance. Under her bed in the sugar bag was a hundred and sixty-nine thousand dollars in cash and four opals. She checked every day to make certain the bag was still there and hoped

Vance would show up soon to relieve her of the responsibility. It was a worry!

Early one afternoon TC was in the laundry folding sheets with the housemaid when Maggie screamed from the dining room door.

'TC, come here now! Hurry!'

TC dropped her end of the half-folded sheet. She ran along the verandah to the dining room to see mostly fifty-dollar notes floating around the room. They were propelled by the ceiling fans, which were whirling at top speed. Junior was sitting on the floor, somewhat enthralled by four small plastic packets, each containing an opal. TC didn't know whether to laugh or cry as she watched Vance's money flying all over the place and heard her son saying repeatedly, 'Opal pretty, Mama,' while Maggie stood still in disbelief.

'For heaven's sake, turn the fans off, Maggie. What the bloody hell happened?'

Maggie quickly switched off the fans and replied, 'Junior was playing with his cars; I was in the kitchen. Next thing, I came out and found this.'

Money was everywhere—under the dining room tables, in the office, on the landing, in the motel's front garden barbeque area, and some notes had found their way into the kitchen and bathroom. After what seemed an eternity, Maggie and TC located all but a hundred and twenty dollars.

'Maggie, please go and help the girl finish folding the sheets,' said TC. 'When finished, tell her she can go for the day. I have to phone the boss.'

'When are you coming to collect your money, Mr Callahan?' demanded TC.

'What's the problem, Little One? Why are you calling me Mr Callahan? As far as I know, I've done nothing of late to upset you,' replied Vance. Vance laughed when TC explained what had happened. 'So where's my hundred and twenty dollars?'

'Probably blew onto the highway. Don't worry, I'll make it good!' replied TC. It was a long silence before Vance spoke.

'That's the least of my worries. I sent Fred Brolga a parcel of stones and he was stupid or smart enough to let some bastard piss off with them. I'll see you in a few days. Know what, Little One? Sometimes I wish I was still a rum-swilling, chain-smoking, pill-pusher. Life seemed simple then!'

'I know what you mean, Boss,' said TC. 'I'll see you when I see you.'

¶

TC was surprised when Keith Dalton whirled his Chevrolet into the motel courtyard much earlier than usual that afternoon.

'Where are you, Carmichael?' he called form the dining room doorway.

'I'm here, Mr D. What is wrong?' replied TC emerging from the bathroom where she had been bathing Junior.

'I want Vance's phone number, Carmichael,' said Mr D. 'Some bastard who calls himself Fred Brolga has been trying to trade opals for a car at my mate's dealership. I think he's the same prick Vance told me about.'

'Sorry, Mr D, the boss is in transit. He'll probably be here in a few days.'

'Give me the bloody number, Carmichael,' demanded Mr D.

'Here it is. You know where the phone is,' replied TC indifferently as she quickly wrote the number. 'I have to go and make sure my child hasn't drowned.'

'Don't be like that, Carmichael,' said KD in his usual dominant manner.

TC shrugged, looked back over her shoulder, and smiled. 'Nothing surprises me anymore, Mr D.'

'What on earth is wrong with you, Carmichael?' demanded KD as he followed TC to the bathroom.

'Every bloody thing is wrong for her, you old bastard,' said Maggie, who appeared from the kitchen. 'Leave the poor little bugger alone! I suggest you sit your arse down and I'll tell you the bits I know of what is wrong with my sister.'

'I'm listening, Maggie!' replied KD impatiently as he pulled up a chair.

'Jake cleaned TC out financially. They had five bank accounts. The bastard left her with a dollar in each one. Today Junior found Callahan's money under her bed. It was flying everywhere. Jake forged TC's signature and cashed in her quarter-of-a-million life insurance policy. He also forged her signature to sell the bloody boat. She spends all bloody day cleaning rooms, washing, and ironing. When you and your mob come to eat, she has to put on a happy face, listen to every bastard's bullshit, and ignore Randy James' unspoken approaches. Unless you haven't noticed, Jake has a couple of his low-life mates parked opposite this joint every night. The latest is the bastard wants to take Junior away from her.'

'When is Callahan coming, Maggie?' asked KD as he got to his feet.

'How the bloody hell do I know?' replied Maggie. 'He probably doesn't know himself!'

'We'll have a drink and a talk after dinner, Maggie,' said KD before hitting the steps, jumping in his Chevy, and blasting off down the highway.

That night, KD and Maggie went to a nearby pub to discuss their mutual concern for TC's and Junior's wellbeing.

TC was surprised when she heard Mr D say, 'Come on, Maggie, I'll buy you a few Scotches at a pub tonight. I'm tired of drinking here. Don't ask me if it's a date, woman. If you do, you'll have to buy your own grog.'

'Don't fight, children,' laughed TC.

'It's difficult not to fight with your sister,' said KD.

'Same goes for you, you old bastard,' snapped Maggie.

Over a few drinks KD and Maggie agreed the best they could do was keep their already-close, protective attitude towards TC and allow her to make her own decisions. They would keep their lips zipped unless they considered her decisions wrong for her.

¶

During his drive east, Vance came to the conclusion he had to let Fred Brolga go. He didn't trust the man! Next thing I know, the bastard will open in opposition to me, thought Vance. Japanese tourists were flocking to the shop; money was rolling in. He appointed Chikako as the new manager of his retail business, knowing in his heart he'd made a mistake. 'Will I ever learn?' he asked himself before reasoning that Chikako was Japanese. She thought the same way the customers did.

Chikako expressed jealously when Vance told her he was going to see TC, that he had to collect some opals. Like all Vance's women, once they had experienced sexual intimacy with him, in their minds he belonged to them.

'I'm coming with you, Vance!' demanded Chikako in her deep, almost masculine voice. Vance laughed.

'Don't be so bloody ridiculous. I'm going to see TC on business.'

'I'm not stupid, Vance! I saw how you were when she didn't come to the opening,' said Chikako.

'I'm going, Chikako! Do your job and mind your own damned business,' replied Vance. He was angry. Vance picked up the telephone and dialled the Pink Brolga. Maggie answered.

'Maggie! Just the girl I wanted,' laughed Vance. 'How about throwing a roast on for dinner. I'll be there around seven.'

'All right, Callahan. Should have known you weren't calling me to tell me you miss me. Be on time. If you're not, you'll wear the bastard roast instead of eating it.' Vance laughed.

'Believe me, Maggie, with that threat hanging over my head, I'll be punctual.'

¶

Vance was there. He almost ran into the dining room, where TC was setting a table and Junior was stringing his guitar, which appeared to be twice the size of the child. Much to TC's surprise, Vance was carrying a huge bunch of yellow roses.

'Don't tell me you bought me flowers, Boss! Wonders will never cease!' said TC. Vance smiled.

'They aren't for you! I brought them for Maggie!'

'What's for Maggie?' called a voice from the kitchen.

'Come and see, "elephant ears",' laughed Vance. 'Bring a big vase with you.' Maggie burst into tears when Vance thrust the roses at her.

'These are for the best roast cook in the world, Maggie,' said Vance. 'What's for dessert?'

'You, you mad bastard, if you don't let me hug you,' whimpered Maggie.

'Come on, then. Hurry up,' laughed Vance as he stretched out his arms.

'Why are you crying, Auntie Maggie?' asked Junior with great concern.

'That's right, Maggie! You not only get roses, you get a hug as well,' said TC feigning hurt. 'I don't even get a peck on the cheek.' Maggie stepped back from Vance, pointed to a square plastic dressing on his neck, and laughed.

'Did a large mosquito bite you, Callahan?' Vance cracked up.

'More like a vampire, Maggie. Last night was a rough one.'

'Why are you setting only one table, Little One?' enquired Vance after he finally pecked her on the cheek.

'You chose a good night, Boss,' replied TC. 'Apart from Mr D and Randy James, everyone else is going over the border to play poker machines and whatever else they do.'

'Your opals are pretty, Mr Callahan,' said Junior from the floor. 'Mama and Auntie Maggie found your money. They ran around and made me laugh.'

'Talking of money, Boss, I want you to count it now,' said TC as she passed the sugar bag to Vance. 'I've replaced the hundred and twenty. Suggest you count it in the kitchen in case any of the men wander in for one reason or another.'

'Come on, Callahan,' invited Maggie, who had finished arranging the roses to her satisfaction. 'I'll make you fresh coffee.'

'Maggie, you're my kind of woman,' laughed Vance. Bag under his arm, he followed Maggie to the kitchen.

¶

When KD told Randy James that Vance would be there, Randy decided he'd join his work mates and go over the border with them. He knew there was no point in pitching for TC when Vance was around. Vance was too protective.

That bastard can see right through me, thought Randy. I can see through him, too. We're the same. Both love women, any size, any shape, anywhere.

¶

Over dinner, KD told Vance about Fred Brolga approaching the Chevy dealer to trade an opal for a car.

'Probably your opal or your money paid for it,' said Mr D.

'I agree, Keith,' said Vance. 'Doesn't matter anymore; I fired the prick. Why isn't Randy James here?' Everyone laughed.

'I think he's frightened of you, Boss,' replied TC. 'Birds of a feather, you know the deal.'

'I need a coffee, Maggie,' smiled Vance.

'Eat your roast, Callahan,' replied Maggie. 'Then you can have a coffee. After that, you'll eat your dessert, then you can have as many coffees as your little heart desires.'

The second coffee after dessert and Vance abruptly declared he was leaving for Brolga, shook hands with KD, hugged Maggie, pecked TC on the cheek, and he was gone.

'That was sudden,' commented KD.

'I know the boss, Mr D,' said TC. 'He suddenly thought of something he needs to do back in Brolga.'

'Hope the darling bastard comes up with a credible excuse for the vampire bite on his neck,' added Maggie. 'By the way, TC, Callahan left the hundred and twenty we lost to the highway. It's in the kitchen. He said to tell you to buy a pair of stilettos.'

¶

Days turned into weeks, and time seemed to fly by.

'I'm thinner than I've ever been,' laughed Maggie. 'Between guarding Junior and cooking for the mob, I don't have time for any other bloody thing. If weight keeps falling off me, I'll need a new wardrobe.' TC immediately extracted a thousand dollars from the pillowcase under Junior's bed and gave it to her sister.

'Buy yourself some new clothes, Maggie.'

'Don't be so bloody ridiculous!' said Maggie. 'You already buy my grog and food and house me.' TC smiled and shook her head.

'It's not enough, Maggie! If I didn't have you here to babysit and cook, I wouldn't be able to do my trips for the boss. In future, whatever you need, you'll get.'

¶

Jake won his way regarding Junior. He had an old school mate who was a lawyer. Jake got Junior every second weekend. Junior didn't want to go and would cry every second Friday when told his father was coming to collect him. Both TC and Maggie always wound up crying with him.

His grandmother, Thel Carmichael, was beside herself with concern for her grandchild. Nothing anyone could do!

Late on a Saturday morning when TC was at the end of a trip south, Maggie and the housemaid were shopping for motel provisions and all guests were working on the airstrip. Jake put Junior through his open bedroom window at the motel.

'Go on, mate,' urged Jake. 'Climb on a chair and open the door for me.' Junior did as instructed by his father, who took anything and everything of value he could find. His loot included TC's stones and specimens. Jake had one of his mates keep watch as he packed his car in front of the office.

Maggie, with the housemaid, drove around the motel corner as Jake pulled out of the courtyard, saw them, and, as per Jake of old, jammed his foot on the accelerator. It didn't worry him Junior was in the car with him.

TC arrived home late afternoon. 'At least the bastard didn't take the cash from under Junior's bed,' said Maggie after explaining the chain of events and circumstances.

'Only because he didn't know it was there, Maggie,' sighed TC in disbelief and utter bewilderment. 'I'd best put the money in the bank. There's even more after this trip.'

'Why don't you hire some bastard to drown Jake Carmichael in the effing ocean, TC?' said Maggie, doing a Con Kara deal by throwing her arms into the air.

'Because Jake's not worth it, Maggie,' replied TC in a whisper.

'Call Callahan, TC,' suggested Maggie.

'The boss doesn't need to know about this, Maggie,' replied TC. 'What's done is done!'

¶

Sammy L had TC select two more large parcels for him. He didn't bother pushing for discount; he was doing fine with the prices he paid.

¶

Numerous females called the Pink Brolga every night. The men were in great demand. Keith Dalton and Randall James were obviously the most popular. They both gave TC instructions to tell their callers they were not there.

'If I want a woman, I'll call her,' said KD.

'I have a self-imposed rule never to see the same woman twice,' said Randall.

'Unless it takes you more than one "go" to get your way with her, Randy,' quipped one of the men. Everyone laughed except Randy.

¶

On completion of stage one of the airstrip, the men went on two weeks' leave and flew off in different directions all over the continent.

During the first couple of days, TC and the housemaid detailed every unit. Then TC told the housemaid to take a break until the men returned. TC was surprised when the housemaid burst into tears and confessed she'd been having an affair with one of the men and was now heartbroken because he'd gone home to see his wife and children.

'I'll pretend you didn't tell me about this,' said TC with compassion. 'Off you go. I'll call you when the men start arriving back.'

'Now the mob have gone, TC, tell Callahan to come and get his money,' said Maggie. 'I'm sick and tired of watching you worry about it, check on it, shift it from place to place, and sometimes sleep with it.'

'Of course, I'm worried about the boss' money, Maggie,' replied TC. 'After Junior finding the sugar bag under my bed and Jake stealing my opals, I'm paranoid!'

'Tell the bastard I'll cook him a roast,' said Maggie. 'That should get him here!'

'The Boss will be here night after tomorrow, Maggie,' advised TC after making the call. 'He said to tell you not to expect yellow roses this time because you invited him.'

'Smart bastard!' laughed Maggie.

Vance arrived all smiles. He was early by a couple of hours.

'Straight from the bush, Maggie!' he said when Maggie commented on his appearance.

'Doesn't matter, I'll hug you, anyway, Callahan,' replied Maggie. 'Bit of red dirt never hurt any of us.' Vance laughed.

'Heard a song about Maggie on the car radio a few minutes ago. Sounded like she was a tough, old bird just like you.' Maggie laughed, too.

'Never judge a book by its cover, Callahan.'

'Where's TC? Where's Junior?' asked Vance.

'They went for a walk. Your money is in the kitchen. Thank heavens, you've come to collect it,' replied Maggie. 'Come on, I'll make you fresh coffee while you count it. You can get yourself cleaned up before dinner.'

'Yes, Boss, whatever you say,' laughed Vance, giving a mock salute. 'You've lost weight, Maggie,' remarked Vance as he followed Maggie into the kitchen.

'Who wouldn't lose weight in this place,' replied Maggie matter-of-factly. 'My clothes were falling off me. TC gave me a thousand dollars to buy new ones that fit. She said if it wasn't for me being here, she wouldn't be able to do trips.' Vance smiled. 'Here's your money,' said Maggie as she opened a cupboard and pulled out a taped-all-over-the-place cushion cover containing Vance's cash, half a dozen or so opals, and stock list.

§

Vance finished counting after drinking two coffees while Maggie was busy preparing cooking for dinner. He thought momentarily before placing the last rubber-banded bundle of ten thousand in the cushion cover, then turned to Maggie while extracting one thousand from the top.

'Here, Maggie, build on your new wardrobe. Everything goes two ways, Maggie. If it wasn't for you looking after Junior and this joint, I wouldn't be here counting this money.' Maggie was in shock, then procrastination. When tears began glimmering, Vance smiled.

'Think I'll get myself cleaned up now, Maggie!'

§

A red-dust-free, straight-from-the-bush version of Vance stood by the motel's laundry door chatting with Maggie when TC and Junior returned from their walk.

'Did you forget I was coming, Butterball?' called Vance.

'How could she bloody forget that!' said Maggie as she removed Vance's now dust-free clothes from the washing machine and threw them into the dryer.

'Mother took me for a walk, Mr Callahan,' complained Junior seeking sympathy. 'I have to wait while people talk to her.'

'Mothers are like that, mate,' said Vance with pretend sympathy as he patted Junior's shoulder, then kissed TC on the cheek.

'Good to see you, Little One.'

'You, too, Boss!' smiled TC. 'Did Maggie give you your money? Sorry I didn't sell everything. There were a few stones left over.'

'Come on, Junior,' said Maggie, 'We'll get you bathed, fed, and in bed before Cranky Mr D comes for dinner. In the meantime, Mother and Mr Callahan can have a talk.'

'Don't worry about me, Maggie,' said Vance when they entered the dining room. 'I'll get my own coffee.'

'Too right you bloody will, Callahan,' replied Maggie over her shoulder as she propelled Junior towards the bathroom.

§

'How are you Little One?' asked Vance after pouring himself a coffee and they were both seated at the kitchen table.

'Not good, Boss,' replied TC after a few seconds of silence. 'I think I'm becoming attracted to Randy James. At first it was because his looks remind me of Graham's. Now it's because he makes me laugh. Randy could never be the wonderful person Graham was, hopefully still is. I'm not stupid, Boss. I'm still sure Randy James has the same effect on all women as he has on me. Don't worry, I'm awake to him, Boss. How are things going with you and your women?'

'Don't ask, Little One!' replied Vance. 'You know what I'm like! Somehow I have to do something about Almut. She's making a play for Jonathon. I feel like wringing her effing throat. The bitch sucks up to Delores every chance she gets, struts around half-naked whenever Jonathon is around. Without uttering a word, dares me with her glares to do anything except shut my mouth, sit back, tolerate, and see what happens.'

'Almut always strutted around half-naked, Boss,' reflected TC. 'Now she realises she can't get you, she's going after Jonathon.'

§

Halfway through dinner KD, excused himself. 'I'll be back in a few minutes. There's something I have to do,' he said. True to his word he soon returned, all smiles.

'Sorry about that. I felt I needed to tell Jake's mates to quit their surveillance of the joint till the mob comes back. Nothing here to see except us!'

'What was their reaction, Keith?' enquired Vance.

'They heeded my advice and took off,' replied KD. 'Now I suggest we continue doing justice to Maggie's roast and everything that goes with it.'

TC surprised even herself by saying, 'When the airstrip is finished, I want to sell this place, Boss. I want to go as far away from Jake Carmichael as possible.' After what seemed an eternity, Maggie broke the silence.

'Come on, eat! Our tucker is getting cold. I didn't go to all this trouble for my health!'

Between roast and Maggie's illustrious "meant to impress Vance" dessert, TC and Maggie were in the kitchen while Vance and KD talked in the dining room. As usual, Vance drank coffee and KD a Bourbon.

'How is TC holding up, Keith?' asked Vance.

'Her suntan is beginning to look good,' replied KD lightly.

'I noticed,' laughed Vance. 'I mean, how is she?'

'You know Jake pinched her opal? Put Junior through his bedroom window and told the lad to open the door.' Vance threw back his chair and began pacing around the dining room. He was furious.

'No, Keith! She neglected to tell me about that incident. Where was TC?'

'On a trip for you. It's not your fault, Vance,' replied KD as he lifted his glass of Bourbon to sip from it. 'Along with her opal, the bastard took everything else of value he could lay his hands on. Thank heavens, she was smart enough to hang the paintings in the units, and he didn't know about her money under Junior's bed.'

'You don't know how hard she worked to get that opal, Keith,' said Vance in disgust as he resumed sitting. 'Poor little bugger was pregnant, working in a tin shed! At times, the heat was effing terrible.'

'Yesterday's crap, Vance,' said KD. 'From my observations, Randall James is beginning to gain ground with Carmichael. He's a silver-tongued bastard! He makes her laugh every chance he gets. The other men call him Randy because he struts around with a perpetual hard-on.' Vance spat coffee all over the tablecloth, then laughed.

'Bloody hell, Keith, I think you just described me.'

'Forget it!' said KD. 'I suppose Carmichael deserves some laughter in her life. I know she didn't get much with Jake.'

'What are you two up to?' demanded Maggie from the kitchen doorway. 'Want more coffee before dessert, Callahan?'

'Yes, and I think Keith needs another Bourbon,' laughed Vance. 'After the money I spent on those roses last time I was here, I expect speedy service.'

'Both of you can go to buggery,' said Maggie. 'I'll be there when I'm ready! By the way, KD, Callahan gave me a thousand bucks today.'

¶

Later KD drove off to the nearest pub to secure another bottle of Bourbon before closing time, and Maggie went to the laundry to iron Vance's shirt and blue jeans. Vance and TC were left alone.

'Did you mean what you said about going away, Little One?' asked Vance.

'Yes, Boss, I did,' replied TC.

'Where will you go?'

'I don't know. As far away from Jake as I can, while still remaining in Australia, Boss. Not sure how I'll do it. All I know is I will do it!'

'Andrew and Marla are getting married, TC. I want you to be there. They want you there, too. I'm inviting you now. No space for repetition of the shop opening.'

'Promise, I'll be there, Boss,' smiled TC. 'Give Andrew my love.'

'A few days after I left here last time, I fired one of my mine managers, TC. Too many Bert Blacks in this world.'

'I knew something was wrong, Boss.'

'Little One, there's always something wrong,' replied Vance. 'Money brings out the worst in most people. It happened to me for a while. It took Faith's death to bring me back to reality.'

❡

The first Sunday barbeque after the crew returned, TC realised most of the crew had girlfriends. They brought them as guests. Only Mr D, his son, Anton, who was a new recruit, another young, fresh starter, and Randy James were unaccompanied by a female.

'Hope we have enough food, Maggie,' said TC anxiously as she looked out over the seemingly sea of faces in the barbeque area.

'Don't worry, TC' replied Maggie. 'The bastards are all on the piss. If we are short on steaks, sausages, and rissoles, I'll fill them up on corned beef sandwiches. In future they'll have to tell us when they are bringing their floosies.'

'None of our business, Maggie,' said TC.

'It's my bloody business, TC. I'm the poor bitch who has to cater for them,' replied Maggie. 'Help me by taking those trays outside. While you're at it, ask KD or lover-boy Randy to start cooking. I'll need you here to make another fruit salad.'

Maggie was right. There was ample food because most were too busy drinking, flirting, and laughing while Bob Seger and his Silver Bullet Band belted out songs in the background. From that night on, Maggie was pre-warned of extras attending dinners and barbeques. Maggie's other rule was she also would like to be advised if anyone was not going to be eating or was going to be eating late.

❡

TC and Maggie warmed to Anton Dalton the instant they met him. He was twenty-one and a carbon copy of Mr D's wartime photograph of himself that he kept on a shelf in his unit.

A couple of months after Anton came to live and work with his dad, his father chastised him for not coming home for dinner and not telling Maggie he'd be late. She had put a meal aside for him. Poor young Anton stood outside the dining room door. He looked dreadful, was unsteady on his feet, and gingerly called to TC.

'TC, it's Anton. I'm sorry I didn't get here on time.' TC opened the door.

'What's wrong, sweetie?'

'I'm drunk, TC. I feel sick. I drank too much alcohol, TC. I'm sorry! Tell Maggie I'll eat tonight's dinner tomorrow night if that's okay by her.' Maggie came to the door.

'You go to bed, darling. Don't worry about dinner. Wash your face, brush your teeth, and drink some water. If your dad starts on you again, tell the old bastard to see me.'

¶

Andrew and Marla married.

Vance delayed the ceremony for almost half an hour because TC was stupid enough to get lost. No matter which corner she turned, she couldn't find the church. When TC eventually did find the church, she manoeuvred her hired car into a "just fit" parking space opposite.

TC smiled inwardly as Vance, attired in a grey suit, white shirt, dark-grey tie, and shoes, raced across the road. He literally pulled her towards the white-gowned and veiled Marla plus entourage standing on the church porch. They were waiting to walk down the aisle.

'Do I look all right, Little One?' asked Vance urgently as TC and Marla were about to share a brief hug.

'Come on!' commanded Vance as he quickly preceded TC into the front pew, where he sat himself down alongside Delores, who was dressed elegantly and wore a frown.

Who could blame her!

You look great, Boss, thought TC. So does Mrs Callahan. Here comes the bride.

¶

Between then and when the airstrip was finished many things occurred, some humorous, some sad, and some dramatic.

'Emblazoned memories for as long as we live,' said Maggie.

'Never forget these times, Carmichael,' said Mr D.

'I love you but you are too hard to get,' said Randy James to TC many times. 'Maybe we'll meet again in another world.'

On the final day of airstrip construction, the crew partied as if there were no tomorrow. For the umpteenth time in almost two years, they were going home. This time for good!

'No point in cooking dinner tonight, TC,' said Maggie. 'Last day on the job, they'll be too busy getting pissed to eat.'

'Point taken, Maggie. Still, their company pays us to feed them; so we better have some food ready anyway.'

The end-of-the-job grog-up began at two in the afternoon. Around six, KD arrived at the Pink Brolga and announced to Maggie and TC in a somewhat disorientated manner, 'All the bastards are drunk. They'll be hungry, some of them, anyway, that is, if they haven't passed out or been arrested before they get here.'

'You sound funny, Cranky Mr D,' said Junior.

'I feel funny, too, lad,' replied KD. 'I'm going to bed.'

A few minutes later, the personnel carrier pulled into the courtyard, closely followed by Anton Dalton's almost-replica of his dad's Chevy. While men in the personnel carrier bus staggered willy-nilly to their units. Anton, followed by Randy James, stumbled to the dining room door. Maggie, Scotch-on-ice in hand, was on the other side of the door.

'Sorry, Maggie,' said Anton. 'I won't be eating dinner. I feel sick.'

'I'm sorry, too, Maggie,' mumbled Randy James. 'I think I ate a bad piece of pork. I need to throw up.'

TC and Junior stood beside Maggie as the three of them watched Anton and Randy make their way along to the far end of the verandah before throwing up, then collapsing under a huge garden gum tree.

'Stupid, drunken bastards, let them rot there,' said Maggie.

'No! No! No, Auntie Maggie, the wild animals will get Anton and Randy!' cried Junior before flinging the door open and racing along the verandah towards the gum tree and rescuing Anton and Randy.

'Junior has a lot to learn,' said Maggie.

'Let's hope he doesn't learn too soon, Maggie,' replied TC as she ran along the verandah after her son.

One by one, the crew said thanks and goodbye to Maggie, TC, and Junior. Maggie burst into tears when she opened a card containing four fifty-dollar notes. The card was signed by all the men and contained a handwritten message of thanks.

To Maggie (Best cook in the Universe),

Most of us wish we could take you home with us so you could teach our wives how to cook. Especially your condensed milk, banana cream, and crushed nut pie.

Thank you, Maggie.

Randy James was the last to say goodbye. He was immaculately attired and, as almost always, looked as if he had just completed a shoot in a Hollywood film.

'Hello, ladies! Couldn't leave without saying goodbye to the lovely TC and her sister. I'll remember you always as the one who got away, TC.' TC laughed.

'It wasn't easy, Randy! You are a slightly shorter version of a young man I knew years ago. First time I saw you, my heartbeat went wild. After observing you for a few weeks, I came to the conclusion that the only similarity between you and him is appearance. You are too much of a charmer, Randy. Worse still, you know it!' Randy smiled.

'You're too wide awake, TC! Pity! Maybe one day we'll meet again, one day when I'm more grown up and you are not so perceptive.'

'Get out of here, you gorgeous bastard,' said Maggie. Randy winked at TC, then was gone.

¶

Only Mr D and Anton remained after the airport runway construction workers left the Pink Brolga. Huge pink-on-black "For Sale" signs were erected on the highway and side-street footpaths alongside the motel.

TC and Maggie were sitting in the dining room reflecting on this and that when they heard a car suddenly brake on the highway, turn the corner, courtyard gravel flying every which way and brakes screeching opposite the office.

'Who the bloody hell!' said Maggie.

'I don't know!' replied TC. 'Whoever it is, they are obviously in a hurry.' Car door slammed, footsteps on the stairs, and Vance burst through the door.

'Maggie, make yourself scarce. I need to talk to TC.'

'Consider me gone, Vance,' said Maggie as she all but ran along the verandah towards the laundry.

'What on earth is the problem, Boss?' asked TC urgently. 'You look terrible! You're as white as a sheet!'

'I know, TC! I know! I know! I know!' he said as he fell to his knees and hugged TC's legs. Head on her lap, Vance began crying.

'What's wrong, Boss?' asked TC. 'I've never seen you like this!'

'Everything is wrong, Little One! Everything!' sobbed Vance. 'I was in the shop today. Chikako was hanging off me like a rat off a rope, gushing all over me when Anna walked in. Oh, shit, TC! I just about died when I saw her. I wanted to cry for what could have been. Anna and I looked each other in the eyes and smiled. We didn't speak to each other. We said nothing! What happened next was mind-blowing, TC. A younger version of me walked into the shop, put his arm around Anna, and said, 'Come on, Mum, seen enough,' and they left. He's my son! I don't even know his name! Not only that, TC, but Almut is after Jonathon. What on earth am I going to do about that?'

'I don't know, Boss. I don't know,' replied TC as she attempted to straighten Vance's wayward hair and wipe tears from his face.

'I know!' said Maggie from the doorway. 'Callahan needs a coffee.'

Junior appeared from the hallway adjoining his bedroom, where he'd been napping.

'Why are you crying, Mr Callahan?' he asked with wide-open eyes and obvious concern.

Vance jumped to his feet, blinked a few times, patted Junior on the head, and replied, 'I'm not crying, mate. Had dust in my eyes, that's all.'

When a private, top-dollar offer was submitted on the Pink Brolga a couple of weeks later, TC called Vance to tell him.

'Where are you planning to go? What are you going to do?' asked Vance after agreeing to the profitable offer on the motel.

'I've looked at the map of Australia, Boss,' replied TC. 'I'm going to Perth! I want to open an opal shop there! How about giving me a few stones on consignment?'

'No problem!' replied Vance before calmly putting down the telephone and thinking. He called TC a little later.

'Don't want you to open your own shop in Perth, TC. I'll put in twenty-five thousand and minimal stock if you open a Brolga Opals Perth retail shop, and I'll put you on twenty-five percent, as usual. Send me the paperwork on the motel so Delores and I can sign.'

'After Jake signs, Boss,' replied TC. 'I'm seeing him and his solicitor mate tomorrow.'

Next day TC looked at Jake in disbelief as his lawyer friend laid down the rules.

'Jake gets a quarter of the net sale price of the motel, he pays no maintenance for the child, who must attend a private Catholic college and, at your expense, TC, the said child must spend every second school holiday period with his father.

'This is wrong!' said TC, shaking her head. 'Jake bashed me in front of our son! He took all the money, my opal collection, forged my signature on my own insurance policy, sold the boat, and even took the car! I can't believe it!'

'Agree to Jake's requirements or you can't take the child interstate, TC,' said the lawyer factually without any emotion whatsoever.

'Consider it done,' said TC. 'Anything as long as my son doesn't grow up to be like his lying, stealing, mongrel, bastard father.'

Jake signed the paperwork on the motel transaction. TC signed it herself in front of Jake's lawyer. On the way back to the Pink Brolga, she mailed it to Vance by registered post.

You won again, Jake, thought TC as she left the post office and walked to the nearest cab rank.

TC asked Maggie if she would like to go to Perth in Western Australia with Junior and herself.

'No!' replied Maggie. 'I'm a Queenslander. I'll live and die here. If you want to do anything for me, buy me a caravan.'

'Consider it done, Maggie! You find the caravan and I'll buy it for you.'

'I'll start looking!' said Maggie excitedly. 'Bloody hell, I'm going to have something of my own.'

During dinner with Maggie, Mr D and Anton, TC was surprised when a Slim Dusty song came on the radio.

'Slim Dusty songs remind me of Brolga. Never heard one of his songs on this radio station before.' As Slim sang, "Lights coming over the hill are blinding me", TC thought of the truckies loading opposite Auntie Flo and Uncle Doug's house in what seemed like a hundred years ago, Lou, Graham, the police sergeant, Old Jess, Lisa, Con, and the men slumped against the wall behind the pharmacy. She became misty-eyed.

'That's you, Carmichael' said Mr D. 'Anton is out of here, heading in the direction of the North Sea off Scotland in the next few days. What about Maggie, minding Junior for a few days while you and I go and see Vance in Brolga?' KD looked across the table at Maggie for a nod of agreement. He got it!

'Come on, Carmichael, I'll drive you to Brolga. We'll see Callahan, his mines, and everyone, and anything else you want to see before heading west.'

'Sounds good, Mr D!' agreed TC. 'I'd like to see the men before I go away. I'll probably never get the opportunity again.'

❡

Anton sold his car and flew off to Scotland. Next morning before daylight, KD and TC left the Pink Brolga, heading west towards the end of the line. KD drove so fast that on one occasion TC demanded he stop the car so they could talk. KD screeched his car to a halt on the side of the road; TC jumped out, and slammed the car door behind her. KD did the same on the driver's side.

'What the bloody hell is wrong with you, Carmichael?' he yelled.

'You and your driving, Mr D!' TC yelled back. 'All right for you. Your children are all grown up as far as I know! My son is still a little boy. He's got no one but me! If you want to kill yourself, do it! I'd rather walk than die because of your death-wish, dangerous driving.' KD strode around his car a couple or three times before facing TC.

'I'll drive carefully and slower, Carmichael. If we are lucky, perhaps we'll get to Brolga Christmas after next! Okay?'

'Thank you, Mr D,' replied TC calmly before getting back into the car.

❡

'So, you finally get to see the pink outhouse, Little Flower,' said Yappy two days later when Vance surprised mine number one workers with a visit from TC. Of course, KD was there, too. Vance showed him around the site while TC enjoyed the attention of Yappy, Neil, and Little Jo.

565

'Doesn't seem the same seeing you men without Faith here with us,' said TC while they all squatted on haunches outside the illustrious pink toilet.

'Faith is here in spirit, Little Flower,' said Yappy. 'Vance made sure Faith got the best headstone on this bloody earth.'

'Vance also paid for the house my mum has rented since I was a kid,' said Neil. 'He bought it for her!'

'He also gave opal panels to the Catholic Church,' said Little Jo.

'He didn't give any to the Anglican mob,' said Yappy.

'That's probably because the Bush Brother didn't ask him for any,' retorted Neil in Vance's defence.

'He's helped a lot of people, Little Flower,' said Little Jo.

'I believe it!' said TC as she stood up. 'I'm going to Western Australia soon. I probably will not see you men again. I want to hug you all!' One by one, the men hugged TC and told her they would never forget her.

'I'll never forget you, either!' said TC. Against her will, she found herself crying. These were true-blue men. She knew she would not meet the likes of them very often in the future.

¶

While in Brolga, TC introduced Mr D to Jess via the Empire window, ate lunch with Lisa and Con at the café, saw Sam, called in on Lou's parents, and signed directorship papers of Vance's company, witnessed by KD.

After dinner with Vance and Delores, neither KD nor TC could wait to be on the road heading east. They wanted to be back at the Pink Brolga with Junior and Maggie.

'Brolga should be called Crapsville,' said KD as he drove his Chevy across the bridge over the creek.

'That's not fair, Mr D,' said TC. 'There are a lot of great people in Brolga. I'll remember them always.'

'Fair enough, Carmichael,' replied Mr D, who hit the accelerator as his Chevrolet hit the red dirt.

SUCCESS –
THE GOOD LIFE

In less than a month, the new owners took possession of the Pink Brolga, and Mr D moved to a motel opposite because he didn't want to live at the Pink Brolga if TC didn't own it. Maggie moved into a caravan park in her own caravan. TC and Junior headed west across the Nullarbor Plain in a sports car TC purchased from a friend. As TC drove into the hills east of Perth, she fiddled with the car radio dial.

'Welcome to 6iX,' said the radio announcer. 'Also welcome to the U.S. aircraft carrier group, which pulled into the Port of Fremantle today.'

Wish I had the shop open already, thought TC. Most Americans love opals. 'Have to catch you next time, my darlings,' she said aloud to herself.

'Catch who, Mother?' asked Junior.

'Some friends of ours, sweetie,' replied TC with a smile. 'First, we have to find somewhere to live, get you started in a nice school, and find you a nanny.'

'What is a nanny, mother?' asked Junior. TC smiled and ruffled Junior's blonde, curly hair.

'A nanny is someone like Auntie Maggie and grandma. She will love you, collect you from school, and take care of you while I find us a shop, then go to work.'

'I hope you find me a nanny I can love back, Mother,' said Junior, who was in ultra-serious mode.

'I'll make sure I do, darling,' replied TC with more confidence than she felt.

Half an hour or less later, TC and Junior were checking into a motel on Perth's Great Eastern Highway. They were no more than a hundred yards from the beautiful Swan River, on the other side of which was located the lovely city of Perth, Western Australia, which is the most isolated city in the nation.

'How do you like W.A. so far?' asked the motel manager.

'Breathtaking!' replied TC. 'The view of the city from the hills made me feel happy that I've come here to live.'

'See you've got Queensland plates on your car,' said the motel man.

'Yes, we've come a long way,' replied TC. 'Can you recommend a nice suburb where I should seek permanent accommodation. It also needs to have a reputable Catholic Junior School in close proximity.'

'South Perth is great,' suggested the man. 'Safe suburb. There's an old, white church with a school perched on a hill overlooking the Swan River. I'm pretty sure it's a Catholic Church and the school is run by nuns.'

'Thank you,' replied TC. 'In the meantime, we'll stay here indefinitely until I find somewhere permanent.'

By the end of her second week in beautiful Perth, TC had leased a townhouse in South Perth and enrolled Junior at St. Columbia's, the church school overlooking the Swan River and city from a hill on the South Side.

Radio Station 6iX kept TC going day after day as she drove here and there doing this and that in her car.

TC brought with her only ten thousand cash. The rest was in the bank. She took Junior to town. They had to buy everything from a potato peeler to a T.V. All, apart from an electric frypan and a couple of blankets she carried with her from the department store, were to be delivered.

'I start school tomorrow, Mother. What are we going to eat tonight?' said Junior on the afternoon they vacated the motel on Great Eastern Highway.

'Don't know, darling,' replied TC as she pulled her sports car to a halt outside a deli opposite a butcher's shop which displayed an illustrious sign "Clayton's Quality Meats".

'We'll buy bread at the deli, then some meat at the butcher's.' TC purchased bread from the deli, put it in her car, then guided Junior across the road to Clayton's Quality Meats, where she emptied the contents of her purse onto the counter.

Carefully she counted, then announced to the man behind the counter, 'My name is TC Carmichael. Just counted so you know I have only six dollars and ninety-five cents. I have a small child, an electric fry pan, a loaf of bread, and my son starts school at Saint Columbia's tomorrow. What meat can I get for six dollars ninety-five that will feed my son tonight and suffice for a sandwich at school tomorrow?'

'You look like an honest lady!' said the man. 'You can have whatever you want. I know by your eyes you'll pay me. My name is Geoff. I own this place.'

'What about me, Dad?' asked a smiling young man hacking meat on a wooden block behind where his father stood.

'This is Trevor, TC. He's my son,' said Geoff Clayton. 'Little bugger likes the limelight!'

'I can see that, Geoff. I think I'll be shopping here for meat a long, long time. You remind me of old friends back in Queensland.

'What's the limelight, Mother?' asked Junior.

'Your little guy is pretty formal, TC,' laughed Geoff. TC laughed also.

'Yes, he has mood swings; calls me mama for months, then mother for a few weeks before switching back to mama. I've leased a place a few doors down the street. I need a Nanny for my son. If you know anyone who might be interested in being auntie or grandmother to him, I would appreciate you introducing me.'

'I think I know the perfect lady for you,' smiled Geoff. 'I'll tell her about you.'

§

'Perth is pretty, Mother,' said Junior early evening as they stood on the upstairs balcony and looked across the Swan River at the city skyline ablaze with lights, many of which reflected in multi-colours.

'It is pretty, darling,' agreed TC. 'I read somewhere Perth is called the City of Lights—now we know why!'

❦

By Friday afternoon Junior was settled in school. He loved it! The school principal, Sister Patricia, said that was probably due to the fact that all staff including herself tended to fuss over him. Not only was he a newcomer, he was the smallest child in the school. Junior also possessed the widest vocabulary and command of the English language they had ever encountered in a child his age.

TC smiled. 'I imagine that's because he's spent most of his time with adults.' Sister Patricia laughed.

'Not any more, TC. Two little girls have taken a liking to him. They follow his every move.' TC nodded and smiled.

'Perhaps that's a sign of what's to come, Sister.'

❦

Geoff from "Clayton's Quality Meats" arranged for TC and Junior to meet an elderly lady who was indeed perfect. She was a replica of Thel Carmichael and Auntie Maggie combined. Junior bonded with her the instant they met. TC felt blessed! Her son was in a school he enjoyed, had a Nanny from heaven, the townhouse was set up nicely, and now all she had to do was find an affordable location for what she envisioned as a high-profile, high-quality opal outlet. TC knew the majority of her future customers would be tourists or corporate clients all from overseas.

Most Australians don't appreciate our national gemstone, she thought as she concentrated on what would be the right next thing to do and recalled a conversation in the dispensary which now seemed an eternity ago. Vance, Neil, Yappy, Faith, Little Joe, and TC were there. It was in the early days, long before TC had gone to the U.S.

'We're wasting our time here in Australia,' said Vance in one of his depressed moments.

'It's the Aussie bloody syndrome, mate,' said Neil, who was also obviously depressed. 'Most of us think if it's Australian, it's no good,' said Faith. He was also feeling defeated.

'We're Australians. Don't know what we've got until it's gone,' added Neil.

'Some bastards think all they have to do is walk around in the bush, bend down, and scoop opal out of the dirt. Bloody hell! They are wrong!' said Yappy. 'Vance puts his life and money on the line, and you men work your guts out. So does Little Flower.'

'You do, too, Yappy,' said Little Joe. 'It's sad! So sad.'

'Don't know about you mongrels. I'm proud to be an Aussie,' proclaimed Yappy. 'What about you, Little Flower. Vance? Neil? Faith?'

'I'm proud with you, Yappy!' replied TC.

'We all are!' said Vance.

'Even me!' said Little Joe. He was not a legal Australian.

TC felt lonely and lost. She missed Mr D, Maggie, Thel Carmichael, and the security of familiarity with her surroundings on the Gold Coast. Her son's future and well-being depended on her making unregrettable decisions there and then. After a couple of hours of deep thinking, TC decided she needed to acquire as much knowledge as possible about Perth and Fremantle before she committed to a shop lease. Her future customers would be mostly international tourists, and she needed the ability to answer questions as to where to go and what to see.

A decision made, TC arranged for Junior to be with his nanny from eight till four the next day, then booked a cab to collect her and take her everywhere previously red-pen-highlighted by her in the tourism booklets and brochures she had gathered at the Great Eastern Highway Motel.

¶

After chatting for a few minutes to her cab driver, who arrived punctually, TC was elated to be told he was Perth-born and bred. In his words, he 'knew the city and surrounds backwards'.

'You are exactly the person I need,' laughed TC. 'Please show me what you think tourists would like to see.'

'That will take quite a while,' replied the owner-driver.

'I understand,' said TC. 'I have to collect my son at four this afternoon.

If I haven't seen everything of interest by then, I'd like to hire you for tomorrow, as well.'

'Sounds good to me!' replied the cabbie, who immediately turned off the clicking gadget on his cab's dashboard. 'Two hundred including fuel until four today, and you buy lunch, which will be a hamburger in Fremantle.'

'Deal!' agreed TC as she reached out her right hand to the cab owner. 'My name is TC Carmichael.'

'I'm Harry. My mates call me Harry the Cabbie,' 'laughed the Mr D–type man. 'May I ask what you are doing here, TC?'

'I'm researching!' replied TC. 'Hopefully, I'm going to open the best opal shop this state has ever seen!' The cabbie laughed.

'With your attitude, I'm sure you'll do it, TC. Let's go to Kings Park first. It's pretty and the view is magnificent.'

Harry the Cabbie did not lie! TC decided Kings Park was much more than pretty. It was beautiful! Trees to the sky; bush gardens; happy, laughing, eyes-glistening-with-excitement groups of four on bicycles negotiating winding paths; families settling for picnics on the lawns; and couples walking hand-in-hand or sitting, cuddling close as they overlooked the breathtaking view. North, south, east and west—it was wonderful! TC was happy.

'Where to now, Harry the Cabbie? So far, I'm more than impressed!'

By four that afternoon TC had seen, been informed about, and absorbed historical facts about Perth and the adjoining port of Fremantle located at the mouth of the Swan River, which flowed into the Indian Ocean.

'I feel like a tour conductor,' said Harry when he dropped TC off.

'A good one, too, Harry,' replied TC. 'Thank you. I'll find a shop. While it's being fitted out, I'll call you again to take me down south, see the wine country you talked about.'

'The wild flowers will be blooming by then, TC,' said Harry as TC passed him his two hundred.

'Great, Harry! I'll call you as soon as I organise things. Once again, thank you.'

¶

TC searched relentlessly for almost two weeks. Finally she decided on a tiny shop in a new arcade close to her dream location on The Terrace. After signing a lease on the premises, she felt relieved that her first steps to opening for business were over and done.

TC spoke to a cabinetmaker working in a shop opposite. After introducing herself, she asked if he was interested in fitting out for her.

'Sure,' he replied. 'I'll have a look and measure up now. We can also arrange signs, electrics, and everything else. All you have to do, TC, is decide on colours and approve our design.'

TC liked the man; he had an open, honest face, dressed in khaki work clothes, and hair all over the place. The second she noticed one side of his shirt pocket falling down and the cigarette packet within, she trusted him and so passed him her shop key.

'You've got the job!' said TC as she reached out to shake his hand.

'Here's my card. Call me Monday. I'll come up with a couple of designs over the weekend,' said the surprised cabinetmaker with a broad smile.

¶

Meanwhile Vance was at mine number one advising the men they were moving.

'I bought the German's lease, men. Think we've mined out here.'

'What do you mean, Vance?' asked Yappy. 'Is that your way of telling us we've got the bloody sack?' Vance laughed.

'No, Yappy, it's my way of telling you we are moving.'

'Leave this beautiful place?! I'll be heartbroken,' said Neil. 'It's taken years to establish this desert.' Little Joe thought momentarily.

'Wish Faith was here. He'd be happy. He hated this place.'

'We all wish he was here, Little Joe,' said Vance with more than a little emotion. 'I'm also temporarily shutting down mine number three. Two of the men will work with you; the others will go to mine number two. We'll start pulling down and relocating after the break. One last thing;

there will be no more managers.'

'So you've woken up at bloody last,' said Yappy. 'It's about bloody time!'

'Give me your mail order, Yappy,' said Vance. 'I have to drive east in the morning and make sure the shop is still there.'

'How is Little Flower doing in the West?' enquired Little Joe.

'I know she got there safely,' smiled Vance. 'She'll be all right! She knows how to handle herself.'

As Vance drove away from camp, he thought of TC. He knew she'd be moving fast to open a shop as soon as possible. He had avoided calling her and knew she wouldn't call him unless absolutely necessary.

'Bloody hell, I'm a prick,' he told himself. 'She worked her guts out in the Pink Brolga; never drew a dollar in wages. Phone, food, and shelter were all she got. I gave her a lousy twenty-five thousand budget to open a shop. Soon I'll have to tell her I've got little or no stock to send her because I allowed another Bert Black- and Fred Brolga-type bastard to rob me.'

'Apart from that, she didn't ask me to open a shop in W.A. All she asked for was a few stones on consignment. Me being me, I couldn't let her go because I know she'll do what she always has for me— work her heart out and make money.

'Yes, Little one,' he said aloud. 'I've treated you like crap from day one. Some things never change! I'm sorry!'

¶

When the shop fit out was underway, TC called an old customer who was a jeweller in Sydney. He advised her what she would need in the way of packaging and the best place to buy it. He also wished her good luck before adding, 'TC, quote me as a reference. I know they'll require one.'

Her order placed per telephone, she phoned Harry the Cabbie and booked him for the following day.

'Where do you want to go, TC?' enquired Harry.

'Not sure, Harry; here, there, and everywhere. I need to buy a safe,' replied a laughing TC. 'Also would like you to show me the easiest, uncomplicated routes to Fremantle, Kings Park, and the suburban shopping centre closest to where I live.'

'Sounds good, TC,' replied Harry. 'Nine o'clock?'

'Done, Harry. See you then.'

※

'I'm almost there,' sighed TC as she slumped into a lounge chair. 'All I need now is stock. Wish the boss would call. Something is wrong; otherwise, he would have contacted me by now. Perhaps he's called when I've been out,' she reasoned while knowing full well that wasn't the case.

TC picked up the phone and she dialled Lou. They hadn't talked since the night before TC left the Gold Coast.

'I've been worried about you, TC. I'm glad you called. At last I'll have an address and phone number.'

'No need to worry about me, Lou. It's not been that long. I've been a busy girl.'

'Seems like you are as far away as you were in America,' said Lou.

'Might as well be, Lou.'

After a long conversation catching up with Lou, TC wrote five letters—one to Mr D, one for Maggie, another to the men at camp, and one each to Lisa and Jess.

※

Harry the Cabbie collected TC at exactly 9 a.m.

'You look very business-like, TC,' laughed Harry when TC got in his cab clutching a Yellow Pages L-Z business telephone directory with a folded piece of newspaper protruding as a marker.

'Very funny, Harry,' replied TC lightly as she opened the directory at Safes, then passed it to him.

'I'd like to check out the places I've marked with an X. After we find a safe, I need to buy a bicycle for my son and bring it back here and hide it. Then, if there's time, you can show me the easy routes to Fremantle and Kings Park.'

'Consider it done, TC!' said Harry. 'Who's buying lunch?' he added as they drove off. TC laughed.

'I haven't got a clue, Harry; not lunch time yet.'

§

'What? No tip!' said Harry, pretending surprise when TC paid him two hundred late in the afternoon. TC also laughed.

'Don't push it, Harry. You got a hamburger and a milk shake for lunch.'

'Keep my card, TC, in case you need me again.'

'Thank you, Harry,' smiled TC. 'You are a gentleman. Believe me, when I need a cab, I'll call you.'

§

The moment TC opened the door Junior raced to greet her.

'Go on, little man, tell your mother your news,' said Gracie beaming from ear to ear.

'What news do you have, darling?' asked TC as she squatted on her haunches to hug and kiss her son.

'I like my name now, Mother,' he whispered in her ear. 'Sister Patricia told me Robert and John are good names. I love you, Mama.'

Tears of love and relief streaming, TC whispered back, 'Mama loves you, too, Robert John.' He abruptly pulled away from TC, cupped her face in his little hands, and looked her directly in the eyes.

'Mother, you can't call me Robert John, only Robert. My friends at school will laugh at me.'

'I understand, Robert,' said TC seriously.

'Isn't he a good boy, Mother?' praised Gracie. TC nodded proudly, patted Robert's cop of curly, blonde hair and replied.

'He certainly is. Grandma, Auntie Maggie, and Mr D will be proud of you, Robert.'

'What about Mr Callahan, Mama?' asked Robert.

'Yes, I'm sure Mr Callahan will be, too,' replied TC while thinking, That is, if he ever gets around to calling me.

§

While waiting for the shop to be finished, TC wanted to spend every waking hour, except when he was at school, with Robert. She knew once the shop was open, she'd be working long hours, six days a week, possibly sometimes seven.

TC was thankful to the Lord for directing her into Clayton's Butcher Shop, for Geoff directing her to Gracie, and for being in a financial position to afford a nanny. Realisation came upon her how disastrous must be the reality of being a lone working parent without Gracie or the means to hire one. Her heart went out to the countless thousands of them she imagined there were.

§

Robert's eyes were wide with disbelief when Gracie brought him home from school the day after he decided he liked his name. Not only was TC there, but beside her was a sparkling blue-and-white chrome bike. He was speechless as he stood still.

'Aren't you going to hug Mother?' said Gracie.

'I'll hug him, Gracie,' said TC as she sat down on the floor next to the bike.

'Come on, darling, Mama needs a hug.'

Robert ran to TC and threw his arms around her and whispered, 'Why are you here, Mama?'

'Because I love you,' TC whispered back. 'Do you like your bike?'

'Is that bike for me, Mother?' he asked, still whispering.

TC wanted to laugh. Who else did he think it was for? Instead, she whispered, 'Yes. I hope you like it.'

The time TC had to share with her son passed quickly, too quickly. She enjoyed being a normal mother for the very first time and probably the last—taking him to school; chatting with his teacher and Sister Patricia; collecting him from school; sharing an afternoon snack; watching him ride his bike in the park by the river; exchanging lots of cuddles; reading bedtime stories; the lot!

The first weekend they took a ferryboat ride to Fremantle, went to the puppet theatre, and ate hot dogs in the park. Next Saturday they went to the movies in the city, and TC showed him where the shop was located. The cabinetmakers were working inside.

TC's heart sank when she looked through the window. A feeling of loathing for Jake overwhelmed her. If he hadn't cleaned her out financially, she would be in a position to be a real mother to her son.

'Where are we going next week, Mama?' asked Robert as they walked away hand-in-hand.

'Maybe we won't have to wait until next week, darling,' replied TC. 'Tomorrow is Sunday, and if you have a good sleep tonight, we can have a picnic by the river. You can feed the ducks. I'll call Gracie and see if she'd like to come with us.'

'I promise I'll have lots of sleep, Mama,' replied Robert as he squeezed his mother's hand.'

After Robert was asleep anticipating seeing Gracie and feeding the ducks, TC sat deep in thought. She still hadn't heard from Vance. The shop was almost done and the twenty-five thousand budget would be almost, if not entirely, gone when she paid the shop-fitters, not to mention incidentals. The safe alone had cost almost six thousand even though it was a year-old, second-hand one. Harry the Cabbie she had paid with her own funds, of which she'd spent almost thirteen thousand; about ten of which went on furniture.

She thought of Vance. I wish I'd never asked him for consignment stones. I should have told him I didn't want to own only twenty-five percent; I want to own the lot. At least I'd know where I stand. As it is, I haven't got any stones, consignment or not. No other stock, either.

I'll call you on Monday, Mr Callahan! decided TC. As far as I'm concerned, you can have your lousy twenty-five thousand dollars back and shove it. You've taken me for granted for the last time!

TC showered, then turned on the T.V. She couldn't believe it. A Steve McQueen movie was playing. Everyone in Brolga thought Vance resembled the famous actor. TC shook her head in disbelief, sat back, and enjoyed the movie. She was still angry with Vance.

¶

Immediately TC returned home after taking Robert to school on Monday morning, she phoned Vance's shop in Queensland. She was livid! She would phone Brolga only if absolutely necessary. She had no wish to hear Almut's voice. TC was well aware of the fact that Delores loathed and resented her because, in her mind, TC was or had been Vance's girlfriend. Too close to the forest to see the trees, thought TC. One day she'll wake up. TC dialled.

'Good morning, Brolga Opals,' answered Chikako's deep Japanese voice.

'Mr Callahan, please,' requested TC.

'Who's speaking,' came from Chikako. It wasn't a question; it was a demand.

'Mind your own business,' replied TC. 'If he's there, give him the telephone. If you don't, I promise, you will regret it.' Almost instantly Vance came on the phone.

'Hello.'

'So, you're still alive,' snapped TC. 'Thought you must have screwed yourself into the next world.'

'Don't be like that,' replied Vance calmly.

'Don't be like what?' snapped TC. 'I suggest you tell your girlfriend to take a hike out of earshot or go to a phone box and call me.'

'The latter is fine,' replied Vance.

'Great! Make it soon! I mean in minutes, not hours or days!'

¶

'That was quick!' snapped TC when she heard Vance's voice.

'I'm calling you from the hotel lobby,' replied Vance. 'How are you, Little One?'

'Don't "little one" me, Mr Callahan. "Used and abused slave" would be a more fitting title for me. I've been here forever and you haven't called me even once. You wouldn't know I was here if I hadn't rung and told you. The shop is all but ready and you haven't sent me so much as one stone.'

'Let me get a word in, Little One,' interrupted Vance.

'Be quiet!' snapped TC. 'If you want to get a word in, go and whisper in one of your girlfriend's ears. I want to break our deal! I never should have told you I wanted to open my own shop, let alone ask for consignment stones. I'm going to return your lousy twenty-five thousand dollars. By the way, I'd bet thieving Fred Brolga wasn't on such a paltry budget. Probably no budget at all. The sky was the limit!'

'TC, stop, please,' interrupted Vance.

'No, I won't stop! I'm returning your money and opening Carmichael Opals as I originally planned. I've worked like a drover's dog for you all those years. Since I began doing trips, I saved you a fortune by not giving discounts. My pay was a thousand here and there and a couple of pairs of shoes now and then as a bonus. Big deal, Mr Callahan! Big deal.'

'TC, please,' from Vance. TC ignored him.

'Another thing! It might be a good idea if you come clean with your wife and clear me as being one of your sluts. Please delete me as a director of your company. Goodbye!'

TC slammed down the telephone, then immediately went upstairs to shower and dress. She needed to go to the city, change the details on the lease documents, then go to the bank to transfer Vance his money.

¶

Vance put down the telephone. He knew if he went back to the shop not more than twenty feet away, he would probably smash a counter or two and most definitely smash Chikako when she began interrogating him. He left the hotel via the rear exit, went downstairs to his four-wheel drive, kicked the tyres, then slammed the door after getting inside, re-opened it, then slammed it again before slumping over the steering wheel.

'Effing everything she said is right! I should have called her; I should have done a lot of things. What on earth am I going to do?'

❡

TC heard the telephone ringing from upstairs. She ignored it, thinking it was Vance. It kept ringing; so she ran downstairs to answer it. If it was Vance, she would hang up. She was calm now. She'd said what she needed to say and it was done. TC picked up the phone and answered. It was the cabinetmaker.

'TC, your shop is almost done. We need the safe delivered so we can erect the walls and door surrounds. Sometime today would be great. Five cartons were delivered from some place in Sydney a little while ago. I took the liberty of signing for them.'

'Thank you. I'll call the safe people now,' said TC. 'How long before it's done?' asked TC.

'If the safe comes today, we'll be finished day after tomorrow, signs and carpet next morning, and it's done.'

Thursday, thought TC as she dialled the safe company.

'Where on earth am I going to get stock? I shouldn't have relied on Vance for anything. Damn it! I forgot about the signs; they read Brolga Opals; the stationery and business cards are the same, the boxes, telephone, the lease, too. Everything!'

❡

After arranging for the safe to be delivered, TC threw herself on the couch and cried tears of frustration.

The telephone rang on the coffee table beside her and she automatically picked it up.

583

'Yes, TC Carmichael speaking.' It was Vance.

'Little One, it's me.'

'Go away. Leave me alone,' replied TC. 'I don't want to talk to you anymore. I've said all I had to say.'

'Are you crying, Little One?'

'None of your business! Goodbye!'

The phone rang. It was Vance again.

'Please don't hang up. What if I give you that money to make up for past commissions?'

'Jam it, Mr Callahan! You didn't give it to me then. Why give it to me now? I'm not for sale!'

'How about forty percent instead of twenty-five?'

'Jam that, too!' replied TC. 'For a while I thought you had reverted back to a time when money wasn't your god. Obviously, that was only temporary. This isn't about money; it's about appreciation, respect, honesty and sincerity. Commodities you've misplaced.'

'TC, I told you a long time ago, I respect you more than any other woman on earth.'

'Sure! That's why you've allowed your wife and sluts to treat me like a doormat all these years. I don't want to talk anymore.'

'Please don't put the phone down, Little One. I want to explain the reason I haven't been in touch with you,' replied Vance. He was pleading.

'I'm listening. It had better be good.'

'I haven't got anything to send you. I was relying on stock I had on consignment with a jeweller in Sydney.'

'Don't go any further!' interrupted TC. 'He disappeared and the stock went with him? No point in sympathy-seeking from me. You sure know how to pick dishonest people. I thought you would have learned your lesson way back with Bert Black. It only took him and the confidence guy in the U.S. to teach me.' Vance sighed.

'Not only that. The so-called managers I hired for two of the mines have been robbing me blind.'

'Perhaps you attract thieves the way you attract loose women,' said TC matter-of-factly. 'Why didn't you tell me before instead of leaving me stranded?' continued TC. 'The shop will be ready in three days and I haven't got so much as a safety pin to display.'

'I'm sorry, TC! Please don't break the deal. You're better than that!'

'I don't know about better. I was out of my mind even to have made it.'

'I'll see what I can rake up in the shop.'

'Thank you, but I'm not stupid. If you rake anything up in the shop, it will only be the dregs your manager-girlfriend doesn't want. By the way, you're sounding so humble; is there anything else I should know?'

'Little Joe asked about you,' replied Vance. TC smiled.

'How are my favourite trio?'

'They are moving camp after next break. I bought the lease on the old German mine, but got screwed to high heaven on the price.'

'You must have appeared too eager.'

'Almut is coming on strong to Jonathon. I'm worried witless about that. Don't know what I'll do if he falls for the bitch.'

'Have you finished with her?' asked TC.

'Not really. She's a bitch and so bloody pal-sey with Delores it makes me want to puke. If I tell her to piss off, she's likely to blab to Delores. Then I'll be on my arse. She wanted me to leave Delores for her. I told her not to be so bloody ridiculous. Since then, she's been after Jonathon like a rat up a rope every chance she gets. I'd like to choke her.'

'Seems to me she wants a Callahan. If she can't get the Big Shot, she'll go for next in line,' surmised TC. 'Pity Jonathon isn't as streetwise as his little brother. Call me tomorrow, Mr Callahan. I have some thinking to do.'

'Please don't go it alone, TC. I don't want to lose you.'

'We both know what you mean is you don't want to lose out on the money you know I'm going to make. Call me tomorrow after ten.'

TC looked up jewellery wholesalers in the yellow pages. There were only two. She phoned both and made appointments, drove into the city, dropped by to take a look at the shop and say hello to the cabinetmaker. To her surprise, the safe was already there, one neon sign was already in place, and the telephone was connected. They were busy working, so TC waved through the window, then moved on.

The first wholesaler had only costume jewellery; nothing of interest to TC. When she asked the second about opal jewellery, his face lit up.

'As a matter of fact, I do. One week each month I wholesale jewellery for an opal dealer in Sydney. It arrived this morning. Some of it are very nice; most of it are ordinary; no colour.' TC purchased all the very nice pieces, totalling twenty-three.

'As soon as I know my phone number, I'll let you know,' said TC. 'Perhaps you could call me when you get next month's consignment in.'

At least, it's a start, thought TC as she walked to the car park.

That afternoon while watching Robert ride his little bike in the park, TC decided what she was going to do.

Vance called early.

'Have you decided?'

'It's only seven. We haven't had breakfast yet,' replied TC. 'There's a two-hour time difference. Phone back in two hours.'

He did in exactly two hours. 'Have you decided?'

'Yes, I want you to know if it wasn't for the fact the shop is a day away from being finished and anything and everything is branded Brolga Opals, I probably would have broken my deal. I want not only twenty-five per cent of the take; I want twenty-five percent of the business. You've put in twenty-five thousand; I'll put in six thousand two hundred and fifty. Until the business is properly established, the shop will pay you cost only on any stock you supply. The same goes for me. Once the business is established, we'll talk again. I actually bought some stock yesterday. By the looks of things, I'll have to buy a lot more.'

'Done! Do you want it in writing?' laughed Vance.

'That's up to you,' replied TC seriously.

'I'm sending you fifty stones and fourteen pendants this afternoon,' said Vance. 'If you don't like them, send them back.'

'Don't worry, I'll do just that,' replied TC.

'I know you will, Little One. Talk to you soon.'

¶

One day early, on Wednesday afternoon, TC took possession after paying the cabinetmaker. She then looked around with admiration. The finished shop looked lovely. The fitout was elegant—W.A. jarrah with glass showcases and wall features, peach-coloured carpet to contrast with the dark jarrah cabinets and stools. Proudly displayed on the front and side windows were Aussie colours–green and gold neon signs announcing Brolga Opals Perth. Everything was in order except stock. She needed stock! She was frantic for some when she heard via 6iX early on Thursday morning that a U.S. aircraft carrier group would dock in the Port of Fremantle next day.

After dropping Robert off at school, she went to the shop and boxed the twenty-three pieces she'd purchased earlier in the week. Vance's fifty stones and fourteen pendants had not as yet arrived.

What on earth am I going to do? thought TC. Please, Lord, tell me what to do! What to do? There's probably five or six thousand potential customers arriving here, and I've got sweet bugger-all to sell them except twenty-three pieces.

TC threw her head into her folded arms on the counter and cried. She now felt defeated as well as lost and alone. After a brief spate of tears, she told herself, 'I'm going to do it!' TC stood upright, shook her head, opened the door to the small, behind-the-counter room which housed the safe and sink, turned on the tap, washed her face, thought of her son, and said aloud to herself, 'I'll be successful! I know it!'

Her feelings of positivity paid off. Only minutes after drying her face, applying fresh lipstick, and tidying her hair, two young men introducing themselves as self-proclaimed Christians representing an Eastern States opal jewellery manufacturing company entered the shop. They had crystal opal in sterling silver settings for sale.

'Would you like to have a look?' enquired one of the well-spoken, clean-cut, immaculately attired two.

'You came to the right place at the right time,' laughed TC. She carefully selected from their large range of earrings, pendants, and rings.

'You are the most discerning buyer we've ever struck,' commented one salesman with a smile as he invoiced her selections and his friend bagged them.

'I hope so!' replied TC while still concentrating on her purchases. 'I learned a long time ago, if I don't like my stock, my customers won't like it.'

'Done deal!' said TC as she placed the last of her selection on the counter. 'I hope a personal cheque is okay. I spent all my boss' money on the fitout, safe, and other necessities.'

'That's fine,' replied one.

'Beautiful fitout, too,' said the other as he looked around, admiring the cabinetmaker's professional finish.

'All I need now is a salesman with gold opal and jewellery to walk through that door and I'll be elated,' said TC seriously.

'There's one in town, TC. We said hello to him on the mall when we were looking for you.'

'There you go, TC,' said the two young men in unison. 'Do you want to count them?' asked one.

'The three of us will do it together,' replied TC.

¶

A few minutes later, TC had her stock and invoice and the men had their cheque and left only to return a little later with a trembling, very young, handsome man attired in a dark suit complete with white shirt and tie. With a black leather flight bag in each hand, he reminded TC of herself all those years ago when Vance had sent her on her first trip. Terrified!

'We found him, TC. See you next time,' came from the silver wholesalers.

'Thank you very much,' smiled TC with gratitude and relief.

'My name is Pete,' said the still-trembling, young man.

'I'm TC Carmichael,' replied TC. 'I'm pleased, I'm also relieved, to meet and see you. Stop shaking, Peter. I'm not as tough as I look,' laughed TC. Peter sighed as he sat down.

'I've been trying to find you for hours.'

'It's not the best location, Peter. Don't have any advertising yet. Not even in the telephone directory. The phone was connected only a few days ago.'

'My father always says, 'We have to start somewhere,'' replied shy Peter.

'Your father is exactly right,' said TC. 'I heard there's an aircraft carrier and other ships coming tomorrow. I'm hoping desperately some of the people on board happen to find me.'

In TC's mind, the law of averages told TC at least a few of the thousands of visitors would find her tiny shop and her. TC smiled.

'You calmed down now, Peter?' she asked.

Peter smiled and nodded, 'Yes, I'm fine! I've heard a lot about you for a lot of years; didn't know what to expect.'

'All good, I hope!' laughed TC. 'Come on, show me what you have to sell.'

Peter opened one of his two bags and placed his opal jewellery trays on the desk for TC to peruse.

'You have some lovely stock,' said an obviously impressed TC while wondering which way to go with her selections. She wished she knew the visitors' budgets.

'I'm going to take a punt and buy across the board,' she told herself. 'If I'm wrong, I'll be wrong!' A couple of hours later, TC was content with her choices.

'Add that up and I'll pay with my personal cheque; afraid I've overspent Mr Callahan's budget.' Peter smiled and placed his father's business card on the desk.

'My father knows you, TC. He said to wish you luck and you can have credit if you want it.' TC picked up the card and immediately recognised the name of one of her old customers in the east, not with Peter's business name.

'Please tell your dad I appreciate the offer, but I never gave him credit when he bought from me. Perhaps one day I'll take him up on it, Peter. I need to see how things go first. Does your dad have two businesses?' enquired TC curiously.

'Yes. This is a new one. He told me not to tell you I'm his son until I saw your reaction to the stock.'

'Tell your father I'm most impressed,' laughed TC. 'Not only with his stock but also with his gorgeous son.'

Peter repacked his stock trays; TC passed him the cheque, then patted his hand and smiled.

'Next time, don't be afraid of me, okay? Take care of yourself, Peter. I'll call you when I need more stock. Our opal world sure is small; I'm not opened yet and already today two wholesalers from the east have found me! I'm blessed you found me before the ships arrive tomorrow.'

'Thank you. Good luck!' They shook hands and Peter was leaving. Unbeknown to him, his father's offer of credit had secured TC as a loyal customer for as long as she remained in the business.

The arcade was deserted; every other shop in it was closed. TC quickly locked the doors then phoned home to apologise to Gracie for being so late and not calling earlier.

'I'm sorry, Gracie. Time got away, and I was too carried away choosing stock to think of the time.'

'That's all right, darlin,' replied Gracie with her soft, sweet, Cockney voice.

Bob Segar was singing, 'Against the Wind' on 6iX as TC gathered the bags of new stock, price tags et cetera. 'You're not wrong there, Bob. I'll be up all night marking,' she said to herself.

As the song continued, TC's thoughts went back in time to the Pink Brolga. Every Saturday night barbeque, this one and Del Shannon's 'Wanderer' were usually the first two played and often a couple or three times more. The men, including Mr D, identified with them. TC herself did now!

Damn it! thought TC when she realised she had nothing in which to carry boxes. Oh, well, can't be helped! With two striped, plastic bags filled with stock, her handbag stuffed with pens and tags, she locked the shop, then hurried to the car park.

¶

Closely followed by Gracie, Robert greeted TC by running out to the garage.

'You are late, Mother. Why are you late?' TC knelt down on her haunches and hugged him.

'I'm sorry, darling.'

'Don't be late again, Mother. I was worried about you,' he whimpered as he clung to TC. TC hugged him tighter.

'I'll try not to be, sweetheart.'

'I told you Mother would be home soon, didn't I, darling?' said Gracie.

'Yes,' replied Robert softly.

'Gracie, would you mind staying a little longer?' enquired TC as they went inside. 'I need to grab my bags, go to the shop, and collect some boxes. There's an aircraft carrier arriving tomorrow, and I need to be ready. The Lord smiled on me today, Gracie; I'm a lucky girl.'

'That's because you're a good girl, darlin',' said Gracie. 'I'll call Brian, my husband; then I'll drive you, save you parking.'

'Can I come, too?' asked Junior. Both Gracie and TC cracked up.

'Of course, you can,' they replied in unison.

Gracie didn't leave until midnight. She insisted on staying to help TC just as she insisted on being there to take Robert to school next morning so TC wouldn't have to rush.

'Thanks to you, it's half finished, Gracie,' said TC. 'I won't forget this!'

'Don't worry about it, darlin',' replied Gracie. 'I'll see you in the morning.'

¶

It was 4 a.m. when TC threw in the towel.

'Better pack it in. Still got a lot to do. It can wait. Doubt I'll be rushed off my feet. If I'm lucky enough to get even one customer, I'd hate to be asleep when they walk in.'

¶

TC was dressed and ready to go when Gracie returned from taking Robert to school.

'You look lovely, darlin',' said Gracie as she gave TC the once-over. 'Where did you get your yellow suit and matching yellow shoes? I love the way you've done your lovely, blonde hair.'

'Stop it, Gracie; you're embarrassing me,' laughed TC. 'This is my business look.'

'Oh, I like it,' rambled Gracie as she spotted TC's yellow handbag on the table. 'You look like a movie star.'

'Stop it, Gracie! I'm going to call Harry the Cabbie. He can drop me off at the end of the arcade so I don't have to walk from the parking station. The bags are too heavy.'

'Bugger Harry the Cabbie! I'll drive you. I want people to see you get out of my car.'

'Enough, Gracie! If you keep on, I'll have to find another nanny!'

'You wouldn't do that; you're too nice.'

'Let's go, Gracie,' laughed TC as she threw her handbag over her arm and picked up the bag.

Once displayed, the stock did not look nearly as sparse as TC had feared. She knew there'd be gaps everywhere if she was fortunate enough to have a rush, so went to a department store on the mall where she purchased a couple of brightly-coloured, silk scarves and a few silk flowers with which to camouflage gaps if necessary.

The decorative tubs with indoor plants were delivered mid-morning as TC was draping one of the scarves within a wall unit.

'That looks pretty', said the delivery man, aged mid-thirties. 'Almost as pretty as you are,' he flirted.

A second Randy James, thought TC as she smiled sweetly. All W.A. men must be the same.

'Love your smooth hands and long, pale-pink fingernails,' he persisted as TC signed the delivery slip. TC burst into laughter and pointed at the door and said, 'Get out of here.'

'Why? What did I do wrong?' he asked while wearing an expression of shocked horror.

'You've been seeing too many movies,' laughed TC.

'Well, can't blame a man for trying. See you next time, I hope.'

¶

Vance's parcel arrived. While the stones were nice, TC rejected all but three of the pendants.

Why am I not surprised? she thought as she dumped the rejects in the safe. Wouldn't sell these to my worst enemy.

It was late morning when TC saw two U.S. naval Officers pass by the shop. They were attired in their verging-on-black, winter dress uniforms. Their black-and-white caps cum hats were gold-braid-adorned along with silver eagle and shield, plus, gold anchor insignia. TC eventually learned the officers referred to their elaborate headwear as a cover. TC instantly recalled a childhood memory. A friend of her mother's was visiting. The friend had met and fallen in love with an American naval officer in Sydney during the war. They married after it was over; she moved to the U.S. and had returned to Australia for a holiday ten years later. On seeing the naval officers walk by, TC could all but hear her mother's friend talking about her husband way back then. 'I fell in love with his uniform first; you haven't seen a man really dressed until you see a Yank naval officer in full regalia.' Now TC knew what she meant.

Although multitudes of officers made their way through the arcade it was mid-afternoon before one entered the shop. Elbows on her desk, pen in her right hand, and chin cupped in her left, TC sat staring into space when the tall, dark, handsome young man wandered in.

'Good afternoon, Ma'am. I've been watching you through the side window. You look as lonely as I feel.'

'I'll have to lift my act,' laughed TC as she got to her feet and held out her hand. 'I'm TC Carmichael.'

'I'm James,' replied the young officer with a smile to die for as they shook hands.

'Some smile you've got there, James!' said TC.

'I'll buy an opal for my mother and sister while I'm in port. Not today, though; perhaps tomorrow.'

'Seeing as you feel lonely and I look lonely, would you like a cup of coffee, James?' asked TC. 'I'm locked in here till five-thirty.'

❡

When it came to closing time, TC knew James was a pilot, twenty-four years of age; his father was an accountant in downtown Chicago; he had an eighteen-year-old sister who was in college; and he loved his mother more than life itself. James had been feeling lonely that day because his two best friends had duty and wouldn't get off the ship until evening.

Thanks to James, TC was made aware that four to six carrier groups visited Fremantle Port annually; very few shopped on their first day in port; duration of the visits was usually five days; there was some sort of friendship club hosting a welcoming function for three hundred officers that night, and uniforms were compulsory first day in port or for official functions.

James walked TC to the car park, which was in the direction of his hotel. TC sensed people scrutinising them as they made their way along the footpath. She laughed when James explained they probably surmised he had "picked her up".

'If you like, I'll drop you off at your hotel, James. It's on my way,' offered TC. When TC pulled her white, two-door sports car to a stop outside James' hotel, a group of his fellow officers were standing on the footpath.

'I'll bring my friends by to meet you tomorrow, TC,' said James as he opened the door to leave. He stepped out. TC heard one of the group say, 'You're a fast worker, pal,' and another say, 'Not only is she blonde, she's got a great car.' TC sped off wondering why most people jumped to conclusions.

Next morning, true to his word, James returned to the shop with his friends, both of whom were as handsome as he. One was early twenties; the other was more TC's age.

After introductions, TC said jokingly, 'I think they must send you people to beauty school before they ordain you pilots.'

'I told you, TC's got a sense of humour,' beamed James as they all laughed. 'I want to by an opal pendant for my mother and earrings for my sister.'

'Me, too,' said the other younger man.

'Earrings and pendants for my wife,' said the one of TC's vintage, who winked at TC as he spoke.

TC learned during the conversation the two lieutenants and the lieutenant commander all hailed from Chicago and were members of the same squadron.

'Wish I'd known you were in Chicago, TC,' said the lieutenant commander when told she had lived there for three months.

'I wish you had, too,' replied TC. 'I was so lonely at times I would have befriended Jack the Ripper if he'd fronted at my door.' Much laughter.

Within an hour, the three pilots had made their selections. It was time for TC to write invoices.

'Because you are my very first customers and have spent quite a lot, I think I should give you a discount.'

'Is that so, TC?' said the lieutenant commander. 'In that case, I'll take a bracelet to go with the pendant and earrings. Go ahead, I'll have a look around while you take care of my friends.'

When leaving, James and his friends promised to tell the other members of their squadron about TC and her shop. TC was surprised when the lieutenant commander returned within minutes.

'Don't tell me you've changed your mind already,' laughed TC.

'No, TC, not at all,' was the reply. 'I'm hoping you'll join me for dinner tonight, then go to my squadron party at the hotel.'

TC was caught off-guard. Her mind raced. If he hadn't purchased a pendant, earrings, and bracelet for his wife, she wouldn't have known he was married. She knew she would have accepted his invitation if he were single. He certainly was handsome and very charming.

How would I feel, she thought, if I was his wife and he was on the other side of the world taking another woman to dinner and a party?

I'd hate it! TC sighed and smiled before replying softly.

'Thank you for your invitation; I'm flattered. I don't think your wife would be happy about my going with you to dinner and a party. My conscience tells me I must decline.'

'Fair enough, TC, you're quite a lady,' said the lieutenant commander as he leaned down and kissed TC lightly on the cheek before leaving.

Business was steady all day everyone who entered the shop made a purchase and they also said they would send their friends.

Thus began TC's long-term business relationship with U.S. military personnel.

By mid-afternoon of the carrier group's last day in port, TC was out of stock apart from twenty-seven of Vance's stones, a few rings, and a couple of brooches. Her feet ached and she felt exhausted. She was embarrassed when people kept coming and she had nothing to sell them. She told herself she'd be better prepared next time, then counted her blessings that she'd had any stock at all to sell them this time.

TC decided to close early. She was printing a sign, 'CLOSED EARLY. SOLD OUT,' when the lieutenant commander walked into the shop and presented her with a bunch of yellow roses.

'These are for you, TC. James told me you were wearing the colour when he met you first day in port, so I assumed you like yellow.'

'It's my favourite colour,' admitted TC after a few moments of silent surprise. 'Thank you. This is the first bunch of flowers I have ever been given. Not only that, they are roses; very beautiful.'

The lieutenant commander smiled.

'It's been a first for both of us, TC. You are the first woman on all my tours ever to have said no to a dinner date with me. I've called my wife four times since then. I have something else for you,' he said as he opened his duffle bag. 'I told the captain what a good deal you've given our people. He said to give you this.'

TC was speechless as he produced a shiny, wooden wall plaque with the aircraft carrier's name and insignia boldly proclaimed in shiny brass beneath which was a small rectangular brass stick-on plate engraved with the words—

Presented

By Officers and Crew

'Most of us show our friends what we buy, TC. We also often discuss the price paid,' said the lieutenant commander seriously. 'Suffice to say, everyone who shopped with you is very happy.'

'I'm pleased to know that,' said TC. 'Please thank the captain for the plaque. I'll hang it in the wall and treasure it. Also thank you for the flowers. I shall always remember you and your gift of yellow roses.'

A soft kiss on TC's cheek, a farewell of, 'I'll come see you if I'm ever back this way,' and the officer was gone.

TC immediately closed the shop and went to buy an appropriate vase in which to display her dozen roses.

¶

Both Robert and Gracie were surprised to see TC home early.

'You're home early, darlin',' said a smiling Gracie as Robert quit what he was doing and ran to his mother for hugs and kisses while Gracie took charge of the vase and flowers.

'I sold almost everything, Gracie. I'm tired, happy, and my feet hurt. If I'd had more stock, I would have stayed till midnight if customers kept coming. The captain of the ship sent me a wall plaque in appreciation for giving his people a good deal. I brought it home to show you.'

Gracie examined the gift in awe.

'I knew a lovely Yank in England during the war,' she said wistfully. 'I was desperately in love with him; he was in love with me, too. At least, I hope that was the case. Broke my heart when the darlin' young man confessed to me that he was married. Cried my heart out, I did.'

TC instantly thought of Graham and long ago.

'Being in love does that to people, Gracie. Think I'll be avoiding it. I read somewhere it's only a state of mind.'

'Don't be like that, darlin'. You're too young to be saying such things,' said Gracie with concern.

¶

After taking Robert to school and prior to going to the shop next morning, TC phoned Peter in Sydney.

'I sold the lot, Peter. I need more stock.'

'Incredible!' replied Peter. 'I'll put dad on.' A few moments later, Peter's father spoke.

'So, you sold the lot, young lady? Looks like you'll be as good in retail as you were at wholesale. Congratulations, TC.'

'I'm not that good,' replied TC. 'I didn't buy enough stock.'

'No, but you picked the eye out of what Peter showed you. Peter will be there Monday morning. If you like more than you can afford, pay me at a later date.'

¶

Vance decided to move camps immediately instead of waiting until after the men's break, when they would be tired and hung over. Consequently, the move was in full swing.

'Don't know what's bloody worse,' mumbled Yappy to himself as he slammed pots, pans, and cooking utensils into a wooden tea chest in camp number one's kitchen, 'setting up or bloody moving. It all breaks a man's routine. Don't know what or how I'll feed the poor bastards the next couple of days till the move is over and done. They better not forget to take my pink shithouse. If they try to leave it behind, I'll bloody kill them.'

Little Joe, Neil, and his brother were disassembling the marquee.

'Looks like we'll be sleeping under the stars tonight,' said Neil.

'Hope one of the bastards doesn't fall on us,' said his brother.

Little Joe shook his head in disbelief. He said nothing.

¶

Vance was in his Brolga cutting room. He was standing a couple of yards behind Delores, Almut, and Marla, who was pregnant as they sat at their grinding wheels working on matrix from mine number two. His Italian terrazzo specialist had completed his one hundred table tops and one hundred rough wall features from that mine, so now they were cutting the opal that ran everywhere through the boulders into matrix stones. It made him sick with disgust to see and hear Almut perpetually yapping and sucking up to Delores. Not only was Almut the most manipulative, bullshitting bitch he had ever known, poor bloody Delores must be blind, stupid, or both.

The night before, Vance and Almut had had a raging exchange of words when he warned her off Jonathon. He stormed out of her upstairs flat when she pulled her usual blackmail antics.

As he stood there observing her interaction with his wife, he wanted to choke her. Instead, he racked his brain for a less violent means of ridding his son, wife, and himself of her forever. Vance knew it wouldn't be easy; still, hopefully he'd come up with something.

Without saying a word, he walked past the women, went outside to his ute, and headed for mine number one. He wanted to check on the men and their progress with the move. He also had to deliver TC's letter. Not only that, but he wanted to get away from the two yapping women. Marla rarely said anything. She was smart. She listened and absorbed. She was nobody's fool. She also knew exactly what was going on.

While walking from the car park to Brolga Opals, TC purchased a radio. Prior to the ship's personnel shopping with her, she had noticed that the monotony of silence in the shop made her feel lonely and depressed. Hopefully, her future customers would feel more comfortable with background music courtesy of her favourite Perth radio station, 6iX.

TC was amazed when she tallied up the invoices. She'd made sales to a hundred and forty-nine people. More than half had made multiple purchases. No wonder she was out of stock. After doing the banking, TC printed a new sign for the front door proclaiming she would re-open on Monday, then went home, called Lou, did her housework, went grocery shopping, then surprised Robert by collecting him from school.

'Where's Gracie, Mother?' he enquired when they were seated in the car.

'Gracie is at home making you a snack,' replied TC, feeling more than a little hurt that her son hadn't shown more enthusiasm about her being there instead of Gracie.

'Good! She promised to take me to feed the ducks at the river. Will you come, too, Mother?' TC laughed.

'Of course, I will, darling. Not only will I go with you and Gracie to feed the ducks, I'll be home all weekend; so, we'll be able to do other things, as well.'

'I love you, Mama,' declared Robert as he threw his arms around TC's neck and smothered her cheek with kisses.

¶

Young Peter from Sydney was waiting out front of Brolga Opals when TC arrived Monday morning.

'Did you wet the bed, sweetie?' laughed TC. Peter laughed, too.

'No. Gave that up many years ago, TC. I got in last midnight. Dad told me I'd best be here early before the vultures swoop on you.'

'Don't know where the vultures are but your dad's a smart man, Peter,' laughed TC. 'I'm happy to see you're not shaking this time.'

Before looking at Peter's stock, TC made a mental note not to have the shop repay her the twenty thousand plus she'd spent on stock as yet. She would re-spend that along with the profits on more stock. After all, the right stock—and lots of it—was of utmost importance. No stock or wrong stock meant no sales. The six thousand-plus she had thrown in had been allocated to prepaid rent. So far, TC had put in more than Vance. As yet, she had not stopped kicking herself for requesting consignment stones. 'Never mind, what's done is done,' she told herself.

Peter began placing trays on the desk. TC stopped him.

'I saw most of this stock last week, Peter. I didn't buy it then and I'm not interested in buying it now.'

'Dad said you'd say that, TC,' laughed Peter. 'I'll show you the trays with new stock only. My dad sent a few bags full, as well.'

It was a little after one in the afternoon when TC passed Peter a cheque.

'Thank you for coming, Peter. Hopefully, I'll be in touch again soon. Tell your dad I said hello. Also thank him for sending the extra bags of stock.'

'You wouldn't have bought much if he hadn't,' said Peter. TC smiled at the young man.

'That's right, I wouldn't have.'

TC began recording, marking and boxing her purchases. She was busy at it when, a while later, a well-dressed and well-spoken middle-aged man came into the shop.

'Are you TC?' he asked in a friendly manner.

'Yes, I am,' replied TC as she held out her hand.

'My name is Barney,' as they shook. 'I'm vice president of a friendship group that quite a few others and myself have going here. We are mostly busy when the U.S. fleet is in port.'

'We throw a welcoming party, barbeques, that sort of thing. Last week I was talking to a group of pilots. All of them had bought opals from you and were raving about how friendly you are. I thought you might like to join our club.'

'That's very nice of you, Barney. Apart from my son's nanny and the corner butcher, I know nobody in Perth.' Barney smiled.

'Good. So I'll count you in. The president knows about you already. I'll tell him you are interested. There's a submarine expected next month. I'll contact you with where and when we'll have a function for its crew. Hopefully you'll be free to come along.'

'Sure, as long as I have a couple of days' notice to arrange for my son's nanny to be available.'

By week's end, TC knew what Peter's dad had meant about vultures swooping. It seemed opal people were appearing out of thin air. TC soon realised this always occurred after a carrier group visit. She purchased a few pieces here and there, mostly crystal opal stones from a Coober Pedy miner and black opal stones from a Lightning Ridge miner. Next, she had to find a reputable jeweller to set them.

Looks pretty damned good, thought TC after completing her display of new stock. The cases are full, plus I have back-up stock in the safe. The boss must have drifted off the planet again; he's not called in two weeks.

The first advertisements in the tour guidebooks were due next week. She hoped they would lure a few customers to her. She was optimistic. The shop was beautiful; the stock was beautiful; and, thanks to the Lord, most people warmed to her personality.

¶

TC took Robert to the shop with her that Saturday. She needed to see how he'd handle a five-hour stint in the confined space so as to allow Gracie full weekends free. By half-past ten, he was tired from drawing and practicing writing and spelling at TC's desk. With a cushion under his head, he fell asleep under the sink in the limited space of the safe room.

'I loathe you, Jake Carmichael,' said TC silently. 'Because you are a thieving, woman-bashing bastard, my little boy has to spend part of his Saturday sleeping on the floor under a sink in a tiny black hole with a safe his only company. You'll get yours one day, Jake!'

Come closing time at 1 pm, TC woke Robert. After he washed his face, she hugged him and told him what a good boy he was.

'I'm hungry, Mama,' said Robert as he hugged TC's legs.

'I heard about a restaurant where the chef puts clown faces on children's sandwiches and hamburgers. They also have clown-face biscuits and ice cream dipped in pretty things called hundreds and thousands.'

'I think I'd like that, Mama. Can we go there sometime?'

'What about now, darling?' asked TC. 'Would you like to go there now?' Robert's eyes gleamed with enthusiasm.

'I'd love to go there now. I love you, Mama.' TC patted her son's head.

'I love you, too, darling.'

'More than life itself,' she added silently.

¶

Vance finally phoned TC late in the afternoon.

'So, you finally found time to make a call,' said TC, oozing sarcasm. 'Life must be hectic at the top.'

'Please don't be like that!' replied Vance. 'I've got a lot of things going on.'

'Sure. I'd bet London to a brick that most of what's got you absorbed revolves around a woman or women.'

'You sound like a bookie,' laughed Vance.

'Why wouldn't I? Stands to reason I'm lumbered with one or two of Jake's sayings.'

'I gave the men your letter. It was addressed to all of them, so Yappy insisted I read it out aloud when they were together at smoko time. Even Little Joe cracked up when I read the bit about you not having spotted any real men of their calibre in W.A. so far. Neil said to ask you if you meant when they were in town drunk or at the mine working.'

'Tell him neither,' laughed TC. 'I received fourteen pendants. I sold two and will post the other twelve back. I didn't bother displaying eleven of them. Tell your girlfriend if she can't send something nice, don't send anything. As a matter of fact, I'd prefer you to choose what I get. It will save a lot on postage. I know you won't bother me with junk.' Vance sighed.

'Keep them there, Little One. Put them out at cost. How did you do with the Americans?'

'Sold everything except twenty-seven of your stones, a few silver rings, and a couple of brooches. I didn't open for the best part of three days. I had nothing to sell.' Silence. 'What's the problem?' asked TC.

'No problem at all. I'm surprised, that's all,' replied Vance.

TC went on to explain she had reinvested her twenty thousand and the profits in more stock, the shop looked great, et cetera.

'I suppose you reinvested the cost of my three stones and two pendants?' asked Vance. TC was furious.

'No! Wouldn't dare. I've sent you a cheque for six hundred and twenty dollars. You need the money. Before you ask, I've taken nothing for myself—no wages, no commission, nothing. I'm living on my own money until the shop gets going to my satisfaction. That may take a while or could happen soon.' On the other end of the phone, Vance was feeling like a real prick.

'Why the eff did I ask her about money for a lousy three stones and two cheap pendants.'

'I'm sorry little one.'

'My name is TC! No, you're no sorry. You're paranoid because you were stupid enough to hire thieves. Let me assure, you Mr Callahan, if I were going to rob you, I would have done it long before now. I could have taken you for bags full of stones and a fortune in dollars. If you were here, I'd punch you.' Vance began talking. TC ignored him. She continued. 'By the way, Mr Callahan, it's not too late for me to return your money, stones, and twelve crappy pendants. Take less than a month to change the name on everything. Call me when you've decided. I'm going now.'

'Are you angry, Mother?' asked Robert, who was colouring in at the dining room table.

'Not really, darling,' replied TC. 'Certainly not with you.'

Hurt and disgusted is more like it! she thought as she joined her son to admire his colouring expertise.

§

As always on Saturday and other movie nights, Old Jock and Brolga's elder mates sat observing goings- on and chatting on the Seat of knowledge.

'What's the latest, Jock?' enquired one of the number.

'Same as it was when we were here last night,' replied Jock in his dry, slow, matter-of-fact way. Ten or so minutes of silence later, Jock spoke again.

'Heard Callahan opened a shop in Western Australia.'

'Why the bloody hell would he open a shop way-to-buggery over there?' asked someone.

'Heard young TC is going to run it. She wanted to get as far away from Jake as she could. Told Callahan she wanted to open her own shop. He must have talked her into staying working for him. Can't say I blame him. We all know she toils like a drover's dog.' The other elders nodded. Silence resumed.

¶

Shortly after opening the following Tuesday, TC got her first customers as a result of her advertising. They had seen her ad in a hard-covered, glossy, in-room, tourist magazine in Western Australia's most luxurious hotel. A man with a familiar face, around forty years of age, dark-haired, lean, maybe five-ten or -eleven, entered the shop flanked by two much younger, broad-shouldered men well over six feet.

'Are you TC Carmichael?' asked the familiar-faced one with a British accent.

'I am,' replied TC with her usual smile.

'I've been reading about you in the hotel room,' came again from familiar-face, who smiled at his companions. 'Told you we wouldn't be disappointed.'

'I'm glad about that,' laughed TC, who had already concluded the man must be someone of importance and extremely wealthy. The younger men had to be bodyguards. Friends wouldn't smother him by such constant close proximity. Every time he moved, they moved. If she were him, she would feel claustrophobic.

'He wants to buy an opal,' said one of the two. TC smiled and looked the man directly in the eyes.

'Does he want a pendant, ring, brooch, bracelet, earrings, or a cut stone?' The man grinned.

'He is not sure yet.' It was then the bodyguards began steering their employer around the shop. 'Your darlin' would like that one. No! Your darlin' wouldn't like this one.' They must have spoken the words, 'Your darlin'' a squillion times. TC got the distinct message it was their way of letting her know their boss was off limits. He was taken. He had a darlin'.

Perhaps I should have told them about my unwritten business and pleasure rule, thought TC while smiling within. TC still couldn't place the man. All she knew was she felt sad for him. She didn't know why, she just did. No way could she cope with these two heavies hovering around her every move. Finally, a decision was made. TC wrote the invoice, then asked the gentleman to write his name and address on the top. She also requested his passport from which she needed details for tax and customs reasons.

'Why do you want his name, address, and passport?' demanded the minders almost in unison.

'Because it's the law,' replied TC calmly. 'I don't make the laws; I must abide by them; I have no choice.'

'You two go,' directed the man purchasing the opal. 'I'll catch up later.'

'Are you sure?'

'I'm sure!!'

'Don't lose your darlin's opal,' from one of them as they walked out the door. TC laughed as she slid the invoice across the counter. 'I felt the urge to tell them not to waste their time warning me off.'

'More likely they were reminding me I have commitments back home. Sorry about that. Sometimes they take their jobs too seriously.'

'I don't know how you stand it. I feel for you,' said TC with genuine pity.

'The price of being famous!' was the reply as he turned his invoice around to TC and fished in his jacket for his passport. TC read the name and realised the reason for the cloak-and-dagger goings-on of his bodyguards. TC smiled.

'Nice to meet you, 'He'.' She instinctively held out her hand.

'Nice to meet you, too, TC,' was the reply as they shook hands. 'Nice to meet a woman who doesn't scream, turn to jelly, or gush all over me on sight.'

'I used to be a fan of yours,' admitted TC softly as she copied his passport details. 'Probably still am,' she added just as softly. 'I imagined you'd be taller,' as she returned his passport. 'At least you looked taller on television.' He laughed.

'That's because they used to have me stand on a barrel. Wonder I didn't fall off the thing.'

'So, what brings you to Perth, He?' enquired TC with interest.

'I'm going south to look at an island off Esperance. I've always wanted to own an island. I hear it's very windy down that way, so perhaps I won't buy this one. Where would you buy an island?'

'I don't have to think about that question,' replied TC without hesitation. 'In the blue Pacific Ocean off the cost of North Queensland. If I was buying an island, that is where I would buy.'

'I'll keep that in mind,' was the reply. 'I appreciate you speaking to me like I'm a normal person.' TC smiled.

'You look pretty normal to me. The way I see things, we are all the same. You got a break and became a world-famous rock star, as did your friends. On a much lower scale, I got a break and became an opal dealer. We come into the world the same way and we all face the destiny of death.'

'I could talk to you all day, TC. Unfortunately, you have more people at the door. I don't want to be recognised. I'll take a look for an island off North Queensland.' He left via the side door as a couple entered by the front.

'Was that who we think it was?' enquired the woman.

'That depends on who you think it was,' replied TC sweetly. 'Please have a look around. I shan't be a minute.'

As TC pinned the rock star's paperwork together, she felt an aura of being watched. She looked up to see him staring at her through the side window. He smiled, waved, and was gone.

Incredible! thought TC as she turned towards her waiting customers. Despite his fame and fortune, he remains totally non-pretentious and a nice person! A while down the track the world was told he had married someone named Olivia. TC assumed this was his darlin'. It was his second marriage. Silently she wished him better luck with this one than the first, and then smiled as she wondered what his protectors might have done to amuse themselves while their boss and his bride were on their honeymoon.

TC wrote and posted Vance's cheque for his stones before she went home late afternoon. He had not called her back as yet. She wasn't surprised; she knew him too well.

§

During the following weeks, rarely a day passed without a sale. Although they were mostly small sales, they were still sales. Thanks to a flyer being placed under her door by a lady who had recently opened a small jewellery shop a couple of blocks away, TC now had someone to do ring sizing and set her stones. The lady was not a jeweller herself; she employed a young man not long out of his apprenticeship. His work was very nice.

Barney of the friendship group called to tell TC the submarine visit had been cancelled. He would contact her in the future.

For work, TC wore business suits with her blouse fastened to the top or second-top button. It was a habit she had developed during her sales-trip days in order to send her male customers the message she was prim and proper, definitely NOT available. Consequently, TC was in stark contrast to a middle-aged, scantily clad German woman who visited the shop on one late morning.

With her low-cut blouse revealing not only her cleavage but half her breasts as well, she wore the tightest white pants imaginable under which she obviously wore nothing. There was no tell-tale panty line. She had a gold bag slung over her shoulder with high-heeled gold sandals on her feet and smelled like a perfume factory.

'I love opals, darling. I'd like to look around,' said the tallish, medium-sized blonde.

'Sure!' said TC while thinking, Don't know how you're going to see the colour of the opals with your hair hanging over your sunglass-covered eyes. The woman went from case to case. After what seemed an eternity, she turned to TC with a sickly-sweet smile.

'Thank you, darling; you have lovely stock. I'll come back.'

TC wanted to say, 'Imagine how much lovelier my stock would look without your black sunglasses. No way are you coming back.' Instead, she smiled and said, 'Thank you. Bye, now.'

Two local opal cutters showed up that afternoon. Nice, down-to-earth men, one of whom had been cutting opal for as long as TC. Only difference was he worked on Coober Pedy opal mostly whereas TC had worked boulder only. His name was Jerry; his mate was Ray. Both were Vance's age. After a few minutes' conversation, TC was reminded of bush people with whom these two men would fit in fine.

'We know your boss,' said Jerry. 'He tried to sell us rough boulder a few weeks back. Beautiful colour.'

TC was confused. 'That's strange. Did he call you from Brolga?'

'No, he came to see us,' replied Jerry. TC shook her head. She was adamant.

'It wouldn't be him! I would know if he was here. Apart from that, he rarely sells rough; almost everything gets cut.'

'His wife was with him,' said Ray. 'His name is Stan and his wife is Clarice. They told us they own Brolga Opals and will be holidaying for six months at Margaret River.' TC laughed.

'My boss is Vance Callahan and he wouldn't holiday for an hour, let alone six months. I'll tell him. He'll get to the bottom of it. Show me your stones. Perhaps I'll buy a few.' Their stones were great. A long-term business relationship began.

Immediately after Jerry and Ray left, TC picked up the phone and dialled Brolga.

'He's not here!' screeched Almut. 'He's away at the shop.' TC steeled herself for Chikako to answer the shop phone and was surprised when Vance did.

'Hello, Mr Callahan. Your abandoned slave calling.' Vance laughed.

'You're not abandoned. I've simply been avoiding you.'

'Yes, I know, for a month to the day,' replied TC dryly.

'How is business?' asked Vance.

'Hit-and-miss, like your love life,' replied TC. 'Thanks for asking how I am. Do you know a couple named Stan and Clarice?'

'Yes, what about them?' asked Vance.

'I heard they are peddling rough boulders under the guise of being the owners of Brolga Opals. A couple of local opal cutters told me an hour or so ago. They said it's beautiful colour.'

'Why wouldn't the colour be beautiful? The bastards probably picked the eye out of the heap.'

'Who are these people?' asked TC.

'He was the manager of mine three. He drove the machine. She was the cook. I fired them last month. He didn't seem like a bad man, but she's a manipulative, avaricious bitch. She probably raided the heap while the men and he were working the cut.'

'How's your German mine going?'

'Nothing! The men are demoralised. It's worse than when we started at mine one. Because the site has been worked before, there are tunnels and holes there and everywhere. Perhaps I rushed in!'

'How is everything else?'

'I have to go now. I'll call you tonight. You understand!'

TC understood. Chikako was probably hanging on his every word, curious as to whom he was speaking to for so long.

He won't call tonight, thought TC. She was right!

¶

Time passed quickly. Robert settled into the routine of spending Saturdays until one o'clock at the shop. Without having been told by TC, he developed a routine of disappearing into the safe-and-sink room every time a customer appeared. On one occasion, she opened the door to retrieve stock from the safe when she heard him softly reciting her 'TC to customer' explanation regarding characteristics of different types of opal and their area of origin. She couldn't believe it! There was her little boy hunched under the sink staring into space. He ignored her presence and continued word for word.

Right! thought TC, as she grabbed a bag of stock from the open safe. Time I gave him some opals to practice with. He's got the words. All he needs now is to know what he's talking about. From then on Robert's knowledge of Australia's national gemstone broadened from week to week. TC gave him tests to make sure he was on the right track. He never faltered, rarely was wrong, and when he was, TC would explain, knowing he wouldn't make the mistake again.

To prevent Robert from becoming bored during his Saturday stints in the shop, TC allocated him jobs. One week he would polish rings, next week he'd straighten pendants in their boxes or trays, and so on. He was on the payroll at five dollars per week. On Mondays he would deposit it in his school bank account.

¶

Barney eventually contacted TC again. The friendship group was staging a welcome party for the new U.S. Navy representative. They had stationed a captain this time due to reasons Barney carried on to explain. TC didn't bother absorbing much of the explanation. It sounded too much like vicious gossip. Apart from that, TC didn't consider it her business. Her objective was to secure as much business as she could from U.S. military personnel, give them the highest quality at the best possible prices, and have her customers refer their friends. She was convinced word-of-mouth and friend-to-friend were worth many times over the money spent on advertising.

TC accepted the invitation. She also made a decision there and then. No matter where her pending attendance at the friendship group's welcoming parties lead her, she would not get caught up in the gossip, back-biting, or bitchiness usually equated with committees and large groups of people. She also knew that if she became involved with the friendship group, she would meet many American men, and from what she'd seen so far, they were all well-mannered, charming, and mostly drop-dead gorgeous. TC made a second on-the-spot decision—no matter how attracted she was to anyone she may meet in relation to the group, she would keep them at arm's length. Mentally, she drew a thick, black line between business and pleasure. The line was permanently fixed.

On party night, TC presented herself at the address Barney had given her, which was located not far from where she lived, so she had very little trouble finding it.

Won't have far to go home if I feel out of place, thought TC as she pressed the doorbell once, then waited. She could hear music and a lot of voices emanating from within. Probably drowning out the sound of the buzzer, thought TC as she pushed the button and held it. All smiles, Barney opened the door.

'Glad you made it, TC. Come in.' Barney led TC through to a large room at the rear of the house where fifty or so people, mostly women, were gathered. Elvis was singing, 'Are you lonesome tonight?' on the stereo when Barney ushered her through the door.

Yes, I sure am, Elvis, thought TC as conversations came to a halt and every eye in the room turned towards her. TC wanted to disappear. She wore a purple pantsuit, pale-grey, ruffled-neck blouse, silver high-heeled sandals, and matching silver bag with silver hoop earrings and chain around her neck. Her hair was pulled back and up and secured with a silver clip. She felt overdressed. Even though the nights were still cool, most of the women in the room wore strapless or low-cut, summer dresses or blouses with pants or jeans. None wore heels like hers.

'Allow me to introduce TC Carmichael, everyone,' said Barney as if she were chairing a meeting. 'TC is the new opal lady some of our last visitors were talking about. Please make her feel welcome. I'm hoping TC will become a member of our friendship group.'

By the looks on these women's faces, thought TC, I think you are a minority, Barney.

'Our president and his wife couldn't be here tonight,' continued Barney. 'They look forward to meeting you in the near future.'

TC smiled. 'Thank you, Barney. I am happy to be here. You all know who I am. Should you not want me to get to know who you are, please tell me and I'll leave now.' Every man, but only a few women, in the room laughed.

'I'm Len, Barney's counterpart, the other vice president. I speak for my wife, Lisa, as well. Please stay.' That was that! TC stayed. The music and conversation resumed.

Len, with his instantly friendly wife, Lisa, along with Barney, introduced TC to Captain Russ, the new U.S. naval representative, who seemed to be a very nice man. His wife was Australian. She and their daughter had not arrived in Perth as yet. TC and Captain Russ chatted for a while after Len, Lisa and Barney got cornered by a couple of committee members.

'You'll get along well with my wife,' said Captain Russ. 'She's blonde, too, and so is our daughter.' He then leaned his head closer to TC's and whispered, 'She's also usually the best-dressed woman wherever we go.' TC relaxed and laughed.

'So, she'd know how I feel tonight.'

'Happens all the time,' laughed Captain Russ.

One of the female committee members stormed over to TC.

'Do you realise Captain Russ is a married man?' she demanded.

'Yes, I do,' replied TC sweetly.

'I was just telling TC I think my wife and she will more than likely become good friends,' said Captain Russ with a broad smile. 'They dress similarly, too; always classy.'

'Oh!' from the committee woman, who made a hasty retreat.

'Nice to meet you, Captain Russ. I look forward to meeting your wife in the future,' said TC before thanking Barney, Len, and Lisa for their warm welcome, then leaving.

⁋

Jerry and Ray, the opal cutters, told TC another opal shop had opened around the corner. TC decided to go and introduce herself and wish the owner good luck. As they were both new to Perth, perhaps they could help each other down the track. TC closed half an hour early, found the new shop, which was set up very nicely, and waited for the owner to emerge from behind a partition. To her surprise and the owner's embarrassment, it was the scantily clad, sexy, German woman who had spent forever in Brolga Opals the previous month.

'I knew you wouldn't come back,' said TC with a counterfeit smile. 'I came to introduce myself and wish you luck.'

'I'm Heidi. I'm sorry. Surely, you checked out the other opal shops before you opened?'

'No!' replied TC. 'Their stock might be better than mine.'

'I don't think so,' said Heidi. 'I went to them all.'

'Good luck, Heidi! I must go. Your shop is lovely.'

Another lesson learned, thought TC after leaving Heidi's. Beware of sexy blondes wearing large black sunglasses.

§

It was dinnertime at the Old German mine camp.

'I hate this bastard of a place,' complained Neil.

'We all do, mate,' agreed Yappy. Neil's brother and two locals imported from mine number three all mumbled in agreement. Little Joe said nothing.

'Holes, pits and tunnels all over the bloody place,' said Neil. 'Wonder some poor bastard didn't die digging them.'

'Shut your bloody mouth and eat your tucker,' commanded Yappy. 'We're depressed enough without your blabbing. Makes us feel worse. We don't bloody-well need it.'

§

Vance was parked at his favourite spot down by the creek. His latest barmaid conquest had left town the previous week. They had been an item on and off for the past three-plus years. She finally gave up on him. The day she reluctantly admitted to herself there was no way Vance would divorce Delores to marry her, she gave Jack Romeo her notice. The next weekend she was aboard the Flea.

That's it as far as barmaids are concerned, thought Vance. Got no way to meet them now the pharmacy is extinct. Will need to hire more staff for the shop soon; can't believe the amount of Japanese business we're getting. How am I going to get rid of Almut! I know this latest mine is going to be a disaster. Lord, I miss having TC to run my troubles by. Wonder how the poor little bugger is coping. Why on earth did she have to go so far away? A voice from within told him she was only a phone call away, always had been. He turned the ignition key and drove towards town.

'This is a surprise,' said TC when she answered her phone minutes later.

'I need to talk to you. I've come to the conclusion within the last hour that I've avoided calling you because I'm pissed off you left Queensland for what might as well be the other side of the world. I thought I'd lost easy access to you; then I realised I can corner you anytime I wish by picking up the telephone.'

'That's about it,' laughed TC.

During the next hour Vance shared with TC his problems, concerns, frustrations, anything and everything he felt was wrong with his life. He concluded the one-way conversation.

'Thank you for listening, Little One. I feel better now. From here on in, I intend to call you every day except when I don't have access to a phone. Talk to you tomorrow!'

'Poor Boss!' sighed TC as she began climbing the stairs to check on Robert, who was sleeping soundly.

TC was amused when the shop phone rang next morning at one minute past nine.

'Just checking to make sure you haven't closed early,' then he was gone.

True to his word, Vance called TC every working day except when he was without a phone. Usually he called at one minute past nine in the morning, sometimes at twenty-nine minutes past five in the afternoon, often both.

¶

One day Barney came out to tell TC an aircraft carrier visit was pending. He gave her a date for the group's welcoming function only a couple of weeks away.

'I don't know, Barney,' said TC. 'Apart from you, Len, Lisa and Captain Russ, I felt like a leper at the party.'

'Stuff them. They're a mob of jealous bitches. I mean ninety percent of them are! I think about ten percent aren't. It'll cost you twenty-five dollars to attend.'

'I'll pay you now, then it's done,' said TC.

'Good. They'll give you a name badge at the door,' advised Barney as he took the money. 'I'll see you then.' Immediately he was gone, TC took a long, hard look at her stock. It was all very nice but would she have enough? She had twice as much as last time; still, she was concerned about running short. A call to Peter, a short conversation with his dad, and her worries disappeared. Without TC asking, he offered to send a large parcel of assorted stock.

'Pay me for what you sell and send the rest back,' was the deal.

Vance sent TC fifty matrix stones and half a dozen strands of matrix beads, his latest processing idea for the yield from mine number two. Although they had a large ironstone content, the fine veins of colour were beautiful.

I can sell these, thought TC as she listed them in the stock book. I like them.

TC was half-heartedly looking forward to attending the friendship group's welcoming party. With a little luck, perhaps she'd meet one or two people with whom she would become friends. She was lonely. Nights after Robert was asleep were the worst. She recalled Mr D once saying, 'Solitude sucks, TC!' She had to agree now that she was experiencing it seven nights a week. At the motel there'd never been time to feel lonely, there was always something to do after Robert's bedtime. Then Maggie and Mr D came on the scene. They kept her company most nights. Of late, Gracie had everything done before TC came home from the shop. While TC appreciated Gracie's unrequested thoughtfulness beyond belief, she had bugger-all, as Yappy would say, to do at nights except shower, pile cream on her body and face, then watch T.V. or go to bed, where she usually lay wide awake for hours. Twice a week she broke the monotony by pampering and painting her nails.

Weekends with Robert were what kept TC functioning. She loved every moment of precious time spent with her son.

The Saturday before the U.S. ships were to arrive the following Monday morning, TC took Robert to dinner at a seafood restaurant she'd seen advertised in one of the tourist magazines. They had not eaten fish since they had left the Gold Coast. Apart from that, TC thought it would do them both good to get out of the house for a change.

When Gracie commented, 'Perhaps Robert is a little young to be going to fancy restaurants,' TC replied, 'The sooner the better, Gracie. I didn't see the inside of a restaurant until I was nineteen. If my friend, Lou, hadn't been with her now-husband Colin, we wouldn't have had a clue as to how to order, let alone which cutlery to use for what. We followed Colin's every move for the duration of the meal. I want Robert to acquire social graces early to enable him to fit in wherever life takes him.'

'You look very nice, Mother,' said Robert as they left their parked car.

'Thank you, darling,' replied TC. 'And you look extremely handsome in your suit and tie.'

I'm glad I chose this restaurant, thought TC as they entered. Feels nice. She was more convinced she'd made the right choice when a Greek gentleman reminiscent of Con approached them, introduced himself as Bill, I'm the owner, collected two menus from the reception counter, smiled at TC, then looked down at Robert.

'Table for two, sir?'

'Thank you, Bill,' replied Robert, relaying the impression he'd been frequenting restaurants since birth. Bill led them to a side-curved booth towards the rear of the restaurant.

'You can see all the action from here,' said Bill as he flicked open a linen napkin and passed it to TC. 'A waiter will be with you soon,' he continued while repeating the napkin-flicking procedure for Robert. The restaurant filled quickly. By the time TC and Robert's meals were served, there wasn't an empty chair to be seen.

'I like being out on Saturday night,' said Robert. 'Can we come here again?' TC smiled.

'I'm sure that's a possibility.'

After their meal came the bill. As TC removed money from her wallet, Robert observed her closely.

'Will you let me pay, Mama?'

'Sure. Why not?' replied TC. She slid the notes across the table to her son.

'Did you enjoy your dinner?' TC asked.

'Yes, it was very good,' came the enthusiastic reply.

'In that case, give five dollars extra as a tip.'

'What is a tip?' asked Robert.

'It's something I learned in America,' replied TC. 'There, it's the expected done thing. Here in Australia, so far we tip only when we feel like it. Tonight the food was great, the service was, too, so, we tip.' Robert nodded.

'I understand, Mama. It's like a present for being good.'

'Exactly!' laughed TC. 'You catch on quickly, young man. Let's go.'

Side by side, they made their way to the reception area near the restaurant's entry-exit door. They had all but reached their destination when TC found herself looking directly into the eyes of Captain Russ seated at the first table and facing the rear of the restaurant from where Robert and she had emerged. He was accompanied by three men whom TC decided, due to their haircuts, were probably U.S. Navy personnel. Captain Russ was instantly on his feet.

'What a coincidence seeing you here, TC. Not five minutes ago we were talking about you.'

'All good, I hope,' laughed TC. Captain Russ turned to introduce his companions, who all began to stand up.

'Don't worry, it's all right,' smiled TC. 'It's a bit difficult to stand in these fixed-booth areas.'

Robert stood quietly during the introductions, then said, 'I'm Robert Carmichael,' which gained him the undivided attention of Captain Russ and the other men. Bill, the restaurant owner, had observed and overheard from his location behind the reception counter. He was most amused.

'You go and pay Mr Bill for our meal, Robert,' instructed TC. 'I'll be right behind you.'

'The reason we were talking about you, TC, is that we want to buy opals,' said one of the men. 'Captain Russ told us he'd heard you had many satisfied customers from the last fleet visit.' TC smiled.

'I'm pleased to say I heard that myself.' Within minutes, it was explained that these men were members of the advance party for the carrier group. Eight of their members wished to purchase opal jewellery while in Perth. TC gave them her business card, and it was arranged they would meet her at the shop at eleven next morning because they would all be busy Monday when and after the ships berthed. Although open trading was not permissible on Sundays, the couple who owned the shop opposite TC in the arcade often opened by appointment behind closed doors because a number of their customers couldn't make it any other time.

Robert and Bill were in deep conversation when TC finished with Captain Russ and his friends.

'All paid up, Robert?' interrupted TC when she joined them.

'All done and done well, if I may say so, Robert's mother,' replied Bill.

'Sorry, Bill; I'm TC Carmichael. Please call me TC.' 'Judging by the already-developed comradeship between you and my son, looks like we'll be seeing a lot of each other.'

'I hope so,' replied Bill. 'See you next time, Robert.'

'I'll tell Mother I want to come and see you again soon, Mr Bill.'

TC drove home via Kings Park. They had not yet experienced the view from there by night. It was not disappointing. Even more breathtaking by night, than day. People were everywhere. It was a beautiful night.

'It's pretty, Mama. Can we stop for a little while?' asked Robert.

'Not tonight, darling; maybe next time. You need to get lots of sleep so you can help me in the shop tomorrow.'

¶

By one o'clock that Sunday afternoon, TC had taken in eleven thousand dollars. The ship wasn't in yet. TC was elated. She couldn't believe it, but the invoices didn't lie. Her advance party customers told her to brace herself. She'd be very busy. The Aussie dollar was way down against the greenback, and the ships' crews had received their pay but a couple of days previously.

Robert wasn't interested in riding his bike by the river; he wanted to practice spelling and writing. TC spent the afternoon selecting, pressing where necessary, and arranging in her wardrobe her outfits for work for day one through to day five of the carrier group's stay. Once appropriate shoes and handbags were in line on the wardrobe floor beneath her hanging business suits, she concentrated on what she should wear to the friendship group's function. She concluded it would almost have to be after-five formal. In that case, TC's decision was easily made. She owned only one after-five. It was a simple black almost-to-the-ankle-length sheath with a conservative slit at the back and a short bolero-style jacket with medium-length sleeves. She chose gold, stiletto sandals with a flower on one side of the front and a matching evening bag purchased in Sydney years before but as yet not put to use.

TC felt confident. The stock was great! She had plenty of it. Gracie had agreed to stay with Robert as late as necessary during the next five days. She'd already sold to the advance party and hopefully they would pass the word to others. Once again, TC felt blessed. She sent a silent prayer of thanks to the Lord.

Vance didn't make his one-minute-past-nine call on Monday morning.

Pity, thought TC. I wanted to tell him about yesterday.

To TC's surprise, customers began coming in late morning and didn't stop coming till late. A lot said they would return next morning because she couldn't serve them. Two at a time she could handle, not three or four. She needed help. Where on earth could she find it? This time the officers were wearing their summer whites. Looked like they'd stepped down from a movie screen. With no time to tally the day's takings, TC closed the shop, went home, quickly showered, and dressed for the welcome party. She panicked.

'Hope I'm not over-dressed, Grace.'

'You look lovely, darlin',' said Gracie. 'Remember always, it's better to be the best than the worst.'

TC didn't have a clue in which direction the function was taking place, let alone how to find it while driving. Harry the Cabbie was booked for seven-fifteen. He arrived spot-on time.

'Got a date, TC?' said Harry. 'Whoever he is, he's a lucky man.'

'No dates for me, Harry,' replied TC with a smile. 'I've been invited to a welcoming party for the U.S. military.'

'They are nice people,' said Harry. 'Had my cab full of them all day; probably will all night, too. Never had trouble with any of them. You are a different matter, TC. Before you let them charm you, remember they are here today, gone tomorrow.' TC shook her head and smiled.

'I'm not stupid, Harry. Business and pleasure don't mix. I'll keep the beautiful creatures at arm's length. I've got 'unavailable' stamped all over me.'

'Won't be easy, TC.'

'I'll manage.'

'There they are, ice cream suits everywhere,' said Harry after turning his cab around a corner and to a halt outside the club where the function was being held. 'Still want me to collect you at ten?' TC nodded.

'Pay me for both trips when I take you home, TC.'

'I'm scared, Harry,' admitted TC. 'I know only about three people in there. I hardly know them.'

'That doesn't sound like the TC I drove around a while back,' said Harry seriously. 'Go on, kid, get out of the cab and get yourself inside. You'll cream it!'

'See you at ten, Harry,' said TC. Without hesitation, she stepped out of the cab. Making certain there was no eye contact whatsoever, she zig-zagged her way through the crowd of American officers to the stairs leading to the club's entrance. Once in the foyer, TC went to a table manned by two committee members she recognised from Barney's party. One of them was the woman who had reminded TC that Captain Russ was a married man. Without looking at TC, she crossed her name off the list of attendees. Without speaking, the woman next to her handed TC a stick-on name tag.

As TC moved towards the hall entry, she heard one say to the other, 'Stuck-up bitch.' TC was going to let it go, but she decided against doing so. She stepped back to the table.'

'Excuse me, ladies,' she almost whispered ever so sweetly. 'You don't know me! You have no right to call me a stuck-up bitch. If you must say it, at least have the intestinal fortitude to say it to my face. Thank you, ladies.' TC quickly entered the crowded hall, leaving the two women sitting at the table with their mouths gaping.

Barney, Len, and Lisa were standing only a couple of feet from the door. The three of them welcomed TC.

'Glad you could make it, TC,' said Lisa. 'I'll have someone to talk to. Most of the others will be busy looking for a Yank to take home.' TC couldn't help but laugh at Lisa's bluntness.

'So that's how it is?'

'Afraid so!' TC decided she liked Lisa. She was straight to the point, no messing around. Black was black and white was white. That was it! TC glanced around the packed-to-the-rafters hall, humming with conversation, some serious, some humorous, many flirtatious.

No wonder all those officers were standing outside, thought TC. No way they'd fit in here. Suddenly TC felt a tap on the shoulder. She quickly turned to look up at one of her advance party customers. With him was a group of seven or so other officers spilling into the lobby.

'Hello, TC,' said the advance party man. 'Saw you get out of the cab and rush inside. Tried to catch your attention but no hope.' TC smiled.

'My first time here. I'm more than a little nervous, feeling out of place.'

'That's understandable. Don't know what you said to the women at the welcome desk, but it must have been good, from the expression on their faces when you finished telling the story.' TC felt her face flush with embarrassment.

'You were watching me?'

'We all were,' said one of the group.

'We want to buy opal from you,' said another. TC stepped into the lobby.

'Will you all be shopping at the same time?'

'Yes,' was the reply from all the men. TC thought momentarily. All these people together, probably better do it behind closed shop doors again. 'I'll have to make a phone call to confirm my availability. Would eight tomorrow morning be okay?'

All nodded. One said, 'Perfect. We're going horseback riding at ten.'

There was a pay phone in the lobby. TC called Gracie to check if she would come in the morning by seven-thirty.

'No problem, darlin',' was the reply. TC re-joined the group.

'Eight at the shop it is, gentlemen. Here's my card. I'll see you then.'

Speeches were about to begin when TC returned to the hall door. On the podium, Len and Barney stood on either side of a tall, silver-haired, distinguished gentleman who introduced himself as Ken Smythe, the president of the friendship group. TC was impressed when he spoke; his command of the English language was flawless. Very much like Mr D's.

After the group's president concluded his welcoming speech, he stepped aside. The admiral of the fleet then took the microphone, announced to the crowd how great it was to be in Western Australia again, thanked all for the warm welcome extended to his people and himself, then presented a wall plaque similar to the one TC had hanging on the wall in her shop, but with a different carrier, emblem and battle group number.

TC checked her watch; almost an hour before Harry would collect her.

'Can't wait to get out of here, darling?' asked a tall, slim, elegantly attired, middle-aged lady who appeared beside her with beautiful, thick, almost-black hair, perfect make-up and manicure. 'I'm Fiona Smythe. Ken, the president, is my husband.' TC smiled.

'TC Carmichael, Mrs Smythe.'

'I know who you are, TC. Please don't call me Mrs Smythe; makes me feel old. Call me Fiona. I've been making my way through the crowd to talk with you since I saw you arrive.'

'Why is that, Fiona?' asked TC.

'Come outside with me while I have a cigarette, darling. I'll tell you out there. I'll also give you the low-down on the group. You're everything Ken and I heard you were. I hope you become a member.'

'How did you know I am me, Fiona?' enquired TC once they were seated on a bench at the top of the club's front steps. Fiona exhaled after the first puff on her cigarette before replying.

'Because you fit Barney's description of being blonde, well-dressed; you wear stilettos and you are definitely not ugly.' TC laughed. She liked Fiona immediately just as she had liked Lisa, who had disappeared into the crowd when TC moved into the lobby to talk with tomorrow morning's customers. Fiona took another puff on her cigarette before continuing.

'You probably don't realise it, darling, but you were hiding by the door.' Fiona's voice changed to a whisper. 'You wouldn't have had the opportunity to notice we are the only women present in this establishment tonight with tits enough to wear stilettos.' TC suppressed a giggle. This elegant, well-spoken woman and oozing-class lady was down-to-earth human. TC was certain they would become true friends.

'I have an obsession where shoes are concerned,' admitted TC. 'I attribute it to not having had any as a child.'

'Don't tell anyone else here you grew up poor, darling,' advised Fiona. 'Instead of calling you a stuck-up bitch, they'll refer to you as a jumped-up bitch.' TC was surprised to say the least.

'You've heard about that already?'

'I certainly have, darling. You sure put those two in their place,' replied Fiona. 'You're only half their size, but you threw a verbal punch strong enough to scare them off. They're frightened our visitors will zero in on you and they'll miss out on fornicating with a member of the 'cream of the crop' for a few days.' TC laughed.

'You sure have a way with words, Fiona. They needn't worry about me. I've drawn myself an imaginary thick, black line between business and pleasure.'

'Ken and I thought as much, darling,' said Fiona. TC was confused. This was the first time she'd met Fiona and, as yet, she'd not so much as spoken to her husband.

'How do you know so much about me, Fiona?' asked TC.

'Let me explain, darling,' replied Fiona as she was about to light another cigarette. TC listened intently for the duration of Fiona's interesting monologue.

Her husband, Ken, had retired from a high-ranking position in the world of commerce only eighteen months prior. Six months previously he had been convinced by friends to run for presidency of the friendship group, which had a foul reputation amongst the upper crust of Perth society as being nothing but an easy pick-up point for visiting U.S. military personnel.

Ken, his vice presidents, and a dozen or so others desperately wanted to change that image. There were two sub-committees other than the decision and policy-making ones. As far as the president and his people were concerned, the sub-committees were being run by the wrong types, who had a habit of throwing raunchy parties rather than acceptable-to-society functions, which would encourage respectable membership and hopefully change the unsavoury image the group presently portrayed.

It was at a sub-committee shindig during the previous carrier group's visit that they had heard about TC. To escape the hub of the party Ken, Fiona and Barney joined a couple of pilots who were sitting aside from the goings-on, introduced themselves, and consequently a conversation took place.

'That's when we heard about you, TC,' concluded Fiona. 'I asked if they were enjoying themselves. They said yes; what else could they say? It was written all over their faces that they were as miserable as we were at being at that ridiculous party. I'd asked a stupid question. Their faces lit up when Barney had the common sense to ask them what they'd been doing so far during their stay. Both of them had bought an opal from you. One of them had invited you to dinner; you had declined, and reminded him he had a wife back home whom he couldn't stop thinking about since. Then a couple of their mates joined us; they had bought opal from you, too. Anyway, to cut a long story short, the report on you was a glowing one, so Barney paid you a visit and here we are. We need people like you in the group.'

'There's my cab, Fiona,' said TC as she saw Harry drive around the corner. 'Please say goodnight for me to Barney, Len, and Lisa. I'm very glad I met you.' As an afterthought TC added, 'If you know or can think of anyone suitable to help me out in the shop for a few days, please tell them to show up tomorrow or call me. Barney has my numbers.'

'Bye, darling,' said Fiona as she stood to return inside, thinking, I'd help the girl myself if I were a few years younger.

A little later, as TC was arranging with Harry the Cabbie to collect her next morning at seven-thirty, Fiona was talking to a relatively new group member named Blanche. Blanche was an extremely attractive young mother of two small children; a boy and a girl. Her high-flying, rat husband had found it fitting to announce to Blanche he was leaving her for another woman the day after her youngest was born.

'I thought due to your circumstances you could probably do with the money,' said Fiona.

'You're not wrong there, Mrs Smythe,' agreed Blanche. 'I'll call my mum now and see if she will babysit. If she says okay, I'll get your friend's number and call her tonight.' Fiona went in search of Barney and TC's number while Blanche made her way through the by-now loud, no-holds-barred, sexually aggressive women and their officer prey, filled with anticipation as to how the rest of their night would go. The majority of them felt confident they'd be into wet and war before midnight. Who could blame the poor buggers? Only difference between most of the women remaining in the room and hookers was these didn't charge.

Fiona found Barney and her husband in deep discussion. Both had their backs turned to the crowd as they stood in the bar-room doorway. Len, Lisa, and a dozen or so other members were seated at tables within, drinking coffee.

'Barney, I need TC's phone numbers,' interrupted Fiona. 'She needs help at her shop. I've asked that new girl, Blanche, if she's interested. She's calling her mother regarding babysitting now.'

'Fiona, I've told the bar people to cut off the grog,' said Ken nodding his head backwards. 'The way those women are carrying on is downright disgusting. No wonder the club has a bad reputation. I don't want our visitors to go away thinking we're running a meat house.'

'Simple, Ken,' smiled Fiona. 'You are the president. Grab the microphone, thank everyone for coming, then announce it's time to leave.'

'Here're those numbers, Fiona,' said a somewhat relieved Barney.

Blanche hastily returned from the lobby phone.

'I can do it, Mrs Smythe. Do you have the number? What is your friend's name?'

'She's not my friend yet,' replied Fiona. 'I only met her tonight. I know she is going to be my friend. Her name is TC Carmichael. Here're the numbers.'

Five minutes later, TC felt relieved she had someone to help her.

TC's customers were early; they were waiting for her when she arrived at a quarter-to-eight.

'You're early,' said TC as she quickly opened the main door, switched on the air conditioning and lights, then opened the safe.

'Couldn't wait to see your pretty face,' said one cutie-pie.

'Flattery won't get you a better deal,' laughed TC as she placed her keys on the counter. 'Would someone please relock the door for me?'

'She's locking us in; that sounds interesting,' from someone amongst them.

'Don't get carried away, gentlemen,' laughed TC as she quickly unloaded trays from the safe and placed them on the counters.

'I suggest I first explain about opals to you, then you have a good look around before making your selections. Don't be afraid to ask questions.'

A sweetheart among her customers spoke, 'Before you start, TC, I have a question for you. Would you like to come horseback riding with us?'

TC gave an exaggerated sigh, 'I'm sorry! I can't let your friends down by not being here when they come to buy opal for their loved ones. Thank you for the thought,' she said with a sincere smile.

It was almost exactly nine-thirty when TC handed over the last of her early customers' purchases, then thanked them all for shopping with her.

'Hope you enjoy the horse riding,' she said as they left. Silently she said, 'Thank you, gorgeous darlings; there're gaps everywhere. Best start filing them.'

'Good morning, TC. I'm Blanche,' came a voice from the filling doorway.

Perfect, thought TC as she looked at Blanche for the first time. She was much taller than TC with a full, but not overweight, figure. Her voice was silky and pleasant to the ear.

'I'm so pleased you could help me, Blanche. My first customers for the day left a few minutes ago. The trays are a bit messy. First thing we'll do is fill the gaps.' Blanche was a natural. Only had to show her once; she cottoned on immediately. At the same time, she was more than a little daunted about selling as she neither knew, nor could be expected to know, anything whatsoever about opals.

'You'll be all right,' encouraged TC. 'Look, listen, and learn. If you're stuck, ask me. I'll teach you between customers.' Needless to say, Blanche didn't receive much tutoring that day. Too busy. Customers kept coming all day long. They were still busy when Vance called at five-twenty-nine.

'Go away, too busy!' answered TC. She had heard this was only a four-day visit, which explained the rush from day one. That was, of course, along with the fact the visit took place immediately after pay day.

'I'm buggered,' said Blanche after the last customer left around six-thirty. 'Hungry, too.'

'Me, too,' sighed TC. 'Sorry you didn't get a lunch break.'

'Do me good,' smiled Blanche. 'Same time tomorrow?'

TC nodded. 'See you then,' she called out as she locked the main door behind Blanche, then watched her walk away. In TC's opinion, Blanche possessed an aura about her TC had never recognised in another woman previously. Although Blanche was a big girl, conservatively dressed, her silky voice, mannerisms and way of moving exuded feminine sexuality. It didn't matter if Blanche was walking around the shop, opening a showcase, or kneeling down to select a pouch or box from under the counter, it was there.

Good luck to you, Blanche, thought TC. Whatever it is, you've got it. Special! I wish I had a bit of it. As for me, I'm too business-like. Wouldn't know how to be sexy if I tried.

¶

The third day and fourth days were hectic as well.

'You've been hit in the butt by an Angel's arrow,' remarked the woman from the shop opposite when they crossed paths in the restroom. 'I'm glad you're close to me; I'm picking up quite a few of your leftovers.'

The admiral, his wife, and the admiral's aides visited the shop afternoon of the third day. Lovely, friendly people they were. Blanche attended to the aides while TC took care of the admiral's wife, who left the shop happy and proudly wearing her husband's gift, a beautiful matching set of earrings, pendant, bracelet and ring.

'You'd think the admiral is a normal business man,' said Blanche after they had gone. 'He didn't come across as someone in command of thousands of lives.'

'Isn't that great! Power very obviously hasn't gone to that gentleman's head,' agreed TC.

¶

Vance phoned three times on the third day. TC told him to leave her alone until Friday, when the ships had gone. It was almost 8 pm on day four when Blanche and TC farewelled the last of their 'leave it till the last for shopping' customers. The lady across the way had stayed open, too. She was happy as she did well by doing so, too.

'I'm pretty sure we've both lost weight during the past few days,' said Blanche.

'Yes, I know,' said TC as she pulled up her jacket to expose a nappy pin in the waistband of her skirt. 'Do you think you could put up with me again tomorrow? There's a lot of cleaning up to be done. I haven't got a clue as to how much we've taken in as yet. The truth is, I don't care at the moment; all I want to do is go home, see my son, take a bath, and go to bed.

'Me, too,' said Blanche. 'Of course, I'll help you tomorrow. Mum won't mind having the children another day. I've enjoyed working here, TC. Some of those Americans are drop-dead something, aren't they?'

'I know,' replied TC with a sigh. 'I told a few of them a while back that attending beauty school must be part of their training.'

'You did not!' laughed Blanche.

'I did so!'

'What did they say?' TC shrugged as she replied, 'They could hardly agree with me. I think the poor darlings were embarrassed.'

§

'How did you do?' were the first and only words out of Vance's mouth at 9.01 am on Friday.

'How would I know?' replied TC bluntly. 'Ask me if my feet hurt, I'll say yes. Ask me if I have a nappy pin holding my skirt up, I'll say yes. Ask me if the girl I was lucky enough to have help me was of great assistance, I'll say yes. Call me again at five twenty-nine for the answer to the only question of interest to you. Bye now!'

'When will I learn?' Vance asked himself as he hung up. He was depressed about anything and everything. Needed to unload on TC. Blew his chance. Now he'd have to wait all day.

Stuff it, he thought. I may as well drive out to the worst mine we've ever had. See if I can cheer up the poor bloody men.

§

Captain Russ and Blanche walked into the shop simultaneously, Blanche through the side door, the captain via the front. They all but collided in the middle.

'That's quite a greeting,' laughed Captain Russ.

'Blanche knocks victims down, then she robs them,' laughed TC.

'Unfortunately, I didn't quite make it this time. Damn it! I'll have to practice more.'

'That explains why your shop is so popular,' said Captain Russ. 'The admiral asked me to give you this. He said to hang it next to the one you already have. He also wants you to know his wife loves opal. I have to rush. I'll bring my wife to meet you soon. Bye, TC. Bye, Blanche. Keep working on your tackling technique.'

Incredible! thought TC.

'You must be doing something right,' said Blanche. 'Two carrier groups and two wall plaques.'

'I'm blessed, Blanche, really blessed,' replied TC softly. 'Every day I'm thankful for the way things have fallen into place for me. What I have to do is keep going and never take anything for granted. We'd best get to work. I have to sort the aftermath. Sounds terrible, but I hope we don't get any customers until we're done.'

'I was thinking exactly the same,' admitted Blanche. 'They can come after we've sorted the mess.'

Sort it they did. By 2 pm, TC knew what they'd sold, how much they'd taken, asked Blanche to make the deposit at the bank, and fetch back lunch while she was at it.

'Here's the money, Blanche. Choose us something befitting a labourer's lunch.'

TC made a call to Peter and his dad to tell them she owed them a lot of money. She also needed to buy more stock. Peter would be there on Monday.

One by one, TC contacted the handful of suppliers she knew, made appointments for the following week, wrote Vance's cheque for his stock sold, then began writing him a detailed list on the shop's exact financial situation.

'Here we go, two labourers' lunches coming up,' announced Blanche on her return.

'Looks like it,' laughed TC when she saw the size of the open-topped box Blanche was carrying. It was loaded with brown paper bags containing she-didn't-know what, with two large milk-shake containers protruding into space.

'Let's eat I'm starving,' said Blanche.

'Me, too,' said TC. 'As the men at camp would say, I could eat a horse, then chase the rider.'

'They sound like an interesting lot,' said Blanche.

'They are, Blanche. They are also good men. More like them and the world is a better place. Only weakness the poor souls have is booze. They drink to escape reality.'

'Do you drink, TC?' asked Blanche.

'No! That's not to say I never will!' replied TC. 'I suppose I haven't, to date, been so desperate for an escape route that I've deemed it necessary to turn to the bottle.'

'I did it myself for a little while,' confessed Blanche. 'I thought my heart was broken; the pain was unbearable. I searched for escape in a brandy bottle. One day I woke up to myself and thought of my children. Thank God, I had my mother to help me through.'

¶

When it was closing time, TC was sorry to see Blanche about to leave.

'That's too much,' said Blanche when she was handed her pay.

'No, it's not, Blanche,' replied TC. 'Where would I have been without you? Is it all right if I call on you from time to time?'

'Sure!' agreed Blanche. 'On Saturday nights my girlfriend and I occasionally go to a nightclub in one of the hotels. Would you like to come with us sometime?'

'I'd love to, Blanche, but depends on Gracie's and Robert's schedules.'

'Done! I'll call you soon.' Blanche was gone in a heartbeat. TC felt lonely again. Vance didn't call. She started home to Gracie and Robert, who would undoubtedly nag her as to when they were going to Mr Bill's restaurant again. The little darling would be excited when she told him it would be tomorrow night. He deserved it. She'd hardly seen him during waking hours for the past five days. Lord only knew how they would handle things when she had to send him to Jake for the Christmas holidays, which were fast approaching. The mere thought of putting Robert on a plane and sending him off to a father who bothered to call his son only once a month, sometimes not even that, made TC shiver with cold.

¶

Vance was at the camp of the worst mine he had, having an after-evening-meal talk with the men, who were all, including Yappy, feeling defeated, demoralised, and depressed.

'I think you've done your dough on this site, mate,' said Neil. 'I know there's supposed to be opal here, but I'm buggered if we can find it.'

'The bastards ripped you off, Vance,' said Yappy.

'I think I have to agree,' surprisingly came from Little Joe. The other men nodded.

'It's eating up money, all right,' admitted Vance. 'I've spent more here already than it cost me all up on mine number one. I don't know what the bloody hell we're going to do. Keep shovelling money in, or pull out and cut the losses.'

'Is it possible it was bullshit about the countless tonnes of magnificently beautiful opal they supposedly mined here?' asked Neil. 'I haven't met anyone who ever saw so much as one bloody boulder come out of the place.'

'That's right,' agreed Yappy. 'Not even the elders can recall seeing any of it.'

'I heard they were private people, kept to themselves,' rationalised Vance.

'Bloody hole and tunnels all over the place, but not so much as a chip off a boulder,' said Neil. 'At least at the other mines, there were surface traces, but not here.'

¶

Vance sighed heavily. He thought momentarily before speaking. 'We'll keep going until the Christmas break. I'll drive one way or the other then. I'm driving east tomorrow. I'll see you in about a week. In the meantime, Jonathon will be around; he's working on a machine at mine two. Should have that tied up in a day or so.'

'How's young Andrew?' enquired Neil with genuine interest.

'He's fossicking. Hopefully he'll come up with a new site. He'll be a father soon.'

'Yes, and you'll be a bloody grandfather,' quipped Yappy.

'Yes, I know! I'll see you men next week.' Vance drove towards town thinking, Bugger it! I'll leave tonight. I won't be able to sleep, so I may as well be driving. I'll call TC tomorrow from the shop. I'll have to send Chikako on a message so she can't earwig.

Vance was kidding himself. From the moment he set foot in the shop next morning, Chikako was glued to him like tarpaper to a concrete pole. It didn't worry her she looked like crap and was covered in red dust. She was sending the all-female staff, including a soft, gently-spoken, pretty Japanese woman named Ayako, employed only a week previously, a firm message to keep their distance from Vance. He was hers! Stay away!

It's downright bloody embarrassing, thought Vance. Where on earth has my stiff prick led me this time? Chikako instructed the staff in her directorial manner to busy themselves in the shop; Vance and she had business to discuss in the office, where she cornered him after firmly closing the door behind her.

'My darling, it seems an eternity since we were alone together,' murmured Chikako in her somewhat masculine interpretation of sultry and seductive as she began unfastening Vance's shirt buttons. Vance pushed Chikako's hands away.

'Don't be ridiculous, Chikako. We are hardly alone now.'

'They wouldn't dare come in here,' replied Chikako while attempting to resume her objective by unfastening Vance's belt. Vance was furious. He grabbed her hands in his and glared into her eyes.

'Chikako, not now!' he whispered angrily. 'If you persist, it will be never.' Not to be perturbed, Chikako smiled coquettishly.

'I can't wait till closing time when they go.'

Vance shook his head in disbelief, stepped past Chikako, opened the office door, then made an effort to chat with the other staff. By closing time, Vance found himself extremely attracted to Ayako, the new Japanese staff member. She was the most feminine woman he had ever met; the total opposite to Chikako. Ayako was married. So, what! Chikako was married, too. Come to think of it, he was married himself.

Better play it cool, thought Vance as one by one the staff departed. Chikako knows more about the damned shop than I do. Better not upset her. she could easily become another Fred Brolga. Without my being any the wiser, she's in the position to rob me blind. Can't afford to lose her at the moment. The only customers we have are Japanese, and there are plenty of them. Best I play the pretend game for a while.

'I'll get a room in the hotel,' said Vance when all except Chikako had gone. 'Give me a chance to take a shower; I'll call you from upstairs with the room number.'

❡

After a few days of pretend passion with Chikako every time she saw an opportunity for them to disappear, her constant nagging him as to when he was going to tell Delores about them, and his growing attraction towards Ayako, Vance decided to escape to Brolga.

If it were the old days, I'd be swimming in half a dozen rum bottles, he reminded himself. Seems I get myself into deeper trouble with women sober than I did when I was a drunk. Perhaps I should have quit women instead of booze. It would have to be less complicated. While thinking of his mess with women, the Almut-Jonathon situation came to mind. 'What the bloody hell am I going to do about that?' Vance knew Jonathon deserved better than Almut. How could he possibly bring himself to say, 'She's not for you, son; she's been on with your old man—for years.' Even if that weren't the fact, which it was, Almut still wasn't good enough for Jonathon. She was a conniving bitch, whereas Jonathon was a well-mannered, well-spoken, intelligent young man, always respectful to his elders, including the men working the mines. He

635

loved and always looked out for his younger brother, who had dropped his education early and therefore had not been afforded the breaks and opportunities Jonathon himself had enjoyed.

Before departing for Brolga, Vance impressed his shop staff by buying them cakes for afternoon tea. He was amused when Ayako chose a pretty pink one. How fitting, he thought. She's fragile; can't weigh more than ninety pounds. I must be debauched. Is it she herself, or the fact she's so incredibly tiny, the reason I'm attracted?'

'All right, ladies. I'm out of here. See you next time. Happy selling.' Chikako moved towards him. His glare warned her off.

After a few hours driving towards Brolga, Vance called TC from a phone booth at a service station. It was 5.25 pm her time.

'You're four days late and four minutes early,' said TC when she heard his voice.

'I got tied up,' laughed Vance.

'In more ways than one, I'm sure.'

'How are you, TC?'

'You're finally learning, Mr Callahan,' replied TC. She was laughing inside. 'I'm fine, thank you. So is Robert. How are you?'

'Honestly, Little One, I'm buggered,' replied Vance. 'Women will be the end of me.'

'Is Chikako giving you a hard time?' Vance laughed.

'You might say that.' Then he became serious. 'She's asking the same question they all do. Only difference with her is she has it set in her mind I'm going to confess to Delores.'

'Sure. Pigs might fly, too. Perhaps you should bottle what you've got and sell it. I'm certain there's a few million or so men who'd rush to buy it.'

'Don't be clever, Little One,' reprimanded Vance seriously. 'It's a real problem! If I tell her to piss off, she'll probably rob me. If I don't, she's likely to blab to Delores.' TC sighed heavily. She was stuck for words. 'Are you there, TC?' asked Vance as TC heard more coins being inserted in the slot.

'Yes, of course I'm still here. I don't think Chikako would say anything to Delores; that would be stupid! Reading between the lines, I'd say she's after money. In Chikako's eyes, you equate to exactly that— money, money, money! If your wife divorced you, only half of what you have now would be your net worth. You're better set to pay her off like you did that other floozy years ago.'

'Oh, shit! I hope it doesn't come to that. I'll find a way if I have to.'

'We did well with the ships. I sent you a list and a cheque for your stock, which was a few pieces of matrix, four stones, and the last of your three decent pendants. I've repaid myself the money I spent on stock when we opened, drawn my wages from day dot, apart from that, the shop owns all the stock and I have a small float.'

'That's good, Little One. Well done. Tell me, did you lose your heart to a Yank?'

'Don't be ridiculous! Unlike you, from whose mistakes I have learned. Business and pleasure do not mix.' Vance laughed.

'Smart girl!' Then a hang-up.

¶

Time passed quickly. The shop was busy as peak season approached. Also closing in was the day TC would have to put Robert on a plane flying east to Jake. Although she phoned and literally begged for their son to stay with her, Jake wouldn't budge.

'That was the effing deal, TC. I'll come over there and wring your effing neck if the kid's not on the plane. Don't stuff me around! Put him on that effing plane, TC, or I'll effing-will kill you.'

Since their first visit to Mr Bill's seafood restaurant, it had become a part of TC and Robert's routine to eat there every Saturday night. Mr Bill treated Robert as a young adult and always chatted with him at bill-paying time. Robert adored Mr Bill.

It was en route home from Mr Bill's a couple of weeks before Russell had to go to his father when TC decided to broach the matter.

'How would you like to spend Christmas with your father?' asked TC.

'No, I want to stay with you, Mother,' replied Robert bluntly.

'He wants to see you, darling.' Robert was on the verge of tears.

'I don't want to see him, Mother. I want to stay with you and Gracie.'

'I know you do, darling. I want you to stay with Gracie and me, too.' Robert was crying.

'Please don't make me go, Mama.' Tears silently streamed down TC's cheeks.

'I can't promise you that, sweetheart. Would you like to go to Kings Park before we go home?'

'No!' sobbed Robert. 'I want to go home, Mama.'

The moment TC pulled into their garage, Robert climbed on her lap and hugged her tightly while continuing to sob.

'Please don't make me go, Mama,' he pleaded repeatedly. TC endeavoured to soothe him by hugging him with one arm and gently patting his head with her free hand.

'Come on, darling; we'll go inside. We can cuddle on the couch.'

'Will you carry me, Mama?' whispered Robert between sniffles.

'Of course, I will as long as you unlock the door for me.' With lips quivering, Robert attempted to smile.

'Deal, Mama!'

Out of the car, TC picked her son up to carry him inside. He spotted her wet face in the light cast by the garage ceiling fluorescent tube.

'Are you crying, too, Mother?' TC smiled at her shaking child.

'No! I've got dust in my eyes.'

Robert wiped his mother's cheeks, then whispered in her ear, 'Like Mr Callahan did at the motel?'

'That's right,' whispered TC back. 'You have a very good memory.'

Robert insisted on sleeping in TC's bed that night. She didn't have the heart to refuse. He was hugging her tightly when he eventually fell asleep before a restless night of tossing and turning. The first words he uttered on waking early morning were, 'Please don't make me go to him, Mother.'

TC wanted to scream, It's not me making you go. It's your lying, thieving, wife-bashing father. Instead, she ruffled Robert's curls. 'What would Robert Carmichael like to do today?'

'Be with you, Mama,' was the reply as he nestled close to his mother.

'Of course, you'll be with me, darling,' assured TC.

Between then and when it was time to fly east, Robert repeatedly begged TC not to make him go. He sought assistance from Gracie with whom TC shared countless long conversations regarding the sad predicament. Gracie suggested Robert tell his father he didn't want to go. He did. After dialling Jake's number himself, Gracie and TC heard him say,

'I don't want to come to you. I want to stay with mother and Gracie.' Within seconds, he burst into tears, dropped the phone on the floor, and rushed to TC.

'He said I'm a sook. I'm going! If I don't, my mother knows what will happen. What will happen, Mother?' Robert clung to TC. He was crying uncontrollably. Gracie was crying; so was TC, whose mind was racing.

It's inhumane to do this to children, Jake. TC was silently answering Jake. You're doing this to get at me. You don't care what it's doing to Robert. This must be happening to little ones all over the world, children being treated like rag dolls in a tug of war. It's wrong, so wrong! My heart goes out to everyone facing the dilemma. It's uncivilised. Suddenly a voice from within told TC to straighten herself up and be strong. She wasn't helping her son by being a wimp. The never-forgotten passage from Vance's AA Bible came to mind—"Courage to accept the things we cannot change, change the things we can, and the wisdom to know the difference". Realisation came upon TC that she couldn't change the fact that Robert was going to his father. She had no choice other than to accept it, as did Robert. She hugged her son tightly, then kissed his forehead.

'Come on, no more tears. Let's wash our faces. That means you, too, Gracie. Perhaps your dad will take you to see grandma, auntie Maggie, and Mr D while you're away,' continued TC as they climbed the stairs to the bathroom.

'I'd like that. I hope I see Mr Callahan, too; he makes me laugh.'

'Maybe you will,' replied TC with zeal, while knowing full well there was as much chance of Jake taking Robert to see Maggie and Mr D or arranging for him to see Vance, as there was of a snow flake surviving a trip on the back of a truck across the Nullarbor Plains. Robert would be lucky if Jake so much as made the effort to take him for a visit with his grandmother.

'Perhaps you should make a list of things you'd like to do, darlin',' said Gracie.

'The Koala Park would be my favourite,' replied Robert with enthusiasm.

Sure! thought TC while knowing full well her son would not be taken to the Koala Park. Jake's gambling and boozing routine couldn't be interrupted for such a mundane outing. Regardless of how much his son wanted to see the koalas, it wouldn't happen.

*

Although TC and Gracie relentlessly encouraged Robert regarding his upcoming trip, he was obviously still feeling anxious. Every night since TC had broached the subject and had allowed him to sleep in her bed, he would settle in his own, but somehow find his way into hers during the night, snuggle close, then wake her in the mornings before the alarm sounded by patting her head until she opened her eyes; then he would say, 'I love you, Mama.' The moment TC would reply, 'I love you, too, darling,' Robert would hug her, then jump off the bed. 'Come on, Mama. Time to get up. Gracie says we don't spend enough awake time together.'

*

The first morning he did and said this, TC wanted to choke Gracie. Immediately she realised it was true. She bounded out of bed, switched on the radio, and did a little jig, which caused Robert to laugh. It was now an every-morning occurrence.

*

The dreaded day, which TC would always remember as one of the worst in her life, finally arrived. It was a Sunday. Robert's flight departure time was scheduled for 10 pm.

'Darling, you choose what you want to take. Mama will help you pack,' suggested TC after performing her morning jig and breakfast was out of the way. 'You'll be able to sleep on the plane. When you wake up, you'll be there, and your dad will meet you.'

'Tell me the shop phone number and address, then the same for here where we live.'

'Spot on,' smiled TC when Robert completed reciting it.

'Do you want your Christmas presents today, sweetheart?' asked TC.

'No, thank you; I'll wait till I come back home,' was Robert's flat reply.

'Okay, that sounds good. Apart from your Christmas presents, I bought you a wallet to take with you,' said TC. Robert's eyes lit up fleetingly.

'I can use that when I pay Mr Bill next time.'

'That's right,' agreed TC. 'Here it is.' She produced his small wallet from a drawer.'

'There's fifty dollars in there, so don't lose it. Your initials are on the front.'

'I love it! I'm glad there's a picture of us inside.'

'There's also a card in there with our address and phone numbers,' said TC. 'Your father's is on it, too. Want to go for a ride on your bike?'

'No, I'd like to go to Kings Park and have a hot dog and Coke.'

¶

They arrived at the airport an hour before the flight time. TC checked in his small bag. Robert stood close to her and took in her every word and move.

'Want to go upstairs where you can see the planes through the windows?' asked TC. Robert nodded. He had not uttered a word since they had gotten in the car at home.

'They're big, aren't they?' said TC. They were upstairs overlooking half a dozen or so parked planes. 'They're very safe, too.' No reply from Robert, who was squeezing his mother's hand so tightly it was numb. A voice on the public address system announced it was boarding time for his flight.

TC stood aside with Robert until the last person in the queue was gone. She then approached the gate. Robert wrapped his arms around her legs. He was shaking uncontrollably; his eyes were wide with terror as he looked up at her, begging to stay. The flight attendant was lovely; she understood.

'Your mummy can go with you to the plane, little man. I'm coming, too; be right behind you.'

'Thank you, thank you very much,' said TC while willing herself to restrain a flow of tears. They reached the plane door as the engines started up. TC kneeled down and hugged Robert tightly.

'I don't want to go, Mama,' he cried.

'I know, darling; the nice ladies will look after you.' TC stood up and turned away. It was breaking her heart to let him go.

'Mama, please don't leave me,' screamed Robert. TC turned quickly to see her son with his arms outstretched towards her. He looked so tiny and vulnerable. His eyes were imploring her not to walk away.

'He'll be all right. You go,' assured the flight attendant softly. 'Broken marriage?' TC nodded.

'Rips your heart out, doesn't it,' continued the nice lady. 'In similar circumstances myself. It's the little ones who are the victims.'

TC went upstairs, watched the plane taxi to the end of the runway, slowly turn, then take off. She all but ran to her car, where she cried until there were no tears left to shed. With every tear, she hated Jake more.

※

TC didn't sleep a wink that night during which the message once again came through to her loud and clear—Robert was, indeed, her reason for her living. Without him in it, her life would be but a void.

※

Robert engulfed her when the telephone rang early morning and she picked it up to hear his voice.

'I'm here, Mother. I cried. The ladies were nice to me. I had a sleep. I love you, Mama. I miss you.'

'I love and miss you, too, darling,' replied TC, once again holding back tears. 'You be good and try to have a happy time.'

'I'm worried about you, Mother.'

'Don't worry about me, sweetheart. You know the numbers. You can call me whenever you want.'

'Dad said I have to go now, Mama. I love you.'

'You, too, darling. Talk to you soon.'

'Pull yourself together, TC,' she told herself immediately after putting down the phone. 'Quit the self-pity. Get yourself to work.'

❡

'How goes it, Little One?' asked Vance when he called at one minute past nine. 'Has Robert gone?'

'Yes. I don't want to discuss it,' replied TC.

'Sorry. I haven't been much help to you during the past couple of months,' apologised Vance.

'Don't worry about it, Boss. You did all you could. You listened to my worries. After all, that's about the limit of what I can ever do to help with your problems.'

'What are you going to do while Robert's away?'

'Work, of course!' replied TC. 'It's summer. The tourist season is in full swing. I aim to get my fair share of customers and hopefully a few more. I'm going to start looking for a house to buy on Saturday afternoons and Sundays. Prices here are amazingly low. New three-bedroom, double-brick homes close to the city are going from around fifty thousand.'

'Sounds like a good idea, Little One; they can only go up. Talk to you soon.'

❡

TC had her first unforgettable experience with Japanese tourists that day. Late in the morning, a tiny, soft-spoken Japanese woman visited the shop. After slowly moving around and closely examining the stock and sticker prices, she advised TC she was escorting a group of Japanese tourists in the afternoon.

'Is it all right if I bring the people here?' enquired the lady ever so politely. 'Your stock is very beautiful.'

TC smiled. 'Of course! I'm afraid I don't speak Japanese. Please bring them if you wish.'

These were the days prior to Japanese tour operators establishing their own offices in Western Australia and directing their guides to escort groups of herded-around-like-cattle tourists to allocated, contracted, commission-paying shops only. For the time being, the guides could take their people wherever they wished.

TC was speechless a few hours later when the tiny guide arrived back at the shop with a group so large only half of them could fit packed shoulder-to-shoulder inside while the rest remained outside in the arcade. It was an impossible situation.

Even if I spoke fluent Japanese, thought TC, I wouldn't be able to sell in this instance. All I can do is smile. She did exactly that—stood and smiled while the tour guide told the crowd in Japanese, 'Now you know where Brolga Opals is located. Please come back in your free time if you wish to make a purchase.'

Unbelievable, thought TC as the crowd left the shop to join the other half in the arcade, then moved off to follow the guide, who led their way to the mall. Poor souls are like sheep.

A little before closing time, TC was surprised to receive a call from the guide lady, who wanted to arrange bringing the eager-to-buy-opal members of the group next morning. When TC explained verbal communication was impossible, the guide replied, 'No problem. I'll be interpreter for you.'

'Thank you. I'll pay you for your trouble,' assured TC. The arrangement was made and so began TC's business dealings with Japanese tourists.

§

'So, they're coming there, too?' asked Vance in surprise when TC told him about her day during his five-twenty-nine call.

'Looks like it!' replied TC. 'If all their groups are that big, I'll need a lot more space and Japanese-speaking staff. I'll see what happens tomorrow.'

'I'm starting to realise we'll have to pay to have the poor buggers shop with us,' said Vance. 'Hasn't happened here yet; I hear that's the go in Sydney and Melbourne.'

'Aren't they allowed to shop at their own will?' asked TC in shock.

'I'm sure they can, but I hear the tour companies tell them there's no certainty of quality, value, and after-sales service unless they shop at allocated outlets.'

'That's unfair. I'd rather give the customer a discount than pay commission to a tour company. Surely they've made money by arranging the trips.'

'You're still innocent, Little One,' laughed Vance. 'You haven't learned about the love of money and what people will do to acquire it, as yet'

'Perhaps I'm better off being innocent than avaricious' was TC's curt reply. 'I'll talk to you in the morning.'

§

TC was in no hurry to get home. There was no one there to greet her; so, why hurry. As she wandered slowly through the mall, pausing occasionally to look in the store windows, she made a positive decision not to be miserable during the month Robert was with Jake. She would curb loneliness by at last going to a nightclub with Blanche and her friend on Saturday night.

I'll also contact Fiona Smythe and accept the invitation to her New Year's party, thought TC. Both women had called TC frequently. Both understood her need to spend as much time as possible with Robert prior to his departure.

It was now time to socialise!

'If I'm going night-clubbing, I'll need a couple more after-five outfits,' she told herself as she ceased dawdling and started walking quickly towards her car. 'I'll call Blanche the second I get home. I'll phone Fiona tomorrow.'

'TC Carmichael, wait,' called a male voice from the entrance to a hotel she had passed a few seconds back.

'I know it's you, TC. I'd know that walk anywhere.'

'It's her all right, mate,' said another male voice. TC turned on her heels to look directly into the face of Randy James. With him was one of the younger men who had worked on Mr D's job and lived at the Pink Brolga. TC was surprised, to say the least, as she shook her head in disbelief.

'It's obviously a small world.'

'Thank heaven for that,' said Randy James, who had obviously had a couple or three too many of whatever he'd been drinking.

'We've had a big day out, TC,' beamed the younger man.

'I don't need to be told. It's obvious,' laughed TC.

'I've been dreaming about you ever since I left the Pink Brolga, TC,' said Randy.

'Sure, Randy,' laughed his companion. 'That's why every time the other men on the job and I turn around you've cottoned on to a different bird.'

'Yes, mate, but they're not TC. She's the one who got away,' replied Randy seriously.

'That's exactly what she is going to continue to do, Randy James,' laughed TC.

'How about joining us for a meal, TC,' invited Randy, who was, along with his mate, trying desperately to retain body balance as they swayed forwards, then straightened themselves repeatedly.

'Yes, TC, how about coming and having a feed with us,' slurred the mate.

'Thank you, but no thank you,' declined a smiling TC. 'While you are both immaculately attired and ruggedly handsome, you are also extremely drunk. Perhaps some other time when you're not plastered. I am surprised to see you. I must go.' As TC hurried away, Randy called after her.

'Where do I find you when I'm not drunk?'

TC kept walking. Without turning, she raised one arm above her shoulder and waved goodbye while silently replying, That depends on how desperate you are to find me, drunken, womanising Mr James. I hope you don't!

The first nightclub outing with Blanche and her girlfriend was interesting with more than a few amusing highlights. Apart from the bar area, the lighting was dimmed to almost dark.

'They keep it dark so even the ugly people appear attractive,' quipped Blanche.

'At least until the lights go on at closing time,' added her friend.

'I understand now, Blanche, why you insisted we arrive early to get a table,' remarked TC while looking around at the way-over-capacity, tightly-packed crowd. 'The males must love it! They can accidentally rub against the girls without fear of a face-slapping reaction.'

'You watch, TC,' laughed Blanche. 'Some of the females are worse than the blokes.' TC smiled.

'I've seen that before,' she replied while thinking back to the Pink Brolga, the night of the friendship group's welcome function, and most of all the antics of Vance's girlfriends in the dispensary. Blanche giggled.

'Of course, you have. Who could forget those poor Yanks cornered by the horny tarts at the friendship 'do'. Poor buggers had no chance; they'd been at sea for Lord knows how long.'

The background music abruptly ended and the DJ's voice sounded loud and clear over the laughter and noise of the multitudes conversing.

'Hello, everyone. It's Saturday night and time to Rock with the King, Jerry Lee, Chubby, Dion, and the Belmonts, plus a dozen or so other legends. We'll leave the slow, romantic numbers until you guys have had your last sherbet and are looking for a victim to take home. Just joking! Here we go with Bobby Freeman's 'Do You Wanna Dance?'

'I know I'll love the music,' said TC.

'That's what we come here for,' smiled Blanche.

'You're spot-on there,' came from her friend. 'Hope you dance, TC.' TC smiled and nodded.

'Where I grew up, just about everyone learned to dance; nothing else to do.'

'Let's do it,' said Blanche as Elvis sang, 'Lord Almighty, I feel my temperature rising.'

Four songs later, perspiring and thirsty, they returned to their table to find their purses piled in the centre and three men sitting on their chairs.

'We've been watching you dance,' said one.

'Easy on the eyes,' said another.

'Can we buy you ladies a drink?' from the third.

'Not for me, thank you, but my feet are tired,' replied TC softly with a smile.

'Mine, too,' sighed Blanche.

'We'd like our seats back please,' added the friend.

'You can sit on our laps,' suggested the obviously more outgoing of the trio.

'Can't do that; you might get carried away by our closeness,' smiled Blanche in her silky, sexy voice.

'We were hoping we would have that effect on you,' replied the outgoing one.

'I suggest you move off our chairs,' said TC sweetly. 'If you don't, I shall have to deck the three of you. By doing so, I would cause you great embarrassment and humiliation.'

Mouths open in disbelief, the three gazed at TC in silence.

'Don't let her size fool you, gentlemen,' added Blanche. 'She's the featherweight female boxing champion of Queensland.'

The three were off the chairs instantly. Within seconds they had disappeared into the crowd while the girls launched into laughter and resumed their seats.

'Poor buggers believed us,' said Blanche.

'You two should be on the stage,' said her friend.

They danced off and on until the music slowed getting towards that last sherbet time.

'This is when we bow out,' said Blanche.

'Sounds good,' replied TC. 'Thank you for inviting me. I've had a great time.'

'We all have,' chorused Blanche and friend.

As they fought their way through the hordes, they heard the outgoing one say to whomever he was with, 'There she is. Wouldn't bloody believe it, would you? She's a boxing champion from Queensland.'

After leaving the nightclub, TC followed the others to an all-night hamburger shop. It was across the river, virtually on Perth's doorstep. Partway through their food, TC decided, due to close proximity to the city, this was the area in which she should look to buy a house.

'Is there's a residential suburb close by here?' she enquired of Blanche and her friend, who both went silent.

'I think I'd like to live around here. It's close to the shop. I could probably walk there in fifteen to twenty minutes.'

'You could also walk to the Perth dump; it's a hundred yards that way,' laughed the friend while pointing left from the hamburger shop.

TC sighed sadly. 'I see.'

'TC's right; it is very close to her work,' said Blanche.

'Talk to you soon.' They went their separate ways.

As TC drove home, she decided to return to the area near the hamburger place next day. She knew she was meant to live there, dump or no dump.

¶

'What are you going to do today, Mama?' enquired Robert when he made his daily, early-morning call. 'It's Sunday. You and I always do things together. I'm not there; so, I'm worried about you.'

'Don't worry about me, sweetheart,' replied TC. 'I think I'll go searching for a new place to live.'

'Will we live there when I come home, Mother?'

'Maybe. Depends on whether or not I find somewhere by then.'

TC could tell Robert was on the verge of tears when he said, 'I miss you, Mama.'

'One week gone; only three to go,' she replied lightly, hoping to curtail his near-tearful state.

'I love you, Mama. I'll call you tomorrow.'

'I love you, too, Robert Carmichael. Talk to you then,' replied TC.

I know Jake hangs on Robert's every word, she thought as she hung up. I'd lay London to a brick that he hasn't so much as taken the child anywhere yet.

With that, TC called Thel Carmichael, who eagerly volunteered to phone Jake and remind him that she was Robert's grandmother and expected to see her grandson very soon.

¶

Vance was checking on the crews from both mines behind the Majestic. All except Yappy and Ted's wife were still drunk from Saturday night's non-stop drinking spree.

'These are a bright-looking mob, aren't they, Yappy? What do you think?'

'I'll wring Ted's neck when the mongrel sobers up,' snapped his wife before turning and striding off towards her room.

'They're as hung-over as fifteen bastards after a three-day Two-Up game,' said Yappy.

'Get stuffed, Yappy,' mumbled Neil as he lifted a flagon of red to his lips. 'I'm not effing hung over; I'm still drinkin'.'

'You tell him, Neil,' laughed Vance. 'How about you, Little Joe? You're looking pretty second-hand flat-out there on the bare concrete. Perhaps you should find a bed?'

No reply.

'They all look like crap,' said Yappy.

'Bloody feel like it, too,' came from one of Neil's brothers, who sat leaning against a verandah post with his head cupped in his hands.

'Piss off, Callahan. You too, Yappy,' came from now-slurring Neil. 'If you're not going to drink with me, go to buggery, both of you.'

'Come on, Yappy, mate; we've been told,' laughed Vance.

'I'm going to Con's for a feed,' said Yappy as they turned to leave.

'Sounds good. I'll join you,' said Vance.

¶

By early afternoon that Sunday, TC had found a new home for Robert and herself. It was a not-quite-finished duplex in a tiny suburb across the highway from the hamburger place. All but a few dwellings in the area were pre-war or wartime built. TC didn't care; most of them were neat and well maintained. It was the location which appealed to her.

After driving down, up, and around, TC had spotted but a few 'for sale' signs. None of the properties with such appealed to her. Then she spotted the near-complete home with a small truck parked in the driveway. The sign on the truck announced it belonged to an independent builder.

I like that house. I can only ask, she thought as she pulled to a stop, then left her car to find the builder or the person who drove the truck.

TC was in luck. A few minutes later, she was looking through the as-yet not-advertised-for-sale property with the builder.

It's perfect for Robert and me, thought TC as she noted the three bedrooms, lovely bathroom, separate laundry, family room, huge kitchen, two fireplaces, and formal dining and lounge rooms.

'You can choose your own floor covering and light fittings to the value of two-and-a-half thousand,' said the builder. 'Anything over that you'll have to cough up yourself. There's also a six-foot fence with gates to be added yet.'

'How much is the asking price?' enquired TC gingerly. The builder thought as he looked around and calculated his costs.

'As there's no agent involved, no advertising to be done, I'll take fifty-two, including the two-and-a-half for the floors and lights plus the brick fence and gates.'

'Done deal,' said TC as she reached out her hand. 'I'll get money from my bank tomorrow.'

'Yes, okay,' agreed the builder. 'Give me half when I've got the paperwork in order and the other half when the place is finished. Should be no longer than a couple of weeks after New Year's.'

'That's right,' said TC. 'It's Christmas one week from today. Thank you for reminding me.'

'My wife and kids do nothing else but remind me,' laughed the builder.

'Here's my card. Give me a call when you have the paperwork. I hope it's this week. The house can be my Christmas present to myself.'

'I'll call you on Tuesday. My wife will probably have half your deposit spent by the big day,' complained the builder with a heavy sigh.

'I love the house,' said TC as she left, bursting with inner excitement.

❡

The week prior to Christmas passed quickly. The shop was busy. To TC's surprise, she sold opals to a few locals for their loved ones born in October, the month of opal. Blanche called. There would be no nightclubbing for her on Saturday—it was Christmas Eve, so she would stay home with the children. Fiona Smythe popped into the shop to invite TC to Christmas lunch with her family, who were coming from interstate. TC declined.

'Thank you for the thought, Fiona. I feel Christmas is a private time for families, especially when yours don't see you too often. I'd feel like a third arm.'

'You are coming to our New Year's Eve party?' asked Francis.

'Of course! That's different.'

'Great! Ken and I want you to meet some people. Would you like to bring a friend?'

'Don't know many people. Thank you, anyway,' replied TC. 'On second thought, I get along well with Blanche.'

'Good. I have her number,' smiled Fiona. 'I'll call her. Happy Christmas, darling. See you New Year's Eve.'

¶

The builder brought the house papers to the shop once, signed and witnessed by his J.P. friend who accompanied him. TC paid his deposit. After shaking hands and exchanging Christmas greetings, it was done. TC felt secure with the knowledge that she and Robert would soon be living in their very own home.'

Robert's calls were happy since talking to his grandmother and knowing he would be staying with her for a few days. Obviously Jake's mother got her message through.

Vance's calls, on the other hand, were entwined with unexplained innuendos regarding his future plans. After four days of such 'go nowhere, say nothing' conversations, TC was tired of wasting time listening to his dribble.

'Mr Callahan, if you have many things you wish to discuss, tell me what they are. While I know you almost as well as I know myself, I'm not yet equipped to read your mind. You're obviously miserable! Join the club of millions! Please don't bother me again until you have something decipherable to say.'

Vance phoned at closing time on Christmas Eve.

'I've made some big decisions this past week, Little One.'

'I'm listening' replied TC.

'I'm quitting on the last mine. I know the opal is there, but buggered if we can find it. I've blown more money than I knew I had on that site. Hopefully, I'll sell the lease to someone who'll have more luck. At least I'll get some of my money back.'

'What about the men?'

'They'll be all right. I'll keep mine two going and resume operating number three.'

'So that's what's been worrying you? Now I understand,' said TC.

'There's more. Almut is a done deal! Jonathon started flinging the word marriage around whenever her name came up. I had to move fast to get her out of town before he proposed. Poor bugger will most likely be confused and heartbroken for a while. That's got to be better than marrying a bitch like her.'

'I can't believe she went,' said TC. 'I'm surprised, to say the least.'

'I offered her two hundred and fifty thousand. She laughed in my face. 'Surely your darling son is worth more than that,' is what she said. She told me she wanted a Callahan. If she couldn't have me, Jonathon suited her fine. I upped the ante to half a million and told her if she didn't take it and piss off, I'd tell Delores and Jonathan about our relationship myself. She would get nothing. I also wrote a letter detailing our affair from day dot, then had her write on the bottom in her own handwriting that it was all true. If the bitch ever comes back after Jonathan again, I'll show him. Anyway, Almut left on this morning's plane. Hopefully none of us will ever see the conniving bitch again. I'm signing the leases and machinery over to Jonathan. Delores and I are moving east. We want to be close to the shop.'

'And Chikako, I imagine,' remarked TC lightly. 'Careful you don't jump out of the frying pan onto the fire.'

'Come on,' replied Vance. 'What could be worse than the thought of my son marrying some bitch I've been screwing for years?'

'Happy Christmas, Boss,' said TC. 'Be grateful she took the money.'

With the stock and shop secured, TC headed home to loneliness.

Thought after America you'd never spend another Christmas in solitude, she told herself. Wrong! Stop wallowing in self-pity, TC. Snap out of it! Millions of people are worse off than you' from the voice within. 'Robert will be back in a couple of weeks. Soon after that, you'll be moving into your new home.

After an afternoon on the phone to Maggie, Lou, Mr D, Gracie, and Jake's mother, TC piled Robert's already-wrapped Christmas gifts around the tiny tree on a corner coffee table. While doing so, she made a snap decision to get herself dolled up and go to Mr Bill's for dinner.

A few hours later she wished she hadn't. She was in the process of paying Mr Bill for her meal when she heard Randy James' unmistakable voice behind her.

'TC Carmichael, we meet again.'

"Looks like it, Randy,' said TC as she turned to face him. He looked good, too good.

This time Randy's companion was a female, who stared daggers at TC as Randy ignored her and focused his attention on TC.

'I'm not as drunk this time as I was last time we met.'

'Not quite, Randy, although I'd wager you've had a few,' replied TC with a knowing smile.

'How's Junior?' enquired Randy.

'He likes his name now. Robert is in Queensland with his father.'

'So, are you having Christmas by yourself?' asked Randy with interest. Randy's well-dressed, over-made-up date coughed.

TC said, 'I have to go now.'

'Do you have a booking, sir?' asked Bill as TC made her escape.

If I was that woman, I would have punched him, thought TC as she hurried to her car. He pretended she wasn't there! Serves him right if he gets a knock-back tonight.

¶

TC and Blanche attended the Smythes' New Year's Eve party together. Their home was lovely, filled with old-world charm. While most of the guests were many years senior to Blanche and TC, both felt comfortable being there.

'So, you're the girl Fiona and Ken have been talking about,' said one refined gentleman when introduced to TC.

'I'm not sure what you mean, sir?' asked TC.

'They want you on their friendship group committee, my dear,' was his reply.

During the evening, TC realised everyone at the party had heard about her, whereas she knew nothing about them apart from her limited knowledge regarding Ken and Fiona, Len, Lisa, and, of course, Barney.

Although she had worked only a few days with Blanche, been once to a nightclub with her, and shared a few phone calls, TC felt she knew Blanche better than all the others rolled together.

'I'm not committee material,' said TC towards the end of the evening when in a three-way conversation with Fiona, Blanche, and herself.

'Yes, you are, darling,' replied Fiona. 'I know it!'

'What about me, Mrs Smythe?' laughed Blanche.

'You can be, too,' replied Fiona. 'I want you both to attend a meeting with Ken and myself towards the end of the month. We desperately need to change the group's image. You girls can help us do that.'

'I'll give it a go if TC does,' offered Blanche.

'I'll think about it,' sighed TC.

'You'll do it, darling,' said Fiona confidently. 'I'll harass you until you see the light.'

❡

The Japanese tour escort had been bringing customers once, sometimes twice, a week since the first incident. TC gave her fifty dollars as an interpreting fee each time. They were both happy with the arrangement. The first business day after New Year the guide called TC.

'I'll keep bringing you Japanese tourists while I can. By next year I think the companies will have their own offices here. Have you heard about contracts?'

'My boss mentioned something about them once,' replied TC. 'I can't say I like the idea of shopping contracts too much myself. If push comes to shove, I'll have to do as I'm told by him.'

'I see. I thought I'd pre-warn you they are on the horizon. If you don't have contracts, you can forget about doing business with Japanese tourists.'

'Thanks for the warning,' said TC. 'My boss will most likely agree to sign on the dotted line.'

True to her word, Fiona Smythe harassed TC about the committee deal by calling every night at exactly 7 pm. TC was growing to love Fiona as a friend. While Fiona dripped high society and class, she had a wonderful personality, a sense of humour to die for, and called a spade a spade. TC had no doubt in her mind Fiona would talk her around and she would wind up on the committee whether she liked it or not.

¶

It was Saturday night after New Year. The Empire bar was full to overflowing with rowdy drinkers. Brolga elders sat on the sacred seat observing the goings-on.

'I wish I was in there with the drunken bastards,' said old Jock. 'Hot as bloody Hades tonight.'

'It has been for weeks,' said one of Jock's mates. 'No wonder the pill-pusher's mob are drinking themselves witless.'

'Not Yappy!' interjected Jock. 'He's as sober as a judge. I heard he won a heap on the horses. Lucky bastard! Also heard the pill-pusher is pissing off east. Young Jonathon will run the show.'

'Don't know how he'll go,' remarked someone.

'None of our bloody business,' said Jock flatly. 'Look at those mad bastards fighting in the pub; might be an interesting night,' he continued as a brawl erupted in the Empire and Jess picked up a broom with which she began hitting the two drunken fighters over their heads.

'Old Jess hasn't lost her spirit. She's giving the poor bastards one hell of a thrashing. Serves them right.' All on the seat laughed and nodded in agreement.

¶

Robert and TC's reunion was tearful and joyful, millions of hugs and kisses, lots of whispered 'I've missed you' and 'I love you', then home to open Christmas presents, after opening only one of which Robert fell asleep. TC carried him to his bed, thinking, Poor darling has probably been awake since daybreak. It's two in the morning in Queensland. No wonder he's asleep. I wish I could spend the day with him tomorrow. I can't. I have to go to work. He'll be happy with Gracie; she'll keep him amused. I loathe you, Jake. You could have sent him home yesterday like I asked. You know I have to work all week. At least you might have put him on an earlier flight today.

After removing Robert's boots, she put him to bed still fully clothed in his denim suit, kissed him on the forehead, patted his curls, whispered, 'I love you, darling,' then added, 'You're back with Mama now, and that's all that matters.'

Gracie had arrived and TC gone to work before Robert stirred next morning. He phoned his mother the moment he ventured downstairs.

'Am I allowed to open my presents without you being here, Mother?'

'Sure! They're yours. I hope you like them,' replied TC.

'Can we get a cat, Mother, and can we go to Mr Bill's tonight? There's no school tomorrow.' TC laughed at her son's combination of requests.

'Perhaps we'll get a cat after we move into our house. Yes, we will go to Mr Bill's tonight. By the way, I love you.'

'I know that, Mama. Bye now.'

Vance and Delores settled into city suburbia. The more time Vance spent in his shop, the less he was attracted to Chikako and the more he was attracted to Ayako. Somehow he had to get rid of Chikako. It wouldn't be easy. She had a fixation in her mind that Vance would divorce Delores and marry her. The only threat she foresaw was TC, the unknown and unseen quantity. Chikako couldn't figure out where TC fitted into Vance's life. She was determined to find out. She didn't know how but felt confident she'd come up with a plan. In the meantime, Chikako was so busy throwing her weight around and lording it over the other staff. She was blind to the chemistry between Vance and Ayako.

TC and Robert moved into their new home the weekend prior to the friendship group's annual general meeting, which was chaired by Ken Smythe, the president. Blanche and TC sat on either side of Fiona in the small, crowded, rented-for-the-evening suburban hall. Both noticed there was a lot of bitching going on as the meeting progressed, with this one, then that one, airing their mostly petty gripes.

'I wish Ken would make them quit whinging,' whispered Fiona. 'At this rate, the sane people will be asleep before they get a say.'

Suddenly an extremely elderly, very well-dressed lady repeatedly thumped her walking stick on the wooden floor.

'Excuse me, everyone. I thought the item on top of our agenda was to discuss ways of cleaning up the group's somewhat tarnished reputation of being a pick-up joint. I've seen the way most of you conduct yourselves when our visitors are here. Disgusting, to say the least. All I've heard so far tonight is pure garbage. We won't solve our problem by ignoring it, We have to act. What on earth are we going to do, Mr President?'

'We need new blood, more members and class,' replied Ken. 'If we want to attract the right type of membership, we must smarten our act by gaining respectability.'

'How do we do that?' yelled a man in the crowd.

'One step at a time,' replied Ken Smythe.

Many 'go nowhere' discussions and suggestions later, he declared the meeting terminated.

'Boring,' whispered Blanche.

'I couldn't agree more,' whispered Fiona Smythe. 'Don't be put off. It's early days yet.' TC shrugged and remained silent.

¶

Not more than a few nights after the meeting, Fiona announced a carrier group was a couple of weeks away. 'Get yourself organised, darling. It's a big one,' said Fiona. 'I know you'll be busy, but I still want you to make time to attend every function, large or small, that the group hosts. Changes need to be made. We need people like you and

Blanche to observe and be constructively critical. We'll discuss your thoughts after the visit. Hopefully you'll come up with some ideas on how to make things better. A few others have been recruited to do the same. We all know it can't be achieved overnight, just as we are aware we have to start somewhere.'

'I'll try,' agreed TC. 'Depends on Gracie's availability. I'll also need a schedule as soon as possible.'

'Good. I'll call Blanche now,' replied Fiona. 'Thank you, darling.'

Blanche eagerly jumped at the opportunity to assist TC in the shop. She also accepted Fiona's invitation to come up with fresh ideas for the group's advancement towards social acceptance.

The visit was a full five days and hectic. Both Blanche and TC were on the verge of collapse by clean-up time the morning after the ships sailed.

'Don't know about you, TC, but as for me, I feel buggered,' said Blanche.

'I feel the same,' replied TC.

'We've been busier than a hundred horny rabbits on the job,' laughed Blanche. 'Working all day, the welcoming function, two barbeques, and one party have worn me out. I hope Fiona appreciates I knocked back five dinner invitations in order to be an observer. It wasn't easy! I still can't get over how scrumptious some of those Yanks are.'

'I know,' sighed TC. 'And so well mannered. Can you imagine our average Aussie guy taking as much time selecting, then spending as much money on gifts for their wives or girlfriends?'

'No way!' laughed Blanche. 'They'd think it would be time lost with their mates and less to spend on booze.'

'I'm sure not every Australian man falls into that category, Blanche. Overall, though, think I have to agree with you.'

Captain Russ called. 'I've got another piece for your wall. I think I'll have to start charging you delivery fees. I don't know what you're doing, but whatever it is, you're doing it well. I'll drop it in to you next week.'

'Captain Russ said we're doing a good job,' said TC after hanging up.

'Glad to know we're good for something,' laughed Blanche.

It's strange Vance hasn't called to ask how we went, thought TC. He's obviously busy or avoiding me. Time will tell.

TC phoned Peter. 'Better beat the vultures here.' Peter promised to see TC on Monday.

'Looks like we've done better than last time,' said Blanche when TC had finished the tally.

'Bigger carrier, more people, more sales,' replied TC. 'We'll have to get a third person to help us next time. If we can find anyone.'

'I wish I could work here all the time,' sighed Blanche.

'Who knows!' replied TC with confidence. 'I plan on having a much bigger shop on the Terrace in the not-too-distant future. You can have a full-time job there if you want.'

'You say that as if you know it's going to happen,' laughed Blanche.

'That's because I know it will happen,' replied TC matter-of-factly.

Desperate to fill gaps until the cases were replenished with stock, TC asked Blanche to hang the 'let them go at cost' silver pendants in one of the wall displays.

'They could do with a clean,' remarked TC. 'I threw them in the safe when the shop first opened. Hang them now. They won't be there, the long, ugly damned things.' Blanche frowned.

'They are awful, aren't they?'

'Let's go to the nightclub again soon,' suggested Blanche at closing time. 'Not this weekend, but perhaps the next.'

'If Robert and Gracie agree, then it's a deal,' replied TC. 'We'll see each other at Fiona and Ken's meeting through the week. What are you going to say?'

'The truth!' replied Blanche. TC nodded and smiled.

'Me, too!'

¶

Due to countless interruptions, Peter and TC didn't finish their dealings until late Monday. TC decided to mark and list the new stock at home that night. Vance still hadn't called.

By Tuesday morning, she was busy displaying the new stock on trays in boxes and wall cases. There was stuff everywhere when a small Japanese woman stepped into the shop. She was dressed in what TC imagined was women's country garb in Japan—white socks, black slippers, ankle-length, black cotton skirt, white blouse, and crinkled, black cotton, ankle-length coat with three-quarter sleeves. She wore no make-up whatsoever, not even lipstick. In one hand, she carried a thick fabric handbag; in the other, she carried a small, obviously expensive leather suitcase, which stood out in stark contrast to her attire. TC's eyes were riveted on a blazing-red, opal pendant which adorned the stranger's neck. It was magnificent. TC was taken aback when the woman spoke. It was the deepest female voice she had ever heard. TC knew this was Chikako. This was the voice she'd encountered on the telephone when calling for Vance.

'I said I'm Chikako! How many times do I have to tell you?' snapped the intruder as she brushed past TC, placed her handbag on the desk, then opened the door to the safe room, where she dumped her suitcase under the sink.

'I heard you the first time, Chikako. Please make yourself at home. I'm surprised you're here without my prior knowledge,' replied TC with as much calm as she could muster.

'This shop is a mess!' snarled Chikako as she unplugged the radio. 'No music when conducting business!'

'I'm aware the shop's untidy,' replied TC while endeavouring to control her tongue and re-plugging the radio. 'I also happen to like music.'

Chikako looked around the shop, pointing at the tarnished silver pendants on the wall.

'Clean those pendants,' she commanded as if talking to a mongrel dog. 'No wonder Vance wanted me to come and check on you.' TC saw red.

'Is that so!' she flung open the glass doors of the wall case. With both hands, she grabbed the pendants, ripped them all off the wall hooks, and then threw the whole lot at Chikako. 'Clean the bastards yourself!'

Chikako was in shock as she looked down at the pieces scattered on the floor near her feet.

'So! Vance sent you to here to check on me? We'll see about that! I'll lock us in, then call him.'

'Put Callahan on the phone,' demanded TC when a soft Japanese voice answered.

'Who's speaking, please?'

'It doesn't matter, and it's none of your business! Give him the telephone!'

'Hello,' from Vance.

'What's this crap? Sending your dictatorial concubine to check on me! In case you've forgotten, we have a business deal. Why didn't you send her last week so she could see how effing hard I work?!'

'Don't use that language,' from Vance.

'Get knotted!'

'I sent her there because she wanted to meet you.'

'Bullshit! She wanted to see me because, like Delores, she probably thinks I've been one of your sluts. I'll put her on the phone. Tell her not to pull her Gestapo garbage with me unless she wants to leave here with a cracked jaw.' Vance laughed nervously. 'Stop laughing! It's anything but funny. Here's your girlfriend,' finished TC as she thrust the telephone towards Chikako. 'Here! Talk to your boyfriend.' After thirty seconds of deep-voiced whispering, TC grabbed the telephone from Chikako and yelled into it. 'I'm leaving the premises so she doesn't have to whisper. Fix it or I'm out of here! This is the final straw!' With that, TC passed the telephone to Chikako. In doing so, she noticed the red opal ring on Chikako's hand. It matched the pendant.

TC sat in the shop across the arcade, chatting with the owner. Chikako's conversation with Vance seemed to go on forever.

I could be in there working on my display, thought TC as she pretended to make interesting conversation. This Chikako must really have Vance by his testicles. Gutless prick! Fancy not letting me know she was coming. Now I know why he hasn't phoned for a hundred years. Finally Chikako put down the telephone, then walked to the shop's main door and began looking up and down the arcade. TC was watching her, so she returned to the shop.

'Vance wants to talk to you,' said a somewhat subdued Chikako.

'Is that so, Chikako? Because I don't wish to speak with him,' replied TC with a smile.

'He'll be angry,' said Chikako.

'Do I look scared?' replied TC as she hurried to the desk where she picked up the phone and placed it gently on its cradle. 'Now tell me, Chikako, did Vance really send you to check on me?'

'He didn't exactly tell me to check on you. I wanted to meet you,' replied a now timid Chikako.

'Good. You've seen me,' said TC. 'You can go now! As you said earlier, I need to tidy the shop. By the way, take those disgustingly ugly pendants with you.'

'I'm going out for a little while,' said Chikako.

'Make it forever!' replied TC as she slammed a tray of pendants in a case. The phone rang seconds after Chikako was gone. It was Vance.

'I told you to get knotted, Mr Callahan,' snapped TC on hearing his voice. 'It'll probably be a great idea; might curtail your illicit sexual activities with other men's wives. Goodbye!' The telephone immediately rang again. TC knew it was Vance. 'What?'

'Please listen to me. Don't hang up,' pleaded Vance. 'I know Chikako is overbearing. She doesn't realise you're part-owner of the Perth shop or a director of the company.'

'Good. I like it that way!'

'As she's already there, perhaps it's a good time for you to employ someone to help you with the Japanese tour business.'

'The season's over,' replied TC.

'I know, but it will give Chikako a reason to be there. She can help you find the right person.'

'I want to choose my own people, Mr Callahan. If I'm still here, I'm the one who has to work with them.'

'Of course, you can pick the one you want. Chikako can help you.' TC shook her head and sighed.

'You're frightened of Chikako, aren't you, Mr Callahan? You must be! Will you ever learn? I don't think so!'

'I was hoping Chikako could stay with you,' said Vance.

'Leave me alone, Mr Callahan. I have work to do,' replied TC in exasperation.

Stock displayed to satisfaction, it was closing time and TC was vacuuming the floor when Chikako returned.

'I have to find somewhere to stay,' said Chikako.

'Don't worry. Vance wants me to accommodate you at my place,' replied TC as she calmly placed the vacuum cleaner in the safe room. Grab your gear. Let's go.'

'Nice car,' remarked Chikako when they reached the parking station and TC unlocked her vehicle. 'How did you afford it?'

'I stole it from a Japanese tourist,' TC said lightly. 'Please put yourself and your gear inside.'

'Who's that lady, Mama?' asked Robert when he, as usual, rushed to the garage to greet TC.

'A friend of Mr Callahan's, sweetie. Her name is Ms Chikako.

Gracie was close behind Robert.

'Hello! What's your name?' enquired Gracie of Chikako. 'Are you Japanese?'

'Yes!' replied Chikako in her deep voice, accompanied by a scowl. 'My name is Chikako.'

'TC, I need to speak with you alone,' said Gracie with urgency as she led the way to the footpath away from the garage. Once out of earshot, Gracie continued. 'I don't want that woman here!' TC sighed heavily.

'I know, Gracie. Neither do I. Don't think we have much choice. She's Mr Callahan's friend, so I took a wild guess, and I'd say she doesn't want to be here. Let's do the best we can to be nice.'

'All right, darlin',' replied Gracie. 'Robert has been fed; corned beef and vegetables are warming. See you tomorrow. Don't let her stay too long.' Gracie was gone within minutes after hugging and kissing Robert goodbye. Chikako settled into her room and showered while TC spent precious time with Robert until he went to sleep.

'Don't you like corned beef?' asked TC later when she placed Chikako's meal of overcooked meat and vegetables on the dining room table.

'Your house is nice. How did you afford it?' enquired Chikako.

'Like my car, I stole it from a Japanese tourist,' replied TC as she spooned pickles onto her plate.

'When Vance and I get married, I'll check you out,' said Chikako, who had her knife and fork in hand while looking at the food on her plate with obvious distaste. TC burst into laughter, pushed her food aside, laughed more, then became silent and solemn as she realised Chikako was serious.

'Why were you laughing?' enquired Chikako.

'I'm not laughing now, Chikako,' replied TC. 'I feel sorry for you. Over the years, I've seen women come and go, and they all wanted the boss to leave Delores for them. Forget it! It will not happen. Sorry, Chikako, I suggest you settle for the red opals and expensive leather suitcase. You won't get Vance!'

'Yes, I will!' declared Chikako. 'He loves me!'

'I'm sure he does,' agreed TC while thinking, You poor woman. You poor fool.

'How long have you known Vance, TC?' asked Chikako.

'A long time,' replied TC. 'Since I was a girl. I'm not hungry. I think I'll go to bed.'

'Vance loves me, TC. I will be his wife,' declared Chikako with utmost confidence.

'That's good, Chikako,' replied TC indifferently. 'Whatever you say. As for me, I'm taking a shower, then going to bed. See you in the morning. We leave at eight.'

Poor thing, thought TC, as she turfed her dinner into the bin.

※

'I'm going to collect the mail,' said TC after setup next morning. 'Be back soon.'

'Take time,' said Chikako.

TC returned not ten minutes later to find Chikako engrossed in examining the sales ledger.

'Find what you're looking for?' Chikako quickly closed the ledger and looked guiltily at TC.

'Just checking.'

'Checking for what? I've already sent the sales records to Vance. I think I need to call him on this one.'

'I've placed an ad in the paper for Japanese staff,' said Chikako.

'Faster than greased lightning, you are,' said TC. 'I'm gone a few minutes, and you've called the newspaper people and perused the ledger. How did you pay for the advertisement?'

'I used my company credit card,' replied Chikako.

'You have a company credit card? Interesting!'

'Yes. Vance gave it to me in case I need accommodation or anything else I require.'

'How lovely,' remarked TC. 'Please tell me the credit limit.'

'Three thousand dollars,' replied Chikako.

'Really? Is that all?' said TC as she began dialling the Queensland shop. Once again the soft, sweet Japanese voiced answered.

'Put Mr Callahan on,' demanded TC.

'Hello, Butterball,' said Vance after a few seconds. 'I knew it was you by the terrified expression on Ayako's face.'

'Screw you. Mr Callahan,' replied TC in a controlled tone of voice. 'A short while ago, I returned from the post office to find your girlfriend looking through my ledger. Please lie to me again by telling me you didn't send her here to check on me. Without any discussion whatsoever with me, she placed an advertisement for Japanese staff in the newspaper. When I enquired as to how she paid for the advertisement, Chikako told me she used a credit card you gave her for accommodation or anything else she needed. You bastard! I holed up in a hotel on the other side of the world and lived on crackers until Sammy L organised a customer for me. Where the hell was a credit card for me?'

'Don't, Little One. I'm sorry!'

'Don't "Little One" me! I'm putting your girlfriend on the phone. Tell her it's okay to max out her credit card. Pity it's not enough to buy me a mink. Never mind. I'll find a way to spend it.' TC smiled at Chikako, who stood nervously listening. 'Here you go, Chikako. I believe Mr Callahan has some instructions for you.' Within seconds, Chikako was off the telephone.

'Where do you want to spend the money, TC?' she asked demurely. TC thought momentarily.

'Come on. Let's go before I change my mind. There's a shop called The Perfumery a block away.'

'Good morning,' the gentleman in The Perfumery said when TC, tailed by Chikako, entered his place of business.

'Good morning,' replied TC. 'Please tell me the price of the most expensive perfume you stock.

'Do you mean concentrate?' asked the man.

'I don't care, as long as it's the highest-priced item you stock.'

'Eleven hundred dollars,' was the serious reply. TC sighed.

'I was hoping it was more. I'll take two.'

'Sorry, Madam, I have only one in stock,' replied the obviously disappointed perfume salesman.

'Okay. Gift wrap it, please,' requested TC with a shrug. 'What are you having Chikako?'

'I don't want any,' was the nervous reply.

'Of course, you do!' insisted TC. 'After all, you're the one paying.'

'Do you have anything around fifty dollars,' enquired Chikako.

'Not really. I have a nice one for seventy-five,' replied the man.

'That will be fine,' agreed Chikako reluctantly.

'You'll make my uncle a fine wife, Chikako,' laughed TC. 'You are so frugal with his money. I'll see you back at the shop.' TC then turned to the gentleman, who was busy gift wrapping his best single sale in months.

'Thank you, sir. I do wish you'd had two of those.'

'So do I,' was the reply.

¶

'How much did you do me for?' laughed Vance when TC phoned him immediately after her return to the shop.

'You're off the hook for the bargain basement price of one thousand, one hundred and seventy-five dollars,' replied TC flippantly. Vance's sigh of relief was audible through the telephone.

'Serves me right for playing two sides against the middle.'

'Yes, it does!' agreed TC. 'Must go. I have a customer.'

'Vance is going to be angry!' said Chikako when she finally returned and all but threw TC's beautifully gift-wrapped perfume on her desk.

'No, he won't be,' replied TC, to whose relief the telephone rang.

'The meeting planned for tomorrow night is cancelled, darling,' apologised Fiona Smythe. 'Unfortunately, a few people are unable to attend. Ken and I have rescheduled it for next Monday night at eight.'

'Suits me fine, Fiona,' replied TC. 'I have a visitor, so the time slot works for me.'

'We have visitors, too, darling. That's why I haven't called you the last few nights. Makes me angry the way some people simply show up out of the blue.'

'Believe me, Fiona, I know exactly what you mean. I'll call you after my guest leaves.'

TC was amused that evening by the expression of disbelief on Chikako's face when Gracie was about to leave. TC produced the gift-wrapped perfume from her handbag and passed it to Gracie.

'Mr Callahan bought you this, Gracie. It's a sign of appreciation for your long hours when the ships were in.'

'What is it?' asked Gracie with obvious curiosity as she hugged TC tightly.

'No need to hug me, Gracie,' laughed TC. 'It's from Mr Callahan. Wait until you get home to your place, then open it. I hope you like it. Mr Callahan is a very generous man.'

'Thank him for me darlin',' beamed Gracie as she hurried outside to her car.

'You never wanted that perfume for yourself, did you?' said Chikako.

'Not my brand,' replied TC lightly with a smile, then fluttering of her eyelids. 'It's all about principles, Chikako. Robert likes pizza once in a while. Tonight's the night. Hope you're hungry.' Chikako glared at TC before storming to her room.

'Why did Mr Callahan send Gracie a present, Mother?' asked Robert, who was obviously hurt by feeling left out.

'I'm sure Mr Callahan will bring you a present when he comes to visit, sweetheart,' soothed TC while thinking, If he ever does, that is.

¶

The shop telephone started ringing next morning with people enquiring about the advertised Japanese-speaking sales assistant position. Chikako answered every call because, from the moment TC and she arrived, she strategically located herself at the desk within inches of the phone. All conversations were conducted in Japanese, so TC had no idea whatsoever of what was being said or arranged. The calls finally ceased around noon.

'What's happening, Chikako?' asked TC bluntly.

'Oh! I told five people not to bother coming. They weren't Japanese. Six Japanese are coming for me to interview this afternoon. The first one will be here in half an hour, then one every forty-five minutes until I've finished.'

'What do you mean until you have finished? I am the person who has to work with them.'

'Don't worry, you'll be all right,' replied Chikako offhandedly.

TC became more and more furious as the afternoon progressed. She was ignored, not even afforded introductions. Not once did Chikako give her an opportunity to ask a question or have an input. All interviews were in Japanese. TC was completely in the dark. TC was taken aback when the fourth interviewee showed up. She was a silver-haired lady of around seventy-five years of age who bowed and smiled at TC when she entered the shop. Chikako quickly took control.

Poor lady, thought TC. Fancy having to look for a job at her age. TC noticed Chikako laugh a few times during the conversation with the woman. She hadn't done that with the others.

It was like a breath of fresh spring air to TC when the last applicant arrived punctually at a quarter past four. She was young, smartly dressed, wore heels, and smiled as she introduced herself to TC while Chikako was rinsing her hands over the sink in the safe cubicle.

'Good afternoon. My name is Kayoko. I'm here about your sales position,' announced the pretty Japanese girl in near-perfect English.

This is the one I want, thought TC as Chikako snarled a command in Japanese. Kayoko became serious and bowed.

Talk about opposites, thought TC as she observed Chikako seat herself at the desk and begin her interrogation of the girl for whom she felt extreme pity.

'Don't worry, luv, you've got the job,' said TC silently as she walked to the door and looked down the arcade. To TC's utter surprise, Chikako's time with Kayoko was brief, less than a few minutes.

'Nice to have met you,' said Kayoko as she paused beside TC at the door.

'That was quick,' smiled TC. 'I'll see you soon.'

'I don't think so,' replied Kayoko very softly with sadness in her eyes. TC patted the girl's shoulder. 'We'll see!' Kayoko hurried away, then TC turned back into the shop and addressed Chikako.

'That's the girl I want.'

'She's not suitable!' snapped Chikako.

'Could that possibly be because she's young, pretty, well dressed, smiles, and speaks English?' replied TC angrily.

'I told the senior lady, Eri, she can start tomorrow while I'm here to train her.'

'You upstart bitch! You have got to be joking! I bet the lady can hardly speak English.' Chikako did not reply. She collected her handbag and left the shop. TC checked the time. It was way past trading hours in the east. She dialled, anyway, on the off-chance Vance was still there.

He was! Unbeknown to TC, the ringing of the telephone put paid to a moment of passion Vance was sharing with Ayako.

'You're there late. Hope I'm not interrupting anything,' said TC when he answered. Vance laughed.

'Think you must have a camera on me.'

'I'd like to know what on earth is really going on with you and Chikako,' demanded TC. 'She acts like she is already your wife and owns the joint. She interviewed six Japanese females today. Everything was done in Japanese. I might as well not exist. I like the last girl; she's everything I need, seeing you say I need to have someone.'

'Well, that's the one you hire,' said Vance.

'How can I? When I told Chikako she advised me she'd already promised the job to a nice, old lady, Eri, who was in earlier. How can I tell someone my grandmother's age to go to the bank or run to the jeweller? I doubt the poor woman can speak English. Quite honestly, Mr Callahan, I've had a gutful of your women. I believe Chikako gave Eri the job without my knowledge because she's downright frightened I'll be more successful than she. She's got you cornered and knows you won't disagree with her again.'

'Chikako will lose face if I pull rank on her again,' replied Vance.

'I don't care if her whole head falls off and gets lost,' retaliated TC. 'What about poor Eri losing face when she realises she can't handle the job?' Silence.

'Hire both of them. That's all you can do,' said Vance. 'Put Chikako on the phone.'

'She's not here. She took off when I fronted her about hiring Eri without my knowledge.'

'I'll wait here,' replied Vance. 'Tell her to call me the second she comes back.'

'Mr Callahan, don't send your girlfriends here ever again,' said TC seriously. 'If you feel the need to check up on me, do it yourself!'

'It wasn't like that, TC.'

'I don't care what it was like! No more!'

TC examined Chikako's notes on the applicants, saw Kayoko's name and number at the bottom of the list, phoned the girl, and told her she had a job.

'Would I have to work with that mean Japanese woman?' asked Kayoko timidly.

'No, not at all. She'll be gone back east before you start. How about

8.30 next Monday morning?'

'Thank you so much. I will be there,' replied Kayoko.

'Vance wants you to call him,' said TC shortly when Chikako returned from wherever. 'He's waiting. I'll make myself scarce while you talk.'

'I'm leaving tomorrow night,' announced Chikako on TC's return.

'Good! If it's an early enough flight, I'll drive you to the airport. No doubt we both want to see the last of each other as soon as possible.'

'I'll make a booking while you put the stock away,' replied Chikako eagerly.

TC delivered Chikako to the airport immediately after work next day in the afternoon.

'Here we are,' said TC as she stopped her car outside the terminal. 'This hasn't been an easy time for either of us. Perhaps we'll like each other more with you on the other side of the continent and me here.'

'I hope so,' replied Chikako with her deep voice and a sincere smile.

Poor woman, thought TC as she started the car and drove off. She's crazy about the boss.

¶

A lot happened during the next few months.

Ken and Fiona had their meeting at which Blanche, Lisa, and TC were convinced to nominate as committee members at the forthcoming annual elections. When the time came, it became obvious the executives and long term, more senior club members had put both time and effort into behind-the-scenes lobbying. TC was elected president of both sub-committees, which automatically deemed membership of the executive committee that made decisions as to which paths should be followed for advancement of the group. Blanche was voted secretary of one sub-committee and member of the other, and Lisa a member of both.

Not long into the first meeting of the ladies sub-committee group, TC realised she had full support of all present, including the more senior members, who had been involved with the group since day one. On the other hand, the first meeting of the functions group was fairly tense.

Most were newly elected members filled with enthusiasm while the others were re-elected members of the former functions group committee with obvious chips on their shoulders regarding the newcomers. Two of these were the women from the reception-desk episode way back. TC knew they loathed her. Almost every time she spoke, they smirked at each other.

'Ignore them,' suggested Lisa.

'It's jealousy because they know we'll do a better job than they did,' said Blanche.

'Don't worry about them, darling,' advised Fiona. 'Tell them to get stuffed under your breath. Smile at the bitches. Show them up by your accomplishments. Concentrate on lifting the image and attracting new members. You have more support than you realise.'

'The first ship's visit will be the big test,' said TC. 'I'm terrified and so are the other new people.'

'You'll all be fine. Remember, you'll have a couple of weeks warning, plenty of time to work out your strategy for success. Now get back to running your opal business, darling. Stop worrying!'

§

Gracie's ageing mother in England had not been well for some time. Gracie warned TC she intended to visit England to spend time with her mum before it was too late.

'I'm telling you now, darlin',' said Gracie. 'I didn't want to pop it on you at the last minute. I'm leaving a month from now and plan to stay for around six weeks. Don't know what you'll do about the little fellow. I feel bad, but it's my mum. I'll never forgive myself if I don't go and see her.'

'I understand, Gracie,' agreed TC while doing a good job at concealing her panic. 'I'll work something out,' she continued while thinking, I don't have a clue what or how.

§

The men were content with their transition to mine number three. Although not gem quality, the site was yielding good commercial colour. Vance rarely made the trip from the Big Smoke. It didn't matter. All in all, they were happy working with Jonathon, who was still licking his wounds over Almut. Andrew continued fossicking, and when not doing so, he spent time in Brolga with Marla and their baby girl.

¶

At the shop TC and Kayoko made Eri's workload as light as possible. Kayoko ran most errands and interpreted for TC and Eri when necessary, which was almost all the time. Eri was a lovely, kind lady who had been a prisoner of her own countrymen during the war. It was during her incarceration that she met her husband, who was many years her senior. Now he was too aged to work. One of Eri's grandchildren was in trouble, which was the reason Eri had sought employment. Two months into Eri's employment, she wrote a letter in Japanese and had Kayoko translate it into English before giving it to TC.

> Dear TC,
> Thank you for your kindness. I shall never forget. My feet hurt even though you have given me a comfortable chair in which I spend a lot of my time while you and Kayoko do work. I cannot come here anymore. I am too tired because I am old. Thank you, TC, you are a good person. Hope you like good luck present.
> Eri

Tears streaming, TC hugged Eri, who pointed to a package on the desk as she spoke in Japanese. 'Open, TC. Put on front counter for luck,' interpreted Kayoko. 'Beautiful Japanese doll.' The doll was indeed beautiful. Silent tears still flowing, TC placed it on the counter closest to the main door, then turned and hugged Eri again. Eri grabbed her handbag. She was on the verge of crying.

'I can go now,' she smiled and was gone.

'Why did Eri leave so quickly, Kayoko? I need to pay her.'

'It's the Japanese way,' replied Kayoko. 'Eri was about to cry. If she cried in front of us, she would lose face.'

'I had tears falling everywhere,' argued TC.

'That's different,' replied Kayoko. 'You are not Japanese. Send her money by mail.'

Vance announced his intention to open a shop in the coastal tourist mecca.

'Who will run it for you, Boss?' asked TC.

'I'll send Chikako there,' was the reluctant reply.

'Out of sight, out of your hair?' laughed TC.

'Yes! Something like that.'

'Better give her more stock than you've sent me,' remarked TC.

'There's too much stock in this shop, so I'll split it. When's your next lot of ships due?' replied Vance.

'Quick change of subject there, Mr Callahan,' laughed TC. 'Don't know about ships, but I do know that if we do okay, I'm going after that bigger shop. This place is like a can of sardines when we're busy.'

'All right, do whatever you want to do. I'm not interfering. I've learned my lesson.'

'I'm curious. I reckon you have another woman on the go. That's probably the reason you're sending Chikako to manage the new shop when it opens.'

'Have to give you credit where it's due, Little One,' replied Vance light-heartedly. 'As usual, you're on the ball. Bye, now!'

It was three weeks prior to Gracie's planned departure for England when TC was told an aircraft carrier group visit was pending.

'Best call your meeting and get yourselves organised, darling,' suggested Fiona. 'Our friends arrive two weeks from today.' TC called Blanche as secretary of the functions group and requested she advise there'd be a meeting the following night.

'Will that mean I'll have a few days' work at the shop?' asked Blanche.

'I was about to run that by you,' replied TC.

'Wouldn't miss it for the world!' was the immediate reply.

'Blanche, I know it's short notice, but if you've got time, would you throw together something about a dress code for the welcoming party? I was thinking along the lines of coat and tie for men and after-five wear for women.'

'Consider it done,' replied Blanche eagerly. 'You know some people won't be happy.'

'I know! We can only try. I'll see you tomorrow night.'

⁋

TC felt somewhat of an alien when she sat to chair the meeting. At the same time, she was secretly amused to note the members of the former committee were grouped to her left while the newcomers like herself were on her right where Blanche was busily jotting down names of attendees.

'Good evening, ladies,' said TC. 'Thank you for coming at such short notice. As we are all aware, along with those of you seated on the right, I am a newcomer.' TC smiled and looked to the left. 'Compared to us, the ladies seated to my left are veterans who share much more knowledge regarding the mechanism of the group. I'm sure we all share the same goal where the overall friendship group is concerned, the goal being to lift our image by giving our guests a memorable evening without that memory necessarily including a hot chick they picked up to play with for a few days.' Stifled giggles came from a few. Dropped jaws and scowls from a few others.

'Who do you think you are; the bloody Virgin Mary?' yelled a scowler. TC retained composure as she calmly replied.

'Not at all! The Virgin Mary is the mother of our Lord. I have no way of knowing if she was ever bloodied. As for me, I'm not a virgin; I have a child.' Silence. 'As I was about to say before being interrupted, we are hosting a welcoming function in the very near future. Let's make it a good one! Positive suggestions and constructive criticism only, please. Who's first?'

So began TC's long-term commitment to the friendship group, as was that of Blanche, Lisa, and a lot of others dedicated to the cause and eager to participate.

TC called Ken Smythe the day prior to the function to voice her concern and that of her committee members.

'That hall is not large enough, Ken. I've noticed at both functions I've attended that a great number of our visitors stand outside because it's too cramped inside. My committee ladies agree.'

'I must say the executive committee members have said the same. I'll ask the president of the hall-owner's association to remove the dividing panels. That will double the size.'

'That would be great!'

Ken Smythe's request was granted. The extra space made a difference. About half the locals attending dressed as requested. It was a start! While the function was good, it wasn't great.

'We'll get there, darling,' whispered Fiona. 'At least most of your committee girls are doing the right thing. You wait and see; they'll come around.' Out of the corner of her eye, TC noticed Heidi, well-dressed, but then again, hardly dressed at all. She was smiling alluringly into Captain Russ' eyes. Heidi was dripping opal. This was Heidi's fist attendance at a welcoming function. She obviously thought Captain Russ was one of the visitors. TC had no idea how Heidi got to be at the party. She wasn't a member. TC turned as she felt a tap on her shoulder, to look into the eyes of an extremely attractive, beautifully attired, petite, blonde woman around her own age.

'Someone told me you are the organiser of this party?'

'Yes, I'm one of them,' replied TC with a smile. Fiona interrupted.

'I'm Fiona Smythe, and this is TC Carmichael. I know who you are. You're Captain Russ' wife, Marjorie.'

'Nice to meet you both,' replied Marjorie. 'Please tell me what the half-naked bitch who has my husband cornered thinks she is doing? She's had him cornered for half an hour.'

'I know who she is. I'll fix it, Marjorie. Let's go,' offered TC.

'You go, TC,' replied Marjorie, who was in a foul mood. 'If I go, I'm likely to knock her down.'

'I can't say I blame you,' came separately from both Fiona and TC.

TC walked casually across the hall. On her face was fixed a smile. Captain Russ saw her first and breathed an inward sigh of relief as he greeted TC.

'TC, how nice to see you again.'

'Same here, Captain Russ,' replied TC sugar-sweetly while continuing to smile. Heidi said nothing. She simply glared.

'Captain Russ, your lovely wife, Marjorie, is waiting for you over by the door.'

'She is? Thank you, TC,' replied Captain Russ. 'I'd best go!' He nodded and smiled at Heidi before hurrying away.

'I didn't know his wife was here!' snapped Heidi.

'They live here, Heidi,' replied TC. 'You've wasted half the night on the wrong man. Better get on the prowl.' Heidi remained silent as TC continued. 'Should you wish to attend these functions in the future, pay your membership fee and don't arrive looking like a high-class hooker. A lot of people are working hard to gain respectability.' Heidi threw her head in the air and merged with the crowd. Towards the end of the evening she left with a pilot half her age.

From that night on, Captain Russ' wife, Marjorie, and TC became friends.

¶

Gracie went off to England and spent time with her ill mother. She was away three months. Seemed like an eternity to TC and particularly to Robert, whom Harry the Cabbie collected from school in the afternoons before dropping the little boy off in a busy street at one end of the arcade, then stopping a couple of blocks away to call TC to verify her son had followed his instructions by running like buggery until he was safe in his mum's arms. They somehow survived day to day until Gracie returned when they both all but begged her not to leave them again.

⁊

Vance opened a magnificent shop on the coast. No expense was spared on fit out, all done to extremes to induce Chikako to happily leave the city and him in the arms of Ayako. Chikako felt with all her heart that Vance would dump Delores as his wife. The opal king was her husband-to-be. All Chikako needed to do in order to achieve her goal was work, work, work, and make money hand over first. That's what she thought, anyway! Then, only then, would she acquire her crown as Opal Queen. Unfortunately for Chikako, she was so blinded by her obsession with making Vance her husband that she didn't see the forest for the trees where Ayako was concerned. Poor Chikako!

⁊

Jake remarried, to a woman who did her best to tolerate and be kind to Robert during his 'had to be' visits to his father. She obviously cared more for her dogs than Robert. Once she drove at break-neck speed to the vet with her sick dog restrained by a seatbelt while Robert was not. TC felt nothing but pity for the poor woman. Fancy being married to Jake!

⁊

Life went on as usual at the mines. The men worked their hearts out, looked forward to breaks, during which all except Yappy blew their money on booze. Yappy won even more often than he lost on the horses.

¶

The Seat of Knowledge met as usual. Vance had been gone from Brolga, apart from the occasional visit, for a long time; they'd forgotten when. Still, on every occasion they gathered on the Sacred Seat, old Jock would remark, 'Brolga doesn't seem the same without the pill-pusher. He doesn't come through too often these days. Even though he's as rich as Midas, he hasn't changed from being a good bloke.'

Always one of Jock's mates would say, 'He was nothing but a bloody drunk,' while another would add, 'Weren't we all!'

¶

TC and Robert dined at Mr Bill's Seafood Restaurant every Saturday night except when Robert was in Queensland with Jake and once a month when TC went out with Blanche.

'Mother is moving into a huge shop, Mr Bill,' announced Robert proudly while settling the account one night. 'I won't ever have to sit under the sink after she does.' Mr Bill looked at TC in surprised disbelief. TC smiled and shrugged.

'That's true, Mr Bill, depending on who's in the shop; it's only occasionally on Saturdays these days. He used to be there a lot in the beginning. Believe me, it was not easy for either of us.' Mr Bill looked down at Robert.

'I'm sorry to hear you had to sit under a sink, Robert. I'm happy to hear you won't have to do it much longer.'

'We'll be in the new shop next week,' volunteered Robert.

'Perhaps your mother would like to consider putting a showcase advertising your new, big shop here in my restaurant?' Robert glanced up at TC and smiled.

'You would like to do that, wouldn't you, Mother?' he enquired seriously. 'Please make it a deal!' Both Mr Bill and TC laughed as they shook hands.

'Thank you for the opportunity,' said TC. 'I'll ask the cabinet maker when we could come by. You tell him where you want it.'

By this time TC had three Japanese staff. Kayoko was still there full-time, two others part-time whenever required, and Blanche during the U.S. Navy visits. It was now off-season for Japanese tour groups, so a perfect time to relocate.

The move to TC's dream shop on The Terrace was made possible by the booming Japanese tour industry and her shop's expanding reputation as 'the place to shop for opals' among the U.S. military, plus, of course, the premises became vacant.

⁋

Vance eventually became more generous with his supply of cut stones. Although TC was well aware she was getting only the scraps after Ayako and Chikako had chosen theirs, she said nothing and began buying stones of her liking from other miners. The colour was better, the prices were better, and she got what she wanted, not what Chikako and Ayako didn't want.

Vance still called, usually to relieve himself of his guilt regarding his predicament, and Delores was still spending money as if it was going out of fashion. Every time he complained, TC would reply, 'What do you expect, Boss? Your wife is obviously in denial. So are you! Let her spend the money! So what! She deserves it for tolerating your infidelity.' Vance would either hang up or reply, 'Delores doesn't know!' causing TC to reply, 'Or perhaps the poor woman doesn't want to know.'

⁋

Mr D drove across the Nullarbor twice to see TC and Robert. Both times, he had whirled into their driveway in an identical manner to that in which he used to make his presence known at the Pink Brolga. Both times he arrived unannounced and in a different imported, top-of-the-range Chevrolet. Robert was fascinated by the cars and waited hopefully each week day morning for Mr D to say, 'Come on, Robert,

I'll drive you to school.' Having been in the British Navy during the Second World War, Mr Dutton commented many times he'd like to be visiting some time when a carrier group was in port, depending, of course, on his job obligations in the east.

'It'll work out one day, Mr D,' assured TC.

'I'll let you know when I'm between contracts,' said Mr D. 'If one of the huge, beautiful pieces of machinery becomes due, I'll fly over.'

¶

TC received three unexpected calls the Sunday morning after Mr Bill's offer to locate a display case in his restaurant. The first was from Vance, who rarely phoned on Sundays.

It must be important, thought TC when she heard his voice. 'What's wrong, Boss,' enquired TC with some urgency.

'Nothing! Quite the opposite,' laughed Vance. 'Looks as if Jonathon has finally gotten over Almut.'

'That's wonderful!' replied TC excitedly. 'How, where, and when?'

'Jonathon and I were in the shop yesterday discussing seriously which or what direction he should pursue with a new mining lease. It's a miracle he was even in the shop. He had brought a load of opal from Brolga and just happened to be there.'

'What happened? I'm curious, very curious; hurry up and tell me,' said TC.

'Little One, you should have seen his face when a beautiful Italian girl walked in. His eyes lit up. So did hers, for that matter.'

'So? So tell me,' persisted TC. 'Why was she there? What's her name? What does she look like?'

'She works for an advertising agency and dropped into the shop hoping to make an appointment for next week. Her name is Lolita, which sounds more Spanish or Mexican than Italian to Jonathon and me.'

'To me, too!' agreed TC. 'Let's face it, Boss, if he's over Almut, who cares if Lolita is a Martian? Tell me what she looks like.'

'She's Italian, long, dark hair, big eyes,' laughed Vance. 'She dresses sexy. Great figure.'

'That's enough! Stop now! Lolita is Jonathon's!'

'Don't worry. She is Jonathon's! I'm not going through that again! Seriously, Little One, I feel as if a semi-trailer filled with boulders has been lifted off my shoulders. My conscience over my relationship with Almut has been a damned heavy load.'

'I know,' replied TC. 'Let's hope it works out. I'm happy for both you and Jonathon, and also lovely Lolita, if things go the way you think. Great!'

TC's second surprising phone call was from Fiona, who usually didn't call till 7 pm.

'Hello, darling. When will your new shop be open?'

'Hopefully, by the end of next week,' replied TC. 'Why? Do I detect urgency in your voice?'

'Better pray your shop is ready. We'll have guests in at the end of the following week.'

'Not again! This happened when I first opened the existing shop. It's a mess; the safe has already been moved into the new one so the cabinetmakers can build the office around it.'

'I thought I'd let you know, darling. See if you can hurry up your shopfitters.'

'I'll do my best,' sighed TC. 'Thank you. I'll talk to you later.'

TC immediately contacted Blanche and asked her to call a meeting of the committee for the following night.

'Oh, well, at least this time you've got stock,' TC told herself. 'Lots of it, too. 'You also have staff. Count your blessings and be positive. The new shop will be finished. If not, you'll find a way to cope.' TC was about to join Robert, who was playing with his cat in the garden, when the phone rang again. To her surprise, it was Lou. They had not communicated for far too long. Lou put it down to TC's work schedule while TC accredited it to Lou being busy with Colin's family and new friends.

'Hello, TC. It's Lou.'

'Hello, stranger. This is a surprise,' replied TC. 'Thought I'd never hear from you again, and you'd scrapped me as a friend.'

'TC, you will never hear from me again after this,' replied Lou in a soft, feeble tone of voice.

'What's wrong, Lou?' asked TC in alarm.

'I'm dying. This will be the last phone call I'll ever make. I wanted it to be to you.' TC was speechless with shock. She wanted to scream 'No' and throw the phone at the wall.

'I've got cancer,' continued Lou. 'They didn't find it until too late.'

'I'm coming, Lou,' promised TC with tears streaming.

'Don't. You'll be too late,' replied Lou, whose voice was becoming weaker with every word. 'I want you to stop crying because you'll make me cry. I've already done enough of that. I wanted to make this call to tell you that you are the best friend I have ever had. I've had others since I've lived in Sydney, but none like you. Please make something of yourself, TC. Be successful. I love you, my friend.'

'I love you, too, Lou,' sobbed TC.

'I know,' replied Lou almost inaudibly. She was gone. TC sobbed uncontrollably. With a million memories, what ifs and whys racing through her mind, she switched off the radio, then inserted an Elvis cassette tape into the machine, turned up the volume, ran to her bedroom, threw herself on her bed, and cried and cried. When 'Loving You' came on the tape, she screamed into her pillow and punched it repeatedly. Suddenly, she thought of Robert, stopped sobbing, and went to check on him.

'You all right, sweetheart?' enquired TC from the doorway.

'Thank you for playing Elvis, Mama,' he replied without looking up at TC. 'I think my cat likes Elvis, too.'

TC thought of Lou and tears flowed heavier as she turned towards the bathroom to wash her face. In an instant her son was in front of her.

'I love you, Mama. I want to hug you.' TC leaned down to hug him.

'I love you, too, darling.'

'Why are you crying, Mama?' enquired Robert with intense concern as he wiped tears from TC's cheeks.

'I got dust in my eyes, sweetheart,' replied TC with a forced smiled. Robert hugged TC tightly and whispered in her ear.

'There's no dust here, Mama.'

TC whispered in reply, 'Yes, there is. We just can't see it.'

⸙

Lou passed away that afternoon. TC's best memories of the best part of her life went with her best friend, who was also the best person she had ever known. She was in denial and could think of no words or actions to sufficiently express her sorrow for Colin and her godson, so she said and did nothing. She hoped they would understand.

⸙

The new shop was ready three days prior to the fleet's arrival. The display case had also been installed at Mr Bill's. The girls, along with Blanche, worked till midnight two nights to help TC get the displays in order. This shop could cope with eighty- to a hundred-customer capacity. TC couldn't guarantee they'd all get served, but space sure was in abundance.

By this stage welcoming functions had become one of the places for more than a few members of Western Australia's up-and-coming parliamentarians and aristocracy to be seen and hopefully heard. Perhaps the media would be present to quote and photograph. These people would attend by formal invitation only and were chosen at random by the executive committee prior to visits. Often Ken Smythe would receive calls from this one or that asking as to why they had not yet been invited. Ken's standard reply was always the same.

'Sorry. Perhaps next time. Membership has grown to over three hundred. Combine that number with a hundred visitors, and the hall is full, which means we are limited as to how many dignitaries we can invite.'

⸙

Early in TC's role as president of the sub-committee, Fiona had warned her, 'The cats will say you are only there to make money, darling. Keep your opal business low key. That will shut the bitches up.' Consequently, TC never wore an opal to any function, nor did she carry business cards. Anonymously, she donated double high-grade sheepskins, large koala and wombat toys as door prizes, and the four-chances-for-a-dollar raffle tickets which were for visitors only. On the other hand, should any visitor mention opals to Fiona, Blanche, Lisa, or women of the ladies group, along with most who had now come to know TC, they would refer the enquiring visitor to Brolga Opals. TC was well aware there was still some animosity felt towards her by two or three, who referred to her as Miss Lily Milk White, Stuck-Up Bitch, or Miss Purity.

'Better than being tagged a slut, darling,' advised Fiona. 'Ignore them!'

On this visit, immediately after the shop was finished, the shop telephone rang at exactly nine o'clock. TC answered, thinking it was Vance. It wasn't. It was an admiral's aide, calling from the carrier.

'Yes, Ma'am. Is TC Carmichael available, please?'

'Speaking.'

'Will you be there all day, Ma'am?'

'Of course,' replied TC.

'The admiral wants to buy a beautiful opal pendant for his wife. He asked me to make sure you'd be there around eleven this morning. He wants to deal with you personally.'

'I'll see you then,' replied TC.

The admiral and his aides arrived at exactly eleven. His aides shopped with Blanche while TC attended to the admiral.

'How did you hear about me, admiral?' enquired TC.

'A friend of mine and his wife shopped with you a couple of years back,' replied the admiral. 'He gave you a plaque; that's it there on your wall.'

'I remember well,' smiled TC. 'His wife loved her pendant earrings and bracelet.'

'That's it. My wife is a friend of his wife, so she wants something just as beautiful. My wife doesn't want earrings or a bracelet, just a pendant. It has to be very beautiful. You know what women are like, always competing.'

'I understand,' smiled TC as she produced her top-shelf pendants and displayed them on the counter for the admiral's perusal. The admiral narrowed his maybes down to three.

'Which one do you like, TC?'

'Admiral, I don't know your wife, so how can I know her taste?' replied TC with a smile.

'Well done,' laughed the admiral. 'That means I can't blame you if I make the wrong decision.'

'Exactly,' laughed TC.

The admiral settled on a beautiful boulder pendant. It was green-orange in a classic eighteen-carat yellow-gold, wear-day-or-night setting. He spent nine thousand dollars.

'If my wife doesn't like it, I'll divorce her,' laughed the admiral as he paid TC. 'By the way, we brought something for you,' he beckoned to one of his aides, who was waiting patiently while chatting with Blanche.

'Give TC that packet,' he directed. 'Can't have my old friend outdoing me. TC, stick that on your wall slightly higher than his.' Everyone laughed as TC retrieved a beautiful plaque from the bag. Her eyes were like saucers with surprise.

'Thank you very much, Admiral. I'll figure out something.'

The admiral then addressed his aides. 'Are you men happy with your purchases?'

'Yes, sir,' was the reply.

'Happy with the service?'

'Yes, sir.'

'Good. Let's go. We'll tell everyone we know who wants opals to come here, TC,' continued the admiral. 'After all, you do have our ship's plaque.' They all laughed and they left.

That night when the admiral was leaving the welcoming party, Heidi was standing very close to him as he waited for his vehicle to collect him. Immediately behind them stood one of the admiral's aides, Blanche, and TC. Behind them to the right were Ken and Fiona Smythe. Heidi had obviously had more than enough to drink. She was talking a little too loudly as she gazed adoringly up into the tall admiral's eyes.

'Yes, darling, I'd love to come to your room, but I won't shower with you unless you buy an opal for your wife from me.'

'I can't do that, Heidi,' replied the admiral just audibly enough for his aides, Blanche, and TC to hear.

'Why, darling? Why not?' pleaded Heidi.

'Because I have already bought one today,' replied the admiral.

'Where did you buy an opal today, darling?' enquired Heidi in disbelief.

'I bought it from TC Carmichael,' was the reply. The aide looked at TC, then at Blanche as they waited for Heidi's reaction. It was quick. Heidi threw her head back and stepped aside.

'Well, Admiral, darling, I know TC Carmichael won't take a shower with you. She wouldn't even go into your room with you.' The aide smiled and winked at TC as she and Blanche suppressed giggles.

'Here's my car now,' announced the admiral as he descended the stairs, closely followed by his aide.

'Admiral, darling, what about me?' called Heidi. 'Don't you want me to come to your room? I'll still do that.' The admiral did not respond. He was in his car and gone in seconds.

'Looks like you frightened the admiral away, Heidi,' said an official standing behind Ken and Fiona. Ken and Fiona turned back inside the building in disgust. Blanche and TC remained. Both felt inward pity for Heidi. TC was about to step forward and ask Heidi if she needed a cab called when two officers passed and began chatting with Heidi, who was immediately gushing all over them.

'If I were Heidi, I'd be hiding under a big rock by now,' whispered Blanche as she and TC turned back inside.

'Poor Heidi, sure can pick them,' replied TC. 'A while back it was Captain Russ, who lives here. Tonight it was the admiral, who already bought his opal.'

'TC, you'll have to do something about that woman,' commanded Ken Smythe the moment TC and Blanche stepped back into the hall.

'Her behaviour is unacceptable! It is downright disgusting!'

'I can't do anything, Ken,' replied TC.

'TC's right,' agreed Len and Barney.

'Too many people have worked too hard to stamp out that type of behaviour under our banner,' persisted Ken.

'I'm going home now. So I must say goodnight,' said TC.

'Me, too. Goodnight, everyone,' said Blanche.

'Good luck tomorrow, darlings,' wished Fiona. She kissed both on their cheeks.

'I'm hungry,' said TC as they walked downstairs to the car park.

'Me, too,' agreed Blanche. 'Funny, isn't it? We walk around all night with trays of food to feed other people and don't get a morsel ourselves.' TC checked her watch.

'It's only a quarter to ten. I feel like going to Mr Bill's for a fish meal? He opens late on Friday and Saturday nights.'

'Sure,' agreed Blanche as they reached their cars. 'See you there soon.'

Blanche and TC were laughing as they entered Mr Bill's.

'Well, if it isn't TC Carmichael. I'd know that laugh anywhere,' said Randy James, who was in the process of paying Mr Bill. TC was surprised, to say the least. This was the third time they'd met by coincidence. Hard to believe in a city the size of Perth. As usual, Randy was immaculately attired, drunk, and handsome.

'Hello, Randy. We meet again. A lot of people know my laugh. Unfortunately, I can't change that.'

'You two ladies look beautiful,' complimented Randy. It didn't bother him his date was two feet away. 'You've both got class. Not every woman has that. Introduce me to your friend, TC.'

'Some other time, Randy,' replied TC. 'Your lady is waiting, and we are in a hurry to eat. Perhaps we'll run into you some time when you're sober.'

'Go through, TC' smiled Mr Bill.

'I'm sure you will,' laughed Randy with one of his winks reminiscent of the Pink Brolga.

It wouldn't have been normal if Randy's tarty-looking date hadn't glared at them as they passed by. She did. Both Blanche and TC smiled sweetly.

'Who was that?' enquired Blanche.

'Randall James,' replied TC with a heavy sigh. 'He was with a construction crew who lived at the Pink Brolga. Pursued me relentlessly until he threw me in the too-hard basket.'

'Pity he's a drunk,' said Blanche.

'And a womaniser,' added TC. 'I'm having dhufish.'

'Me, too,' agreed Blanche. 'Tomorrow night is going to be interesting with the fleet in town.'

'Perhaps you'll find a man of your dreams, Blanche,' laughed TC.

'You might, too,' replied Blanche.

'No chance of that,' replied TC. 'I have my 'business and pleasure don't mix' rule to keep in mind.'

'Thank God, I don't,' laughed Blanche. 'These Yanks get more beautiful every visit.'

§

Saturday at the shop was hectic. The three Japanese girls, Blanche, and TC didn't stop. By mid-afternoon, TC and Blanche traded their heels for sheepskin slippers.

'Very glamorous,' laughed Blanche. 'Perhaps we should wear these to the nightclub tonight.'

As always on their monthly nightclub outing, Blanche and TC arrived early to secure a table or the booth they had come to prefer.

'Obviously we didn't come early enough tonight' laughed Blanche. 'Looks as if we should have camped outside all day. The joint is full.'

'All women, Blanche,' replied TC. 'Probably hoping to meet their dream man, too. Let's check our usual booth. Perhaps Disco Danny got here before the multitudes.' Disco Danny was a tall, extremely thin, not-at-all-attractive, thirty-year-old who loved to dance or at least attempt to dance. While Danny wasn't quite the full quid, he was a harmless soul who had cottoned onto Blanche and TC because they were nice to him and didn't ignore him like ninety-nine percent of other nightclub regulars. Blanche and TC had dubbed him Disco Danny because he was always attired in a replica white-shirt outfit worn by John Travolta in Saturday Night Fever, and had even dyed his hair black in an attempt to imitate his Saturday night dancing idol.

'Thank heavens, you got here,' said a relieved, somewhat agitated Danny when he spotted them emerge from the crowd to find him spread out at the booth. Danny was sitting in the corner of the booth with one leg stretched along one side of the seating and his other to the opposite side with his arms outstretched on the table.

'Everyone's been trying to take over our booth,' complained Danny as he sat correctly and moved to one side so TC and Blanche could be seated.

'Some girls ignored me and sat down. I was very rude to them, so they left. One called me an idiot pervert. I didn't care. I knew you'd be here tonight. You're my friends.'

'Thank you, Danny. You're our friend, too,' acknowledged Blanche.

'You certainly are,' added TC. 'I'll tell you what, Danny. The way you were around the table, with a bit more practice you will be able to dance like John T!'

'I practice in front of the mirror,' replied Danny seriously. 'That's why I can spread my legs like his.' TC smiled.

'I think my boss' petty cash can buy your drinks tonight, Danny. Yours, too, Blanche. I think I'll even risk a couple of drinks myself tonight. Might loosen me up a bit.' Blanche looked at TC in surprise.

'You're joking!'

'No!'

'Good. It's about time,' said Blanche with a broad smile.

'Can we have champagne, TC?' asked Danny. 'I've never had champagne.'

'Me, neither,' smiled TC.

'Champagne's fine with me,' laughed Blanche. 'If the boss is paying, why not?'

'I'll make a deal with both of you,' laughed TC as she opened her purse and extracted a hundred-dollar bill. 'I'll hand over Callahan's money; you guys cooperate by fighting your way through the crowd to buy the goods.'

'Deal!' said Blanche. 'Come on, Danny, let's go!'

When they returned, what seemed an eternity later, Blanche's eyes lit up to see two of the day's customers seated in the booth, chatting with TC. Both were drop-dead gorgeous.

'Look at you, TC! I leave you alone for five minutes, and you've found not one, but two men.'

'It's my hidden charm,' laughed TC. 'By the way, it's been at least twenty minutes, and I'm not that fast a worker.' Blanche placed the tray of champagne flutes on the table while Danny followed her with the ice bucket and champagne. The incredulous expression on the faces of Chad and James, the two officers seated at the table, was more than a little amusing when they saw Danny in his disco outfit.

'This is Danny. He's our friend,' said TC. 'Isn't that right, Danny?'

'Yes, I am,' replied Danny. 'TC and Blanche are nice to me.' Chad and James twigged immediately as both stepped out from the booth to shake hands with Danny after he placed the bucket on the table.

'You can sit with us if you like,' said Disco Danny. 'I saved the table.'

'Thank you, Danny. That would be great. I'm James and this is Chad.' TC had noted James wore a wedding ring. Chad did not. She needed to think quickly regarding seating arrangements.

'I've got an idea about our seating. Let's make it Danny, Blanche, Chad, myself, then James. That way Blanche and I have a man on each side of us.' Everyone was happy.

'Would you gentlemen like some champagne?' asked Blanche as she began pouring. 'Our boss is buying.'

'Sure,' replied Chad and James as they placed their empty glasses in front of Blanche.

'We saw you ladies at the party last night,' said James. 'I tried to catch you, but you were moving around.'

'That's for sure,' laughed Blanche.

'It's our job,' smiled TC.

'There you go. We all have a drink,' said Blanche as she raised her glass and all followed suit. 'Here's to what?'

'Having a good time tonight,' said Danny.

'Sounds good, Danny,' laughed Blanche. They all clicked then sipped.

Chad and Blanche immediately got into a conversation. He was a pilot and had shopped today for his mother.

'So, do you own the opal shop, TC?' enquired James.

'Manage it,' replied TC. 'What do you do, James?'

'I'm with an attack squadron.'

'He's my boss,' laughed Chad.

Danny kept checking his watch, waiting anxiously for the DJ to play loud music. Blanche passed the change from the hundred to Danny.

'Danny, get another bottle, huh?' then looked at TC. 'Make it two and another bucket?' TC nodded. One bottle didn't go far with five people drinking it.

'I'll go with you, Danny. Get a couple more appropriate glasses.' TC looked at James as he stood and collected the empty bottle and bucket.

'I know what your intentions are, James. Please don't pay. It's my boss' shout. You men spent a lot of money with us today. Simply help Danny, okay?'

'See you're drinking a lot as usual, TC,' laughed Blanche as she looked at TC's still half-full glass. Chad laughed, too.

'I'll catch up. I'm a slow drinker as you know, Blanche,' smiled TC, who didn't care much for the taste and didn't want to drink it too quickly in case she got sick. 'You two continue chatting. Pretend I'm not here.'

The DJ started up as Danny and James returned with three bottles in ice buckets along with two fresh flutes. Danny plonked a bucket and ten dollars change on the table. He all but ran to the dance floor. TC looked at James and rolled her eyes as he placed two buckets on the table. James smiled as he sat down.

'If it weren't for you, Blanche, and Danny, we'd be standing all night or going to our rooms. Surely the seats are worth a bottle of champagne.'

Why does he have to be married, thought TC. She immediately thought of Graham Sandler way back when. Why did I have to be married?

'Do you dance?' asked James as he began filling flutes. 'I hope so. Do you?' TC laughed.

'Very clever, James.'

'What music do you like?' asked James.

'Rock.'

'Heavy or soft?'

'Both'.

'Good. Me, too,' smiled James.

'What sort of music does your wife like, James?' asked TC. James quit pouring and burst into laughter.

'How did I know you were going to ask that? Finish your drinks; you're one behind.'

'What's so funny?' asked Blanche.

'TC. She's on the ball and straight to the point,' laughed James. 'She's also a very slow drinker.'

'Right on both counts,' laughed Blanche.

'Oh, all right!' TC picked up her glass and swallowed the remaining contents. 'There. I hope you're happy now.'

'Big green eyes and feisty, to boot,' laughed James as he began to refill her glass. 'Before you ask, my wife's eyes are not green.'

'Very clever, James,' replied TC with a sarcastic smile. 'You can quit flirting with me. If you want more than to share light or interesting conversation over a couple of drinks, I suggest you move on now. I'm certain you'll find a hundred or more willing participants in this crowd. Another thing, should you think getting me drunk by pushing me to finish my drinks I'll change my mind. Think again!'

James saluted.

'Yes, Ma'am, I understand. This is a good song. Do you want to dance? Promise I won't hurt you.' TC shook her head in exasperation.

'Sure, why not,' as she got to her feet.

Three songs later, the music changed to disco. Danny bounded onto the dance floor from the sidelines where he had been waiting and observing. He virtually had the floor to himself after all the rockers left. James and TC returned to the booth to find Chad and Blanche were at the 'whispering in each other's ears' stage.

'That's enough of that, you two,' laughed James. 'Don't you know this is a public place.' They ignored him. James picked up his glass.

'Let's drink a toast to us both being good rockers, TC.'

'Sure!'

'Where did you learn to dance?' asked James.

'In Queensland with my brother. We grew up with rock and roll.'

'Same here. I learned to dance in high school.'

'We're going for a walk,' said Chad. 'Afraid we knocked off a bottle and a half while you guys were dancing. We need some air, don't we, Blanche?'

'Yes,' replied Blanche softly.

'See you then,' said James.

TC smiled at Blanche, who looked serenely happy as she stood beside Chad.

'If you don't come back, I'll talk to you tomorrow. Failing that, I'll see you eight-thirty Monday morning. Please don't drive tonight.' Blanche leaned forward and kissed TC on the cheek.

'Thank you.' Chad followed suit.

'Glad we met up with you, TC.'

'Same here, Chad. Please look out for Blanche.'

'They look like lovers, don't they?' laughed James as they watched Chad and Blanche move away with their arms around each other.

I wouldn't know, thought TC. No one's ever walked like that with me. Perhaps it's because I've never been drunk.

'Yes,' she replied.

'Have you got a man in your life, TC?' asked James.

'My son. He's eight. His name is Robert,' replied TC. 'Before you ask any more questions about my personal life, I think we should change the subject.'

'Why is that?' asked James seriously.

'Because you're a married man, James. I grew up by the Bible. You know, do unto others, et cetera. I don't want to get too close. James looked wistful and nodded before speaking.

'Let's have a few more sips while we wait for the DJ to play more of our kind of music.' James and TC discussed his career in the navy, hers in the opal business, and danced when the rock music was played. TC refused to dance to the soft rock numbers—too romantic, too close.

Danny returned to the table only once or twice. When the champagne was finished, James wanted to buy more. TC said no, she'd had more than enough already.

'I'm going home now, James.'

'I'm hungry,' said James. 'Let's go to my room. We'll get room service.' TC shook her head.

'No way.'

'Do you have food at your place?' asked James.

'Of course!'

'Can I come to your place, have something to eat, then catch a cab back here?'

'What if I live a hundred miles away?' laughed TC.

'Doesn't matter! Where do you live?'

'Just across the river,' laughed TC. 'Come on, let's go. My son's nannie is sleeping over, so you'll be safe.'

'I have to collect something from my room. Will you come with me?'

'No! I'll wait in the lobby. Please don't be too long.'

'Okay, in a flash,' replied James as he rushed towards the lift.

'Eight minutes flat,' laughed James when he arrived back, puffing and panting and carrying a canvas-type bag.

'Did you run?' laughed TC.

'Along the corridors I did,' he replied. 'I was lucky the elevators weren't busy.'

'Come on, there're cabs out front,' said TC. 'I don't drive here because I live so close and parking is a hassle.' The cabbie gave TC a foul look when they got into the cab. She knew what he was thinking. She didn't care, but just gave him her address and suppressed a giggle. James wanted to pay the cabbie when they reached her house.

'No!' said TC. 'You were kind enough to see me home.' She passed a note to the cabbie. 'Keep the change. You can take care of your fare back to the hotel after we have a cup of coffee with my mother.' The cabbie's attitude changed immediately.

'Thank you, dear.'

'Thank you. Goodnight,' said both James and TC.

'Don't know whether it was the tip or the mention of your mother that made him call you 'dear',' laughed James as TC fiddled with the key to unlock the gate. 'Here, let me do that,' said James. TC handed him her keys.

'I think I'm a little tipsy.' James laughed and opened the gate, then locked it behind them.

'The door key is the big one.'

'Got it!' They were inside immediately.

'Don't make too much noise,' said TC. 'Might wake Gracie and Robert.' She closed the hallway door to the bedrooms.

'Lovely place you have,' said James as he looked around the family room.

'Robert and I are happy here,' replied TC as she switched on the kitchen light and opened the fridge door. 'What would you like to eat?' James came up behind TC and put his arms around her waist.

'You.'

'James, don't be ridiculous!' said TC angrily. 'Remove your arms or I'll scream. Gracie keeps a loaded gun under her pillow. If I scream, she'll come running out and shoot you. She'll think you're an intruder trying to molest me.' James moved away.

'You're having me on.'

'Wouldn't take the risk if I were you,' laughed TC. 'I asked you what you would like to eat.'

'And I told you,' answered James softly with a look that would melt a thousand hearts.

'No way! You know, James, I didn't realise you were as handsome as you are until you looked at me like that. I mean, I thought you were handsome when you were in the shop today, but didn't notice your eyes and other features. I didn't have time. The nightclub is so dark, one can hardly see anything. Come to think of it, how could you see my eyes are green in the dark?'

'I saw them in your shop today,' replied James softly. 'I saw everything about you in the shop today.' TC closed the fridge door and looked up at him looking down at her. Tall, black hair, huge eyes, long lashes, movie-star face, he was a man to fill every woman's dreams. She hadn't felt like this since Graham. Her heart was racing.

'I said no, James! You are a married man! I'll call you a cab.'

'TC, Chad took an instant liking to Blanche in the shop. I couldn't believe it when I saw you. My heart began pounding on sight. We couldn't believe our luck tonight when we were sitting in the hotel lobby and saw you and Blanche go into the nightclub.'

'So, you came in there looking for us.'

'Sure did,' replied James as he walked towards the chair where he'd placed his bag from which he produced three miniature bottles of champagne. 'Well, my beautiful, feisty, green-eyed, blond, petite, 'morals beyond belief' girl, if you won't let me make love to you, please have a couple more glasses of champagne with me.' TC sighed, then spoke softly, also matter-of-factly.

'It wouldn't be love, James. It would be sexual relief for you because you've been at sea. I've already told you, I'm tipsy. If you want me to drink more so I'll change my mind, forget it. You are still a married man.' James said nothing. He opened the refrigerator door and placed two bottles inside before speaking.

'Where are your glasses?' TC pointed to a cupboard.

'Do you have any music?'

'In the lounge,' replied TC, resigned to the fact he wasn't leaving. 'Why don't you put some on while I get our drinks?'

TC shrugged, 'Sure,' and moved into the next room, turned on 6iX, and slumped on the couch. James followed her a couple of minutes later, placed the glasses on the coffee table, switched on the corner lamp, then switched off the overhead lights.

'Won't do you any good,' sighed TC. As James sat on the couch beside her, Louis Armstrong's 'Wonderful World' song came on the radio. 'Is it a wonderful world, James?'

'Overall, I guess so,' replied James. 'There are some injustices, like me meeting you when I'm married.' TC sensed sincerity in his words.

'That will pass. Once you're back at sea and on your way home, I'll be but a memory.'

'I have two daughters, TC. I'm not happily married. If it weren't for them, I would have said 'stuff it' years ago.'

'That shows responsibility. I feel sorry for both you and your wife and also for your girls. When parents are unhappy, the children sense it. After all, they didn't ask to be born. They deserve the security of a sound home environment.'

'I know. I'm happy I'm away most of the time because of that very reason. When I'm home, there's constant friction between their mother and me.' James picked up his glass.

'Let's drink to happy children.'

'Let's do that.'

'Were you married, TC?'

'Yes! To Robert's father. It was hell and not worth talking about.'

'TC, may I kiss you?' TC smiled and shook her head.

'No, James. We both know that would more than likely lead to a second kiss, then a third, then the whole deal. Whether you are unhappily married or not, you are still married. There was a supply ship through here a year ago. One of the ladies on my committee fell in love with the captain, who romanced her for almost a month while the ship was undergoing maintenance work. He proposed to her. She said 'Yes' and bought a wedding dress and all the trimmings. They planned to marry in Hawaii two months after the ship pulled out of here. She flew to Hawaii for the wedding, which her fiancé told her he would arrange. She thought she'd surprise him by arriving a week early. She was the one who was surprised. He was married and still living with his wife!' James was in disbelief.

'You're kidding! What did the woman do?'

'What could she do? She hightailed it out of Hawaii and came back here to mend her broken heart. The mending is still in the process. It would probably take years.'

'That makes us all look like a mob of assholes.' TC shook her head.

'Not necessarily. It simply means when people are far away from home, sometimes they do and say things that might not be quite the truth. They say what they would like to be the truth to suit their present circumstances.'

'How old are you, TC?' asked James as he reached over and touched her cheek.

'Same age as you. You're ten days my senior. It caught my attention on your I.D. I wouldn't have a clue what your name is, but I know your age.'

'You're wise beyond your years, TC Carmichael.' TC smiled.

'My boss told me that when I was sixteen.' 'Love Me Tender' came on the radio.

'Please, TC,' said James stroking her cheek.

'Please stop doing that, and the answer is still 'no'. Let's finish this drink; then you have to go home. It's one o'clock in the morning.'

'That's early. Anyway, I'm not going home,' softly and seductively.

'You are! Stop stroking my cheek!' said TC as she pushed his hand away, then collected her glass from the table.

'You're not tipsy anymore?' asked James.

'I don't know. I probably am, but I'm too wary to show it. Please, James, go home. I want to go to bed.'

'I want to come with you,' he pleaded.

'That's it! I'm calling you a cab,' said TC. She placed her glass firmly on the table, spilling some as she did so, stood up quickly and caught her heel in the rug, causing her to fall backwards. James put his arms out to catch her, and she landed in his lap with them around her.

'Now I've got you,' whispered James. 'God, you smell beautiful.' TC's heart was racing out of control again.

'I'll give you the name of my perfume. You can buy a bottle for your wife.'

'Forget my wife, I'm with you,' he whispered back in her ear.'

'Please let me get up, James. I can't forget your wife. If you don't let me go, I'll scream.'

'No, you won't, TC Carmichael. Tell me you don't want me to make love with you.'

'I didn't say that, James. I said I won't because you're married. Please stop whispering in my ear, and take your arms away.'

In a split second, James turned TC to the side and was kissing her. It was the first real kiss she had ever experienced in her life. Tender, yet passionate at the same time. Lord, how she wished he didn't have a wife and children. Without realising it, she put her arms around him. She wanted that kiss to last forever. It did until reality struck and she pulled away. James was heavy-breathing and so was she as she disentangled herself from him.

'Don't tell me you didn't enjoy that, sweetheart,' gasped James softly.

TC said nothing. She picked up her glass and gulped down the contents, then carefully this time stood up and walked to the kitchen, where she leaned against the bench until she regained control of her breathing. She then opened the fridge, grabbed another bottle, and returned to the couch and James.

'Open this please, James. I need to get drunk so I can go to sleep. When I do go to sleep, leave me here. You can sleep in my room. It's the first door on the right down the hallway. Should you need the bathroom, it's to the left at the end. Both light switches are halfway down the wall inside the doorway. Please hurry and open that bottle.'

'I find you incredible, TC.'

'Yes, I feel the same about you. Please pour that champagne, or I'll drink it from the bottle. Seems I've become a drunk in just one night. God help me. God forgive me, I almost let it happen.'

'I'm sorry, TC,' said James softly as he gently stroked her hair and she took her first gulp.

'No, you're not, James. Neither am I,' replied TC also softly, almost a whisper. 'Some of the women on my welcoming committee refer to me as Miss Lily Milk White, and the others, Miss Purity. I've had sex with one man in my life and very little of that. It was loveless. Your kiss is the first real kiss I have experienced in my entire life. My body has never felt the way it did during that kiss. Why the bloody hell do you have to be married!? Why did you have to follow me into the nightclub?' She gulped more champagne.

'Please put that glass down and let me hold you.'

'No, you lovely man, you can't hold me. I will put the glass down. I'm very tired.' TC was asleep in a heartbeat. James removed her stilettos and laid her on the couch with a cushion under her head. He then sat beside the couch, running his fingers through her hair with one hand while he rested his other on her shoulder. The radio was still playing softly in the background, but James couldn't hear it—he was deep in thought.

On Sunday morning TC woke to hear Gracie's voice, 'Come on, you two. Get off that bed,' then Robert ask, 'Mama, who is that man?' TC sat bolt upright, felt overwhelming relief when she saw she was still fully clothed.

'I've got a headache,' she complained as she cupped her head in her hands.

'Judging by those empty bottles in the lounge, it's no wonder,' scolded Gracie.

TC then felt movement on the bed beside her and heard James' voice.

'Hello. I'm James. You must be Gracie, and you, young man, must be Robert.'

'Why were you on mother's bed, Mr James?'

'I was guarding her for you, Robert, and you don't have to call me Mr James. James will do nicely. Mr James makes me feel old. Gracie, TC didn't drink all of that. I drank most of it. She drank one glass too quickly, then fell asleep.'

TC looked towards the doorway to see James clad in white undershorts and shirt towering over Gracie and Robert.

'Thought I told you to leave me on the couch,' mumbled TC.

'Is it all right if I use the bathroom, Gracie?' asked James.

'Of course, darlin'. I'll get you a fresh towel.'

TC moaned as she thought, That'll be right. Ten seconds and Gracie is calling him darlin'.

Robert quickly jumped on the bed and hugged his mother.

'I love you, Mama.'

'I love you, too, darling,' she replied as she hugged him back.

'Mama, why do you still have your dress on?'

'I fell asleep in it, sweetie,' replied TC while thinking, One more kiss and I wouldn't have.

'Is James an American, Mother?' enquired Robert ever so seriously.

'Yes, darling. You should ask him what he does. Mama needs to get out of these clothes and get ready to have a shower after James is finished in the bathroom.'

'I'll go and play with the cat while I wait to ask James what he does.'

'Close the door behind you, please, darling.'

TC straightened the bedspread, undressed, put on a short, cotton house coat with tiny yellow roses on a white background and yellow slippers with bows on the front, brushed her hair, then went to the kitchen to face Gracie for the inquisition, a couple of Aspros, and a large glass of water.

The first thing TC saw when she entered the family room were James' trousers, shirt, tie and jacket neatly placed on a coat hanger attached to the back of a kitchen stool.

'Poor darlin' folded his clothes over a lounge chair,' explained Gracie. 'I hung up them properly for him.'

'How do you know he's a darlin', Gracie,' laughed TC as she fumbled in a drawer for her headache relievers. 'He wanted me to have sex with him.'

'Well, why didn't you? He's lovely.'

'Because he's married,' said James, who emerged from the hallway dressed in walking shorts, short-sleeved, striped shirt, and sports shoes. He spotted the look of confusion on TC's face.

'I brought them in this.' He held up the canvas bag before dropping it on the sofa. TC rolled her eyes.

'I suppose you brought your toothbrush, razor and aftershave as well?'

'Of course.'

'You packed a lot and covered a lot of ground in eight minutes, or do you always have your overnight gear at the ready.'

'Leave him alone, TC,' said Gracie. 'James, would you like some breakfast, darlin'?' TC swallowed her Aspros followed by a glass of water, then another glass.

'Doesn't TC look cute in her yellow roses and bowed slippers, Gracie?' teased James.

'Yes,' replied Gracie. 'Yellow is her favourite colour. She likes pink, too.'

'That's right, talk about me as if I'm not here. I'm going for a shower.'

TC returned to find James and Robert deep in conversation at the dining room table. Gracie was standing alongside, listening intently while gazing at James in adoration.

I can't say I blame her, thought TC. It also probably brings back painful memories of the American lover she had during the war. He was married, too.

TC joined them. James looked her up and down.

'Well, here she is, the lady who looks great in everything, be it a black, cocktail dress, yellow slippers with bows, or blue jeans and a shirt.'

'Flattery won't get you far, James,' laughed TC. 'Quit while you're ahead.'

'We're taking James to the lakes for a picnic, Mother. He's going to take me rowing in a canoe. Gracie has the picnic basket almost ready.'

'Thank you for letting me know. I suppose James is doing the driving.'

'That was the idea,' smiled James. 'I'd like to know what it's like to drive here. If it's okay with you, TC?'

'Are you coming, Gracie?'

'No, thank you, darlin'. I have to see my grandchildren.'

James drove the sports car faster than TC had ever dared. She wasn't afraid. She figured if he could pilot an attack plane, he'd have to be an expert driver, even if it was on the opposite side of the road to America.

Robert had the best time she'd ever seen him enjoy. James and he were in and out of a canoe on the water for hours. TC relaxed on a blanket under a shady tree. Her headache hung around forever. She thought it served her right. No more champagne. None! Observing James's interaction with Robert convinced her he must be a great dad to his daughters and possibly was sticking with his marriage for them. Who would know except him?

⁋

TC ordered pizzas after they returned to the house. James drank a couple of beers purchased en route.

'Are you staying tonight, James?' asked Robert hopefully.

'No. I have to go to work tomorrow, Robert,' said TC.

'I didn't ask you, Mother. I asked James.'

James looked at TC and smiled wistfully, patted Robert on the head, and replied, 'No, pal, I don't think that would be a good idea.'

'I hope I see you again, James,' pleaded Robert. Once again James looked at TC, this time with intensity.

'Perhaps your mother will let me take you guys to dinner tomorrow night?' How could TC refuse? The message emanating from his beautiful eyes told her James wanted to see her again, even if it was in a crowded restaurant.

'That will be fine,' she nodded and smiled. 'It can't be late. Robert has school on Tuesday, and I have work.' Relief flooded James' face, and Robert hugged TC.

'Thank you, thank you, thank you, Mama.'

'We'll drive you back to your hotel, James,' said TC.

'Are you sure?' replied James softly. TC sighed.

'It's safer that way,' was her reply.

⁋

At eight-thirty on Monday morning, Blanche arrived at work looking as if she had been to hell and back.

'What have you been up to?' laughed TC.

'Please! Don't ask!' replied Blanche as she threw her bag on the desk and slumped into one of the two office desk chairs. 'I've got two nights to go yet and I'm already exhausted.'

'Two nights of what?' kidded TC. Blanche sighed heavily and cupped her chin in her hands.

'I'm not telling you, Miss Lily Milk White. I wouldn't want you to faint from shock. How did you go with James?'

'He's married, unfortunately,' replied TC.

'I knew you'd say that! You're too pure for your own good!'

'Probably,' agreed TC as she glanced towards the street and the front of the shop. 'Smarten yourself up, Blanche. We've got customers waiting outside already, and it's only twenty to nine. Looks like another busy day.'

TC hurried to open the doors through which entered almost an entire squadron of pilots.

'Are we too early, ma'am?' enquired one.

'Never too early,' laughed TC. 'Only Blanche and myself are here for a little while yet, so we'll put the trays on the counters. You can help yourselves. Any questions, please ask. If you make a mistake, I'll tell you.'

'Are you TC Carmichael?' enquired one young man.

'That's me,' laughed TC. 'Have I done something wrong?'

'Not at all. Quite the contrary. We heard this is the place to buy opals, so here we are.'

Blanche appeared via the office door and TC introduced her. The Japanese girls came at nine, and by ten-thirty, the happy customers were leaving. Again, Blanche and TC donned the sheepskin slippers mid-afternoon. As always with every sale, TC said a silent prayer of thanks to the Lord for her reputation with the U.S. Navy visitors.

James phoned a little after five.

'Do you want to eat in the hotel, TC?'

'No, too expensive! If you like fish, Robert loves going to a restaurant called Mr Bill's. Smart, casual attire.'

'Sounds good. Can't wait to see you.'

'Thank you. I have to admit, I feel a bit the same. Do you want us to collect you around seven?'

'Is it okay if I come to your house and we go from there? I don't care to hang around in my room until seven.'

'Sure.'

TC called Mr Bill's and made a reservation. She knew he'd be busy with the fleet in port.

§

TC was surprised to see that Gracie's Fairlane was not in the driveway. It was only six-thirty. She hoped nothing was wrong as she hurried inside to find James and Robert laughing in the family room.

'Gracie has gone home to get changed,' said Robert as he ran to hug TC.

'I invited her to dinner with us,' said James as he moved slowly towards TC, then leaned over and kissed her on the side of her neck.

'Stop it!' whispered TC, who began shaking and quickly stepped away. 'I'd best change.'

'You don't need to; you look lovely as you are. Yellow again, I see. Very business-like but lovely.'

'It's Mother's favourite colour,' explained Robert.

'James knows, darling. Gracie already told him. Right, if I don't need to change, I'll brush my teeth and apply fresh lipstick.'

'Perhaps a touch more of that perfume,' James hinted.

'Consider it done!'

§

Dinner was great. Gracie was dressed like the English flower she was and bathed in the attention afforded by all, in particular James.

'I feel like I'm reliving my young days,' beamed Gracie. 'All these lovely Americans.'

'I bet you were a wild girl in those days, Gracie, and beautiful, too,' said James.

'Yes, I was. Don't know about the beautiful, but I did have a lot of fun. We used to go dancing and get up to all sorts of nonsense.'

'In other words, you were a naughty girl,' teased James.

'Oh, yes, I was! So were my friends. We'd never had so much fun in our lives as we did when you Yanks were in England. We cried and cried when you left.'

'Shh, Gracie,' whispered TC. 'You might give away too many secrets from the past.'

'Doesn't matter now, darlin'. What with the goings-on today; we did nothing.'

'I wish Mother would have more fun,' said Robert.

So do I, thought James.

'Mother works too hard to have fun, darlin'. She's got no time,' said Gracie.

When they were leaving, Mr Bill was beaming.

'How's business, TC?'

'Flat out, thank heavens.'

'Mine, too. Look around. I love it when these Yanks are in town.' TC smiled, and so did James.

'Aren't they lovely?' said Gracie.

'Mr Bill, this is Gracie,' announced Robert with pride. 'Gracie takes care of me when Mother works. And Mr Bill, this is James. He's my friend. James is American and he flies jet planes.' Mr Bill laughed.

'As I said, I love it when you people are in town. Did you enjoy your meals?' enquired Mr Bill as he took James' money.

'Great, thank you,' from James.

'Oh, yes,' from Gracie. 'I hope TC and Robert bring me here some time when they come Saturday nights.' Mr Bill, James, and TC laughed.

'That's a subtle hint if ever I heard one,' said James.

'Don't worry, Gracie, of course, we'll bring you,' promised TC. 'You're welcome whenever we come.'

Gracie had insisted on taking her car because it was bigger.

'I don't want to be squeezed up in that tiny little thing,' she'd complained.

When she dropped James, Robert, and TC back at the house, she jumped out of the car and hugged James like there was no tomorrow.

'Thank you for dinner, you darlin', beautiful Yank. I'll never forget you. I promise! I won't!'

'I won't forget you, either, Gracie,' laughed James. 'What man could?'

'Oh! I hope you're right,' said Gracie, then she was in her car and gone.

'Don't worry about us, Gracie,' laughed TC.

❡

Once inside, TC instructed Robert to brush his teeth, put on his pyjamas, and go to bed.

'I want to sit up and talk to James,' complained Robert.

'No, sweetie, it's nine o'clock. School tomorrow.'

'How about you do as your mother said, then I'll come say goodnight to you before I go?' bargained James.

'Promise?'

'I promise.'

'It's a good thing you're not staying long, James,' commented TC.

'Is it? Why?'

'Robert is getting too attached to you.'

'What about Robert's mother?'

'That, too! I'll go and see that he's in bed, then you can say goodbye to him before you leave.'

'You're right, TC. It will be goodbye. I have to be back on the ship midnight or so tomorrow night.'

TC was back in minutes. 'Robert's in bed. He's waiting for you.' James went to talk with Robert. TC went to get out of her business suit and heels. A little while later she was in the bathroom brushing her teeth when James came to the door.

'He's asleep, TC. I'll wait in the lounge for you. Glad to see you've got your yellow roses outfit on. It's so cute.'

'James, I'm way past the age of cute.'

'It's still cute,' insisted James. 'Okay if I turn those other lights off?'

he said as he moved towards the kitchen/family room dual switches.

'You have to go, James. I have to work tomorrow.'

'I'll go soon, but I want to talk with you for a little while first. After tonight, we'll probably never see each other again. I have some things to say to you. Firstly, since cheap champagne gave you a headache, I got us some fine white wine, guaranteed not to do the same. Please sit down while I pour.'

'Please, dear Lord, let me be strong,' prayed TC silently. 'Why does he have to be such a gentleman and beautiful, to boot.' James returned with two chilled wine glasses filled with the finest white wine he'd been able to locate.

'Here's to you, TC Carmichael.'

'Here's to you, James. I don't even know your surname.' Silent tears began falling from TC's eyes. James put down his glass and wiped her tears across her cheeks.

'Yes, you do. It's on my I.D. You have a copy. Please don't cry. You'll have me crying, too.

'I'm not crying, James. It's dust in my eyes.' James put his arms around TC and held her.

'Oh, sweetheart, you're one in a million.'

'Thank you, I think you are, too. I'm all right, darling man. Let's start again.'

'Are you sure?' asked James tenderly. TC nodded and forced a smile.

'Here's to you, TC Carmichael.'

'Here's to you, James I-have-a-copy-of-your-I.D.' They intertwined their arms and drank from their glasses.

'Now we drink to a promise we'll never forget each other,' said James. 'I promise I'll never forget you, TC Carmichael.'

'I promise I'll never forget you, James I-have-a-copy-of-your-I.D.'

'Now can I kiss you?'

'Yes, but we're not making love.'

'I know that, sweetheart, and I know why. It's not only because I'm married anymore. I know it's because we're in love.'

'That's right, James. It seems crazy two people can fall in love so quickly. Someone told me a long time ago that with unrequited love the mystery will forever remain and the loved one always remembered.'

'Who told you that?'

'Probably my boss. I can't remember. As I said, it was a long time ago.'

James and TC were there until two in the morning. They kissed a lot, held each other tightly, whispered, and even laughed occasionally. TC called his cab.

'I left some things with Gracie, sweetheart. Don't open them until the ship has sailed. I don't want to leave you, TC Carmichael.'

'I know. I also know you have to.'

By the time the cab came they were both crying. One last kiss, a hug to last forever, and James was gone.

¶

Next morning at the shop, Blanche asked TC what was wrong. TC burst into tears, but didn't say a word as she searched through the invoices for James' I.D. Eleven o'clock that night she heard a horn beeping outside her house. It was a cab. James was at the gate.

'TC, open your garage door.'

She did.

'I couldn't leave without seeing and holding you one more time. TC, I love you. Please always remember that. I'm running late, sweetheart. I have to go.'

'I love you too, James, have a good life. God bless you and your girls.'

This time he was gone forever except in her memory.

Tears streaming again, TC poured herself a glass of wine left over from the night before while thinking, I thought I promised myself some years ago the only tears I'd shed would be for Robert. Just goes to show we can't always keep our promises, not even to ourselves. All I seem to do of late is cry. She then went into the lounge room and opened a letter James had left with Gracie.

My Darling TC Carmichael,

As I told you on Saturday night, the moment I saw you in your shop, my heart began pounding. When we kissed in the early hours of Sunday, I felt more tenderness combined with passion than I have ever experienced in my life. My heart told me you felt the same. I hope that was the case.

After you fell asleep, I stroked your hair and watched you breathe. You looked so vulnerable, soft, and innocent. No fieriness whatsoever. Not that there's anything wrong with being fiery.

I believe I fell I love with you right then while your invisible wall of self-protection was absent. With every breath you took, I wanted more to call my wife and tell her our marriage was over. I've had enough of plastic happiness. That is why I drank all the champagne. I did that as a substitute for the call.

I carried you to your bedroom because I wanted to be near you, which I was until Gracie and Robert woke us.

Yesterday I fell for Robert. He is the most well-mannered, well-spoken child I have ever met. It's hard to believe he's only eight. His vocabulary and worldly intelligence is far beyond his years. Be proud of him, TC. He sure is proud of you!

Please remember me as I shall remember you. Everything about you, your green eyes, the softness of your hair, smile, frown, voice, walk, laugh, and fragrance of your perfume.

Take care of yourself, TC Carmichael.

James.

After reading the letter, TC went to the bathroom and washed her face. She then sat back in the lounge room and stared into space as she drank the wine.

James is the first person in my life to recognise my invisible wall, she thought.

The gifts James left were a small, yellow, porcelain rose in a brushed-pewter holder. It was beautiful. TC shed a bucket of tears. For Robert, a large, framed picture of James' ship with his plane flying above it, and the inscription, Robert, keep charging. James.

TC's invisible wall became more impenetrable. She felt numb and desperately needed to talk to Vance. He had moulded her into being as he was. He would understand! Then again, what was the point? After all, she'd broken her business-and-pleasure rule by inviting James to her home. She could have avoided the heartache for both of them had she adhered to her rule. She knew in her heart James was hurting, too. He was trapped by his love for his girls. She respected him for that. If nothing else, she'd always have the yellow porcelain rose and her memories of their brief time together. TC made a vow to herself there and then, 'No more socialising with visitors unless in crowd scenes.' She sat on her lounge room couch until daylight. Thinking. Thinking about anything and everything.

'I shall concentrate on nothing except business. Obviously, I'm a failure in the romance department. Twice I've fallen in love! Both times bad news! James' ship is probably sailing now,' she told herself. 'Get yourself together. Go and be a success. Do it for Lou! Do it to forget what could have been. Love and happiness never happen! Not for people like you! Live with the fact you have missed the fairy-tale deal.' Making money is all I'm good for, thought TC. Better do that or I'll be good for nothing. She threw three Vitamin B effervescent pills into a glass of water, then headed for the shower.

Half an hour later she called Gracie as Gracie walked through the door. TC put the phone down.

'I'm early, darlin',' said Gracie.

'I'm glad you are, Gracie darling. I was calling you. I need to go to the shop early.'

'Gee, that James is nice,' said Gracie.

'I know, Gracie,' TC replied. 'So are you. Tell Robert I love him. Don't give him James' present until this afternoon.'

'What is it?'

'You know very well what it is, Gracie. He gave it to you to put behind the couch,' laughed TC.

'Oh! That's right! It's a picture of his ship and a plane. James gave me some chocolates, you know.' TC smiled.

'No! I didn't know. That was nice of him. He's a nice man.'

'Yes! He gave them to me yesterday afternoon before he invited me to dinner.'

'I have to go now, Gracie. I'll see you around six. Thank you and, by the way, you looked gorgeous last night.'

'Thank you, darlin'!'

¶

At eight-thirty, Blanche wandered in, bubbly and starry eyed. TC had the display organised, lights and counters cleaned, and floors vacuumed. She was on the telephone with Vance, who was complaining about Chikako not being happy because she wasn't seeing enough of him.

'Tell it to someone who cares, Boss,' said TC. 'You get yourself into these situations, then whinge to me.'

'What's changed about you, Little One?' asked Vance with the most concern TC had ever heard him send in her direction.

'Just about everything, Boss. I'm no longer a 'little girl'! You made me what I am. All you ever do is ask how much money I've taken in, complain about your wife spending money, or your love life triangles, quadrangles, or whatever. We've been over this a million times! You! You! You, and bloody you! I'll send you a report. By the way, I'm employing an Australian girl!'

Five minutes after the doors were opened at nine, Clarice, wife of Stan, who used to be manager of one of the mines, came charging into the shop. These were the people Lenny and Ray had told TC to be careful about.

'Where's TC?' demanded Clarice. TC smiled sincerely.

'I'm right here.'

'Suppose you had to screw Callahan to get this shop!' snarled Clarice.

'If I did, I didn't screw him to take a six-month vacation down south,' replied TC while remaining calm with sickly sweetness additives.

'Oh!' Clarice disappeared, never to front up again. Not at the shop anyway.

Blanche, with her soft, silky voice, looked at TC in a different light from that moment on. Seemed that way.

'I don't believe it,' said Blanche.

'Anything is believable, Blanche,' smiled TC. 'As long as it's the truth, that is. Do you still want a permanent job?'

'Of course, I do.'

'Good. You start next Monday. Let's get started on the tally. Kayoko can fill the gaps after she gets here at nine-thirty.'

Kayoko did not get there at nine-thirty. Instead of filling gaps, she told TC she was pregnant and was going east to get married. She and her husband-to-be were leaving that afternoon. She had come to collect her pay.

'So that's the Japanese way of doing things?' said Blanche. TC shrugged.

'How would I know? Looks like it!'

'Were you sad to see James go?' asked Blanche.

'Probably. Let's get on with the tally. Peter from Sydney will be here in the morning. We need to know what we sold so we can replace it. If it's okay with you, perhaps you start permanent as of today.'

'Suits me.'

⁋

With Kayoko gone, the two part-time Japanese girls split the week as neither wished to have full-time positions. This meant that TC needed to find a replacement for Kayoko before the season began, which was in the very near future. After interviewing the half dozen who applied for the position, TC settled on a very attractive woman of her own age named Hideko.

There was something about Hideko which bothered TC, who couldn't quite figure out what it was. Time would tell.

⁋

TC received a letter from Lisa to advise her that Con and she had sold the café to Lena and Jack. Con and she had finished with café work. They were retiring and hoped to enjoy life in Sydney. If they didn't like Sydney, they would move somewhere else, perhaps the Gold Coast. Lisa wrote——

We're free at last, TC. It's been a long time coming. I'll keep in touch.

Not a week had passed when she received another letter. This one was from Jess. She wrote—

Had enough of this place, young TC. Should have thrown in the towel years ago. My feet are buggered, luv, probably because I'm so damned old. I heard about lovely Lou going to our Lord. Must say I was sad. I'll never forget you kids. Talk about peas in a pod. Heard you're doing well. Good on you, luv. Just goes to show what a girl can do with the right push. Glad I pushed you.

Old Jock and his mates reckoned the scenery from the sacred seat would never be the same with Jess gone.

'She's been here for bloody ever,' said Jock.

'Longer,' said one man.

'That's for bloody sure,' said another.

¶

It was international tour season 1983. Perth, Western Australia, was on the map due to Australia winning the America's Cup in September of that year. It was hectic!

Vance hired a Japanese lady named Emi to portray the role of public relations for Brolga Opals. Not only was she beautiful, Emi was a relentless hard worker. She took her job seriously. Emi was principled to the eyebrow, plus some. She managed to avoid Vance's approaches. After all, she had an extremely handsome Aussie husband and son. As far as Emi was concerned, Vance was a dreamer. A good boss, and that was it. Emi was absorbed in her job. Her enthusiasm was obviously contagious. Pretty soon, huge buses filled with Japanese tourists were pulling to a halt in front of all Brolga Opal outlets.

Money, mostly cash, kept rolling in. If TC didn't take a hundred thousand by the end of every week, Vance told her she wasn't working hard enough. Staff volume became eight full-timers plus the couple who worked only when necessary. Business was booming.

The ships kept coming. Prior to arrival, once word was out, TC received phone calls up till 3 am from eager women hopeful of attending welcoming functions. She turned more away then could be accommodated.

Consequently, TC would sleep under her office desk from around nine till twelve while her staff answered calls of enquiry and took care of the shop. Blanche was wonderful. Hideko was jealous of Blanche's relationship with TC. In her mind it wasn't fair—they could socialise, be close friends as well as work together. She had to go home to her husband, a fact she resented.

Randall James dropped by the shop every six weeks or so, always sober and dressed immaculately. He knew where TC worked after collecting one of her business cards from atop the shop's display case at Mr Bill's. Randy worked in the state's north and was in Perth on leave one week in seven. On every occasion he presented himself, he enquired about Robert, Mr D and Vance before then asking TC out to dinner. TC always declined.

❡

Jonathan married lovely Lolita. They lived in Brolga. Although Lolita tried hard, she could not adjust to living in an isolated, bush-country town. Most of all, she loathed the dust and flies. Jonathan was in a dilemma. He loved his dad, but by the same token, he loved Lolita. He had to make a huge decision. He knew if he sold the leases and machinery, he would break his father's heart. He also knew, if he didn't, he would lose Lolita. It was tough-decision time. He sold the leases and most of the machinery. When Vance called TC, he was near to tears.

'This is another one of the worst days in my life.'

'What's wrong now, Boss?'

'I'm an opal miner, Little One. That's what I do best. Jonathan has sold the whole bloody lot. Doesn't he know ME? Doesn't he know what I'm all about? What about the MEN? What about every bloody thing?' Apart from when Anna and his unknown son had surprised him at the shop the day he came to the Pink Brolga and cried, TC had never heard Vance sound so desolate.

'Are you crying, Boss?'

'Just about am, Little One; just about am.'

'Nothing you can do about it, Boss. Have to accept the things we can't change.'

'I know,' sighed Vance. 'I'll talk to you soon.'

Vance's diehard loyalists-to-the-end dispersed in different directions. Yappy returned to central-western Queensland. One night he got drunk, then climbed onto the pub roof from which he jumped. Yappy died from a broken neck and multiple other injuries. The fact was, Yappy didn't wish to live any longer——threw the towel in, so to speak. Neil stayed in Brolga, worked for the council, as did his brothers. They missed the seclusion and safety of being at the opal mines. Afternoons when their workday was over, they headed to the Majestic, where they would drink until closing time at ten. Little Joe went north to Winton, where he found employment with another opal miner. As always, he worked his heart out and said very little.

Mr D and Vance drove across the Nullarbor to surprise TC and Robert. They timed their visit to coincide with a carrier group.

'I'll be very busy, so you'll both have to help me by taking care of yourselves,' declared TC.

'I'm not going to anything, including the shop,' laughed Vance. 'I brought Robert a tape of a movie I like. He can laugh at other people dancing. I'll laugh with him.'

'Only place I'm going,' announced Mr D, 'is to the Yanks' welcoming do. The rest of the time I'll help Gracie with whatever she does. She'll probably boss me around like the last time I came here.'

'No whinging, Mr D,' laughed TC. 'Any whinging about anything, you can stay in a hotel.' Both Vance and Mr D cracked up. They knew all too well TC would never carry through with her threat. Robert and she loved their presence. So did Gracie, for that matter. Both men had a knack of making Gracie feel important, like the 'queen of the manor'. Gracie bathed in the limelight! Who could blame her?

Mr D consumed more than a few bourbons the day of the first-night welcoming function. He phoned TC mid-afternoon.

'I don't want to go to this thing tonight, Carmichael.'

'Okay, don't go!' replied TC. 'I'll take your name off the dignitary list.' She didn't. Mr D was already in his suit when TC arrived home from the shop.

'Hurry and get yourself dressed, Carmichael. We mustn't be late.'

'I deleted your name, Mr D,' laughed TC. 'You said you didn't want to go.'

'I've changed my mind, so get yourself ready, lass,' was the arrogant, commanding reply.

'Consider yourself told, Little One,' laughed Vance. 'Robert and I want to watch the dancing movie.'

TC rolled her eyes as Gracie said, 'Oh, yes, I do, too.'

¶

Mr D and TC parted ways at the reception hall door.
'You're on your own, Mr D,' said TC. 'I have work to do. Please be a good, darling man and refer to the visitors as fine, young Americans instead of bloody Yanks.'

'Bye, Carmichael. I'll do my best,' replied Mr D as he merged confidently with the early arrivals.

Later, TC spotted Mr D taking the floor while surrounded by a group of young officer pilots, all of whom appeared to be listening intently to his every word. By the end of the evening, four of them approached TC. They congratulated her on what a 'great father' she had.

'We haven't spoken to anyone else all evening,' commented one.

'Your dad is intriguing. He knows everything about everything.'

'Especially to do with ships,' added another.

'Thank you. I'm proud of him. He's one in a million,' laughed TC. TC went to find Mr D, who was in deep conversation with Captain Russ, his wife Marjorie, and a couple of senior officers.

'Time to go, Mr D. Some of us have work in the morning.'

'Please don't drag your dad away yet, TC,' said Marjorie. 'We're interested in hearing the end of his story.'

'That's right!' said Captain Russ while the officers nodded in agreement. TC shrugged and smiled.

'Okay. I'll be at the door with Ken, Fiona, Len, and Lisa. Perhaps I'll find Blanche, too.' Blanche had left a message with Lisa.

'Tell TC I've gone to a squadron party and not to worry as I'll be on time for work tomorrow morning.'

'That'd be right,' laughed TC. 'Looks like we won't be going nightclubbing tomorrow night. She'll already have a date.'

'You should get yourself a date, too, darling,' suggested Fiona. TC knew Fiona was testing her.

'I'll be fine, Fiona. My boss and Mr Dalton will keep me company.'

'Smart girl,' smiled Fiona with obvious affection.

When Mr D and TC finally left, Mr D was on a high.

'Wonderful night, Carmichael. Great lads, those young pilots. That Marjorie is a lovely woman; her husband's a good man, too.'

'So, you're not my dad now?' laughed TC.

'No! Not at the moment. I'll be your father again on Sunday. I invited five pilots, a chaplain, Captain Russ and his lovely wife to a barbeque at the house. I told the pilots they were welcome to bring female companions if they got lucky in the meantime.' TC was surprised to say the least.

'Thank you for asking me, Mr D.'

'I'm telling you now, lass!' was the reply. 'All you do is go to work and go home. You need some fun. It'll be like back at the Pink Brolga.'

'Perhaps for you, Mr D, but I don't recall having much fun at the Pink Brolga.'

'I've got it all worked out, Carmichael. While you're at work tomorrow, Callahan and I will go shopping. I'll buy the booze. Callahan can pay for the meat and trimmings. You can compile a list of what we'll need.'

'Sounds like I don't have any choice other than to agree. As it's my house, you and the boss are paying. I reserve the right to invite half a dozen or so others—the Smythes, a couple of other committee members, and Blanche.'

'Consider it a done deal, Carmichael,' laughed Mr D. 'What choice do I have?'

'None!' was TC's firm reply.

¶

Robert was in the garage before TC had turned off the motor.

'Mother! Mr Dalton! Gracie, Mr Callahan, and I watched the dancing movie three times. Mr Callahan and I both danced while Gracie made us hamburgers. We've had a great night!'

I wish I had, thought TC as she slowly got out of the car to hug her son.

'So have I, lad,' added Mr D. 'Let's go inside. I need a Bourbon.'

'Mr Dalton, did you meet any pilots? I can't wait to be old enough to meet a pilot. I had a friend. His name is James. I'll show you a huge picture he gave me. It's on the wall in my room. He gave it to me when I was eight.'

'Is that so?' asked Mr D. 'That's nice. You'll have to show me.'

'Come on, Robert, let's get inside,' directed TC while thinking, Please, my darling son, don't say another word.

'We've had a wonderful time,' exclaimed Gracie.

'How did it go?' enquired Vance with a laugh.

'Mr D has planned a barbeque for here on Sunday,' replied TC. 'He'll tell you about it while I get changed.'

'I need a Bourbon,' from Mr D. 'What will you have, Gracie?'

'Oh, lovely, I'll have a Bailey's,' replied Gracie. 'TC keeps it for me in the cupboard with the Scotch whiskey. I'll get it out.'

'Does TC drink Scotch?' asked Vance in shock, horror, and alarm.

'Only sometimes,' replied Gracie as she opened the cupboard door. 'She only started having a couple since she got really sick on champagne and felt she didn't fit in at the nightclub and the few parties she attends.'

Vance said nothing. Instead he fell into deep thought. Haven't I taught her anything? Surely, Little One should have learned from what she saw me do years ago. Bloody hell!' Mr D noted the expression on Vance's face.

'Come on, Callahan. Let the lass have a life. She's a grown woman!'

'I'll have a Coke with you, Mr Callahan,' said the now-almost-eleven-year-old Robert.

'Sounds good, mate, but I think you've had enough fun tonight,' said Vance. 'Go to bed, okay? I want to spend some time with Mr D, Gracie, and your mother.'

Gracie left a half hour later. Mr D went to bed soon after. He'd had one too many Bourbons. It had been a long day. Vance was seated on a chair in the family room. TC was positioned opposite him on a kitchen bar stool.

'How many drinks have you had, Little One?' asked Vance. He sounded serious and concerned.

'I have had three glasses of water at the shop today, two at the party tonight, and I've almost finished the Scotch and dry I am holding in my hand as we talk,' replied TC.

'I don't want you to be a drunk, Little One.'

'I don't want to be one, either,' replied TC matter-of-factly.

'What's wrong with you?' asked Vance with great concern.

'Everything!' replied TC. 'Everything is wrong with me, Boss. Everything! I'm lonely. I have a wall around me. I'm a money-making machine for you. You rarely praise me. You take me for granted.' Vance sighed deeply.

'You're right, Little One. I'm sorry!'

'No! You are NOT sorry, Mr Callahan,' replied TC as she got off the stool. 'I'm going to bed! I suggest you do the same. Mr D has a big weekend planned.'

'Little One, please don't go to bed. I want to talk,' pleaded Vance.

TC stood straight and placed her hands on her hips, reminiscent of pub-window days. She threw her head back and asked, 'About what!? Your beloved money, girlfriends, or your wife's spending habits? You rarely tell me about your kids. I've known them since they were babies. You remembered to ask about Robert perhaps once a year, if that.'

'Listen to me,' interrupted Vance.

'I don't want to listen to you!' snapped TC in a controlled tone of voice. 'You are besotted by money, Mr Callahan! It can't keep you warm and you can't take it with you. It can't buy you love, health, or happiness. I still liked you better when you were a drunk. Goodnight! I'm going to bed! You're my boss and my best friend, now Lou has gone. By the way, you hardly bothered to mention her. Couldn't spare the time.'

She's right, as usual, thought Vance. Poor little bugger has been right since day dot. I'll have to tell her, next opportunity I get.

TC kissed Vance on the cheek. 'I'll see you in the morning, Boss. I'm glad you drove across with Mr D. I love both of you and so does Robert.' Vance smiled and TC was off to bed.

¶

Chaos was the only way to describe what took place at the shop that Saturday. It was late morning. There were Americans wall to wall. Every staff member, including the part-timers, were rushed off their feet when two unscheduled tour buses pulled up out the front. Blanche sidled up to TC and whispered.

'Bloody hell! Look what we have! They're about to step off and inside.' TC threw her hands in the air after a quick glance towards The Terrace door.

'Great!' she sighed heavily. 'Think quick!' she told herself as the door was opened and the mostly elderly Japanese tourists filed inside. Some bowed, uttering 'so sorry' to the young Americans, who stepped backwards to allow the tourists closer access to the counters. TC directed her attention to the Americans, most of whom were holding intended-to-purchase goods.

'We should wait in the hallway, TC?' enquired a man who appeared more senior to most of the others.

'If so, that would be good,' replied TC with a smile. 'Please take whatever you have in your hands with you. We'll take care of that later. Thank you!'

It doesn't matter, thought TC. I have to keep everyone happy. It's not easy sometimes.

Blanche backed into the office and turned up the radio. The King was singing 'I feel my temperature rising.'

'Mine, too,' laughed Blanche as she clasped her hands behind her back after returning to stand beside TC.

'I know exactly what you mean,' replied TC as she glanced towards the hallway filled with patiently- waiting Americans, observing while Hideko gave her explanatory talk about opals to the tour group. It was a spending frenzy! Whatever the Japanese ladies chose, they got. Price was obviously not a factor. The Japanese staff made the sales before literally flinging the selected stock and paperwork at TC and Blanche to be packaged, photocopied, or whatever. The deals were done when money changed hands after the Japanese gentlemen found a secluded spot between the souvenir shelves from where they extracted cash from their packed-to-capacity money belts before passing some to Blanche or TC.

'Don't you just love those old folk,' laughed Blanche as the tour group heeded their guide's instructions and filed in an orderly manner towards the door while bowing and saying, 'Arigato' to the Americans waiting in the hallway.

'Yes! I do!' replied TC as she beckoned to the hallway U.S. fleet personnel by waving her hand and smiling.

'Poor buggers have been waiting forever!' said Blanche. TC checked the clock before replying.

'Twenty-eight minutes. Give them fifteen percent extra discount. The usual, then deduct fifteen from that.'

'I know what you're doing,' said Blanche.

'I know, too!' replied TC. 'The tour company picked up fifteen percent for directing their passengers here. These people deserve to keep the equivalent in their pockets because they waited.' TC noted dissatisfaction written all over Hideko's face and wanted to say something, but didn't bother. There was no point, at least not to Hideko. She obviously loathed Americans. Instead, TC waited until they were all back inside the shop after their time in the hallway.

'My boss and self-professed father are in town. There'll be a barbeque at my home tomorrow. Any of you who would like to attend are more than welcome to do so. Any of you interested, please ask for the phone number and address.'

§

A hundred and four attended the barbeque. Mr D and Vance were the cooks. Thanks to Clayton's Quality Meats, who made an after-hours delivery of fine steaks, everyone was well fed.

'We don't have proper cutlery,' complained Gracie when informed of the great numbers.

'Gracie, make a few salad plates. Everyone can throw their steaks and whatever between a couple of slices of bread,' commanded Mr D. 'As long as we have enough grog, everything will be okay.' Mr D was right, although a little worried when Gracie retorted, 'Where's the bread, Mr D? We'll need a lot!' Mr D and Vance looked at each other.

'I suggest we go and find some,' laughed Vance.

'You're right there, mate!' replied Mr D, who grabbed his Chevy keys before embarking on their mission to find bread. 'Because bread is in the food department, you pay! By the way, we'll need more booze. I'll pay!'

When it was dark, the party raged with the assistance of rock-and-roll mixed with country blasting from within the house, all guests helping themselves to beers from ice-filled eskies or top-shelf mixers covering two outdoor tables.

The steaks were sizzling. Vance laughed a lot. So did most others when Mr D confessed, 'I'm not Carmichael's dad! Let's drink to that!'

Robert felt and acted like a prince while enjoying more attention than he had ever collectively received in the past. It was his mum's house, and he was the only underage person in the crowd.

§

The party ended at 2 am with the departure of what seemed to Gracie, Vance, and TC the last of the millionth cab collections for guests, all of whom departed happy and in high spirits. Even the chaplain appeared tipsy.

'I love those bloody Yanks!' proclaimed Mr D.

'Oh, I do, too. They're so lovely,' added Gracie.

'I have to work tomorrow,' said TC.

'They're a nice lot,' admitted Vance.

'Mother, I don't want to go to school tomorrow,' moaned Robert from the couch on which he was curled in a ball, clutching his stomach. 'I ate too much, drank too many colas, and had too much fun. I'm tired.' Vance, Mr D, and Gracie looked at Robert, then at TC.

¶

'Please, darlin'. It's only one day,' pleaded Gracie.

'Come on, Carmichael, give the lad a break,' said Mr D.

'Don't know when we'll all be together again,' said Vance. 'Let him off a day of school. KD and I will take him driving. We'll have fun.' TC thought momentarily before looking at one, then the other.

'You're a convincing lot. I'm going to bed!' She then leaned and whispered in Robert's ear. 'Okay, you've got what you wanted. I love you. Have fun with cranky Mr D and Mr Callahan.'

A few hours later TC was woken by Vance.

'Come on, Little One, wake up. I need to talk to you,' he said repeatedly while sitting on the edge of her bed, shaking her shoulders until her eyes were wide open.

'What's wrong, Boss?' TC all but yelled in alarm. 'Is Robert all right?'

'Yes! Robert is fine. He's asleep in his bed. I need to talk to you while there's no one around.' TC sat up, rubbed her eyes, and yawned repeatedly before replying.

'Put the kettle on. I'll be with you in a few minutes.'

'What is wrong, Boss?' asked a now-wide awake TC shortly after Vance and she were seated at the kitchen counter. Vance sipped his coffee before replying.

'Everything and nothing. I bought myself a Mercedes Benz; I have race horses in New Zealand; got two shops in the east; thinking of opening another further north; a TV mob have made a documentary about me. Tell me, why do I still feel like crap? Sometimes I even feel lonely.'

'You forgot a faithful wife, children, and grandchildren, plus women falling all over you, Boss,' replied TC as she sighed heavily. Why do you feel like crap with everything you have? I don't know why. Perhaps you want to feel that way.' Vance was silent. He sipped coffee and stared at the ceiling before replying.

'As always, you are probably right. No one on earth knows me as well as you do. Chikako will quit soon; she's tired of waiting to become Mrs Callahan.'

'Who can blame her, Boss? You lead her on!'

'That's not all. There's another one. Her name is Tsune. She's married to a politician. That's not all, either.'

'What!?'

'There's another. Carla!' replied Vance. 'I'm opening an office on the coast. After Chikako leaves, I'll give Ayako the job of manager at that shop. Tsune will work with me in the office, and the Carla look-alike will run the shop from which Ayako has been transferred.'

'You make me sick! Too much for me, Boss! Give up on searching for another Anna! You'll never find one!'

'I know that,' replied Vance, who was resigned to the fact. 'I'm juggling women like a clown in a bloody circus. Sometimes I get their names confused, have to look at the red opal jewellery they wear to remind me of where, when, and why.'

'I have nothing to say to you. I can't fix your life for you. I can't even fix my own. I have to take a shower, then go to work and make some money. That is what I do best.'

'Yes! It is,' replied Vance. 'In case I forget to tell you later, I am proud of you.' TC smiled as she stepped down from her stool and kissed Vance's cheek.

'I'm proud of you, too, Boss. You made me what I am. Good or bad, we're stuck with it.'

Vance grasped TC's wrists and looked directly into her eyes.

'No bad in you, Little One! I made sure of that!' TC sighed.

'Sometimes I've wished you hadn't done such a good job. Please release my wrists so I can get ready for work.' Vance laughed.

'Off you go. By the way, can you still sign my signature?'

'Of course! As I recall, you made me practice over and over every day for what seemed forever. I got fired over it once. How could I forget?'

¶

Referred business was in abundance all day at the shop. Calls were received from Fiona, Lisa, and Marjorie, thanking TC for the hospitality.

'A few of you had to work bloody hard,' said Lisa. 'Anyway, it was worth the effort. The poor buggers had a good time. That's what matters when you're a long way from home. The steaks were great!'

'You, Gracie, Keith Dalton, and your boss worked yourselves witless, darling,' said Fiona. 'Good show! Call you later.'

'I love Mr Dalton. He sure is a character,' said Marjorie. 'He thinks you and I are a good team. You should offer me a job.'

'It's there if you want it,' replied TC seriously.

¶

Vance left on a midnight flight. Mr D drove off with a hiss and a roar five hours later. Robert and TC were both sad.

'Why do people we love live so far away, Mother?' asked Robert.

'Because we came far away from them, darling,' replied TC.

¶

A couple of days later, a short, small Japanese gentleman came to the shop. He was well dressed, confident, a man who exuded importance. This was perceived by the manner in which he carried himself. He had an air of graciousness about him as well.

In perfect Queen's English, he requested to speak with TC, who

Hideko immediately summoned from the office to hear him announce, 'I am Japanese Consul General. I love colour of opals. Please may I photograph?'

'Of course, sir,' agreed TC before instructing Hideko and other staff members to oblige by pulling out trays, specimens, et cetera from the showcases while she herself stood back at the ready for any questions.

After photographing a dozen or so pieces, the Consul General folded his camera in its case, stood away from the counter, and bowed while saying, 'Arigato, TC-san, I'll be back.'

'Who was that?' enquired Blanche when TC returned to the office.

'The Japanese Consul General,' replied TC. 'Seems like a nice man! He loves the colours in opals!'

The Japanese Consul General returned again and again and again. Every time, he took a few more photographs and every time he made a purchase. TC and her staff were impressed. He had the first gold credit cards they'd ever seen. Seemed to them these cards had no limit as some of the purchases made went into tens of thousands plus and were a regular occurrence.

'Wonder what he does with all this opal he's buying?' asked Vance, Blanche, and the other staff.

'None of our business!' was TC's reply to all.

It really got up Hideko's nose that the Consul General always dealt with TC. In Hideko's eyes, he was Japanese and so was she. Why did he prefer TC? It wasn't right! Blanche was on the ball.

'I think Hideko hates your guts, TC.' TC laughed then agreed.

'You're right. Probably hates yours, too. We're free as birds and don't have to report to husbands. Apart from that, she can't boss us around the way she does the young Japanese staff.'

§

Time rolled on and money kept rolling in, as did tourists and the carrier groups.

One night, two of her committee members complained to TC about the four-chances-for-a-dollar raffle tickets being sold to the visitors.

'Where's the money going, TC?' asked one. 'The poor buggers are paying ten dollars to come here. Surely they shouldn't have to spend money on raffle tickets.'

'What do you mean, they pay to come here?' asked TC in great surprise. 'I thought the money we locals paid covered the costs for the visitors, and the raffle money helped.'

'What's all this about?' asked Fiona, who as always was accompanying TC, carrying trays of food to offer the guests.

'They want to know where the money goes,' replied TC. 'How would I know? I have absolutely nothing to do with the money. All I do is organise and provide door and raffle prizes.'

'Anonymously, at that!' said Fiona. 'If you ladies want to know where the money goes, I suggest you ask the treasurer.'

'Yes, I think you should do that, too,' agreed TC. 'At the moment we have a lot of people to feed.'

Most members wore a friendship pin. All committee members wore one. Less than five minutes after the money question, TC decided she'd had enough. She no longer wished to be involved with the friendship group.

'Come on, darling,' said Fiona. 'I see the governor's wife over there. She's my friend. We're members of a lot of the same clubs. I'll introduce you to her.' TC looked in the direction indicated by Fiona to see an elegantly attired woman of Fiona's vintage talking to a tall, way-overweight man in a grey suit. He had one side of the suit jacket pulled back with his hand in his trouser pocket. In his other hand, he held a glass of red wine.

'Who is that man, Fiona?' enquired TC.

'He's a big, fat would-be politician,' whispered Fiona. 'Everybody hates him, including my friend, whom he's got cornered. Come on, darling.' As they got closer, TC could see the man's white shirt was open, exposing his fat, white, hairy stomach. The buttons had obviously burst because his shirt was too small to accommodate his bulging girth.

'Disgusting!' whispered Fiona before gushing, 'Jill, how lovely to see you,' to our governor's wife. TC stood beside her. She could see the politician was extremely annoyed that Fiona had interrupted his conversation. Trying not to look at his exposed, revolting stomach, TC held the tray of assorted canapés towards him.

'Would you care for some food, sir?' He looked TC up and down with an expression of disgust on his face. He zeroed in on the friendship group pin.

'No! You're one of the girls, aren't you? I thought you'd be too busy chasing a Yank to be carting food around.' Fiona heard him and immediately accidentally-on-purpose turned her tray to collide with his glass of red wine, which spilled onto his hairy, fat, white gut.

'Oh! I'm so sorry!' said Fiona.

'So you should be!' snarled the politician.

'Fiona is my friend. Accidents happen,' said the governor's wife calmly.

'That's it! I've had enough! I'm out of here!' Without a word, TC placed the tray of food on a table, collected her purse, and was out of there after mouthing, 'I'll see you later,' to Fiona, who nodded with an understanding look in her eyes. In a way, TC was relieved as she left, then drove home. No more calls at all hours of the night and morning. No more sleeping under the office desk. Not only that, she'd have a lot more time to spend with Robert. The shop would save a fortune on sheepskins! Definitely no more Miss Lily Milk White. Two weeks later TC presented her written resignation along with her verbal reasons for doing so to the executive committee. She was certain she was not imagining it when she noted an expression of guilt on the executive treasurer's face. It turned out the very night TC had left the hall function, Blanche had found the man of her dreams. He also found her. He was not an American. He was an Australian naval lieutenant based a little south of Perth who just happened to be in the right place at the right time to meet his future wife. His name was Tony.

'See what happens when I leave you alone in a hall packed with men,' laughed TC.

'He's a little younger than I,' sighed Blanche. 'That's a bit of a worry.'

'Don't worry about that, and please don't tell me the age difference,' replied TC seriously. 'If you clicked, you clicked. Don't wind up like me. It's too lonely. I suppose this puts paid to nightclubbing,' she smiled.

'Probably,' agreed Blanche with a sigh and shrug.

⁋

After Captain Russ enquired of his superiors any possibility of conflict of interests arising should his wife work for an opal shop, Marjorie happily began working at Brolga Opals. One, it got her out of the house, and two, it gave her a personal income. Never once did Captain Russ recommend the shop. On occasions when he was asked about where to purchase opals, his stock-in-trade answer was, 'Go everywhere else first, then perhaps try Brolga's on The Terrace.'

Blanche and Marjorie got along like a house on fire. Often when the shop wasn't busy, while waiting for tour groups, they would get up to mischief by standing giggling in the souvenir section and teasing TC by continuously hurling cling-koalas or kangaroo earrings over the office wall. They had uncanny aim because the fluffy little things always landed on TC's paperwork on which she was attempting to concentrate. TC usually ignored them. One day a six-inch stuffed koala landed in her coffee, which splashed all over her ledger. TC jumped to her feet and threw open the office door to confront the two ladies. Blanche and Marjorie were at opposite ends of a souvenir isle with their backs to the office and a feather duster in their hands, pretending to dust shelves while shaking with silent laughter.

'No point in asking which one of you threw the koala?' demanded TC. 'I didn't think so,' laughed TC as Blanche and Marjorie turned to her with innocent smiles. 'It landed in my coffee and splashed my ledger! Why don't you two be good and go wait down the front of the shop with Hideko and the others?' TC cracked up as both their expressions turned to indignance, and they silently mouthed 'No!'

⁋

Chikako quit. She grew tired of waiting for Vance. Soon after, she opened her own shop. She called it the Opal Empress. TC and Chikako became friends years later.

'I should have listened to you way back then,' confessed Chikako.

'I know,' replied TC.

¶

Ayako happily moved to the coast to replace Chikako. Her husband and son went with her.

¶

Vance was the luckiest man where women were concerned. Delores was happy spending money. He had his beloved Ayako in the coast shop close to where he now lived. Tsune worked in his office with him, which was convenient. When in the original shop, he had the Carla look-alike. Emi he couldn't get! Vance offered Emi the general manager's job. She flew to Perth, where she broke the news to TC, who surprised Emi by not batting an eyelid.

'How does Vance pay you, TC?' enquired Emi.

'I've been on two hundred and fifty dollars as week plus part profits since I came here,' replied TC. 'How much does the boss pay you, Emi?'

'I don't want to tell you,' replied Emi reluctantly.

'Okay, that's all right,' shrugged TC. 'That's between you and Vance.'

'You are a director of the company,' said Emi. 'You're entitled to much, much more, directors fees, et cetera.'

'I know nothing about such things. I signed the directorship papers because the boss told me to sign them. I've been doing as he tells me since the first day he employed me. I guess I've always felt grateful because he rescued me from a pub. Who knows?!'

'TC, I'm not taking the job,' announced Emi seriously after a lengthy silence. 'If anyone gets that job, it should be you.' TC was shocked.

'I don't want that job, Emi. I don't want to live on the east coast again.

Mrs Callahan thinks I'm a threat, and the boss' girlfriends would hate me.'

'TC, my pay is a thousand dollars a week plus all expenses,' said Emi.

'I see,' replied TC. 'You must be worth it. In season, you keep those tour-bus people coming in droves. I'd be worth a fortune if the boss sent me my share of the profits every month. Occasionally, he does! Usually, after I prompt his memory he owes me from forever ago, he'll send me a cheque for a couple of the quietest months. That's why I put as much money as I dare into stock. I hear the boss is kind to lots of people, but I'm not one of them, Emi.' TC laughed mischievously. 'Obviously, you're not one, either, Emi. I don't see any blazing red opal on you.' Emi laughed, too.

'Don't see any on you, either.'

'I got a green stone after I'd been working with him ten years,' replied TC. 'It was a nice one. I had it set in a ring. It got stolen.'

'I bought a beautiful green stone,' said Emi. 'It took me ages to pay off.'

'Hope you got it at the wholesalers,' laughed TC. From that moment on, Emi and TC were close friends. They had something in common. They weren't red-opal women. They didn't want to be, either. Emi and TC chatted for hours about anything and everything. They both agreed they were happy Vance had offered Emi the general manager's job. If he hadn't, they probably wouldn't have met. On parting company, TC laughed.

'Once you're in that job, Emi, I refuse to call you 'Boss'. One of them is enough!'

Emi replied, 'I couldn't agree more!'

When Vance made one of his regular calls a few days later, he sounded angry.

'What did you say to Emi?' he demanded. 'She turned down the job!'

'I also noted she's obviously not one of your girlfriends due to her lack of wearing blazing red opals. I told her, on request, that my pay is two hundred and fifty dollars per week; that you owe me back profit-sharing, and send me as little as possible when I remind you.' Vance burst into laughter.

'Who can argue the truth?'

'Not you, obviously,' replied TC. 'I work my heart out here and you know it. You taught me to keep deals. Surely that applies to you too, Boss. I'd be happy to go back to our original agreement of me extracting my share before I send yours. If you want it to stay the way it is at the moment, I'll continue to buy stock. That way, I'll end up with something.' Vance laughed again.

'I'm going now!'

A few days later TC received a cheque for two dollars and fifty cents. Vance also included a scribbled note: Don't spend it all at once! She hung it on the office wall, then called Vance, who was laughing when he answered. TC then heard female giggling.

'Do you have one of your women on your lap, Mr Callahan?'

'Something like that,' laughed Vance. 'I'll call you back.' He did so a few minutes later.

'Sorry about that, Little One. I was busy.'

'I can imagine,' replied TC. 'What's this nonsense, sending a cheque for two dollars and fifty cents?' Vance laughed.

'You reminded me that when I send you any of your twenty-five percent, I send as little as possible. That's what I did!'

'Very clever!' replied TC before slamming down the telephone.

'What's the problem, TC?' enquired Marjorie, who quickly opened the office door.

'Nothing! The boss is being a smart-ass, to quote our American friends.'

'What are we going to do about the missing stock?' asked Marjorie with concern. TC frowned and shrugged.

'We can't do a thing until we pinpoint the culprit or culprits. Can't accuse everyone!' Marjorie sighed.

'Neither can we allow it to keep happening.'

'I know it's not you or Blanche,' replied TC. 'Had I thought that for an instant, I wouldn't have told you it's happening. As I said before, I've noticed a few good pieces, which haven't been sold, are missing. I guarantee, I know every fine piece in the shop and would be aware if one is sold, let alone three.'

'What did Vance say you should do?' asked Marjorie.

'As I said before, he told me to make sure I know who it is. We'll have to be alert. Perhaps we'll install a security camera.'

⁋

TC remained close friends with Ken and Fiona, Lisa, Len, and most of the more senior ladies on the previous committees she'd chaired. Whenever the friendship business came up, TC changed the subject. She had wiped her hands of it when she submitted her resignation and reasons why. Ken didn't bother to nominate at the next general election, neither did Len and Lisa, plus most of the members of the executive committee. One of the few elderly darlings who'd been a member since day one called Fiona.

'It's not the same anymore with you all gone.'

'It can't be any worse than it was before we started there,' was Fiona's frank reply.

'It is!' replied the dear lady.

⁋

Blanche and Tony had a lovely wedding, shortly after which they moved to Sydney where Tony completed his naval career. Blanche gave birth to a baby girl, who was a much-loved little sister to Blanche's two children from her former marriage.

Good for you, Blanche, thought TC. You got the whole deal. It couldn't have happened to a better person. With a fine husband like Tony, you'll have hearts and flowers forever. Marjorie thought the same and told TC, who agreed. While being happy for Blanche, both of them missed her being at the shop, with her laughter, sense of humour, and general presence.

⁋

One Friday winter's morning, only TC and one Japanese part-time girl were at the shop. Everyone else was sick or on holidays. It was pouring rain outside, windy and cold. TC had been up all night with Robert, who was suffering similar symptoms as herself. Gracie took him to the doctor. TC wished Gracie could have taken her to the doctor too, but it was out of the question to leave only one staff member in the shop alone. Too dangerous! TC had to be there. She was curled up between a couple of sheepskin rugs under the office desk when the Japanese girl came to tell her she was wanted in the shop.

'Who is it?' asked TC softly. 'I hope it's not the Consul General.' The girl shook her head.

'No!' With her hair all over the place, sniffling, no make-up, not even lipstick, sheepskin slippers on her feet, and a large sheepskin wrapped around her shoulders, TC entered the shop to see a middle-aged, handsome, smiling couple.

'Hello. I'm TC. Sorry, I'm a bit sick. Sorry, also, for the way I look.'

'A friend of yours asked us to call on you,' beamed the American lady.

'He's our son!' added the gentleman. 'My wife also wants to buy an opal.'

'He sent you a note,' interrupted the lady. TC took the note.

'What type of opal did you want, Ma'am? I feel embarrassed presenting myself like this. I'll ask my girl to get you started while I go and fix myself up.'

'You look and sound sick,' commented the man. TC forced a smile.

'I am, but I promise I won't sneeze or cough without a couple of tissues protecting you. I'll be back in a few minutes.' TC then turned to her youngest, tiniest staff member, who was waiting for direction.

'Show these nice people whatever they wish to see, please, Mini. I won't be long.' TC quickly brushed her hair, then clipped it up, applied lipstick, straightened her clothes, put on her stilettos, and hurried back into the shop.

'Did you read our son's note?' enquired the gentleman.

'Oh, no. It's on the desk. I'll get it,' smiled TC. 'That was silly of me.' TC recognised the handwriting on the envelope. It was from James. Lord knew she'd read his letter often enough to know this was from him. Why today of all days did his parents have to visit the shop when she felt and looked like hell? She wasn't game to read the note. She might start crying, so she decided to bluff it through.

'Very nice of James to send you here,' said TC while holding tissues to her face. 'Sorry I have to be in this condition. Your son is a very nice man. You must be proud of him.'

'We are!' was the reply in unison.

'From memory, he has two daughters?' smiled TC.

'That's right. They're growing up quickly,' replied James' Dad, who looked at TC knowingly.

'I can't decide on a ring or a pendant,' said James' mother.

'Take both,' smiled TC. 'I promise you'll get the best price possible.'

'James told us you'd look after us,' came from the father.

Why wouldn't I, thought TC as she went in search of a gift to send James. It was only fair. He'd left gifts for both Robert and herself. It had to be something impersonal! TC chose a small, polished, boulder specimen with an inlaid opal yacht. Although small, it was beautiful. She had done a deal of a lifetime in acquiring this one and a few similar, which she'd hoped would have sold earlier in the year when the America's Cup yacht race took place out at Fremantle. TC need not have bothered. Although Perth and Fremantle were packed with tourists, the shop had the quietest time on record. The race was over in the blink of an eye, with the Stars and Stripes victorious over Kookaburra III.

TC gave James' parents cost price on their purchases. She'd tell Vance they were 'special customers' in her report--mates' rates, so to speak.

'Please don't tell James about the deal you got,' she laughed. 'He didn't get anywhere near that when he shopped with us. I've wrapped a little gift for him. I hope he likes it. Please give him my best regards.' James' Dad took the package and once again gave TC that knowing smile.

'Don't worry, TC, we won't tell anyone what we paid. I'd give you a hug, but you're too sick,' came from James' mother.

'Have a safe trip home. Lovely to have met you,' called TC as she waved them out the door before rewrapping the sheepskin around herself, having a coughing fit, kicking off her shoes, putting on the sheepskin slippers, and positioning herself back under the desk, where she opened James' note, which was more like a short letter.

Dear TC Carmichael,

I told you I'd always remember you. Hope you're doing the same where I'm concerned. When my parents told me they were visiting Perth, I asked that they call on you. My mom wants to buy opal. I know you'll take care of her.

I told my dad about you, TC. I had to tell someone. I hope you understand. By the way, I guess the world is still all in all wonderful. Mine would be a much happier place if you were in it. Hi to Robert.

James.

'I know exactly what you mean, James I-have-your-name-on-your-I.D.' murmured TC before experiencing a coughing spasm. This is ridiculous, she thought. I don't want that dear little girl working in the shop to wind up with whatever it is. TC got out from under the desk and told Mini to pack up.

'I don't want you to catch this cough. We'll go home. I won't be opening tomorrow, either. You'll be paid for your lost time. It's only fair.'

'Are you sure, TC?' enquired the young Japanese girl in disbelief. TC had nicknamed this girl Mini because she was very tiny. TC also tended to favour her because she was sweet.

'Only fair, sweetie. Hurry on, let's get out of here.'

'I won't tell Hideko about you paying me because you're sick.'

'Tell no one, Mini. It's none of their business. Now hurry up so we can go.'

The telephone rang. It was Gracie.

'Robert has influenza, darlin'. It's not too bad. I told the doctor you are sick. He said you need to see him. I made you an appointment for one this afternoon.'

'You read my mind, Gracie. I was about to call his surgery.' Cough, cough, cough. 'We're closing the shop now. I haven't told Vance yet. I rarely get sick.' More coughing. 'I've never closed the shop early before.'

¶

TC had a severe case of a new strain of influenza.

'You probably picked it up in your shop,' explained the doctor. 'Only needs one carrier to sneeze or cough in an enclosed area.'

'You could be right,' replied TC. 'Three of my staff are already off sick.'

Marjorie cut her holiday short to run the shop with Mini and another part-time girl who agreed to work whatever hours necessary. TC wasn't worried. She knew the business was safe in Marjorie's hands.

Gracie took care of everything at the house and got Robert to school the following Tuesday when he recovered. She nursed TC as if she were a child. Vance phoned twice—three times on one occasion, four times in one day to check on TC's health. Gracie asked him not to call so often as the phone ringing disturbed TC.

After days in bed, TC felt well enough to get up for a while. The first thing she did was phone Vance.

'Thank God, you're all right! You should have a telephone in your bedroom!'

'I'm okay, Boss,' sighed TC. 'I should have a lot of things. My doctor told me I need a holiday. I'm run down. We both know that's not on, so I'll count these sick days as my holiday.'

'Is Marjorie keeping an eye on the stock?' asked Vance seriously.

'She is like myself. She doubts very much that either of the two young girls working with her are the guilty party. We'll find out. Robert was sick, too, but nowhere near as bad as me, thank heavens.'

'I know. Gracie told me. You have to take care of yourself, Little One.'

'Listen to who's giving lectures,' laughed TC. 'How's business over your way?'

'You know the deal! It's winter time.'

'I'm going back to work on Saturday,' said TC.

'Why bother? Spend the weekend with Robert. Go back on Monday. I'm sure Marjorie and the two girls won't mind working Saturday. It's a short day.'

'Thank you. That would be nice,' replied TC. 'By the way, I promised to pay Mini the hours she lost because I closed the shop early on Friday plus Saturday morning.'

'That was kind of you,' said Vance, his words loaded with sarcasm.

'Take it out of whatever you owe me, Mr Callahan. It's eighty-two dollars! Bye now!'

'How can the boss be thoughtful one second, then a prick the next?' TC asked herself as she hung the phone on the wall. It rang immediately. She knew it was Vance with the guilts.

'I'm still not well. Leave me alone,' said TC before Vance could speak. Once again, she hung up before settling on a couch in the warmth created by the family room fireplace.

Desolate! thought TC. There's no other word to describe the way I feel. Perhaps I made the wrong decision coming here. It's so far away. I have Robert and the shop. Robert has Gracie and me. Not twelve yet, and he's flown alone across Australia and back eleven times. Another trip coming up at Christmas! Lord, I'm a terrible mother!' Suddenly a voice from within said, 'Stop it! What's done is done! You can't change yesterdays! Call Marjorie! See how she's going. Poor darling must feel abandoned.'

'Hello, stranger,' laughed Marjorie. 'Glad to know you're still in the land of the living.'

'I feel like a wimp. Can't believe I allowed myself to get sick,' replied TC. 'Thanks for filling in for me.'

'Happy I could do it,' replied Marjorie. 'Everything's okay here. Not much business. I had three low-life in, checking the place out. I smiled at them, looked at my watch, then complained loudly and seriously, 'I don't know why I was silly enough to marry a senior police detective. He's five minutes late.' The would-be thugs were out of there like rats up a rope. I doubt they'll bother coming back.' TC's laughter caused a bout of coughing, which quickly subsided.

'You should have been an actress, Marjorie.'

'So should you, TC' laughed Marjorie. 'This was the first occasion that I've been faced with that type of situation. Every other time, you've been the front woman.' TC became serious.

'Often I appear braver than I feel.'

Shop arrangements made with Marjorie, TC called Fiona, who insisted on visiting to see for herself that TC was getting well.

'You sound terrible, darling. I've been very worried about you. I'll be there in an hour.'

TC wanted to say, 'Please don't come to visit. I'd prefer to be alone.' She didn't get the opportunity as Fiona was gone. As promised, she arrived at TC's home exactly one hour later. It took Fiona less than a minute to see through TC's façade of plastic smiles and false bravado.

'What on earth is wrong, darling?' asked Fiona with utmost concern. 'You look terrible.' TC forced a smile.

'Thank you, Fiona. I've been sick. I'm still not right.'

'I know, darling. I also know there's more than that wrong. I can see it in your eyes.' TC sighed.

'I'm that transparent? Obviously, I've been kidding myself by believing I'm stronger than I actually am.'

'Something like that, darling,' agreed Fiona. 'Make me a coffee. I'll drink it and smoke a couple of fags while you tell me what on earth is wrong with you, apart from feeling crook.'

'Now! Tell me everything, darling,' said Fiona after relaxing in a lounge chair, lighting a cigarette, and blowing smoke in the air.

'That's exactly it, Fiona. Almost everything is wrong. At least, that's the way I feel. I don't know why. This is the first time in forever that I've been too sick to go to work. I had one sick day a long, long time ago. My boss brought me chocolates and magazines. I think he thought I wasn't sick. Overall, I'm healthy and Robert is healthy. I'm lucky.'

'All right, darling,' said Fiona. 'We've eliminated health issues.' TC shrugged.

'I don't want to talk about it, Fiona. I don't know what my problem is. Perhaps it's a combination of a lot of things. Then again, there's a strong possibility I'm suffering from a severe case of 'poor me'. I'm depressed as buggery and can't pinpoint why.' Fiona lit another cigarette.

'Tell me the possibilities. I don't know if I can fix things for you, darling, but it might do you good to talk about it.' TC ran her fingers through her hair, frowned, grimaced, and shook her head.

'I don't know where to start.'

'Start anywhere, darling,' urged Fiona. 'The important thing is you get it off your chest, out in the open, so you can deal with it.'

'I suppose loneliness is one of my problems, Fiona, especially nights after Robert has gone to bed. Radio Station 6iX and I have become best friends. When Robert is away in Queensland, Sundays are the pits, definitely the loneliest day of the week. I find myself having one-way conversations with the cat. I'm already conditioning myself for when he leaves when Christmas school holidays come around.

'Then there's my guilt that he has to fly across the continent and back by himself. He's become accustomed to it by now, and the airline staff are lovely to him, but those factors do very little to soothe my conscience.' Fiona's expression was one of sympathy.

'You can't do anything about that, darling. Years ago, you made a decision and now you're stuck with it.'

'I know that, Fiona. I said almost exactly that to myself this morning. Would you like another coffee?'

'Don't change the subject, darling,' replied Fiona. 'If I want coffee, I'll tell you. You can empty the ash tray. I hate being reminded of how many cigarettes I've smoked. Do you like the opal industry?' TC collected the ashtray off the coffee table.

'I love opals. As far as I'm concerned, their beauty runs rings around other gemstones. Opals are like people—all have individual character. There're a few humans in the industry that I would like to do to what I'm doing with your cigarette butts, though,' said TC seriously as she upturned the ashtray over the kitchen tidy bin. 'Probably only a ten percent minority, if that. My boss says, 'Where there's money, there are also mongrels.' The lure of the dollar brings out the worst in many people.'

'Your boss is right, darling,' said Fiona. 'I'll have another coffee now.' TC waited for the electric kettle to boil, emptied the ashtray, went outside to cough, then presented Fiona with her fresh coffee before sitting down to resume talking.

'On the other hand, Fiona, I respect the opal miners, ninety-nine percent of whom endure hard, dirty work, which is often more disappointing than rewarding. Most of them are 'give their guts for garters, help their mate when he's down' type of people. I know an opal mining family in Queensland who have been at it day after day for years. They've found hardly anything but they keep trying.'

TC sat in silence as she thought of a friend who was killed in a car accident while driving to a mining town to buy opal a few months earlier and another man she'd heard about who had died while mining just a few days after his first strike in years. Visions of Yappy and Faith also flashed through her mind. TC silently asked herself, 'What right do you have to feel sorry for yourself?' Her unspoken reply was, 'None! Those poor people are dead. Wake up to yourself. Count your blessings.'

'What on earth is wrong, darling?' asked Fiona. 'What are you thinking about?' TC smiled.

'Nothing! Nothing is wrong, Fiona. I was thinking how blessed I am. I didn't get to air almost everything bugging me. I didn't have to. I'm fine now.'

'Good girl! We'll have to do something to get you out and about more. I'm going home now. I'll call you tonight.'

From that day forward, TC was privileged to be under Fiona's wing. Every social function Fiona attended, so did TC––cocktail and dinner parties, and luncheons when business allowed. Fiona was the president of three charity committees, the Ladies Liberal Party Support Group for Perth's most prestigious suburbs, and a member of Perth's exclusive ladies clubs. She knew everyone who was anyone and proudly introduced TC to all and sundry. It didn't worry TC that most people she met were many years her senior; they were all courteous and friendly.

¶

Vance's attitude towards TC changed somewhat when she returned to work after her time off sick. He sent her a cheque for ten thousand dollars with a note.

Not much, but it's a start. Try not to be crook again. I missed your lectures.

Every time they spoke on the telephone, his first question was, 'How are you? How is Robert?' He waited for TC to talk about business. Often, he sounded tired. TC guessed that was because of his business, plus juggling three girlfriends and a wife. Couldn't be easy! Deep down, TC pitied Vance––he had everything, while at the same time, to her way of thinking, he had nothing.

¶

Randy James was persistent. He continued to drop by the shop whenever in Perth. A couple of times, TC was more than a little tempted to accept his invitation to dinner. Something inside warned her to continue declining. She did.

¶

It was the Saturday night before Robert flew east to his father for the Christmas holidays. Robert and TC were at Mr Bill's restaurant as was their routine. They had ordered and were waiting for their meal when Robert looked up and smiled as TC felt a tap on the shoulder. She immediately turned her head to see Randy and a younger ex-Pink Brolga resident.

'Mind if we join you?' asked Randy.

'Please, Mother,' urged Robert, who had gotten along extremely well with the younger man years before at the motel. TC had also liked him way back then.

'Sure. Please do,' she replied. 'This is a surprise.' Both men laughed.

'Not really,' said Randy. 'I did some detective work and knew you'd be here. It's Saturday night and it's seven-thirty.'

'How did you find that out?' enquired Robert curiously.

'That's my secret, mate,' replied Randy.

'He obviously asked Mr Bill, sweetheart,' interrupted TC.

'That's exactly what he did, Robert,' laughed Randy's mate. 'He dragged me along in case you weren't here. He didn't want to be embarrassed by eating alone. That wouldn't fit Randy's silver-tongue image, especially on a Saturday night.'

'What does that mean?' asked Robert ever so seriously.

'He's having a go at me, Robert. I usually have a date on Saturday nights.'

The waitress came to take the new arrivals' orders. The men ordered beers. Randy looked at TC.

'Would you like some wine, elusive one?' TC smiled sweetly.

'No, thank you. I have to drive.'

'Mother has to drive me to the airport. I'm going to Queensland,' declared Robert. 'I don't like leaving mother alone.'

'I'll take care of your mother,' offered Randy.

'I'll be fine, Mr James,' said TC. 'You're flat-out taking care of yourself. By the way, must say I'm surprised to see you sober.' Randy's mate laughed again.

'Old Silver Tongue has been hanging out for booze all day, TC, but he's so damned eager to impress you, he's been dry till now. Been bloody torture for me, putting up with his bad mood.'

Randall James' silver tongue motored throughout dinner. With every drink, he became more loose-lipped and humorous. His mate laughed with every outrageous sentence Randy uttered. Robert laughed at the jokes he grasped. TC sat stone-faced.

'Takes a lot to impress you, doesn't it, Miss Elusive?' said Randy after TC announced it was time for Robert and her to go and they stood to leave. TC sent Robert off to pay Mr Bill, then looked Randy directly in his eyes.

'Suffice to say, it takes more than a man like you, Randy. You're far too smooth; at least you think you are.' She then smiled at the younger man. 'Don't let Mr James lead you astray. Nice seeing you again. Have a nice night, gentlemen,' as she moved off to meet Robert at Mr Bill's reception counter.

'Cold bloody bitch if ever I've met one,' complained Randy.

'Not necessarily,' remarked his mate. 'She went to hell and back with that bastard, Jake. Can't blame her for being on guard.'

'Oh, stuff it,' laughed Randy. 'Let's get out of here. I know a sure thing and her sister. They'll be in anything. I'll give them a call.'

¶

Two weeks to the day before Christmas, an impeccably dressed business man of Latin appearance visited the shop with two male companions. TC got the impression they were his minders. He chose items, all top-shelf, to the value of a hundred and forty-two thousand after discount. He also selected an exquisite, very large, black opal loose stone which he wanted set in a mounting of his own design. TC was excited! Beyond her wildest expectations, the sale would total a hundred and sixty thousand after rounding off. It would be the biggest sale ever for the shop. While the customer waited in the shop, she called the jeweller to make certain he could make the piece for the following Thursday afternoon.

'No problem!' promised the young jeweller, who used to work for the lady who had introduced herself to TC years before. That woman had since sold her business, so he was self-employed.

'I'll be back on Thursday at three,' promised the businessman.

TC phoned the jeweller on Thursday morning.

'Yes, it's ready, TC,' he advised.

'Good. I'll collect it,' replied TC.

'No. I've given it to my girlfriend. She'll drop it in during her lunch hour.' TC was in shock.

'You what?! Do you know what that piece is worth?'

'I have a fair idea,' was the reply. 'Don't worry, she's a smart girl. She works for a lawyer.'

'I'll go collect it from the office,' insisted TC.

'No! You can't do that. You'll get her in trouble.'

'What time does she take her lunch break?' demanded TC as politely as she could handle while her heart raced erratically in alarm.

'Don't stress, TC' replied the jeweller. 'She'll have it there around one.'

'She'd better!' TC put down the telephone, then turned towards Marjorie, who had been listening to TC's side of the conversation.

'Problem?'

'I think so,' replied TC, who was shaking uncontrollably. 'I have a gut feeling we're not going to see the pendant, which will mean we've lost face and blown the deal. This has never happened before! He always delivers and collects his cheque. Something is very wrong!!'

TC's gut feeling didn't lie! The little blonde, bimbo girlfriend of the jeweller strolled leisurely into the shop at almost one-thirty. She was enjoying a milkshake in a plastic container when TC greeted her and eyed the girl's shoulder bag.

'You've brought the pendant. Thank you.' The nineteen-year-old stopped sucking on her straw and smiled.

'I lost it,' she said casually. TC gasped.

'You what? You'd better be joking!' With wide, innocent eyes, the girl resumed drawing milkshake through the straw. TC was beside herself.

'Don't give me that look, and STOP with your drink before I smash it out of your hand!'

'No need to speak to me like that,' purred the girl.

'How, when and where did you lose it?' demanded TC, who was experiencing great difficulty in restraining herself from grabbing the little bitch and shaking her.

'I took it out of my bag and put it on the counter where I bought my milkshake,' was the 'I couldn't care less' reply. 'When I remembered to put it back in my bag, it was gone.'

'She's lying,' said Marjorie, who was, like TC, in a state of disbelief.

'I know she is,' agreed TC while glaring the girl in the face. 'You expect us to believe you are intelligent enough to work for a law firm, yet stupid enough to put a twenty-thousand-dollar piece of jewellery on a milk bar counter while you wait for a milkshake. Bullshit!'

'It was wrapped in a tissue,' was the reasoning reply.

'Did you look for it at all?' demanded TC.

'No point. It was gone.' TC shook her head in disbelief.

'I've heard the lot now! You and your boyfriend are in this together! That's why he didn't deliver as he always does. That's why he didn't want me to collect it. You didn't lose it. Between you both, you cooked up this 'I lost it' scheme to rob me. You have an hour to produce it! Before you go, I want to talk to him,' continued TC as she dialled his number.

'Why am I not surprised there's no answer?' snapped TC. 'Be back with the pendant within an hour!'

Exactly one hour to the second later, TC phoned the police to report the issue. She was too late.

'I'm sorry, Ms. Carmichael,' said the police officer TC spoke with. 'Your jeweller and his girlfriend left five minutes ago after reporting the piece lost. Unfortunately, we can only accept one report in circumstances like this. They reported it as lost before you called to report it stolen.' TC couldn't believe what she was hearing.

'The perfect crime. They had it planned right down to the last detail,' said TC. 'Obviously, my ex-jeweller's girlfriend has learned a lot while working for a lawyer.'

'Looks like it,' agreed the police officer, who sounded genuinely sympathetic. 'I don't know if you are aware of it, but they are flying out of Perth to London this afternoon.' TC sighed heavily in despair.

'No, I didn't know. Now that I do, it makes perfect sense. London is an ideal place to unload my piece of jewellery.'

'I'm sorry, Ms Carmichael,' apologised the police officer.

'So am I,' replied TC. 'Thank you.' White as a sheet and feeling defeated, TC looked at Marjorie.

'What on earth am I going to tell our Latin customer?'

'Buggered if I know,' replied Marjorie. 'He'll be here in less than ten minutes.'

'They reported the pendant as lost, Marjorie. They must have gone directly to the police station after she left here.'

'I gathered something like that from hearing your side of the conversation with the police,' replied Marjorie while patting TC's shoulder.

The Latin-looking gentleman and his companions arrived at exactly three o'clock.

'Show me my piece, please. I know my mother will love it.'

TC gingerly explained to him what had happened. He didn't believe her. He was furious, and rightly so.

'It's so beautiful you want to keep it to sell for more money!' he yelled.

'That's not the case, sir. I wish I had it here as much as you do, if not more than you do,' replied TC.

'You must be stupid, woman, to employ a thief as your jeweller.'

'I certainly feel stupid, sir. I'm also embarrassed and extremely sorry.'

'I'll buy nothing from you! You lie. You didn't have it made. I thought you were a good businesswoman. I was a fool!'

'I'm sad you feel that way, sir,' replied TC softly as the three men stormed out of the shop.

'He didn't mean that, TC,' comforted Marjorie.

'Yes, he did Marjorie. Who could blame him? I'm certain I've wrecked his plans for family Christmas gifts.'

'It wasn't your fault,' said Marjorie.

'Yes, it was. One, I trusted the wrong jeweller. Two, I should have called the police while his girlfriend was here. I don't know how I'll tell the boss I've managed to lose the biggest retail sale we would have ever made. On the bright side, I'm thankful there're no tour groups today. Hideko and the girls weren't here to witness the goings-on. Hideko would have revelled in it!' Marjorie agreed wholeheartedly.

'You can say that again!'

That night when Fiona made her seven o'clock call, she immediately realised TC was despondent and not her usual self.

'Something is wrong, darling? I can hear it in your voice.'

'Dear Fiona, remind me never to attempt to pull the wool over your eyes,' replied TC lightly.

'What's the problem?' insisted Fiona, who then listened without interruption while TC explained. After a brief silence, Fiona abruptly terminated the call.

'I'll get back to you later, darling. I need to discuss something with Ken.'

Fiona called later as promised.

'I've been talking with Ken about what happened with your jeweller, darling. We agree in some areas you are too naïve for your own good. You think others are as honest and open as yourself. Surely you should know that! You did tell me there's an element of crooks in the opal industry.'

'Yes, I did. Of those I have met, I know who they are, so I'm very wary.'

'Con men, thieves, and corruption exist is every walk of life, darling. Instead of trusting everyone until you discover you can't, turn it around—trust no bastard until you find out you can.'

'I understand,' replied TC while thinking, Ken and Fiona are spot-on. It's about time I rid myself of the sitting duck syndrome.

'Someone told me a few years back I have an invisible wall around myself, Fiona. After that person brought it to my attention, the wall was reinforced. Obviously, it's time I have it steel-clad.'

'You do exactly that, darling,' urged Fiona. 'Both Ken and I love you like a daughter. We don't want to sit by and see anyone hurt you in any way.'

Tears welling, TC replied, 'Thank you, Fiona. The love is mutual. I'll talk to you tomorrow night.'

Vance called at nine the next morning. TC explained what had happened. To her surprise and relief, he was not angry with her.

'Who the hell am I to criticise any poor bugger about getting robbed? Look how many times it's happened to me. Truth be known, some bastard is probably robbing me as we speak.' TC was more confused.

'You're not minding who's robbing you?'

'Come on, Little One, don't tell me you think the women I've got in tow love me for my good looks,' laughed Vance. 'I'm damned sure Carla's look-alike and Tsune are in it for what they can get. Ayako—she's another story.'

'I'd like you to deduct the cost of the stone from what you owe me, Boss. That's fair.'

'We'll worry about that when I get around to paying you. As a matter of fact, I posted you another instalment this morning.'

'Thank you, Boss.'

'Ken and Fiona are right—trust nobody, including me.'

'That's taking it a bit far.'

'Try to catch the thief you have in the shop. I'll talk to you soon.'

Two large tour groups shopped in the afternoon. It was extremely busy. While setting up the display next morning, TC noted a one-off boulder opal, eighteen carat, yellow-gold lady's belt buckle was missing. She scoured through the previous day's invoices, searched the safe, under the counters and everywhere. It was nowhere to be found. TC decided she'd had enough. Being robbed twice in two days was the last straw. There was a large tour group scheduled for mid-morning, so all Japanese staff would be on board at nine-thirty.

TC waited until everyone was present before broaching the matter of the belt buckle and other missing items. TC braced herself to remain calm.

'I'm happy you are all here at the same time, ladies. I'm wondering if someone knows the whereabouts of the gold-and-boulder belt buckle and these three pieces.' She held up photographs of the jewellery in question. No verbal response, but there were surprised expressions on the faces of Mini and two younger staff members.

'Nobody has any ideas?' continued TC. Hideko threw her head back and shrugged.

'Customers probably stole them.'

'The belt buckle disappeared yesterday, Hideko. The only customers we had were Japanese tourists. Are you telling me one of them helped themselves to the buckle?'

'TC-san, that couldn't happen,' said Mini. 'I was working the front end of the shop. The showcases holding the really lovely pieces weren't unlocked for either tour group.'

'That is true!' agreed one of the senior, part-time ladies. 'I worked beside Mini.'

'I see. That means only one thing, ladies. We have a thief or thieves in our midst. Should the guilty party or parties feel even the slightest consideration for their fellow staff members, I urge them to return the pieces to stock as soon as possible. There'll be no questions asked. Simply put them back where they belong. I suggest you take care of the problem on Monday or Tuesday. Video surveillance cameras will be installed on Wednesday.'

'You should tell Marjorie about this, too,' said Hideko. TC remained calm.

'Marjorie is not a suspect, Hideko.' Once again, Hideko threw back her head.

'Of course not! She's Australian—like you.' TC smiled.

'That's right, Hideko. I don't forget that insignificant factor.'

¶

When setting up the shop the following Tuesday morning, TC was not surprised to find the three originally missing pieces of jewellery on a tray at the top of the safe. No belt buckle!

'Three out of four is not too bad,' was Vance's comment. 'Unfortunately, you're still harbouring a thief. We'll eventually find out who.'

'I got the cheque, Boss. Thank you.'

'Yeah, it's only ten thousand. As you know, there's a long way to go.'

'I trust you. I'll get it eventually.' Vance laughed.

'I told you before, I agree with your friends—trust no bastard.'

¶

Although she'd made many friends since moving to Perth, most were transient people within the opal industry who came to town four to six times per year. Len, Lisa, Captain Russ, and Marjorie were married couples. They had their own things to do. Fiona's social calendar had subsided until well after New Year came and went. So, apart from going to the shop, TC had very little to do and no company apart from her good old faithful radio and Robert's cat. She had dinner with Ken and Fiona at their home a couple of times before Christmas, which they invited her to spend with them. TC declined. Their son and his family were coming from the east.

¶

TC's telephone rang at six on Christmas morning. She was out of bed in a flash and ran to answer it, thinking Robert was the caller.

It wasn't. It was a business call diverted to the house via the shop's main line.

'Thank God, I got you,' said a somewhat anxious male American voice. 'I'm sorry to call you so early, especially on Christmas Day. I was in your shop a couple of weeks ago and saw a ring I want to buy as a Christmas gift for my wife.'

'I understand. Please don't worry, sir. It's okay,' interrupted TC. 'Where are you?'

'I'm at my hotel. It's not far from your shop,' was the reply.

'I'll be there in twenty minutes,' promised TC.

'Thank you, thank you!'

TC quickly dressed, then drove to the shop. She did not see another moving vehicle on the bridge or streets. Everything was quiet and still. She recognised the man who was standing in front of the shop door.

'I remember you, sir. You're an oil man from Texas.'

'That's right, and you're an angel for doing this.'

'Can't recall being called that before,' laughed TC as she unlocked the door.

'I thought I'd be back two days ago,' explained the man. 'I got delayed on company business. I flew in last midnight, fly out for Sydney in a couple of hours, then home to Houston. My family are delaying Christmas for a day for me.'

'That's lovely,' said TC.

'Nothing more important than family and friends, especially at Christmas time,' said the Texan.

That's for sure, agreed TC silently as she turned the safe's combination dial.

The man purchased a ring and bracelet for his wife, matching pendant and earring sets for each of his three daughters, a brooch for his mother, also one for his wife's mother, and boulder opal cufflinks for himself. He requested that TC gift-wrap and mark everything except the cufflinks.

'Would you like a lift to the airport?' enquired TC. 'I live on that side of the river, so it's no problem.'

'That would be great. Thank you.' TC smiled.

'The least I can do. You've just given Brolga Opals a seventeen-thousand-dollar Christmas gift. The oil man looked at his watch.

'My plane leaves for Sydney in an hour.'

'No problem,' said TC. 'Perhaps you go back to the hotel while I put my stock away and lock up. I'll meet you out the front of your hotel in ten minutes.'

'Great! My bags are packed and in the hotel lobby with the porter. I'll see you then!'

As TC drove the happy-to-be-heading-home Texan to the airport, he told her his company was establishing an office in Perth the following February. He promised to send her some business.

'What's your name, by the way?' he asked. TC laughed.

'Did I forget to tell you? Sorry about that. My name is TC Carmichael.'

'What does 'TC' stand for?' TC laughed again.

'My mother made a mistake when naming me. Here we are. This is where I drop you off,' she added as she pulled in out front of the Qantas terminal.

'I can't thank you enough, TC,' he said as she watched him collect his bags. 'Six women in Houston are going to be wearing happy faces the day after tomorrow.'

'My pleasure,' smiled TC. 'Have a great trip home and Happy Christmas. I'll see you next year.'

§

The phone was ringing when TC opened her front door a little later. It was Robert.

'I called to tell you I love you, Mama. I won't say "Have a Happy Christmas" because I know you won't. You're by yourself.'

'That's life, baby,' laughed TC. 'I love you, too, my darling.' TC shared a long conversation with Robert. He was amused when she told him about the gentleman from Houston.

'You need one of those signs like that auto place. It says, "We never close".'

She then called Gracie, whom she hadn't seen since Robert left, Thel Carmichael at the retirement home, Mr D in Sydney, Emi in Brisbane, and Maggie in North Queensland. Maggie finally had a telephone installed after years of badgering by TC.

TC checked the clock. It was almost midday. She then spoke to the cat.

'Wonder my voice box hasn't thrown in the towel. I've been talking for hours. I'll take a bath, then we'll have chicken for our lunch and watch some video movies. It's a tough life, my darling, little, furry friend.'

¶

TC was happy to see Christmas and New Year's Day over and done with. After much thought, she reached the conclusion special festive-season days were by far lonelier for people who were alone than a year of Sundays combined.

Days seemed to fly by once business trading was back to normal. Fiona insisted TC spend Sundays with her and Ken. 'Can't have you sitting at home like a shag on a rock, darling,' said Fiona. 'You come over to our place late morning and go home after dinner.'

It was good! Although decades apart in age, they never ran short of conversation. Similar likes and dislikes were in abundance. They had much more in common than their preference for stiletto-heeled shoes.

Robert's thirteenth birthday fell on the Saturday after he came home from Queensland. TC invited Ken and Fiona, Gracie and her husband, Brian, Captain Russ, whom Robert asked, and Marjorie to a birthday dinner at Mr Bill's. Robert thought only TC and he would be there. He was speechless when they arrived, and he saw everyone waiting at a special table Mr Bill had arranged. Captain Russ was the first to stand and shake Robert's hand.

'Congratulations, pal. You're a teenager. Stay cool and enjoy.'

'I will, Captain Russ,' promised Robert.

After handshakes from Ken and Brian plus hugs and kisses from Marjorie, Fiona, and Gracie, it was sit-down and present-giving time. Ken and Fiona gave him an engraved pen; Gracie and Brian, a model car. While he loved both, his eyes lit with joy when he opened his gift from Captain Russ and Marjorie. It was a photograph of two U.S. Navy jet planes in flight through clouds.

'Those are the planes I used to fly, Robert,' said Captain Russ. 'I can see you like the photo.'

'I do, Captain Russ, I really do. I'll put it in my bedroom with the one my friend, James, gave me when I was eight.'

'I remember him. He was lovely,' said Gracie. TC changed the subject instantly.

'I'm pretty sure this is the best fish restaurant in Perth. It may not be the flashiest in décor, but the food is great.'

'I agree,' said Captain Russ. 'I come here quite often when we have ships coming or in port. I recall running into you and Robert here years ago when you'd just opened your first shop.'

'That's right, I remember, Captain Russ,' said Robert. 'You were with other officers who wanted to buy opals from mother. They did, too, didn't they, Mother?' TC smiled.

'Sure did, sweetheart. That was the very beginning of our relationship with the U.S. Navy. Been a long time now.'

'It sure has,' said Captain Russ. 'I think the navy will put me out to pasture soon. I expect to be told any day.' Captain Russ noted the bewildered expression on Robert's face.

'Marjorie will fill you in, TC. What are you going to have to eat, Robert?'

'Fish! There're also prawns, oysters, or crab,' replied Robert confidently. 'Mother and I come here most Saturday nights when I'm not away. I know the menu without looking at it.'

Mr Bill provided a birthday cake free of charge for dessert. A great evening was had by all, especially the teenager who insisted on going to Kings Park, where he and TC sat overlooking the city and its dazzling array of lights for as far as the eye could see.

'It's been my best birthday ever, Mama,' said Robert matter-of-factly. 'All the people I love have called, sent me cards, money, or presents. Mr Callahan said it's time you give me a raise for Saturdays in the shop.'

'Is that so? I don't suppose he mentioned a figure?'

'He said he thinks I must be worth at least fifteen dollars.' TC smiled.

'He's the Boss. Fifteen it is.'

'I took grandma into Mr Callahan's shop when I was at dad's. Grandma loved a strand of boulder opal beads, so I bought them for her.' This was news to TC.

'You what? Where did you get the money? They are at least five hundred dollars.'

'The one I got for grandma was one thousand and two hundred dollars.'

'I'm listening.'

'I asked Mr Callahan if I could give him a deposit and send him the balance after I came home and asked you to take it out of my bank.'

'And?'

'Mr Callahan asked me how much money I had on me. I told him I had two hundred and fifty dollars. Mr Callahan asked me where I got so much money.'

'Where did you?'

'Dad gave me a hundred and fifty for Christmas, and I had the hundred you gave me. Mr Callahan said good people never took their mate's last dollars, especially when they needed money to take their grandmother to lunch and a movie. He sold me the beads for a hundred and fifty dollars.' TC was touched and amused simultaneously.

'You need to send Mr Callahan a card and thank him for his generosity, Robert.'

'I already did, Mother. I bought him a card and a box of chocolates straight away, then took them back to him. He was surprised and happy.'

'That's good. He loves chocolates. Let's go home.'

❡

'What's your caper, doing deals with Robert without my knowledge?' asked TC when Vance called the shop on Monday afternoon.

'That's between Robert and me. Nothing to do with you,' laughed Vance. 'He's a good kid, like his mother. He's principled to the eyebrows. Could have gone the other way and taken after Jake.' TC shuddered.

'Please! Don't even think it! The young jeweller who robbed us came to see me this morning, Boss.'

'You're joking!'

'No, I'm not joking. I thought he'd brought the pendant back. That's the only reason I allowed him in the office.'

'Did he?' asked Vance hopefully.

'No! I couldn't believe it! He asked me if he could resume doing our work. He even turned on the waterworks after I told him not to be ridiculous. He told me his girlfriend made him do it. He even got on his knees and begged me to forgive him. What concerns me, Boss, is I felt no compassion for him whatsoever.'

'How the bloody hell could you?! I would have throttled the thieving bastard.'

'The truth is I wanted to kill him myself,' replied TC. 'Instead, I told him to stop blubbering, get up off his knees, be a man, never to darken our doorstep again, and enjoy his life of crime.'

'Hopefully, he'll end up in the slammer some time down the road,' said Vance. 'He steals once and gets away with it, he's sure to do it again. How are the German jeweller brothers treating you?'

'Great! Their work is beautiful. I'm blessed they heard about what happened with the thief and his girlfriend. Prompted them to come see me. Seems like something good comes out of everything.'

'Hope you're right, Little One. Talk to you later.'

¶

Amongst the day's mail collected in the afternoon were two envelopes addressed to TC in Vance's handwriting. In large block letters in the top left-hand corner of one was written: Open this one first. Try not to cry.

Very clever, thought a laughing TC. When she opened it to find a cheque for one dollar made out to: Relentless, Loyal, Hard-Working Confidante. The attached note read: Please be certain to deduct this from the dollars I owe you in shared profits. The second envelope contained a cheque for twenty thousand dollars. TC was more than a little surprised. The note: Don't bother to deduct this. It's such a paltry amount. JUST JOKING!

Mini came into the office.

'Why are you laughing, TC?'

'Mr Callahan's sense of humour, that's all, darling.'

§

In early February, TC's most consistent customer, the Japanese Consul General, requested a private meeting with her.

'My cousin owns a females' clothing factory in Japan, TC-san. He wants to come to Perth to buy opals from you. I imagine you are curious why I buy so many beautiful ones. Most of them I buy for him. He is impressed. That is why he will visit himself. With him, he will bring one hundred of his best customers. I ask you now, TC-san, to have the most beautiful opals in the whole of Australia to show him. I need you to promise me you will. I must not lose face!'

TC assured him, 'I understand! I promise!'

'Good, TC-san. I trust your word. They will come in early December.' A handshake and the deal was set.

§

'TC-san please don't say anything to Japanese staff. Not yet. Hideko is not good Japanese woman. She has big mouth.' TC smiled.

'I understand.'

By the end of February, TC had made arrangements with the best of her old customers from her wholesaling days. All agreed to send her stock in the last week in November.

Marjorie and TC were in the shop in mid-March when the Texan customer TC had driven to the airport on Christmas morning came in. His company office was set up and operating. He was accompanied by three other gentlemen from Houston.

'Here she is, TC Carmichael. I told you I'd fetch you some business, TC.'

'You did, indeed, sir. Did the ladies in your family like their Christmas presents?'

'They sure did. I had trouble convincing them you got out of bed at six on Christmas morning so I could buy them. I need to get a few more things. My friends here are eager to buy, too.' TC smiled and nodded.

'Suits us. This is Marjorie, my friend and partner in crime.' The four men laughed.

'Let's get out of here now,' said one.

'We have no chance,' said another.

'Victims to two beautiful Aussie women. Suits me,' said another. Mini came from the office, where she'd been eating her lunch.

'What about me, gentlemen? I am not an Aussie. I am Japanese.' Everyone except Mini burst into gales of laughter.

'Why are you laughing, TC?' she asked in her sweet, barely-audible voice.

'Because, darling Mini, everyone can see you are Japanese.'

'Oh, I forgot!' More laughter; this time Mini laughed, too. She recognised the humour.

⸿

A lot happened quickly.

Captain Russ retired from the U.S. Navy. His replacement was a commander, a very nice, family man with a lovely wife and four children. TC liked both him and his wife on sight. After retirement, Captain Russ took a temporary job within a friend's company until he and Marjorie decided which direction to take regarding their future. Marjorie continued to work in the shop. TC and she became closer every day they spent together.

When Fiona's social life resumed after the annual break, she insisted TC have lunch as her guest once a fortnight at her exclusive ladies' club.

'I want you to meet people, darling. I want you to become a member of the club. You haven't made it in Perth unless you're accepted there. When it is time for the annual nominations for new memberships, my friend and I will do the honours for you. You'll probably be the youngest club member for quite a while. That doesn't matter.'

'What if I don't fit in, Fiona?'

'Don't be ridiculous, darling. Of course you'll fit in.'

The first time TC went with Fiona to the club, she was taken aback, in awe of the old-world charm the décor exuded. It was beautiful; like stepping into another era.

Carrier group visits had begun to wane down to three a year. People involved within the tourism industry were disappointed. Many had come to rely on regular visits for their livelihood. Ken said it was because of the Green Peace activists' outrageous demonstrations which greeted the American naval vessels every time they pulled into port.

'Those Greenies would be the first to holler, "Help us, America," if we were ever threatened by an invasion. They forget Australia wouldn't be the wonderful country it is today if it hadn't been for General MacArthur's proclamation of, "I shall return".'

The Consul General of Japan visited the shop once weekly to remind TC of his promise to have the best opals Australia had to offer when his cousin and entourage visited in December, which seemed an eternity away. TC reassured him every time, 'I'll have them here and set up a week prior to your cousin's arrival. I promise.'

¶

Vance had rarely mentioned Delores or his girlfriends since the time TC was sick during the previous winter. TC didn't enquire. He was also sending regular cheques, sometimes two thousand, sometimes five or ten. One day, out of the blue, he rang the shop mid-afternoon. Not his usual routine. TC knew something was bugging him.

'What's wrong, Boss?' asked TC with obvious urgency.

'You know me too well, Little One,' was Vance's serious reply.

'No way would you call me this time of day if something wasn't wrong.'

'I'm pretty sure Carla look-alike is robbing me for money and stock. Tsune is more than likely into me for stock.'

'Front them and get rid of them.'

'I can't bloody well do that! They'll blab to Delores I've been screwing them.'

'I'm sure she already knows you've got at least one on the side.'

'No, she doesn't! Ayako is her biggest threat, as far as I'm concerned. Delores is forever in the coast shop yapping with her. It seems that way to me.'

'That's your guilt, Boss! I have no idea how often Delores talks with Ayako. Knowing you as I do, I believe if they chatted once a month, it would be too often as far as you are concerned. You are terrified Delores will pick up on Ayako's love for you. How she hasn't already is beyond me. I don't know how many reps I've told to mind their own business when they've mentioned the adoring manner in which you and Ayako look lovingly at each other. At least from my point of view, I doubt she will rob you. The poor woman loves you too much.'

'I'm not worried about Ayako robbing me, TC Carmichael. It's the other two molls!'

He is in a foul mood, thought TC. He's never called me that before. TC sighed with sadness for Vance. 'How are they robbing you, Boss?' she asked.

'I heard Carla-moll stays back at night after the other staff have gone for the day. I think she's messing with the computer, destroying cash invoices, confiscating the cash, and thieving stock.'

'I see! I heard your other staff had concerns about that. Emi told me you have a Japanese lady named Aiko in that shop. Perhaps you should have appointed her as manager.'

'Don't eff with "should have". I should have and should not have done a million effing things!'

'Stop! Don't use that language to me, Mr Callahan,' commanded TC. 'Save the f-word for your sluts!' Silence.

'I'm still here,' announced TC. 'How is Tsune robbing you?'

'You know me, Little One,' replied a now-much-calmer Vance. 'I think with my dick. She's such a good lay, I created the position of Stock Controller for her. She's thieving stock! There's a lot missing! It wouldn't surprise me if some time in the future she opens her own shop with my stock. She's already scammed me for the best painting I had of mine number one and the most beautiful red ring we've had for years.' TC sighed heavily.

'I don't know what to say. No pun intended, Boss. It was more years ago than I can recall when you mentioned you should have your appendage removed. Perhaps you should have gone ahead and done it. That thing, combined with your lack of control over it, has cost you a fortune. Not only where money and red opals are concerned, but you have to take into consideration the stress and emotional turbulence your girlfriends have caused you over the years. I wish I could fix it for you, darling Boss, but, unfortunately, I can't.'

'I know, Little One. Thanks for listening.'

TC put down the telephone and stared silently at the wall in front of her.

'Are you all right, TC?' enquired Marjorie, who as always disappeared from the office and into the shop when Vance called.

'Yes. Thank you, Marjorie,' smiled TC in reply. 'Sometimes I wonder who I worry about most; Robert or the boss. I think I can safely say it's the boss.'

'Hideko is at the front end of the shop abusing Mini,' said Marjorie. 'I thought you'd like to know.'

'Is that so!' TC immediately left the office and approached Hideko and Mini, who was crying.

'What is going on?' she demanded, looking directly at Hideko.

'I was telling her she's dressed like a little girl,' snapped Hideko.

'I think she looks lovely,' snapped TC in return. 'Don't tell me you are jealous of her, Hideko? Could it be you wish you were young, beautiful, and free again yourself?' TC patted Mini on the shoulder.

'You go and wash your face, darling. As far as I know, I'm the boss. I say you look gorgeous in your cute, bowed shoes and pretty dress. I love bows on shoes myself. I doubt I look like a little girl.' Mini hurried to the office to wash her face while TC spoke to Hideko. 'I know you loathe me, Hideko. You probably feel the same about Marjorie. I'm certain you can't stand Mini and the other young ones. You probably dislike the senior part-timers, too. Jealousy is a curse. Be careful it doesn't catch up with you one of these days.'

Hideko threw her head back and glared momentarily at TC before brushing past her.

'I'm going for a walk,' she announced as she flung open the door onto The Terrace.

'Hope it takes forever,' said TC under her breath, seconded by Marjorie.

§

With winter looming, TC made certain to get flu shots for Robert and herself. She couldn't believe her eyes when they went to the doctor late one afternoon. Randy James was sitting in the doctor's waiting room when Robert and she entered it. Randy was obviously surprised, too.

'Small world, isn't it, TC.' TC nodded.

'Sure is! Surely, I couldn't be blamed for thinking you're stalking me.'

'Hello, Randy,' said Robert. 'This is twice you are at the same place at the same time as Mother and I.'

'Are you sick, Robert?' asked Randy while TC checked in with the doctor's receptionist.

'No. Mother and I got sick last winter. We're here to get flu needles so we don't get sick again this year. Why are you here?'

'I have to get a check-up. The company I work for wants a health clearance every year. Do you live near here, Robert?'

'Yes! About five minutes away by car, near the new casino, where the dump used to be.'

'How is Mr D, Robert?'

'He's fine. Mother and I talk to him on the phone every week.'

'How about Mr Callahan?'

'He's fine, too.'

'Mr James,' called the doctor. Randy got to his feet and followed the doctor into one of the rooms. A couple of minutes later, the doctor beckoned Robert and TC into another room.

'Yours will be quick. I'll fix you both up now to save you waiting.'

§

An aircraft carrier group came in July. It broke the monotony of the quiet, slow-for-business winter. TC felt lucky Marjorie had delayed her holidays until Captain Russ got a break after six months in his new job. Hideko was on holiday. It didn't worry TC. It depended on Hideko's mood, whether or not she was nice to their American customers. All the better if she wasn't there as far as TC was concerned. As in the past, the shop was extremely busy during the visit. As always, TC felt blessed to receive the Americans' business, this time in particular because it was mid-winter. They needed the turnover.

Vance had not mentioned his pilfering girlfriends again, and TC didn't broach the subject. She knew he would talk with her if and when he wanted to discuss it. The cheques had stopped coming in a couple of months earlier. TC didn't mention that issue, either. She felt it was demeaning to remind him and that he would pay her one day soon.

§

Prior to the secret-ballots-being-cast membership of Fiona's exclusive ladies' club, Lisa told TC in conversation, 'One black cross against your name by any member, and you're out of the running. Not only that, but you can never apply for membership again.'

'Good heavens above, I didn't know that! Fiona will be beside herself if anyone gives me a black cross.'

'I'm not saying it will happen, TC,' said Lisa. 'I am asking you to prepare yourself. 'I wouldn't know how many women's applications for membership have been rejected. It's a lot.'

TC was on edge until ten days later when she received her letter of acceptance as a member of the club. She immediately called Fiona, who did not seem at all surprised.

'Good, darling, very good. You can take me to our club tomorrow for lunch. It's only fifty yards from your shop. I suggest you walk across and make a booking instead of phoning.'

'All right, Fiona. I'll do just that,' agreed TC. 'Thank you, Fiona.'

§

Suddenly it was mid-November. TC began preparing for the Japanese Consul General's cousin and entourage. Vance and Delores were coming to Perth for the occasion. They were bringing stock for Brolga Opals from the east coast. Packages began arriving from TC's contacts. No doubt about it—the bulk of the jewellery was magnificent. The stones were too.

Instead of checking once weekly, the darling little Consul General came every day, sometimes twice a day. His cousin wanted to shop after hours on December first. He would shop himself with his wife first at 6 pm. His ten best clients would shop from six-forty-five, fifteen more at seven-thirty, twenty at eight-thirty, and the remaining fifty-five from nine-thirty on.

'Talk about bloody pecking order,' said Marjorie. 'We'll be run off our feet, girl.'

'The king's temperature will rise through the roof on this deal. Wish Blanche could be here to see it.'

On November twenty-ninth, the Consul General hurried into the shop and walked around the shop looking carefully down at every showcase.

'TC-san, you promised beautiful stock. I thought everywhere you would have it. The people coming are very wealthy.'

'I know that, Mr Consul General,' replied TC. 'Unfortunately, not all the customers we might have today, tomorrow, and until six when your cousin comes to shop the day after, are as wealthy as him and his friends. We have to display lower-price-range items for them.'

'I understand, TC-san. I'm worried I'll lose face,' was the somewhat shaky reply.

'Come into my office, Mr Consul General,' invited TC. 'I'll show you. The trays are all prepared. My boss, Mr Callahan, and his wife are flying in late this afternoon. They are bringing many more beautiful pieces.' One by one, TC placed the trays on the desk for his perusal.

'Oh, TC-san, beautiful! Very beautiful! Lovely, all lovely!' TC smiled.

'Happy now, Mr Consul General?'

'Hi, TC-san, very happy. So sorry I was worried.'

'You come tomorrow. We'll have more for you to see.'

'Thank you, TC-san, thank you,' said the Consul General, who gave TC the full treatment. The dear man bowed.

§

Vance called TC after he and Delores were settled in their hotel accommodation. 'We're here safely. See you in the morning.' No further conversation. That was it.'

§

A group with a high number of tourists was scheduled for 9 a.m. Consequently, all staff were busily preparing the shop for the influx at eight-thirty. TC and Marjorie were in the office adjusting tray displays, when Mini gingerly opened the door.

'TC, there are strange people, a lady and a man, peering through the front door. They are dressed funny.' TC looked through the glass-partition office window and laughed as she opened the office door.

'They're strange all right, Mini. That's the boss and Mrs Callahan.' Mini's expression was one of surprised while Marjorie smiled.

'They live on the Gold Coast, Mini. They are wearing tourist garb.' Mini was shaking.

'I hope I won't be in trouble, Marjorie.' Marjorie laughed and hugged Mini.

'No way, Mini, not with TC and me here to protect you. Go back to work in the shop.'

TC unlocked the front door.

'Hello, strange-looking people. What are you doing scaring my staff? Come in so you can frighten them more.' Vance laughed, while Delores appeared confused. TC, being TC, kissed Vance on the cheek as she always had. She then turned to Delores with the intention of kissing her cheek as well. It seemed the right thing to do.

'I'll be right, TC,' said Delores, who after all these years still didn't realise TC was an open book. What you saw was what you got. TC relocked the door and turned to the staff. One by one she introduced them to Vance and Delores.

'I have no hope of remembering all your names,' said Delores nervously. Vance stood in silence while nodding and smiling.

'Come in the office and meet Marjorie,' said TC. 'I have her slaving away behind the scenes.'

After a few words of greeting Marjorie made herself scarce by joining the others in the showroom.

'They are all very attractive,' said Delores as TC filled the kettle for coffees.

'I figure I might as well be surrounded by beauty,' replied TC. 'The staff complement the stock. The opposite also applies. It helps!'

'Talking of stock, here's more,' said Vance as he plonked a lettered briefcase on the office desk.

'Is it all marked, Boss?' asked TC.

'Some are, but most aren't.'

'Great! Guess I know what I'll be doing all day.'

⁋

The morning tour group came on time. After half an hour of shopping frenzy, they left. As usual, a lot would return after hotel check-in to shop in a less hurried, more relaxed atmosphere.

TC returned to the office, where Delores was sitting at her desk while Vance was observing the activity in the shop with Marjorie collating invoices with takings and the others tidying up and filling gaps.

'Who's the older one in the white dress?' enquired Vance.

'That's Hideko. She loathes me and gives the young ones a hard time every chance she gets.'

'I don't like her,' said Vance flatly.

'You haven't so much as spoken to the woman yet, Vance,' commented Delores matter-of-factly.

'Okay, we'll go and do the tourist thing,' said Vance. 'TC has stock to mark. Let's go.'

'Right!' replied Delores as she collected her bag and got to her feet. TC smiled.

'Speaking of tourists, you look the part? You in particular, Boss. Never seen you in midcalf shorts and Roman sandals before.' Vance grimaced.

'Yes! Come on, Delores. TC has things to do.'

TC stood at the office door as Vance paused to tell the staff he'd see them later. Delores waited for him at the front door while his departure was delayed by Hideko's grovelling behaviour, which was so obvious TC had difficulty believing her eyes.

So there's another side to you, Hideko, thought TC as she closed the office door, then opened the old briefcase containing stock. As per Vance of the old days, the stock had been literally thrown into the bag with no sorting, no listing, no paperwork, nothing except stock, lots of it.

Don't know what his stock controller, Tsune, does with her time, thought TC as she began grouping the jewellery. It sure as hell isn't keeping the stock in order. Obviously, she must concentrate only on satisfying the boss and helping herself to whatever takes her fancy.

Vance phoned at closing time. He and Delores had been to the beach.

'The ocean is green here,' he said with as much surprise as TC had experienced years before.

'I know!'

'Did you finish marking the stock?'

'Don't ask! Marjorie and I have been at it most of the day. I'll take home what's left and do it tonight.'

'Okay. I'll see you tomorrow some time. Delores and I are probably touristing again.'

'I need you here by five-thirty, Boss. The Consul General's cousin and his wife will be here at six sharp. Speaking of the Consul General, the dear man is nervous as I imagine a person facing the gallows would be. He's been in three times today.'

'Is that so? See you tomorrow.' TC left the phone thinking how distant and cold Vance was when in Delores' company.

He's on guard with every word he utters. Surely Delores doesn't still think I'm one of his conquests? Oh, well! Nothing I can do about it.

At five the next afternoon, the display was ready, vibrant colour literally jumping out of every showcase. The Consul General had done his final inspection. He was bursting with pride. His cousin and friends were in for a once-in-a-lifetime experience.

'Looks beautiful, TC,' said Marjorie and everyone else, except Hideko, who simply threw her head back and raised her eyebrows.

'Don't know where you got all this stock, TC.' TC smiled.

'That's right, Hideko. You don't.'

Vance wandered in a little before five-thirty. TC couldn't believe what she saw. He was dressed in long denim shorts and a T-shirt and was wearing the brown, heavy-leather Roman sandals.

'Are you going to a fancy-dress party, Boss? Have you lost your faculties! Where's your suit?'

'I didn't bring a suit. What do I need a suit for?'

'Bloody hell, you're going to meet a hundred rich businessmen and women coming to buy opal, and you rock up looking like an aged surfie.' TC raced to the front door. She looked north across the street to an exclusive menswear shop, noted the telephone number on their sign, rushed back to the office, dialled the number, and all but begged the man who answered to stay open for Vance.

'We're already closed, Ma'am. If the gentleman comes immediately, I'll meet him at the door.'

'Come on, Mr Callahan. I'll be your guide,' offered Marjorie.

Twenty minutes later Vance returned with a large gents' boutique bag, which contained a grey business suit, white shirt, and dark grey tie.

'Hurry up, Boss. Change in the office,' directed TC. 'We'll wait in the shop.'

'I'm ready,' came Vance's summons from the office.' TC looked him over.

'The trousers are too long, the legs are dragging on the floor. I'll have to pin them up. No, that will take too long. I'll staple them.' As TC turned up the hem of the first leg, she couldn't help but notice Vance's bare feet. 'Don't suppose you bought a pair of socks.'

'No, didn't think of it.'

'Okay, Boss. I'll leave your trouser legs as long as I can without them dragging. Marjorie, would you please hold them in place while I staple?' Mini opened the office door.

'They are here, TC, waiting for you inside the door.' TC passed the stapling machine to Marjorie.

'You finish. Make it quick!' She then took a deep breath, put on a beaming smile, and hurried to greet the VIPs. Hideko and the other staff were lined up like soldiers along the other side of the counters as the Consul General introduced TC to his cousin and wife, both of whom bowed in the traditional Japanese style. Both also spoke English. This was a bonus factor. It put Hideko's nose out of joint because it meant TC would be handling the deal without her assistance. The Consul General looked confused.

'TC-san, where is Mr Callahan? You said he would be here.'

'I'm right here,' said Vance as he appeared in the office doorway, then stepped forward. TC shuddered when she spotted the pearl head of a pin protruding from Vance's shirt collar. More introductions and bowing, then down to business. While her customers were discussing a particular piece which caught their eye with the Consul General, TC excused herself momentarily, touched Vance's ankle with the tip of her shoe, and indicated to him to go to the office via eye contact.

'You've got a pin sticking out of your collar,' she whispered quickly as she pulled on the tiny, fake pearl.

'Don't move around too much. They might spot your bare toes and sandals. Come on, let's get back in there.'

It was close to midnight when the staff, apart from Marjorie, finally got to leave. The Captain was coming to collect Marjorie, who asked Vance if he would like a coffee. While TC totalled the invoices, Marjorie made coffee and chatted with Vance.

'I was serving two ladies up the front. They were looking at twenty-thousand-dollar pieces when Hideko actually picked me up and moved me away. It wasn't as if I couldn't communicate with them. They both spoke English very well.'

'I saw that happen, Marjorie,' said Vance seriously. 'I couldn't believe it! Probably cost you the sales by butting in like that.'

'I don't know,' replied Marjorie. 'I moved on to other customers. I must admit that by doing it, Hideko made me see red. I wanted to deck the bitch.'

'I can't say I blame you,' said Vance. 'Did that belt buckle ever surface?'

'No! The three other pieces reappeared, not the buckle,' replied Marjorie. Vance put down his coffee cup before looking briefly at the ceiling, then speaking.

'I'd bet my balls Hideko has got that belt buckle.'

'That's a risky wager,' said Marjorie seriously.

'I know!' replied Vance. 'That's how sure I am.'

'There you go,' interrupted TC as she finished calculating.

'Five hundred and twenty-one thousand, six hundred and thirty dollars. The Consul's cousin spent sixty-one thousand of that.'

'Cash or credit cards?' asked Vance, whose eyes were wide open and gleaming.

'All cash,' said TC.

After Captain Russ came to collect Marjorie, he dropped Vance off at his hotel, then gave TC a lift to her house. Her car was locked in a parking station which closed at midnight.

TC didn't know when she called it a night after seeing Gracie off home and spending a few minutes sitting on the edge of Robert's bed watching him sleep, that the next day held in store for her a couple or three incidents she neither expected nor needed.

The shop had been open a couple of hours. TC, Marjorie, and Mini were in the office sorting and packing stock for return to TC's old acquaintances. At least two pieces of each consignment parcel had sold. This factor made TC happy and confident she could call on them again should the need ever arise. Hideko came into the office.

'The tour guides are here to collect their sales report.'

'What sales report?' asked TC.

'I don't know. You'll have to ask them,' replied Hideko.

TC went to speak with the tour guides.

'You must be referring to the day-before-yesterday's tour group? One of the guides already collected the sales report.'

'No! Our group shopped last night,' was the reply.

'I'm sorry,' said TC while shaking her head in denial. 'That was a private group. The Japanese Consul General has been organising their shopping with us since the beginning of last February.'

'Our company still needs sales report,' persisted the male of the duo.

'I'm sorry, no. We gave the people more discount instead of paying tour commission.'

'We need sales report,' repeated the guide.

'Not this time,' said TC. 'If your boss is unhappy, tell him to contact me.'

'We NEED sales report,' demanded both guides in unison.

'Sorry, you're not getting one,' replied TC before turning back towards the office and hearing Hideko begin speaking to the guides in Japanese.

God only knows what she's arranging, thought TC as she sat down at the office desk to resume her work.

Five minutes later, Marjorie said, 'Look, TC. Hideko is still talking to those guides.'

'Probably plotting our demise,' replied TC lightly.

Vance showed up a little before lunch.

'Where's Delores?' enquired TC, who was surprised to see him alone.

'I gave her some money and told her to go shopping. She's an expert shopper.' He hadn't been there more than a few minutes when Hideko came to the office door.

'Mr Callahan, I need to see you alone. Could we please go for a coffee?' Before Vance had the opportunity to reply, Hideko was halfway down the shop towards the door.

'Wonder what the bloody hell this is about,' said Vance before following her.

'Lunch time, Mini,' said TC. 'I'll tell the girls to join you. Marjorie and I will watch the shop.'

'Why do you think Hideko wanted to see the boss by himself?' asked Marjorie.

'I have no idea, Marjorie,' replied TC nonchalantly.

'I think she's going to ask him for your job, TC,' said Marjorie. TC found Marjorie's words amusing while probably right on the ball.

¶

'Most likely you are spot-on, my dear friend. I assure you, if that is, indeed, her plot, she's got no hope. It'll be like pushing wet mud uphill with her bare hands.'

'If Hideko gets your job, TC, I'll leave. I think everyone will,' said Marjorie.

'Let's see what happens first. No point in worrying about something that's not going to happen. After all, I do recall overhearing the boss say he'd bet his balls she's got the belt buckle. Believe me, he wouldn't do that lightly.'

Hideko and Vance returned after having been gone for an hour. Marjorie and TC were serving a couple of oil men referred by the Christmas Texan who had certainly remained true to his word. Not a month passed when he didn't send a customer or two, sometime more. By coincidence, both oil men, Marjorie, and TC were laughing when Vance and Hideko entered via the hallway door.

'This sounds good,' said Vance, who paused while Hideko hightailed it for the office. 'Let me in on the joke.' TC gave an exaggerated sigh.

'These gentlemen wanted more discount. I told them to look at our feet. We can't even afford shoes, so how can we give more discount?'

Vance walked behind the counter to see both Marjorie and TC standing in stockinged feet with their shoes pushed under the counter ledge. One of the Texans spoke up.

'We told them we'd buy them a pair of shoes each if they'd come to dinner with us tonight. Marjorie said while she'd love a pair of shoes, she would have to get her husband's permission.'

'These ladies are too alert,' added the other man. 'TC said she couldn't dream of eating dinner with me, knowing the opal I'd bought for my wife is in my briefcase.'

'This is our boss,' said Marjorie.

'Yes! He'll fire us if we give you more discount,' said TC seriously.

'You'd be mad to fire these two,' said one man while the other nodded in agreement. Vance laughed.

'I don't think there's much chance of that. I'll leave you in their capable hands.'

The Texans left happy after promising they'd return for another laugh the next time they visited Perth. TC and Marjorie entered the office as Hideko went into the shop. She stood by the front counters and stared out onto The Terrace. Mini went to collect the mail, Marjorie to purchase her lunch, and the two younger staff members to prepare for a scheduled afternoon tour group. Vance told TC to sit down beside him at the desk.

'Hideko asked me to get rid of you and give her your job, Little One.' TC nodded resignedly.

'Not at all surprising. Boss. You'd need a chainsaw to penetrate the hatred and jealousy she harbours regarding me. I've sensed it since day one. Anyway, what did you tell her? Am I fired? Are you buying me out? What's the deal?'

'I told her, no. It blew her away when I told her I couldn't fire you even if I wanted to, as you're part owner. She was surprised. Get RID of the bitch! The sooner the better!'

'It shouldn't take long. I saw one of the so-called Sydney 'big shots' in the shop with a woman and a couple of male cronies last week. They were talking to Hideko for ages. He gave her a card with something on the back of it. Probably a phone number. He didn't think I recognised him with his shades on. The next day our landlord called. He told me he'd sold one of his buildings around the corner to an east coast opal dealer and thought he'd warn me that we'd have more opposition in the near future.'

'Who is it?' TC told Vance the man's name. 'Let the bastard have her. They deserve each other,' said Vance. 'She tried it on me first. She didn't want to accept his offer of a job if she could get rid of you. She'll contact him tonight and take the job because she'll be the head honcho. He'll be over the moon because with her she'll take knowledge of all our Japanese tour and corporate contacts. A deal made in heaven for both of them. They are both thieves! She steals stock and he steals staff. In this instance, it's lucky for us. We don't want the staff he's stolen.'

Marjorie with her lunch and Mini with the mail, returned together.

'That was quick!' said Vance. 'TC and I will leave the place in your capable hands, Marjorie. We'll go around the corner for a coffee and sandwich if that's okay with you?'

'Take your time,' replied Marjorie with her usual lovely smile.

In a quiet walkway near the shop was a partly secluded park bench.

'You don't really want coffee and food, do you, Little One?' asked Vance.

'Not really. Not after the Hideko deal plus tour guides looking for sales reports on last night's VIPs.'

'Let's sit on this bench,' suggested Vance. They sat down.

'What's this about tour guides and sales reports?' TC explained. Vance was angry. 'Stuff them! Guess they can't be blamed for trying. They're only doing their jobs.'

'I've told you before, Boss, I feel sorry for the Japanese tourists. Poor buggers are herded around like cattle and only allowed to shop at contracted shops. Do you know they are told if they shop anywhere else, they'll be ripped off? We both know where the rip-offs are.'

'I feel sorry for the poor bastards, too. At least when they shop with us, we don't inflate prices to cover the commission. A lot do!'

'I know! A few of the wholesalers have told me about some of the goings-on over in the east.'

'Mongrels and money, Little One!' said Vance.

'Hope I never become one. I want to be able to sleep at night. Unfortunately, some people would rob their own mother and not think twice.'

'Speaking about ripping off,' said Vance seriously. 'I told Delores I think you're robbing me.' Simultaneously TC was speechless in shock, turned white, angry, and hurt beyond belief. After what seemed like an eternity of silence, during which time TC glared at Vance looking directly into his eyes, she smacked his face so hard the imprint of her hand turned red while the rest of his face was ghostly white. Still looking into his eyes, TC spoke with a controlled voice.

'You effing bastard! You have me confused with your molls and past mine and shop managers. I know who's robbing whom! After last night's trading with the Consul's cousin and his friends, you owe me four hundred and twenty-one thousand dollars, less, of course, one cheque for two dollars, fifty cents, one for one dollar, seventy-five percent on the stone the jeweller stole, and the balance on the beads you sold to Robert for nearly nothing.'

'I have to admit, you're a great face slapper,' said Vance lightly.

'Don't you dare try to gloss it over, Mr Callahan! You told your wife you think I'm robbing you?! Screw you! There's a fortune in stock in that shop. Not bad considering it began with a few crappy pendants and a handful of stones as your input. That's all your girlfriend at the time could spare. Oh! I forgot your huge investment of twenty-five thousand.'

'No need to be sarcastic, Little One.'

'Don't you dare "Little One" me!'

'It's because you plan on having a new house built.'

'So!' demanded TC.

'Delores doesn't know what our deal is,' reasoned Vance. 'She knows we have an arrangement! I haven't told her exactly what.'

'So, she's wondering how I can afford a new house? You're pretending you're wondering, too? That figures! Lay the crap on me to keep the heat off your sluts.'

'I suppose it's something like that,' replied Vance.

'SCREW YOU!' snarled TC venomously while, with difficulty, she managed to control her voice level. 'So, Delores thinks I came over here broke? She doesn't know I did trips for you after Jake cleaned me out?'

'She knows you have your share of the motel,' interrupted Vance.

'Big bloody deal! I don't suppose she knows I put my money into kick-starting the shop here, or I own twenty-five percent of it? I draw a lousy two hundred and fifty dollars a week, and until recently you have sent me bugger-all regarding my share of profits ever since we got involved in the Japanese tour business!' After a long silence, TC sighed heavily.

'I think it's time I get out, Boss. I should have stuck to my initial idea and opened my own shop. I never should have asked you for consignment stones. Anyway, that's yesterday. No point dwelling on past mistakes.'

'I'm sorry, Little One.'

'I told you to quit on the "Little One". Surely, "I'm sorry my wife and I think you're a thief" would be more appropriate. I have two hundred and eighty thousand. I own my house plus what you owe me in my share of profits along with twenty-five percent of the stock. I suggest you tell Hideko she can have my job. Robert and I will go back to Queensland. I'll open my own shop there.' TC stood, then walked slowly back to the shop. Vance remained sitting on the park bench staring into space and thinking for ages before heading for his hotel room and Delores.

Immediately TC returned to the shop, Hideko, without so much as glancing at TC, announced she wasn't feeling well, and she was going home.

'Sorry about that, Hideko,' said TC, knowing full well Hideko needed to get away to contact her soon-to-be new employer.'

You shouldn't rush, thought TC. I'm going! Perhaps you'll get from Vance what you wanted.

After the small afternoon tour group had come and gone, TC sent Mini to post return stock, cheques, and letters of thanks to her east coast contacts while Marjorie and she sorted and re-bagged stock Vance had brought with him.

'It's all priced now, Marjorie,' remarked TC. 'It will make the boss' and the stock controller's job lighter; give her more time to spend on whatever else it is she does.' Marjorie laughed.

'Did I detect a hint of sarcasm in those words?'

'Yes, my dear, you were meant to,' replied TC.

'What's bugging you, TC?'

'Just about everything, Marjorie,' replied TC. 'Sometimes we associate with people forever and we think we know them. It's a shock when we discover we don't know them at all.'

'So far that hasn't happened to me,' said Marjorie seriously.

'That's good! For your sake, I hope it stays that way,' replied TC.

'Did Hideko ask the boss for your job?' enquired Marjorie.

'She did! He said no. I'm ninety-nine-point-nine percent certain she'll be running the opposition shop about to open half a block down and one block over.'

Vance phoned at closing time. TC answered. Marjorie, Mini, and the other two young girls were clearing the showcases.

'Delores is taking a shower,' said Vance. 'How are you?'

'Me? I'm floating on effing clover.'

'Don't speak like that. It's not you,' chastised Vance.

'Why not! I'm sure thieves use foul language.'

'I'll come and see you in the morning' said Vance.

'I can hardly wait. Have a nice evening,' replied TC.

TC mentioned none of her day's occurrences to Fiona during their usual seven o'clock telephone conversation. Fiona, being Fiona, detected something was bothering TC, who managed to ward off questions by laughing and telling Fiona not to be concerned about anything.

'I'm fine, my darling friend,' assured TC. 'Of course, I'll go with you next week.' No point in causing Fiona concern until the dust settles and I have a firm plan, thought TC.

'Is Mr Callahan coming to see me, Mother?' asked Robert hopefully.

'I don't think so, darling. He and Mrs Callahan are busy doing touristy things. If they are still here on Saturday, perhaps you'll see him in the shop.'

'I hope so. I hope they will be here.'

'How would you feel about moving back to Queensland, sweetheart?' asked TC during a later discussion with Robert about Mr D and Auntie Maggie. Robert thought for a minute or so while silently weighing pros and cons within his mind.

'I don't know, Mama; not until I finish college. I don't fancy the thought of changing places until then.'

'That's all right; not long to go,' replied TC while thinking she could obtain a job in a department store or such until Robert had completed his University Entrance Examination. It was only twenty-two months.

'Why did you ask?' enquired Robert seriously.

'No reason in particular, sweetie. It simply sprung into my mind.'

After Robert went to bed, TC sat in silence for hours. She felt numb with hurt combined with spasms of anger.

I could have robbed him a thousand times for opal and money, she thought. Perhaps I should have. Thieves seem to prosper more than honest fools. As for Delores, not only does she have a fixation I have been or still am one of Vance's concubines, she'll now be thinking I'm a thief, to boot. If it was true, it wouldn't hurt. It's because it's not true it's tearing me to pieces. Never mind. What's done is done. Once words are spoken, they can't be retracted. Vance's words of today will remain with me forever. Unfortunate but I know they will.

§

As per TC's routine, she arrived at the shop at eight-thirty after dropping Robert at college. Vance was waiting on a seat at a bus stop close by. He looked miserable.

'You're here!' he said.

'No, it's my twin sister,' was TC's terse reply.

'Don't be like that, Little One.'

'I told you yesterday to quit calling me "Little One". Refer to me as

TC or nothing.' Vance followed TC into the office, where she dumped her bag on the desk before beginning to unlock the safe.

'Make yourself coffee if you like.'

'That's all right. I don't feel like anything,' replied Vance as he observed TC going about her morning routine. 'I feel as if I'm seeing you for the first time,' said Vance with a hint of sadness in his voice.

'Really! What? As a woman or a thief?'

'I'm sorry, Little One. I shouldn't have said what I did,' he sounded sincere. TC ignored Vance as she extracted heaped trays of stock from the confines of the safe before putting them on the desk. Instead of issuing a command, Vance made a request--humbly, at that.

'Please stop that! I want to have a talk.' TC's cold attitude did not falter.

'I can't stop. I have to organise the cases before Marjorie and Mini arrive at nine. The doors are opened then. I doubt Hideko will be here today. If she does show, she's got more hide than a rhino.' Vance followed TC around the shop in silence as she arranged the displays. When finished to her satisfaction, TC turned towards him. 'All done. Mini can vacuum the carpets and clean the windows today.'

'Can we please talk now?' asked Vance.

'While I don't particularly want to talk, I understand we have to. I may be a thief and in Delores' eyes one of your sluts, but I'm not stupid.'

'Stop it! Stop it now! I'm imploring you!' TC smiled.

'Now, there's a word I've not heard you use before, Mr Callahan. I imagine it's usually reserved for your tarts.' Vance sighed. He appeared forlorn.

'I imagine you are right. You usually are.'

❡

Marjorie and Mini arrived simultaneously at exactly nine. Hideko didn't front. No surprise to all, except for Mini. None of them, particularly Mini, gave a tinker.

The moment Marjorie saw Vance, she commented 'You don't look well, Boss.' Vance smiled.

'Very observant of you, Marjorie. I didn't sleep too well last night.'

'You look a bit rough about the edges, too, TC,' came once again from Marjorie.

'I sat up most of the night thinking about business,' said TC, who didn't bother to mention it was her own future business she'd been thinking about.

Mini, who had begun vacuuming the serving area, tapped on the glass office-door window and nodded towards the door. The Consul General had walked in. He was carrying a huge, beautiful, floral arrangement, which hid from view his face and body above his waist.

'Where is TC-san?'

'I'm here Mr Consul General,' said TC. 'You can't see me because of the flowers.'

'Silly me,' he said as he deposited the huge vase on the counter. 'TC-san, my cousin and friends sent these for you and staff to enjoy. I hope you like them.'

'They are very beautiful, Mr Consul General.'

'Yes, like your opals. Difference is flowers will die like people when they are old. Opals will last forever.'

'As long as we take care of them, they will,' agreed TC. 'Please thank your cousin and his friends for us for the very much appreciated lovely thought.'

'He said you opened your shop night time for him, so they appreciated, too. I'll come again soon, TC-san.'

'Most impressive,' said Vance, who had been observing via the office window.

'I'll display them on the front counter, TC,' said Marjorie. 'They certainly are beautiful.'

'Sure are,' agreed TC while feeling sad she wouldn't be seeing Mr Consul General too many more times.

'Marjorie,' said Vance. 'Would you please mind the shop while TC and I go for a coffee and talk?'

'No problem!' replied Marjorie. 'Mini and I will be fine'.

¶

'Let's sit where we did yesterday,' suggested Vance. 'It's a pretty private spot.'

'Sure. Whatever you say,' replied TC. When they were seated on the park bench, Vance spoke first.

'I want you to know I'm sorry for what I said. I'm sorry!'

'You listen to me, Mr Callahan. If you think I've been robbing you, why the bloody hell didn't you front me? No, you know it's not true! You're pissed off because I'm going to have a new home built, something you've never done, something you've never given Delores. Let me tell you now. If you'd paid me my money to plan, I would have had the bastard built three years ago. Why don't you go ahead and plan one now that you're withholding enough of my money to pay for it?!'

'You know I'll pay you eventually, Little One.' TC shook her head in denial that he'd called her that again.

'Sure! When? You can start by giving me the sixty-nine-and-a-half thousand which is my share from the Consul's deal.'

'I don't know. It's a lot of money,' stalled Vance.

'So is it three times that amount you'll get?' snapped TC. 'Plus the cost of your stock sold. I'm the one who has the contacts and did all the work. I said in the shop an hour ago I'm not stupid. I realised an instant ago, I am stupid! I should have insisted on our deal being written in blood.'

'I'll send you money when I can,' insisted Vance.

'Why can't I have my share of this deal now?' Vance became extremely serious.

'TC, I want you never to tell Delores where you got your money. Lie to her if you have to. Don't tell her.'

'Why! I earned it! We have a deal! At least, I thought we did! Putting it bluntly, I do believe I'm screwed. I don't know why you're so worried about me telling Delores where I got my money. We rarely speak to each other.'

'I know. Keep it that way! Surely you don't expect me to pay you your money, let you quit, then open in opposition to me in Queensland?' reasoned Vance.

'Why not? Competition never hurt anyone. Look at the competition I've got here. I've lost count of how many opal shops there are in Perth, and another one about to open. Are you afraid I'd cream you?'

'Probably! Are you and Emi still friendly?'

'Of course! When I open my own shop, I might steal her from you.'

'That's what I'm afraid of. I don't think you'd steal her; she would offer her services willingly.'

'You have another Japanese lady who answers the telephone sometimes. Her name is Aiko. I think she'd leave you in a flash. From what I hear, she's awake to your Carla clone, and feels uncomfortable working under a thieving, conniving slut who also happens to be one of her boss' mistresses.'

'You certainly have a way with words, Little One,' laughed Vance.

'Don't blame me! I had a good teacher,' replied TC bluntly. 'By the way, Marjorie is right. You don't look well. You're white! Don't you die!'

'You mean, don't die before you get your money,' laughed Vance.

'No! I don't mean that at all, and you know it. While I will never forgive you for telling Delores you think I'm a thief, I don't want you to die, money or no money. You're my father, mother, big brother, friend and mentor rolled into one.' There was a long silence before Vance spoke. He was more serious than TC could ever recall.

'Remember what I've always told you, Little One. Do as I say, NEVER do as I do. Listen carefully now while I tell you what to do should I die.' TC didn't interrupt as Vance predicted what would happen and what she should do to counteract and protect herself. He ended by saying, 'No matter what, you must keep the Brolga name. You've earned it and deserve it more than anyone else who might outlive me. Should I die, do exactly as I've told you and be on guard. Trust no bastard!' TC was starry-eyed, close to tears.

'Do you know something you're not telling me?' Vance was adamant.

'No! I'm simply preparing you for if and when I go before you. Promise me you'll remember every word I said.'

'I will, I promise,' replied TC seriously.

'Good! Quit being soppy. We'll go back to the shop and sort out my stock.'

'Already done. All you have to do is count it.' Vance looked at TC, shrugged, and smiled.

'How the bloody hell would I know how many pieces I brought?' TC rolled her eyes and shook her head in exasperation.

'Some things never change! No wonder your molls are robbing you.' Vance laughed.

'Now! Now!'

§

At closing time, Vance once again told TC he was sorry before hugging her lightly and kissing her on the cheek.

'Where's mine, Boss?' teased Marjorie. Vance laughed.

'Can't hug and kiss you, Marjorie; you might lead me astray.'

§

Vance and Delores flew back to Queensland a few hours later. Vance left TC nine-and-a-half thousand of her profit share on the VIP deal. He said he'd send her more when he could. TC knew in her heart he would hold out and pay her in dribs and drabs, because he was afraid if he paid her straight up, she would follow through and open in opposition to him back in Queensland. She also knew, without any doubt whatsoever, in the very near future he would announce he was building a grand, new home.

§

Two weeks later TC received a cheque for five thousand. This time the note read: I know you'll never forgive me. I'm still sorry. TC threw the cheque on the desk, scrunched the note, and flung it in the bin while thinking, You're not wrong there, Boss.

That same day Marjorie and Mini were out buying their lunches when they saw Hideko in the mall. Mini literally ran back to the shop.

'TC, Marjorie and I saw Hideko. She's wearing the stolen belt buckle!'

'Calm down, darling. Stop panting and puffing.'

'She saw us, TC. I'm sure she knows we saw the belt buckle. She didn't speak, put her head back the way she does, and passed us by. Aren't you surprised?'

'No, Mini, not in the least. The boss, Marjorie, and myself were sure she had it. She must have started her new job. She's showing it off.' Marjorie came back wearing a suspicious look.

'I knew that bitch pinched the buckle. I have to tell the boss his balls are safe.' Mini appeared confused.

'Does Mr Callahan play tennis?' Marjorie and TC cracked up inside.

'No, Mini. Think he prefers cricket,' said Marjorie. 'Isn't that right, TC?' TC nodded.

'Yes! Cricket is his game. He likes bowling overs.'

While Marjorie and Mini ate their lunches, TC phoned Vance at his office.

'Did you get my note?' were his first words.

'Yes. I'm not calling about that,' replied TC. 'Marjorie and Mini saw Hideko in the mall. She was sporting our belt buckle.'

'Thank God for that! I get to retain my testicles.'

'Marjorie said the same thing. Should I contact the police, or let her get away with it? Up to you. Personally, I'd like to go around the corner, choke her, then rip the thing off the bitch.'

'I would, too, Boss,' called Marjorie from the background.

'Let me think about it. I'll call you back,' said Vance.

Vance did phone back.

'I've been thinking. Have decided to let Hideko think she's gotten away with her crime.'

'Which she has if we do nothing.'

'That's exactly my point,' explained Vance. 'Let her rob the prick she's working for now. She won't be able to help herself. She'll think she's gotten away with it once, so she'll do it again. Do we care? No!'

'You're the boss,' said TC.

⁋

A few days later Mr Japanese Consul General came to see TC, who immediately picked up he was in an agitated state.

'TC-san, I came to apologise for wicked Japanese woman. Hideko-san is telling all Japanese people you sell only cracked opal. I know that is not true.' TC was not surprised, neither was Marjorie, who was standing beside her.

'That is the important factor, Mr Consul General,' said TC. 'We know she is lying to steal our business and will stop at nothing to ruin our reputation.' Marjorie joined in the conversation.

'Hideko asked Mr Callahan for TC's job, Mr Consul General. She hates us because he didn't give it to her. That is why she is working around the corner.' The Consul General was obviously in shock.

'No! Japanese women should not do that. So sorry, TC-san. Very, very sorry. You are my friend.' TC smiled.

'It's not your fault. Please don't worry. Put it out of your mind.'

'Thank you, TC-san. I'll not forget. I will always buy opal from you.'

'That bloody Hideko must be the biggest bitch I've ever known,' exploded Marjorie after the Consul General had gone. 'Not only is she a thief, she's also a lying, sly, manipulative piece of slime, to boot.'

'She'll get hers, Marjorie,' replied TC. 'Might take a while, but I assure you the day will come when she'll be exposed for what she is.'

'Wish it was yesterday,' sighed Marjorie.

⁋

It was the busiest time of the year. Thanks to Emi's dedicated commitment to her job, Japanese tour groups arrived every other day. That factor, combined with the annual influx of tourists from other parts of the world who came to Australia to escape winter in their homeland, meant TC and her staff were run ragged, all buggered at closing time each day's end.

After her experience with Hideko, TC had no intention ever again of hiring the 'best of a bad lot'. Sooner or later the right senior Japanese sales lady would present herself. TC wished Emi lived in Perth.

Christmas was on the doorstep. Mr D and Maggie were due to arrive in a couple of days. Robert was excited about spending time with them. Fiona was disappointed, yet understanding, because TC had not been in the position to attend any of her end-of-year social functions. Captain Russ and Marjorie were flying east to spend the festive season with Marjorie's family. Vance announced he had land on the coast north of Brisbane and he was going to have the house of the century built for Delores.

'Delores and I like it there,' he said. 'Not only that, living there will remove Delores from those other women's environments.'

'Good for both of you,' agreed TC. 'Please be selective about how you spend my money.' Vance laughed.

'I will. By the way, I posted you ten thousand yesterday.'

'How generous of you,' replied TC. 'When you get this month's report, you'll be owing me for at least twice that on top of what it is already.' Vance laughed again.

'Be thankful for small mercies, Little One. Do you forgive me yet?'

'Never! And you know it! You expect too much!'

It was Saturday two days before Christmas when Randy James appeared at the shop. Last time TC had seen him was at the doctor's surgery way back before winter. Randy was carrying a bunch of red roses.

'Well, look who's here,' said TC. 'Red doesn't suit your complexion, Randall James.'

'Don't be like that, TC Carmichael. Be nice. It's Christmas. These are for you.' TC was surprised, to say the least, as Randy held the roses out towards her. TC was confused and reluctant to accept them.

'What on earth for?'

'God strike me pink, if it's not Randy bloody James,' said Mr D as he and Maggie entered the shop from The Terrace.

'Take the bloody roses, TC' said Maggie. 'If you don't, I sure as buggery will. How are you, Randy?' Amid greetings and handshaking, TC directed them into the office because customers were coming in. She was about to enquire as to Robert's whereabouts when Mr D preempted her.

'Robert is off buying his mother a Christmas present. I think Maggie and I were slowing him down, so we came back here.'

With Marjorie away and Mini and the others off for Christmas, TC remained busy until closing time, when Robert staggered in loaded with bags and packages. KD, Maggie, and Randy James were still catching up on old times at the Pink Brolga amidst gales of laughter, which reverberated throughout the shop.

'Did you buy the city out, darling?' laughed TC as Robert struggled not to drop his purchases.

'I spent all the money I drew out of my bank, Mama. Please lend me five dollars. I told the lady in the arcade shop I'd bring it back to her straight away.'

'My wallet is in my purse. She must be a nice lady. She trusted you.'

'She knows you, Mama. She's a friend of Mrs Smythe,' replied Robert as he gently placed his packages on the floor before heading for the rowdy office and TC's purse. Robert nodded hello to Randy James, extracted a five-dollar note from TC's wallet and rushed out to pay Fiona's friend before she closed. He was back in minutes to help TC clear the cases and secure the stock in the safe.

'I'm excited, Mama,' said Robert as they busily stacked trays. 'I'll have you, Mr D, and Auntie Maggie for three-and-a-half days.' TC smiled. She was happy he was happy.

'Don't forget your cat.'

'I didn't forget him. I bought him a new collar for Christmas,' replied Robert.

The three former Pink Brolga residents were still yapping forty to the dozen when TC and Robert were ready to leave.

'I don't know about you lot,' said TC. 'Robert and I are ready to go home.'

'We're coming, too, Carmichael,' said Mr D.

'Of course, we bloody well are,' said Maggie. 'I'll carry your roses, Randy.'

'Thank you, Maggie. Doesn't appear your little sister wants them.' TC ignored their comments as she helped Robert load his packages into a huge Brolga Opals bag usually utilised to accommodate large sheepskins.

'We've invited Randy home for a few drinks and dinner tonight,' announced Mr D.

'I see,' said TC while concealing her disapproval and thinking, Thank you, Mr D. The last thing I need is Randy James knowing where Robert and I live.

'We won't all fit in your car, Mother; it's too small,' said Robert.

'That's right. Someone will have to take a cab.'

'I will. I'm an intruder,' volunteered Randy.

'I'll come with you,' said Mr D.

❡

'Who invited Randy James to the house, Maggie?' enquired TC as Maggie, Robert, and she walked to the car park.

'We both did,' replied Maggie defensively. 'He's all right, TC. I can tell by the way he looks at you, he's crazy about you.'

'Sure, along with anything else in a skirt,' replied TC off-handedly. 'It's the challenge, Maggie! Nothing else! The only reason he wants me is because he can't have me.'

'Well, TC, he's coming to the house and that is that.'

'Yes, I guess so.'

'Randy is all right, Mother,' said Robert. 'Sometimes he is amusing.' TC sighed in surrender.

'Okay, appears I'm outnumbered.'

'Give me a vase for the roses,' said Maggie the second they entered the house. 'A dozen red roses. Must have cost the poor bastard a fortune.'

'I'm glad you're impressed, Maggie. I'm going to get changed out of these shop clothes,' said TC.

§

Christmas break was over in a flash. The only time Randy James left TC's house was when he went to his motel on the highway a few blocks away to shower and change. From the first night, on Mr D's and Maggie's combined, while extremely inebriated, invitation, he took to sleeping on the couch in the family room.

TC listened a lot, as did Robert. They laughed a lot too. Neither of them spoke often. It was almost impossible to get a word in even if they wanted. As in the past Pink Brolga days, once Maggie and Mr D consumed a couple of drinks past what should have been their cut-off point, their clashing personalities rose to the forefront. Randy tried hard to impress TC, who came to realise he was an extremely intelligent man while sober. The silver-tongued bullshit artist emerged after his sixth beer and loitered till pass-out.

Great shame, thought TC. So did Robert, who remained wise and perceptive beyond his years.

A few days back at work, and it was New Year's Eve. Fiona and Ken and Gracie and Brian came for a barbecue. The weather was perfect— clear sky and millions of twinkling stars, which, after a half bottle of Irish Cream, Gracie tried to count. Consumption of excess alcohol that New Year's Eve was not restricted to Mr D, Maggie, and Randy James, who began drinking mid-afternoon. After the guests arrived at seven, Ken and TC drank Scotches and dry with Maggie, who was on her usual Scotch and water. Mr D stuck to Wild Turkey; Brian, vodka and tonic; and Fiona, gin and tonic. Randy James was dubbed by Mr D as drinking double, full-strength beers because all night he had two beers on the go at the same time. After Gracie's attempt at counting the stars, she knocked off another half bottle of Baileys.

TC and Maggie had prepared food platters, salads, and dessert during the afternoon. Mr D and Randy James had nominated themselves as barbecue cooks. TC badgered them to begin cooking at eight. Everyone howled her down.

'There's plenty left here to eat yet, darling' said Fiona, indicating the assortment of food on the table at which they were all seated.

'Yes, leave it for a while,' agreed the others.

TC tried again at nine. No! Nobody was interested. With Louis Armstrong, Tony Bennett, and Elvis providing background music via tapes in the lounge room and everyone in conversation, time passed quickly. Fiona spotted Randy eyeing off TC a little before midnight.

'Keep your eyes away from her. She's too good for a drunken, smooth-talker like you. Don't dare to attempt to kiss her when the sirens sound.'

'Fiona, please!' said Ken.

'You mind your own business, Ken. I've been watching him looking at TC.'

'Come on, everyone. Let's be nice,' said Mr D.

'I'll drink to that!' said Maggie.

'We all will,' said Gracie.

'I think I've had enough,' said TC. 'I'm tipsy.'

'We're all tipsy, darling,' stammered Gracie, whose face was very red.

'Don't be such a bloody wimp, Carmichael,' said Mr D.

'No, have another one with me, darling,' urged Fiona.

'Fiona, you're drunk. Leave TC alone. The girl will drink if she wants to,' said Ken.

'Ken, in case you haven't noticed, we are all drunk, and that includes you,' replied Fiona to her husband's chastisement.

The sirens sounded and the fireworks began exploding over the river a couple of blocks away. The eight of them jumped to their feet and began shaking hands, hugging, laughing, kissing and clinking glasses. Robert came running from his room to be hugged and kissed to the point of embarrassment for someone his age by TC, Gracie, Maggie, and Fiona. He was obviously relieved to get the fawning females out of the way and move on to Happy-New-Yearing the men, who shook his hand and patted him on his shoulders. With that out of the way, Robert stood beside TC.

'Are you drunk, Mother?' he asked seriously.

'I think so, darling,' was TC's reply.

'We all are, Robert,' came officiously from Fiona. 'Even Mr Smythe and myself.'

'It's New Year, darling,' said Gracie.

'We all love you, sweetie,' proclaimed Maggie.

'I love you all, too,' smiled Robert. 'Haven't Mr D and Randy cooked yet, Mother?'

'No, darling. Are you hungry?'

'Not at all. I've been watching my new videos in my room. I've had heaps of Cokes and lots of food. Excuse me, everyone. I'm going to watch more movies.'

After five minutes of Robert-praising by all, Mr D said, 'Raise your glasses, everyone. We'll drink to the lad. Years ago as a tiny boy he went to hell and back with his mother. Now, thanks to herself, he's a fine, young man. Principled to the core and honest as the day he was born.'

'You're bloody spot-on there, KD,' agreed Maggie.

TC wiped away a couple of stray tears, then joined Mr D, her sister and friends in toasting her son.

'Say a few words, Carmichael,' suggested Mr D. 'This is your opportunity to speak. Lord knows, you've not had much chance to be heard since Maggie and myself teamed up with Randy. You haven't been able to get a word in edgewise with three drunks yapping all the time.'

'Speak for yourself, you old bastard,' said Maggie indignantly.

'Come on, be nice to each other,' slurred Randy. Maggie gave Randy a foul glance.

'Im-bloody-possible!'

'Come on, lass. It's New Year. Say a few words,' insisted Mr D.

'All right, Mr D. Stop nagging,' said TC, pretending she was irritated. 'To begin, I want you to know how much I appreciate your company on this special occasion. As I speak, another year has begun. Nineteen hundred and eighty-nine is upon us. Let's hope it's a good one. Not only for us, but for everyone, everywhere.'

'Every bloody year's a good one as long as we're alive and got our bloody wits about us,' said Maggie. Mr D was angry.

'Maggie! Shut up, woman! You never stop! Yap, yap, yap, yap all the bloody time.'

'I think both of you should be quiet,' interjected Ken with authority. 'You are both acting like children. 'Please continue, TC.'

'In response to your kind words regarding Robert, I need you to know I am fully aware he is as he is not due to my influence alone. I spend too much time working to take the credit.

'Robert's integrity is the result of examples set for him by the people he loves most, the people who taught him right from wrong. They are his grandmother; Mr D, or, as Robert used to call him, Kranky Mr D; his Auntie Maggie; my boss, Vance Callahan; and Gracie, who in the others' absence has been all of them rolled into one since we left Queensland to live here.' Gracie tapped TC's shoulder.

'Are we allowed to drink to ourselves, darling?'

'Of course,' laughed TC. Gracie giggled.

'Oh, I like drinking to myself.'

'Come on, everyone let's drink,' from Randy James. They all did as instructed.

§

TC called cabs for Ken and Fiona and Gracie and Brian. It was almost half-past-three in the morning. They had ended the night by dancing to a Tony Bennett record in the lounge while Maggie and TC watched on, both thinking how lovely it was to see couples dancing together after being married forever.

Mr D and Randy were still in the garden discussing whatever it was, when TC called them to bid farewell to the others.

'And a good time was had by all. Thank you, darling,' said Fiona as she leaned to kiss TC.

'Fiona, you almost fell, darling,' said Ken, who was more than a little wobbly himself as he turned to TC and kissed her cheek.

'Damned good night, TC, darling. Thank you.'

'Lovely to have you. Sorry about the barbecue, Ken.'

'Don't worry about it, darling. We had plenty to eat. We had plenty to drink, too.'

Poor Gracie's face was now red.

'Love you darling.'

'Goes for me, too, luv,' said Brian.

There was the wishing of good nights all round; then the cabs came one behind the other, and New Year's Eve was almost over.

'I thought you'd be drunk by now, Carmichael,' said Mr D. Randy James spoke up.

'How could she be, Keith? She's been on water since we toasted Robert and you guys. She's had four Scotches and dry all night.'

'None of your business what I drink or don't drink, Randy,' retaliated TC.

'I could have sworn I saw a couple of sparks fly off TC then,' said Randy. 'Did you see them, Keith?'

'Leave the lass alone, Randy. You've obviously been watching her all night if you know what and how many she drank.'

'I'm not denying that, Keith. She's easy on the eye.'

'Stop now! Both of you leave her alone,' commanded Maggie, who, like KD and Randy, was as drunk as drunk could be.

'I think I'll go to bed everyone,' announced TC.

'Can I come with you?' called out Randy. TC glared at him.

'You must be insane!'

'Don't go to bed yet, Carmichael,' said Mr D. He handed TC a drink.

'Have this one with just us while we sit in the garden and watch the sun come up.' TC smiled. She loved Mr D.

'How can I refuse? Guess I'll cancel bed until after an early breakfast. Come on, let's hit the garden.'

TC cooked breakfast at six. When she checked on Robert, he was still awake with eyes glued to the T.V. screen.

'Looks like we'll all be sleeping through the day,' said TC. 'Come and have some breakfast with everyone else, darling.'

'Those videos I got from Auntie Maggie and Mr D are GREAT, Mother,' he said after hugging TC good morning.

'That's good, darling. Perhaps I'll watch them myself sometime, if you don't mind.'

'Of course, I won't mind, Mother. If it's a weekend, I'll watch with you.'

❡

Randy James flew to Darwin where his then-current job was based two days after New Year's Day. Mr D and Maggie returned to Queensland three days later. Robert went to the shop with TC every workday after they left. The house was lonely after having had company for a couple of weeks.

❡

January in the shop was busy as usual that time of year. TC was grateful to have Robert as an extra presence. He did all the necessary errands, cleaned windows and other glass, of which there were a lot, kept the souvenir shelves stocked and in order, plus anything else thrown in his direction by TC, Marjorie, and the others. He certainly earned his fifteen dollars per day.

The morning after his fourteenth birthday Robert did an excellent job of serving two Western businessmen when everyone else was busy with other customers. Everyone except TC was surprised at his sales ability.

'Why should I be surprised?' explained TC. 'He's been watching and listening to me sell opals for most of his life.'

'Mother is right,' said Robert. 'If I haven't learned by now, I never will.'

TC still hadn't found a replacement for Hideko. To date, they were managing things as they were.

Vance sent TC twenty thousand dollars towards the end of January. She was surprised, as rarely did he send twenty. She was grateful and thanked him.

'A long way to go yet, Little One. Mustn't spoil you by sending twenties too often.'

It was the first Friday in February when he made one of his regular almost-closing-time calls. Marjorie answered the telephone.

'It's the boss, TC.'

'Tell him we need some red opals,' said TC from her desk before standing to take the phone.

She heard Marjorie say, 'TC said to ask you to send red opals, Boss.' Marjorie was laughing by the time TC took the telephone.

'What are you up to, Boss? Marjorie is giggling like a teenager.' Vance laughed.

'I told her you know what you have to do to get red opals from me.' TC laughed herself.

'Sorry! Too high a price! You know that! Don't know why you bothered to mention it!' Vance laughed again.

'Can't blame a man for trying. I'm serious. Tell me you'll pay the price and I'll fly over tonight and bring red opals with me, promise.'

'Are you drunk, Boss?' asked TC seriously.

'No! Don't be silly, Little One. I'm in a good mood, that's all.' Business talk for a minute, if that.

'All right, I'll go now,' said Vance, then mischievously, 'Sure you won't take me up on the red opal deal? I can be on a plane in an hour.' More laughing from TC.

'No, Boss. I've got this far without one. I'll be right. Talk to you soon.' He was gone.

'Great, Marjorie. I haven't heard the boss sound so happy for a long time,' remarked TC.

¶

It was ten-past-twelve Perth time the following Sunday when TC's phone rang. She was surprised to hear Emi's voice. They usually spoke via the shop telephone.

'TC,' said Emi. 'Please sit down if you're not already.'

'You sound so serious, Emi. What is it?' No response.

'Emi, what is it?' repeated TC urgently.

'TC, Vance is dead! Vance is dead, TC. I thought I should tell you.' TC's body went cold and began shaking in shock.

'No, Emi! No! Not the boss! He's only fifty-five years old!'

'I'm sorry, TC. He died this morning. He had a heart attack while walking on a Sunshine Coast beach.'

'I'm having difficulty accepting it, Emi. He was really happy when I talked to him on Friday afternoon. He was joking with Marjorie and me.'

'He was happy yesterday, too, TC,' replied Emi. 'I had the biggest single we've ever had. I sold to a hundred-and-forty-thousand-dollar customer.'

'That would have made him very happy, Emi,' agreed TC. 'Seems incredible, even to me. When he was here in early December, he told me what would happen and what I should do if he died before me. His first prediction has already come to fruition. He told me I'd first hear about his death from someone outside his family.'

'I wonder how long it will be until you're told?'

'Who knows?' replied TC. 'Thank you for calling me.'

TC sat staring at nothing as a million memories flooded her mind. As if programmed to delete the bad, she recalled only good ones with intermittent flashes of sad. TC felt alone! Not lonely! For the first time in her life, she realised there was a vast difference between the two.

'I can't believe he's gone!' she said to the silence surrounding her. 'Why? Apart from women, he's been living a clean life for what seems an eternity.'

'It was a long time to go,' replied a voice from within. The telephone rang. It was Emi again.

'Are you all right, TC?'

'Not really, Emi. Guess I'm in shock. I mean, it's so sudden. Seems like a huge chunk of my life has gone with him.'

'Have you been officially told yet?' enquired Emi.

'No! What time did the boss die? Was Delores with him?' replied TC. 'She must be a mess.'

'It was early morning. He was by himself,' replied Emi. 'Some people saw him stop, turn around, and fall down. He was dead. They called an ambulance. That's all I know.'

'I see.'

'When are you coming out here, TC?' TC sighed heavily.

'The boss predicted I would be told not to come until the funeral. Guess I will fly out of here the day before.'

'I can't believe it's six o'clock in Queensland and you haven't been told yet.'

'Don't worry about it,' replied TC. 'The boss did pre-warn me. Apart from that, due to your thoughtfulness, I already know. Thank you, Emi. I'll never forget it.'

Jonathan Callahan called TC an hour later.

'TC, I have some bad news for you.'

'I already know, Jonathan,' replied TC. 'Emi told me.'

'I see!'

'How is your mother holding up?'

'As can be expected. It's a shock to all of us,' replied Jonathan. 'Mum said not to rush over. I'll let you know once the funeral arrangements are made.'

'Okay,' agreed TC, who put down the telephone while thinking, No doubt about you, Boss. You knew exactly what would happen. Spot on! TC wanted to cry again. She didn't. She recalled every word Vance had said to her that second day on the park bench.

'Whatever you do, Little One, don't fall to pieces. Keep your wits about you,' having been part of his instructions.

When Robert came home from a car show he had attended with a friend and his parents, TC gently broke the news about Vance's passing. Robert was distraught. He insisted TC and he go to seven o'clock mass to pray.

'It's important we ask our Lord to save Mr Callahan's soul, Mother.' TC agreed—how could she not!

Marjorie cried when TC told her about Vance. The Japanese girls and women bowed and said, 'So sorry.' Marjorie agreed wholeheartedly to mind the shop while TC went to Vance's funeral, as did Gracie to moving in with Robert during TC's absence.

As per Vance's instructions of the prior December, TC applied for a new company title under which she registered a new trading name containing the word Brolga. She realised it was Vance's way of making sure she would always retain the Brolga name.

After taking a midnight flight out of Perth, TC was on the ground in Queensland at seven the morning before Vance's funeral.

'Good to see you again,' greeted Emi, who had insisted on them meeting at the airport.

'Wish it was under different circumstances, Emi, my friend.'

'I know. It's still hard to believe Vance has gone,' replied Emi.

'I know, Emi, I know. There's my bag. Grab it,' said TC as she saw her piece of luggage appear on the moving roundabout.

'Carla has told the staff they are not allowed to go to Vance's funeral,' explained Emi.

'Probably came from higher up. It's something to do with Carla as to who attends the boss' funeral. Surely, he'd expect them all to be there.'

'I don't think Delores or Jonathan said they're not to go,' insisted Emi.

'If they didn't, I'd say Carla is pulling rank because she's been illicitly fornicating with the boss, getting away with robbing him because of the fact, and is now under the illusion she is in command.'

'Yes, you are probably right,' agreed Emi after a few moments in thought.

After leaving the airport neither Emi nor TC spoke until Emi drove her car into the lane behind the hotel which housed Brolga Opals' first shop. They'd both been deep in thought.

'You take your bag and check in,' suggested Emi. 'I'll Park the car underneath and meet you in the lobby.'

¶

TC smiled to herself when she saw two partly-enclosed telephone booths against the wall a little way past reception.

'That must be where the Boss used to call me from in the early

Chikako days. I can imagine him standing there, feeling like a fool while the hotel staff, who would know him, were wondering why on earth he wasn't using his shop phone.'

Emi went off to do business after seeing TC to her room. TC phoned home in order to catch Robert before Gracie drove him to college.

'I'm here in one piece, darling. I know you're halfway out the door. I'll call you tonight. Love you.'

'You, too, Mama.'

She unpacked, took a shower, then sat down and looked out through her hotel room window. Once again, old memories of Vance reappeared in her mind. They lingered until Emi knocked on her door hours later.

TC took a cab to Vance's funeral service. It took place at a small suburban church, which was full near to capacity when TC finally arrived after the cab driver temporarily getting them lost en route. TC noticed a vacant spot in the second last pew at the rear of the church. She squeezed past a half dozen or so strangers to reach it. Once seated, her eyes were fixed on Vance's coffin. People were a blur. The coffin was the only thing of significance to her because she knew Vance lay within. She wondered if he was wearing a suit. Visions of him covered in dust with his hair flying off to one side while in his jeans and shirt with torn pocket, his Gold Coast tourist outfits, stapled trouser legs and his Roman sandals, all ran through her mind.

TC was switched off during the clergy's sermon and hymns. She became wide awake and listened intently when Jonathan began his eulogy. Jonathan was halfway through speaking when TC heard a vaguely familiar voice directly behind her. 'That's one of his girlfriends there,' said the voice. TC had no idea whom the voice was referring to. Knowing Vance as she had, she wouldn't be surprised if half the females in the church had at one time or another been one of his tarts. She didn't know who was there; she hadn't bothered to look.

'There's another one over there,' said the voice. TC turned around in disgust to see Cane Toad's head and one of his mates from Melbourne. She glared into Cowlegg's eyes.

'Don't you dare point that finger at me!' His face turned red. He'd been caught out by not realising the woman in front of him was TC.

Jonathan finished speaking. One more hymn and the pall-bearers picked up his coffin. TC desperately wanted to touch it. By the time she filed out of the church, it was too late. Vance's coffin was in the hearse. Her heart sank an instant later when the hearse pulled away, closely followed by the other cars in the funeral procession.

'Looks like you missed the boat, TC,' said an old Brolgaite, who tapped her on the shoulder.

'What's new?' smiled TC.

'Nothing, by the looks of things, luv,' was the reply. They chatted until Emi interrupted from behind.

'TC, I've been looking for you. I thought you must have gone to the cemetery.'

'No, I don't have a car, and no one offered to give me a lift,' replied TC. 'I'll go to the cemetery and say goodbye to him before I fly home.'

'Come on, we'll go there now,' said Emi. 'We'll be too late, but Vance would understand.'

'You're right, the boss would understand,' replied TC. 'It's the thought that counts.'

Confirmation of Vance's sudden demise had filtered through to everyone in Brolga and surrounding district. All who knew him were in shock and denial, while those who knew of him felt sad because Brolga had lost a much-proclaimed, legendary man who had put everything on the line in order to successfully find his beloved opal. By persevering and succeeding, he put Brolga on the map.

Being Friday night, Brolga's Elders congregated on the sacred seat. They had just settled when Neil approached them.

'Mind if I join you tonight?' he asked as he sat down on the grass beside the seat.

'I thought you'd be in the Majestic on the piss,' said Old Jock.

'Not tonight,' replied Neil. 'They shoved Vance in the dirt today. I decided to skip grog as a sign of respect. Poor bugger had my interests at heart when he kept me off it for years. The least I can do is turn my back on the effing stuff for one lousy night.'

'The pill-pusher would be proud of you, mate,' said one Elder.

'Yeah, yeah,' agreed all.

'Can't believe the poor bastard is gone,' said Jock. 'Didn't bloody believe it when I first heard. Still have trouble even though I know it's true.'

'How old was he, Neil?' enquired one of Jock's friends.

'Wouldn't have a bloody clue,' replied Neil. 'Isn't that bloody awful? I worked for the man for effing years, and I don't even know how bloody old he was when he died.'

'Poor bastard was fifty-five,' said Jock with a faraway, remembering-yester-years look in his eyes. 'I know that because we talked about ages back when I lost my wife.'

'That was sad, Jock. She was a good woman,' said Neil sincerely. All agreed.

'Anyway,' said Jock. 'I know Callahan was fifty-five.'

'That's young!' said someone.

'Yeah! Yeah!' from all.

'Tell you what, my friends,' added Jock. 'Goes to show getting off the piss and quitting death sticks doesn't make us live longer. I'm calling it a night. I'm going home.'

'I'm going to the Majestic. I need a drink,' said Neil, who got quickly to his feet and hurried off towards the pub.

'It's too early,' complained Jock's mates.

'I don't give a stuff,' replied Jock. 'Life's too short for me to waste mine sitting here with you bastards. Jock stood and stretched, then looked at his mates.

'See you tomorrow night! Hopefully, we'll all still be alive.'

EPILOGUE

Vance's sons took the reins of their father's opal empire. They continued fossicking and mining. They were successful.

Tsune and Carla disappeared without advising.

Aiko was appointed manager of the original shop.

Captain Russ and Marjorie moved east.

Gracie retired when Robert turned sixteen.

Mr D retired to live in an apartment overlooking the Sydney Harbour.

Ken Smythe passed away. Fiona followed him soon after.

Len and Lisa spend much of their retirement travelling the world and enjoying each other's company.